CRIK

KARL BEER

Illustrated by Mark Beer

CRIK © 2015 Karl Beer
Cover © 2015 Karl Beer
All Rights Reserved
This book or any portion thereof may not be reproduced or used in any manner whatsoever without the express written permission of the publisher except for the use of brief quotations in a book review.
Printed in the United Kingdom

First printing, 2015
EBook ISBN:1508988498
Paperback ISBN: 978-1508988496

For my Dad for sharing his love of books

My Mother with love and admiration

For my Wife, Helen for always believing in me,
My guiding light

Contents

1. YING AND YANG
2. BENEATH THE ROSEBUSH
3. A GRAVE, MR HASSELTOPE
4. PUPPETS IN THE DARK
5. HOP, SKIP AND JUMP
6. SOMEWHERE WARM
7. A FAMILIAR STRANGER
8. AMONGST THE TREES
9. ALL YOU COULD WISH FOR
10. THE MARSH HOUSE
11. STAY AWHILE …. I'LL KEEP YOU FOREVER
12. WHAT IS YOUR NAME?
13. GO AND HIDE SEEK
14. LINDRE REMEMBERED
15. AWAKENED
16. A LIFE TAKEN
17. GREY DIRECTIONS FROM A BLACK HEART
18. FORESHADOWING
19. A SHARED LIGHT
20. HELLO, GOODBYE, AND HOW WE GOT THERE.
21. A THORN IN THEIR SIDES
22. BLACKTHORN TUNNEL
23. THE RED WOOD
24. NORTH BY NORTHWEST
25. IF I ONLY HAD A HEART
26. A REMINDER OF HOME
27. SINS OF THE FATHER
28. PARSNIPS AND RUST
29. A GLIMMER OF GOLD IN THE MORNING
30. NEW LIFE
31. WHEN THE DEAD WALK THE WOLD
32. SHADOW MIMES
33. THE HANGMAN'S NOOSE
34. THE GHOSTS AMONGST US
35. ANGRY WORDS
36. STAMPEDE
37. AS THE NOOSE TIGHTENS
38. A HELPING HAND
39. WHAT GOES UP, MUST EVENTUALLY COME DOWN
40. WHAT CAME NEXT
41. THE CAT AND THE MOUSE
42. HERE'S LOOKING AT YOU KIDS
43. THE WRITINGS ON THE WALL
44. THE DEMONS WITHIN US
45. WITHOUT A PADDLE
46. SCORN SCAR
47. BEHIND THE VEIL

48. THE PRICE
49. A HUSHED EXCHANGE
50. FADE TO BLACK
51. THE CURTAIN CALL
52. HOMECOMING
53. ON THE OTHER SIDE
54. REUNION
55. CONVERGENCE
56. THEM AND US
57. THEM OR US: PART ONE
58. THEM OR US: PART TWO
59. WITHIN THE SHROUD
60. GRAVES END
61. EXODUS

1. YING AND YANG

THE HANGING TREE dominated the skyline. Sat astride two stone hills it loomed over the other trees in the valley. A tall figure, with slumped shoulders and a hunched back, contemplated the ancient wood as he stepped along the country lane. Bark, like cracked leather, funnelled the rain into thousands of small tributaries. Twisted gnarled roots formed a canopy over the path, offering respite from the downpour. Hunching down, the traveller entered the tunnel. Wood thrummed to the sound of the pounding rain. Leaning against the cold rock that supported the tree, the figure scanned the bent boughs through the nest of roots. Generations of children from the nearby village had played unmercifully on the branches. Tied to the tree hung a long knotted rope. With each gust, the rope swung into the air, threatening to loop over a branch, or snag the many scraggly twigs adorning the outer appendages. Despite a hundred bowed branches, some falling so low from the trunk they appeared broken, the old wood remained strong. Leaves rustled as the traveller found what he sought. Swinging from an upper branch, well away from where the children played, fell another rope, its weave frayed by the passage of time. A spark of lightning illuminated the noose that gave the tree its name, and its true purpose.

Grunting, the traveller pushed away from the wet rock and stepped from under the roots. Rain went through his worn white shirt, peppering skin as thick and gnarled as the Hanging Tree he left behind.

Passed the hangman's tree, the slopes disappeared into a wide valley, surrounded by other, less impressive trees. With all the rain over the last weeks, the foliage had grown thick, darkening the woods even during the day. They shepherded the valley, with only a high snow-capped mountain visible over the dense canopy.

A fast river cut close to the wood before turning inward across the gentle rolling hills. The water met the road at a stone bridge, where the roiling depths frothed with furious abandon beneath the arch. On the far bank, stood an aged pub, a sign above the door, showing a frothing pint of ale, identified both the pub, and the village that came into sight, as Crik.

Despite the small size of the village, the cemetery on its outskirts held far more occupants than most towns. Various sized and shaped tombstones sat

CRIK

atop a high hill, surrounded by stone woodland creatures. Granite foxes, hawks, and an occasional wolf, occupied this high ground. Simple sticks, with names long faded from the wood, peppered the poor soil closer to the riverbank. After floods, it was common to find an arm protruding from the ground, even a whole corpse drifting with the current. An epitaph of the buried person resided beneath their name, "Jack Smill, hanged by mistake". Another read, "Here lies Margery Bremp, she said she'd live to see a hundred, but died at ninety nine instead".

The village, sitting alongside so many graves, took on an unwarranted gloomy persona. All the homes were in good repair, and the gardens, both front and back, tended with care, the hedges neat and trim, and the grass not too long. Two roads intersected at a cross within the village. The larger, better-paved road, led from the Hanging Tree. A house stood at the end of the shorter road, its white boards pale in the darkness, with four windows downstairs and a further three above. Heavy curtains, pulled tight against the continuing downpour, darkened two of the larger upstairs windows. Inside the highest window, set within reach of the curved roof, and its overflowing gutter, shone a gentle light. Despite the dim glow, it gleamed conspicuously in the darkened village.

Behind the window sat a boy, staring out at the rivulets of water streaming down the glass. Tracking individual droplets wind down the pane, he muttered under his breath. His count reached eleven when another spark lit up the sky. The storm was getting closer, not fading. At his elbow, the candle, already short, dripped red wax on the small saucer.

Heaped around the desk where he sat was an assortment of oddities and discarded toys. Everything from taxidermy animals, to miniature battlegrounds, where elves fought goblins amongst huge war engines constructed from twigs and twine. Landscape paintings, featuring mountains, fields, and wooded glades, dotted the walls. Pencil drawings of exotic creatures, both real and imagined, covered every other available surface. Amongst the clutter on the floor, and on his bed, were scraps of black and white comics. A fearsome image of a crazed bear attacking a half dressed man holding a small knife, peered up from the floor. In the next panel, the man stood over the dead predator, his knife jutting from the wild animal's neck.

Turning from the storm, he studied a small framed picture of a handsome man with a proud moustache. His father's image meant less to him than it once had, the man sketched in charcoal was only that, a sketch in his memory, with time as the eraser. Although he never knew who drew the picture, he knew his mother had written "To Jack," in the bottom right corner. It was his name, but his friends called him Ying. The flickering light from the candle revealed Yang.

Yang moved stuffed sparrows and a robin to a high shelf, where they peered down with gold-speckled eyes. Displeased by having the small birds in place of

YING AND YANG

honour, he replaced them with a barn owl. Satisfied with the owl, Yang sought something else to rearrange. In bored amusement, Jack watched Yang stuff a field mouse into the gaping jaws of a grey fox. Yang made Jack unique in the village, though not the oddest member of their small community, for Yang was Jack's shadow. Without doubt, no one else had ever had such an independent shadow, and he was sure Yang's ability to move things around was particular to him. While a light shone, Jack was never alone; something that brought trouble down on him nearly everyday, for Yang, being a mischievous sort, often did things that got him into trouble. Noticing Jack's attention, Yang spread his fingers across the wall. Three of the elongated fingers striped a curved shield. Jack thought Yang held his hand in greeting, before noticing the black insubstantial fingers closing off one at a time. Only two shadowed fingers remained when Jack realised Yang counted. As the hand closed into a fist, a flash of white light enveloped the room; illuminated, Yang grew to giant proportions. Standing upright, his hair spiked around his head, Yang lifted one stiff arm and then fell on the bed. Patting his head, Jack felt his mop of sandy hair flat against his skull.

Tired of his shadow's antics, he returned to his vigil in time to see movement down in the street. The lack of streetlamps in the village spoiled his chance of identifying the stranger. Only the white cloth the figure wore, standing in stark contrast to its surroundings, gave him any guidance. Close to Bill's house, beside the rosebush Bill's grandparents had planted the summer before, leaned the stranger. From the size of the white shirt, he knew the stranger dwarfed anyone in the village. At once, he recognised one of the woodland folk, who grew to immense size, lurking outside. Scared, he doused the candle, dispelling Yang, who had come wandering over to look. With the dying light, a row of pale houses bloomed in the night. Below, the figure grew more distinct, revealing for the first time a large sack slung over a humped shoulder. A hand, far larger than the proportion of the arm, swept great clumps of wet dirt onto the road.

Jack hoped his night vision improved before the Wood Giant found what he looked for. Eager to see, he rested his head against the cold glass, the thumping rain tickled his brow. The Giant, oblivious to Jack's scrutiny, continued with its digging. Briefly, Jack thought the long fingers, coated with earth and torn grass, was the Giant's shovel. No matter what it looked for, Bill's grandparents would be furious come morning when they saw the damage wrought to their beloved roses. Especially Grandma Poulis, whose scathing tongue, had touched many in Crik, particularly himself, who had the misfortune to carry Yang along with him. Looking down, he did not think the Giant cared what Grandma Poulis would say or do.

As the storm worsened, the thunderous downpour hid the sounds of the excavation. Heavy rain pummelled the collection of homes and made a river of

CRIK

the road. Returning lightning brought the misshapen features of the Giant into vivid detail. The light afforded him only a moment to inspect the long face of the Giant, yet the vision remained secure in his mind's eye, where he groped for every detail. Woodland folk had no hair, only branches as fine as silk, dotted with growths of red and gold leaves covering a high-rise brow. From the numerous tales his mother told him, Jack knew the longer the branches and the fatter the leaves the older the Giant. Even from the distance he sat from Bill's house, he saw ropes of tangled leaves dropping down below the open shirt. He turned his attention to the black eyes. An unblinking cluster, scattered over the cheekbones, varied in size, some no larger than coat buttons, while others equalled a prize-fighter's fist. Looking at each orb swayed him from wariness, to full comfort. Each eye portrayed a different emotion. One deep-set eye surrounded by great rings of thoughtful conjecture, instilled calmness, and great introspection. Another, above the skin, scrutinised with a maddening keenness that placed him at nerves end. Brown skin, with many cracks and growths, appeared thick and rough, not at all like the smooth skin of smaller people, whose joy of running and bathing contrasted the Giants' fondness of darkened dells and rocks. Twisted roots dangled from the long face. Jack's mother had told him, the roots, hiding the mouth, siphoned minerals out of the rock water they drank. She later said, when threatened they could pull back the roots, to uncover their mouths. His probing for a description of the mouth went unanswered, his mother had never seen a Giant with the roots pulled back, and she knew no one who had. He felt disappointment again as the roots remained in place over the Giant's chin.

Finished with its digging, the Giant pulled a sack from its shoulder to place it on the cobblestones. Surprised, Jack saw the bottom of the bag bulged with hidden content. He had it wrong, the Giant did not dig to find something; it dug to leave something behind. The neck of the sack, tied with thick cord, flopped over to one side. With slow measured movements, the Giant first regarded the hole, then Bill's house, and finally the sack itself. Continuing to tilt its head the Giant remained unhurried, not troubled by standing at the centre of the village.

The humped back made it difficult for the Giant to lower itself to work at the cords; eventually the thick fingers loosened the knots, and the neck of the sack opened. Bending did not come easy to the wood folk, preferring as they did to stand tall and proud, and move as little as possible. Jack, prepared to see what lay within the bag, felt his stomach sink. The colossal hand, which delved inside, withdrew, obscuring the object it carried behind fingers as broad as the root of an oak tree. Taking its time the Giant moved the mysterious object to the expectant hole.

Shifting position, Jack accidentally knocked over the picture of his father. In hopes of gaining a better advantage, he never noticed the cracked frame.

YING AND YANG

Frustrated, he scrambled atop his desk, planting his hands and face against the topmost edge of the glass.

Taking less time to cover the hole than it had to dig, the Giant, after retrieving the empty bag, walked from Grandma Poulis's rosebush. The huge form marched down the street, toward Jack's house.

Alarmed, Jack wanted to jump away from the window, only his great curiosity kept him at the glass. As far as he knew this was the first time one of the woodland folk had ever entered Crik, and for it to leave something behind, only made the adventure more appealing. The Giant carried on in its lumbering gait; its broad and powerful legs more squat than tall, reminded Jack of the foundations of a house.

Just beyond the shelter of Jack's home, it stopped. Tipping back its head, the Giant peered up at the highest window. Unblinking eyes held Jack prisoner. Scared witless, Jack locked his gaze with the Giant. The pointed fence circling his home only managed to reach the Giant's knees, offering no barrier to the night prowler, and the front door would not withstand one knock from the dirty hands swaying at its sides. His hurried breath fogged the window, obscuring the Giant for seconds while the white mist dissipated to a small area before his open mouth.

What felt an hour, certainly only took a few minutes; after watching Jack, the Giant continued on its way, leaving behind the frightened boy. Unwilling to light the candle to have Yang with him, for fear of the light bringing back the Giant, Jack sat down at his desk to wait for dawn.

CRIK

2. BENEATH THE ROSEBUSH

WHEN MORNING BROKE, it found Crik bathed in sunlight, the storm of the previous night had passed, leaving behind a few scattered clouds. Still wet from the downpour, the ground glistened with the reflective sun, making it hard not to squint against the glare. The curved roofs, benefiting from the first rays, were more than half-dried, and the once overflowing gutters ran empty.

A shaft of light caught Jack's face. Trying to hold onto the wisps of his dream, he found it too hard to hold onto the elusive imagery. Missing the darkness, he lifted his hand as though warding off an attack.

Disoriented, he found himself sprawled across his desk, with one arm tucked under him. Memory of the previous night crashed back, snapping him awake. The encounter with the Giant seemed unreal in the dawn, though he did not doubt his recollection. Once the Giant had left, he remained by the window, making sure that it did not return; or try to enter the house. After the Giant had spotted him, he feared he would never again close his eyes, so it was with surprise that he had fallen asleep. It took until the early hours before he had grown weary of his vigil.

His thoughts turned away from the appearance of the Giant, to what it had hidden. Looking outside, he saw the rain had washed away the dirt the Giant had thrown onto the road, together with all other tell-tale signs of its work. Dwayne Blizzard stood close to Bill's house talking with Liza Manfry. Dwayne's Talent allowed him to see things others would miss. Leaning closer to the glass, Jack willed them to move down the street away from the buried secret. Come on, his lips serving action to his will. Liza said something, making Dwayne blush, and skipped down the road. Remaining by the bush, the boy looked down at his boots abashed. A torn flower lay under Dwayne's heel. Frantic, Jack feared Dwayne would see the tell-tale sign and discover whatever lay under the bush. Shouting over her shoulder, Liza called for the blushing boy. Reminding Jack of a yo-yo, Dwayne leapt forward, and followed her down the street. Jack eased his grip on the desk.

Sparing only a fleeting glance at the other children running toward the cemetery, he swung himself off his chair. Already dressed, he dashed across the room. Caught by surprise, his shadow stopped fiddling with a toy catapult, and followed. Opening the door, he heard his mother humming in the kitchen. She busied herself with frying his eggs and making his toast, burning the bread black, the way he liked it.

His bedroom, once being the family attic, led out onto a narrow stair, with not much of a landing. A board, nailed into the post and wall, fenced off the drop to the first floor. He almost crashed into the ornament case his mother had placed on the landing the day before. She had put it there to alleviate the gloom; like painting the walls white or hanging a few paintings, it did nothing to brighten the upper stairwell. Jack approved of the darkness. At least she gave up with filling the space with potted plants. Deprived of sunlight they died, and Yang took them to add to his collection of dead things.

The wood creaked as he took the stairs two steps at a time. He passed his mother's room, the door open wide enough for him to see the large double bed, with the turned down top sheet. Flowers lined the bedroom wall, filling the house with their sweet scent. A thick blue carpet masked his second descent.

The living room was both the largest and the most often changed in the house. Only a week ago, he helped his mother move the high backed chairs away from the window to stand closer to the fireplace, and with far more difficulty the sideboard and two more of her display cases to take their place. Bright sunshine lit up the ornaments wonderfully in their new home, though no doubt his mother already had plans where to place them next. Beside the kitchen rested a long black wooden table, a silver candelabrum stood on elaborate crochet at its centre, with four newly placed candles.

Pushing through to the kitchen he almost collided with his mother.

'I heard you coming,' she said, blowing a curl of black hair from her face. 'Here are your toast and eggs.'

How his mother could look so smart first thing in the morning never ceased to amaze him. Other mothers still wore nightclothes at midday, with their hair in disarray, complaining all the while that they were not morning people. Here his mother stood, wearing a purple dress, frills on the hem and arms, with white birds spreading their wings as they took flight up the sides. A pink apron, sprinkled with crumbs from his toast, wrapped her waist. She had brushed her long hair into waves that nestled her shoulders and cascaded down her back. She put plenty of powder on her face, in an attempt to hide the burns that disfigured her.

A glass of fresh juice sat next to a plate on a yellow tablecloth. Behind him, his mother had placed a second plate for Yang, filled with sliced apple and pears. Despite not having to eat, Yang attacked his plate, leaving the dropped fruit for his mother to pick up.

'You're in a hurry this morning.' His mother watched him devour his toast, with a generous helping of egg.

'Got things to do,' he mumbled around the food.

CRIK

'Can't say that I blame you, all this rain we've had, must be torture not being able to leave the house.'

Eating, he gave a shrug.

He dismissed the idea of asking whether she had heard or seen anything last night. If she knew about the Giant, she would have mentioned it by now, besides he did not want to upset her. The woodland folk never entered the village; if she knew any different, she would keep a tighter rein on him.

'I grew a new plant this morning.' His mother pointed to a pot near the sink.

Most members of Crik had a Talent; his mother's was the ability to grow things. She only needed to concentrate on a seed to make it grow in moments. The sight of a flower blooming in seconds never ceased to amaze Jack. All the flowers in the house grew that way. Every new flower, or plant, made his mother happy. He liked it when she smiled. This morning she beamed with pride as he moved closer to the pot.

The pot, no larger than a coffee mug, held a small purple tree. It looked different to other plants. Spear shaped leaves filled its branches, each etched with dark red veins, like blood. Moist wood yielded at his slightest touch.

'Careful,' his mother warned, 'I don't think that's wood.'

He agreed, it felt warm, almost as though he ran his finger down the spine of a rabbit.

'Where'd you find this?'

'I found the seed resting on the windowsill this morning.' She moved to the oval window, laying her hand on the dark wood outside. 'Being of an odd shape and colour I had to see what it grew into.'

His heart quickened. 'You took it from outside.' He rushed passed his mother to poke his head out the window. Studiously he scanned the grass bordering the house for any sign of the Giant. The wet ground yielded no evidence of the Giant having left the seed. Someone of his size surely would have left behind a footprint in the damp soil. Remembering how the Giant used its hands to dig, he hunted for soil on the sill, but saw none.

'You're very pale, are you unwell?'

He ducked beneath his mother's hand as she tried to feel his forehead, mumbling that he felt fine. With a hurried promise to be back in time for dinner, he headed for the door.

An appreciative gust of wind welcomed him as he left the warm kitchen. Ignoring his tingling nerves, he paused. Trapped in the house for days had him draw in a long breath. Satisfied he allowed his impatience to resurface. He trotted along the garden path watchful for any sign that the Giant had revisited his home after he had fallen asleep. Did the Giant leave that seed for his mother to find? If not it was a strange coincidence that she should find it this morning.

At the end of his garden, he clenched his hands in excitement when he saw the deserted street. He wanted to run up the cobbles to the rosebush, but

BENEATH THE ROSEBUSH

before he could take another step, he spotted Dwayne and Liza. Hoping neither would see him, he carefully opened his gate, with the intention of cutting across Miss Mistletoe's backyard. Having pointed his boots in that direction, Yang slammed the gate, alerting them to his presence.

Dwayne's huge eyes swivelled around, catching Jack in a glare. A rash of gooseflesh always coursed up Jack's arms when Dwayne focused on him, and again he felt the accustomed roughening of his skin. The boy's stare reminded him of painted eyes that followed you around a room. Uncomfortable, he turned his attention to Liza. With her upturned chin, she looked down at him with suspicion. Yang liked nothing more than to lift her skirt and hear her wail. Fearing his wayward shadow, Liza clasped her hands tight against her thighs.

'I suppose, like everyone else, you want to run off to the river and gawp at the body.' Disgust laced her remark.

Following a storm the bloated Tristle River tended to break its bank, flooding Long Sleep. The loose soil gave up graves easier than an old man coughing up a clod of phlegm. Only the tombs set high up on the hill were safe from the water. Yang would be eager to see the body and anything else the rain had disturbed. His shadow had a knack for finding some artefact to add to his collection; Mr Bane's canteen, half filled with whiskey, being his favourite. Where the other half of the drink had gone, following Mr Bane's burial to his untimely excavation, remained a mystery. A shiver ran down his spine.

'I won't bother.' Noticing a suspicious glance between them, Jack added, 'Seeing the body will only excite Yang. If we went to the river he'd cause trouble.'

'We all know you control your shadow Ying,' said Dwayne, 'so stop trying to pretend otherwise.'

'Crows eat your eyes.'

Although Dwayne took a step closer, he was bigger than Jack and liked to use his fists, the sight of Yang extending himself from the fence made him take two hasty steps back. One advantage of having a living shadow was he never fought alone.

'The body isn't from one of the riverside graves,' Liza interjected. 'Someone opened one of the tombs.'

This declaration sent ice fingers playing a discordant rhythm up along Jack's spine. The memory of the Giant's huge hands, filled with gnarled roots, made his breath rattle in his throat.

Dwayne scratched his red hair. 'I bet it was a grave robber from Grenville. They must've used a sledgehammer to knock in the stone door.'

'What tomb?'

'The one overlooking the deep well; you know, the cloaked figure holding the noose.'

CRIK

'We saw it earlier.' Liza gave him a smile as though she had a slice of a birthday cake that had all gone by the time he had gotten to the table. 'We decided it would be bad taste to go looking at the body.'

'Besides, the adults kept us away from the river,' said Dwayne.

This remark drew an agitated glance from Liza. 'Be that as it may Dwayne,' she said, 'I would not have liked to ogle some poor soul floating in the muddy waters of Tristle River.'

The plant Jack's mother found must have absorbed her attention, or she would have mentioned the commotion to him. Bill and he often went to the well beside the statue holding the hangman's noose. The other statues were all animals, foxes, wolves, a few birds; their favourite was the cloaked figure with the skeletal hand. They always shared an uncomfortable feeling in the waning light, as the hangman's shadow lengthened over them, as though it judged them as they played, which only added to its attraction.

'I can see you're like all the rest,' said Liza. 'No doubt that freak, you hang around with, is already up at Long Sleep. With his head always in a book, he acts innocent. Give him a chance however, and the freak,' her emphasis on the epithet made her teeth click together, 'would gawp at the body like everyone else.'

Taking a step closer, Jack said, 'There's nothing wrong with Bill. Just because he can't annoy people like you, doesn't make him any different.'

'Liza has another Talent too,' said Dwayne, oblivious to the scornful look the girl gave him.

'You should run and hide Liza, before I have my shadow do something - unpleasant.' This time Jack smiled, as the self-satisfied smirk left Liza's face.

'Why don't you and your shadow run along with the rest of the rubberneckers? Come Dwayne, I do not fancy wasting the first dry day in a week on the muddy slopes of the Tristle. Let's go to the meadow.' She snapped her fingers, and with a haughty twirl of her skirt left.

Jack spotted the look of disappointment in Dwayne's large eyes and could not stop from grinning. It was his own fault, why would Dwayne want to hang around with a girl. They were never fun. Why head for the meadow when he could explore the woods, or, now that no one else was around, use the swing tied to the Hangman's Tree.

Extended to twice his length Yang slipped his hands into a dirty puddle and, ignoring Jack's waving arms, threw the water over Liza's white skirt. She wailed in disgust and outrage, before disappearing in a ground hugging mist.

'I'll get you Ying,' she cried from the departing cloud.

'Liza, wait for me,' called Dwayne, trailing after the fleeing mist that sped toward the meadow.

Shaking his head Jack wanted to admonish his wayward twin, useless as that would prove. At least they were now alone in the street. With a quickened heart,

BENEATH THE ROSEBUSH

he marched from his gate and up the road. He began to jog outside Miss Mistletoe's house, and was running by the time he passed the rundown Space house, with the rotting wheelbarrow leaning against the gap-toothed fence. His eyes fastened on the rosebush.

Hoping Liza was right, that Bill's grandparents were by the river, he stopped beside the red and white flowers. Beneath the thorns and twisted stems, he looked at the earth, seeing no sign of the disturbance the Giant had wrought the previous night. Perturbed by the lack of evidence he turned. Only one torn flower lay on the cobblestones. Picking up the rose, he knew anyone else would presume the storm had caused it to fall.

Jack did not know whether Yang had seen the night visitor before he had extinguished the light. Glancing at Yang he hoped his shadow did not call attention to them; he needed to know what the Giant had left here. On hands and knees, he pushed his fingers into the yielding soil. He buried the Blue Leaf, Grandma Poulis used in her tea, in handfuls of dirt. With cold sweat already dampening his hairline he peered up at the windows of the house. The curtains were open, though no doubt Bill, sleeping at the back of the house, still had his shut. Bill always slept late; his grandparents were early risers, with Grandpa Poulis taking their dog Wolfen, known as Wolf to everyone else, out for a walk as far as the surrounding wood. As he continued to dig, Jack hoped Grandpa Poulis, after hearing about the body floating in the Tristle, had returned to fetch his wife.

Yang helped, using his dark fingers to delve beneath Jack's own. Perhaps his own strange actions piqued his shadow's curiosity, or had Yang sensed something buried deep in the ground? Knowing his twin's propensity toward the macabre perturbed his thoughts. Instead of handfuls of wet earth, he now slackened his pace, scraping the dirt back with wary fingers, unsure whether he wished to discover what lay beneath the sodden ground.

With a troubled brow, he touched an object. Although the smooth round surface could belong to a hidden stone, the warmth emanating from its touch belayed any illusion; this was what the Giant had left. Yang moved back as Jack carefully brushed away a thin layer of dirt, revealing a golden sphere, no larger than a cricket ball. It looked precious. With shaking fingers, he removed more grime from the sphere.

With the ball out in the open, Jack fell back onto his haunches, scrutinising the golden globe. By its shape and size, he guessed it to be either an egg or a nut. His mother would know; she understood seeds, and nuts, only he did not want to show it to her. She may want to grow it, as she had done with the seed she had found, and he was not entirely sure he wanted to see what grew from the nut the Giant had planted.

CRIK

A narrow silver line zigzagged down its centre, splitting the gold in two. If not for the rising sun striking the silver, he would have missed the singular difference in the outer gold shell.

Shadow hands crept closer, nudging the side of the sphere. Alarmed, Jack sprang forward taking the object for himself.

His breath caught in his throat, not only from the sudden rush of heat against his palms, but he also felt something within the orb move.

3. A GRAVE, MR HASSELTOPE

ONCE HE HAD FILLED in the hole, Jack headed home with the golden orb secure in his pocket. Through his jacket's thick wool, he felt the furtive movement of the presence inhabiting the egg. He no longer regarded the orb as a nut, because plants do not move.

His eyes roved from one side of the street to the other, checking the windows and the open doorways. He expected a furious Mr Space, his hair in disarray, to appear, cursing him for messing with Grandma Poulis's roses. Thankfully, no one came accusing him. The news of the floater had emptied the streets quicker than a plague of rats.

Fear dampened his upper lip, as the egg again shifted in his pocket. Forcing his gaze downwards, he saw Yang had risen up his body, without his realising, to cradle the egg with caring hands. Horrified, he slapped his shadow's hands away.

Disturbed by Yang's interest in the egg he failed to notice the figure running up behind him. He let out a cry as a hand smacked his back. When he doubled over in fright, he almost let the egg slip from his pocket. Hearing laughter, he turned angrily on Bill, his heart hammering against his ribs.

'Damn it Bill, you almost gave me a heart attack!'

Bill's grin pushed his glasses higher. Through the thick lenses, his brown eyes appeared huge, and the golden burst of colour near the left pupil beamed bright.

'Will you look at him,' Jack said, looking with disgust at his double. Yang rolled in the street holding his stomach, kicking his phantom legs into the bright sky. 'You'd swear I pissed my pants the way he's reacting.'

'I did call your name twice,' said Bill. 'Remember, I'm the daydreamer.' He held up a worn copy of "The Nymph and the Willow," or as the subtitle below read, "Fun Times in the Wood". A provocative picture of a half-dressed girl hugging a tree adorned the cover.

Cracking a smile, Jack took the book from Bill. 'Does your grandma know what you're reading?'

Wrenching the book from Jack's grip, Bill held it to his podgy stomach. 'Grandpa gave it to me. He said there was nothing wrong with a bit of fantasy. There must be something naughty in these pages; he made me promise not to

CRIK

show it to Grandma.' A pink tongue explored Bill's lips as he fingered the book's spine.

'Are your grandparents over at Long Sleep?'

Scratching his head, Bill for the first time took in the deserted village. 'Is that where everyone is? What's happening over there?'

Eager to get the egg to his room, Jack at first didn't want to go to the cemetery. He was about to show his disinterest when he paused. Could there be a connection between the egg and the open crypt? The coincidence of the Giant and the torn open door happening on the same stormy night demanded investigation. Besides, Bill would be suspicious if he didn't go with him.

'Liza said someone broke into a tomb last night. They found the body in the river.'

'What and you didn't come to get me? Come on Ying, it's not everyday that we can see inside a tomb.'

Jack hadn't thought of it, preoccupied with the idea of the body, the open crypt never entered his mind. Coerced by his curiosity, he allowed Bill to lead him along Brandy Road to the graveyard.

Despite having nearly the entire population of Crik at Long Sleep, the graveyard was curiously hushed when Jack and Bill stepped around the first wooden crosses littering the bottom of the hill. A few young children remained close to the village, happy to let the adults congregate by the riverbank. They ran between the wooden markers, laughing as they tried to catch one another. Jack envied them, he wanted to be as carefree as them - his sighting of the Giant, and the weight in his pocket, ended any hope of that happening.

An old path, overgrown with tangled weeds and coarse grass, wound up the slope, bypassing the humped earth where coffins rotted out of sight. Both boys followed the crumbling flagstones. Now higher, they saw Mr Gasthem, the Village Elder, standing on the bridge on the far side of the hill. His Talent allowed him to talk with creatures, not horses, or wolves, or anything as interesting as that, but common slugs and cockroaches. Jack often wondered what, if anything, a bug could say of interest. Despite having a rather unfortunate Talent, Mr Gasthem always knew what happened in Crik, far quicker and in more detail than did anyone else in the village. Close to the corner of Crik pub, stood three solemn men; Bill's grandfather amongst them.

'They must be fishing out the floater,' said Bill. 'You don't want a body to stay in the river for too long, otherwise it'll poison the drink.'

Deciding to check out the tomb later, they followed the bank down to the bridge. They came to a stop amongst tall reeds. The familiar smell of malted barley, used to make the pub's famous thick black ale, drifted over to them. Jack's mother blamed the drink for drawing in so many people to the village every weekend. It was common for the population of Crik to swell to the thrice

A GRAVE, MR HASSELTOPE

its number on market days - more on special holidays. Many farmers enjoyed Crik pub more than, perhaps, they should.

Eager to see the body, Yang stretched himself toward the bridge; for once Jack shared his shadow's ghoulish curiosity.

'Okay boys, that's far enough.' Mr Gasthem strode over, his long hooked staff tapping the white stone bridge. 'It's not a pleasant sight we have here.' As his shadow fell over them, he lowered his tone to a whisper. 'His tomb has kept Mr Hasseltope well preserved. It's not like the washed out bodies you've seen before, where there's only rags and bones. He's as fresh as morning-baked bread. I'm afraid animals found him before us.' Two nicotine-stained fingers touched his nose.

Extended beyond Mr Gasthem, Yang peered over the lip of the bridge. Jack wondered what his shadow saw amongst the bloated tide of the Tristle River.

As was customary, Mr Gasthem wore his brown suit, ironed and spotless. Hundreds of insects scurried over his sleeve and turned down collar. Beetles both large and small filled his breast pocket; spiders took residence close to his ears, with their silken threads mingling with his iron-shod hair. An encounter with any one of those bugs would have Liza screaming in dismay. With his concentration squared on Jack and Bill, Mr Gasthem paid the creatures no interest.

'Back to town with you now,' said Mr Gasthem.

'Bill,' called Bill's grandpa, 'heed Mr Gasthem now, go home.'

'You too Ying, and take your bothersome shadow with you,' said Mr Dash.

Yang! With the Village Elder taking his attention, Jack had forgotten about his shadow. Looking toward the bridge, he saw Yang's upper body had slipped over the side. A deep unease settled into the pit of his stomach; he knew his dark twin's intent.

A loud splash turned everyone back to the river where widening rings spread out from beneath the bridge. Realisation hit Grandpa Poulis, Mr Gasthem, Dr Threshum, Crik's only butcher and doctor, and finally the grave keeper Mr Dash, at the same moment. Each mouth formed a large 'O' as Yang pulled one of Mr Hasseltope's dripping legs over the lip of the bridge.

Clothes normally rotted first, and yet the trousers Jack's shadow gripped were, if not for the water pouring through its stitching, in pristine condition.

'Ying, release Mr Hasseltope. Do you want the entire town to see him?'

What did Dr Threshum expected him to do. Despite telling them on numerous occasions that he had no control over Yang, every time his shadow misbehaved, he got the blame.

With anger boiling his blood, he threw up his hands to show them all he had no control over what had happened.

The gutted ruin that was Mr Hasseltope's stomach raised a cry from a few of the girls watching from the hill. In a grisly display, roped intestine bubbled through the shredded black burial shirt, like bloated sausages. Unconcerned with the spectacle he caused, Yang carried on lifting the body, bringing more of the gaping wound into view.

'Damn it boy, throw it back in, we'll retrieve it out of sight of the girls.' Mr Gasthem glowered at Jack; the insects filling his pockets bubbled furiously.

'It's not me,' cried Jack. 'Why doesn't anyone listen to me, I don't control my shadow.'

'If not you, then who?'

The unfairness of the question hit Jack, hard. Unable to find a suitable answer all he could do was keep quiet as Yang threw the drenched body onto the stone at Mr Dash's feet. Feeling faint, Jack noticed a fish caught in an empty eye socket.

Back a few years, when bodies still hung from the branches of the Hanging Tree, Mr Hasseltope took it on himself to tie the noose. He enjoyed it a little too much, Jack's mother always said. Bill's grandparents, who knew Mr Hasseltope the best, said he hanged anyone, whether they deserved to die or not, even children, whispered Grandpa Poulis.

Jack had only seen one man condemned to the tree, a child killer who took kids to his cabin deep in the woods. As a warning, Mr Gasthem left the killer dangling for more than a week. Before the crows came, Jack saw his bulging eyes, and his clenched fists.

Bill had travelled halfway up the hill before Jack noticed. Let them blame him for Yang's behaviour, if they didn't know he was different from his shadow by now, they never would. Wiping away angry tears, he trotted up the path, catching his friend as he reached the hill's crown.

The sight of the body had turned the curiosity of the crowd into disgust. It did not take long for the girls to scamper back around the hill, and the rest followed with hastened footsteps.

'They should've worn black veils,' said Bill, pushing back his glasses with his thumb.

Jack understood his friend's point. Even the hangman deserved to rest in peace. 'We'll light a straw man to guide his spirit.'

Bill nodded.

Despite the sun, they felt cold as they approached the open tomb. With its face hidden within its stone cowl, the statue, holding aloft its rope, welcomed them. The pair shied away from the looming figure as they navigated the broken stone slabs littering the crypt's opening.

Dry dust caught in their throats, making them cough into their hands. A patchwork of cracks on the marble floor, and shards of broken stone, made it awkward for them as they entered. Alcoves lined the walls, welcoming spools of darkness within their recess. The large coffin at the centre crowded the small room.

A GRAVE, MR HASSELTOPE

'Something tore open the door.' Bill blew out his cheeks.

Jack nodded. He had little doubt the Giant had enough power to do that, but what did it want in here. As far as he could tell, the small chamber held nothing bar the coffin and the broken door pieces.

'It smells in here.' Bill's voice echoed as he waved a hand before his face.

It smelled of old cabbage and urine. Doing his best to ignore the foul odour, Jack looked inside the coffin, where his shadow had slipped in unnoticed. Beneath his transparent twin, on a silk pillow, lay the hangman's noose. They buried him with it, he thought with a curious thrill. Beside the noose, a flap of red lining had come away, half hiding the remains of a long dead fox. Looking down at the fur still clinging to the gaping skull turned Jack's stomach. Why a body of a fox laid inside the coffin was anyone's guess. At the foot of the coffin was a piece of white cloth. Mr Hasseltope wore a black burial shirt. Did the torn fabric belong to the Giant? It was here, not down by the river that the Giant had ripped into Mr Hasseltope. Why would the Giant gut him here and then take his body to the river? None of it made any sense.

Hunched over at the far end of the room, Bill waved Jack closer. 'What're these?'

Intrigued, Jack joined his friend and saw a series of small pictures carved into the stonework. The faded lines appeared old. Though crude, the first picture showed a boy standing amongst trees, waving through the stone. A second drawing showed the boy and a second smaller figure. Squinting, he still could not make out what the newcomer was; however, the stance of the boy had changed, reflecting his fear of the smaller shape. A final image revealed the boy as an adult with the little figure perched on his shoulder.

'Wonder what it means?' said Bill, straightening up. 'It looks like a forest sprite with the boy. Why would he fear a sprite?'

Jack had no idea; sprites were annoying, but hardly dangerous. Stepping closer, to inspect the drawings for further detail, he felt the egg inside his pocket give a violent twitch.

4. PUPPETS IN THE DARK

SOMETHING MOVED WITHIN THE EGG. Jack would have dropped it, had he not feared that the outer shell would shatter releasing whatever horror resided within.

The moon cast eerie shadows across his bed. Yang, curling his fingers across the spread, did nothing to alleviate his taught nerves. The shell was hot against his palm. Erratic movement from inside tickled his flesh, raising the hairs along his arms. By cold light, he once more studied his find, curious to see if he could discern any more detail of the shadowy form. An outline at the base of the shell had to be a tail, the shape and length told him that much, though the growths along the tubular body mystified and excited his imagination. Could they be hair, or perhaps feathers? Attempting to answer the riddle, he ran through his meagre knowledge of the local birdlife. Without a doubt, the Raven was the most common bird in Crik. Rooks also took up residence at the graveyard. Neither shared any characteristics with the shape outlined before him. Duck eggs were smaller with darker colouring, and the hawk nested in the loftiest branches far from the ground. Besides, he thought with exasperation, why would the Giant bury a normal bird, it must be something else.

Yang, grown bored with his pantomime, moved closer to the window to peer at the egg. Jack knew Yang wanted to hold it, his shadow had acted more agitated than normal once he got home, even his mother gave a cross word when his shadow danced through the kitchen in Jack's wake.

'You can't hold it,' said Jack, turning his shoulder away from his shadow, 'you'll drop it, and I'm not sure I want to see what lies inside.' Especially tonight, in the day his mother would be up, and others will be about outside his window. One cry and the entire road would be at his doorstep.

Another gentle thump against his hand made his heart hammer. What if it did break through; though small, it could hurt both him and his mother.

Dead eyes watched from the shelves, and for once they did not look at him, the amber and grey stares remained fixed on the egg. Stupid, they are nothing but stuffed fur and feathers, they never watch you, and they definitely have not taken an interest in what's in your hand, he told himself. Yet the feeling refused to leave him, and he didn't relax until he turned his chair to put the stuffed animals to his back. It was only then, with the glow of the moon hitting the shell at a different angle, that he noticed a new silhouette. Appearing like a question mark, he deduced it to be the creature's head.

No larger than a thumb nail it raised over the main mass, swaying toward the edge of the egg before withdrawing. The movement barely registered, the creature moved so slowly. Jack's eyes watered before he dropped his gaze. Flinching, he felt a slight tap on the shell, before his bewilderment had abated two more hits played against his fingertips.

Yang lit a candle. The light flickered at the corner of the desk, illuminating a few metres in a golden nimbus. Glad of the extra light, Jack left it burn, allowing the warm glow to soothe him.

For what purpose had the Giant buried the egg, had it something to do with Grandma Poulis? She was the oldest member of Crik, and stories existed of times past when the wood folk met with people. Many poems and songs recounted tales where a Giant, or a dryad, helped a lost traveller. Other tales told how Giants ate travellers. Yang preferred those. Could it be more than coincidence that the Giant went straight to Grandma Poulis's rosebush?

Through blue drapes, he could see a light burning from the far house, the position of the moon told him the late hour; was Grandma Poulis still awake. It could be nothing more than she wanted to go to the toilet, or read in bed, but the conviction that she knew something about the Giant's visit disquieted him.

Another tap on the shell interrupted his surveillance, this time the pressure managed to make the shell bulge against his skin. Alarmed, he placed the egg on his desk. Pushing back his chair, he watched from arm's length, expecting the shell to break.

The quick moving head thumped the casing that trapped it with more determination. Yang did not attempt to take the egg, preferring to watch from a distance. Jack sighed; at least he had his shadow with him.

A green light spilled from a crack in the egg's exterior, expelling a puff of smoke, which drifted toward the window where it dissipated. The light reminded Jack of swamp gas, though eerier than the light filling the Boswain Bog. Another, larger, crack joined the first, spilling more coloured vapour into his room. Anyone who looked across the road to his house would see him bathed in this sickly hue. He wished someone would see him; whatever lay inside the egg was about to eject itself onto his desk.

Time froze as the eggshell broke away with a sharp crack, granting him the first glimpse of the creature, which lay inside. His immediate conclusion on seeing the scaled beast was that a dragon had hatched. Yet, apart from the tanned scales and the distinct reptilian head, everything else about the Hatchling convinced him that it could not be the fabled winged beast of the old tales. It had two mouths, one beaked, with the second set high on the left cheek, where three teeth bit at the cold air. Protruding golden eyes swivelled to him, catching a moonbeam along its narrow horizontal silver slit. A nose as mismatched as the mouths sucked in air through one huge nostril, while from the other extended a pale green tube that curled almost to its serpentine neck. Along a neck, as long as half its entire length, ran delicate scales. Its body, bloated from eating the sustaining nutrients in the egg, had strange growths along both its back and abdomen. These tube-like protrusions had made the silhouettes seen through the egg. Each autonomous strand filled Jack with loathing; he likened them to poisonous centipedes. Curled around the broken half of the shell, moving in languorous indecency, was the creature's tail. Having no distinguishing feature, other than its ordinariness, the tail appeared to belong more to a rat than some mythic beast.

Jack's chair fell with a clatter to the floor as he bolted away from the creature. Riveted by the beast's first investigations of its surroundings, he failed to see Yang circle closer to the desk. His shadow took a stand beside the desk, his form flickering wildly with the spluttering candle. It seemed Yang reached for the Hatchling, instead the insubstantial fingers entwined, and after some wriggling, Yang made a perfect replica of the beast. Yang's fingers became the tubes along the creature's back and his thumbs formed the beaked head.

Mesmerised by its double, the Hatchling took its first steps away from the egg. The green light, almost gone by this time, flared up once more, dousing the candle before disappearing.

Yang moved to the right, and the creature followed. The golden eyes drank in the moonlight. When Yang wriggled his fingers the tubes along the Hatchling's back perfectly mimicked the movement.

Why was his shadow so bold as to communicate with the thing? Many times Yang did things that baffled Jack. Yang teased Liza horrendously, yet last year when she had lost her cat Yang had comforted her. Bemused by the contrary aspects of his shadow, could not prepare Jack for tonight. He had always known the limits of Yang's actions, for in a sense they were his own. So how, without his own knowledge, could Yang instinctively know how to communicate?

Yang did not stop there; contorting his hands, he formed a small bipedal creature, much like a tiny man, with a long looping tail. For a long moment, the Hatchling stared at the new shape Yang had created, moving its head from one side to the other. Then the tubes along its back flattened against its scales.

Dumbstruck, Jack whimpered as the mysterious creature began to twist and shake. Ripping and popping sounds filled the silence, as four legs became two; the spine straightened, allowing it to stand erect. Its tail thickened like a long leach bloated with blood. Losing two mouths, the creature's face elongated into a fearsome muzzle. The long neck had halved its length and the tanned scales gave way to yellow skin. Large golden eyes stared at him.

'What did you do Yang?' Jack whispered.

5. HOP, SKIP AND JUMP

THE SMALL ROOM CLOSED IN around Jack as the Hatchling stepped up to the edge of the desk. Its new mouth, now filled with rows of pointed teeth, smiled at him across the gap. Ceasing his attempts to communicate with the creature Yang stood back, looking forlorn at having lost the creature's attention.

Only his fear of his mother rushing into the room and seeing the monster for herself stopped Jack from screaming. In despair, he scooted up his bed, dragging his woollen blanket into a ball beneath him.

With its back toward the window, the Hatchling, in near perfect darkness, almost vanished; would have if its eyes didn't glow. A moment lingered in which the two disembodied orbs held Jack. Taught nerves thrummed through him like clashing cymbals. Paralysed with fear, he looked to Yang for help; his shadow remained apart, as watchful as the Hatchling on the desk. Slipping from behind a cloud the moon highlighted the Hatchling in silhouette, altering its long ears into horns. Jack had no idea whether a trick of light fabricated the illusion, or if the Hatchling had once more transformed. Its fingers took on the appearance of five cruel knives.

Why couldn't have Yang created a rabbit with his fingers instead of this monstrosity? Even if he had, Jack had to admit the same feeling of loathing, wriggling in his guts, would remain, his fear of the Hatchling was more than skin deep.

Tired of the stalemate, Yang reached out to grab the creature. With a disgruntled grunt, the Hatchling dove off the desk to the dark floor, evading Jack's shadow.

Jack heard its running feet on the carpeted floor. It ran from the bed, not toward him as he expected. A large catapult he had made from wood and twine crashed to the floor, scattering a group of toy soldiers in its wake. Thankfully, he had closed his bedroom door before bringing the egg out; the last thing he wanted was for his mother to catch him. If it escaped outside it could hurt her. Alarmed, he moved to the edge of the mattress, determined to stop it. Anticipating the creature to head toward the door, he gasped when the noise came from another quarter. Looking high he listened to the sharp cracks punctuate the dark as the creature climbed up the wall.

CRIK

His mother always said if you gave fear a shovel it would keep digging. Fear sank deep into him as the demon scuttled up the white stone. He wanted to move, but where could he go? The room offered no protection, and to get to the landing meant he would have to pass the Hatchling, something that filled him with dread. Drawn away from the window by the climbing creature, Yang had first grown indistinct and then disappeared in the dark. Robbed of his only help, Jack grew more nervous, imagining the little demon attacking him from every side.

Snick. Snick. The fingers gripping the mortar were loud, crunching the stone and sending piles of dust to the floor. In many ways, the soft sound of the falling dust disturbed him more than anything else. Perhaps knowing his mother would have to clean up the crumbs of broken stone made the nightmare more real.

With the creature climbing toward him, Jack decided to move from the bed. Stopping beside Yang's collection of grinning animals he listened to the Hatchling make its way across the wall. Along with his fascination with stuffed animals, Yang also managed to discover gruesome artefacts amongst the hedgerows. Stumbling blindly into the corner Jack laid hands an old battered sword. Lifting the weapon, he doubted the sword's edge would cut paper, yet its weight gave him some much needed courage.

Away from the light, the demon's shining eyes had winked out, and it took time for Jack's vision to accustom itself to the gloom. Casting about he noticed against the pale wall a dark smudge outlining the creature. Leading with the rusted blade, he closed the distance, wanting to confront the beast before it dropped back to the floor, where it would be much harder to track. Not for the first time he found himself wishing he had left the rosebush alone.

'What are you?' His voice came out as a throaty growl.

The Hatchling turned its head in the dark to observe him. 'You understand me, don't you,' said Jack.

Perhaps the stillness that came over the creature as he talked convinced him of the Hatchling's understanding, or the beast's arrival had awakened a feeling lodged deep inside. This latter speculation disturbed him, how would he have some buried connection with the Hatchling, he had never seen anything like it before. The memory of Yang's communication for a second time raised the hairs on the back of his neck. What did his shadow know?

With the Hatchling now motionless, watching him, he found himself at a loss of what to say or do. Grasping the sword, he wondered what good it would do him. He had only ever fenced with Yang, and his shadow always disarmed him with little effort, he had little hope of fending off an assault.

If the Hatchling could understand him, perhaps he would be able to reason with it. Without any other course of action coming to mind he said, 'I mean you

HOP, SKIP AND JUMP

no harm.' Feeling foolish he continued, 'I'm Jack, I brought you here today. You were under the rosebush at the end of the street.'

A change came over the Hatchling, a slight turn of the head toward the window.

'I don't know why you're here. If you want food, I have a couple of biscuits by the bed. Their old and a little hard, but they should taste alright.'

The creature refused to shift its gaze from the window. Jack knew the Hatchling peered out at Grandma Poulis's garden. What was so important about the rosebush? He should have told Bill, the Giant had left the egg outside his home; if he had, he would have someone else with him.

With a quick spring, the Hatchling launched itself from the wall, hitting the desk. Its tail wrapped itself around the back of the chair as it steadied its feet on the wooden top. Amazed at the distance the creature had jumped, Jack could only stare, mouth agape. It cleared the bed with no effort, and he felt sure it could have jumped a lot farther if it were not for the pane of glass now reflecting its hideous demon face.

The talons, still dusted with mortar, tapped the glass, cutting shallow cuts down its length. A wash of moonlight returned, and with it the glow in the Hatchling's eyes and, Yang, who, on his return, rushed the Hatchling. With a sharp intake of breath, the Hatchling dove forward to evade Yang's grasp, breaking the glass in a tinkling shower.

Jack rushed forward, banging his shin on his bed in his haste. Leaning over his desk, he peered out. It lay on the grass with its leg twisted at an awkward angle. Shards of broken glass winked up at him from around the sprawled figure. A mewling cry from below reached his ears, then the Hatchling pushed itself from the ground on shaky arms.

Hoping his mother had not heard the window breaking he went to his bedroom door, releasing the lock. Peering cautiously out, he saw no light and no sign of movement coming from the first floor. Careful of the worn wood that creaked, especially at night when he needed silence, he tiptoed out. Sneaking along the small landing, he gratefully reached the carpeted passage at the foot of the stair. Pausing outside his mother's door, he sighed with relief when he heard her gentle snores.

Picking his way to the front of the dark house, careful not to bang into the furniture his mother had rearranged again that day, he met the door. Passing into the cold night air he saw the garden gate swinging on its worn hinges. Still gripping the sword, he crept toward the street, ignoring the vacant imprint left on the lawn.

The houses along both streets were dark. It seemed no one had heard the commotion. Perturbed that so much noise had not alerted anyone to his misadventure, he followed in the wake of the limping demon.

CRIK

Keeping to the shadows the Hatchling hugged the row of fences, only pausing long enough to glance back at Jack. Its little body, only three feet tall, became increasingly difficult to follow, but Jack knew its target and set off at a brisk trot to reach Grandma Poulis's roses first. The demon realising Jack's intent increased its own pace, its limp now becoming more of a hopping run as it navigated Mr Space's overgrown garden.

After every fourth or fifth jump, the Hatchling turned its misshapen head to see how much distance Jack had caught up. Once it shook a fist in the air and jabbered madly before abandoning the gardens for the cobbled street.

Taking heart that the fall had managed to injure the creature Jack closed the distance, but saw the Hatchling would reach the rosebush before him. With sweat coating his body and greasing his hair he tried to find more speed, but was unable to close the gap.

The large flowers loomed pale against the laced branches. Taking a final backward glance, the Hatchling threw itself into the bush, breaking off a few low roses. Jack arrived as the last of the petals alighted on the floor. With squint eyes, he scrutinised the darkness amongst the branches, but saw no hint of the creature lurking within. Stabbing the dark pockets in frustration only made him more anxious. Yang made no effort to help; he stayed back where the moonlight remained strong. Yang's form, more solid and distinct than at any other time that night, allowed him to create a sword that mirrored the one Jack possessed.

Remembering the light in Grandma Poulis's window Jack stared up; it seemed like everyone else in the village she had gone to sleep. Part of him wanted to shout a warning, to let others know of the Hatchling. That however would mean letting others know about the Giant, and if his mother knew what had come into town she would never allow him to leave the house again. The memory of those long rain swept days was too fresh to ignore. Besides, how could he tell Grandma Poulis that he had dug through her prized garden, she would skin him alive.

A rustle of leaves betrayed the location of the demon. It remained close to the front, much closer to him than Jack guessed. No wonder his stabbing sword never came close to hitting the beast. Black lips, pulling back from razor teeth, smiled up at him from beneath two red rosebuds. Time froze as they locked eyes; Jack's wide and fearful, the demon's narrow and cunning. What the Hatchling did then amazed Jack; it stuck a forked tongue out between its deadly rows of teeth, wagging it at him like a petulant child. Perhaps he should not have been that surprised, after all, the creature was not yet an hour old, but seeing such childish actions from another creature bewildered him completely. Before he had time to react, the Hatchling pulled back into the bush. A series of snaps and cracks followed as it drove through the dense foliage to the other side, where, discovering an open downstairs window, it entered the house.

6. SOMEWHERE WARM

HE NEVER EXPECTED to find a mess, but as Jack entered the window, the clutter at his feet almost sent him crashing to the floor. The room's confusion heightened his tension; only when his hands fell atop a curled head did he remember the dolls Bill's grandmother collected. Like a silent troop, the dolls, whether sporting summer hats, lacy frills, or holding closed umbrellas, watched him through unblinking glass eyes. Preferring Yang's collection of dead squirrels, he moved among the stacks of toys, careful not to snag the flared dresses with the sword. His infrequent visits to Bill's house did not prepare him to navigate in the deep gloom. Each doll, being of a similar height to the Hatchling, sent his heart racing at every silhouette. Once, he almost swung his blade at one holding a sweeping broom, mistaking the miniature household item as the demon's tail. Venturing deeper into the room, he had less light, and Yang grew faint, until finally his twin disappeared.

With nothing but touch and hearing to guide him, he passed the last of the dolls, hoping no one would hear him tread the wooden floor. Using the dark shapes, he drew a vague picture of his surroundings. To his right, still smelling of a cooked roast, was the kitchen; to his other side loomed the stairs. Knowing he had less chance of Bill's grandparents discovering him down here had him move toward the kitchen. Would the smells wafting throughout the house, awaken the Hatchling's hunger? Not liking the idea of the Hatchling feeling hungry, he nevertheless entered the wide room.

The kitchen, both larger and more ordered than was his own, had storage shelves for a myriad of frying pans and pots. Wooden cabinets fit the far wall, and a large marble-topped worktable sat at the centre of the beech floor. Overhead more pans hung from hooks, together with a set of three deadly looking cleavers. He deliberated taking a cleaver instead of the sword; despite the cleaver's advantage of a smaller size, he decided to keep hold of the sword. Having a fighting man's weapon gave him all the false courage he needed to carry on with his search.

Sweat dripped from him. He could not believe his daring in entering the house, if Grandma Poulis discovered him the Hatchling would be the least of his worries. Unlike Bill's grandfather, who always used his Talent to transform himself into a boy, Grandma Poulis kept her Talent hidden, creating wild

CRIK

conjecture amongst Jack and the other children of what it was. To his continued annoyance, Bill refused to relinquish her secret. As far as he knew, Bill was the only member of Crik without a unique Talent. Perhaps that was why his friend read so many books. It couldn't be much fun having Liza Manfry call you a freak every chance she got.

A shape residing in the corner of the kitchen moved. Jack seeing the circumspect shift of weight reluctantly moved toward it, holding the blunt-edged sword high, ready to drive its point into the Hatchling's stomach. When he was no more than a few feet away, he recognised a familiar tail. Relaxing his arm he grinned as Wolf moved in his sleep. He had forgotten about the old dog. Careful not to wake him he tiptoed back to the workbench.

The Hatchling was not in here, unless it hid in the cupboards amongst the pots and pans. His breath faltered as he cast his eye back from where he had come. It would have been too easy if he found it downstairs. Shaking his head, he retraced his steps back to the passage and the pregnant stairs.

The stairs became a mountain face; its steps leading to the dark summit felt as treacherous underfoot as scree-filled slopes, which at any moment could creak, bringing Bill's grandparents down on him. Wishing for a carpet to mask his steps, but instead finding varnished wood, he mounted the first step. Snatching the banister, he clung to the woven wood with tenacious strength. Wooden flowers spiralled up his own staircase, whereas roping vines and small intricate shaped leaves stretched to meet his fingers here. Creeping vines wrapped the entire banister length in loping python coils. Nothing about the aesthetics soothed him, the hardness, and sharp angles, only heightened his tension. Pictures presented themselves as dark squares along the wall. He recalled one of the paintings had red puddles that gradually grew into a lake. Rain swept the scene, rippling the lake's surface in hundreds of small circles. Bill named the painting as "The Blood Storm". Why anyone would want such an image in their home had eluded Jack then and now.

He almost reached the landing when a blue glow filled the house, throwing warped outlines across his path from stationary furniture. Yang spawned across the wall, anchored to Jack's feet. Frantic, Jack caught his shadow's attention and demanded Yang to his side before anyone saw them.

A door, standing ajar down the hallway, allowed the blue light to invade the darkness. The location of the room at the front of the house identified it as the same one Jack had spied illuminated earlier from behind drawn curtains. Bill's room looked over the trees at the back of the house. Ignoring the shot of adrenaline surging through his limbs, he refused to bolt, knowing he couldn't leave while the Hatchling remained in the house.

The door opened on well-oiled hinges.

Vaporous material escaped the room; each thread floating on the air as though cast forward by a sudden gust. It took him a moment to realise light did not shine through the diaphanous garment from some unseen source, but from

SOMEWHERE WARM

within. When more of the coloured cloth floated into the landing, he pressed his cheek against the uppermost wooden vine, knowing that he only had a remote chance of remaining hidden.

A form, brighter than the glowing garment, strode into the doorframe. Recognising Grandma Poulis did not lessen the shock. Her face, smoothed of the ravages of age and worry, became beautiful; heightened cheekbones framed almond shaped eyes, not the dark circles he knew. A full mouth, turned at the corner in a perpetual smile, promised love, laughter, and sorrow in equal measure. Hair, free of its accustomed tight bun, spun down her shoulders in a shower of gold. She glided into the landing, her feet hidden beneath folds of shifting light.

A Ghost Walker. Hard to accept that any still lived after the Cleansing, but he had heard enough stories to recognise one when he saw it. Many women possessed by a woodland spirit had died at the Hanging Tree. That one should still live in the village right under his nose filled him with horror. Seeing how beautiful Grandma Poulis had become discredited the tales of Ghost Walkers consorting with Boguls and Wretches. Then memories of the Giant going straight to her rosebush surfaced. Had the Giant come to visit the Ghost Walker? Why else had it come into the village? Stories told how when the spirit wandered, the body died, and would only awaken once the spirit returned.

Despite his misgivings, the young girl enchanted him. Love for Grandma Poulis spread through him, making him lightheaded. Relaxing his grip on the wood, he felt himself sway forward. No, he couldn't let her see him. If she found him, the Hatchling would escape, or more horrible, attack Grandma Poulis. Yang slipped onto the verge of the landing, his form bold in the dazzling light, leaving Jack to pray his wayward shade would not betray their presence.

The Ghost Walker had not noticed them; in fact, her eyes never left the door at the far end of the hallway. Driven by some invisible force, she effortlessly glided across the wooden floor. Without pause, she passed both Jack and Yang.

As the blue light enveloped him, Jack felt his love deepen for her. He wanted to stand up and go to the Ghost Walker. Tears dropped from his eyes as his hand lifted toward her. Never had he experienced a love so pure, it filled his body with warmth.

Mesmerized by her, he failed to notice Bill's door standing open with the Hatchling peering out, its eyes ablaze in the Ghost Walker's glow. The creature had its tail wrapped about its potbelly, ignoring the Ghost Walker as she reached the door at the far end of the landing.

The door opened without Grandma Poulis reaching for the handle. Aided by her radiance the room sprang into immediate life, revealing an old stool set before a half finished painting. Taking her seat, she began to paint figures on the branches of a golden tree. White light shone upward from the figures to create the drifting clouds.

CRIK

Perturbed by the painting, Jack turned and spotted the Hatchling watching him from Bill's room. He flinched. It was larger, the ears more pointed than he remembered, and the rows of teeth keener to his critical eye. Now the sword no longer felt adequate. The blade had a good weight, but he had no skill with the weapon, if he got into a fight with the creature, those talons, stroking its tail, would rip him to shreds.

The Hatchling, sensing Jack's reluctance to follow, stuck its forked tongue out, taunting him, before disappearing into Bill's room.

Hot anger drove away the warmth imparted by the Ghost Walker. He should have destroyed the egg, he had another chance to kill the creature when Yang communicated with it, and this was how it repaid his mercy? Grinding his teeth, he rose from his haunches, when the task of crossing the landing unseen brought him to an immediate halt.

Grandma Poulis put green bristle to paper. Could he risk crossing? A few seconds would carry him into Bill's room. Finally, knowing his friend was alone with the beast, spurred him from the safety of the stairs. His fleeting glance at the woman at the easel assured him that she had no idea of his trespass.

Enough blue light entered the bedroom for him to avoid the furniture, and Bill's clothes strewn across the floor. A round mat softened his steps as he moved closer to the bed, where Bill snored, oblivious of the two intruders in his room. Branches scraped the window, playing his nerves like a master harpist. Unable to see the Hatchling, he nevertheless heard the demon banging into a cabinet, before careering into a tall bookcase, filled with the leather-bound books. The noise drew him deeper into the room.

Resting his free hand on a carved toad on the bedpost, he waited for the Hatchling to betray its location. His friend's snores frustrated him by masking the demon's whereabouts. Yang, spread across the lighter wall, pointed with a hurried hand at the windowsill. Jack followed his shadow's finger and saw the Hatchling perched on the ledge.

'Come here,' he hissed through gritted teeth. Pulling his hands to his chest, he tried to coax the Hatchling away from the window. If the demon again tried to escape by crashing through the glass, not only would it wake Bill, but the Ghost Walker would also find him.

The demon tilted its head in amusement; much like a grown man humouring a child's tantrum, halting Jack's gesture. If he had some sweets, he would offer them to the demon, though he imagined he would have better success with red meat. Pushing his hands into his pockets, he felt around. All he found was some loose thread pulled into a bundle from the seams of his pants.

Noticing his hesitation, the Hatchling leapt from the windowsill to land on the pillow beside Bill.

Aghast, Jack could only stretch his arm out in silent reproach. The sword, proving more useless by the second, hung forgotten at his side as the demon stroked black talons through Bill's hair.

SOMEWHERE WARM

Opening his mouth, Bill snored loudly. Inexplicably the demon threw its head into the open cavity, bringing a surprised grunt from Bill, and a silent scream from Jack. Remarkably, Bill's eyes remained closed. Diving forward, Jack grabbed the Hatchling's tail, its slippery feel bringing to mind one of Mr Gasthem's blind Milk Worms. Wrestling with the beast, he planted his feet on the mattress ready to yank back with all his strength. Instead of coming out, the demon sank deeper into Bill's mouth. In moments, it had an arm and a shoulder nestled between incisor and molar. Yang, watching from the wall, refused to help. Sending a silent plea filled glance for his shadow to assist him accomplished nothing. Scared of alerting Grandma Poulis, he remained silent, but cast reproachful looks at his immobile twin. How could Bill sleep through this? Fretting over the question, he tugged on the tail once more, shifting the mattress beneath his feet. The creature's chest now flowed into Bill, the ribs snapping and cracking as it fought its way through the wide open lips. With mounting desperation, Jack coiled the tail about his wrist; gaining better anchorage, he arched back in greater effort to get the beast off his friend. It stopped at the midsection, unable to creep any farther down Bill's throat. Elated at his small success, Jack doubled his efforts, grinning with triumph as a snapped rib slipped back into view. Locking his jaw, he prepared to keep pulling until the rest of the Hatchling emerged; then the tail disappeared from his grasp.

He wanted to yell in frustration. The Hatchling had changed its shape.

He tried to grab the flailing feet that beat against his friend's chin, only when he got a hold, they turned into flippers and vanished into the darkness.

Dismayed, he fell back in a huddle, panting from his exertion. Lying in a heap, he heard a croaking laugh, buried deep in his friend's throat.

CRIK

7. A FAMILIAR STRANGER

HIS MOTHER STOOD with her hands on her hips, looking through the broken window. 'Tell me again how this happened?'

Jack tried to remember the lie he had told to cover up the events of the previous night, however, all he could think of was Bill swallowing the Hatchling. 'I fenced with Yang, who ducked my blow,' he said, cringing as his mother's face darkened.

'I told you not to go playing with those weapons, didn't I Jack.'

Jack gave a nod. His mother turned her back on him to finish lining his window frame with seeds from her apron pocket. After counting out twenty, she stood back, and the seeds burst. The stems shot up, blotting out the morning light. The entwining plants filled the entire window.

'Go down to the garden and pick up the glass,' she said. 'You as well Yang, you're as much to blame as my son.'

With a hung head, Jack left his room; he had never seen his mother so angry. He knew, for the next few days, the plants would act as his prison bars.

'Use gloves.' His mother's shout followed him down the stairs. 'You'll find them on the hook on the backdoor.'

At least she bought his lie. If she knew the truth, she would not be so lenient.

He had feared the demon would kill Bill; suffocate him, or worse. Listening to his friend snore deep into the night, he had expected something to happen. Only nothing had. Whatever the Hatchling was doing, it did not want to kill Bill. Jack had hunkered in the dark, waiting for the Ghost Walker to breathe life back into Grandma Poulis. His mind had raced with fears. A Ghost Walker was a woman possessed by a demon. All the stories agreed; a wood demon stole a woman's soul, leaving her dead body each night in her bed. Was that what had happened to Bill? He never heard of a demon possessing a boy. It was close to dawn when Grandma Poulis at last put down her paintbrush. Blue light slipped through the gap under the door touching him; overcome with calm, he had, for the first time since taking the egg, felt at ease. The tales must be wrong; how could someone so wonderful do him harm. Although fearing discovery, he did not fear her. Then, if not a wood demon, what had slipped into Bill? Plagued by doubts he had crept down the stairs and back through the room with the dolls.

A FAMILIAR STRANGER

Now, with the sun shining, he wanted to discard everything he had experienced; the Hatchling, the chase to the Poulis house, the Ghost Walker; all of it. Only, how could he? The Hatchling was inside his best friend.

The village awoke like any other morning, innocent to the events that had unfolded a few hours ago. Miss Mistletoe's cat prowled, holding her tail stiff in the air. Beyond the cat, he spied a few children playing along a beaten track. The Belson twins, having transformed themselves into Grints, chased them. Malcolm wore the lidless eyes and the sharp beak of the night hunter, while Graham waddled around on green mottled legs. Everyone just accepted the twins' sharing of their Talent. Squealing, Tracey Hulme launched herself into the air, hovering just beyond Malcolm's grasping fingers. Beth, Tracey's younger sister, sent blue and red lights into the beaked face, making the boys take after her. She sped down the lane in the direction of the river.

Although the good weather continued, with hardly a cloud to spoil the sky, and the scent of fresh cut grass lingered in the air, Jack could not assuage his foreboding. He spotted Grandma Poulis in her kitchen. Once more age masked her face. Her beautiful golden hair that had spun down her back now fell across her face in a grey web. His longing for her had departed leaving him bereft, as though he had given up a long cherished secret. Silently he wanted Grandpa Poulis to take Wolf for a walk, to show him that everything was normal. Only now, nothing was the same. If he saw the old man, his actions would appear false, an act to deflect any interest in his family. Until he saw Bill, he could not relax.

Nervous sweat greased his palms, making him want to discard the gloves that clung uncomfortably to his skin. When his shoes met the glass shards, he stopped. Anxious, he looked around; positive someone would come and ask about the shallow impression left in the mud. Each bent grass and bruised area of dirt, revealed in stark relief where the Hatchling had landed. Ignoring the glass, he kicked away the tell-tale signs of the demon, first with the toe of his shoe, and then the heel. Hurriedly he obliterated the imprint left by a clawed hand. Stepping back, he noticed, with rising disgust, where the demon had dragged its twisted leg through the grass.

Yang stood off to one side, snatching a fly from the air. Jack neither expected, nor wanted, his shadow's help. In Bill's room, when he needed him the most, Yang refused to move; together they might have pulled off the creature. Many of Yang's recent actions frightened him. How had Yang communicated with the Hatchling? Why had Yang done nothing to help Bill? Although his shadow acted by its own accord, usually against his wishes, he had put that down to a mischievous nature. Last night his shadow went down an unexpected path, and since then he eyed Yang with suspicion.

The sun, glinting off the stacked glass, speared into his eyes. Grimacing, he raised his hand to shield his face. His mind turned reflectively inward. Had the

CRIK

Giant known Grandma Poulis's secret? Why else would it leave the egg at her doorstep? More kids ran hooting and hollering down the street. Tired to the bone he only glanced at them. Hoping to spy Grandma Poulis, wanting to recapture the feeling of ease her light had instilled in him the night before, he looked at Bill's house. The empty kitchen window stared back. Doesn't matter, he thought surly, during the day she was only the old woman who shouted at him for playing ball too close to her house. He ached for that blue light, and part of him hated Bill's grandmother for not sharing it with him.

Disgust, at his own need for comfort, made him turn away from the house. Peeking, beyond the side of his home, he saw strange drooping branches. Forgetting the glass, he drew closer to discover a strange tree growing where none had ever grown. At odds with the tree's grey trunk, which stretched up to the roof, were riotous coloured broad leaves. He ran across the garden. Fine hair, ruffled by the passing wind, covered the trunk. Curious, he discarded his gloves and felt the wood warm to his touch. His mother had grown the strange plant she had discovered; she must have planted it here when it outgrew the kitchen. Walking around the tree, he heard a baby cry. Startled, he pressed his ear to the wood, only to jump back in stunned amazement when he began to sink into the soft down. Yang sprang forward, disappearing inside the trunk. Wondering whether a hole existed within the tree, Jack pushed his hand against the wood, to feel it give under the pressure.

Wind passed through his fingertips making him tug back his hand. Shivered like a wet dog, he stumbled back, his legs feeling like hit wickets. He went around the corner of his home, eager to lose sight of the strange tree. Yang stood in front of him, waving, and then the gate crashed against its jam, making Jack jump. Turning he saw Bill with a flushed face at the end of the garden. A jolt of fear swept through him; what had the demon done?

'You'll never guess what happened!' Bill's chest heaved from running down the road.

The hair on the back of Jack's neck stood on end. Did Bill know about the Hatchling? His friend showed no real sign of distress.

'I'm no longer a freak.' Gasping, Bill fell to his knees.

Such a declaration put Jack further on the back foot; what was this all about?

Out of breath, Bill struggled to get out his words. 'I woke as normal. Tired, but not feeling any different.' Every fibre in Jack screamed for Bill to end the suspense. Had the demon hurt him? 'Then I went downstairs,' continued Bill, oblivious to Jack's concern. 'Grandma had flour up to her elbows, beating out pastry for a pie. Wolf was busy sniffing Grandpa's muddy shoes.' Bill's eyes widened with excitement. 'That's when I felt it.'

'Felt what?' asked Jack, his unease a palpable knot in his throat.

'It's hard to explain, my head began to buzz; and then I heard a snap in my ear.'

Jack gripped Bill by the shoulder. 'What snap?' The Demon must have hurt him, though he saw no outward sign.

'I don't know,' said Bill, 'just a snap. Spotting Wolf I knew I could make him do things.'

'What do you mean, make him do things?'

'Things,' said Bill, waving his arms. 'I called Wolf to me. That old dog won't come on command, not even to Grandpa, so I almost cried when he came over. My grandparents only noticed when I had Wolf stand on his hind legs. You should've seen ol' Wolf standing like a man.' He laughed. 'Grandpa saw him first, dropping his half-filled pipe amongst his tobacco. Grandma turned around to tell him off for messing up the table top when she saw me shaking Wolf's front paw. Grandpa shot up from the table to shake my hand. If not for Grandma, Wolf would still be walking on his hind legs. She was concerned with his age.'

Yang, having taken the shape of Grandpa Poulis, clapped Bill's back, knocking off the blue cap that had sat askance on his head.

Too often, Bill, without a Talent, had felt an outsider, but now that Bill had found his, Jack became disquieted. He tried to force a smile, only for his lips to quiver, betraying his uncertainty.

Bill, having spotted Miss Mistletoe's cat, Gesma, scratching the white fence bordering the garden, failed to notice Jack's reaction. Settling down with his back to Jack, Bill beckoned the black feline away from her rubbing post. Any other day the cat would have given Bill a long disdainful stare and then shot up a tree. This time when Bill hooked his finger, she came running, her tail straight up in the air. With a pounce, the cat sprang onto the offered arm and coiled herself around his shoulders. Peering behind Bill, she blinked at Jack.

Turning, Bill smiled. 'What should I make her do? Something special, I want to test myself.'

Troubled by the morning's turn of events, Jack could think of nothing. Who commanded the animal, his friend, or the demon? Preoccupied by the conundrum he absently watched Bill direct the cat from his shoulder.

'There's one more thing,' said Bill closing his eyes.

'What are you doing?'

'When I close my eyes and concentrate I can see through the eyes of the animal.'

'What do you see?' asked Jack, intrigued despite his foreboding.

'Everything that we can,' answered Bill, 'only in black and white.'

The long grass rose to Gesma's face, her emerald eyes rapt on Bill. Twisting her lithe body, the cat flipped backward, clearing the grass to land on her feet in one smooth motion. Bill clapped his hands in delight. Without pause, she jumped from left to right. When Gesma performed her third flip, Bill stood, looking about with an expectant eye. Scratching his hair, he wondered how best

CRIK

to show off his Talent. Disappointment clouded his face as he discarded one idea after the next. Then he spotted his target walking down the street, wearing a yellow blouse and green skirt. Liza Manfry, ignorant of Bill's interest, wandered down the road, her nose stuck in the air. A crooked grin passed over Bill's face as he turned to Jack, a "watch this" expression if ever Jack had seen one.

Waiting patiently on the grass, purred Gesma, her flanks flexing from the earlier workout. 'Gesma, give Liza a kiss,' laughed Bill. The cat, with her tail swishing behind her, sprang through the fence. In moments a horrified scream shattered the peace of the village, as Gesma, clinging to Liza's yellow blouse, licked the girl's face. It took a loud sneeze to stop Liza from screaming. Another two violent sneezes doubled her over. Either the violent sneezes spooked the cat, or Bill, no longer able to see through his tears, ended the connection between them. Bill and Yang both laughed while Gesma rushed off to her favourite tree, and Liza, still sneezing and blotting her weeping eyes, ran for home.

'This is incredible,' said Bill, pumping his fists in the air. 'We should go to the woods. I wonder what animal I can find. There are wolves in the wood! Imagine that Ying, a real wolf, not an old dog pretending to be one.'

Looking back at the plants hiding his room, Jack shook his head. 'I can't, I broke my window. I'm grounded.'

Bill, picking up his cap, hit him with it. 'Don't wimp out on me Ying. It's not everyday you discover your Talent. You know the woods better than I do; by myself I'd soon lose my way. Come on,' he pleaded, 'imagine the look on everyone's face when I come back to town riding on the back of a wolf!'

Knowing the Hatchling still lay inside Bill; Jack could not let him go off alone. Who knew what the beast would do to him in the woods. He could not protect Bill from his bedroom. Having already tested his mother's temper, he hated going against her wishes; she would lock him up and throw away the key. Checking the house, to make sure his mother did not watch from the kitchen, he gave a quick nod.

'Good, come on, before you're spotted,' said Bill, turning and running for the gate.

Yang stretched toward the road, impatient as Bill to get away. Jack started to follow, when he noticed Bill's footsteps had impressed themselves over the Hatchling's from the previous night, mingling to form a hybrid of the two. Elongating the rounded edge of Bill's shoes were three claws.

8. AMONGST THE TREES

GRANDPA POULIS HAD told Jack that no one knew Crik Village's age, neither in writing nor in memory. The houses held no clue, they had new walls, and the old well was the third to reside within the graveyard. Certain graves gave some insight, with the oldest belonging to the old mayor's son, Strident Castly. His epitaph, immortalised in blackened stone, lay un-mourned for two hundred years.

The wood, surrounding the village, was much older. Harsh seasons had bowed trees, transforming them into grim sculptures to haunt secluded paths. Great roots, burrowing deep underground, like huge wooden worms, churned the earth and broke stone. These aged bastions gave home to the long eared rabbit, sheltering amongst the dark and moist roots, the squirrel ran along its branching paths, and the snake lay in wait to put an end to the scampering feet. Fat staring owls, and cruel crows, watched from hidden perches. Crooked shadows, stretched and skewed, crawled across the leaf-strewn floor, darkening every dell and hill. Gurgling brooks, tumbling over round stones, spread through the wood like arterial blood.

At one time, the wood stretched farther than now, its green and brown swathe ending where the land met the sea. The earliest name man gave to the wood is still spoken of in legend. No one realises that Criklow Wood remains the same dark forest where trees snatched girls and heroes fought scaled demons. Earliest man named the wood Illyarden Forest, a name still whispered in stories. If Grandpa Poulis knew that Criklow was Illyarden, he would forbid Bill from entering the woods. Everyone remembers the cursed name of Illyarden.

The boys rushed into the wood, eager to get beneath the trees to escape prying eyes. They ran to a stop, both panting. Bill sat down, sweat trickling down his broad face. Standing over him, Jack had his breathing under enough control to look around. The tight packed trees darkened the morning to evening, with a few scattered rays of sunlight sprinkling the ground. A small shrew nuzzled at the undergrowth a few paces away, Jack didn't mention it to Bill, afraid his friend would have the critter do somersaults or some such. Being in the woods made Yang happy, despite the poor light, his shadow expanded itself to twice its size, twisting behind every tree and rock. Jack became fond of

CRIK

Criklow Wood, no matter how hard Yang tried; here, his shadow could not get him into trouble.

'Your mother is going to kill you,' said Bill, with little sympathy.

'I know.' The glass from the garden had managed to cut through the discarded gloves to nick his finger. Smearing the drop of blood between his fingertips, made him wish his mother would leave the pile of broken glass where he had left them. 'I shouldn't have come.'

A disdainful look passed over Bill's face. 'You are kidding, right? Sure you're going to get it bad when you go home,' he said getting to his feet, 'but your mother doesn't hold grudges for long. As soon as Grandma hears I talked you into coming with me, I'll get it worst. Wait and see if I don't.'

Jack recognised the truth in Bill's words, and for the first time that morning, he gave his best friend a genuine smile. 'Come on, let's find your wolf.'

This close to the village both knew every gnarled piece of wood, each moss covered rock, and stand of nettles. The remains of an old fort, they had built four years earlier, still stood a dozen paces into the thicket. By craning their necks, the boards crossing the branches came into view.

A small stream cut across their path; a few days earlier rainwater had swelled the water to a torrent, leaving blackened debris along its shore. The murky water brought back images of Mr Hasseltope in the Tristle River. They stepped over the stream, having to go single file to pass the encroaching trees. A small twig snagged Jack's shirt, tearing a small hole in the white fabric. Bill, hating tight places, cursed, muttering all the way through to the small clearing beyond the line of trees.

'When you made Gesma kiss Liza,' said Jack, 'did you talk to the cat, like Mr Gasthem does with his bugs?'

Looking thoughtful, Bill shook his head. 'No, at least I couldn't understand them, I guess they must understand me, otherwise how would they know what I want them to do?'

'You don't speak,' said Jack, 'with Gesma you flicked your hand and she did a somersault.'

'I pictured what I wanted her to do in my mind, and she did it. Perhaps I'll discover more about my Talent with practice. After all, I've only tried it twice.' He paused to brush clinging burs from his jacket; then his expression became sombre. 'Grandpa knew someone who controlled animals. Hardly lifted a finger and any animal he saw did whole sorts of tricks.' Bill, wringing his hands, looked at Jack. 'I don't know if I like that Ying. Sometimes, when I get mad, and sometimes when I'm not, I think bad thoughts,' he confided. 'When Dwayne stares at me with his round eyes I want to give him a bloody nose.' He threw his hands up. 'I get angry. What if something picks up on my mood and attacks him - something larger than Miss Mistletoe's cat.'

AMONGST THE TREES

Jack could sympathise, Yang had gotten him into enough trouble, and he had often wondered whether his subconscious controlled his shadow. That was until the puppet show last night; now he had no idea where Yang's actions came from. 'I guess you won't know, until you test it.'

'I suppose.' Bill shook himself. 'Ying, you're right. All I need is practice, and when I find my wolf I can practice all I want.'

Jack could think of other creatures he would prefer Bill to practice with; only a hedgehog had none of a wolf's awe.

Bill, shrugging off his melancholy with typical aplomb, traipsed ahead, whistling the same tune his grandfather whistled when he took Wolf for a walk.

The larger animals kept to the deeper woods, away from the village. Jack knew of hunting paths leading into the heart of Criklow Wood. The paths were only a few steps wide, and the wood in parts had reclaimed whole sections of the trail. Walking ahead, Bill missed one such path.

Yang threw a small stone, bouncing it off Bill's shoulder. 'Hey!' cried Bill rubbing his hurt shoulder; he cast a baleful glance back at Jack.

'Yang threw it,' explained Jack. 'But look,' he pointed to where hunters' boots had depressed the ground into a snaking trail around a hillock. 'Let's follow this for a while.'

With the track at their feet, the going became easier. They wound around thick copses of trees and missed deep fissures that split the earth without warning. Huge clumps of granite grew from overhanging banks. Jack noticed hunter marks, a series of dots and lines, cut into the stone, the markings were a mystery; he guessed they pointed the way for other hunting parties to follow. An aged tree lay across their path, its skeletal branches snatching at them like pickpockets at a country fair.

A few times, as they travelled, Bill stopped to make some small critter perform simple tricks, or collect a twig, or nut from off the beaten track. No matter how mundane the task he had the animals perform Bill never tired of repeating the chore. Jack threw his hands up in despair after the fifth time Bill had a rabbit hop around in a circle.

'Come on; if you stop every time you see something we'll never make it to your wolf before dark.'

As they roamed deeper into the wood, the spaces among the trees became tighter. A few places appeared like bubbling wooden walls, not separate conifer and spruce. In search of rare shafts of sunlight, smaller plants took odd shapes. Some spread wide across the wood floor, with hundreds of low hanging branches sheltering half-glimpsed eyes. Other trunks were so twisted Jack started, afraid a Wood Giant stood to the side of the path. At the feet of the trees sat brown and grey mushrooms, a few spotted red caps also grew over the humped roots. Mushrooms, needing far less sunlight than flowers, outnumbered the brightly coloured orchids. The Skomuria flower, being the most striking of the hardy flowers, with its white blooms and green tipped sepals, grew on the steep banks.

The trail dipped violently into a dell, where interwoven branches darkened the floor. From the top of the slope, the boys could not see what lay ahead. A few silhouettes of bordering bushes in the darkness gave some insight as to the course the trail took.

'Have you ever been this far into the woods?'

Although he heard Bill's question, at that moment the silence around them occupied Jack's mind. The birdsong that followed them for so long had disappeared, and an hour had passed since the last time Bill had tried his Talent on some unsuspecting creature. Even Yang pulled back from the slope.

'Come on, the hunters use the trail, they must pass through here all the time,' said Bill, eager to continue his search for the elusive wolf.

The well-trodden trail gave credence to Bill's words. Not relishing having to go into the dark, Jack paused. Had the Hatchling brought him here to kill him? A preposterous thought, after all, he, not Bill had led the way through the woods; yet the fear continued to grow. Conscious of wanting to put distance between them, he took the first tentative steps down the slope. The slippery packed earth sent him plunging into the dark. He managed to stay afoot for most of the descent, until a hidden root tripped him. With a cry, he crashed forward, landing hard on his side. Rolling the last few metres, he came to a stop in the gloom.

'Ying, are you still alive?'

Touching his ribs gingerly, Jack checked his new surroundings. Beneath the enveloping canopy, his eyes adjusted to the dark; he saw individual plants, and moist moss clinging to the near rocks. Satisfied that he had only suffered a few minor cuts and bruises, he got to his feet, brushing the dry earth off his trousers.

'I'm fine,' he called up to Bill, who tore at his cap with worry.

Despite thorns having overgrown the boundary into the path, they did not offer much of a challenge to his exploration. Enough light remained to allow Yang by his side.

Bill still stood at the top of the slope, toeing the decline. Jack had time to wonder whether the Hatchling had orchestrated his tumble. Bill could control animals; did that mean he could make people do things? Was the Hatchling responsible for his trip? The absurdity of his own fears made him want to hit his head.

A growl, shed from a mouth filled with sharp teeth, erupted from within the trees. Dense foliage hid the maker of the call. Again, Jack heard a growl, lower than before, and a little closer. Yang retreated from the sound, cringing behind Jack, portraying none of the courage he had shown the previous night.

'I'm coming down,' cried Bill, unaware of the danger.

AMONGST THE TREES

Blue eyes peered through the darkness a few yards from Jack. The beast's girth, evident in the dim light, was twice Jack's own; with the shaggy hair, bristling along the creature's back, making it appear even larger. It no longer growled, instead the silence became ominous, as on padded paws the hunter crept forward, keeping its stare fixed on Jack. A scarred muzzle, pulled back from yellow fangs. Drool slipped from black lips in long silver loops. Two rounded mountains of flesh and muscle worked along its back as it drew closer. Placing one careful leg before the other it got ready to pounce.

The black wolf opened a maw filled with cutting sabres and filleting knives; Jack knew one bite would tear his head off. It sank onto its haunches, its keen eyes surrounded by raised wrinkles of flesh and fur.

Jack, smelling the rank odour of the wolf, stepped back into a protruding branch. The wolf, seeing his retreat, sprang forward, its roar deafening in the tight confines of the forested dell.

Jack screamed, throwing his arms about his face to protect himself as best he could from the ravenous carnivore. The expected impact never came, only the discomfort he felt from the branch pushing into his back. Daring to drop his arms from his face, he looked down and saw Bill scratching the mighty beast under one tufted ear.

'Well done Ying! I was beginning to think we'd never find one.'

Steam rose from the wolf. Its tongue lolled from its open mouth, two lower pointed teeth creasing the red carpet. The beast stood as high as Bill's eye line.

'You stopped him,' said Jack, his voice weak from fear.

'Oh yes, as soon as I saw him I got him under control. Isn't he magnificent!' exclaimed Bill with delight. 'Can you imagine Grandpa's face when I come home with a real wolf?'

Moving closer, Jack reached out; his hand shook as he patted the thick black coat. 'Next time, you go first.'

Working his fingers deeper into the wolf's hair, Jack forgot his fear. He began to relax when he saw two sets of golden eyes watching from the edge of the path. Immediately he knew their mistake, the wolf was not a lone hunter; it belonged to a pack.

CRIK

9. ALL YOU COULD WISH FOR

ANOTHER WOLF LAY PRONE, watching from the tangled weeds. The other wolves circled, wary of the strange behaviour of the large black. These were leaner, their ribs protruding through white and grey fur.

'Bill can you take control of the other three?'

Bill, keeping a firm hold on the large black wolf, shook his head. His face had grown pale. 'I can only concentrate on keeping Black with us. He's the pack leader, but they're starving, they will attack.'

Black would kill any one of the other wolves, though he had little chance against three. The nearest wolf, snapping its jaws, inched closer. Jack braced himself for the assault, when Black bared his sabres. Threatened by the bigger predator, the animal retreated into the trees.

'They are circling,' warned Bill.

Following Bill's wavering finger, Jack spotted another wolf moving toward him through the foliage. Staying low, the wolf moved on silent feet, probing for any lapse in their guard. Black growled from deep in his throat. Showing no sign of his former allegiance to the pack, he forced back the smaller wolf.

'We can't stay here forever,' said Jack. 'Sooner or later they will attack. Black can't fight them all.'

The poor light only allowed Yang to appear as a ghost outline. The shadow rustled a clump of ferns, startling the encroaching beasts.

'I don't know what to do,' Bill cried, 'I only wanted to have a wolf.'

'Well you've got one, and a few more besides. Your wolf scares them; or we'd already be dog meat. He isn't starving like the others.'

'Well they're fed up of going without.'

Two wolves crept forward, their eyes set securely upon Black's hulking, menacing, form.

Bill, tight against Black, fidgeted with his hat.

'Bill, give Black room to fight.' If he didn't move, Bill would get hurt, as well as get in the way of their only protection.

An eerie silence descended; each of the animals bared long teeth, waiting for some subtle sign to attack. Backtracking away from the immediate danger, Bill bumped into Jack. Jack, intent on seeking an avenue of escape, cried out in alarm, breaking the hush.

ALL YOU COULD WISH FOR

Two wolves attacked, the third stayed, waiting for its chance to join the fray. Only Black's quick speed saved his neck from the jaws of the first wolf. The assailant's teeth snapped shut on a hank of fur, tearing long dark hair from the larger wolf's shoulder. From the right, the second wolf arrested Black's attention. Both larger and more aggressive than its cousin, it sought the black wolf's soft underbelly. One huge paw swiped four great furrows across the attacker's muzzle, releasing ribbons of red blood. Clamping his teeth down on the exposed neck, Black punctured an artery. Before the blood had time to clot in the grey fur, Black had dropped the lifeless husk. Standing over his dead opponent, Black turned on the smaller wolf. He towered over his challenger, his head twice the size of the greys; his yellow fangs made the other's canines feeble in comparison.

Jack judged the grey wolf stood thirty inches at the shoulder; Black far outreached that, standing at an impossible forty-five inches. The starved wolf weighed eighty pounds, whereas Black must have a hundred and fifty pounds of flesh and muscle on his bones. Black's pelage contributed to his overall size, with the thick coat creating mounds of knotted hair. Contending with two foes negated his size advantage; keeping the outcome of the fight uncertain.

Snarling, the wolf standing stiff-legged amongst the trees broke through to both wolves. Ignoring his nearer foe, Black locked eyes with the female; they both stood rigid, stretching themselves to their full height. The female, larger than the other attackers, remained smaller than Black. Both wolves held their tails vertical, curling them toward their backs, where the hair bristled.

'What's going on?' asked Jack.

'I read about this. They are staring each other down.' Bill looked excited to see something he had learned come to life. 'Whoever pacifies the other will be the dominant wolf.'

'This will be over when Black wins?' Jack hoped so, his nerves thrummed like tuning forks up his arms.

Black, his coat blending into the shadow of a curled oak, strode forward with erect ears. The wolf, which had bit Black's shoulder, retreated a few paces, watching the contest with intense interest. Unlike the other members of the pack, the female had meat on her lithe frame. Black's blue eyes met the other's golden scrutiny without a flicker as he wound closer on padded paws.

'Is she his mate?'

Bill nodded. 'They are the pack's dominant couple. Grandpa says, during hard times only the alpha pair breed, stopping the others from coupling.'

On reaching her, Black let a growl escape his squared muzzle, intimidating her, the gore colouring his mouth adding to his aggression. The standoff ended when the female lowered her entire body, and drew back her lips and ears. She pointed her tail at the large male in a final act of submission.

'That was close,' Bill observed. 'She looked ready for a fight.'

CRIK

'When the wolves appeared, I couldn't see how we'd ever leave these woods alive.' Jack looked back up the steep slope, his mind conjuring images of his mother receiving his lifeless body from the Village Elders. Distraught with the thought of her going through such heartbreak made him again rethink their expedition. The wolf stood with unnatural patience for Bill's next command. Unnerved by the wolf, he said, 'You best release Black.' Knowing how crestfallen Bill would be returning to Crik Village without the wolf, made it difficult to say. 'You know he belongs here.'

'I'll let him go once everyone has seen him,' promised Bill.

'It's too dangerous; I shouldn't have agreed to help you.'

With a flinch, Jack heard the forgotten wolf howl. It sat on its haunches, away from the hierarchical pair, its head held taught, howling at the half-seen sky. A red bird flew from a lofty branch. Before its wings bore it from sight, answering howls met their ears.

'Oh no,' Bill cried, looking into the woods from where the howls emanated. 'What're we going to do; Black can't protect us from more.'

Five wolves answered the howl; if they stayed, they would never leave the shadowed dell. 'Quick, call Black over here.' Jack heard the frantic pitch in his voice.

'Why, he can't fight those coming.'

'We'll ride him out of here; he's powerful enough to bear our weight. Hurry, while we still have a chance.'

Bill needed no more urging; with a hurried flick of his hand, he called Black to his side. The black wolf leapt away from the female, jumping over tree roots and weed strangled boulders to get to them.

The immense size of the lupine once more impressed itself on Jack. He waited for Bill to mount the wolf, feeling confident with the ease Black took his friend's weight high on his back, that his plan had a chance to work. Settling in behind Bill, he grabbed fistfuls of coarse hair, smelling the musty scent of their unusual mount. Yang took what anchorage he could from the long tail, his shadow fingers coiling over the stiff appendage. Jack doubted his shadow needed to hold on, but felt happier knowing Yang held on tight.

'Ready!' came the muffled shout from the front where Bill buried his face between the broad shoulders of the wolf.

The wolf started to run, startling Jack. Despite having ridden unsaddled horses before, the jostle he endured on the back of Mr Tremle's old steed could not prepare him for the bouncing he now endured. His teeth clattered together at every rise and fall of the four powerful legs carrying him along the winding path. Rounding the first curve in the hunter's path took them away from the slope Jack had fallen down. Frightened, Jack tried to shout, to tell Bill, only for the powerful lunges to upset his every effort. He wanted to go back home, not go farther from it. A backward glance showed him a lone chasing wolf; he recognised it as the one that had howled. The ground sped by at an incredible speed, the brown and greens blending into mingled streaks.

The dark wood tied in with the wolf's colouring, only the boy's clothes gave relief from the pervading darkness. From the lip in the ravine poured white, grey, and brown wolves. More than ten of them chased, their jaws open in hungry anticipation.

Waiting until the pack had passed, the female rose to join the hunt.

Despite the rough ride, the coarse hair provided the boys with adequate anchorage to feel confident in each twist and turn the wolf chose. The thorax, rising and falling, like some huge bellows, gave Jack a sense of elation. He understood his friend's need to show his power off to the rest of the village. However, who commanded the wolf, the boy he had grown up with, or the Hatchling? His fingers loosened their hold at the terrible implications of that question; he managed to regain his grip in time to avoid the branches, which stung his arms and face, from unseating him. Could it be that his friend no longer existed? Had the Hatchling taken command of Bill the same way Black became spellbound? Jack had no doubt that Bill still carried the demon inside him.

Chill water hit them as Black ploughed through a calm river, disturbing a school of salmon beneath the surface. If Jack paid attention, he would have recognised the water for an estuary of the Wednig River, the blue ribbon that fed the foul Boswain Bog.

Raised howls drove them to greater speed. The lush vegetation growing on the riverbanks sped by in a blur of riotous colour and variety. Flowers and fauna not found outside Criklow Wood, fought for the rich soil, taking advantage of the open sky. Stalks of Yapri, rich with sugar, shared land with Norse Brush, and Scraggle Weed.

On they ran with the starving wolves snapping at their heels. The wolves whipped through the foliage, navigating their way over rotting logs and other obstacles with much more agility than did their burdened pack master.

Yang picked up stones to throw at their pursuers. His good aim made a wolf whine, and Jack heard the dull thud of another hitting the heavy pelage of a closing predator.

Criklow Wood seemed bent on hindering their escape. Repeatedly they entered an open glade, with good ground to keep running, when the trees hemmed them in once more. Wiry bushes and nests of thorns changed their direction as the wood continued to throw up unexpected obstructions. The thought that something herded them did not escape Jack; it seemed whenever they turned away from the east something drove them back in that direction.

A wolf leapt, its teeth jutting forward from red gums, intent on hamstringing Black. The animal came within a hairsbreadth of disabling the larger wolf when Yang struck the attacking wolf with an enlarged fist, sending it flipping

CRIK

backward. Jack gave a cheer, Bill, with his head buried in the dense fur, never noticed.

The vibrant land altered to muted tones, with the grass appearing dull and flowers giving way to hardier plants. The spongy ground threw discoloured water over Jack and Bill's knees, and matted Black's fur in tangled ropes. With the change in terrain, the smaller wolves struggled; many sank into the marshland.

Seeing their chance to escape, Jack shouted ahead, urging Bill to command Black to greater effort. Misty breath expelled from the black wolf's open maw as it laboured on, trudging through the filthy pools collected around the field they traversed. Trees dwindled in number, with those that did grow, lacking the thick woodland foliage.

'They've stopped chasing us!'

Jack barely understood the gasped shout from ahead; turning he saw the wolves watching them flee with lowered tails

Laughing, Jack hugged Black. He failed to notice the small hut standing alone among the marsh weeds, with smoke rising from a stumped chimney. He also failed to see an open casket filled with bones, leaning against its crumbling foundations.

10. THE MARSH HOUSE

Black trudged to a stop, his legs submerged in the thick mud; head lowered, breathing hard after the long run. The pack, having given up the chase, slunk back into the woods to disappear from view. Jack wished he could say the sight filled him with joy; instead, a sullen disquiet filled him. Why had the starving beasts given up the chase? Their flight had exhausted Black. To have an easy meal, the pack had only to follow. The wolves' departure increased his unease, with the greater cause of concern before him.

Cracks split every stone of the house, with moss filling the seams where the mortar had rotted away. Mushrooms, large pale umbrellas, with dark undersides, and spotted stems, clustered at the foot of the small dwelling. Stalactites of discoloured water, extended from the reed roof. A cache of bones filled a tall narrow box. Its odd shape, though similar to the caskets found at Long Sleep Cemetery, chilled the air with its ominous remains. Being no expert, Jack could only guess as to what the bones came from. Animal bones, he hoped. Stout bones joined, frail, gangly bones; some had rounded joints, while others had rough edges pitted with dark holes. Neither skulls nor animal horns lay within the odd casket. A small window glowed from the fire that gave birth to the smoke rising from the chimneystack. Focusing his attention on the thin pane of glass, Jack waited to see a silhouette pass, or a white face jump into view.

'I don't like this.' Bill stated the obvious. 'We should go back.'

'We can't, not while those wolves are so close.' Although Jack wished he could tell Bill to turn Black around, to leave this house alone, he knew it would be suicide to go into the woods.

Marshland extended on all fronts. Among the tall reeds, the sun glinted off ponds. Frog song filled the air, while a heron picked its careful way through the bog. A dark, distant line, tantalised with the promise of the wood continuing on the far side. Not keen to try crossing the miles of treacherous ground between here and there, Jack resigned himself to finding the owner of the house.

Having a pet wolf bolstered his courage, so that when he swung down from Black, his knees did not knock together. Mud sucked his feet down to his ankles, filling his shoes and ruining his socks.

'Come down Bill,' he said, 'let Black pull himself out of the bog.'

CRIK

Clutching the wolf's wiry hair in white knuckled fists, Bill looked from Jack to the grey house. Refusing to budge, he sat, mesmerised by the flickering light at the window.

'Black can't run anymore,' said Jack. 'We're lucky he had the strength to bring us this far. Let him rest, if we need him he'll be close enough to help us.' Jack held out his hand.

'I'm not scared.' Bill ignored the offered hand. 'It's higher up here, that's all. I wanted to see if I could spy through that window.'

'Can you?'

'No, the sun is reflecting on the glass.'

As Bill clambered down from Black, movement from the house caught Jack's eye. Spinning around, he only saw swaying rushes growing at the cornerstone.

'It's dragging me down,' cried Bill. The mud had closed around his shoes.

With a helping hand, Jack pulled Bill from the sucking mire.

A steep rise leading to the house, gave them firmer ground underfoot. Arriving at the house, Jack placed his hand on the cold wet stone; he peered around the corner. A wooden wheel with three missing spokes, and a bucket filled with stagnant water, crowded beneath a side window. Though small, the hut had enough space under the makeshift roof for another room. Old stone filled the space where a third window should look out on the grim land.

'See anything?' asked Bill, kicking mud from his shoes. Black stayed at his heel.

Jack stared at the side of the house; he felt the way a rabbit must feel looking up at a clear blue sky, not seeing, but knowing the hawk was there, waiting to strike. He shook his head, as much to answer Bill's query, as to shake himself of the feeling of the blank stone scrutinising him in turn.

'Someone's here, no one would leave a fire burning unattended with a reed roof.' Bill, craning his neck, studied the house. 'Wonder why they haven't come out, we made enough noise for them to know we're here.'

'Perhaps they're shy,' said Jack.

'Yeah right,' laughed Bill.

'Or the sight of two strangers riding a huge black wolf to their doorstep has made them nervous.'

'I guess that could be why. Hey Ying, tell Yang not to touch those.'

Fascinated with the grisly collection, Jack's shadow fingered a long leg bone near the bottom of the casket, turning, and then gently pulling it. Horrified, Jack watched with disbelief as Yang attempt to extract the gruesome artefact. Even out here, his shadow got him in trouble. The pile of bones came clattering down in a deafening roar. Without a face, Yang still managed to look sheepish, holding the femur as the rest of the bones piled through his insubstantial waist.

THE MARSH HOUSE

To make matters worse, the casket, with a creak, toppled over onto its side, splintering the wood to spill its entire content at their feet.

'That's it,' said Bill, 'forget about any warm welcome.'

'Not that I expected one from a place that keeps a stack of bones outside the window.'

'Do you think they're human?'

Looking at his friend, Jack believed Bill hoped the remains did belong to someone, as though this were all part of a story, and not a grim reality. Perhaps a lone traveller, driven to the bog by four legged hunters, sought refuge under the reed roof. With enough bones in the fallen casket for ten bodies, Jack stopped himself from further speculation. Mr Gasthem told of families living among the trees; surviving on whatever, or whomever, they could. He shuddered in revulsion. Bill's eagerness was at odds with his own reticence to the macabre. Having forgotten his earlier fright, Bill stood beside the door, willing it to open.

Bill's mounting excitement troubled Jack, who, not forgetting the demon, feared where this new courage emanated. Terror, that a silver slash would appear in Bill's eyes, drove through him, making his head swoon. He took no notice of Yang handling the femur, until Bill snatched it away.

Inspecting the cracked bone, Bill said, 'It could belong to a man. I've seen enough limbs sticking out of the Tristle riverbank to know that.'

'Put it down, whoever lives here could hear you.'

Bill blanched, which improved Jack's mood a little, at least his friend hadn't fully forgotten their predicament.

Black wandered around, sniffing at the discarded wheel, and licking the water from the bucket. His humped back rose to cover the bottom pane of the window.

'If I saw the wolf, I wouldn't leave the house,' confessed Jack.

'Black?' replied Bill, dumbfounded. 'He's one of us, don't be silly.'

Jack said nothing; remembering the burning blue eyes amongst the trees.

Not wanting to lose that advantage, Jack pointed toward the front window, where the glow of the fire still flickered. Tight against the stone of the house, Jack edged closer to the portal. With the stone rough against the palm of his hand, he counted the inches. Bill crept close behind, his breath raking Jack's nerves more than the disappearing brick. Yang pressed himself hard against the side of the house, his ghostly body finding the nooks in the broken mortar.

Stopping a hands span away from the window, Jack turned, placing a warning finger on his lips for Bill to remain silent. With blood pounding in his ears, he inched nearer. The glass reflected the pale sun, and the trees in a dark abstract line. Filth touched the corners, with dead flies, and dried moths, caught in dusty spider webs. A few jars, filled with amber liquid, each capped with chequered cloth, stood on the windowsill.

CRIK

'Do you see anything?'

Although the question from behind met his ears as a whisper, Jack almost released the contents of his bladder. A maddening laugh threatened to escape, a laugh if let out he would not be able to stop. Regaining his composure, he again pressed his finger to his lips, compressing hard enough to turn his finger white.

Yang looked in with him, he did not mind, his shadow spread himself thin across the outside shelf. Wiping away a layer of grime, he peered into the room. A hole-ridden sheet covered a table, besides which stood a couple of homemade high-backed chairs, with enough splinters and sharp edges to look dangerous. Two coffee stained cups sat on the table. Paintings, bringing to Jack's mind Grandma Poulis sitting at the easel, covered large sections of the grey walls. He could not discern much detail in the work; they looked much like the surrounding landscape, as though the painter never left the window. Logs sat in a stone fire; turned black by licking flames. The room contained two doors, the front door to his right, and a smaller inner door toward the back of the house.

'I can't see anybody.'

'They must be out. Let's knock and see,' said Bill, flush with excitement.

Before Jack could stop him, Bill crossed the window without fear. In his eagerness, Bill had left the large wolf pawing at the corner of the hut. Leaving the windowsill, Yang joined Bill as the young boy struck the warped door.

'Careful, we don't know who lives here,' hissed Jack.

'Whoever does, must know we're here, I'm fed up of tiptoeing around.'

Jack had never known Bill to be so impulsive. The sudden change troubled him. Had finding his Talent imbued new confidence, or had the mischievous demon taken control? If the creature influenced his friend, it must bare bad feeling toward Jack; did it seek a way to repay him for its hurt leg?

A face, distorted by the jars filled with the amber fluid, swam passed.

While Jack looked through the window into the room, the owner had sat quiet, not moving a muscle. If the shock of finding the room occupied had not silenced Jack, the quickness of the man would have made any words of warning useless.

Bill froze with his fist raised. The door flew open, a man dressed in rags glared down with bloodshot eyes. Neither spoke; it took Jack long seconds to approach, his tongue felt swollen as though stung by a bee. When Jack reached Bill, the man, with bloodless lips, raised a bushy eyebrow.

'Took you long enough, I started to think you didn't want to come in,' said the man. 'I poured you some tea, by now its cold.'

The man spoke in a quiet, mellow tone, which was in stark contrast to his rough appearance. Despite the savage kink in his spine, he stood at average height. His bent back forced him to look down at the two boys at an odd angle. However, this deformity did not affect the man's agility; Jack doubted he could

THE MARSH HOUSE

get any faster to the door. Wrinkles etched themselves around his eyes and mouth. Scars, both small and large covered him. The worst scar, a purple swathe falling from his left eye, pulled his lip up into a permanent sneer. A twist of long grass tied back his grey hair.

'Well,' he continued, waving them in. 'I'm not leaving my door open to catch marsh flies.'

'What's your name,' asked Bill.

'Krimble, and you're Bill, and he's Jack.' Krimble's eyes lingered on Jack. 'Or should I call you Ying? Now we know each other, come inside, you too Yang.'

'How'd he know our names?' Bill asked, after Krimble had retreated inside. 'I haven't said your name, and anyway I never call you Jack.'

'Perhaps knowing names is his Talent.'

'What's the use of that out here?' The vast swamp echoed Bill's words. 'I doubt a frog will have any use of a name, and a fly will only buzz at you if you called it by its first name.'

'We aren't going to find out anything by standing here all day. You wanted to go inside, so let's get moving, he seems nice enough.'

Bill looked to where Black sat scratching his neck. 'Can I bring Black,' he asked, wistfully.

'I don't think so,' said Jack, thinking how his mother would react if Bill brought his pet indoors. 'Best leave him outside.' He moved closer to Bill to whisper in his ear, 'Don't let him wander away from the house, we may need him.'

Nodding, Bill signalled for Black to stay, before stepping across the hut's threshold.

A cloying damp smell, no doubt from the scattered ponds metres away, met them as they entered; Jack coughed into his hand. The morose paintings, seen from the window, sprang to colourful life; twisting the dire landscape outside into vivid plains. An extraordinary diversity of life filled the canvass, from the humble frog, to long eared deer, and circling hawks. The depth created invited deeper exploration, intoxicating the senses. When he did look away, Jack noticed Krimble sitting in a worn chair, packed with pillows, under the front window. The man watched him with interest.

'They are good,' said Jack. 'Did you paint them yourself?'

'With instruction from another,' answered Krimble. 'Please sit, you must be exhausted after your near escape from the wolves. I saw your escape from the woods, quite breath-taking. Never seen anyone ride a wolf before, it will make a nice picture. Have a drink.'

Steam rose from two cups; to be polite Jack reached for one. His fingers welcomed the warmth of the porcelain, so he clutched it tight with both hands. Taking the chair beside Bill, he felt the rough grain of the unfinished wood pull at his trousers, making the seating uncomfortable.

CRIK

'It's been a while since I've had anyone new visit,' said Krimble.

Jack smiled, watching Krimble's tongue probe his lips. 'I'm afraid we can't stay long, I shouldn't have left the village at all.'

'It will take hours to get back to your village. Rest here for a while; give the wolves a chance to move on before going back to the wood. Please drink your tea.' Krimble touched his own cup to his withered lips.

Glancing over to Bill, Jack saw his friend had already emptied half his cup. Feeling rude, he drank. The sweetness of the drink surprised him, but it passed down his throat easily enough, and he found himself taking a longer sip.

'I use honey instead of sugar,' explained Krimble, pointing at the jars. 'I find it packs more bite.'

Picking a framed picture from the wall, Yang turned it around, so the sky became the ground and the reflecting water the sky. Upside down, the trees, brush, and birds swooping through the air, looked more like a portrait of a crying face than the marsh.

Unsettled, Jack called out to his shadow, 'Put it back the way you found it.'

His shadow ignored him, studiously admiring the twisted image.

'Hang it up,' said Jack, alarmed that Krimble, not knowing he had no control over his shadow, would blame him if Yang should drop and break the painting.

Grinning, Krimble said, 'Put it back Yang, but before you do, can you clear the dust from the top of the frame. I find it hard to clean these days.'

To Jack's and Bill's immense surprise, Yang at once started to brush the dust bunnies from the pine frame, he even polished the glass before setting the picture back on its nail.

'How'd you make him do that,' asked Jack, his mouth agape.

'You just need to know how to speak to them, that's all,' replied Krimble.

Bill dropped his cup, smashing it across the reed strewn floor, stopping Jack from asking Krimble what he meant by referring to Yang as them. Only a spongy layer of honey lay at the bottom of the shattered cup.

With a muttered apology, Bill bent to pick up the broken pieces. When he got to his knees, his eyes rolled up and he crashed forward into an unconscious heap.

Racing to his aid, Jack failed to notice Krimble rise from his chair, clutching a cudgel in his long fingers. Bill's head lolled in Jack's arms, his skin was as white as papier-mâché, making Jack's pulse quicken in alarm.

'Something's wrong with him,' said Jack, fearing the hand of the Hatchling in Bill's sudden ill turn.

He opened Bill's mouth in an attempt to coax out the demon, when a shadow fell across him, sending a shiver down his spine. Looking back, he saw Krimble standing over him with a cruel grin peeling back his lips, showing for the first time his rotted teeth, and his madness.

11. STAY AWHILE …. I'LL KEEP YOU FOREVER

THE MEAGRE AMBER glow from a lone candle shaded the three people sat at the table, highlighting certain features, while swathes of blackness hid others. A girl, with copper blonde hair, tipped her face forward, revealing sunken cheeks and roving wild eyes. She tapped her chipped fingernails on the wooden table top, watching the two sleeping boys with growing impatience.

Krimble no doubt left her in near darkness as a new torment. He often changed his games, in an attempt to get her to react. Since coming to the Marsh House, she had come to prefer the shadows. Even in this dim light, she refused to look down at herself. A moth circled the candle, drawn by the light before the heat beat it back. She envied the insect, at any moment it could fly into the flame. Having endured timeless misery here, she saw no end to Krimble's imprisonment.

When Krimble first brought in the two boys, she mistook them for stuffed dolls; neither moved in his arms, nor had they stirred when he arranged them on the chairs. Once Krimble had gone, the boys' snores, so like the soft passage of wind through leaves, made her want to cry. The boy, with sandy hair, rapidly moved his eyes beneath his lids. The candle illuminated their tanned skin, which made her inspect her once sun-browned arms; appearing to her now like the underside of gigantic white slugs. Blood matted the boy's fair hair and stained one cheek in maroon swirls. She wanted to reach over, to feel the warmth from another living person.

When he brought the boys in, her captor ignored her, and she ignored him. During her long imprisonment in the windowless room, she could not recall a time Krimble had spoken directly to her. Again, his parting words were not for her ears. The scraps of her last meal spoiled next to her arm. She had picked at the meat, leaving the raw vegetables on the plate; moving the peas around with her fingers. Her stomach ached, but not trusting the food Krimble brought her, she refused to eat more than necessary.

***

A coppery taste filled Jack's mouth. Moving his tongue around, he touched the roof of his mouth, where it clove to his dry pallet. He recalled the tea, he drank earlier, filled with honey; it did not seem so long ago for his mouth to dry

CRIK

out. Images of Bill collapsing, and then Krimble attacking him from behind, roused Jack from his gentle quandary. His head swam when he opened his eyes, making him dizzy and sick to the stomach. Fearing he would throw up, he tried to raise his hands to his face, but coarse rope bound his wrists to a chair. Frightened, he jerked at his bonds, burning his skin.

'He knows how to tie good knots.'

With a start, Jack looked up from his secured arms. At first, he did not see the speaker, only a small candle flickering atop the table. Then he saw a girl half submerged in shadow, watching him through eyes as dark and dazzling as black diamonds.

'Who're you? What's happening here, release me.' He tensed his arms against the rope.

'Release you,' she laughed, throwing back her head. 'Release you,' she repeated, banging the table with the palm of her hand. 'If I could get you out of here, do you think I would be here myself? He has you now, and your podgy friend.'

For the first time Jack noticed Bill sitting next to him.

'Don't worry,' said the girl, 'he's sleeping off Krimble's wonder drug. He'll come around soon enough.'

'He drugged us?'

'He drugged him,' she said, pointing a slender finger at Bill. 'I think with you he had to be a bit blunter. There's blood in your hair, I suppose you didn't drink Krimble's tea as greedily as your friend.' Her voice croaked, as though she had not spoken in a long time, and when she smiled, her chapped lips cracked, drawing a little blood.

'Why has he done this to us, we haven't done anything to him?' said Jack, disbelieving what had happened. 'We only came here to escape the wolves, we meant no harm. We spilt the bones outside by mistake; if he's mad about that I can mend the box and put them all back in.'

'Do you want some food?' She pushed a plate toward him. 'I'll feed you if you like.'

'No, I don't want to eat,' replied Jack, agitated with how passive she took his captivity. 'Untie me.'

She ignored his demands. Leaning back in her chair, she opened her mouth in a wide yawn. 'I wonder what time it is. I tend to lose track in here.'

'What's wrong with you; take these bloody ropes off me before he comes back.'

'I tried to keep count once,' she said, ignoring his struggles. 'I tapped the table every second until my fingertips bled. Another time I repeated my mother's name, until the words became so muddled in my head I don't know what I was saying.'

STAY AWHILE....I'LL KEEP YOU FOREVER

The same damp smell he had smelt when he first entered the house, cloyed the air, making him gag. Peering into the dark room, he spied rags heaped on the floor. White sheets reflected enough candlelight to make out a crude bed. Beside the bed was a rusted basin. He presumed the girl slept on the sheets, and used the large bowl for a toilet.

'I left home to find some mushrooms for my mother.'

Looking back at the girl, Jack noticed, behind the harrowed lines and sunken cheeks, how young she was. Horror, as thick as winter stew, rose up his throat; the girl was only a few years his elder, not a thirty-year-old woman as he had first surmised.

'Storm clouds brewed on the horizon, making me hurry,' she continued, oblivious to his scrutiny. 'I followed an old path my grandfather cleared out; the stone flags he used were still visible after so many years. The path dips, and then skirts a few hills, before leading into a meadow, where I collect mushrooms. This time the path led me astray?' She frowned. 'Instead of leading me south, the stone flags turned to the east. I should've turned back then, but my curiosity got the better of me.'

Remembering how the trees and foliage had negotiated his own path eastward during his escape from the wolves pricked Jack's attention.

'Years of mud and intrusive weeds had half buried the path,' she continued in her vacant, cracking, voice. 'Had my grandfather also placed them? A divergence in the path, which had until then gone unnoticed. It took me through unfamiliar parts of the wood. The animals changed from the small birds and squirrels I befriended near to my home. Larger shapes now swooped through the trees, tracking my every step. Frightened, I wanted to turn back, although when I did, I found the path extended before me, with nothing behind but forest floor. Nightmarish shapes, half glimpsed in the trees, kept me on the path. Stepping from the cobbled stones would have meant sure death. The bog ended the path.' Memories clouded her face. She refused to look at Jack. When she again spoke, her voice clipped the air like shears, 'Smoke rose from the east, drawing me through the wet mud, until I found this house. Krimble opened his door to me, and despite his fearsome appearance, I trusted him enough to enter. He gave me some of his tea, and here I am.'

'Won't your mother be looking for you?'

Anger compressed the girl's lips into a thin line. 'Of course she would.' She leant forward. 'Can you tell me where we are? The path, which led me astray, would appear normal to my parents, leading them to the meadow. My father, with all his tracking skills, could not follow a bewitched route.' She wiped away a tear. 'Your fat friend is stirring.' When she returned her stare to the flickering flame her sorrow dulled the reflected light.

CRIK

Jack turned his head as Bill slowly opened his eyes. Opening his mouth, Bill coughed up tea. With a groan, Bill leant his head back, cracking it against the chair.

'Careful,' said Jack, alarmed.

'What happened?' asked Bill, his skin waxy in the poor light.

'You drank drugged tea,' said Jack.

'The drug will wear off soon,' said the girl, with some sympathy. 'You'll have a headache for a while, but there's no lasting effect. Close your eyes until the dizzy spell passes.'

Surprise at hearing a girl's voice brought Bill forward in his chair. 'Who're you?'

'Inara,' she replied, after a pause, as though trying to recall her name. 'Don't fight against the ropes,' she said as Bill discovered his bound wrists.

'We can't just remain here,' said Jack. 'No one knows where we are; our only chance is to escape.'

'What's going on Ying?' asked Bill.

'I guess it's the upstairs room,' replied Jack, remembering the space beneath the roof of the house. 'I don't know why we're here. Krimble has held Inara captive a lot longer than us.'

Inara scratched her knotted hair; both Jack and Bill waited for her to give them an explanation. 'What's that moving across the table,' she said, drawing back her arms.

'It's Yang!' cried Bill. 'Ying, get him to untie the rope.'

Jack saw his shadow move closer to the candle, his form almost too faint to detect. The flame licked the curled wick with a blue sheen, the yellow fire extended only a little higher, providing the candle with a peaked hood.

Shaking his head, Jack said, 'He's too weak, without a stronger light he won't be able to loosen the ropes. If we had a second candle, he could do it. As it is, he won't be able to grip anything.'

Climbing the white wax, Yang reached for the flame. They held their breath, willing the shadow to gain strength. The shadow's fingers passed through, stirring the candlelight as though disturbed by a breath of wind.

'It's no good,' said Jack when Yang did not solidify. 'How about you Bill, can you get Black to kill Krimble for us?'

Bill shook his head. 'I've needed to see all the animals I've commanded. Locked up her, all I can do is feel Black's presence. He's still outside, obeying my last command. I'll try later, I'm still sick from the poison.'

'Don't try to escape,' warned Inara. 'He will catch you, and then it will be worst.'

Dumbstruck, Jack looked at the girl. 'How can you say that, knowing how sick with worry your parents are? We must get out of here.'

STAY AWHILE....I'LL KEEP YOU FOREVER

'I'm not going to spend my time locked away in this room,' said Bill. 'Black will protect us once we're outside.'

Unshed tears shone through a fan of blonde hair. Inara, her mouth cast into a grimace, said, 'I want to get from here more than you. I have lost everything since coming to this house. Once I escaped from this room.' Her voice, cracking like a castanet, fell silent. She sat, wringing her hands in her lap. 'It was the last time I saw anything other than these walls. He caught me.' Shifting in her seat, she hiked her brown skirt over her knees.

Jack's eyes grew large with horror; Bill vomited the last of the tea onto his shirt. Inara sat on the chair showing how Krimble, after discovering her downstairs, had cut off her legs below the knee. Only two ruined stumps remained; blood soaked through the dirty rags bandaged around her legs.

'You understand why he doesn't bother to tie me to the chair. He doesn't need to, I can't escape.' She banged the table. 'If you attempt to escape, he will catch you, and make you scream.'

The significance of the casket of bones became clear. Suppressing a surge of bitter-tasting bile, Jack remembered his shadow playing with the leg bone. Had that once belonged to Inara? How many people had Krimble mutilated, the casket held enough bones for at least another ten people, had they all once sat up here in the dark?

'I'm sorry Inara,' he said, 'I am, but we must escape. We will take you with us, don't worry, we'll get you out of here.'

He saw Inara about to argue, when they heard the doorknob turn. With an intake of breath, Inara straightened her skirt, hiding her crippled legs. The door opened, bleeding new light into the room.

Krimble stood framed in the doorway, holding a cage full of black rats.

CRIK

12. WHAT IS YOUR NAME?

YELLOW TEETH GNAWED at the cage's wire mesh. Cackling, Krimble set the cage atop the table in front of the children. Inara licked her dry lips. Light ushered in from the open door betrayed the fear in her eyes. Still reeling in shock after discovering Inara had lost her legs, Jack fought against his rising panic. The bloated stomachs forced up against the side of the cage, did not help, he felt weak and disorientated. To make matters worse, the new light had made Yang stronger; delighting his shadow who began rocking the cage; the vermin squealed.

Picking at his scar, Krimble ignored the cage. The wooden chair gave his bent back some trouble; after a few attempts at getting himself comfortable, he finally settled down, his nose hovering a few inches above the wooden top. Glints of light, dancing on wet corneas, peaked through bushy eyebrows, stealing Jack's attention from his wayward twin.

'Leave us go,' Jack told the leering face.

Inara's shrill laugh answered Jack. 'Don't my missing legs tell you anything? Why haven't I asked if he would let me go? How stupid I am.'

'Quiet, you'll upset him,' said Bill, pushing his chair back with his toes, getting as much distance as possible between himself and Krimble.

'Upset this piece of marsh piss,' said Inara, wagging her finger at Krimble. 'Why would I want to do that? He's done nothing to me!'

Krimble remained silent, first looking with longing at Jack, then Bill, and finally Yang. His haggard face lit up when the rats retreated from the fingers Yang fed through the wire mesh.

'I don't think they like you stroking them,' said Krimble. 'Please continue, they are vermin, and what they want doesn't matter. These disease riddled creatures do nothing but pick over my leftovers. However, if you care to keep one, please be my guest, take any you fancy.'

Eager to possess a rat, Yang slipped his hand inside the cage, catching the fattest occupant by its tail. The rat cried in alarm when Yang lifted it over its scrabbling companions.

'Good,' said Krimble, reaching for the lock atop the cage. Yang extracted the rat from the open door. 'Don't let it escape,' warned Krimble.

WHAT IS YOUR NAME?

Jack wanted to tell Yang to put the rat back, not wanting his shadow accepting anything from his captor. To escape, he needed Yang to stay focused, and with the light shining in from the landing, his shadow had the strength to manipulate his bonds. If Bill could distract Krimble long enough, Yang could release him; when Krimble left, Jack would untie Bill and seek a means to leave the room. Without a way to communicate his plan with Yang, he failed to see how to implement it. Inara laughed into her hand, Yang cradled the rat like a doll, swinging its furry body to within inches of the candle's flame.

'It will burn,' said Inara through a wide smile as Yang again swung the rat.

'She's lost her mind,' said Bill.

Jack refused to comment. Considering what had happened to her, who could blame her if she did have a few screws loose. The way Krimble hunched forward over the table made him appear pitiable; another person with a ruined spine and scarred visage would invoke just that reaction from Jack, but the torture he had inflicted upon Inara left no room for sympathy.

'What's your name?'

Jack found Krimble addressed him. 'You know my name; you knew it before I could tell you. Now untie me!'

'What's your name?' Krimble repeated in a beseeching tone.

Incredulous, both Jack and Bill shared a look. Both boys wondered whether during his isolation in the marsh Krimble had grown crazy.

When Krimble asked a third time, Inara said, 'He's not speaking to you.'

'What do you mean he's not speaking to me? He's looking directly at me,' said Jack.

Shaking her head, Inara said, 'What he wants lives inside you. He doesn't care about us; we're the same as that cage. We give home to his desire; nothing more.'

'What're you talking about?' said Bill. 'You aren't making any sense.'

'He doesn't want you; he wants his shadow,' she pointed at Jack, 'and whatever secret you possess. Once he gets it, he will kill you both.'

Krimble continued to ask his question, changing the pitch from a whisper to a shout that reverberated around the room. He cajoled with a smile, moving to pat Yang's arm. At first, long pauses punctuated his words, and then he tumbled them together, so that sentences strung together as a single word.

'Kill us,' cried Bill, twisting in his chair. 'Why do that, we didn't want to come here.'

'Fewer bones than what you saw lay outside when I arrived,' said Inara. 'You are not the first to have shared this room with me. When I opened my eyes after drinking the tea, four others welcomed me to this prison; each missed one limb or another. Huir had all four limbs hacked off; yet he never stopped planning his escape.' Inara laughed, throwing back her head. 'I asked him once

CRIK

why he continued to try, without his arms and legs where could he go, he said he could live without his limbs, he could not live without his ability.'

'His ability?' asked Bill.

Again, Inara grinned. 'He could control the weather. He owned a farm, and his family relied upon him to provide the rain and sunshine needed to grow his crops. Personally I'd miss my arms and legs more than that ability, but he believed his family would starve without it.'

'He wants Yang?' said Jack with incredulity. Smoke curled off the back of the rat Yang played with. 'How, he's as much a part of me as my hand.'

'You know how easy Krimble takes people's hands,' remarked Bill.

'What's your name?'

'I wish he would stop saying that,' continued Bill, shaking his head.

With dawning horror, Jack understood Inara's meaning, when she said Krimble wanted what lived inside them. Bill had no Talent until the Hatchling climbed inside him, the following morning he could control animals. Inara, unaware of Bill's Talent, had called it Bill's secret. Jack's own Talent rocked the rat in front of them. 'Have I got a Hatchling inside me?'

'What's a Hatchling?' asked Bill.

'I've never heard that word,' said Inara. 'A Narmacil lives within you. It gives you your ability. Without it your shadow would be the same as mine.'

'You mean the demon hiding inside Bill is in me as well,' cried Jack, jerking against his restraints.

'Ying, what demon?' said Bill, sweat glistening on his brow. 'What's all this nonsense?'

Clapping her hands, Inara said, 'You don't know about the wood sprites.' She didn't hide her amazement. 'The Narmacil come from the trees to join with you, to make you whole. He,' she pointed at Krimble, 'can speak to our Narmacils, that's why we're here.'

All his life Jack believed Yang belonged to him, that his parents had somehow imparted his shadow to him at birth. If Inara spoke the truth, the black creature with the golden eyes had hitched a ride his whole life; even now, it slunk around inside him, conspiring with Krimble.

'Tell me what's all this talk of demons and Narmacils, you two aren't making any sense. Come on Ying, if you know something, tell me.'

What could Jack tell Bill? He had kept the discovery of the egg in Grandma Poulis's garden from Bill. The demon, after hatching from the egg had jumped into Bill's throat. By knowing, what could Bill do? Sticking his fingers into his mouth would do no good.

Krimble, opening the cage, saved Jack from giving his friend an explanation. Clamping his bony fingers around the swaying belly of a rodent, Krimble lifted it toward Bill. Bill, eyeing the gnashing jaws of the filthy creature, pushed back in his chair. A stone protrusion stopped him from gaining much distance from

WHAT IS YOUR NAME?

his captor. Keeping a tight grip on the rat, so that flesh and black hair bulged between his fingers, Krimble jabbed his arm forward. The creature writhed as though it drowned only a few inches from life giving air. The old man's glee, apparent on his withered features, grew as Bill squealed in distress.

'If I bring the rat closer, it will bite your cheek,' said Krimble with a crooked smile. 'Of course, with your Talent, the likelihood is the vermin would turn against me. It will twist in my grip in a futile attempt to sink its teeth into my thumb; forcing me to break its ribs. That will not happen,' he remarked, showing ruined brown stumps lining his red gums. 'I have an understanding with your buried friend.' He glanced across at Yang, and then gave Jack a wink. 'It won't hurt you,' he assured Bill, 'it will do what I say.' He opened his fingers on the struggling rat, which once released stopped moving; not attempting to flee to the open door only yards away. 'All I want is your power. I would gladly sit astride that black wolf of yours and go everywhere in search of other Talents. Bending the forest to my will, to bring visitors to my remote house, will be unnecessary. Instead, I could visit them, taking what they do not fully appreciate.

'Although I have many Talents, I desire the companionship of my own shadow.' A wolfish hunger made Krimble's mouth gape open as he regarded Jack. 'To never suffer from loneliness is a covetous and a unique gift. You don't value Yang; I saw your silent reprimand when Yang took his present from the cage.' He moved across the table, pushing the rat in front of Jack. 'I could use your friend's Talent to command this beast to tear into your flesh. A deserved punishment for the oppressive years Yang has had to endure with you. With my help he will unlock his full potential, and enjoy a freedom he has never known.'

'He is not talking to you,' Inara told Jack, 'he is coaxing your Narmacil away from you by promising to give your shadow privileges you don't allow. It is a lie,' she continued, now speaking to Yang, who had stopped playing with the fat rat, 'you will be a prisoner amongst those he has already fooled. Trapped inside his crippled body, enslaved to his twisted spirit; he will not leave this place, and you will rot with him.'

'Silence bitch.' Krimble swung his hand around, smacking Inara across the side of her head. 'You speak of things you do not understand. She lies,' he said with madness gleaming in his eyes, 'come to me Yang and we will travel far and wide. Crik is a small, insignificant, village. I will show you sights you could not imagine if you remain with the boy.'

'He promised Huin's Narmacil to spread his influence across the marsh, to brighten the sky, to make the land wholesome and good, instead he only brought more mist and rain.'

'I said be quiet,' said Krimble.

'Yang, you have a connection with Jack, I see it. Don't tell him your true name, once he has that you will belong to him.'

CRIK

Krimble threw the rat at Inara. Hatred for the girl deepened his scars. 'Eat her eyes,' he commanded.

Inara screamed; the rat clung to her golden hair with tiny paws. It scrambled higher as Inara tossed her head from side to side in a futile attempt to dislodge the vermin.

'Bill, stop it, tell it to let go,' said Jack.

'Leave her alone,' cried Bill, tears running down his cheeks.

The rat continued to climb, seeking Inara's eyes, as Krimble commanded.

'I can't stop it,' said Bill, horrified. 'Don't touch her,' he yelled, only for the rat to ignore him.

When the rodent's pink tail whipped across her chin, Inara lost control; her screams became an insane ramble. Her enlarged pupils became dark pools in which the rat grew with every passing moment. Tears wetted her face, while the weight of the hungry rodent pulled her to the left.

'Bill,' cried Jack.

'It won't listen to me Ying,' muttered Bill, hoarse in defeat.

Cackling with glee, Krimble scrutinised the horrified girl's struggles with a disgusting perversity. Ignoring the pain in his back, he hunched forward, eager for the show to continue to its grisly finale. A black fist, shaped like a hammer, smashed into his grinning mouth. Blood sprayed upward as Krimble fell from his perch in a crumpled heap.

Jack looked with disbelief at his shadow, who had discarded the rat it had moments ago been playing with. The urgent screams from Inara brought him back to the immediacy of her plight. The rat still clambered closer to her eyes, hungry to sink its jaws into her yielding flesh.

'Get off her, leave her alone,' commanded Bill.

After falling to the ground with a soft thud, the foul creature scrambled for the open landing.

Ignoring the fleeing rat, Jack raised his voice, over Inara's cries, for Yang to untie his bonds. Familiar with knots, Yang untied the rope with little difficulty. Jack moved to place a comforting hand across the girl's shoulders while his shadow attended to Bill. At that moment, he shared her sorrow; Inara had witnessed Krimble kill the others before turning the knife on her. Unabashed grief overcame him, so that he barely noticed Bill's hand, or Yang wrapping his insubstantial body around them all.

A groan, from the ground, separated them. Looking down Jack saw Krimble had not moved; he remained unconscious, though the groan had reminded them all that Krimble could wake up at any moment.

13. GO AND HIDE SEEK

IN THE TIME IT TOOK them to carry Inara halfway down the worn stairs, she had stopped crying. Struggling with her weight, both boys took the steps slow. Inara burrowed her face into Jack's shoulder. Did she expect to find Krimble at the door, waiting for them? Nothing came from the windowless room. Fed by Inara's shaking body, Jack's relief turned to acute anxiety. Blossoms of brilliant crimson mingled with the maroon and brown swirls staining the rags that bound her legs. Her blood reminded him of crushed roses.

They passed another of Krimble's paintings, the frenzied brush strokes portrayed a field of dying corn, where worms writhed amidst the rotten roots. Narmacils hid amongst the failed harvest, some rolled in the spoilt earth, and others climbed the blackened stalks, while more peppered the distance, indistinct but for the characteristic golden gleam with the dissecting silver bolt. Knowing one lived inside him made Jack ill; nausea, making his stomach roil, hit him like surprise punch.

'Ying, careful,' said Bill, in alarm, as Inara dipped toward the floor.

'Sorry,' muttered Jack, tightening his hold. 'This should lead outside.' He nodded toward a white door, long blackened with mould.

Damp mist trailed into the house through the open door. The night sky shone with constellations. Freezing wind made them shudder as they stepped onto the grass. Despite the biting cold they all welcomed being outside, especially Inara, who peered up at the clear sky, and took a deep breath. Inara became lighter in Jack's arms. Carrying her with less effort around the corner of the house, he came to a sudden, shocked, stop. A looming presence, wreathed in swirling eddies of mist, stood before them.

'Come here Black,' said Bill, with an impatient jerk of his head.

The wolf emerged, big and powerful, from the mist, his blue eyes reflecting starlight. His sodden black fur hung in twisted threads, with the ends of the matted hair trailing across the ground. A low growl escaped the square muzzle; Jack feared the wolf ignored Bill's command, as had the rat.

'Hush,' said Bill, and Black, lowering his head, approached.

Clinging to Jack, so fiercely that she choked him, Inara whimpered. If she had legs she would have ran from the wolf. Pulling her arm from his neck, Jack gasped, 'It's alright, he's with us. We named him Black for his colour, and if it were not for him, we would never have escaped the woods with our lives. Bill has him under control.'

'Like he did with the rat,' said Inara, not won over with the strength of Bill's gift.

'That's not fair, Krimble blocked me,' argued Bill in outrage. 'I got it off you when Yang knocked him out didn't I.'

'It's a lot bigger than a rat,' she said, wary of them carrying her closer to the predator.

'Trust me Inara,' said Jack, 'Bill has him under control. He carried us from danger, and he will again. We can't hold you much longer; quick, climb onto Black's back, before Krimble wakes.'

The threat of Krimble recapturing them spurred Inara into allowing Jack and Bill to lift her onto Black's waiting back. Once perched atop Black she grabbed a hank of hair in closed fists, drawing an agitated growl from the wolf. She dug her knees into the wolf's flank; Bill sat before her and hugged the wolf's powerful neck.

The wolf, though large, could not carry three people. 'I'll walk beside you.' Jack, having the better chance to traverse the wilderness than Bill, who still looked groggy from the drugged tea, took the lead. He strode through the wind-churned mist, eager to be on the move. They had tarried too long, at any moment Krimble could rush through the doors, and this time he had a wolf he could turn on them.

Stagnant pools, surrounded by soft earth, conspired to ensnare Jack's feet. He stumbled from one obstacle to the next. The mist thickened around the group. Visibility reduced to a few feet. Frustrated, he wanted to thump the ground, when he spied a long stick. Taking the wood, he immediately began prodding the soft ground ahead to warn him of any pitfalls. The slow progress frustrated the group. Black navigated the swamp better, circling the sinkholes and water with ease; a few times the wolf had no other option than to traipse, like Jack, through the mire. Whenever her wounds met cold water, Inara cried out. Hearing her painful sobs spurred Jack to lift her legs from the bog.

'Where are we going Ying?' Stars crowned Bill's head, while impenetrable mist clung to his legs.

'I don't fancy making for the near wood, the wolves could still be waiting for us to leave the marsh.' Wanting to get as much possible distance between them and the house Jack had paid little attention to their direction when he started to walk. 'We'll make for the northern woods.' Looking to the heavens, he spotted a red star. 'There's the Maiden, waiting in her tower for her lost love, she'll guide us to the trees.'

'I always enjoyed that story,' remarked Inara, smiling down. 'My mother told me the Maiden's father would not allow any man to see her, and would lock her in the tallest tower, where she grew lonely and sad. She often sat in darkness, looking out at the wild country; then one night she spotted a Huntsman.' She pointed at another group of stars sinking into the western horizon. 'Soot from the castle's forge discoloured the stone of the tower to its roof, so every night it became invisible. To gain the Huntsman's attention she lit a lamp. The rose tinted glass caught the man's eye, and he came to the tower where they fell in love.'

'Didn't he have to outrun a hound with two heads?' asked Bill.

'The white hound, Numo,' she agreed, 'the favourite pet of the Ice Giant Dragonorth.' Inara pointed out a larger constellation.

'They don't look like anything,' remarked Bill, of the sprinkling of lights above them. 'That one looks more like a frying pan than a hound.'

'You have to look with better eyes,' said Inara. 'The handle of your pan is Numo's tail, and there,' she pointed at a cluster of bright stars, 'his legs, and his pricked ears.'

'There's nothing wrong with my eyes; it looks like a frying pan, or perhaps a bedpan.'

Jack let them argue, happy to hear Inara speak of things other than Krimble. Although he also agreed that the stars looked like a frying pan, he preferred Inara's explanation; it reminded him of his mother's stories.

Blisters covered his hands from holding the stick; his fingers jarred each time the end struck the ground. A frog leaping into a pond scared Inara, who broke off her argument with Bill to listen.

Without warning, the mist lifted, allowing them to see the shimmering land by moonlight. Casting his eye back, Jack spotted Krimble's home. Alarm swept through him like a poison that weighed down his already tired legs. 'We should be farther away than this,' he heard himself say.

'He's awake,' whispered Inara.

'The fog confounded us. Krimble used his Talent to make us walk in a circle,' said Jack. A hush fell over them. Exposed, and vulnerable, they each felt the searing stab of panic. Jack wanted to rant against the injustice of their predicament. They had escaped the Marsh House, spent hours walking, only to find themselves back where they had started. Hunkering low across Black, Bill planted his face into the wolf's coarse hair, while Inara hugged his back. Crouching low, Jack clutched his walking stick so tight his blisters burst. Guiding them from the house, Jack hoped Krimble had missed them. Without the mist hampering their sight, they navigated the small ponds with ease, and spotted the larger bodies of water well before stumbling on them.

The spongy ground sapped Jack's strength; he slipped on the wet grass where Black trod with surefootedness. Mud covered him to his waist.

'Oh no,' cried Inara, pointing up at the sky.

Jack followed her wavering hand to billowing storm clouds that obliterated the stars. The Maiden star stood resolute against the storm. Peering up at her

CRIK

light he refused to lower his gaze. A few wisps of cloud obscured the red light for only a moment. She will not abandon us, repeated Jack's racing mind. When an anvil shaped Cumulonimbus cloud rolled in, to hide the Maiden star better than her father's forge had hid her tower from searching eyes, he howled in despair. All turned dark, the still water no longer mirrored the sky, and the grass became a stretch of ink before them. Only silhouettes fed their hungry eyes.

'Where to now,' asked Bill.

'Keep straight, we were heading toward the woods when the clouds appeared,' replied Jack. He did not voice his concern on how to remain in a straight line over a land designed to confound their every step.

A roll of thunder crashed down, to reverberate in the chests of the small group. The wind picked up strength, snapping Inara's skirt and fluttering Jack's collar around his reddened cheeks.

'Keep moving,' cried Jack over the dying thunder.

Knowing the house grew smaller with every step encouraged Jack onward. He took hold of Black's fur, trusting the lupine's keener senses to keep them on track.

A spark of dazzling white lit up the world. In the brilliance, Yang appeared as a giant, towering over them. Jack quailed at the sight; positive the demon meant them harm. He threw his hands up over his face in fear. The vanishing light took Yang with it. Breathing in the night air, Jack kept his eyes fixed on where Yang had sprung above them.

'He's looking for us,' laughed Inara. 'It's his searchlight.'

'Shut up, stop laughing,' Bill shouted, his hands jammed against his ears. The terrible searchlight flashed again, leaving the indelible image of Inara's terror-stricken face to haunt them.

Inara's mad laugh continued in the dark. She expressed her anguish no words could describe.

'She's losing it again,' said Bill.

'Leave her alone,' said Jack, 'she's frightened. She'll calm done in a minute.'

'It's alright for you; you haven't got her shaking on your back. If she continues for much longer, I'm likely to go insane.'

With each flash, the land came into focus, revealing the layout of the marsh for an instant at a time. Rounded grassy knolls, and clumps of reed, made the lumpy terrain difficult to remember when the darkness swept back in. They clambered over small hillocks on hurried feet, seeking lower ground, away from Krimble's searching gaze.

Jack found himself wishing Dwayne Blizzard were with them, they could use Dwayne's Talent to guide them in the dark.

Coming to an especially high hillock, Bill said, 'We shouldn't climb that, Krimble will spot us. Let's walk around.'

'We don't want him to see us,' mirrored Inara.

GO AND HIDE SEEK

Jack shook his head. 'No, if we start to deviate from our path we won't be able to find the woods. We have to climb and hope we're far enough from the house to avoid detection.'

They waited for the next flash of light before starting to climb. Black, carrying Bill and Inara, easily scampered up the slick slope, pulling along Jack, who still held onto the wolf's long hair. They stopped at the summit, looking down the slope at Krimble's home.

'How,' said Jack in amazement. 'We've been walking for over an hour, we can't have circled back to him?'

'This hill was never by his house, I would've remembered it.' Bill shook his head.

Inara chewed her lip.

'He altered it, just like he altered the path by Inara's home,' said Jack. 'Come on, we have to go back.' He turned to retrace his steps, when Black tugged him toward the house. 'Bill, stop him.'

'I can't he's doing it by himself.'

'He's controlling the wolf,' whispered Inara.

With desperation, Jack realized they could not just ditch Black; they needed the wolf to carry Inara, without his help they had no chance of getting out of the swamp. Resolute, he marched beside his friends; no way would he let them face Krimble without him. Grounding his teeth, he readied himself for the confrontation.

The house remained the same; the firelight danced on the window, creating shadows on the glass. Krimble's stooped figure stood before the door, a flash of lightning showing up his scars to great effect. Blood ran from his lip to his chin.

'I got a little excited,' said Krimble, when Black brought them forward, 'so I lost my concentration.' He looked apologetic. He turned to the shadow that appeared in the glow cast from the window. 'I won't make that mistake a second time.'

'We are going home,' cried Jack, 'all of us.' He looked at Inara, who shivered behind Bill. 'Now leave us alone, or you'll suffer more than a busted lip.'

'Your stupidity is infuriating. I could turn that fine beast against you; he would have you strewn across the grass and in a moment. Your friend, atop the wolf, grants me this power, or have you forgotten what happened in the upstairs room?' He smiled at Inara, his wrinkles deepening. 'You should tell me your name, before it's too late. My patience is spent. Give me what I want, or rot in the ground. The same goes for you,' he told the boys. 'Why waste your gift, join me, and together we will accomplish so much; be part of something grander than you are by yourselves, live with your brothers and sisters.'

'We won't listen to you,' shouted Bill, his face pinched white.

'I'm not talking to you,' remarked Krimble, absently.

CRIK

Yang had not moved since coming to the house, locked in place by Krimble's power. Jack dismissed the idea to rush Krimble, he remembered the man's quickness, and though Krimble had a crooked back he was a grown man, he could not overpower him.

'I could maim these two, like I did with this other vessel.' Krimble pointed a crooked finger at the two boys, though his gaze never left the girl. 'I could do that quite easily. My saw is hanging on a nail a few yards behind me. I have lost my patience, so I won't wait any longer, either join me, or drown in the stinking bog. No one will come to retrieve you here.' His grin broadened.

Black turned his blue eyes on Jack, baring his teeth, snarling from deep in his throat. Still carrying Bill and Inara, he moved toward Jack, his hackles rising in thick bristles. The wolf's howl both froze Jack's blood, and turned his legs into a quivering mess. Even when Black's huge paw stepped across him, Yang refused to help. Alone, Jack only half heard the screams from Inara, and the repeated orders from Bill for Black to stop. He wanted to flee into the darkness, only the wolf saw better than him in the dark and could outrun him over any terrain.

'What's your name?' the familiar question passed Krimble's lips in an excited rush.

Bill yanked on Black's ears to no avail, the wolf continued to bear down on Jack. Drool, fed by Krimble's need, poured from the stretched maw.

Preparing himself for the attack, Jack felt movement inside. Touching his stomach, he could feel his skin stretch as whatever lived inside him turned and twisted. Horrified at the proof of a demon living inside him his entire life overrode his fear of the wolf. Although the skin bubbled beneath his hand, he felt no pain. Revulsion, as horrid and invasive as terminal cancer, swept through his system. He shuddered with the profound knowledge that he was not alone in his body. How would it appear? This question brought back the image of the dragon outside the cracked egg. Alternatively, the forked tongued demon could prise his jaws apart and vomit onto the ground. Could it even look different; some new horror concocted to scatter his sanity. Going back a couple of hours, he had regarded his shadow as an extension of himself. All the trouble Yang caused, no matter how buried the origin, came from himself. His shadow acted out his subconscious; or so he had thought. This flawed knowledge, tied him closer to Yang than anyone. Knowing a demon controlled Yang, changed everything. Yang's fascination with dead things, and weapons of war, became sinister in the hands of a demon. When Yang got him into trouble, had the demon done that as a test? At each repeated question, the Narmacil pushed against his hand.

A golden-eyed wolf crept around the house, her tail held high. Jack spotted her, at first mistaking the canine for the demon that still twisted in his gut. The she-wolf, unnoticed by the rest, continued to stalk closer.

GO AND HIDE SEEK

The struggling Narmacil left Jack's stomach, reaching higher, making him cough as it fluttered into his chest. Finding it hard to breathe, he focused on the new arrival. He recognised the she-wolf as the same one Black had cowed back in the trees. If Krimble took notice of Jack's gaze he would have spotted the wolf, but being so obsessed with the emerging Narmacil he failed to spot the new arrival until too late.

The wolf leapt soundlessly, sinking her fangs into Krimble's neck. Krimble crumpled to the ground wrestling with the she-wolf, digging his fingers into her coat. Spurts of blood coated the white fur around the mouth of the wolf, as Krimble's efforts to release himself grew weaker.

'Where'd she come from,' shouted Bill.

The demon slipped from Jack's chest back into his stomach, allowing him to breathe. Sucking in air he looked up and saw Black had lost interest in him, the wolf watched the smaller wolf kill Krimble. Inara whooped her delight at the demise of her tormentor.

Looking around Jack saw no sign of the rest of the pack. 'She must've followed on her own. You said they were the dominant pair, they must share a greater connection to one another than the rest.'

'Well, however she got here, I'm glad she did.' Bill looked up from Krimble's corpse. 'He would have killed you,' he said, patting Black, 'I tried to stop him but he wouldn't listen.'

'I don't blame you, Bill. There's nothing you could've done, he proved that upstairs when he attacked Inara with the rat.'

'I'm not finished with him,' said Inara, her dark eyes set on Krimble's body.

'What do you mean, you aren't finished with him?' asked Bill. 'Even the wolf has finished.'

'He doesn't deserve to rest,' said Inara, curling her lip.

'What do you mean to do Inara?' asked Jack, fearing the answer as though it were a venomous serpent.

'He never gave up on me; he wanted my Talent more than the others.' She smiled. 'I'm sure in time he would've got what he wanted, changing my suffering to something altogether more horrible.'

'What?' Jack hated asking the question, he already had too many disturbing revelations for one day, for one lifetime.

Pointing at Krimble, Inara flicked up her hand, bringing him to his feet. Blood leaking from his ruined neck, turning his groans into a babbling cry. Krimble opened his eyelids, to reveal dead white orbs.

'He belongs to me now,' said Inara.

CRIK

14. LINDRE REMEMBERED

THE GROUP, COMPROMISING of two wolves, two boys, a crippled girl, and a dead man, left the marsh covered in sticky mud and harassed by flies. Sitting on a log, Jack fished a stone from his shoe. He threw it back into the marsh with an irritated grunt. Rubbing the sole he found a blood blister, he wanted to burst it, but mud caked every part of him, and he did not want to infect the cut.

Bill swung down from Black, waving his hand at an annoying fly. 'He's ripe; we should leave him rot in the marsh.' With a sigh, he sat beside Jack. Out of habit, he reached for his lost hat. 'Grandpa's favourite hat,' he moaned when his hand touched only hair. 'He's going to kill me; and if he does, don't you go bringing me back, you hear.' He waved a finger at Inara. 'Not saying you haven't got a great Talent, if I didn't have such a great one myself, I'd love to be able to raise the dead. It's just I don't want to go rotting in front of anyone. Just look at Krimble, the flies have taken his fingers down to the bone, and there's something moving in his trousers; I saw it.'

'He deserves his punishment, I won't release him.' Inara brushed away a cluster of flies hidden in Black's wiry hair. 'You never saw the worst he did, I'm here to make sure he answers for his crimes.'

Looking across at the rambling wreck, Jack wondered whether Krimble could feel the insects eating his eyes, and crawling up his nose to lay their eggs. He hoped so; Inara deserved her retribution, as did Huin, and the other victims.

'Stand back,' said Inara, waving her hand for Krimble to step away. With a stiff-legged gait, Krimble moved back, until his awkward feet fell into a deep puddle. 'That will do.' Krimble worked his silent mouth.

'He took a cloud of flies with him, but not all.'

The flies, not content with Krimble, hung in the air over Bill. Fortunately, the insects left Inara alone. When the bloodsuckers first appeared, Jack feared for her legs. Cringing at the sight of them, still weeping blood, he kept a steady eye on her bandages. So far, no fly had landed on her, and he intended to make sure none had a chance. Flies laid eggs in open wounds. Touching the warm skin of his stomach, he noted the demon had fallen silent. He tried to imagine it had left him, fluttered away when Krimble coaxed it from hiding. Yang, throwing clods of mud at Krimble, did not allow him to entertain that hope for long. The Narmacil burrowed under the skin like a fat maggot. Like all parasites, it fed from its host.

'I'm starving,' said Bill.

Inara watched him, her dark eyes scornful. 'You were just complaining about the smell, and with all those flies circling you it would be anyone's guess whether you'd eat more of them or food.'

Bill ignored her scathing tone. 'I can send Black hunting, if you'd get off him. These woods are teeming with game. We can light a fire to keep the flies away.'

'Send Silver.'

'I told you I can only control one animal at a time.' Bill looked across to where the slender she-wolf sat with her head on her outstretched paws. 'Black would buck you off his back and crush your skull, if I weren't here.'

'Then why isn't she attacking us?'

Bill shrugged. 'Black's the dominant male, she follows him. I guess we're now her pack.'

Jack had listened to them argue all morning. Once they saw a frog, and for the next hour, they argued whether it was a frog, or a toad. Another time, Bill said he had once held his breath for three minutes, Inara argued that he could not. All pointless, and Jack guessed they picked things to argue over to stop dwelling on their march through the bog. Only they were no longer in the bog, and they still bickered.

'We should travel a little farther in before we eat, put distance between the stinking marsh and us. What do you think Jack?'

'We call him Ying, only his mother calls him Jack.'

'She can call me Jack, if she wants.' He would be quite happy to distant himself from his ever-present shadow. 'I don't fancy eating in sight of the bog, I've seen too much of it. We don't have to go far, only let's get under the trees.'

'What's her problem,' said Bill, once they started to move. 'She disagrees with everything I say, and you side with her every time.'

Jack had guessed Bill wanted to walk with him, instead of riding Black, to have this private word. 'I'm not siding with anyone. I'm keen to enter the woods, and not worry whether my next step will go into a puddle, or a sinkhole. Besides, you're arguing with her as much as she's arguing with you.'

'I'm not.'

'I've listened to nothing but you two for hours; believe me you're giving as good as you get.'

Bill scratched his head. 'The cap must've blown off when the wolves chased us.'

'Your grandfather has plenty of hats, he won't miss one.' He took hold of Bill's shoulder and gave it a squeeze. 'Don't worry; we'll be home before long.'

CRIK

Casting his eye over his shoulder he saw Inara was out of earshot. The trees cut out the sun making the wood almost as dark as night. 'Listen,' he said.

Glancing across, Bill noticed Jack's tenseness. 'What's wrong with you?'

'I have something to tell you.' He told Bill everything, from seeing the Giant in the storm, of finding the egg and its hatching. Finally, in a rush of whispered words he divulged how the demon had evaded capture by jumping into Bill's open mouth. Once told, his friend's reaction was startling and worrisome.

'I'm not stupid.' Colour had risen in Bill's cheeks. 'The drugged tea Krimble gave me knocked me out, but it didn't addle my mind. He tried to lure, what you call "our demons", so he could have our Talents. As the creatures bestow our Talents, it makes logical sense that one of them leapt into me the night before we entered the woods.'

Dumbstruck, Jack muttered, 'Aren't you upset? These things are using our bodies like hollowed out trees. It frightens me to death.'

'I'm angrier that my best friend kept what he knew secret from me.'

Undeterred, Jack said, 'There's something alien inside you.' He poked his friend in the stomach. 'Right now it's hiding in there, doing what it wants.'

'Everyone back home has a Talent. The Mayor, my Grandpa, even your mother. Generations have had Talents. All you have to do is read the old headstones at Long Sleep to know that. No harm ever came to them.'

'You didn't see the thing.' Jack wanted to grab his friend's shoulders and shake him until he understood.

'I don't have to see it. Before the other day everyone pitied me. Poor ol' Bill, he can't do a thing.' His face drooped into a sullen sneer. 'Having Yang you never understood how alone I felt.'

'I wish I was alone,' Jack cried. Even in the shade he had caught glimpses of his shadow. 'Each time Yang shows himself I see the forked tongued demon. They are using us!'

'Think what you like Ying; I'm happy. Finally I have my Talent. I will return to the village ahead of Black. None of your tales of demons will stop that from happening.'

Troubled, Jack stopped trying to argue. They both carried on in awkward silence.

After the barren marsh, they found the amount of life on view as they entered the dense woodland obscene. Everywhere grew new fauna, smothered in colour, smelling rich and intoxicating. Yellow-ringed caterpillar ate the leaf of a blue bush. Beside the bush sprouted red fronds, like a creature in a rock pool, snatching any caterpillar that wandered too close. A haze of gnats, stirred in the hot morning air, joined the marsh flies in an agitated cloud. Bees flew by, intent on collecting nectar from the flowers to carry back to their queen. Small birds, with purple breasts, and long beaks, swooped through the air, snatching the insects with practised ease. Squirrels, rabbits, and hedgehogs, crossed each other's paths in the undergrowth. The trees altered from the slender Maple with its broad leaf and musical branches, to the thicker limbed oak. Faces, sunken into the trunks of the oak, stared out in silent reproach. Red sap ran down these humanized knots of wood, giving them tears.

'We should've gone back the way we came.' Bill stamped on a fat root. 'We're lost.'

'That happened when we left the hunter's path, and with Krimble messing with the wood we had no chance of finding it again. Besides, we could not risk running into the wolves; with Inara with us, we had no chance of outrunning them.'

'I guess,' conceded Bill, refusing to acknowledge their earlier disagreement. 'The thing is, by coming north we're taking ourselves farther from Crik. No one will look for us all the way out here. We have to circle back at some point, whether those wolves are there or not; there's no escaping it.'

'We'll get there, only we'll do it by a different route. The first thing we need to do is get Inara back home.' Jack looked back at the girl riding the wolf, who beckoned him.

'There's a clearing passed those trees,' she told him, once he and Bill dropped back to her side. She pointed her chin to where two old oaks pushed away from each other.

Standing on tiptoes, Jack gasped in astonishment. 'What is that?'

'What can you see Ying?'

What he saw defied explanation. Framed by the trees, and cradled by a large glade, stood three stone figures, two women and a man, each wore armour and held a decorated shield. A jade hand held the statues in its palm. The male statue looked to the sky, shielding his blind eyes with the blade of his hand. Grotesque faces carved into the tips of the green fingers grimaced and frowned down at the three statues. One face passed a ragged tongue over bulbous lips, and another gave a sly wink. Emerald light shimmered across the clearing as sunlight shone through the green stone. All the statues took on the hue, their blank faces appearing reptilian. Past the sculptures appeared a small hill, alive with yellow flowers, beyond which ran a gentle stream. Fish, glistening in the water, leapt into the air. An apple tree, its branches full of red fruit, overlooked a circular pond.

'What's that green light?' Bill, lacking Jack's height to see over the intervening foliage, began to jump, gripping Jack for support.

Trapped in his thoughts about Bill, Jack had missed the green light spilling through the trees. Atop Black, Inara had easily spotted the queer light.

Growing tired of jumping, Bill climbed Black, sitting behind Inara where he grew silent as he viewed the clearing with its strange inhabitants.

'It's a safe place, its protected,' said Inara, reading Jack's reticence. 'I've stayed within similar glades with my parents.'

CRIK

'There're other places like this?' whispered Bill, regaining his ability to speak.

'Of course, the woods aren't only home to trees, you know.'

Without offering any further explanation, Inara dug her knees into Black's side, guiding the wolf toward the green light. Clearly not as keen to enter the clearing as the girl, Bill lifted his eyes to Jack, who felt even less sure of the mysterious statues.

Jack's skin tingled as the green light touched him, making him itch; also, his hair lifted as though by a stray gust, but no wind stirred the air? Following behind Inara he took less notice of the peculiar sensation than if he had entered alone. Besides, Inara had assured him it was safe, and he trusted her - didn't he?

The crisp grass underfoot, crackled under their weight. The crunching vegetation made him think of running through a cabbage batch.

Silver trotted ahead, her nose close to the ground. Without her intervention Krimble would have killed him. Yet he must never forget her savagery; if Black kept her in check, what would happen if something befell Bill? Not wanting to dwell on that possibility, he followed the wolf, at a slower pace.

Krimble, dropping decaying flesh wherever he walked, stirred a deep disgust in Jack. The raised body of the marsh man decayed at an accelerated rate; patches of skin peeled back, exposing red bones. Jack could not deny the physical revulsion the zombie stirred in the pit of his stomach, nor could he ignore his greater mental aversion to Krimble the man. Could the demon have twisted Krimble into kidnapping strangers? Who had desired the captive Talents? If the demon had manipulated the man, then would his own demon try to do the same to him? His concern deepened, as with faltering steps he trailed the group.

Black pulled up short of the emerald hand, his tail held stiff. Inara, her interest focused on the sculpture, failed to notice the wolf's reticence. Bill, having gained an appreciation of art from an assortment of books, mirrored her fascination. Thankful for the silence, and an end to the incessant bickering, Jack forced himself closer to the strange artefacts. In the face of new discoveries, he forgot about his tingling skin.

Metal armour wrapped the three stone statues; the women wore bronze breastplates, decorated with a black swirl, and skirts of pleated metal, while the gazing man had tempered gold covering his chest and back, with protective greaves rising to sharp stabbing points. All carried a small shield, with a different picture engraved on its surface. An owl, its head larger than its small body, adorned one woman's shield, while a black bird, a wriggling serpent in its beak, filled the round disc of the second woman. The man bore a clenched fist on his, with a broken spear below the disembodied wrist. A curved dagger, with a white hilt, rode each hip.

'If these are as old as I think they are,' began Jack, 'shouldn't the metal have rusted by now?'

LINDRE REMEMBERED

'They are Lindre,' answered Inara. 'Our laws, and those of nature, do not apply here. Look how the stream starts and ends in this glade.'

The stream Jack first noticed from outside the clearing ran for twenty yards before ending at the deep azure pond. 'How is that possible? Where have the fish come from?' His raised hand pointed out a leaping salmon.

'Enchanted,' said Inara. 'If you ate an apple here, before you got to the core, another fruit would have grown in its place. Those flowers on the hillside,' she stabbed the air with her finger in excitement, 'will never wilt.'

'Well its better than the marsh,' said Bill, unconcerned with his mysterious surroundings. He jumped to the ground. 'I'm famished, how about some fish?'

Inara shook her head. 'Although you can eat the fruit and drink the water, it is forbidden to kill inside a Lindre Circle.'

'Who forbids it?' asked Jack.

'The Lindre won't allow a living creature to come to harm within the clearing.'

Peering at the statues bathed in the green light, Jack could not understand Inara's meaning; why fear stone?

Bill stood off to one side. 'Who are the Lindre? Why can't we go fishing? An apple won't fill me, I'm starving.'

'It's as I told you, the Lindre protect the clearing. They are older than the trees surrounding this glade. Once they walked these woods, nurturing everything within it and creating the hills. Cutting into the mountainside, they formed miles of caves as they explored the mountain's secrets. My father told me the Lindre discovered the Rock Giants under the ground, and brought them into the light.'

Hearing the name brought the Giant back to Jack's mind in vivid detail. Remembering the many-eyed Giant made him uncomfortable. How many secrets did the woods have? Unsettled, he raised his hand. His fingers hovered over his stomach, not wanting to touch his skin out of fear of feeling something beneath. When they delved into the earth, had the Lindre awakened the demons?

'If they were so great, how come no one in Crik has ever heard of them,' asked Bill. 'I've read plenty of books about Crik Wood, and I've never heard them mentioned.'

'You have to leave the safety of your houses to find the truth.'

'We aren't afraid to leave the village, hunting parties are always entering the wood; sometimes for days at a time,' replied Bill, infuriated at Inara's accusation.

'I'm not arguing with you, the truth is here in front of you. I don't need to say anything more.'

Jack sank into a tired silence. He moved from the green hand to sit under the shade of the apple tree. Reaching up he picked a red fruit from a low hanging branch, and bit into it. The juice gushed into his mouth and over his

CRIK

chin. Hunger, released like a captive bird flying from an open cage, surged up from his aching belly. Meaning to clip the wings of his gnawing hunger, he devoured the apple and did not stop eating until he crunched the core of a third fruit. Yang, vibrant in the green light, pulled Krimble's arm, forcing the dead man into a lurching half-run toward the tree. Having Krimble close upset him, but he expected his shadow's fascination with the zombie. Thankfully, the flies had left, though the zombie's pocked white skin showed the ravages done by the foul insects. With Krimble came his smell, and Jack lost his appetite. Disregarding a fourth apple, he turned his back on his shadow, and its obsession, to see Bill marching toward him, his fists pumping at his sides.

'She's insufferable,' Bill muttered. 'She's calling everyone back home dimwits. No one knows anything about the woods, she says. Ignoring me when I tell her about the hunters, to say if we knew nothing of the Lindre, then we knew nothing of Crik Wood. I have a right mind to command Black to dunk her in the water.'

'She has a point. We knew nothing about how we got our Talents. If I hadn't dug up the egg, we'd still have no clue. Everything we believed...'

'I don't want to talk about that.' Bill sounded angrier than before.

'Like me you thought we were born with our Talent,' said Jack refusing to drop the topic. 'I told you how the demon hatched from the egg and disappeared into you.'

'Yeah, thanks again for keeping that from me.' He glowered.

'I kept it from you, scared to tell you, in case the demon hurt you when you found out.' Was he the only one who saw anything wrong with a shape-shifting demon living inside them? Inara saw it as natural. What of the others back home, did his mother know about the Narmacil?

'Think what you like, I can't see anything wrong with allowing something to use my body if I get a Talent in return. You are just like her,' he glared at Inara, 'you never listen to reason.'

Seeing Bill was on the verge of storming off, Jack hurriedly said, 'We can't argue with Inara about the circle.' He spun around. 'This place is a mystery. Your grandfather never mentioned anything like this in his stories. She obviously knows the woods far better than us.'

'I bet she knows nothing about the Hanging Tree,' said Bill, sullen. 'There are plenty of things we know, things we take for granted, which she doesn't have any idea about.'

'You're right.'

'I am, but I don't go rubbing her nose in it.' Bill folded his arms. Inara, oblivious of Bill's rant, scrutinised the Lindre statues. 'The quicker we can return her back to her folks, the better. She can take Krimble too; Yang is taking a liking to the walking corpse, and I don't care if you are my best mate, I don't fancy sticking around him for much longer.'

LINDRE REMEMBERED

'I wish we could get rid of him already,' said Jack, looking across at Krimble's weeping eye. 'The decision is Inara's to make. I won't tell her what to do; he owes her for taking her legs.'

'I can have Black chew his off, if that makes her feel any better.'

'Not letting him die is a worse punishment; she doesn't need to do anything else.'

'I suppose it can't be nice having bits of you falling off.'

The sound of splashing water stopped their conversation. In dismay, Jack watched Silver step out of the river, her grey fur clinging to her ribs in wet tangles. A fish squirmed in her jaws.

'Why'd you let her do that?' Inara shouted at Bill, her face flushed.

'Me, what do you want me to do? I told you I'm holding Black in check, if you had let me send them off hunting when I asked, Silver wouldn't be so hungry now.'

'Quiet,' said Jack. 'Did you hear that?'

'What?'

'Sounded like grinding stone.'

'Oh no,' cried Inara, 'She's awake.'

The female statue, bearing the owl shield, turned her lifeless face toward them, shattering her stone neck in hundreds of fractures. Dark blood, poured from the rents, drenching her bronze armour. Tilting back her head, the Lindre let out a shrill cry.

15. AWAKENED

THE STATUE'S HEAD turned, and the stone cracked. From the broken neck poured blood as thick as crude oil, drowning the intricate swirls on the breastplate. Setting her sights on Inara, who, astride Black, stood the closest, the Lindre lifted her shield. With a sound of tearing leather, the statue pulled her feet free from the green hand, splintering the ancient stone, sending jade jewels into the bordering grass.

Inara threw her hands in front of her face and screamed. Black, whether obeying Bill, or some primal urge, fled deeper into the clearing. He stopped under the leaning apple tree, snarling back at the statue.

On numb legs, Jack closed with Inara, followed by Yang, who towed Krimble behind. 'How can this be possible?'

'I told you not to kill anything in the circle. The Lindre will not stop until she has had a life for a life.'

'Silver killed the fish, we didn't. Tell her.'

Inara rounded on Jack, her dark eyes full and scared. 'How can I tell her? The Lindre have guarded this glade for a thousand years, and you want me to tell her to go back, that it has all been a misunderstanding. Oh Jack, if it was only so simple.'

Holding onto a branch of the apple tree, Bill shouted, 'If she wants a life, give her Krimble, she can do whatever she wants with him.'

'He's already dead,' answered Inara. 'Although he is conscious, it is my ability that animates him.'

The stone covering the joints of the Lindre fell away, revealing a mesh of grey muscle. The other statues remained in their silent repose, leaving their sister to deal with the group. With the owl-adorned shield thrust forward, the Lindre moved off the giant hand, with its many gleeful faces.

Looking back to where they had entered the clearing, Jack saw the foliage had risen up, swallowing their retreat in an unruly nest of thorns and twisted wooden limbs.

Bill, also noticing the imprisoning wall, let out a gasped yell. Hopping down from a bulking tree root, to the grass, he said, 'We're trapped.'

The pleated metal skirt tinkled as it stroked marble thighs. A dispassionate stony stare tracked them as they hedged away from the awakened statue on directionless legs, seeking an avenue of escape from the ringed clearing. The statue's stiff fingers dipped to the floor, flicking the blood away in smoking droplets.

Coming to the mysterious stream, filled with trout, salmon, and whiskered catfish, Jack paused. Ahead, flowers in eternal bloom, with yellow, red, and blue petals, welcomed them with a rich fragrant embrace. Surrounded by such beauty, it both felt unreal, and unfair, that they had escaped one nightmare to find another. His weary spirit faltered; only his fear for his friends' wellbeing stopped him from giving in to full despair. He pondered sacrificing himself to save them. A life for a life, right, he thought with gloomy resignation.

'The trees have moved; there is no way out.'

Listening to Bill, Jack searched the forest wall for any gap, no matter how small, for them to squeeze through. Silver trotted close to the glade's boundary, sniffing the foliage with her sharp nose. Finding no egress either, the she-wolf returned to shadow Black. The Lindre had not gained on them, nor had she dropped back as they tracked through the flowerbeds. Free of the hand's green light, her marbled skin gleamed in the sunlight. The reflected light from the armour forced Jack to shield his eyes as a hundred golden needles glinted with every move. Despite his desire to run, to stretch the distance between them and their hunter, Jack dismissed the idea; the trees imprisoned them in a strangling grasp.

Inara pulled Black to a stop. 'It's no good walking around without a plan of escape. We have to face her.' Her set face demanded respect, Jack had not forgotten her formidable mental fortitude; how else could she have survived her captivity?

'We haven't got a plan.' Bill, disagreeing, made Black continue forward, jostling the girl and making her cry out in surprise. 'If we face her, one of us will die. Do you want to offer yourself?'

'She'll eventually catch us; this is stupid; all we're doing is prolonging the inevitable.'

'She's right Bill, we'll wait for her here.'

'We haven't circled the clearing yet, there may yet be another way out.'

'There's not,' said Inara, yanking on Black's fur to make him stop. 'The trees closed in behind us; what makes you think the Lindre would leave another opening?'

Believing Bill would continue to argue, Jack opened his mouth to lend weight to Inara's counsel, when Bill shocked him by turning to face the approaching guardian.

'A bear would come in handy right about now,' said Bill, clenching his fists. 'What do you think Ying, could a bear break stone?'

'I guess it could,' said Jack, with a surprised smile.

CRIK

Coming to heel beside Jack, Silver snarled, her black lips quivering in rage. Yang, appearing in the guise of a longhaired giant, stroked the wolf's bristling fur.

'Stand in front of us,' Inara commanded Krimble in an emotionless voice.

Their one time captor came to stand two feet in front of Yang, facing the Lindre. The wretch rocked back on his feet, held upright, not by tendon and bone, but from the sheer force of Inara's will.

A Wood Pigeon took flight when the Lindre emitted a loud groan. The statue came to a sudden halt. Black blood no longer pumped from her splintered neck. Tilting her head back, the Lindre forced her mouth open, showering the hillside with alabaster fragments as the stone fell from her fissured cheeks.

'What's her game?' said Bill, touching Black with a restless hand.

'I think she's going to speak,' answered Jack in awe.

'She is our judge and executioner,' Inara said, looking down at the two boys. 'She is about to pass judgement.'

Seeing the Lindre motion toward them, Jack had no doubt what Inara said was about to come to pass, but the hollow voice of the ancient guardian surprised him with her first words:

'Why do the children of Illyarden flee from me? You have entered our circle to enjoy our protection; why then do you fear my coming? Is it my visage that stirs fear in your breast? If that is so, please lay aside any concerns, I come to you now in this stone countenance only through necessity. I am ancient, having slumbered for long years. Tell me of Illyarden, of its troubles, and joys.'

'If you come in peace, why trap us here? You've stalked us from one end of the meadow to the other,' called Bill, in frustration. Under his words, like turbulent water beneath a placid surface, his fright stirred, threatening to pull him down.

The Lindre's laugh that punctuated Bill's challenge echoed inside her stone shell. 'If I wanted to strike you down, I would not need to chase you. We, who saw the birth of your first, will see the last of you leave this world. We do not need to prove our peaceful nature, we who nurtured you when you were infant.'

Jack stepped closer, stopping once Krimble's rotting flesh assailed his nostrils. The blood no longer clung to the Lindre's brass armour; the beating sun dissipated it in a grey steam that bathed the white face. Only the cracks in the stone remained to spoil the beauty of the carven image, and like the moss covering the dulled headstones overlooking the Tristle River back home, they added a weight of passing time. 'If not to punish us for the killing of the fish, why have you come?'

'Doubt riddles you Ying. A newly planted disquiet awakens, making you fear yourself. I have answers to soothe your troubled mind, come to me and you will be eased.'

AWAKENED

Jack could feel Yang behind him, stretching away, but always there, anchored to his feet, even while he slept. He needed to know what the demons were, where they came from, and what they wanted. Inara had called them Narmacil; was that all she knew of them? Only he had seen the demon that entered Bill, the mischievous sprite with its forked tongue and black skin. Jack couldn't imagine the creature could be anything other than evil.

'Ying stop,' shouted Bill.

Although Jack heard his friend's call, once he started forward, he knew he had to know, no matter the risk. If the Lindre could tell him the truth, perhaps she would know how to get rid of it. With Yang drawing up behind him, Jack left behind the flowers, stepping back onto the crisp grass. His friends stirred restlessly, but they did not follow.

'There was a time when you would have come to me, without my asking,' said the Lindre as Jack faced her. 'Your unease is understandable, and unfortunate. We have been gone for a long time. Take my hand, and I will show you the answers you seek.'

He studied the offered hand, seeing the long lifeline imprinted on the palm. He backed away, his fear commanding his steps as surely as though someone held a knife to his exposed throat.

A golden light spilled from the Lindre's eyes as they opened wide. With terrible swiftness, she reached forward, grabbing Jack by the shoulders and hoisted him into the air. Her cold fingers held him tight, while the colour rushing from her face engulfed him. Dimly he heard Inara scream.

CRIK

16. A LIFE TAKEN

A WARM GUST THREW dust across a dirt track, lifting a brown leaf high into the summer sky. A white dog, with a splash of brown over its right eye, watched the errant leaf in bored attention. Dirt smeared the thick rope tethering the mongrel to a leaning post. Written across the post in red chalk, in a child's scrawl, were the words, "Knell tells no lies, so don't ask". Accompanying the post on the dirt track stood two windowless houses; they also had no door. The nearest building had a net thrown over a gaping hole in its side, where a baby's cry rent the air in a siren's call. Dead grass and bald mounds of earth outlaid the gardens. An old metal swing, its frame speckled with rust and the seat damaged by damp, creaked with every gust. A dead tree, its blackened limbs home to blacker birds, overlooked a large hole that dominated the other garden. Red jagged stone poked through the loose earth around the edge of the hole.

Blinking, after the sudden bright light, Jack looked around. His mouth fell open in amazement, and only grew wider as he spotted the dog tied to the leaning post, biting its hind leg. Almost tripping over his feet, he searched for the Lindre, the clearing, and his friends, but only saw the two houses and a hillside rising in a purple swathe of heather. The cawing of a large Rook perched on the dead tree snatched his attention. The cruel grey beak of the carrion bird cracked wide again; its red eye froze Jack to the middle of the track. The other birds paid him no attention, and the dog still busied himself by attacking the fleas on its backside. Ignoring the interest of the bird, Jack regarded the odd houses with no windows. Having never seen homes like them, he had no clue as to his present location. Was he still in Crik Wood? Behind him, an angled stone stood in tall grass. Age had taken away the name carven into the white stone, leaving behind only rounded holes.

The dog barked, but not at him. The mongrel glared at the birds, and they glowered back. Standing apart from the smaller birds, the Rook watched him from the highest branch. The sun beat the back of his neck drawing a line of sweat across his skin. Wiping away the moisture with an irritant hand, Jack crouched down with the idea of freeing the dog, so it could escape to cooler shade, but he found he couldn't undo the knot. Although he pulled the threads apart, the knot remained. After three failed attempts, he gave up. His failure went unnoticed by the dog; it continued to bark at the birds. Disturbed by the

A LIFE TAKEN

dog's lack of curiosity in him drove Jack back a step. Bringing his fingers to his mouth, he licked the tips where the rope had rubbed them raw.

For the first time since coming here, he found himself staring at the dark smudge under his feet. Wherever he had gone before Yang had been there, anchored to him, but here his shadow was the same as everyone else's. It did not move contrary to the position of the sun; it did not change shape. Here his shadow could not get him into trouble; it just was. Extending one leg, he watched his dark outline mirror him over the lumpy ground. Trying to trick his shadow, he shot out an arm, spreading his fingers. The shadow copied him. Kicking the air, he then jumped and waved an arm, and then the other, and always the shadow moved with him. Inexplicability he found himself growing concerned over Yang's absence. Didn't he want Yang to disappear? If his shadow remained in one place, instead of wandering off, the demon would be no more. Then why feel sad? Regardless of his confusion, he could not deny the loneliness pulling him down.

Acrid smoke stung his throat, making him dry swallow. Only dust swirled across the street, no smoke. Confounded he looked again for the fire. In an attempt to build saliva, to clear the taste from his mouth, he moved his tongue, to find it stuck like glue to the roof of his mouth. Chalking the dryness to the hot day, and not the fear coiling around his innards, he continued walking down the track. By the time he had passed the dog, he had dismissed the mysterious smoke. Within the nearest house, rising above the nattering birds, he heard a baby cry. Hair prickled along the back of his head, and the skin along his arms cobbled.

The net covering the side of the house billowed outward, bulging with its invisible catch. Waiting, he held his breath for a repeated cry, and when only the Rook's harsh voice broke the silence, he moved with weighted feet to the grass bordering the property. He wanted to cough, perhaps to make some noise other than the bothersome bird. With his nerves shattered, he kicked a rough stone. It struck the frame of the swing, snapping the dog's attention away from the dead tree and its resident delinquents. Unsure how he could affect the stone and not the slipknot he tried kicking another stone, and watched as it skidded across the straight track. Again, the dog followed the projectile.

Movement from the other side of the net stopped him from further experimentation.

The bulky silhouette, he had spotted, disappeared in an instant. He correlated the outline with that of a flesh-eating ogre, straight from the pages of his favourite comic. The shape however did not fit with his over active imagination, though wide, it did not possess the height required to be a monster. He approached, hoping whomever he saw inside suffered from the same blind spot as the dog.

CRIK

The tickle in his throat increased as his feet drew him nearer. Again, he scanned around for smoke, and again he found none drifting on the winds. Disregarding his discomfort, he proceeded to the side of the house. Through the net, he looked into the room beyond.

The back of a large padded chair, its stuffing spilling from torn seams in yellow balls, covered half of an old cot. A hand rocked the cot, with its gap-toothed bars, while a half remembered lullaby played from the shadows. In one corner stood a broken grandfather clock, stuck at the close of the witching hour. Mushrooms festered on the wet walls, like barnacles on a whale.

At the close of the lullaby, the baby began to scream. Pressing forward, Jack spied the blanket rise at the tail of the cot. A tired sigh, close to the crib, followed.

The chair creaked as the same shape he had earlier seen rose to block his view of the crying baby. Heavy robes accounted for the bulk of the person. From the thick woollen sleeves appeared a slender hand holding a strange flute. Longer than a flute, the instrument also had many more holes. Bending over the cot the figure brought up the musical instrument and played a high-pitched note. An orange glow brightened the room. When the note faded so did the light, allowing the gloom, which was as much a part of the room as the chair, to return. The screams of the baby reached new falsetto heights before subsiding into gentle sobs.

'You can come in now.'

Jack jumped at the female voice.

'She is about to fall into a deep sleep, it will be hours 'till she wakes again.' The husky accent of the woman tasted each word, stretching her speech in a comforting way. 'Careful, do not tear the net, it's old and frayed, but it still keeps out the birds.'

Listening to her warning, Jack looked back at the blackbirds with their yellow beaks. The rook had shifted position; it now perched on the leaning post. Unconcerned with the big bird's proximity, the dog watched the row of blackbirds.

'You can see me?'

'I know you're there,' she responded, drawing out the last word, until it fell into a whispered silence.

Taking care not to pull too hard on the rope, Jack drew aside the net, leaving behind the hot sun. 'What's your name?'

'Names are too powerful to relinquish so hastily. Those who knew my name are gone.' She paused, her hood rising a few inches, tantalising Jack, who fancied having a peek under the drooping fabric at the owner. 'You may call me Knell, for it fits me well.' She dropped her head as though in prayer.

'I'm Jack.'

'Half-truths are always the wisest lie,' responded Knell.

A LIFE TAKEN

The sobs of the child became gentle snores.

'Where are we?'

'As with all old things it has many names; some are beyond my speech, whereas others describe what once was. I knew a hunter, who called these parts "The Scorn Scar," which fits better than you may think.'

Dust bunnies crunched beneath Jack's feet as he trod the warped boards.

'One, both older, and younger than I, brought you here,' she continued without turning from the cot. 'Company is such a rarity these days that when a visitor does drop by, it always comes as a shock. I suppose it's like finding an unexpected love letter on your stoop.'

Unnerved by her reluctance to turn and face him, Jack came to a stop. Though not as tall as the creatures in the pages of his favourite sequential art, she still towered over him. For all the cowl revealed, she could be bald, or have horns. Her squared shoulders were strong. The robe itself bulged at the waist and again high on her back, as though she carried a hundred different items within the blue wool. The hand, clutching the strange flute with long tapered fingers, appeared ghostly white in the gloom. She had chewed her nails, and strips of skin peeled back from the end of her fingers in fine tissue paper coils.

'Am I dead? I saw a blinding light.'

'I've never seen a ghost,' said Knell. 'I suppose there's a first time for everything - but not today.'

Jack sensed her smile.

'Tell me why I'm here?'

'You have many questions,' said Knell, 'of which I know many answers. But the most important question only you can answer.'

'What question?'

'You don't know? It's written all over you boy. Instead of looking outside for answers, try looking within.'

'All I want is to go back to my friends, to get back home.'

'No you don't. Your village is full of secrets, and you will never fit in until you discover all of your little town's clandestine affairs. Having glimpsed the truth behind one lie, you distrust everything, and everyone you have ever known. Your suspicion of your shadow is only the beginning. Who else knows about the little demons? The girl in your party knows. Who else, perhaps your mother kept the truth from you?'

Taking a tentative step, like placing a foot on shifting plates of ice, he moved into the room. Despite the interior gloom wiping away his shadow, he still felt its imprint. He knew the demon that had hatched from the egg in his room, and then jumped into Bill, was evil. The forked tongue, the slanted eyes, the mischievousness of the beast, accounted for his deep-set abhorrence of the Narmacil. How could anyone in Crik live knowing such a loathsome creature existed? His mother would not keep Yang's true nature hidden. If she knew the truth of the demon, she, not he, would be seeking out the answers he sought. Inara's distorted belief in the Narmacil's benign nature, could not dissuade him.

'I want to be rid of the Narmacil.' Nagging him was the single idea that he should leave Yang alone. Aggressively he shut the door on such a poisonous thought, which no doubt came to him from his unwanted hitchhiker. Yet, like a bout of conscience after perpetrating a bad act, he could not fully shake the notion.

'We all have our own personal demons, but sometimes they lend us strength. Are you so sure you want to lose part of yourself?'

Disturbed at how close Knell had come to voicing his own troubled thoughts left him dumbfounded. Instead, he looked back through the net at the watching Rook. Its black feathers, shining with a dark lustre, fluttered with the vagaries of the warm breeze. The bird seemed larger, something its closer proximity could not fully account for.

'If I help you,' said Knell, 'you will only find shades of death. Are you so keen to lose your identity?'

'I want it gone,' replied Jack, not fully understanding her meaning.

'Then go outside and look into the hole, there you will find the pathway to your answer. Return to me once you have seen what lies among the ruined ground and things will become clearer.'

Jack wanted to leave, to discover what mysteries he would find in the ground before the dead tree, but before he could, he had to ask, 'Can I see your face?'

Silence, broken only by the soft sleeping breaths of the baby, met his question. Not daring to ask again, he turned to leave. Spying the large Rook made him pause. Mistaking his hesitation for stubbornness, Knell said, 'I will show you what lies within this cowl when you return to me.' She sounded amused.

The Rook raised an obscene note as Jack pushed aside the net and stepped back into the heat of the day. With the bird only an arms length away, he saw flecks of gold twinkling like stardust in the red irises.

Eating up the ground with swift steps Jack moved around the house. He stopped when he spied the neighbouring garden with its hole exposed like a festering wound. The tree threw down its shadow, sending searching skeletal fingers into the pit. To Jack, the tall tree reminded him of a headstone, wrought in twisted old wood instead of granite. The hole itself then was an open grave. His skin grew tight at the comparison, compressing his lips into a hard line.

The tickle in his throat returned, making him cough.

He passed the creaking swing, missing the doll, with the button eyes, propped up against its frame.

Nearer to the hole, he could smell the earth. It was a good smell. Clods of different coloured mud mingled with the red brick he had earlier noticed.

A LIFE TAKEN

Watching his mother grow things had inured him with enough knowledge to recognise there was too much clay to grow anything besides grass and bramble.

The irritation continued to rise in his throat, burning his lungs and causing his coughs to become more violent.

A sudden cry from the Rook stopped him short of the open ground. Clay crusted his shoes, and the first crumbled stone littered his path. Turning back, he saw the black bird spreading its wings, frantically flapping them, sending pinion feathers high into the air. The bird squawked in great pain, and then its plumage erupted in flames.

Shocked, he cast his eyes away from the burning bird, wanting desperately to see what lay only a few feet away at the bottom of the hole. With faltering steps, he stumbled forward. Ignoring the screaming bird, he looked over the lip of the hole and into an impenetrable black abyss. He looked hard, sure Knell had sent him out here to see something, and he would not look away until he saw it. His intense scrutiny revealed something in the depths. Leaning forward, until his hands sunk into the torn earth, he saw a moon. No, he corrected himself, not a moon, a face, unlike any visage he had ever known. Inexorably it grew closer, as though his being there drew it upward as though he were a magnet and the face a piece of metal. Shallow, quick breaths squeezed from his constricted chest. The hideous grotesquery that resolved itself from the deep made him want to cry out in alarm. Hooked hands groped the air, wanting to snatch him and toss him into the pit. The pallor of the man, if he could think of the rising creature as a man, brought to his mind half cooked egg whites. Despite his tight chest he noticed the stinging acrid smoke wafting off the screaming bird. Now aware of the bird again, he threw himself backward. His back hit the garden hard. Two hands, the fingers broken and bleeding, flew out the hole after him, clutching the brick. Thick clouds formed, blotting out the sun. The blackbirds, which had hung back until that moment, took wing, further darkening the day. A yell of frightful anger tore itself free from Jack as the birds descended, hitting him with wing and beak. He sensed through the crazed birds the figure rise from the hole. Snatching at the blackbirds, Jack continued to scramble back. It took all his effort to draw in breath. A step below his dragging feet he spied the figure. The nightmare face rushed toward him. He could not breathe. Despairing, he felt himself about to lose consciousness, when the face he saw hanging over him materialised into Bill. An instant later, he felt air blown into his mouth.

Coughing, he turned his head, looking for the figure that had lurched up out of the pit. Where was it? He jerked his head to the side and saw Inara, her face as pale as melting candle wax, astride Black. Overhead dark clouds amassed, flickering with electricity.

'What…?' Jack began, and then the question faltered and died.

Jagged lightning screamed down from the sky, striking the Lindre. Sparks flew off her brass armour, and her stone limbs, blackened by the assault,

CRIK

struggled to deflect the web of electricity surrounding her. Blue and red fire fell with awful accuracy. Torched grass led from the bank where Bill stood over Jack, revealing the course the fight had taken. Yang stood to his left, watching the fire flicker across the armour's dark swirls.

'No,' Jack struggled to say, 'stop it, she was helping me.'

'Don't worry,' Bill shouted over the clapping sounds of thunder. 'I thought you were dead, but you were only unconscious. I gave you the kiss of life.'

The Lindre screamed as Krimble called down another bolt.

'Inara, leave her alone!' But the sounds of the storm drowned out his words.

The final flashing strike burnt the image of the Lindre on one knee onto his retinas. With smoke rising from the ruined heap of marble, he saw her ghostly image, dark against the green grass.

17. GREY DIRECTIONS FROM A BLACK HEART

A CRESCENT MOON and a sprinkling of stars filled the sky by the time the small group left the Lindre Clearing. The good mood they felt after finding their way free slowly dissipated as in a halting fashion Jack told them what the Lindre had revealed to him.

'Why look for this cloaked woman?' asked Bill, after Jack had fallen silent. 'We should take Inara back home. The sooner we return to the village, with a hot stew in our bellies the better.'

Aged roots, clothed in green moss, and ill looking flowers, surrounded the group, making the prospect of continuing deeper into Crik Wood fraught with untold dangers. Twisted tree trunks leant close, eavesdropping on their hushed conversation.

'She has the answers,' replied Jack. 'There's something within us, giving us our Talent. I have Yang, you can command animals, and Inara can raise the dead. A desire for more power drove Krimble insane; he wanted more demons. What do the Narmacil get in return?'

'We are not like Krimble,' Inara said. 'He was a murderer.'

'Who controlled who? Did he want to steal the Narmacils from others, or did his demon wish it?'

Draping her fingers over Jack's shoulder, Inara said, 'You have it all wrong. The Narmacils are our friends, our benefactors. The gifts we enjoy, the abilities that define us, are due to them. Are you any different now that you know where Yang comes from?'

'I was foolish and naive to think Yang's actions were my own,' replied Jack, looking over to where his shadow tore open a black pod, scattering tiny seeds over the ground. 'He always got me in trouble – stealing things and upsetting Liza Manfry. An obsession with dead things, stuffed animals and dying plants, I put down to my own interest in the macabre. Knowing his fixations had nothing to do with me makes me question everything.' Looking up sharply, he said, 'I can't say for sure whether my own interests are mine. What if the imp wanted me to like certain stories, or hobbies, to make me more susceptible to its wishes?'

'If it wanted to harm you, it could have,' argued Inara.

CRIK

Jack stabbed his finger against his chest. 'I don't know who I am. Until I get rid of the demon, I will never know whether my actions are my own, or if the Narmacil is making me do it.'

Yang had dropped the pod and stood watching Jack with hands at his sides.

Poking his head around Krimble, Bill looked angry. 'I don't care how I got my Talent. I've waited all my life to find mine, and now that I have I won't give it up.'

'Calm down Bill, I'm not asking you to give up anything. I want to find Knell for myself. You can make up your own mind when you hear what she's got to say.'

'I don't want to hear what she's got to tell you. I'm not going home without my Talent. No one will believe what I can do if I returned alone.'

'Go back then, but I'm going on until I find the answers.'

Heat rose up Bill's neck in a sweeping rash before setting his cheeks aflame. Moving his jaw soundlessly, Bill reminded Jack of a cow chewing grass. Glistening alert eyes peered at him in hurtful reproach.

Jack wanted to smile, to show, despite his harsh words, how much he needed Bill's help, instead his face closed, becoming stern. His cheek muscles bunched in an aching knot. Bill should understand his need to discover all he could about the Narmacil, which after all lived in him too. The prospect of continuing alone with his shadow into the woods sent a cold spray up his spine. Inara wouldn't back him up, her unreasoned view of the harmless demons only fed Bill's own desire to return to the village to show off his Talent. That's all Bill wants, to lead Black passed the Hanging Tree and over the bridge crossing the Tristle River, to rub everyone's nose in his ability to control a wolf. Why shouldn't he, for Bill, the only person in the village without a Talent, life was horrendous. The other kids targeted him with all their jokes; they taunted him by what they could do. Bill, like a man born with two heads, was an outcast. Only didn't he see, raved Jack in his mind, until the night the demon hatched, Bill was the only clean person in the village.

The calm acceptance in which Bill took the existence of the Narmacil made Jack ponder whether his friend had prior knowledge. Consider the secret Bill had kept about his grandmother. Many nights they had sat in the graveyard listening to Mr Dash's warnings about Ghost Walkers. Bill had remained tight-lipped, even when the old grave keeper muttered that; the woman possessed by a Ghost Walker was dead, murdered by the evil spirit. It proved he could keep his mouth shut.

'You want me to go back,' said Bill, his flush attacking his hairline. 'You would see me traipse back through the marsh. I saved your life in the clearing, not to mention from the wolves, and just like that,' he snapped his fingers, making the loose flesh under his arms jiggle, 'you would see me go home alone.'

GREY DIRECTIONS FROM A BLACK HEART

'You're willing to see me set off and find Knell by myself,' retorted Jack. 'I've told you how important it is to find her and you're refusing to help. To have the final laugh, you're letting the demon use your body, just like a snake finding an empty burrow.' Crooked trees framed the woodland trail ahead. Looking along the path he had chosen for himself, accelerated his apprehension of his friends abandoning him to his quest.

'Come on Ying, you're being crazy.' Not liking the idea of backtracking without Jack made Bill try another tack. 'I've seen Yang get you out of tight scrapes before,' he said. 'No one will dare fight you; they all know they'd be fighting Yang as well. Shit Ying,' he cried throwing his hands up as adrenaline pumped through his body, 'why change who you are!'

'I read comics, the grislier the better.' Jack pointed at the jawbone peeking through Krimble's cheek. 'Creatures just like him pulling themselves from coffins, and werewolves lurking in a blanket of fog. Only now I don't know if it's me who likes those stories, or this.' He indicated his stomach.

'You like them Jack,' said Inara. 'Learn to trust yourself.'

'How can I, knowing what's inside me.'

Having Yang stand there watching him played with Jack's nerves, as though a giant claw scraped a field-sized blackboard. Unlike everyone else, his demon was a physical manifestation with its own personality; he could not escape from it. It stood there like a petulant child listening to him voice his fears.

'Listen to her,' urged Bill, who waved away the stench coming off Krimble in a brown haze. 'She knows about the Narmacils. All you've seen is one leap into me.'

Jack's mouth swam with cool saliva, making him want to spit, but he didn't want to show any weakness, seeing Knell was too important. Swallowing he pointed down the trail, still visible among the broad leaves and stalks of the underbrush. 'I'm not arguing anymore, I've got to find her. I want you both to come; I don't like being in the woods. It doesn't mean I won't carry on by myself, only I'd prefer your company.' His heart pounded so hard after giving the ultimatum that he found it hard to breathe.

'You don't know where she is,' said Bill. 'Crik Wood is huge; you'd get yourself lost in no time.'

Jack turned to Inara. 'Do you know where she could be? The woods can't have that many settlements.'

With her blonde hair fanning her dark eyes, Inara shook her head. 'There're a few houses near where I live, but they all have windows, and there's not a hill like the one you described.'

'It's hopeless Ying. You could hunt for years and never meet Knell. Come back home, tell my grandfather about the Narmacils. He knows more than anyone about the woods. He may even know Knell.'

CRIK

That was the last thing Jack wanted to do. If he went back home his mother would never allow him to leave the house. She must already be mad at him for running out after she had ground him. 'No,' he said.

Slipping through the trees Silver returned to the group with blood coating her lips from a fresh kill. Only Black marked her return.

Jack watched Bill, and spotted the subtle change in his countenance, a relaxing of the brow, a new slackness to the lips, and he knew he had won the argument; he would get to see Knell.

Absently scratching the brown cloth bandaging her stunted legs Inara also saw she had lost the argument. Her tremulous sigh, the only sign of her profound disappointment, left her lips unnoticed by the boys.

'How're you going to find her?' asked Bill, beating nettles with a stick he took from Yang's shadowed fingers. 'We can't just walk around, hoping to stumble upon her. The woods are dangerous, or have your forgotten the wolves.'

'I haven't forgotten anything…'

'There're worst things than wolves living amongst the trees,' remarked Inara, 'strange, terrible creatures.' She looked through the bent boughs and at the gaunt branches teased by the passing wind. 'You may have heard of some, thinking they were stories told to scare you. Werebeasts, the tell-tale clanking that warned of the wandering Myrm, the carrion faced Doctors, seeking out spare parts for their bodies. As outlandish as they may seem, they're real, and they roam these hills. Until today you had no idea that the Lindre existed.' Her expression did not change as she craned back her head to look at the stretching branches overhead. 'Secretive creatures, older than the Lindre still live out here, they are always watching.'

'You just want to scare me,' said Jack.

'She's doing a bloody good job too,' said Bill. 'Can you tell us about these things in the morning? I'll be able to handle them better in the light of day.'

'If you aren't scared you are deluding yourself.' Her black eyes, darkened further by the shadow stretching down her white face, held Jack. 'Your village and other settlements are relatively safe from the Myrm. Lone children traipsing through the woods are better sport. Why do you think the hunters of your village stay to their paths? They know what's out here.'

'Stop trying to scare me into changing my mind, I'm not going back.'

The smile Inara showed looked haggard. 'If I thought I could change your mind, I would carry on until you screamed for me to stop.' She tilted forward, feeding her chipped fingernails through Black's shaggy coat. 'You saved me from him,' she tilted her head to Krimble, 'so I'll do what you want. Besides, I see you're set on your mission to find Knell; nothing I say will stop you from going. Only I thought you should be aware of what's awaiting us.'

GREY DIRECTIONS FROM A BLACK HEART

'Thank you Inara,' said Jack. 'I promise you'll see your mother and father before too long.'

'Don't promise things you don't know you can keep,' warned Inara. 'It's good enough for now that I'm coming along.'

Feeling exhausted, all Jack wanted to do was to go to sleep. Rubbing his eyes made them sore and puffy. Bill and Inara, and even the wolves watched him, waiting for him to tell them their next step. Did they think he was the leader of the group? He supposed he was, he wanted to find Knell - no one else cared. Off to the side another figure watched him. Yang, always silent, always there, what must he be thinking? He wanted to ignore his shadow, to forget it was even there, but the moonshine did not allow him that luxury. The spying shadow imparted a feeling of an angry hissing snake, waiting for an opportune moment to strike. Yang frightened him, not Inara's warnings of creatures in the wood.

'Are you sure you haven't heard any stories about Knell?' he asked Inara. 'She may have had a different name. Think about what I told you, the tree, the hill dotted with heather, the road and the houses.'

'I know of no one like her.'

'How about him?' said Bill, pointing at Krimble.

'No,' said Inara.

'Why not, he's lived all his miserable life out here, if anyone would know, it's him,' argued Bill.

'He's right Inara.' Jack's mouth filled with distaste as he spat out his agreement. He never wanted to hear Krimble's voice ever again, but if he knew something, they needed to know. 'Can you make him talk? I mean Silver did a job on his neck; will that stop him from speaking to us?'

'I don't want to Jack.' She touched her legs with a nervous hand. 'He's being punished for what he did to me, and for what he did to the others. My allowing him to speak lessens his punishment. I want him to wallow in silence, to have his thoughts crying out in his head while he feels his body decay and fall apart.'

White-eyes, like two boiled eggs, turned in their sockets. A burrowing worm made Krimble's eyelid flutter.

'You can make him stop speaking once he's told us what we want to know,' said Bill, poking Krimble with the end of his stick.

Understanding Inara's reticence, Jack hated having to press her, but Krimble could know where Knell lived. Without such knowledge, they could spend weeks looking for her, or never find her at all. 'I'm sorry Inara, we've got to try.' He took her hand. 'If he knows the whereabouts of the Scorn Scar it will save us stumbling along blindly.'

'And if he doesn't know, I'll be letting him speak for nothing.'

Her cold hand trembled with fear. Krimble had tortured her in his house for a long time. If not for Bill, Krimble would have made that rat eat her eyes.

CRIK

Jack's throat, taught with sympathy, made him wish he could leave her alone. She had the right to punish Krimble her way. Wanting to back off, he could not, he had to find out what the man knew. 'Let me talk with him. Once I find out what I can, you can silence him.'

Crushing Jack's hand Inara bent forward and whispered into his ear, 'I'll do it Jack, you saved my life and I owe you.' Her voice, carrying no higher than her breath, continued, 'By allowing him to speak you're asking me to break his punishment, and that tears at my heart. Ask him Jack, but I no longer owe you anything, we're even.'

Stepping back from the wolf Jack gave Inara a nod, and then turned to Krimble.

'Speak,' said Inara, from a face drained of all blood.

Krimble's jaw, filled with brown twisted teeth and its blue tongue, fell open on its bone hinge and screamed. The sorrowful sound rose higher, making the wolves shift in alarm. Jack wanted to press his hands against the side of his head to block out the pain of that voice. Bill, dropping his stick, stumbled backward and fell over a root, his face as gaunt as Inara's in the gloom. Sounding like an animal caught in a cruel snare, Krimble cried without taking a breath. Tilting his head back revealed his torn jugular, its severed pipes somehow emitting the sound that hushed the wood.

With shattered nerves at the outpouring of Krimble's grief, Jack waited as the screams subsided into a low continuous moan. 'You speak only to answer my question.'

Krimble ignored him. Fresh blood pumped from his ruined neck, soaking into the maroon splashes already coating his shirt. An earwig passed over a black molar to disappear into his mouth.

'Tell him again Ying,' urged Bill, gaining his feet and coming around to stand behind Jack.

Turning his head on his brittle spine, Krimble looked at Inara. His voice wheezed from his gaping maw, 'I should've torn off your head, not your legs.'

Listening to Krimble's voice reminded Jack of the last gasps of a drowning man. 'Speak to me, leave Inara alone.'

'Why should I answer you,' said Krimble, his colourless orbs swivelling to take in Jack. 'I had everything under control until you turned up.' A sneer folded the decayed flesh under his hooked nose. 'I could feel her Narmacil loosening, only a few more days and I would've had its Talent. Now you want me to tell you how to get rid of your own - your treacherous shadow.' The bruise Yang had given him on the side of his head was still visible amongst his dead skin. 'Ironic how you killed me to keep the demon you now want to get rid of.' His lips twitched. 'Don't you think?'

'Do you know Knell?' asked Jack, ignoring Krimble's attempts to draw him into an argument. 'Where is the Scorn Scar?'

GREY DIRECTIONS FROM A BLACK HEART

'I have heard others speak of her,' responded Krimble, taking a shuffling step closer. 'Are you sure you want to meet her? You didn't take too kindly to my hospitality, what makes you think you'll enjoy hers any better?'

'What does he mean by that,' said Bill.

Pointing a red finger, Krimble said, 'Let me die, and I'll point you in the right direction.'

'No,' shouted Inara in a strained voice. 'I won't let you go; you're going to suffer for a long time. Answer his question.'

Krimble's teeth clashed together in a broad grin as he bent forward in a mock bow. 'The bitch speaks,' he said. 'Tell me you name.' His grin on his cadaver face came from a nightmare.

'Shut up,' Bill shouted, balling his fists.

'What will you do, kill me?' The sardonic laugh that followed sounded hollow.

'I'll find a rat and shove it down the hole in your neck,' threatened Bill. 'You're rather fond of rats aren't you?'

Jack saw Krimble tremble, and got satisfaction from the zombie's reaction. 'Knell,' he repeated, 'where is she?'

'A hunter came to my house a few years back,' said Krimble, through clenched teeth. 'With his Talent he could alter the land, making him a very good hunter.'

Jack sensed Inara stiffen behind him, it was through this Talent that Krimble had ensnared her.

'He told me of a cloaked woman living beside a hole in the ground.'

'Did he say what was in the hole?' asked Jack, eager.

Ignoring a piece of green flesh, waggling from the tip of his chin, Krimble shook his head. He gave a fiendish grin. 'Too frightened to look into the ground, he had said. Sensed something moving within the hole; a something he did not wish to see.'

The figure that rose from the pit and the attacking birds sprang to Jack's mind. Who or what had come for him from the ruptured earth had left an indelible fear. He felt faint. They failed to notice, and he redoubled his effort to remain focused on what Krimble told them.

'He called it the Scorn Scar,' said Krimble. 'It lies to the north, through the Wold.'

Inara gasped. 'The Wold.' She brought her hand to her mouth.

'What's the Wold?' asked Bill.

'That's where the Myrms live,' she muttered, biting her chapped lips.

Tilting back his head Krimble revealed a series of jutting neck bones through his torn throat. The dead man laughed. 'You want to run through the Wold, you don't want the Myrms getting hold of you.'

'Silence,' said Inara.

CRIK

A sneer spread across Krimble's mouth. 'I don't think so, you've given back my voice and I'm keeping it.'

18. FORESHADOWING

THE AIR FELT DAMP. Above the interlaced branches grey clouds brewed, bottling up the impending rain. The small group followed a rock bed through old trees, scaring up thin birds from the bordering brush. Silver, with a growl, leapt after each one, but the sparrows and the wrens flittered away before her agitated jaws.

Jack knew Inara was angry with him. Did he have the right to ask her to make Krimble break his silence? Even if it meant finding Knell? No, he had to find out what the demon inside him wanted. If the woman in the odd house could tell him how to get rid of it, then giving Krimble the ability to talk was worth it. She rode with hunched shoulders, allowing the shambling corpse to walk, with his stiff limbed gait, beside her down the rutted path.

The thick rubbery skin of the mushrooms Jack ate stuck to his teeth, and the stalks and umbrellas were sour, but they sated some of his hunger. He discarded the idea of offering some to Inara; he could not take her accusatory glare any more.

Guilt gnawed at his guts. Guilt for making his friends continue into the dangerous wood, haunted by Myrms and strange creatures called Doctors. Guilt for leaving his mother. What must she think? When he first left the village, he knew she would fret; that was days ago. She would wrap a pale scarf over her face, not to frighten the small kids with her burns, when she went to see the Mr Gasthem. Hundreds, perhaps thousands of beetles, flies, and woodlouse would then spread out from Crik Village. They would search Long Sleep Cemetery, the nearby clearings, even Grenville, in the hope that he and Bill had gone there to sneak a peek at the dancing women, with their high skirts, and low blouses. He wished he could tell his mother that he was fine, that he would return once he found Knell. Instead, a steep decline, strewn with sharp stones, striped with faint daylight and green shade from the trees, brought him to a sudden halt. Beyond the slope lay a wide valley, filled with tall evergreens.

'They'll pull out your tongues,' said Krimble, 'with bone tools. Others just stick their grubby pinkies into your gob and give a yank!'

'You already said that one,' said Bill, sitting in front of Inara. 'I preferred when you said the Myrm would stick our heads on the branch of the highest tree so that we could see for miles.'

CRIK

'So that others would see you for miles,' corrected Krimble, with a narrow glance up at Bill.

'Didn't you say they would imprison us in wooden cages,' asked Bill. 'Or were the cages to keep the boars? You know,' he said, with a wry smile, 'the ones which were going to eat our feet.'

'I'll remind you once we get to the Wold.'

'Make sure that you do,' said Bill, crossing his hands over his belly. 'I want you to eat your words when we travel through without seeing anything larger than a badger.'

'They'll see you, before you see them.'

'I liked you more when you were begging Inara to kill you,' said Bill. 'After hearing so many others beg, it must have seemed to your ears like a well versed prayer. We're as deaf as you, so you're out of luck.'

'Ignore him Bill,' said Jack. His belly gave a flip-flop as his eyes drifted to a silver stream at the bottom of the descent. The others were a few steps behind and had not yet seen the imminent drop. 'You're only encouraging him,' he continued in an attempt to focus on something other than the dizzying height.

Bill kicked out, hitting Krimble a glancing blow on his upper arm, staggering the zombie into the bole of a leaning tree. 'He doesn't need any encouragement. Taunting us is his only source of fun, and I mean to stop him from enjoying himself.'

Yang spread himself across the downward drift like a lizard sunning itself on the sharp rocks. Jack suspected the demon played on his fear at this new unexpected obstacle. If it could speak, no doubt, it would be laughing at him.

'Carry on Bill.' Inara regarded Krimble with a face that looked like it was carved from soapstone. 'Your taunts are humiliating him. Before I allow him to leave this world I want him to learn humility.'

'I'll gut you yet,' said Krimble, pushing off from the tree, leaving a sliver of skin on the rough bark.

Krimble reminded Jack of the horror comics lying in a disordered heap under his bed. Within the painted pages a rotten bride, or a coach load of vampire children, returned to exact grisly retribution against their killer. He could almost see the words "I'll gut you yet," written in italics inside a floating speech bubble.

'I gave you permission to speak,' said Inara, her eyes aflame with black fire, 'so I can't stop you from wagging your tongue, but that doesn't mean I can't control you. I could make it years before I let you rest in the ground. During that time I will make you do things that will drive you insane.'

Beneath his scarred, rotten face, Krimble managed to look sullen, and for the first time his derisive words quietened into grumbles.

Listening to Inara, Jack didn't believe Krimble would remain quiet for long, but at least she had stood up to him. Perhaps now she would speak with him

FORESHADOWING

again. He wanted to breach the silent wall that had erected itself between them, but Inara, seeing his lingering gaze, clamped her lips together, turning her mouth into a thin, cold, scar.

With a heavy sigh, Jack turned once more to look down the hill. Although the group pressed up to him, he only became aware of them standing at the lip when Bill spoke.

'I'm not going to ride Black down there; I'm likely to go headfirst into a rock.' Bill armed sweat from his brow. 'There must be an easier way down.'

Krimble licked his peeling lips. 'If you want to reach the Wold you will have to go down. It lies beyond the mouth of this very broad and long valley. There is no way around.'

'He's right,' said Jack, begrudgingly. 'We must enter the valley. At least here we can see the ground.' He looked into the trees either side of him. 'In the bush, there're hundreds of pitfalls waiting to break a leg.'

'What do you think those stones will do to us,' said Bill, jumping down from Black. 'Don't get me wrong, it could be fun, but it's a long way to fall if you make a mistake.'

Silver pawed at the loose earth. She looked downhill for a long time before turning her nose up to Jack. He watched the wolf retreat behind Bill with a lowered tail. If he had a tail, Jack knew his would also be touching the ground. Seeing no other avenue into the valley, he hung his head.

'If we take it slow, we can make it.' Hoping to inject some enthusiasm into his voice only made Jack sound panic-stricken. Embarrassed by his high-pitched tone he grew more determined to start the descent.

'What're you doing,' said Bill as Jack sat down on the floor with his legs dangling over the drop.

'It'll be easier if we do it this way,' replied Jack with a tongue that felt as rough as caked salt.

'You two may be able to scoot yourselves down there,' said Inara, 'but my legs are not healed.' Frowning, she pointed at her bandaged legs.

Her expression did a good job of impersonating his mother, Jack thought, the one she used whenever he tried to duck a chore to play with Bill, an expression that brooked no argument.

'Black can...'

'I'm not going to ride a wolf down there,' shouted Inara in outrage. 'Bill got off so fast I thought someone had lit a campfire under his ass, and you want me to hold on and hope.'

Jack looked around. There were enough raw materials at hand to make a sled; balancing it once they were underway was the problem. Besides, if Inara couldn't stay on Black, she would never agree to sit on a sled. Other ideas came, and each he shot down before uttering them to the others.

CRIK

'Are you sure you can't give it a try,' said Bill, wanting to fill the awkward silence that had grown into long minutes.

Grateful for his friend's help, but also realising Inara's reticence was turning quickly to anger, caused Jack to bite his tongue and wait for Inara to batter Bill with well-aimed words. Instead, Inara tossed her head back, barking a mirthless laugh to the grey sky.

'If you sit on the floor and keep your legs up,' continued Bill, in hurtful reproach, 'and brace yourself with your arms, your legs won't get hurt. You can go after me; I could stop you if you fell.'

'I'd be safer crawling through the wood on my hands than I am with you two,' she said, waving her arms as though conducting a hundred-piece orchestra.

Only Krimble noticed Yang slip back over the lip of the hill to where the big wolf stood. The zombie scowled down at the shadow. Something crawled inside his ear; he slapped a hand against his withered flesh. When he looked again, Yang had peeled himself from the floor.

'Unless you want me find my own way home, I suggest...' A startled scream broke off Inara's words as Yang wrapped elongated arms around her midriff in three overlapping coils.

'Ying what are you doing?' said Bill as Yang lifted Inara with ease.

Jack ground his teeth. 'For the last time, I don't control Yang. The demon inside me does!'

Held aloft on a dusky pole, the wood clearly visible through its width, struggled Inara. 'You really won't give up will you,' she shouted down at Jack.

'It's not me,' he began, and then threw his hands up. Let them think what they want; nothing he could say would make a blind bit of difference. Even after everything he had told them, they still thought he controlled his shadow. He should be used to it; everyone blamed him for Yang's pranks. That it still managed to irritate him, made him angry.

'You'll be safe up there, Yang won't drop you,' shouted Bill, through cupped hands. He looked at Jack, and for a moment, Jack saw Bill readying himself to ask, "You won't drop her, will you Ying?" If he had, Jack would have hit him flush in the nose.

'There's nothing I can do about it,' said Inara. 'So get going, I don't like heights.'

Taking the lead, Jack pushed himself forward, feeling the loose stones scrape the back of his legs. A cluster of stones shot out before him to tumble into other, larger, boulders, where they broke into halves and splintered quarters. A wave of vertigo swept through him, making him sink his fingers into the rocky soil. With as much grace as a pregnant cow climbing down a ladder, came Bill. Bill's glasses were already askew. He grazed Jack's knuckles with his shoe.

'Hey, be careful,' hissed Jack through gritted teeth.

FORESHADOWING

'You're in my way,' said Bill, kicking up a cloud of dust.

For one dreadful moment, Jack felt his upper body tilt forward, and was sure he was about to cartwheel all the way down the slope, leaving a bloody trail for Bill to follow. Collapsing back, he felt his heart threaten to jump from his chest.

'Careful Ying!' cried Bill. 'You're kicking the stones loose.'

'Don't follow me, go to the left; you'll fall on top of me.'

Looking up Jack saw Inara smiling in Yang's grasp. She used her hands to keep her windblown hair from her eyes. He shook his head; a few moments ago she didn't want his shadow to carry her, now she loved it.

Taking a deep breath, he pushed himself forward, keeping his back against the hillside. He barely noticed the two wolves tearing down the slope. Black led, his pink tongue lolling out from his open jaws with stupid glee.

The trees that had looked tiny from the top of the decline took more shape, with individual branches coming into focus. The rushing water below rang the air with its turbulent beat. Thousands of small cuts scored his fingers by the time he heard the birds nesting in the valley.

Closer to the bottom, the slope became more gradual, allowing him to get to his feet. Bill followed him in a mad dash for the bottom of the hill. Brushing away the dust coating his torn trousers, Jack looked around and spotted Krimble pushing a disjointed shoulder back into place. Looking up the hill, he saw the path Krimble had taken. Strips of skin and chunks of decaying flesh littered the slope. Krimble, having righted his arm, placed his hand against a crack in his skull, fingering globs of yellow fluid pumping from the open seam.

Yang gently placed Inara back on Black. Before he had time to retreat, Inara patted Yang's arm. Jack, irked by this show of affection toward his shadow, jumped to the bottom.

'Told you there was nothing to worry about,' he said, hoping the sheen of sweat bathing his face did not make him look foolish. 'Now that's behind us, things will be a lot easier.'

'Will they,' remarked Inara crossing her arms. 'We don't know what's ahead. Even the birds are strange down here.'

As though to prove her point the beat of leathery wings crashed overhead. Looking up, Jack followed the flight of a large bald bird. It had rows of ivory teeth in a snub beak.

'Well we're down now, so there's no point in worrying. We push on and once we're through the Wold we can think about returning home.'

'Yes Jack,' said Inara, 'you've told us. What happens if Knell tells you to find your answer you have to travel even farther? Will you drag us to Grog Mountain and through the Black Mines? When will it stop?'

'Hey guys, look at this,' shouted Bill, saving Jack from having to answer.

Moving across, he saw Bill standing over a lantern.

CRIK

'Do you think someone lives down here?' asked Bill, gripping the metal casing. 'It still has some oil, that'll come in handy tonight.'

The valley floor, lighter than the jungle above, allowed them to see far ahead. To the east snaked a glistening river; while to the north lay a large open field, dotted with rabbit holes. They saw no other sign of any human inhabitants.

'It could've been left down here a while,' said Jack. 'Take the lantern; only keep your eyes open, I don't fancy finding myself locked in another house.'

Krimble laughed.

'I hate him,' said Bill.

The hard ground took them into the trees toward the river. After the tight trails of the floor above, Jack felt unfettered by the valley, and he took the lead. Not even the weird birds flitting in and out of eyeshot could dampen his rising spirits.

'Ay Ying,' said Bill, rushing to Jack's side, his face flush, his eyes wet and wide, 'remember that vagabond who stumbled into the village last year.'

A small man, wearing rags, and smelling foul, had set up camp on the outskirts of Crik. The dwarf had raved how the woods had turned against him, thwarting his every effort to find his way back to his village. The stranger grew wild when the village hunters offered their help to take him back to his home. He claimed something, or someone, hunted him. Mr Gasthem, seeing the stranger's distress, allowed him to stay within sight of the village. Two nights he stayed camped, never entering the village, but stayed close to the busy street. He disappeared on the third night. The hunters could find no sign of his passing, as though the woods had wiped away all traces of the man.

'What about him,' Jack asked, suppressing a shudder.

'The only thing left behind to show that the dwarf had ever been to Crik was a snake charm. Do you remember?'

Now that Bill mentioned it, Jack recalled the black metal disk found hanging from a bush. A coiled snake, with four feet emerging from a cave, engraved the charm. He nodded, not liking where the conversation was going.

With a shaking hand Bill lifted the lantern and pointed at a serpent climbing out of a cave. 'I think whoever lost this, is still down here.'

19. A SHARED LIGHT

NIGHT FELL QUICK in the valley, and as the sun dipped beyond the distant mountains, eerie calls invaded the spaces amongst the trees. The small group huddled close to the lantern. The light only stretched as far as the ring of stones Bill had placed around the campsite. Only Krimble sat beyond the circle, grumbling to himself.

Bill, chewing his lip, inspected the etched symbol on the lantern. His intense scrutiny, afforded him only the briefest non-committal reply to Inara. She, being so fascinated with the abundance of new creatures within the valley, failed to notice. Earlier, rabbits with whiptails had intrigued her. Moving through a field of the small grazing creatures, she had slowed them with each new discovery. First, how they only ate in pairs, and then, after noticing the small horns peaking through their brown fur, Jack knew she wanted to take one as a pet. Traversing the field should have taken minutes; instead, they spent over an hour picking their way around the burrow entrances. Happy with her lightened mood, Jack had not complained, even when she asked to get down from Black so she could feed the rabbits. Bill, not concerned with getting in her good books, protested at every detour. In silence, Jack ran his tongue over his teeth, as Inara again tried to engage Bill in conversation.

'I wonder why they had those long tails?' she said, drumming her fingers on the ground.

Bill Shrugged. 'Who's to say they were rabbits. For all we know they could be giant gophers. Or rats,' he added.

Inara's horrified reprimand came quick. 'Don't be silly.' She clutched her hands to her chest.

Ignoring her clipped tone, Bill said, 'Why not? I've never seen rabbits with long wormlike tails before. Have you?' He lay back, disengaging his sights from the lantern for the first time since they had made camp. 'The truth is we don't know what they were. What do you think Ying?'

Though obscured in darkness, Jack felt Inara's eyes on him. Close by he heard a shrill cry amongst the trees, tightening his nerves. 'I don't know. We haven't a clue what's living down here.' He looked behind him as a new rustle stirred the undergrowth. He hoped no snakes lived in the valley.

CRIK

'That lantern could've lain in the grass for a long time; it doesn't mean someone is down here.'

'Doesn't mean there aren't,' replied Bill, his face aglow with lantern light.

'Those rabbits,' Inara stressed the classification, 'weren't afraid of us, so I presume there are no hunters. This whole valley looks untouched.'

Jack nodded. 'We would've spotted a settlement from the top of the hill.'

'That doesn't mean no one uses the valley,' argued Bill. 'I for one won't eat those giant rats, and we could've easily missed a house built amongst the trees. Someone left this lantern.' Using the metal handle, he held it aloft. 'By the oil left inside I don't think it was that long ago.'

'Why leave a half full lantern behind?'

'I don't know, ask Ying, he's the one who's always looking for answers.'

'There's no point in speculating until we have further proof that people live down here,' said Jack. 'I'm more concerned with what waits beyond the valley, I don't like the sound of the Myrms one bit, and I'm sure not all of Krimble's stories are lies. Everything is strange down here, and I can't see them getting any more familiar, but nothing has attacked us, so we should rest while we can.'

Bill said, 'How can you think of rest? You just mentioned the Myrms as though they were just a child's tale and not something that we're about to face. If you weren't so obsessed with getting rid of Yang we wouldn't be here.'

'And we wouldn't have to enter the Wold,' added Inara.

A blood moon slipped the cover of the clouds, its cratered surface seeming to stare down upon the small circle with inhuman keenness. Jack glanced at the orbiting sphere. Grandpa Poulis said a blood moon was an evil portent. The thought made him colder than the wind.

'The decision has been made,' he said, ignoring his roving shadow. 'It's not too late for you to turn back.'

'I'm not leaving you out here alone,' replied Bill in a rushed whisper. 'That doesn't mean I have to like where you're taking us. The sooner we can see Knell, and turn our feet back home, the better. I've yet to show Black to anyone, and that just tears a hole in my gut.'

'They'll see Bill, and when they do no one will make fun of you for not having a Talent ever again,' said Inara.

Bill gave a firm nod. 'They can change how they look,' he said. 'They can pick pebbles off the ground with their minds, but none of them will be able to ride a wolf, or make an owl roost in their room. I can't wait to see their faces.' He turned to Jack. 'For that I will gladly allow my Narmacil to remain inside me.'

Narmacil is just a fancy word for demon, thought Jack, sticking his cold hands into his pockets. If only they had seen Bill's demon. He tossed a stick into the darkness, beyond Krimble's hunched form. He had done his part,

A SHARED LIGHT

warned them of the thing lurking within, bestowing gifts to pacify their revulsion at being a host to the creature.

Jack noticed Black's blue eyes studying him. He returned the look, startled by the intelligence in the wolf's gaze. For a moment, as Inara and Bill resumed their argument about the valley, he imagined the great black wolf shared his fear of the demons. Resting on his bent arm, he continued to watch the great lupine. In the torchlight neither blinked. His mouth lacked any moisture, and his tongue felt too large for his mouth. The square muzzle of the wolf parted, wrinkling its flesh. Silver coming into the circle broke the contact, and when his eyes once more settled on Black, the wolf had dropped its gaze.

'You should have Black guard us while we're sleeping,' said Inara.

'Thought you said no one lived down here,' argued Bill. 'Black needs to rest; he's been carrying you for hours. If you hadn't stuck your nose into every hole in the ground, he'd be much more alert.' The wolf's shaggy head nestled into Silver's lighter coat as she lay down beside him. 'Poor thing is exhausted, he can barely stay awake.'

'He's probably bored,' replied Inara, swiping her hair from her face. 'Let him go hunting with Silver. A bit of excitement and something to snack on will put strength back into his limbs.'

'Hunt? So now you're alright with them going and killing a few of the giant gophers?'

Inara chewed her lip. Her expression made it clear she did not like the idea of the two wolves snacking on her new favourite animals.

'You'll be in control of Black the entire time,' interjected Jack, quite happy to have some space between him and Black for a few hours. 'Guide him away from the field. There're plenty of other things to eat in the valley.'

'I hope nothing down here will eat them,' said Bill with a worried frown. 'Or us,' he added in a whisper.

'Keep them close,' said Inara as Black rose to his feet. 'In case we need them.'

Time passed slowly. Bill sat with the lamp on his lap, his finger tracing the etching on the casing. Inara watched Krimble from the corner of her eye, while Jack followed his own shadow, as it too took an interest in the morose corpse that sat with hunched shoulders.

'It's dangerous to take Krimble into the Wold,' said Jack as Krimble waved a hand at his troublesome shadow. 'He'll give us away the first chance he gets.'

The girl regarded him with lazy eyes. The tight lines, bordering her thin lips, deepened into dark tributaries across her chalk white skin.

Blowing out his cheeks, Jack remained silent, waiting for Inara to talk.

'I won't let him go,' she answered, long after the silence had become awkward. 'You have asked too much of me already. I want my heart to grow, but it will remain small and cold until I again see my family.' She placed her

CRIK

hand on Jack's arm. 'Krimble kept me captive by lock and key. You keep me imprisoned by my gratitude towards you.' She let go, leaving small crescents on Jack's skin where her chipped fingernails had dug in. 'Although I'll go through the Wold and see this woman on the far side, I won't allow Krimble's punishment to end. Your distrust of the Narmacils is foolish, Yang saved you in the marsh house, and he has been a constant companion since you can remember. You shouldn't be so suspicious of him.'

'Was it fair that a demon decided to use me?' he retorted. 'If these things are our benefactors why do they hide? Why did the Giant enter my village in the dead of night to leave the egg behind? I'm certain the need for secrecy is to stop people asking what they are, what they want, and where they come from.'

'I knew of them,' said Inara. 'I've told you how innocent you are concerning the woods. That does not make them evil. It was fear that made me destroy the Lindre; only to discover she was helping you.'

Jack spoke through Inara's guilt; he refused to let her feelings fester. 'When you attacked her you thought you had no choice. You did not understand her motives. That is why we need to find Knell, to understand, to question. Perhaps I'm overreacting, but until we know for sure what they want,' he touched his stomach, 'who can say which of us is right?'

'What's that?' Bill looking passed Jack.

'What?' Jack jumped to his feet and around in one motion.

'A light,' said Inara, spying the weaving illumination before Jack had time to locate it.

Following the direction, in which his friends looked, Jack saw a speck of colour, no larger than the stars sprinkling the sky, it shone yellow, blinking as it passed by the intervening trees. It remained close to the ground as it travelled; only rising when the ground itself swelled into a small hillock or a protruding rock.

'It's another lamp,' said Bill.

'Then kill ours,' said Inara, pointing a finger at the lantern. 'Do you want to be found?'

While Bill fumbled with the wheel that controlled the gas, Jack took a step outside the stone circle. No one else had yet heard the whistling, a strange tune that carried on the wind. The haunting melody raised the hairs on the back of his neck. It made the same sound as Knell's flute.

Inara sat up straighter at the sound. 'There's music.'

'What're you talking about, music? It's the wind you're hearing,' said Bill.

'No, I hear it as well.'

Bill pushed his glasses up his nose. 'Do you recognise the song?'

'No, it's not like that,' replied Jack. 'It reminds me of how the wind sounds as it rushes through the eaves of the old church back home.'

'Charming,' said Bill, walking passed Inara.

A SHARED LIGHT

Neither Bill stopping beside him, nor Krimble, with his slouching walk, diverted Jack's attention from the spot of light. It drew closer. Whoever, or whatever, carried it, appeared to be in a rush.

'Call Black,' said Inara.

Neither Bill nor Jack heard her.

The music grew, blowing its haunting melody over the group. It had no effect, other than to herald the coming of the light bearer.

'Whoever's carrying the lamp must be very short,' remarked Bill, watching the bobbing light hug the ground.

Splashes of colour lit up the bushes in yellow and green hues. Together with the hanging red moon, it was a most diverse rainbow. Yang appeared, sitting close to Jack.

Despite the light being so close as to reveal the shadows cast by the lantern housing the flame, they still could not see the actual owner. A lean tree blocked their view for a moment; when the light came back into frame, they saw a small, wizened, old man carrying the lamp. An immense beard hid the man's features.

Soothing music accompanied him as he trudged forward. Stopping, the man blew out his cheeks, and patted his beard with a dirty handkerchief. Turning to Bill, he said, 'Well, what do you want?'

CRIK

20. HELLO, GOODBYE, AND HOW WE GOT THERE.

'WHAT DO YOU MEAN,' said Bill, bewildered, 'what do I want?'

'You lit the bloody thing,' said the little man. 'So, what do you want?'

Jack noticed the eyes of the man were a light shade of pink. Another oddity was the hollow wooden spokes at the heel of his boots; they played a note with every step.

The man's irritated expression darkened; angry lines formed through his nest of a beard. 'The lamp, boy,' he said, clicking his tongue against his front teeth. 'I ran the length of Elysium to get here. Now what is it?'

'Elysium?' remarked Inara, who was the only one at face height with the stranger. 'Is that the name of this valley?'

'Well it's not the Swine River, is it?' He swung around the stick, from which swayed his lantern. 'It'd be manners to offer me something to drink right 'bout now.'

'We've got some water.' Inara moved to retrieve a bottle, fashioned from the hide of one of Silver's kills.

'Blah,' shouted the quarrelsome man, sticking out his tongue. 'Do I look like an otter to you? I expect some rum for running all this way, or if not that then a little beer would go down a treat.'

'We haven't got any,' said Jack.

'Well, that's just dandy.' He planted the lamp on the ground. Free of the weight he sat back on his haunches and shook off the boots. Two mournful notes played as the shoes hit the ground. Tearing a blade of grass, he set it between his teeth. 'Here Miss, rub these for me.' He shook his feet at Inara.

Inara stared at the outstretched feet as though they were a nest of worms. 'I'm not going…'

'He's come a long way,' interrupted Bill.

Her stretching lips skinned back from her teeth. 'You lit the lamp, so you can do it.'

'I'm not having a guy rub my feet,' cried the man, moving the grass from one side of his mouth to the other. 'Now come on, I'm not asking you to give me a bath.' The man gave Jack a wink.

HELLO, GOODBYE, AND HOW WE GOT THERE

'It's not going to happen,' said Inara, narrowing her gaze, as Jack, standing to her side, blinked in astonishment. 'So you may as well stop asking, and take your paws away.'

'Not a particularly hospitable group are you. First, you've no drink waiting for me, and now you're refusing to rub my sore feet, which I suspect have blisters after my run. I've a good mind to turn tail.'

'We didn't ask for your help,' said Bill, hiding the doused lamp with a self-conscious slight of hand.

The man squinted up at Bill. 'Not the sharpest blade of grass, are you?' he muttered. 'It's not hard to see by your tracks that you're headed for the Wold, a dangerous place, mayhap the most dangerous place in Crik Wood. Therefore, you do need my help. Aye, you do.' He gave them all a grin.

Jack, not liking the man's smugness, bent forward. 'Who are you?'

'I'm Llast, and what I am is angry and tired.' Llast turned to Inara. 'And I'm parched.'

'If you're that thirsty then you'd be glad to have this water,' she said, again offering the water skin.

'What's that smell?' said Llast, ignoring the water. 'Smells like fish left to rot.'

'That'd be Krimble,' said Bill, pointing outside the pool of light. 'Believe me he smells worst in the day.'

'Not possible,' said Llast.

Llast chewed on the grass while he observed Krimble limp closer. The left cheek of the zombie had disintegrated into a mushy mess. What remained of his grey hair had balled into isolated humps on his scarred head.

'On second thoughts, I think I will have some water.' Llast snatched the skin from Inara. Pulling the string, that tied the bottle's neck closed, he upended the liquid so that it splashed his face, dampening his beard and making his eyes squint shut. After rubbing his face, he let his hands drop, and looked once more at Krimble, who stood with a sneer. 'I was hoping you were just some dust in my eye. You're one ugly sod. Look at your clothes, all muddy and torn. Count it as a blessing that I don't mention your face. You're lucky there aren't many mirrors in the valley.'

'I'm beginning to like him,' said Bill.

'Thought you might,' said Jack.

'You may fool these,' said Krimble, 'but I know you. I daresay there're more mirrors in Elysium, than there are of your people.'

Llast stared at Krimble as a smirk sloughed across the corpse' mouth. 'There're more of us than you think.'

'Then why the haste?' asked Krimble. 'Where're the others, they would've seen the light as well?'

'Shut up,' Inara warned.

CRIK

'That's ok girl,' said Llast. 'I know who he is now. He's the Marsh Man. I almost stumbled into one of your traps a while ago,' he told Krimble. 'You would've got me if it weren't for my nose. I smelled you then too. I've waited a long time to kill you; it's a shame I waited too long.'

Inara smacked her fist into her palm. 'He's suffering. I can feel his mind crying out for mercy that will not come. He will feel his flesh fall from his bones, and the jelly of his eyes bubble from their sockets before I allow him to rest.'

Llast remained silent, the grass clamped between his teeth drew circles in the air as he mulled over Krimble's fate.

Standing back, Jack watched, expecting the albino to leap from the ground and attack Krimble. He saw such hatred and sadness in those pink eyes. He imagined Llast sinking his two over-sized incisors into Krimble's rotten neck, and he silently urged him to do just that.

After a while, Llast leant forward, and with a hand supporting his chin, said, 'I'm almost glad, I didn't get you. I think this girl has dreamt up a punishment beyond anything I could've done.

'Now go, it's more than your smell that I find offensive.'

'You heard him,' cried Inara. 'Stand back, and don't return until I give you permission.'

'It doesn't matter what he tells you,' said Krimble, swiping at Yang, who stood close, 'there's no hope for any of you once you enter the Wold. The Myrms know every track in their Red Forest.'

'Bugger off,' said Bill, throwing a stone.

With a voice like a barn door, all creaks and groans, Krimble said, 'Don't misunderstand; I want you to enter the Wold, that's my quickest route to peace.' Enjoying their contempt of him, Krimble at first did not notice Yang touching his ribs. When the probing shadow tried putting a finger through a tear in his shirt Krimble flinched as though struck. 'Keep your carrion shadow to yourself,' he warned Jack, swatting his hand at Yang.

He tried not to show the rest, but Yang's continued fascination with Krimble weighed heavily upon Jack. Memories of the stuffed birds in his bedroom no longer seemed like a simple hobby, it had become far more nefarious now that he knew something other than himself controlled his shadow.

'I said leave, sit in the dark and do not disturb us till daybreak,' said Inara, oblivious to Jack's unease.

With his bent back pulling his grey shirt up like a haystack, and his entourage of crawling things, Krimble struck a lonely figure as he walked away from the light. As he was about to leave he turned, and Jack saw the glint of mischief in his ruined eye. The man who had lived alone in the marsh looked happier than he had since Silver had taken a chunk out of his neck.

HELLO, GOODBYE, AND HOW WE GOT THERE

When the sound of Krimble's shuffling feet had died, Llast clicked his tongue. 'Be careful with him, he still has power, I can smell it even under his rotting skin.'

'Inara can control him,' said Jack.

'Like you can control your shadow,' replied Llast.

Hoping the others hadn't noticed the sweat peppering his brow, Jack remained silent, unsure how to answer.

'At one time we used the marsh,' Llast finally said, relieving Jack of his stare. 'We found the soft ground welcome, and it was quite pleasant in the summer; if you ignored the midges. Then he came, and there weren't any more summers. We still went, despite familiar paths leading us into traps. At first, the traps were obvious, steel jaws and rope snares, none of which gave us any problems. His tricks were more of a hindrance than any real threat. The kids sometimes went to the marsh to play a game where they would follow the Marsh Man's routes, stepping as close to the traps as they could before stepping around 'em. They always laughed.

'The kids disappeared first,' he continued in a throaty whisper. 'Guessing they had gone to play their game, we struck out for the marsh. We found the false paths, and the set traps. We never found those kids.'

'If you knew who was responsible, why didn't you go to his house and cut his throat? Would've saved us a whole lot of trouble,' said Bill.

'Steady lad,' said Llast, wagging his finger, his face as stern as a rock bluff. 'Of course we tried. My eldest and a few others went to pay the Marsh Man a visit. They returned a week later, minus my son. The hunting party never found the house, the illusion of the false paths were too crafty, leading them far from his home.'

'What happened to your son?' asked Jack, fearing the worst.

Llast remained silent, his pink eyes half closed as memories swarmed beneath their glassy surface. 'I only tell you this as you seem intent on taking that thing with you. Even now he's dangerous, and you would be best to leave him by himself to wallow in his pain.'

'No,' said Inara. 'He's wronged too many, I want to see him suffer.'

'A dark motive can weigh heavy on your shoulders,' Llast warned.

Inara shook her head, her short blonde hair fanning across her pale skin like a thousand golden needles.

'Okay,' said Llast, snatching the blade of grass from his mouth. 'The path my son and the rest of the party followed took them through the wettest parts of the marsh.'

'Did you take hunting dogs? The wet ground would upset their sense of smell,' interrupted Inara.

CRIK

Llast clicked his fingers. 'Not as dull as you look, which is a pity; I don't like women that are too bright. Women who can think are nothing but trouble,' he said, looking at Bill and Jack with a sage expression.

'Women are just as smart as men,' said Jack, thinking about his mother, and then as an afterthought Grandma Poulis, who had kept her secret in the small village.

'They can be smarter. That's the problem. You're so young,' said Llast, 'you'll learn.'

'What happened to your son,' said Bill, impatient to hear the rest of the story.

'He died boy, just as I told you he did. The how of it is more complicated, as no one there saw him fall. The group were wading through the deep waters, when they heard his surprised yelp. Thinking my son had stepped on a trap the party rushed back, but could not find him.'

Bill gave Jack a knowing glance. Could the man who had appeared at their village, be Llast's son? Krimble, attempting to snare the man, would have turned the woods against him. The serpent charm he wore, mirrored that on the lamp, and Jack had little doubt he had come from this valley. Though not certain that the man was Llast's lost son, he felt positive his assessment was correct. He saw his suspicions in Bill's face too. Should he tell Llast what he knew? To what end, he queried with himself. There would be no relief to Llast's grief, whether he disappeared from here, or back at the village, his son was still lost. If he were to speak of what he knew, he would only re-open old wounds. The decision made, he gave Llast his full attention. Bill, apparently coming to the same conclusion, likewise listened to the old man's tale.

'Others they found,' carried on Llast, ignorant of the look that passed between the boys, and Jack's inner turmoil. 'Each was the same, sitting with their mouth agape, looking as though something had clawed its way up their throat.'

Behind the shield of his hand Bill mouthed the word Narmacil to Jack.

'Did your son have a special Talent?' asked Jack. 'A power that was unique to him.'

'He could speak with the Myrms. Lucky thing too, although I never knew what he told 'em, they never troubled this valley whilst he lived. Lucky thing too, although I never knew what he told 'em, they never troubled this valley whilst he lived.' Llast looked reflectively at the light at his feet. 'Like my son, most were never found,' he eventually continued, sounding gruffer than before. 'Listening to him,' he looked in Krimble's direction, 'they found their way to the marsh house. Those we did find, well, it was never a pretty sight. We would find 'em lying on the ground with their mouths open, as though surprised by something they saw in the sky.'

'I'm sorry,' said Jack.

HELLO, GOODBYE, AND HOW WE GOT THERE

'Nothing for you to be sorry about, lad,' Llast said, leaning back on a crooked arm. 'If it weren't for you lot, the Marsh Man would still be out there laying his traps. I thought about trying to find the marsh house again; looks like you saved me the bother.'

'You said your nose kept you safe,' said Inara, rubbing her bandages from habit. 'What did you mean by that?'

'I've got a nose for trouble, and for keeping out of its way.' Llast scratched his ear, pulling it down to his cheek. 'I told you my son's Talent. Well, I suppose my nose is mine. I know when something isn't right, and I get outta of its way. Pity no one paid any attention to my grumbles, but I have been told that I grumble a lot.'

'We wouldn't have guessed,' said Bill.

'Watch it lad. You don't have my nose, so you should be more careful where you stick yours. A fast mouth will get you into trouble faster than a purse of gold will buy you a girl at a whorehouse.'

Inara said, 'Bill isn't very tactful.'

'Hey!'

Jack placed a quietening hand on his friend's shoulder.

'It's alright Ying,' said Bill, shrugging Jack off. 'People forget that without me we'd all be dead.'

Jack ground his teeth to stop an immediate retort. If it weren't for Bill, he'd be home reading a comic or setting up a battleground on his floor. Yang, perhaps feeling his frustration, stretched out toward Bill in the guise of a wolf. Bill's obsession with getting a wolf had started this whole affair. Had his demon read his thoughts, was that why Yang had changed form? Or did his shadow just react, recreating the alluded to wolves? Either way it didn't matter, it was now his fault they were here – his obsession that took them deeper into the wood.

'You said you could help us,' said Inara, ignoring Bill's crossed arms. 'We have to go through the Wold.'

Knowing Inara looked at him, focused Jack's attention on Llast.

'Why?'

'We need to see a woman called Knell, who lives beyond the Wold,' answered Jack.

'Have you heard of her?' asked Inara.

'Or a place called The Scorn Scar?' added Bill.

'Nothing could be so important as to risk entering the Wold,' replied Llast. 'The best advice I can offer is to turn back. I will take you to my home, where I have honey cakes, and nuts by the dozen. I'll even provide a little rum,' he said, poking the empty water skin with his toe.

'Have you heard of her?' Jack insisted.

CRIK

'Can't say that I 'ave lad. Crik Wood is larger than any one person can know entirely, so my not knowing shouldn't come as a surprise. The parts of it that I do know are enough to keep me awake at night. And my nightmares start at the Thorn Hedge.' He pointed to the west. 'You'll see it in the morning. The hedge reaches into the sky, keeping the Red Forest hidden from Elysium.'

'How'd we get around the hedge?' asked Inara.

'You don't,' said Llast, 'the Blackthorn Tunnel burrows through it. A haunted place, so keep your wits about you when you enter.' Snatching up a discarded shoe, he withdrew a flute from its heel. 'As you enter blow on this,' he said, handing the instrument to Jack. 'It keeps the Vestai from swarming. It's not much, but it's the best I can do.'

Jack looked down at the odd flute with its uneven sized holes and an amber reed filling the hollow. Raising it to his lips, he gave a tentative blow. The low-pitched note that escaped made his head hum.

'Place your finger on the largest hole and the upraised square at the end of the Syll,' instructed Llast.

Pressing down on the square with his small finger and, covering the large hole while he blew, created a strange sound, both high and low, and melodic and jarring. Allowing the flute to drop, Jack tasted a harsh tang on his tongue, not unlike the taste of lemons, which left his mouth a little numb.

Llast grinned. 'Doesn't taste nice, does it,' he said. 'Why'd you think I wear 'em on my feet?'

'And the Myrms, how do we get passed them?' asked Bill.

'No idea,' said Llast. 'I've never wanted to go to the Red Forest, and my nose has kept me safe when they've ventured forth from behind the hedge. You should turn back; the Red Forest isn't a place for travellers, 'specially when one of those travellers can't walk.'

'I don't need to walk,' responded Inara, moving her hands back from her ruined limbs. 'Black carries me where I need to go.'

'I don't know this Black. No matter how you get to the Wold you'll find it far harder leaving than you did entering.'

'We're going,' said Jack.

Llast reached for his shoes, and with much tugging, he placed them on his feet. 'In that case I'll say goodbye. As I told ya, my nose keeps me away from trouble, and its tingling for me to go.' Picking up his lamp, he shooed away the night. He turned to leave. 'My cakes are delicious.'

Jack smiled. 'I'm sure they are, but we've got a long way to go before we can return home.'

Moving slowly, Llast said, 'Why don't kids ever listen? First the kids of my own people got us mixed up with the Marsh Man, and now, despite my warning, you're going to the Wold.'

'Sorry Llast,' said Inara.

HELLO, GOODBYE, AND HOW WE GOT THERE

'You'll be sorry you didn't listening to me. If you come back this way,' said Llast, looking over his shoulder, 'make sure you bring some rum with you.'

'We will,' promised Inara, raising her hand to the retreating man.

'Goodbye,' said Llast. His one remaining flute played as he trudged back over the field, until eventually even the light from his lantern disappeared.

CRIK

21. A THORN IN THEIR SIDES

THEY ALL AWOKE from an unsettled slumber in the pre-dawn. High above them a thin layer of cloud obscured a scattering of stars. At their feet lay the returned wolves, and three dead skunks. They think of us as their pups, mused Jack. After setting a fire, they enjoyed a breakfast of half-charred meat. By the time the wolves roused themselves, the group were licking the fat from their fingers and eyeing a dark line on the horizon.

'I'm surprised we missed seeing it yesterday,' said Bill.

No one answered; the Thorn Hedge cast a heavy pall over the morning feast.

As the morning neared afternoon the featureless sketch grew more distinct, taking shape into a monstrous wall of twig, thorn, and looping vines. The land, which had undulated over gentle hills and slopes, now stretched out before the Thorn Hedge in an unspoilt plain, where only isolated groups of long grass took root.

The faint raucous caws of birds welcomed them to the end of their trek across Elysium. Inara, sensing the mood of the group, hugged Black.

The impossibly huge hedge threw down its shadow across half the plain, expanding its influence much as a haunted castle broods over a small town. Dotted, like cancer through the hedge, grew black flowers with red stems. The thorns, giving the hedge its name, were over three inches in length and dagger sharp. These barbs grew no more than a few inches apart, making the hedge impenetrable to all but the smallest creature.

Silver ran ahead and, stopping shy of the hedge, pulled back her lips and growled at a deep furrow skirting the edge of the plain.

'What's got her tail in a twist?' said Bill.

Unwilling to speculate, Jack remained closed mouthed as they approached the she-wolf. Close to the hedge Silver appeared ghostlike, reminding him of Grandma Poulis as she had looked as she passed him on that long ago night. Not trusting himself to keep his fears in check, he turned from the pale wolf, trying to take his mind off all things supernatural. Instead, the hedge, now filling his sights, increased his trepidation. Had the Lindre erected the Thorn Hedge? It didn't seem possible that it had grown here by itself. Leaning back, he tried to see the top of the hedge, only he now stood too close to judge where the thorns stopped and the sky began. He felt like one of Mr Gasthem's bugs. At least with the wall blocking the sun Yang only appeared as a diffused shade, and was easy to ignore.

Stepping closer, they came to a gaping ditch running the length of the hedge. The trench dwindled in the distance, as a pencil line across green paper. It was two metres wide, and uniform down the line. Dark water ebbed at its bottom, lapping strings of blue beads. The water caressed the stones, like a potter's hands moulding clay.

'What's with the pearls?' asked Bill, as the toes of his boots touched the lip of the trench. 'They couldn't have gotten down there by mistake, someone placed them there.'

'Perhaps Llast, or his people had something to do with them,' said Inara, peering over Black's shaggy head.

'Whatever they are, Silver doesn't like 'em, so we'd best leave 'em alone,' said Jack. 'Let's try and find the tunnel Llast told us about. The quicker we do the more light we'll have.'

All three looked up at the clouds; painting the sky an ashen grey. Little warmth came from the dim sun, dampening their mood as they began to navigate their way along the Thorn Hedge. They kept a metre from the trench.

'Wonder if anyone back at the village knows about this,' said Bill. 'It must be hundreds of years old. Something this large, and this old can't have gone unnoticed.' He tugged at his glasses, smudging the lenses with a careless finger. 'I'm sure one of my grandfather's tales mentioned a great wall. Do you remember the story Ying?'

Looking into his friend's pale moon face, Jack read a silent plea written behind the glasses, a need to connect this place with home. Grandpa Poulis often told stories up by the Hanging Tree – set the mood, he said. Most told of haunted places amongst the woods. A deserted witches' cabin, clustered with cobwebs and dust bunnies the size of small dogs. Trapped in each of the cabin's windows, frozen in time, were the faces of all the evil witch's young victims. His favourite spoke of a hollow where a gang of cutthroats set up camp, only to run away screaming when during the night dark shapes poked them awake. He recalled a dark figure holding a machete watched them flee from atop a bank, his blade glinting in the full moon. The one Bill spoke of didn't have any ghosts, only a wall so huge it darkened the world. A girl told her lover that if he scaled the wall she would marry him, and he would have her farm with its prized horses. Using antlers as climbing axes, the man scaled all the way to the top, once there he saw the world spread out before him. Looking down he saw the girl's farm, and being so small he cast his sights to the other side of the wall where he noticed bigger farms and larger towns. Forgetting the girl, he climbed down to find these bigger places, only to discover when he arrived that he was smaller and less important than everyone else. His clothes were dirty, whereas the townspeople's were rich and lavish; his speech sounded garbled, while theirs

CRIK

sang out. Returning to the wall, he found his antlers worn and useless. Unable to climb the steep surface, he shouted, and through the wall, the girl, hearing him, called back: 'Why didn't you return to me when you reached the top of the wall?' she asked. 'I wished to see more of this side. They have large farms, and their horses are sleek and powerful,' he replied. A lingering silence passed, eventually the girl cried out, 'I know there're richer lands and quicker horses behind the wall, but I am on this side. I sent you to the top of the wall to see what your heart wanted, and it is not me. You only yearned for my farm, to ride its fields on my animals. I will only marry one who loves me.' She fell silent, and no matter how loud the boy shouted she never replied to him again.

'I remember,' said Jack, trying to imagine climbing to the top of the Thorn Hedge. He would see the whole world, Crik Village to one side, with the Scorn Scar on the other.

'You got the Syll safe Jack?'

In answer, Jack waved the instrument at Inara. 'I'm keeping it inside my shirt until we reach the tunnel.'

'It's our only defence against the Vestai,' she reminded him.

'Ying knows that,' said Bill. 'You do remember that...' He stared at the flute, pondering the power within the instrument.

'Damn Bill, of course I know how important it is. I still have the taste of lemons in my mouth. Now will you both relax, I know what I have to do.'

The trench stopped the snaking roots of the hedge clean. Scanning the earthen divide Jack saw no growing vegetation, only hard soil and rough stones. Jagged leaves littered the floor, blown across the rent by the ceaseless wind. The crisp carpet crunched underfoot. Now and then, a dark petal from one of the flowers stood in their path, which the group skirted around, afraid to touch the foul flower.

'Do you think we're headed in the right direction?' asked Bill. 'The hedge goes just as far that way.' He pointed back the way they had come.

'We've come this far, we may as well continue walking this way,' replied Jack.

'Ok, but if your wrong, just remember I told you.'

'I doubt you'd let me forget.'

An impression of something watching them from the cover of the hedge intruded on the group. The wolves kept a wary eye to the left. Krimble, taking his position at the rear, looked into the glooming depths with a crinkled smile.

Jack spotted a protrusion in the hedge. It jutted forward only slightly, but after the straight line they had followed, it called out for attention.

Inara spotted the anomaly too, and brought Black to a sudden halt. 'Is that the tunnel?'

'The hedge comes out far enough to cross the divide.'

Spurred by Bill's observation, Jack took the lead, taking long strides as he went. Silver kept pace; Bill hung back with Inara. The protrusion rose as high as a church spire. Foliage receded at its apex, like an old man's hairline, revealing white gleaming wood. Jack saw the mouth of the tunnel. Its square cut maw was more appropriate for a castle's entrance. Studying the straight lines, he expected to see a drawbridge barring his way. Twenty horses could gallop through in a line and never touch the tunnel walls. He stopped, his mouth suddenly tasting of cotton. Sprinkled across the grass were hundreds of the same blue pearls that littered the trench. The hair on the back of Silver's neck rose in stiff lines.

Approaching Jack, Inara spoke, 'What're we going to do?'

'There won't be another entrance,' said Bill. His hand strayed to his belly. 'Llast only mentioned one tunnel.'

Burning tears stung Jack's eyes. Faced with first crossing the line of pearls and then entering the dark belly of the hedge forced him to concede how selfish his motives were in bringing his friends here. They were all weary from the trek across Elysium, and there was no easy way back. Fingering the Syll, he said, 'Wait here, I'll enter. When I wave, come in after me.'

'Don't be stupid,' said Bill, reaching out to grab Jack's arm.

Pulling back, Jack shook his head. 'I'm the only one who wants to go through the Wold. I should go.' He gave Bill a tired grin. 'I'll be fine, just follow when I say.'

Without waiting, Jack hurried forward. He noticed Yang's weak outline trying to hang back, clawing at the grass, raking the soil with his shadow fingers. He felt the pull of his shadow, slowing his steps. Determined, he gritted his teeth and placed a foot over the thin pearl line. Searing pain lanced up from his belly. Crying out he gripped his abdomen, and, with horror, felt the Narmacil twisting against his fingertips. It writhed in agony. Realising, whoever dropped the blue stones meant to hurt the demon, did not deaden his own pain. Yang changed into a hundred different shapes, birds, beasts, and trees. Some were a myriad of forms, twisted things that thrashed the air. Each movement the Narmacil made within his stomach awoke fresh agony in Jack. Gripping himself, he stumbled beyond the line of pearls. Falling to the ground, he felt the demon thrash for a moment or two before quietening down. With ragged breath, he remained face down on the grass.

'Ying!'

Too weak to respond, Jack drew in a shuddering breath. Nothing moved inside, and for a time he wondered if the stones had killed the Narmacil. Opening his eyes, he saw his shadow sprawled beneath him, unmoving. His breath hurried; was Yang gone? He pressed his hand against the floor and noticed the dark patch beneath him begin to move away from the pearls. He watched as with each agonised inch Yang pulled himself closer to the tunnel. Painful tears spilled from Jack's eyes. With shaking shoulders, he got to his feet. He hated himself for sentencing his friends on this dangerous course. If he could turn aside from his quest, though a part of his mind spoke closer to the

CRIK

truth, his obsession, he would in a heartbeat. Only, he conceded, he could not do that, not even to save them from the imminent pain, or the danger that would surely follow. More than the pain passed on from the injured Narmacil, he felt guilt, twist through him like arthritis.

'Come,' he said, with a laboured wave. 'The pain only lasts for a second. It's the demon the stones hurt.' He could not meet their eyes.

'I don't want to harm it,' said Inara, her cheeks pinched and waxy in the dying light.

Jack shook his head. 'The pain only lasts for a moment. Look, Yang is fine.' He pointed to his moving shadow.

'Yang looks hurt,' said Bill, pushing up his glasses.

His shadow looked better than he had a few seconds ago; already its movements were surer. 'He's fine, it didn't kill him.'

'You sound disappointed,' said Inara.

Instead of answering her, Jack knelt down to pick up the Syll. He gripped the instrument so hard his knuckles turned white. 'Are you coming?'

Bill jumped up onto Black behind Inara. 'I'll have him run us through,' he said, holding onto Inara's shoulder. 'It'll be quick, so they won't feel too much pain.'

Inara, tight lipped and gripping her stomach, gave a stiff nod.

With his eyes boring into Jack's, Bill made Black bound forward. The great wolf rushed the blue line and crossed with a long jump.

Immediately the pair cried out and tumbled from the wolf. Jack rushed forward to Bill who squirmed on the ground. Inara shook beside him, her blonde hair picking up the wet soil. Taking Bill's hand, Jack said, 'It'll pass. The pain is only momen…'

Black's growl stopped him from speaking. Looking up he saw the wolf bearing down upon him. Black lips curdled back from long canines like windblown sheets. Focusing on Bill's hand Jack willed his friend to recover, but he dare not make a sound. Tilting its head back, Black howled, and then bringing its shaggy head down, rushed forward.

'Stop.'

Bill's words had an immediate effect on the wolf, which stopped a metre before Jack. Unable to move, Jack continued to watch the wolf, listening to the wind pass from its laboured lungs.

'I suppose having your own demon can be useful,' said Bill, pushing himself up from the ground.

Bill moved to take Inara's hand. 'Help me get her on Black.'

Not wanting to approach the large predator, Jack advanced tentatively. Fighting down his fear, he helped Bill lift Inara. With a familiar heave, they got her up onto the wolf's back.

A THORN IN THEIR SIDES

Noticing Inara's penetrating stare fixed across the blue stones, Jack saw Krimble standing back looking more uncomfortable than at any other time he had known him, alive or as an animated corpse.

Pencil thin lips cracked open as Inara spoke in a whisper that reminded Jack of little boys pulling legs off spiders. 'Come here,' she said. 'Walk slowly across the line.'

The zombie on stiff legs stumbled up to the line, his yellow tinted eyes wide with terror. His mouth hung open revealing the root of his decayed tongue.

'I said come here,' she repeated, ignoring the expression of panic painted on his face.

As soon as he reached the line, Krimble gripped his head, pushing his half-eaten fingers into the flesh of his cheeks. Blood coursed in thick streams down his front, colouring his grey flesh crimson. Beneath the blood, shapes began to move in a jittering dance. Flesh bubbled across his chest, pulsating with hidden shapes. Black faces, with wide golden eyes, peered out through Krimble's ravaged body. Fingers spread through the decayed flesh, only for Krimble to push them back with a horrified cry. More strove against their prison walls. Little impressions pushed against the soft belly. Even Krimble's arms convulsed with trapped Narmacils.

'Have mercy, how many Narmacils has he got,' said Bill taking a step back.

'He brought this on himself,' replied Inara. 'Every one of those came from someone Krimble tortured and killed. How do you like them now?' she shouted at Krimble. 'Who died so that one could writhe inside your leg? Huir? Remember how you cut off his arms and legs? Do you remember cutting off mine! I screamed, just as loud as you are now, but you didn't care, after you were done, you went back downstairs and drank tea. I heard the whistle of the kettle!'

Krimble had fallen to the ground, his back bubbling from the encased demons.

Jack turned, unable to watch.

Only Yang moved closer, holding out his shadowed hand to the struggling Narmacils.

'I should order you through the line a hundred more times.' Inara's voice was as dry as a snapping twig.

With his back to them, Jack faced the hedge. The branches that made up the walls of the tunnel moved, writhing together like a nest of snakes. Large branches as thick as his leg rubbed up against smaller wood, scraping off bark in long strips. The sound reminded him of the faulty step outside his bedroom door, only a thousand times louder.

With the sound drowning out Krimble's screams, the others faced the moving tunnel. The sun sank behind them, and in the dying red light, their elongated shadows touched the dark mouth.

22. BLACKTHORN TUNNEL

'THE WOOD'S MOVING.' Bill removed his glasses, wiped the lens, and replaced them back on the bridge of his nose. 'How's it doing that?'

If anything, the wood moved faster, splintering the limbs in furious rushing strokes. Broken branches and stripped bark littered the ground, adding to the continuous shower of leaves from above.

'It's only moving at the tunnel entrance.' Inara peered down the length of the hedge. 'I can't see another way through the hedge.'

Jack let some of his tension into his voice. 'Well there's not. You don't want to go back across the beads do you? We have to go through the Wold, and this is the only place we can do it.' He pointed a trembling finger toward the tunnel. 'Look, we can walk inside without going close to the hedge walls. An army could. Just stay to the centre and we'll be fine.'

Swaying, Inara rode forward. 'Can you promise our safety now Jack?' She looked down at him, and shook her head. 'No, you can't. The truth is you don't know what's happening.'

'We have no other choice.' Looking up at the girl, whose imprisonment had aged her, Jack felt the air drain from his lungs. He hated himself for adding to her misery. 'Tell me Inara.' Waving his arms around, he took in the rest of the countryside. 'Please, tell me, what else can we do? If there's an easier way, one without danger, then I need you to tell me.'

'Our path was set the moment you learnt about the Narmacil. Knell is all that matters now. Getting to her, so you can rid yourself of Yang.'

Her words alarmed him more than the tunnel. Reflecting on his choice brought a second, more powerful bout of shame. Her gratitude for her rescue from the Marsh House was the only reason she agreed to travel with him. 'I'm sorry Inara,' he replied. 'It's too late to turn back.' With his mouth set in a grim line, he took a step toward the tunnel, and its moving wall.

'It's moving faster,' cried Bill. 'It reacted to your approach.'

Without its bark, the wood appeared to be a nest of flailing white worms.

'The mouth of the tunnel is still as wide as before,' answered Jack. 'Stay to the middle.' His fingers crept to the instrument hidden inside his shirt. Hoping to find courage, he explored the Syll, touching the holes as though they were magical incantations of protection.

BLACKTHORN TUNNEL

The twigs, carpeting the floor, crunched underfoot.

'Ying, hold on,' said Bill, fumbling with the lantern. 'There's no way I'm following you into the dark.'

'Don't be in such a rush all the time,' warned Inara. 'Just because we have to go this way, doesn't mean we've got to stumble blindly forward.'

Feeling his cheeks burn, Jack relented, and then saw his shadow in the gloom. A peculiarity concerning Yang. Another abnormality, Jack corrected the singular, was his shadow's ability to be present on a cloud heavy day. One lone shadow amongst a world made up of none. True, rather than the fully formed entity presented on a sunny day, the demon appeared as a faint outline, like a drawing faded by time. How about the night, he mused, did the darkness hide Yang? On those rare occasions he could not sleep, he pondered what happened to Yang in the dark. Did the shadow cease to be, only for the morning to make him whole? Questions such as these had plagued him. Turning on his bedside lamp would make Yang reappear. Yang always looked as though he expected the sudden light, as though he kept watch in the dark. Jack shivered at the thought. Bill lit the lantern, focusing Yang in stark relief against the backdrop of the hedge. Let him watch, thought Jack, whatever nefarious activity occupied the demon's time in the dark could remain hidden. Despite his conviction, a seed of doubt remained to trouble him. Did the darkness dispel Yang, or not?

Holding the lantern aloft, Bill watched the rustling hedge with wide roving eyes. Cracks followed snaps, and splinters clouded the air as they stepped into the entrance. The vibrating wood settled into the pits of their stomach. Feeling like he had eaten a hive of bees, Bill wanted to vomit. The world lost all other sound; they jammed their fingers into their ears to block the deafening clamour of breaking wood.

Hurrying their steps, the group passed under the entrance. Bill, having kept his face upturned, was black from the falling dust before they had entered the tunnel proper. Once away from the entrance, the tunnel walls shook with less force. Here foliage rustled, yet the bark remained on the branches. The tunnel muted a lot of the sound, allowing them to lower their hands.

'I'm deaf in one ear,' complained Bill, digging his finger into his right ear.

'If you had waited to light the lamp you could've used both of your hands,' said Jack.

If Bill heard him, he didn't reply. Most likely, the black flowers shielding the tunnel walls kept him quiet. Like the others, Jack disliked the look of the flower. A flower with black petals went against everything he knew. His mother had grown all sorts of plants, his house looked more like a garden than a home; he had never seen anything like these before. Even Inara, who had remained calm in the Lindre Clearing, looked anxiously about. The thrashing wood made the flowers shimmer, reminding him of little talking heads, as though he were the one under inspection.

CRIK

'Let's keep moving,' shouted Inara. 'We're still too close to the entrance.'

The tunnel remained straight, and they had no trouble in keeping away from the hedge as they forged ahead. The sooner they were away from the dark blossoms the better. Pitch-black spaces shared the tunnel with the flowers, and the sense of something watching them flooded through Jack, turning his blood to water.

The wolves tucked in close, treading the same ground as the boys. Only Krimble walked close to the flowers, stroking them with his fingers. They rustled under his teasing touch. The red stems, which Krimble's fingers uncovered, reminded Jack of veins; he shivered at the comparison. Yang stayed close, twisting his entire agitated length to look back at the entrance whenever the plants rustled. Jack had never seen his shadow so nervous.

'I'd wish he'd stop doing that.' Bill watched Krimble with mounting unease.

'Ignore him,' said Inara. 'The more we take notice of him the more he likes it. As far as you're concerned, Krimble is not here. He's nothing more than a shadow.' She looked around. 'Sorry Yang, I didn't mean that we'd ignore you, just a poor choice of words.' Yang dismissed her anxiety with a wave of an arm. 'He'll be with us until his punishment is done.'

'When will that be?' asked Bill.

'I suppose when his rotting legs no longer hold him up.'

Wiping the grime from his face, Bill said, 'Remind me not to get on your bad side...and I thought my grandmother held a grudge.'

How could they ignore Krimble, at any time the zombie could bring death upon them? Even here, perceived Jack, he threatened them by stroking the flowers. When they got to the Red Wood, Krimble would give away their location the first chance he got. Krimble's rotting stench combined with the sick perfume of the flowers, each threatening to suffocate him. Scratching his nose with an absent finger, he bit his tongue from telling Inara to make Krimble go back, or die, or whatever else she wanted, just as long as he didn't have to worry about him any longer. Appraising Bill, he was aware of his friend's shared opinion. Wanting Bill to voice his objections did not make it right; Jack forced them down this path, not Bill, and as such, he couldn't expect anyone else to speak for him. Swallowing his protestation, he marched on, keeping his attention on both the tunnel and their sly companion.

How could things have changed so much in a week? Hard to believe, only a few days ago his biggest concern was whether his mother would again rearrange the furniture. Now, far from home, having survived meeting ancient statues and packs of wolves, he wondered what else waited ahead. No one else from the village had witnessed such sights, and for that, his chest swelled with pride. Such emotion passed like an errant leaf caught in a sudden cold updraft. His mother would be frantic. Wanting to cry he pictured her forced into stepping outside to raise the alarm; something she hated to do because of her burns. The plants in

BLACKTHORN TUNNEL

the house were her way to bring the outside world to her. Not doubting the tracking skill of the village hunters, he knew they would find where he and Bill had met the wolves. Finding only wolf tracks leading away from the path, they'd conclude the wolves had eaten them. A cold sweat broke out. Oh, he wished Knell lived close; he had to get back and tell his mother he was all right.

The air within the tunnel thinned.

'Are the walls getting closer?' asked Bill, moving the lantern from one side to the other.

The beam of light had shortened.

'Jack!' cried Inara.

Turned by Inara's frightened tone, Jack glimpsed a shape clinging to the roof of the Blackthorn Tunnel. It hung in view for only a moment before scurrying into the wood. The leather strap bit into his neck as he pulled the Syll from his shirt. Clutching the instrument, he looked around for the figure.

'What'd you see?' asked Bill, spinning around.

'I'm not sure.' Her eyes shifted between the walls. 'I thought I saw something watching us from above. I didn't get a good look at it. How about you Jack? I saw your face when I called out. You saw it didn't you.'

'There was something,' agreed Jack. 'It went into the wood. Let's group up, we don't want any stragglers whilst we're in here.'

'Get ready to play the flute,' said Inara. 'Remember what Llast told us.'

'I haven't forgotten.' Jack waved the Syll.

'How about blowing a note,' urged Bill.

Shaking his head, Jack said, 'We don't know how long this tunnel goes on for. When Llast asked me to try it my mouth grew numb, I'm not sure how long I can play it.' In readiness, he placed his finger atop the square and the largest hole. 'Shout if you see the Vestai, and I'll start.'

'With the flowers shivering it'll be hard for us to see them coming,' said Inara. 'It's as though the Blackthorn is the gullet of some immense monster.'

Bill nodded his agreement. 'Yeah and we're marching to its stomach.'

'Stop trying to scare each other. Keep the lantern high,' instructed Jack. 'It's the only thing in this forsaken place that isn't painted in shades of black.'

Only Yang saw the Vestai sneak forward from the tunnel wall. Large wings, covered in black feathers, shielded its pale body. Jack's shadow grew large, transforming into a bear. Yang rushed the Vestai, who let a shriek escape ruby lips.

Following the rushing bear, Jack spotted a girl in a bloodied dress standing to one side of the tunnel. Black wings spread out, stirring the air with a smell that reminded him of old attics. Yang launched himself, knocking the frightful girl to the ground.

'Its one of them,' shouted Bill.

CRIK

Shadow and Vestai wrestled on the ground. Although Yang's bear form covered the Vestai, through his body, the party could see the shrieking woman. Ferocious beating wings drove them back to the opposite side of the Blackthorn. The human face of the Vestai stared through Yang, holding Jack prisoner with colourless eyes. They appeared so large, so frantic to him that Jack believed the woman had no eyelids. Her slender nose came to a snub end before a nightmare mouth filled with wooden stakes.

Yang's heavy paws kept her imprisoned beneath him. Her brown hair whipped across her cut cheeks in untidy swirls. Repeatedly she plunged her wooden teeth into Yang, but each bite met with empty air. Blood gushed from her gums as the stakes splintered apart in her mouth.

'The Syll, Jack,' shouted Inara.

'Yes, of course,' he said dumbly, breaking his connection with the Vestai.

The taste of lemons filled his mouth as he wrapped his lips around the flute, making saliva collect beneath his tongue. The tune, which was both melodic and harsh, broke through the Vestai's screams, silencing her. Under Yang, she grew limp, and her eyes sunk deep into her skeletal face, until only pools of inky blackness remained.

Yang slowly withdrew from the Vestai.

Silver sniffed the wings splayed out on the floor. Snarling, the brave wolf retreated. The others encroached closer to the prone Vestai as the music played.

'She looks almost human,' said Inara.

'With vulture wings and a garden fence for a mouth,' replied Bill.

'I said almost human.'

'Make sure you keep playing,' Bill cautioned Jack as he knelt down. His fingers shook as he touched the dress. 'I wonder whose blood this belongs to? It looks old. Now that her wings have stopped flapping, she looks smaller. About as large as Liza Manfry, and about as ugly,' he added.

'Look at her arms,' said Inara, pointing down from Black. 'What're those welts?'

'They aren't welts,' answered Bill. His fingers brushed up against the Vestai's elbow where the largest dark splotch appeared. 'It's the same damn flower that grows on the wall.'

'Why'd she stick those on her arm?' asked Inara.

Jack could only feel his tongue if he pressed it against his teeth. Another minute or two playing and he will lose even that sensation.

Bill looked back, his face slack. 'She didn't stick them to herself. They're growing out of her arm.' He lifted her shoulder, pulling part of the wing up from the ground as he examined her. 'Her back is plastered with them.'

Jack let the Syll drop from his mouth. The flowers didn't just grow on the Vestai -the flowers were the Vestai. He yelled in fright as pale arms threaded through the hedge behind him. Long tapered hands reached out to snatch the air with hooked nails. The blackness between the flowers lifted as midnight wings parted, revealing horrid white faces.

The women stepping from the Blackthorn wore the same bloodied dress as the first Vestai. Fabric, matted in dried blood, clung to their forms like resin. Men also stepped out, their sunken chests dotted with the black flower, and children, their faces stretched into masks of torment.

'Ying!' cried Bill as the woman on the floor clutched at his collar, bringing his face down toward her gaping mouth.

Yang kept the nearest Vestai away from Jack with oversized fists. Bodies flew back from the impact of the shadow's hits, but more came through the hedge. The wolves were going crazy, snapping at anything that came close. Inara only saved herself from falling by ringing her arms around the wolf's neck. Silver, her eyes rolling back into her head sank her teeth into Krimble, who let out a gurgled scream.

The splintered wood filling the Vestai's mouth touched Bill's cheek when Jack blew into the Syll.

Although Jack failed to notice a small child crawl beneath Yang's wild defence, the first musical notes stopped it, and all the other Vestai, who collapsed onto the floor. The weight of the child on his legs made Jack's breath falter for a moment. It had come so close to biting him, another second and those barbed teeth would've been tearing into the flesh of his leg.

'Why'd you stop playing,' asked Bill, diverting Jack's attention away from the child with the sunken eyes. 'No,' said Bill, holding up a hand, 'don't answer me. Just play, and don't stop for anything.'

Bill fiddled with his torn collar for an instant, before turning to Inara. 'I'm sorry I lost control of Black, my mind just went crazy when she had a hold of me.'

Inara had her teeth clenched together, and her knuckles were white from gripping Black's fur. 'Forget about it,' she said, without moving her lips. 'Can we just go now; I really don't like this place.'

Bill nodded his emphatic agreement.

'I've got the lamp, so I'll take the lead,' said Bill, lifting the lantern to lend weight to his words. 'Make sure you don't step on any of them.' He looked down at the silent bodies surrounding them.

As though he has to tell us, thought Jack, as he followed behind.

The Syll felt hot in Jack's hands, and as he blew, he felt the vibrations of the reed inside, tickling his fingers. Struggling to balance the instrument, he tiptoed around the winged bodies. The movement made it harder to play than when he had stood still, and a few times the piping music blew a dud note. Each time the music died Bill threw a dark backward glance, and Jack knew Inara did the same from behind.

CRIK

'Don't you dare step on any of them, you hear me,' Inara told Krimble. 'Grab Black's tail if you're having trouble following us,' she added after Krimble's garbled reply.

The wings splayed out on the ground however made it impossible not to tread on the Vestai. Crunching the feathers underfoot sent shivers up Jack's spine, making the Syll produce high-pitched notes. Already his chest strained with the effort of blowing into the flute, and his mouth continued to lose feeling.

The walls of the Blackthorn encroached upon them as they proceeded, making it harder to step around the bodies. Most of the Vestai were women. The few men lying on the floor were larger with much of their face rotted away. Their skin looked wet, reminding Jack of slime on stone. The children were the hardest to look upon; they appeared normal, apart from their sunken eyes.

His chest ached and his gums were sore. Exhausted from playing, Jack stumbled after Bill, conscious of the large wolf padding close behind. Having to escape the tunnel before he lost the ability to play stopped all other stimuli; he no longer noticed the bodies lining the tunnel floor. His mind swirled, he imagined the upturned faces of the women were winking up at him. One Vestai, who would've been attractive if not for the wooden teeth sticking through her cheek, seemed to motion him closer with a curled finger.

'Careful Jack,' said Inara, gripping his arm as he bowed closer to the prone woman on the floor. 'I don't think you should get that close.'

Despite his mouth losing feeling, his chest took up the slack. It burned, and with each blow his body tightened, until it felt as though his skin sank between his ribs. With each inhalation, the pain increased.

'Give up boy,' called Krimble. 'Just let the instrument drop from your lips, it'll be so easy. Relax; take a moment to gather your strength. It's a long way to go; you can't possibly keep it up all the way.'

Krimble's words had a different effect than what the zombie had intended. Hardening himself against the strain, Jack strove onward. Krimble's whispery tones, like a whip at a horse's back, pushed him through the pain.

If the tunnel deviated from its straight route none noticed, and though the ground was far from level it never threw a sudden slope in their way. In the distance, a bluish haze heralded a change in the Blackthorn and with it a cool breeze that rustled their clothes.

'It's the way out,' cried Inara.

It was too much to hope for, but as they continued Jack saw the hedge give way to an open expanse.

What lay beyond the Blackthorn Tunnel stopped them in their tracks.

23. THE RED WOOD

CUMULUS CLOUDS STOOD to the north like great mountains, shining rose pink in the morning sun. A cool breeze ruffled the collars of the bedraggled group's shirts. They stood in the open, their expressions showing surprise, and a complete lack of understanding. At their front, Jack allowed the Syll to drop from his tired lips. His relief after escaping the tunnel faltered and died. He expected green lands; instead, a land filled with red hues greeted them. Everywhere his eyes touched lay crimsons, maroons, sangria, and carmine. Gulping in air as dry as sun-baked hay, he tried to make sense of a land covered in blood. Black's movement stirred red dust in small swirls; before long, the dust coated the great wolf's tail and underside. Amongst this wash of harsh colour rose pillars of slender metal. Some twisted spires curled inward, creating abstract shapes akin to some awesome unknown art. Rising above these warped constructs sprang spear points, stabbing the overcrowded skyline.

It's not blood, Jack realised with no small measure of relief. The aged metal waged an intolerable war against the elements, and with each season, they shed a little more of their skin. Rust covered everything like flour on freshly made bread.

'Where're the trees?' asked Bill.

'I don't think there are any,' replied Inara. 'There's nothing here but dead metal. No bushes or flowers.'

'But there're bugs.' Cupping his hand to his mouth Bill drew their attention to a hovering swarm of brown insects. 'They're disgusting. Look,' he observed, 'they aren't flying, they're leaping like fleas.'

Against his own revulsion, Jack stepped through the haze of insects. The fleas, batting against his calf, made him want to shriek. Refusing to look down, he carried on.

'Pity Mr Gasthem isn't with us; he could ask the flies for directions,' said Bill.

A scream from the Blackthorn Tunnel rent the air. In the darkness, they could make out the white fabric the Vestai wore; they stopped short of the sunlight. There were hundreds of the horrid creatures, snapping the air in frustration with their sharpened stakes.

CRIK

'I don't need any bugs to tell me we have to get away from here,' said Inara, spurring Black toward a hill rising to the east.

While the others scampered into the Wold, Jack stayed. The tormented faces of the child Vestai held him. A macabre thought teased him with delicious horror. Had the children come from the hedge, or had something taken them to the damned tunnel? Grandpa Poulis told stories of children going missing in the wood. He thought Bill's grandfather had made them up to frighten them from playing too far from home, now he wondered. Burdened by the question, he left to follow his friends.

Metal, imitating shrubbery, littered the path, making it feel as though he trod on sharp stones whilst wearing slippers. The cruel, unpredictability of the terrain made progress slow and treacherous. Not troubled by the new terrain the wolves threaded through the iron with uncanny agility. Without Inara's added weight, Silver ran ahead, marking the territory. Remaining apart from the group, Krimble stumbled from one hazard to the next. Within the first mile, he had lost three toes, with a fourth attached only by sinew. Evidence of Krimble's passage littered their back trail. A blind child could follow them by smell alone, mused Jack, his patience already spent.

Atop a rise, the air grew thin, Bill already gasping from the ascent, staggered to a slab of rock, where he sat with a grunt. From their elevated position, they could see the immense size of the Red Wood. Copper domes reflected golden light over the ground like sunlight on wet stones. Silver wire, as though spun by some monstrous spider, threaded through an intricate steel lattice. Caves speckled the side of mountainous heaps of lead like air pockets in a sponge. Although their initial reaction to the sight stirred wonder, they soon found, on closer inspection, a plague of rust in every quarter of the Wold. It brought to mind a full sink, where a drop of blood had spoiled the purity of the water.

Fingernails, caked with dirt, scraped across Inara's dirtier cheek. She no longer noticed the grime. 'It'll take days, if not weeks to reach the other side.' She didn't expect an answer; the truth of her statement lay before them, in an undulating map.

Despite the obvious evidence, Bill answered with a furious nod, dislodging his glasses. 'I'd say months.' He bent to retrieve his spectacles. 'The metal on the floor will slow us down. We can't run, that's for sure. You could not push a 'barrow more than a few yards without puncturing its tyre.'

'Doesn't matter,' said Krimble. His lips peeled back from his teeth like a tide scraping a beach. 'It's not like any of you are going to survive a meeting with the Myrms. They won't like you invading their home. You are intruders, insects in their larder. When they see you they'll squash you all.' Old hands came up to touch his sunken chest where grey hair grew in an untidy thatch. Perhaps the fingers creasing his pale skin sought the Narmacils housed within. 'When you came to my house, I took you in, kept you alive. The demons,' his accusing

THE RED WOOD

yellow eyes swivelled to Jack, 'saved your lives. I wanted to unfetter your demons; help them reach their full potential. Instead, you trap them in your stupid pursuit of a meaningless truth. The girl had it right Ying; your Narmacil, with its spiny tail wrapped around your heart, is as much a part of you as your shadow.

'The Myrms don't care for the Narmacil. They have evolved without knowing those gifts most of you enjoy.' He paused, allowing his statement to percolate. 'Best you sacrifice yourselves in the tunnel than go forward.'

Bill's lower lip trembled at the mention of returning to the Blackthorn Tunnel. The boy, who had read books until his eyes had grown weak, showed through his mud-streaked face. Jack understood. For the first time since leaving the village, they could not turn back. Before now, they had the option to cross the marsh, and try to find the hunter's path back to the village.

Krimble also recognised the cause of Bill's faltering courage. 'No one from your small village will find you here. There was a chance they would have if you stopped at the marsh.' He looked around. 'No one comes here. I daresay you are the first people to set eyes on the Red Wood for a hundred years. It is a pity your demons could not make you fly. It would be so much easier if you could float above the clouds. Who knows, if you flew high enough you may be able to see, far away, smoke rising from your homes' chimneys. And Inara my dear,' his words slipped into a sympathetic patter, 'would you spy your papa out in the wild, still hollering your name?'

Anger shot through Jack; focusing his mind on Krimble with single-minded hate. He balled his hand into a fist, and had taken it back only a few inches when Bill stepped passed him; and smacked the zombie in the nose.

'Sorry,' said Bill, looking both abashed and pleased. 'I've been itching to do that for days.' He stumbled back, jamming his hands into his pockets.

Krimble cackled on the floor. With his bent back, his hands waving in the air, he looked like a flipped crab. 'Fear is like swamp water boy, it'll suck you in slow, dragging you deeper, and before you realise it you're in over your head. Best turn back and try your luck with the Vestai; at least they'll eat you fast.'

Jack gritted his teeth against Krimble's mad cackle. To look into those sallow eyes, the full moon lunacy of them is to welcome nightmares. He knew then Krimble's mind, if not already gone, was fast slipping away, decaying faster than his body. Madness had its allure; such a filthy curtain would hide a thousand torments, a multitude of unforgivable sin.

Inara remained silent. The shimmer of light from the metal forest glanced across her angular features, revealing in that moment the beautiful woman she would become. Her blond hair, now a copper gold, fanned her brow like a metal comb, hiding an eye pregnant with heavy sorrow. 'I will not allow him to go unpunished.' Entranced by the scope of the vista, she refused to look away. 'I have decided what must be done.' She hedged off Bill, seeing the boy about

CRIK

to intrude. 'You have done me – and others – a great harm.' She locked Krimble with a look of terrible loathing. 'The physical scarring you have left on me is nothing compared to what you have done to my mind.' She smiled. 'I recognise your lunacy; it is also a part of me. No longer will I be able to take pleasure from a morning stroll, or laugh at an innocent thing. I am bereft of warmth; I feel ice water running through my veins instead of blood. This is unforgivable.' She reached down from where she sat upon the great wolf, and with tender fingers, stroked Krimble's scarred face. He flinched from her touch, and within that moment, his yellow eyes cleared, and feelings as harsh as a pinch poured in. Inara grinned, her small white teeth showing for the first time in memory. 'Strange how you wanted my gift, but once I gave it to you, you howled in despair. Sometimes what we want is not what we should have.

'Our path,' she commenced, straightening her back, 'is fraught with danger. We were lucky to get through the tunnel unscathed. I don't know what is before us.' She turned from the Red Wood with its dancing light. 'The little we do know is that you are a danger we cannot afford. Bill is right, you must go.'

Krimble's jaw yawned open, as dumbstruck as were the boys. 'You're letting me die. You're going to end this?' He looked down at his mottled flesh with disgust. 'You will let me rest.' A weak smile, cradled his mouth.

Inara's smile broadened. 'I'm banishing you from the group,' she replied. 'This does not mean your punishment has ended. You cannot die until I wish it, and that will never be. You shall roam these lands, alone and hated. Shunned by man and bird; you will know no rest. Your body will continue to decay, the blood in your limbs will congeal until it is a yellow poison, but still you will live. No doubt, your eyes will become dim, until you cannot see, and even then, you will have to find your way. This is your punishment, Krimble of the Marsh House.'

'Wha...,' Krimble said, his arms swaying useless at his side. 'You can't do this.'

'Yes she can,' Bill said rushing forward. Pushing Krimble, he knocked him once more to the ground. 'You have stayed with us for too long. Your dark speech will be your only company from this moment.'

'You said it yourself,' Inara said, looking down as Krimble squirmed back on scathed elbows, 'no one has been here for a hundred years. There is no turning back. Your attic was our prison, welcome to yours. Enjoy it.'

'How will we find Knell without him?' asked Jack. 'He's the only one in the group who knows of whom I speak.'

'He told us everything that the hunter had to say,' replied Inara.

'North beyond the Wold,' said Bill. 'We've found the Wold; all we need to do is keep heading north.'

Beseeching fingers, their skin peeled back from tendon and bone, reached up to Inara's back. 'Don't do this. I know many things.' He swung his head

THE RED WOOD

around on brittle bones to look at Jack. 'The bitch with the birds will be impossible to find without my help. Listen to me,' he said, his stained teeth biting off each syllable. 'What do you think happened to the others living in the Scorn Scar? Knell didn't always live by herself. There were others in that small town. They gave me their marvellous gifts.'

'Don't listen to him Jack,' Inara said, laying a hand on Jack's chest as he took a step toward Krimble, 'he's full of lies. His deception caught me once; I will not fall for it again.' She regarded Krimble. 'You brought this upon yourself.'

With his mouth sagged open Krimble looked up at them. 'You can't just leave me here.'

'Yes, we can,' said Bill.

Reaching out, Yang laid his hands on Krimble. Incredulous, Jack watched, sure Yang wanted to give Krimble a hug. Instead, Yang stood still, his palms pressed against Krimble's ravaged flesh. Furtive movement, seen through his dark twin, raised the hackles on Jack's neck. The shapes were vague, elusive, like ghosts trapped beneath layers of ice. The sight of them made his skin crawl with spindly spiders, the kind normally reserved for dusty shed corners. Even without a face, Yang manages to portray deep sorrow.

With an impatient grunt, Krimble strode through Yang and reached out to snag Inara's top. Before his fingers touched the worn fabric, Yang grabbed him, dragging him away. Struggling with the dark arms entwining his body, Krimble groaned; his eyes continued to look around for help. The zombie even sent an imploring glance toward Silver, who sat on her haunches licking her paw.

'Let go of m...' Krimble cried as Yang, who had grown strong in the multihued light, yanked him backward and down the slope.

Jack watched as his shadow carried Krimble away. Yang's shadow legs were pencil thin by the time he let go of Krimble; even then, they all heard the man shout back up the hill. Closing off the pleas for mercy Jack laid a hand on Inara's shaking shoulder. Struggling to contain her composure, at Jack's comforting hand, she bit her lip, but in the end, she could not stop the laughter pouring out of her. The metal hills echoed to the sound, until it seemed the entire forest laughed with her.

On his return, Yang did not share Inara's mirth; he looked worried with his head bowed. Did Yang want Krimble out of the group? Perhaps his shadow regretted his choice to remain with him. After all, Jack mused, he wanted freedom from the Narmacil, whereas Krimble had begged for a union.

'Let's go before he has a chance to climb the hill.' Bill threw an uneasy glance at Inara as she sniggered into her cupped hands.

Taking a last look, Jack wondered whether Krimble knew something more about Knell. He did see another home in the Lindre's vision. Again, the awful spectre of the figure rising from the hole threatened to eclipse his rationale. Having kept the figure a secret from the group, he now regretted his decision. If

CRIK

anyone could shed light onto the menacing shape, he was no longer part of the group.

24. NORTH BY NORTHWEST

KNEE HIGH COPPER SWIRLS snagged Jack's woollen trousers, their sharp edges left shallow cuts on his skin. Thankfully, only a few bled, nothing serious. Yang pushed the more dangerous protrusions out of his way. With ferocious strength, Yang drove a silver shard, the size of a broadsword, into the ground.

The Red Wood continued to dazzle with unexpected beauty. The metal forest had more variety than Criklow Wood could ever hope to equal. Here the land ignored the laws of nature. Shards, sticking from the ground, did not vie for the sun's attention. Iron mixed with veins of copper, zinc-splashed colour on steel. Big spires, and aged shavings, shared the same hillside. No two things looked alike. Whether the shapes were marvellous or muted, it did not matter as the next view held more wonders to behold.

'Look what I found,' said Bill, rushing from behind a stone boulder, that looked out of place amongst the sea of red, brandishing a long spike. Clothe torn from his sleeve bound the base of the two foot long weapon. 'We could equip an army with what's left here to rot.'

'It's no good,' said Jack. 'It's covered in rust, one smack and it'll break.'

'It's strong, and sharp. I'd like to see the Vestai try clawing at me with their dirty fingernails now.'

Even rusted it looked a fearsome weapon when Bill, with bravado, sliced the air. Since leaving Krimble, they had travelled for hours, and Jack saw the confidence, Bill had gained with his Talent, return. Allowing him his fun Jack turned and saw Inara some way off gripping Yang's hand. She smiled at his shadow, and confided with the demon in a conspiratorial whisper. His good humour evaporated.

He walked under rusted blades, not letting Inara know he had seen her clandestine meeting. How she kept overlooking the cunning demon's true nature frustrated him no end. Her deliberate disregard for his warnings, would eventually land her, and probably each of them, in trouble. Rust clogged water trickled alongside his route, reminding him sharply of arterial blood.

He wanted nothing more than to be in his room, playing toy soldiers. A sudden jolt of pain hit his chest. Clutching his ribs, he expected to find the Narmacil trying to break free. Only after his initial panic subsided did he realise the pain he felt was brought on by homesickness. Thoughts of his mother

CRIK

sparked new aching waves. Things had happened so fast since leaving the hunter's path that he had given his mother little thought. Shame bowed his head. He hoped, though he knew it to be futile, that she did not worry overmuch. A weak smile parted his lips as his attention reverted to the Red Wood. What was there to worry about? He almost laughed aloud at his own absurd question. Yang sensing his shift in mood drifted closer, falling back into his accustomed role as silent companion, of protector, and friend.

'Get away,' Jack barked, waving his arm in a furious strike that passed through Yang. 'You aren't part of me. You never were!'

Instead of hunching his shoulders as Jack expected, Yang stood tall, then gave a stiff nod. He pointed first at himself and then at Jack.

'Why lie, I know what you are. As soon as I find Knell, you'll be gone for good.' A wolfish grin, that would have made Black proud, accentuated his threat.

'You shouldn't talk to him like that,' said Inara. 'He has always been there for you. Without him we would never have escaped Krimble's house.'

He looked over at the girl perched on a grey arch, banging her mutilated legs against the metal. 'If we didn't have demons inside of us we wouldn't have been imprisoned in the first place. The false path that took you away from your parents, or the reason why Bill and I went into the woods to look for a wolf, would not have happened. Krimble's mind was like an apple left to rot in the sun, but the Narmacil gave him the tools he needed to capture others.'

Biting her nails, with a series of ferocious snicks, stretched out Jack's observations, lending them both time to digest what he said. Spitting the half-moon slivers into her dirty palm, Inara said, without looking up, 'You can't blame the Sprites for what he did. If a dog bites you, do you then distrust all dogs? Or do you see just one mean mutt with a foul temper? The way I understand things,' she continued, moving the cut nails around the lines of her hand, 'the Narmacil within us follow our actions, our choices shape them. Have you ever witnessed Yang do anything mean, or criminal?'

'Of course, he got me into trouble daily.' His arms came up in exasperation. 'Grandma Poulis grew hoarse shouting our names. Once he stole half the town's clothes. Everyone came to our house in the rain, wearing nothing but his or her bedclothes. When my mother found the clothes stuffed in my cupboard she grounded me for two weeks.'

To his consternation Inara laughed.

'It's not funny,' he told her. 'My mother was furious. To teach me a lesson she took away all my clothes; I could only wear pyjamas for days on end.'

'You see,' she said as her shoulders shook with laughter, 'there was nothing evil in what Yang did. I guess you'd call it a prank, nothing more.'

Fine for her to say thought Jack, crushing rust beneath his heel, she didn't have the entire town blame him for everything that went wrong. He almost told her about the time Yang had dyed the river red making it look like a ribbon of blood. He bit his tongue, no doubt that would make her laugh harder and she'd fall off her branch. Besides, he thought looking down at the discoloured stream; if that was a prank, it was a prophetic one.

'You and Bill seem to be better friends than when we started out.'

'Hmmm, we have a common goal. He still doesn't want me along though,' she observed.

'Why'd you think that?'

'Quite simple Jack, he wants to ride his wolf by himself. I take up too much room for both of us to ride comfortably. It doesn't worry me, he needs the exercise. Walking instead of riding will get rid of his belly quicker than any diet.'

'He's not fat.'

'No,' Inara agreed. 'I'd call him podgy. Look.' She held her hand out to Jack, showing the nails she had bitten off arranged into the shape of a man. 'It's you,' she said, 'as you are right now.'

'It could be anyone,' said Jack, cocking an eyebrow.

'No it's you,' said Inara checking her palm. 'Look.' She offered her hand once more. 'I gave him an unhappy mouth.'

Jack saw the downward facing nail. Tilting her hand Inara stretched the small crescent shadows across her lifeline. Unnerved, Jack moved back from the darkening image.

'What's the matter?' she asked.

'I don't like pictures,' he replied, remembering the pictures in Mr Hasseltope's tomb. 'Especially ones of me,' he added when he saw the question in Inara's silent stare. 'I read that if someone had a picture of you they could harm you.'

'You think I would harm you Jack?'

He shook his head. It was a silly thing to say, he once read a comic in which an old witch killed someone by just having a drawing of his face. Absurd. Yet Inara watched him with such an earnest intent that he felt obliged to answer. 'Not yet, but another weeklong trek and you just might.'

He meant it as a joke, but it felt stiff and awkward on his tongue, robbing it of its intended wit.

'That depends on where your quest leads us next.'

A pretty turn of her mouth put Jack at ease. What a remarkable girl she was. If he had gone through half of what she had, if Krimble had so much as cut a toe from his foot, he would be as bitter as a dry tablet. Walking over he sat beside her, letting his legs dangle above the ground. He wanted to hold her hand, to let her know through action how much he appreciated her company. He started to reach across when he lost his nerve; instead, he stuffed his hands deep into his pockets. Finding a piece of string, he wrestled it between his

CRIK

fingers. Her eyes reflected the sun's bathing glow like a spring brook, only deeper inspection betrayed no light of their own.

'Is everything alright?' asked Inara. 'You're looking at me like I'm a porcelain doll.'

Jack felt his face grow numb. Bill's grandmother had dolls with eyes just like hers. 'Don't be silly,' he mouthed, unsure whether he spoke or not. For a moment, he had the temptation to reach out and touch her skin, to see whether it would pimple under his finger or remain firm. Don't be stupid, he told himself, she isn't a bloody doll.

Yang reached out and pinched Inara's arm, causing her to cry out.

'Hey, what's the deal?'

'I don't know why he did that,' said Jack when Inara rubbed her arm.

His gaze shifted to his dark twin. Had Yang pinched her to satisfy his curiosity? Or just to get him into trouble? If the former, then it proved the demon could read his thoughts.

'That wasn't very nice of you Yang, it hurt,' said Inara with rising colour in her cheeks.

'I told you, he has a mind of his own,' Jack said meekly. 'Doesn't seem so funny now, does it,' he whispered.

'Not at all,' agreed Inara. 'Bill,' she called out, waving to him through a gap in the iron trees. 'Call Black, I think we'd better be off.'

'He's hunting,' Bill answered. 'He's caught the scent of his prey. He won't be long.'

'Prey?' Jack looked around. 'Apart from these blasted bugs I haven't seen a single living thing since we entered the Wold. What has he found?'

'Beats me,' said Bill coming closer. 'It's got him pretty excited whatever it is. Poor thing is almost as hungry as I am. And I'm starving.'

'Let's hope the wolves have some luck, just make sure Black doesn't eat it all.'

'We also need clean water,' added Inara.

Where can we find clean water here, pondered Jack as flakes of rust drifted passed his nose from an overhead branch?

'It's a problem for another time,' said Bill in alarm.

'Why, what's happened?' asked Jack looking around, but saw no threat.

'Whatever Black was hunting,' said Bill, gripping Jack's shoulder, 'is now hunting the wolf. They are coming this way.'

'Black wouldn't run from anything,' said Inara, lending voice to Jack's reaction.

'I can feel Black's terror. Whatever follows him is something that he has learnt to fear.'

Even the constant buzz from the insects seemed muted as they waited to hear signs of pursuit. Black had been gone for at least twenty minutes, at a gallop the wolf could arrive back at any moment. Bill, still gripping his makeshift weapon, trembled with his legs apart. Inara gripped the iron branch she sat upon, her cheekbones etched sharply under her drawn skin. Jack saw all this while his pulse pounded away unchecked.

'We have to draw the enemy away,' said Jack, licking his lips. 'Make Black run away from us.'

'I won't let Black face whatever it is alone,' cried Bill. 'He's always been there for us. He's our friend.'

'We have no weapons,' said Jack. 'At least Black has a chance to outrun his pursuer. Keep hold of your connection with him, when he escapes bring him back to us.'

'We have to leave as well,' said Inara. 'If the thing hunting Black follows his back trail he will follow it back to us.'

'How?' asked Bill, turning on her. 'You have no legs to run with, Black always carried you. Without him you can't go anywhere.'

'We're going to carry her,' said Jack.

'You're crazy Ying, bang out of your head. How're we going to carry her through this metal forest by ourselves?'

'We haven't got a choice.'

'Yang can carry me without much effort,' said Inara.

'Ok,' said Bill. 'We'll have to leave you behind if you slow us down though. No point in all of us getting caught, you understand.'

'Shut up Bill,' said Jack. 'We aren't leaving anyone behind.'

'Tell that to Black.'

Ignoring Bill, as Yang lifted Inara from the branch, Jack looked to the north where something pursued the wolves. What could scare them so much? The wolf was a predator, they ran from nothing. The Red Wood had turned nature on its ear. Not even seeing a bird burrowing into the hard ground would surprise him now.

Scores of cuts criss-crossed their arms and legs as they ran through the metal twigs. One long metal thorn struck Bill above his eye; the resulting blood blinded him, forcing them to halt to wrap the wound.

'I haven't heard anything behind us,' said Inara, sweating despite Yang carrying her. 'Are the wolves far away?'

Fidgeting with the blood soaked bandage Bill gave a nod.

'Best if we carry on this way,' suggested Jack. 'I don't want to turn north just yet. The wolves went that way; we could end up crossing the path of whatever is chasing them. If we keep going west and then turn north we won't have gone too far from our path.'

'He's still scared.'

CRIK

Jack looked at Bill, and for a moment, he recognised some of Black in his friend's expression. The way Bill's jaw had hardened into a firm line, and his studying eyes.

'There's nothing we can do to help,' repeated Jack. 'As soon as they shake the pursuit you can bring them back to us.'

Bobbing in the air, with only two shadow arms supporting her, Inara said, 'They are protecting us, just like they have in the past.'

'I wish I could see what Black sees,' said Bill. 'All I know is what he feels, and it's tearing me up inside.'

Swarms of Insects wrapped around their legs as they moved, masking their footfalls in a constant buzzing. The dense hovering cloud swirled above the ground like a flock of starlings.

'I can't keep going like this,' said Bill coming to a halt. Sweat bathed his hot flushed face. 'The wolves are far enough away. We won't be found here.'

'Here,' said Inara, looking around at hanging gold thread, 'where's here?'

The ground, beneath the swarm, sucked at Jack's feet. Fearing they had stepped into a bog drove him back, where he collided with Bill. His feet came free, but muddy. Something had turned the earth.

'Something has dug the ground.' He voiced his findings in a rush.

'Why?' asked Bill.

'Over there.'

Jack looked to where Inara pointed and saw a young tree uprooted and tossed to one side. The roots, pointing toward the grey sky, still held clumps of earth. The trunk, broken in two, yawned widely, giving the wood the look of a screaming animal.

'So trees do grow here,' said Bill.

'Doesn't look as though they are allowed to grow for long,' observed Inara. 'Whoever did this prefers cold metal to living wood. All this gold,' she reached up touching the precious metal with her fingers, 'is hard, unyielding. It's not natural what's happened here.'

'Not natural, wow, I thought copper thorns and iron trees as high as towers grew from nuts,' said Bill. He hit the bark of the fallen tree with his makeshift weapon, chipping the wood.

Yang moved Inara closer to the felled tree. 'Since leaving the marsh we've seen statues come to life, an old man wearing flutes as shoes, and a hedge attack us. None of that should be natural, but it is. We can't say for sure how the Red Wood became as it is.'

'Until now,' said Jack. 'Whatever killed the tree is probably the same something that is running after the wolves.'

'Well it's not these bugs,' muttered Bill.

'There're more of them here than elsewhere in the wood,' remarked Jack. 'Perhaps the churned earth attracts them? I don't care why, I don't fancy sticking around. Whatever uprooted the tree may come back.'

'And cut us down,' finished Bill.

'Walk around the disturbed ground,' said Inara, 'you don't want to leave footprints behind.'

Glad one of us has some sense, thought Jack.

A sound of metal striking metal rang through the air. It didn't sound like a hammer strike in a forge, it felt deeper. A second sound soon followed, reverberating in their chests. Yang lowered Inara to the ground; the insects reached her waist. Jack hunched down. Bill, with mouth agape, looked around, his eyes, through his spectacles, appeared huge.

Clenching his teeth Jack grabbed hold of Bill, tugging him to the floor.

Bill cried out in surprise.

The noise of metal upon metal immediately stopped. The insect sounds continued, and Bill's whispered apology was all Jack heard. Long minutes went by. The Red Wood retained a pregnant silence. Behind him, Inara bit her lip so hard she drew blood.

'Is it gone?' asked Bill.

Clang, then a hollow bong, broke the stillness. The party froze, as with horror they heard the hastening approach of the hunter.

25. IF IT ONLY HAD A HEART

Rushing legs snapped through the underbrush, then stopped. A dull thud, like a drum hit with a flat palm, followed. Before the punctuating noise had Jack crane his neck upward, Yang had spread himself over the group, covering them in a thin obscuring layer. Above him, clinging to the tree like a boy at play, was the oddest beast Jack had ever seen. Its skin matched the forest in hue, blending in despite its righteous colour of cobalt blue, rustic red, and worn yellow. An impossibly broad face, peered down. It was a frog, a giant amphibian, complete with webbed feet and hands. Though to Jack it appeared more like a puppet without its string. The whole body, being bipedal and tall, jarred with the head. An artist's impression, other than what nature intended. Like this entire place, he mused. The sun slipped by a slow moving cloud, affording greater light. Sunlight glinted like coins off the creature. Jack's heart quickened, it was metal, the same as everything else in the Wold.

Huddled under Yang's body they remained undetected. From above they must appear as nothing more than part of the shadow of the felled tree. Each held their breath, enduring the swarming insects covering their lower bodies with stiff resolve.

A deafening sound, as the creature descended, had Jack clench his fist until his knuckles turned white. The armoured wrists, of the first denizen of the Red Wood they had laid eyes upon, sported long jagged spikes. An especially cruel shard of hammered tin sprang from its right elbow, reaching back as far as its cobalt shoulder. Despite the webbing between its fingers, the creature did not grip the trunk, preferring to lay its hand flat to the replicated plant.

Grandpa Poulis's stories of Myrm attacks came rushing back to hit Jack like a fall through an icy river. Myrms attacked lone travellers, stealing their weapons and possessions. One story in particular came rushing back, causing him to squeeze his eyes shut to dispel it from his mind. Instead, shutting his eyes brought it back in vivid detail.

'The house where Elisa lived, with her little brother and father, stood apart from the rest of town,' Grandpa Poulis had said, setting himself down beside a roaring campfire. He appeared as a boy, with his tell-tale mop of grey hair. A pipe, dangling comically from his small lips, also set him apart from the other boys. 'Her father, being the town's only blacksmith could do what he wanted.

IF IT ONLY HAD A HEART

After all, if he didn't want to fix your horses' hooves, or your broken wheelbarrow, who would fix it. When he wanted his house a couple of miles up the road in the meadow overlooking the stream, no one argued. And no doubt if he wanted a bridge over that stream, he would've got that too,' Grandpa Poulis remarked, switching his pipe to the other side of his mouth.

'Elisa was a beautiful girl,' he continued, 'but this isn't one of those tales my boys.' His eyes gleamed in the firelight. 'This story doesn't have some guy turn up to save the day, or any of that other tripe my wife would prefer me to tell. And if she asks,' he said fixing his gaze onto Bill, 'you tell her I told you about a princess kissing a frog that turned into a prince. That way I sleep in my bed tonight, not in the kitchen with Wolf.' Wolf coughed, making the boys laugh. 'No, this story is a warning.

'The sound of her father's hammer was a constant in the meadow. One day he would be making a wheel, or a fence for the town's church. Being a master of his craft, he would always strive to improve on everything asked of him. If you asked him to make a horseshoe he would do it, and then go to the trouble of trying to improve its design. He changed the horseshoe from an O, to a U.' His finger traced the patterns in the air. 'The welding on the church fence would be so precise you would never see its joining.

'Elisa was only six when they moved into the meadow, but the night she woke to hear her father's hammer she was fourteen. The ice creeping up her window did not dissuade her from leaving her room. Scared to disturb her brother she snuck passed his room and left the house. Warped shadows danced across the wall of the forge, illuminated by the roaring fire within. One of them, she presumed her father, held a hammer. Just like that,' Grandpa Poulis commented as Yang grew, arching his back to hang over their heads, his hand becoming a hammer which he beat the ground. Jack laughed at his shadow.

'She counted at least three figures. Standing closest to the anvil was her father, with the other two nearby. Closing her collar, she proceeded closer, but came to a stop when she failed to hear any voices. Being outside the village her father always wanted to hear the latest gossip. If he wasn't asking about someone, he invariably explained his work. Many times Elisa walked from the forge with a headache, not from the ringing hammer, but her father's constant questions. So the quiet unsettled her. The shadows also struck her as odd. Unlike her father's erect shape, the stooped and crooked silhouettes made her uneasy. Stepping around the back of the forge, Elisa looked through a small window and spied the creatures surrounding her father. They wore skins of recently killed animals beneath crude metal armour. Their bare faces struck fear into her heart, freezing her to the spot more than the winter air. Immediately she recognised them as Myrms. The vile creatures had brought heaps of iron, which they had piled in the corner. Her father worked furiously, beating the metal into shape. She stayed there for a long time, watching her father work, as she had done countless times before. As night gave way to dawn, she saw movement in the corner of the forge. Her little brother, bound in rough rope, lay beside the now dwindling supply of metal, and she knew then why her father worked so diligently.'

'Grandpa, what was the blacksmith making?' asked Bill.

'I don't know,' Grandpa Poulis admitted, 'if I were to hazard a guess I'd say they forced him to make weapons. That's what their kind is normally after.' Drifting smoke from his pipe, closed one of his eyes, adding weight to what he said. 'Seeing her brother in trouble broke the spell that had frozen Elisa to the spot and she set off for the town. It took a while for her to reach the town, and longer still for anyone to understand what she was trying to say. Wasted time,' he whispered with regret, 'by the time we arrived the Myrms had taken both her father and brother.'

'You were there?'

'Aye, I followed a party of hunters. I was a little younger than your parents are now. Not that much younger, you understand. I'd say it happened about fifty years ago.'

'The Myrms killed them?' asked Jack.

Grandpa Poulis emptied his pipe on the round stones ringing the fire. 'We found no trace of the boy or his father. The pile of metal Elisa mentioned had also vanished; that at least left tracks. Not one hunter who followed those tracks returned. No doubt in my mind, those beasts led our men into an ambush.' He shook his pipe. 'I reckon they caught up to the Myrms.' He sat quiet, glancing at the boys around the fire. 'Childish fancy, perhaps, no evidence proves me right, but I like to think our hunters got a scalp or two before the end.

'Elisa never returned to her house, preferring to stay in town. The foundations of the house and forge are still in the meadow, hidden by tall grass.'

'You said the story was a warning,' said Jack.

The wizened eyes set in the small face always unsettled Jack when they focused on him, and none more than that night. 'It's a warning alright,' Grandpa Poulis said. 'Elisa's dad made the mistake of wanting to live alone. He wanted to build his house away from the town in the meadow. If he remained in the village, the Myrms wouldn't have come to him as they did. There's safety in numbers, and don't you boys forget it.'

Doubting three, four if you counted Yang, constituted as safety in numbers, kept Jack still, in the hope the thin shadow would hide them until the Myrm left. Inara reached over to grip his hand, which he squeezed in return. They had no chance of fighting the Myrm, and seeing how swift it moved down the metal he knew they had little hope of fleeing from it.

The Myrm landed two yards from Jack. Its long legs looked awkward, as though it had one too many kinks, making the Myrm hunch as it moved toward the root end of the felled tree. The sure motion it possessed above, vanished as

IF IT ONLY HAD A HEART

it stumbled over the uneven floor. It more snatched at the roots than took hold of them, crunching the dried mud between its fingers. An echo resounded within the head of the frog as the beast sniffed the dry dirt and sneezed. Jack had a maddening urge to say bless you, and literally had to bite down on his tongue to stop himself.

The flies that dogged the company shied away from the Myrm, allowing sections of the ground to become visible amidst the swarm. Hoping the Myrm wouldn't discover their footprints, added pressure on Jack's heart. It stood close to the muddy section that had sucked at his shoe. He must have left an imprint; by the time he had pulled his foot out, the mud had risen to his ankle. The insects still obscured the area, another step and they would leave.

The Myrm hit the fallen trunk with an agitated open palm, breaking the bark and splintering the white wood beneath. The group felt the ferocious impact deep in their chests, scaring them with its raw power. Guttural noises, sounding like a pregnant sow, issued from the static alien stare. Despite its aggression, it continued to move slowly, staying close to the dead wood.

In many ways playing hide and seek with a monster was no different from playing with friends. Dwayne, with his wide eyes, would have already spotted them through Yang. The shadow's deception would work against most. The twins would no doubt make themselves look gruesome to scare kids from hiding. Good practice for the real thing, reflected Jack. Thinking of hiding from the Myrm as a game helped calm his nerves. The secret remained the same, keep still, and do not let those hunting you spook you from hiding. He drew in a steadying breath, knowing sounds often gave people away, and though his legs ached, he ignored the need to flex them.

A more unsettling thought came to him as Yang darkened his image. His life and the lives of those with him depended on his demon. It could at any moment lift the shadow, and with a forked tongue pressed firmly between phantom teeth blow him a raspberry.

The insects dispersed from the ruined ground left by the uprooted tree. Jack saw his footprint, so did his friends. A muddy hole to the side of the larger hole, filled with dirty water.

The Myrm scanned the heights of the Red Wood, arching its neck back to an impossible angle. Its feet continued to move until its toes crested Jack's footprint; an iron shod toenail made small ripples in the water. Its fingers skittered impulsively over a small disc held in its open palm. Scrapes and abrasions marring the disc's surface drank in the sunlight. Closing fingers hid the disc.

The beast swung around.

The Myrm's erratic movement reminded Jack of the game again. When playing he had spun around, hoping to spy kids, who thinking themselves safe, had crept out of hiding to get to the safe house. Only now, there was no safe

CRIK

house, and they would not be creeping out of hiding until the Myrm was long gone.

Despite its agitation, the Myrm remained over the large hole, with the smaller print now at its heel. Satisfied nothing moved behind it the armoured figure returned to its original stance. Bowed head, it clicked its fingers on the tree trunk, muttering odd sounds to itself.

It is brooding. The observation leapfrogged from Jack to Bill and Inara, who watched in mute horror.

The grunts coming from the Myrm were beyond comprehension, and yet the tone conveyed bafflement and a tired resignation. Bronze and zinc cuttings caught the monster's attention. Mesmerised by the glint, it allowed its shoulders to sag. To those watching, the creature almost looked comedic. Turning from the entrancing light the yellow eyes, seen through eyeholes cut into the frog mask, widened.

It has seen my footprint, Jack's mind screamed.

The rotting wood hid the Myrm as it bent down. They heard great inhalations of breath as the creature sniffed with an animalistic eagerness. When it rose, it carried a torn piece of clothing in its mailed fist. Though muddy, they recognised the piece of shirt Bill had used to wrap around his weapon.

Ashen faced, Bill moved his hand so that they could all see the naked metal shard resting on his knees. The sharp instrument looked ineffectual now faced with a real adversary.

Excited, the Myrm moved down the tree, using the wood to balance itself. Despite its exhilaration at finding evidence that they had been in the clearing, the Myrm still had no definite idea where to look first. For all the creature knew they could have left the area an hour ago. The creature moved steadily away from them, until it dropped from sight.

Inara squeezed Jack's hand, grinding his knuckles together in an agonising pinch. He welcomed the contact.

A distant thrum of metal echoed across the clearing. They heard a responding grunt from the Myrm. This time the guttural growl carried notes of speech. None of the huddled children could understand the barbaric words, Grushni kurazan, arran. What those syllables meant was up for conjecture. What was not up for speculation was the sound of the approaching second Myrm. The familiar clang grew louder, until the air reverberated like a war drum.

When listening to the first Myrm making its way toward them, the noise had sounded softer, yet quicker than the new arrival.

Fixated by the sound, they missed Yang take one of the rawhide bags they had fashioned into the surrounding foliage. The brown bag almost passed out of sight when Jack saw it from the corner of his eye.

'I knew he would give us up,' he said with a start.

IF IT ONLY HAD A HEART

Inara clamped her hand over his mouth. She bit her lip.

The crescendo coming from the Wold must have hid his voice, as the Myrm did not react to the noise. Inara's hand remained covering half his face. He tracked the long thin arm of his shadow. Gun grey slabs of iron hid the bag. Had she seen Yang take the bag? Her dark eyes, like scorch marks in a white sheet, stopped him cold. He relaxed, but she still kept her hand over his mouth. Bill too ignored Yang's action preferring to mouth obscenities at him.

Inara waited for the next deafening crash before whispering in his ear, 'If your shadow wanted to give us up, all he would have to do is disappear. His body is still shielding us.'

Jack only then noticed, with Inara pointing upward with one long finger, the world had not brightened around them. What was Yang doing?

The arm now extended so far its width did not exceed that of a blade of grass.

The giant frog stepped back into view on the far side of the hole. The insects had now swarmed back over Jack's footprint, alleviating his concerns only slightly. The torn shirt held in a clenched fist remained all the proof the Myrm required to continue its search.

'Yang must be hiding our scent,' Inara whispered. 'That creature doesn't look that clean to me, but even when it stood over us I couldn't smell it. Your shadow is full of surprises.'

'Let's hope he doesn't have any unpleasant ones for us.'

Inara gave him a reproachful glance before returning her attention to the Myrm. It walked around the clearing, not knowing where they were, but unwilling to leave. In desperation to find them, the Myrm began looking behind everything, whether the obstruction could hide them or not. Once it returned to the tree it would find them for sure, thought Jack in panic.

Jack mistook movement behind the Myrm as the arrival of the second hunter, instead he saw the bag Yang carried snake into view. His shadow held the bag close to the ground, dragging it over the uneven ground. The insects hid the lower half of the bag so that the raised leather appeared to the watchful group like a tortoise shell. So far, the Myrm failed to notice the pack, even when a shard sticking from the ground snagged a strap.

What his demon attempted eluded Jack. If Yang needed a weapon, something to strike the beast over the head, he could have picked something more deadly than a half-empty bag. Any one of the shards of metal lying around would work nicely.

The bag began to rise. Inch by inch it rose from the insect swarm until it was free. Yang's appendage was so thin it looked as though nothing held the bag. Yang took it higher, and as it came to shoulder height, the shadow looped the strap over an iron branch at the far end of the clearing. There it remained, sawing back and forth in the wind.

CRIK

An instant later, just as a thin black line dropped to the ground, the Myrm noticed the bag. With a howl, it raced to its discovery. Snatching the bag, it tore the strap from the branch and brought it to its face. The chosen tree marked the entrance to a narrow meandering path out of the clearing. After only a slight pause, in which the Myrm cast its eye back toward the felled tree, it entered the passage.

A thundering crash from above spoilt any hope the group had of relaxing. Following the sound, a half-glimpsed figure, bulkier than the first Myrm, swung into the path after its fellow.

In many ways, the following silence was louder than the arrival of the Myrms. At least when they were crashing through the Red Wood the group knew how far away the hunters were. Wrapped in pregnant silence they twitched with every stimuli apprehended by their heightened senses.

The three jumped, as though jabbed in the ribs, when a voice echoed across the clearing. 'No, no, you're going the wrong way.' The voice cried in evident annoyance. Another, caustic, language wrapped each syllable, as though two people spoke at once. 'I can hear them chattering away.' The first words were understandable, yet the accompanying dialect shared the harsh tongue used by the Myrm.

They knew the speaker, and when the Myrm stepped from the passage, they saw Krimble holding onto its back. The old man pointed toward them, a maniacal grin twisting his face.

'They are always yapping away,' the zombie continued to say in a hurried, gleeful shout. 'Some nights I couldn't get to sleep; they wouldn't shut up.'

Bile seared Jack's throat as Krimble guided the Myrms around the hole toward the tree. Their one time captor, and captive, pointed a rotted finger and the Myrms followed.

'What can we do?' hissed Inara.

What could they do? They would never outrun the hunters through the metal underbrush. Yang's trick had no chance of deceiving Krimble. All they could do was wait for the Myrms to find them.

26. A REMINDER OF HOME

FOR A MAD MOMENT Jack wanted to take up a weapon against the Myrms, he gripped an iron bar rooted to the floor before dismissing the act as pointless. The creatures, he knew from the old stories, were ferocious fighters; he wouldn't stand a chance. He dared not to look over the tree at the encroaching group with the cackling monster hitching a ride. He could picture Krimble without having to see him; a wide smile, pulling pallid skin back from brown teeth, a damning finger pointing to where they lay.

The excited blabbering from the zombie did not cease as he closed the distance. 'I can hear them. They belong to me,' he cried. 'They want me to take them to my bosom. Shout for me, I'm almost there to free you from the frail children. They don't know you as I do, they can't understand how they are wasting your lives.'

In the end, Jack stopped listening to the man from the marsh. Yang had sunk to the ground, dissolving the dark shield. Without his shadow covering him, he felt the harsh sun. Yang remained below him, a dark puddle, sinking slowly out of sight. Despite his shadow's earlier help, he wanted to strike out, to wrap his hands around Yang's arm to make him defend them, to play another demon trick. Instead, he only looked, and wished he could also dissolve into the ground.

'How about the wolves?' whispered Inara.

Bill looked at the girl. 'What about them? They are far away, still running for their lives. Besides, they can't do anything for us here.' His resignation twisted like a plough through Jack's guts.

'The demons are calling out to him,' said Jack as Krimble continued to speak. 'They're giving us away.'

Inara gave him a withering look. Before he could argue against her stare, the Myrm carrying Krimble peered over the log.

'You shouldn't have left me behind,' said Krimble, his yellow eyes bright. 'Or had you forgotten your friend's tale?'

'What friend?' Bill fell back from the Myrm's stinking breath. Unlike the first beast, this took on the form of a monstrous wild boar, complete with curled silver tusks.

CRIK

'Llast of course,' said Krimble. 'You remember, the stupid fellow with his fluted shoes. He told you that I acquired his son's gift to talk to the Myrms.'

'Stole the gift,' said Inara.

'Liberated,' countered Krimble. The zombie clashed his teeth together in a snarl. 'I could have these two tear your arms off, and then all you'd be is an annoying talking head.' As though to accentuate his words the hideous frog appeared. The foreboding beast moved from right to left in agitation. 'Alas, they have other orders.' Krimble, with a frown, glanced behind him. 'It seems they've been hot on your trail ever since you left the Blackthorn. They are impatient to get their hands on you.'

'And you led them straight to us,' said Bill.

Krimble clenched his fist until it shook. 'You shouldn't have sent me away.'

'I prefer to deal with them, than you,' said Bill, shifting his glasses.

'We'll see if you feel the same way, once we arrive at our destination.'

'And where's that?' asked Jack.

'To their home of course,' replied the zombie. 'I would help you out, but seeing as how you left me behind, I don't think I will.'

'We'd never ask for your help,' said Inara.

'You might,' said Krimble, a slow smile growing. 'Given time you may beg me to help you.'

Krimble turned to address the second Myrm. 'You'll have to carry the girl, she's a cripple.' He looked to the waiting frog's blank face. 'If the other two try to escape, kill them.' The Myrm's harsh language echoed his every word.

The hunter's awkward stance belied its speed; it leapt seven feet into the air, passing over Jack. A cloud of reddish dirt rose as it landed, and then, with outstretched arms, it snatched Inara under her arms.

A surprised gasp left her. If the creature had taken hold of him, Jack knew he would be screaming and hitting out with his fists. The futility of that action would have eventually made him stop. Inara suffered the crude grasp in stoic silence; she already knew struggling would be useless. Even if the beast let her go, she couldn't escape.

With a yell, Bill charged the Myrm. The Myrm first knocked away the metal spike Bill brandished, and then hit him to the floor, where he lay in a dazed heap.

'Bill,' cried Jack rushing to his friend's side.

The mailed fist reopened Bill's head wound, soaking the makeshift bandage with fresh blood. 'I'm alright Ying,' he replied, touching his head with a tender hand. He tried to get to his feet when Jack laid a hand on his chest.

'Best stay down until you feel better,' said Jack.

'No time,' shouted Krimble. 'Get to your feet. We have a long way to go. Hurry now.'

A REMINDER OF HOME

The Myrm, with Krimble's arm nestled around its neck, hunched over them. Its snarls reminded Jack of a bad tempered dog as it drove Bill to his feet.

'Ok, ok, I'm up,' said Bill, holding his head and looking as though he had just rolled out of bed.

Despite the awkward gait of the two Myrms keeping the pace slow they covered a great distance in a short period. The hulking brutes navigated the metal jungle with ease, veering them away from obstacles and taking the boys down half-seen tracks. Occasionally Jack saw Inara watching him from over the crook of the Myrm's arm.

Yang appeared periodically during the arduous trek, and each time he did Krimble watched him close, going so far as to lean over the top of the Myrm's head to keep the shadow in view. Jack never failed to notice Krimble's renewed interest in his demon. Whether the zombie still yearned to possess the shadow for himself, or if he feared a trick from the troublesome demon, he could only speculate. Perhaps they communed with each other. The unbidden thought sent a shudder up his spine.

Flowers of beaten gold filled a hollow. The Myrms skirted the flowers, heading toward an imposing wall of steel trees, whose trunks reached as high as the few low hanging clouds. The tightly packed trees made an almost perfect circle. As they drew closer, Jack noticed paper-thin sheets of silver cut and shaped into leaves hanging from the branches. Someone had even taken the time to make a bronze squirrel, complete with an obligatory acorn.

'What do they want with us?' Bill asked, stumbling beside Jack.

Krimble turned an appraising eye on Bill. 'They don't like trespassers. I presume they intend to kill you. The stories I've heard about those captured within the Wold are quite bloody. How else do you think people started calling this place the "Red Wood"?'

Rust gave it that name, thought Jack, kicking up a cloud of the stuff.

The bronze squirrel sitting on the branch dropped the acorn, and then turned its steady gaze on the approaching group. In a high-pitched tone, it began to taunt them.

'I know why you've come here' it cried out. 'The unwinding of long days, without a twist or a knot has caused many to stick their nose out of their doors.' The bronze animal rushed over the branch, keeping track with Jack. 'Most times they return home with a bloodied nose, sometimes they don't return at all.'

'Leave me alone,' said Jack, unimpressed with the squirrel, or its taunts.

The squirrel ignored his plea. 'You keep strange friends. Two are flesh that want to be more; another is losing his skin until there is no more. Then there are more, a girl without feet, where have they gone? Did they walk away down the street?'

'Quiet,' said Jack, throwing a handful of dust at the troublesome rodent.

CRIK

The squirrel stopped a moment to brush off the flecks of metal dulling its hide. 'I struck a nerve, plucked like a hair from your head.'

'Get away,' said Bill, peering around Jack's back at the scurrying squirrel. 'Go on,' he said waving his hand at the squirrel, 'we have enough trouble without you harrying our every step.'

The squirrel flattened out its bushy tail. 'I'm no ordinary animal; you can't make me do anything that I don't want to do myself.'

The Myrms ignored the bronze squirrel, and Krimble only passed a fleeting glance over the creature before returning his attention to Yang who slipped over the uneven ground. Although Inara tried to keep track of the strange rodent, the Myrm's jostling gait beat her every effort.

The squirrel, with the lone attention of the two boys, called out a challenge. 'If you answer a riddle, then I will go. Answer me wrong and I'll come along.'

'It's a trick,' said Bill beneath his beetled brow. 'You'll ask something without an answer and we'll be stuck with you.'

'If you don't want to try, I will remain with you till you die,' answered the metal squirrel.

'Where we're headed I doubt that will be long,' said Bill.

'What harm is there in asking,' said Jack. Glad of the distraction from the oppressive trees bending off to his left, he gave the squirrel a nod.

The squirrel closed one eye. 'What has fingers, top and bottom and has rings that tighten and burn?'

Now Jack's brow drew down in a frown of concentration. He repeated the riddle to himself. Did toes count as fingers? He looked over at the rodent, whose front paws were much like its back pair. Even if that were the case, they didn't possess rings that burned. Nothing about the riddle made any sense, and in time, his thoughts became frayed. Giving up on what the fingers could be, he instead tried to puzzle out what ring tightened and burned. A ring of fire would expand outward, as did the heat of the sun. Preoccupied with the riddle, he failed to notice a glade appear through the widening gaps between the steel trees.

'I see my question has you both stumped,' said the Squirrel, leaping increasingly long distances to the next tree. 'Are you so puzzled, that you can't answer? What a shame, you'll never guess its name.'

'It doesn't make any sense,' said Bill, almost tripping over his own feet. 'Nothing has fingers top and bottom. I've gone through all the animals I know. I haven't a clue. It could be anything in this crazy place. For all we know you could be friends with a rat who has a hand for an ass.'

'Then you admit defeat, and will be having me keep up with your feet.'

'I didn't say that,' said Bill. 'I just want a fair riddle, that's all.'

'As fair as fair can be,' the squirrel replied.

'Coming from something screwed together I doubt that.'

A REMINDER OF HOME

The squirrel puffed out its cheeks. 'You won't find no screws, bolts, or nuts on me; at least, none that you'll ever see.'

'I don't doubt that you're missing a few screws,' retorted Bill.

A gentle lake came into view between the trees, its water lapping the rough shore of the glade. Golden swans, and grey and black Moorhens, swam on its surface. Its colour swirled with purple, green, and yellow, like a rainbow caught in a bubble.

'It's beautiful,' exclaimed Inara spotting the lake.

The metal clad frog grunted something to the silvered boar. With no further communication, the boar turned into the glade.

'You'll be pleased to know that we're almost at our journey's end,' said Krimble.

Freeing his mind from the riddle, Jack looked into the glade, and what he saw resting between two banks made his feet falter. The trunk had a red crust, not the brown bark he knew, and the roots anchored on either hill were metal, not the life giving roots of the real thing. 'The Hanging Tree,' he and Bill both exclaimed together.

'What!' shouted the squirrel, skidding to a halt as the Myrms stopped the group with a series of barking grunts. 'How'd you know the answer to the riddle?'

'Riddle,' said Jack, transfixed by the sight of the tree he had known all his life.

'The Hanging Tree, of course. The reaching branches are its topmost fingers, the dangling roots are its lower,' said the squirrel wiggling its toes.

The branches were just how Jack remembered them; they even bowed toward the ground like the real thing. From every height, a hangman noose fell, peppering the ground with their grim shadow.

'The rings that tighten and burn,' said Jack spying the swaying rope.

A few brutes, encased in metal armour made to look like animals, roamed around the tree. Their long arms dragged the pitted ground, throwing red dust up as far as their knees. On seeing the captives, they rushed forward in a frenzied knot. One exuberant youth, with a goat's head, launched into the branches of the Hanging Tree. The magnets pinned to his knees and arms clanged as they stuck to the rigid frame.

Listening to the ruckus their arrival had caused, Jack missed the squirrel jump down. The small rodent danced around the heavy boots of the Myrms. A brute stamped down, missing the squirrel by inches. After his narrow escape, the squirrel dashed for the great tree, and disappeared.

Inara screamed as a Myrm, wearing an ornate helmet crafted to look like an owl, charged into the group, dislodging her from her captor's arms. She fell with a heavy thud.

CRIK

Outraged, Jack shot forward, not caring how close he came to the two Myrms. The owl Myrm smacked his gauntlet against the frog, cracking the lime green helmet. The aggressor, being much larger, dropped his opponent to its knees.

'You alright?'

Coughing up red dust, Inara gave a quick nod. 'Feels like someone threw me off a cliff.' She batted dust off her thigh. 'I'll be fine.' The dazed Myrm crouched in the shadow of the giant. 'I feel a little sad for him. Forgetting the fall, he was gentler than I expected.'

'They're all savages,' said Bill, hunkering down beside them.

Glowering bloodshot eyes set deep within the owl helmet demanded their attention. Another hole, half hidden by the curved beak, revealed a set of blunt slab-like teeth. From this opening issued a series of threatening sounds. The children dared not move, fearing the behemoth would attack.

Now amongst larger and fiercer residence of the Wold, Krimble kept himself as low as possible, while interpreting the barbaric speech for them. 'Raglor,' he looked toward the menacing Myrm, 'is a great hunter, and First Fist of the Feylr Clan.'

Unlike the milling crowd, Raglor kept still, watching them with interest. An etching of the Hanging Tree adorned his dented gauntlet.

'What does he want with us?' asked Inara, sitting up. 'We were only trying to get out of the Wold, not trespass on his land.'

'He can't just allow people to come as they please,' argued Krimble. 'If he did, it wouldn't take long before people started to take advantage of his lenience. A few campsites would give way to more permanent dwellings. Given time, whole settlements will start to spring up, to mine all this magnificent iron.'

'Well we won't,' shouted Bill. 'You know we only want to get away from here.'

Impatient, Raglor raged forward. His shoulders bunched into tight knots behind his head like iron mountains. He reached out to snatch Bill's shirt, only to roar in outrage as the boy ducked under his grasping fingers.

'Careful Bill,' cried Inara as Raglor strode forward.

'I'm not going to just let him grab me,' said Bill, backing away until a tree brought him to a sudden stop.

'Where can you go,' called out Krimble in hysterical delight.

'Take control of him,' called Jack.

'I tried already,' answered Bill. 'They only look like animals...'

Raglor drove his fist into Bill's stomach, doubling the boy over in pain. Blinking away tears, Bill managed, between mouthfuls of air, to say, 'Animals have more sense,' before collapsing to the ground.

'He has magic that he wants to use against you,' said Krimble, crowding behind Raglor. 'Quick stop him before he has a chance to hurt you.'

A REMINDER OF HOME

Krimble flew back. Raglor's fist had broken two of the zombie's ribs with a sickening crunch. As the zombie lay on the ground, touching the bone splintering from his chest, the Myrm took a step toward him.

Krimble listened to the grunts of the First Fist. When the chieftain had finished, he answered in a staccato voice. 'I never meant he could beat you in a fight. I only wanted to warn you, that he has hidden dangers. They all have. Look.' He pointed toward Yang, who had Inara circled protectively. 'That shadow is treacherous, and will try to trick you.'

Raglor glowered at Yang. The shadow, contrary to the strong sunlight, remained in place. Noticing this anomaly for himself set Raglor over to investigate. Raising his boot, he brought it down with all his might. The ground cracked under his heel. Yang, having moved from the attack, swam back in to snatch Raglor's foot. The hunter let out a surprised gasp, as too did the other Myrms gathered around. The muscles along Raglor's thighs bunched and strained, groaning against the armour casing. Eventually he peeled the stubborn shadow from the ground. It appeared as though Raglor pulled himself from sticky tar. With an earth-shattering roar, Raglor smashed his fist into the shadow, only for Yang to secure his hand. Tying himself to the brute's other appendages; Yang pulled the Myrm to the ground.

The other Myrms stayed clear of the fight. Only the headdress of their leader escaped Yang's embrace. The black mass writhed as Raglor continued to fight. Bolstered by the hot sun, Yang threw a dark wave over the roaring hunter.

The Myrms ringed around the conflict hollered their outrage. The First Fist's armour cracked, revealing a raging white haired beast beneath the ornamental layers. With a twist of a hand, Yang threw off the owl helmet, unmasking a grizzled, scarred, creature. A stone flew from out of the throng. Yang dissolved away from the striking stone, allowing the projectile to hit the jaw of the Great Hunter with a sickening thud. Blood spurted from rubbery black lips. Yelling in pain, Raglor renewed his efforts to escape. Straightening up Raglor stretched Yang, from a low-lying mound, to a tall black monolith. For a time it looked as though Raglor had the strength to pull free, and the other Myrms expected their chief to do just that. A collective groan escaped when Yang, rushing up Raglor's chest, drove the chieftain back down to one knee.

Bill, having moved close to Inara and Jack, cowered with them just outside the frenzied mob. They could have tried to escape if Inara could walk, but they were stuck to the spot just as surely as Raglor.

'The children control the shadow,' cried out Krimble. 'Kill the children to free Raglor, Fist of the Feylr Clan!'

Jack felt the blood drain from his face. The sly zombie had hobbled over, and with a word condemned them all.

Two brutes closest to the children turned. One held an iron club; the other flexed its fingers ready to tear them apart.

CRIK

'Free Raglor,' called Krimble through a sneer. 'Free your leader!'
The raised iron cudgel hung over the trio, ready to fall.

27. SINS OF THE FATHER

ALTHOUGH THE CUDGEL'S shadow moved, like a sundial, from Jack to Inara, the hand holding the weapon never shifted. Jack traced the clockwise shift of the shade. He assumed his demon had another trick up its sleeve and had taken charge of the weapon, yet all his shadow's attention remained on Raglor. Switching his focus from the weapon, he saw the Myrm's bloodshot orbs looking off to the left to where approached tendrils of light.

'What's coming?' Inara asked, clutching his arm.

The light spread out like windblown ribbons of cloth. The Myrms backed away from the radiance; some took to the trees, clamouring for the high branches. Although a few of the larger clan members grunted amongst themselves, to show they were not as afraid as the younger brutes, they too eventually stepped out of the light's path

'There's more than one coming,' said Jack, spying other light from behind the Hanging Tree.

'And there's another on the far side of the lake,' reported Bill.

Lowering his arm, the creature with the club, with an impatient snort, retreated. His companion sprang upward, snatching an overhead branch with a thunderous clang, breaking loose a few silver leaves.

Inara snatched back her hand as the serrated edges of the metal shards punctured the ground around her. 'They're scared,' she said. 'None of them will face the light. I bet they'd kill one another to get out of its way.'

'Is that a good thing?' asked Bill.

Jack wondered. If the demon living within him hadn't protected itself, Raglor would've hurt them, even killed them. This new danger, presented a more alarming peril. He knew the Myrms physical threat; he had faced such dangers during the wolf attack. The looming light had the same effect on him as a fire had on a cornered animal. Sweat beaded his upper lip, and his heart no longer thumped against his chest, it thrummed like a guitar string.

The core burned brightest amongst the billowing filaments of light. Shielding his eyes with the blade of his hand, he attempted to discern some detail, when his watering eyes smudged the bright centre of the wandering light. Before his vision dissolved, he spotted a figure gliding toward them.

'There's something in the light,' he told the others. 'It's female.'

CRIK

Bill turned to him, his face slick with sweat beneath his bloodied rag. 'How can you be sure?'

With a shrug, Jack replied, 'There's a silhouette within the light. Tall, narrow legged and full at the hip. It's feminine.'

'You're wrong.'

'Not bloody likely. Why'd you care if it's a woman or not?' said Jack, feeling his anger growing.

'I don't think you need argue,' said Inara. She bit her lip. 'Whatever it is, it'll be here soon enough.'

Raglor's roars only grew at the appearance of the newcomers. Held prisoner by Yang, the chieftain, with stubborn fury, struggled against his bonds. Yang's stranglehold showed no sign of weakening until a wisp of light touched him. Immediately the shadow recoiled from the caress. The spreading light pushed Yang back, so that he fell from the white fur like melting snow. Freed first were the chieftain's large biceps and angular triceps, and then his shoulder and a portion of his thigh. Torn armour lay in a ruined heap at his feet. Feeling the warm contact of the sun spurred Raglor to greater effort. As his head appeared, his triumphant roar deafened the children. Continuing to pull away, Yang dripped from the Myrm like raindrops on glass.

'He's going to come for me again,' said Bill. 'They always come for me.'

Watching his shadow return to his side, Jack doubted the chieftain wanted anything more to do with them. So he let out a gasp when Raglor hurled himself after Yang.

His fearsome mouth opened to an incredible girth as Raglor hurled a fearsome challenge. Standing his ground, Yang remained with his arms planted on his hips. Dust swirled up from the boots of the chieftain, and his driving fist cracked the ground.

Stretching his arms and splaying out his fingers, Yang rushed Raglor. With a howl, the Myrm skipped back, almost tripping over in his alarm.

Although he had nowhere to go, Jack wanted to retreat from the light. Holding his breath, the light washed over the bewildered chieftain, before bathing him and his friends. He expected its touch to be searing hot, not cold and withering. Shivering, he wrapped his arms around his chest and stared into the face of a woman. Sorrow painted her face heavier than any makeup. A deep loss, casting her mouth down, and creating impenetrable pits for her eyes, dulled her light into autumnal shades.

In straight lines, her lank, dispirited hair, framed her cheeks. 'You've come a long way from Crik Village,' she said, reaching out to touch Jack's chin.

Jack imagined a lizard's tongue would feel like her fingers. 'How'd you know that?' he asked. Had she heard the revulsion in his voice?

'You have its taint,' she responded, pinching his skin. 'Its shame.'

SINS OF THE FATHER

'There's no shame in living in the village.' He pulled back from her grasp. 'Only good decent people live there,' he said, picturing the Hulme sisters playing in the street. Tommen Guild, one hot summer's day, iced the pond so whole families could skate. Above all, he saw his mother, kneading bread with flour up to her elbows. He decided it wasn't the right time to add a quip about Dwayne Blizzard, her dislike for Crik Village had nothing to do with his own childish aversions. 'No one from back home has ever entered the Wold.'

'Until now,' she said. 'You passed the blue stones. We placed them to stop you from trespassing. You risked killing your Narmacils by coming here. Why have you come into our retreat?'

Walking up to Jack's shoulder Bill looked at the woman. With his eyes half shut, he pursed his lips. 'You're a Ghost Walker.'

At once, her features changed from sorrow, to one filled with anger. Black pools developed under her eyes, blotting out the light. Tributaries flowed from the crepuscule concavities down her smooth skin. Her lank hair blew back from small ears as she crowded the boys, enveloping them in a cold that sank bone deep.

'That was a name given to us; one we have not heard for many years,' she said.

The breath caught in Jack's throat. These were not the first Ghost Walkers he had seen, another much closer to home walked night-time boards.

The Ghost Walker, looming large, said, 'Does the village think so little of us that they have given our eradication over to the children? Do they think your Narmacils are powerful enough to combat us? Your shadow has shown its worth against the Clan Chief.' She tilted her chin toward a knot of three Myrms, where Raglor stood in evident distress. The First Fist, shielded its broad face from the Ghost Walker's inspection. 'What impressive Talents have the fat boy and the girl to warrant such overconfidence?'

'Don't give them a chance to use their abilities, Justice.' said a second Ghost Walker, who came to stand behind Bill. 'We should kill them now; let them swing from the Hanging Tree. The wind stirs the rope in anticipation. Give them to the hemp.'

'Your words remind me of laying in a thicket, watching a line of torchlight weave a path toward the first Hanging Tree,' replied Justice. 'Are you so eager to pick up the torch yourself, sister?'

'Kyla's words reflect all of our feelings,' spoke a third woman. 'We are the persecuted, not the persecutors. We must defend ourselves. Why else would they go through the agony of crossing the stones if they did not want to hunt us down?'

'We aren't hunting anyone,' said Jack, looking at all three women. 'We didn't know you were here. Until a few days ago we thought the Red Wood only existed in stories.'

CRIK

'The Myrms carried us here, taking us from the path that would lead us from the Wold,' added Inara.

'Only one exit from the Wold,' said Kyla. 'The Blackthorn Tunnel is to your backs, as you well know.'

The news that the Blackthorn Tunnel was the only way in or out of the Red Wood rocked Jack. He couldn't face returning to that horror. Terror clouded his mind when he thought of the creatures covered in black flowers. He knew he could not survive going through there again. His friends mirrored his fears.

'You must help us,' Bill suddenly cried out, falling to his knees. 'My grandmother is one of you. That is how I knew you were Ghost Walkers. She leaves her body every night.'

Bill's words had revealed a long kept secret. Bill knew about his grandmother being a Ghost Walker. For years, he had kept the truth hidden. Being Bill's closest friend, Jack had expected no such secret to exist between them.

'The child lies,' said Kyla.

'He's not,' said Jack. 'I've seen her myself. She paints in her room.' He ignored the amazement on Bill's upturned face. He had also kept secrets from Bill, more than one. His sense of Bill's betrayal dissipated, leaving room for a sea of guilt. 'What you suffered in the village ended a long time ago.'

'We should be free to wander, to share our light,' said Justice. 'Not to dream of other places while clutching at brushes. If what you say is true, then your grandmother,' she looked down at Bill, 'is a prisoner within the village. In case the villagers discover and destroy her sleeping body, she will not risk venturing into the woods.'

'No, she is happy,' argued Bill, shaking his head vigorously. 'She lives with my grandpa, and there aren't two happier people in the whole village. Most fear crossing her; you can't say she is a prisoner.'

Nodding his agreement, Jack said, in a breathless rush, 'She's always yelling at me. One time she left my ears ringing for hours cos I hit her roses with my ball.'

Justice ignored his outburst. 'If safe, why hide her true self? Why else does she remain inside?'

'The villagers are as small minded as they were in our day,' said Kyla. 'If they found out about her, her spirit would wander alone in Crik Wood. The fear of the men of her village unearthing her secret is terrorising the poor woman.'

They wouldn't think that if they knew Grandma Poulis, thought Jack. Then why not reveal herself to the village? Why did his closest friend keep the fact from him? The poem he knew about the Ghost Walkers did not come from Grandpa Poulis, that night Mr Dash, the grave keeper of "Long Sleep" Cemetery, sat in the fire's glow. His eyes shone like rubies, and his voice took on a serious tone as he began:

SINS OF THE FATHER

The wood's secrets are strange and accursed,
Whistling wind shapes its crooked curse.
An icy call passes on its fell light.
Heeding the ancient voice, the lady, alights.

From haunted land, and unbeaten track, she comes.
A mischievous smile, plays across greying gums.
To plant a poison kiss, she comes.
Beware her light or you will succumb.

The slumber of innocence, taken with a kiss.
Beware the Lady, her poison lips.
Your life she wishes to eclipse.
Beware the Lady's possessive grip.

Her house of blood and bone, talks,
Loved ones unbeknown fall for this horrid faux.
Amongst the sun and fields, she walks,
Wrapped in disguise, the innocence she stalks.

On blackest night, she roams,
Stepping from her house of bones.
She schemes and plots our demise,
While her house falls and dies.

The ancient voice has its own expression.
From which spells tales of woe and depression.
Lies and warped truth she tells,
This we must all repel.

Her deceit caught, her guise revealed.
Her lifeless host, no longer concealed.
With solemn hearts, we compose,
To end such a dire pose.

To break the shackle, and remove the curse,
The Hanging Tree concludes this epic verse.
Swinging from wood, we drop the rope,
We can only offer this one hope.

Without a place to hide, without a body to wear,

CRIK

We must conclude this awful affair.
The Lady disappears with despair,
Her dire light held by our prayer.

After hearing the poem, it had taken Jack a month to sleep without first checking the bolt on his window.

'You shouldn't hang them,' spoke Krimble, shuffling close. 'They hate you, this is true. They lied about this supposed grandmother to weasel into your trust. Don't listen to them; that's how they trapped me.' He kicked dust in Inara's direction. 'Her Narmacil is the most dangerous. Look at me, I am proof.' He thumped his chest so hard his bent form rocked back. 'A week ago I lived a quiet life in the marsh, now I am here, rotting in the sun. Before you hand out your judgement, you should find out why they have come here.'

'There you are sister,' said Kyla, 'what more proof do you need. They reveal their cruelty by tormenting this man.'

'His power of words over the Myrms does not impress me,' said Justice. 'Perhaps his crookedness runs deeper than his crooked spine.'

The tenseness of Inara's body against him told Jack how much she wanted to shout, curse and deny everything Krimble said about them. He knew, as well as she did, that Krimble wanted them to do just that. By remaining silent, they offered no further opportunity for the zombie to spread his lies. Besides, the Ghost Walkers had no interest in what they had to say.

Kyla had murder within her. Their past haunted Justice and the other Ghost Walkers, terrorising them. Kyla's memories fed her anger until it lay bloated like a full leach about to explode.

'You have travelled a great distance from Crik Village,' said Justice, drawing Jack's attention from Kyla's green gaze. 'The wood is no place for children; it is dark and very dangerous; even haunted.'

'Haunted by us, Justice,' said Kyla. 'That is why the people we trusted, and loved, took us to the tree.'

'I speak of older things than us,' said Justice. 'Time is ever moving, but not all things move with the times.' She looked at the children. 'You took a great risk in coming this far. The wood has no compassion, and the mire you traversed is treacherous, taking lives, as you would swallow a breath.' At mention of the marsh, Jack ignored his compulsion to glance over at Krimble. He refused to give the zombie any satisfaction, no matter how small. 'So,' continued Justice, 'why have you risked your lives to come so far?'

Jack knew Bill's eyes bore hot holes into the back of his neck. They wouldn't be here if not for him. All the dangers Justice mentioned were avoidable, only his desire to make his forked tongued imp disappear kept them on this long dangerous road. Even now, Yang flitted around the edge of his vision, reminding him of what hitched a ride inside.

SINS OF THE FATHER

'We've come to see Knell,' said Inara, before Jack had time to speak, 'we would like to speak with her about getting me back home.'

Justice turned to Inara for the first time. 'You are not from Crik Village?'

'He,' Inara said, pointing a finger caked in dust at Krimble, 'took me from my parents. He used a stolen Narmacil to alter the path leading from my home until I became totally lost. It is my hope that the woman Knell will know the way back to them. Jack and Bill rescued me from the marsh house, and have helped me ever since.'

'The only ones living between the wall and the swamp are the folk of Elysium,' said Kyla. 'And you,' she said, edging up to Inara, bathing her in cold light, 'aren't one of them. So why travel east from the swamp?'

'Wolves chased us,' volunteered Bill. 'If we returned to the wood they would've eaten us all.'

'Don't listen to him,' whispered Krimble. 'He commands the wild dogs. Ask the Myrms, they chased away the wolves the children used as mounts. Look at the girl, she has no legs, how do you think she came so far?'

'I have lived here for a century,' said Kyla. 'You,' she continued, looking at Justice, 'have lived here longer than that. In all that time, no one has disturbed our sanctuary. If we allow the children to leave, they will tell tales of the Wold, and soon after the village hunters will seek us out.'

'Kyla is right Justice,' said the third Ghost Walker.

Justice shook her head. 'If we hang them, we then become the executioner.'

'Then you will let us go,' said Jack, but his gratitude only lasted a moment. His terror-filled eyes grew and he let out a gasping cry. Justice had turned to him, the light pulled back from her face. He wanted to look away while his mind scrambled furiously for some distant refuge, only it found none, only a dark place where a bleached skull screamed shrilly from a mouthful of aged teeth.

'We're undying.' Justice's jawbone swung open like a windblown barn door. 'The people of your village cursed us to this damned existence. That is why I cannot allow you three to leave the Red Wood. You will remain here until the day you die.'

CRIK

28. PARSNIPS AND RUST

SLEEP CAME SURPRISINGLY easy to Jack. The Myrms had carried them to a mound of reddish dirt, which obscured the crafted Hanging Tree. Two Myrms carried a squirming Bill, whilst he and Inara allowed the brutes, armoured in their animal disguises, to carry them without objection. Anytime Yang revealed himself, the Myrm carrying him grew agitated; by the time he dropped Jack, a damp musty odour rose up and through the beast's armour. Relief after the day's sojourn swept through Jack as soon as he hit the dirt and he closed his eyes as though he had drank a barrel of ale.

All thought of the Ghost Walkers and the Wold fled as he dreamed of fields of cabbage, parsnips, and runner beans. He recognised Farmer Vine's land, even the old swing hung where he remembered it. The boy, whose swing it was, had died so young Jack couldn't recall his name. It made him feel sad that he couldn't. A dog's bark had him choke back a sob. Some time had passed since he had heard something as mundane as a dog's bark. Taking a deep breath, he stepped through the cabbage batch, relishing the crunch of the leaves underfoot. The farmhouse, and its rickety old windmill, remained hidden by the wooded knoll that sat dead centre within the field. Hearing the wooden slats of the windmill turning drew him forward. Quickening his steps, he broke into a run. Within moments, he gained the summit of the knoll, coming face to face with the weathered face of Farmer Vine. Farmer Vine clutched a dirty parsnip in one hand, and a pitchfork in the other. At first, the farmer ignored him, satisfying himself with the look and smell of his crop. When he acknowledged Jack's presence, he cast a quick glance over Jack before dropping his gaze to the ground at Jack's feet.

'I'm sorry,' said Jack, fearing the farmer spied ruined vegetables mashed to the leather of his shoes.

Instead, Farmer Vine gave a perplexed half smile, and hit Jack over the head with the parsnip.

'Hey, why'd you hit me?'

'Your mother isn't here to do it for me,' drawled the farmer. 'She's worried about you, you know.'

'It's none of your business,' retorted Jack, taking a backward step.

PARSNIPS AND RUST

'It became my business when she came out here to visit me. Crying she was, hysterical with worry. I doubt a day has passed since you left that she hasn't cried. Poor dear. You should be ashamed of yourself.'

Blushing under the weight of the stern words, Jack said, 'I only meant to enter the wood. I planned on returning home before she noticed that I had gone.'

'Oh, she noticed alright,' said the farmer. 'Soon after the entire village knew about your leaving. You and your friend stirred things up right proper. Every hunter in the village has followed your trail. They think the wolves killed you.'

'We escaped them,' said Jack.

Farmer Vine smacked him over the head with the parsnip a second time. 'I know they didn't eat you boy, or I wouldn't be talking with you now.'

Jack rubbed his head, feeling a lump beneath his hair. 'How are you talking with me?' Was he still asleep? The smack on the head felt real, and the pain still lingered, not at all like a dream.

'I can step into another's dream. That's my Talent. Haven't done it for so long I almost forgot how,' said the farmer dropping to a knee. 'I'm out of practice, so I don't know how long I can keep our connection, so answer me quickly boy. Are you and Bill well?'

Thoughts of his capture swirled through Jack's mind. Everything he and Bill had experienced since leaving home was both fascinating and horrible. How could he share his tales of meeting the Lindre, they belonged in fairy tales, not out in the open. The Wold itself, with its fabled Hedge Wall, lived in Grandpa Poulis's stories, not as a physical reality. Yet the Red Wood existed. He wanted to tell the farmer everything, only if he did people from the village would come. Trembling, he pictured his mother entering the Blackthorn Tunnel. Nightmarish images of black flowers growing from her skin left him with only one choice.

'We're fine,' he said, wishing he didn't have to lie. 'Bill has found his Talent. Being able to control animals is very handy when you're out in the woods.'

The smile left the farmer as he looked back down at Jack's feet. 'I don't think your telling me everything Jack. You're called Ying back at the village, aren't you?'

Jack nodded.

'Yang is your shadow. As I hear it,' continued Farmer Vine, 'he used to get you in trouble. Now I come to think of it, didn't you two steal mushrooms from my garden a few years back?'

Jack had forgotten about that. Farmer Vine had set his dog, a huge Irish wolfhound with tangled grey fur called Jaffer, after him. Yang held the dog back on that day, letting Jack escape.

'Well boy, where's your shadow?'

CRIK

Looking down, Jack for the first time noticed Yang missing. 'It's a dream; I suppose I didn't dream him, that's all.'

The farmer shook his head. 'Who you are in life carries forward into your dream. Has something happened to your shadow since leaving the village?' A worried frown creased the farmer's weathered brow.

Shaking his head, Jack said, 'Nothing.' However, as he said it, he also pondered the meaning of Yang's absence. Could the reason his shadow didn't follow him in his dreams have anything to do with how he now viewed himself and Yang as two separate beings? The Narmacil shared his body like a parasite, something he had to eradicate. Did this explain his shadow's absence?

'I think you know more than you're telling me boy,' said the farmer, resting his weight on his pitchfork. 'It's something we can discuss when you're back home. What's important is where you are. Tell me and I'll send out a posse to come and bring you safely home.'

Again, visions of anyone entering the Blackthorn stopped him from talking. How could he allow anyone else to face the dangers he had already subjected his friends to. Bill and Inara are his responsibility, he got them into this mess, and he would find a way to get them out. He refused to be accountable for anyone else.

'I don't know where we are.' The lie caught in his throat. 'We're lost; all we can see are trees.'

'Any landmarks? Anything at all,' said Farmer Vine, eager for any useful information he could report to the village. 'A hill; a strange looking rock? There must be something, no matter how small that someone back here may recognise.'

How could anyone help them where they were? Even if they passed through the tunnel, the Myrms would hunt them down and hang them from the metal tree. He sympathised with the farmer, and he wanted desperately to see his mother again, only he refused to place them in danger.

'There's nothing,' he replied, tipping his head down to his chest. 'Tell my mother that we're safe, and we will get back home. I promise.' His eyes sparkled as he regarded Farmer Vine. 'I will return with Bill as soon as we can. Don't come looking for us, I don't want anyone else to get lost for our sakes.'

Farmer Vine reached out to grab Jack's shoulder...

Jack opened his eyes to the sound of a hammer beating metal. Night had fallen, leaching the warmth from a nearby fire. To his left rested Inara, her gentle rhythmic breathing making her chest rise and fall. A worn brown blanket covered her shoulders, whilst her arm cradled her head.

'How you two can sleep is beyond me.'

Startled, Jack almost sprained his neck as he swung his attention over to Bill, who sat with his knees drawn up beneath his chin.

PARSNIPS AND RUST

'I thought you'd banged your head when that brute dropped you,' continued Bill, his teeth chattering from the cold. 'If they left us some water to drink I'd have thrown it over you.'

'I'm glad you didn't.'

'Did you dream of having a hot meal back home?'

Jack shook his head. 'Why'd you ask?'

'You kept mentioning parsnips.'

'Did I,' said Jack, feeling guilty for keeping quiet about meeting Farmer Vine. He knew Bill would like to hear from back home, he also knew if he told Bill about his encounter he would also have to explain why he didn't tell the farmer where they were.

Looking toward a second more distant fire, Bill said, 'Made me quite hungry to be honest. I'd give anything to have a bowl of stew right about now.'

'With a chunk of bread to dunk,' replied Jack, ignoring the pang of hunger throttling his stomach.

'Now you're talking. My grandma always gave me a glass of ginger beer when she made her stew. It was almost as thick as the stew itself, just the thing on a cold night like this.'

Looking around at the clearing, Jack couldn't see any Myrm. The darkness made it impossible to gauge the size of the land; any number of enemies could lay in wait out there.

Bill saw him looking around. 'I haven't seen them since they dumped us here. There's something by that other fire; it's not a Myrm.'

'What makes you say that?'

'Saw a silhouette in front of the fire a couple of times. It walked differently to the Myrms. You know how the Myrms walk bent over like they're always looking at the ground for dropped pennies.' Jack nodded. 'Well, whoever is over there walks upright, like us.'

Intrigued, Jack looked over to the distant flames, and again heard the ringing of metal upon metal. Who was over there? Not a Ghost Walker, they would light up half the night. He kept staring at the distant flames, in the hope of spotting the mysterious figure. A few minutes lapsed in silence before a large figure with jagged wings sweeping back over its shoulders appeared.

'You didn't mention it had wings,' said Jack, rising to his knees in wonder.

'Whoooaaa, I didn't see those before.'

'It must be our jailer,' said Jack. 'Why else would the Myrms leave us?'

'You could be right. We wouldn't get far with a flying demon on our tail. Not that we can go very far with,' he pointed toward Inara, mouthing her name.

No wonder the Ghost Walkers had no use for bars to make their jail. They had little chance of outrunning the Myrms, and with a winged jailer, and a girl missing her legs in tow, they had no hope of escape. Again, Jack felt his heart plummet. He told Farmer Vine he would find his way home. His mother will

CRIK

hear those words soon, only how could he return home? Tracking back through the Blackthorn Tunnel held little appeal even if they managed to getaway from the Myrms. Alarmed, he spotted Bill crawl toward the second fire.

'What're you doing?' Jack grabbed Bill's arm. 'If you go over there you'll upset it. For all we know it could drink blood - our blood.'

'You don't know that.' Bill pulled away.

'Exactly, we don't know anything about it at all. Wouldn't it be better to wait for daytime? I know I'd feel more confident.'

'You've slept Ying, you were snoring your head off a few minutes back. I've yet to shut my eyes, and I don't intend to until I know what's over by the other fire. I'm knackered, so the sooner we know what it is, the quicker I can rest.'

'Ok,' Jack relented. 'Let's take things easy though, I don't want to startle whatever that is, by us suddenly appearing at its fire.'

'Yeah, we'll be the ones startling it.'

Jack started to follow Bill when he remembered Inara. 'Should we wake her?'

'We'll only be a few minutes, let her sleep.'

With a glance back at the sleeping girl, Jack left the relative warmth of the fire. Already a score of small nicks peppered his palms as he crawled after Bill. At least the insects of the Wold gave this place a wide berth. The cold bit deep, clamping down on his thighs like a bear trap, and leaving his elbows and knees feeling exposed and bruised.

'Get up Bill,' whispered Jack. 'We'll scrape our skin off crawling all the way.' He stood, eager to relieve the weight from his arms. 'It's going to notice us, whether we're on all fours or not.'

Bill rose rather sheepishly. 'I wish Black was here with us.'

'Where is he now?'

Bill shook his head. 'I lost contact with him when the Myrm hit my head. It took all my concentration to keep track of him. Now,' he shrugged, 'he could be anywhere. I just hope he and Silver are alright.'

Probably doing better than us, thought Jack. At any time, Kyla could persuade the others to hang them by their necks. Her hatred of them scared him more than the image of Justice's skin peeling away from her face. He had little doubt that Krimble further poisoned her thoughts toward them. The last time he saw the zombie he stalked off behind Kyla, his rotted features alight with mischief.

The crackle of wood burning broke the silence of the night. Fiery embers scattered by the wind drifted close, before disappearing in a blink. He had not seen the creature since they had left their own fire. The feeling that it had left the fireside to stalk them, crept into his mind, making him jump at every touch of wind, and at Bill's every movement. Wanting desperately to retreat to where Inara slept slowed his pace, leaving Bill to take the lead.

'Try to use your demon to take control of it,' whispered Jack.

PARSNIPS AND RUST

Bill showed no sign that he had heard him. Instead, his friend stepped closer, to where the flames highlighted him in red and wavering yellow. Still, the winged beast refused to show itself. This is madness, what did they hope would happen by confronting this thing here tonight? The question plagued Jack's mind, when a sharp retort of struck metal shivered through the air. A shower of rising sparks lit the night to the right of them. The fleeting light failed to illuminate the winged demon.

Bill stepped back. 'I don't think this is such a good idea.'

'You think?' said Jack, punching Bill in the arm. 'We could die out here. This isn't our back garden. This is the Red Wood, and everything in it wants us dead.'

Another clash of metal, followed by a flash of light muted the pair. For a brief moment, they saw a hunched figure, with an upraised hand holding a devastating club.

'I've seen enough,' whispered Jack, pulling away from the intruding light.

'Me too,' agreed Bill, following him.

'Strange, two come out into the cold to seek the truth, and turn aside when they should be a sleuth.'

'Oh no,' whispered Bill.

'It's no fun to turn around and run. Come back into the light, it'll be fun.'

Also recognising the voice of the squirrel set Jack's spirits plummeting. Any more shocks and he wondered whether his heart would drop into his belly. Turning back, he spied the small metal squirrel sitting on a log before the fire. The squirrel had a paw raised, waving at them in a slow arc.

'I thought we were shot of him when we answered his riddle,' said Bill.

There was no riddle here, the squirrel by calling out to them left no doubt in Jack's mind, the winged demon knew they were here. Leaving now would only show how frightened of it they were. Trudging forward he and Bill moved into the light, where Yang appeared. He couldn't deny the appearance of his shadow lifted his flagging courage.

'Don't go doing anything rash, I don't want to get into deeper trouble.'

Bill looked shocked. 'Of course I'm not going to do anything stupid. I'm wetting my pants here.'

'Not you.' He pointed at Yang stretching toward the fire. 'Don't go grabbing anything, or making rude gestures. This is serious; I want to leave as soon as we can.'

Jack did not know whether the demon inside listened to him or not. For now, Yang enjoyed the life giving light.

'Friends lost and friends found, it's all the same to my beaten crown. Copper and tin make my skin. Flick me and you'll hear me ding!'

'Silence Herm, your incessant yammering is giving me a headache.'

CRIK

The squirrel regarded the far side of the clearing where the dry heavy voice originated. 'Your hammering has nothing to do with the state of your head, or your mood then,' retorted the squirrel.

An angry sounding hiss, and a sudden flare of orange, answered the squirrel.

The boys stopped. What is that thing, wondered Jack. Did it breathe fire as well? What horror awaited them on the far side of the fire? White billowing smoke drifted up to the sky; a dragon he thought.

Now they were here Bill lagged behind Jack. The heat of the flames did nothing to warm Jack as he passed the squirrel. He saw the demon sat on a three-legged stool; he had his toes planted on the ground so the soles of his feet were facing them. A dirty leather jacket hung on his back, and hard as Jack looked, he could not see the demon's wings. An unruly mop of shaggy hair framed its bent head as it worked over something in its lap.

'Sorry to come to your fire,' said Jack. 'The Myrms brought us here, and we saw you…'

The head, wreathed in rising steam, twitched to the right. 'We were all brought here. All apart from Herm. Though I guess, he's here because of me.'

'Dink, dink, do you think,' said Herm, jumping down from his perch to scamper over to sit beside the stool.

'Quiet Herm, as always you get over excited. Rest your paws, and your wagging tongue for a few minutes, or I'll douse your head in a bucket of water.'

Herm ran up a jagged metal sculpture, his bronze paws clinking as he went.

'My companion can be a little troublesome,' said the seated figure. 'I'm Huckney.'

When Jack saw an old man, not a gruesome monster, sat before him, he almost collapsed in relief. This was no demon set to guard them. Grey eyebrows, grown unruly and thick, cascaded over crystal blue eyes.

'Where're your wings?' asked Bill. 'We saw them on you not ten minutes ago.'

Jack wanted to hit Bill over the head. He shot an agitated glance back to his friend.

'Wings?' replied Huckney, perplexed. 'Why'd you think I've got wings?'

'We saw you walking, and saw them as you passed the fire,' said Bill.

Huckney tilted his head back and barked out a laugh. 'You mistook those shards of metal,' he pointed to two curved iron sheets, 'for wings. I'm no more a demon than you, or your cautious friend.'

We already have plenty of demons with us, thought Jack. He noticed a smith's hammer held in Huckney's hand, not the deadly cudgel he had presumed the old man held. 'You're a blacksmith.'

'The only one in the Wold, which makes me the best, I guess,' said Huckney. 'At least since my father passed away. Most of the trees and metal scrub you've seen through the Wold came from my father. For decades, this place rang to the sound of his hammer. He made the domes and the spinnerets that cluster the basin floor. I've carried on; the steel trees surrounding the lake are mine.'

'Not forgetting me,' said Herm, wrapping a knuckle against his metal head.

'You wouldn't let me forget you,' Huckney sighed.

'Why would you want to?' queried the squirrel.

Ignoring the squirrel's quick fire question Huckney laid down his hammer, before throwing a satchel of water to Jack. 'You'll find the Myrms won't give you much to drink. So enjoy it while you can. I saw them bringing you to the clearing; I wanted to introduce myself then, only I thought it wiser to wait until you had rested. Besides, I believe the time for introductions is best done during the day. I'm less frightening in the morning.' He laughed.

Savouring the water, Jack kept one eye on his shadow, who had taken a renewed interest in the metal rodent, and the other on the old man. The man had a kindly face, one that engendered a quick trust. Still, perhaps the way Huckney had kept his distance from them, or the work he performed for the Myrms, kept him on guard.

'You say you and your father made everything in the Wold,' said Bill. 'From the trees, to the copper grass, that cuts into my shoes. Yet the Red Wood is huge, how could you outfit this entire place? It'd be impossible.'

The man wore a weary grin. 'In the morning I'll show you what I can do. In the meantime, go back to your beds. You best get all the rest you can. The Ladies won't like you leaving your fire.' He leaned in close. 'Bad things happen to those who don't play by their rules. Be careful lads.'

CRIK

29. A GLIMMER OF GOLD IN THE MORNING

COLOUR SEEPED BACK into the sky. First only a faint blush on the horizon, mixing with the dark blue of the pre-dawn. It didn't take long for the sunrise to burn off the last wisps of cloud. Jack sat watching the dawn in mute wonder. Strange, he thought, how he and his mother shared the same sky. The village of Crik seemed to belong to a different planet; a place of warmth and colour, where soft vegetation met gentle streams, unlike the harsh browns and jagged metal besieging him on all sides. Propping himself up on the crook of his arm, he gave silent thanks that Farmer Vine did not visit him again. Lying to him once had been bad enough.

With his legs crossed and his arms folded over his chest sat Yang. The shadow didn't share Jack's appreciation of the new day, instead Yang studied him. He turned away from his shadow.

'How long have you been there?' He asked, keeping Yang in the corner of his eye. 'Haven't you got anything better to do than to watch me sleep?'

Yang shook his head.

His demon's intense scrutiny took all the warmth from the morning, leaving a cold lump in the pit of his stomach, where he knew the creature resided. His hand strayed to his belly. He felt skin and the muscle beneath, nothing else, no furtive shift of an arm or leg, nor the rounded crown of the demon's head. Pushing his fingers into his flesh, he explored, waiting for some clue as to where the demon now sat. Yang, sitting in front of him, wasn't the demon, just a manifestation of it. When Grandpa Poulis turned into a boy, the face he showed wasn't that of his demon.

'Why are you in here?' he asked. 'Why'd you pick me? Did the Giant bring you as well?' He had so many questions. Where did they come from? Bill's demon hatched from an egg, had something laid that egg? If so, what could lay such an egg? A monstrous hag perhaps, with folds of fat hanging from her bloated body. He no longer doubted that such a creature could live amongst the trees of Crik Wood. He knew that within its dark confines his shadow grinned at him.

Inara still slept beside him. He could hear her grinding her teeth in her sleep, and he had little doubt that in her dreams she never escaped the Marsh House.

A GLIMMER OF GOLD IN THE MORNING

An urge to touch the hair covering her dark eyes swept through him, he leant in close, only to stop when she flinched in her sleep. Shying back, he wondered what dark memory she relived. Suddenly he realised that he had never asked her parents' names. Not having to ponder why he hadn't, he withdrew farther from the girl. He lived with his guilt, as surely as he lived with the knowledge of the demon inside of him. Knowing his desire to get rid of the demon, outweighed his guilt, making each stronger.

'Stop looking at me,' he said, exacerbated with his shadow. Yang's immobility held the same sense of scrutiny he got when he studied his own reflection in a mirror. 'You're not with me in my dreams anymore,' he said, not bothering to hide his grin. 'I'm winning aren't I? You know, once we leave the Wold, you won't be able to hide anymore.'

Yang, shaking his head, got to his feet. Sweeping out his arm, he pointed to where the Myrms delivered them to the Ghost Walkers. Extending farther, the shadowed arm indicated the metal branches of the Hanging Tree that towered over smaller constructs.

Did his shadow threaten that only death would separate them? He recalled discovering how the Giant had smashed its way into Mr Hasseltope's tomb; and then the strange drawings scrawled on its walls. Three drawings, one of a boy standing alone, a second revealed a demon and the terror-struck boy, the last showed a man with the demon perched on his shoulder. Should a fourth sketch exist, showing the body of an old man and the demon leaving the corpse to find a new host? Was that the only way he would be free of Yang?

'Your shadow worries about the Hanging Tree.'

Turning to the gruff voice Jack looked up into Huckney's kind face.

'I didn't notice your approach,' said Jack.

'He misses a lot.' Bill, shifting his glasses, spoke to Huckney. 'I bet he didn't even notice that I wasn't here when he woke up.'

In truth, Jack had not noticed his friend's absence, but he refused to admit that. 'Where have you been?' he asked.

Bill smiled. 'Huckney showed me what he can do. It's amazing.'

Kneeling down Huckney took fruit from a bag he had slung over his shoulder. He laid down red and green apples, a couple of plums, an orange, and a few pears. Finally, he retrieved a sack full of water, which he passed to Jack.

Taking the offered drink Jack brought the bottle to his parched mouth. 'Where did these come from?' he asked, looking around at the barren wilderness around him.

'The Ladies allowed me to keep my father's garden. I grow my food there, and the rust which rains down across the rest of the Wold doesn't contaminate the water,' answered Huckney. 'You should eat; build up your strength before the Ladies come for you.'

CRIK

Reaching across, Huckney rested a huge hand on Inara's shoulder, waking her in an instant.

Inara had barely opened her eyes before demanding Huckney's name.

After the introduction Bill laughed. 'Tell them what you can do.'

'It's easier to show,' replied the big man.

Stretching, Inara sat up. 'I feel as though I've stepped into a play that's halfway through. You all seem to be fast friends, and all I know is your name is Huckney.'

Believing he was the only one who heard the suspicion coating Inara's words Jack watched her closely. Being older than either he or Bill, and knowing more of the world than them gave Inara some authority amongst their group. The blacksmith seemed pleasant enough. Perhaps Inara distrusted all men after Krimble.

'I met your friends by my fire last night,' said Huckney. 'They thought at first that I was a demon with huge sweeping wings.' He tilted back his head and laughed. The laugh being both warm and infectious spread to both Jack and Bill. 'I'm sorry,' he said wiping away his tears. 'I've been alone so long, and to be mistaken for a creature after all that time is quite amusing.'

'It seems,' remarked Inara, biting off each word, 'all we meet are monsters. The Myrms are mindless brutes controlled by ghosts of dead women. Others only look human so they can manipulate us.' Her accusatory glance at Jack stopped his giggles. Slow hurt played over his face, like a reflection of crows on a cold window. Unable to bear that look, she added, 'I do mean Krimble.' Her tone, which had softened to a patter, now hardened. Her distrust was a bitter taste on her tongue she had to spit out. 'Who's to say he's,' she pointed a finger at Huckney, 'isn't just as bad as Krimble. At least the Myrms look like monsters.'

Raising his hands, Huckney said, 'I don't intend on hurting any of you. We're here all together. This is my home, that doesn't mean I belong here. Take an apple and enjoy the morning air.'

'The air is noxious,' said Inara, 'as is everything in the Wold. At least the bugs haven't followed us to this wretched glade.'

'Give him a break Inara,' said Bill, adjusting his glasses. 'You can trust Huckney. If it weren't for him, we wouldn't have anything to eat for breakfast. He told us that the Myrms kidnapped him and his dad and brought them to the Red Wood a long time ago.'

Picking an apple, Inara first looked at the fruit then tossed it at Jack. 'This fruit could be a trick, like Krimble's honeyed tea. If you trust him,' she said to Jack, 'if you believe the Myrms kidnapped him, take a bite.'

The apple that Jack clutched invited him to sink his teeth into its bright red skin. The water slacked his thirst, but his stomach still groaned for food.

'Eat it Ying,' said Bill. 'I've had two already.'

A GLIMMER OF GOLD IN THE MORNING

'I won't be fooled again,' said Inara.

Looking from Inara's blunt stare, to Bill's incredulous face, Jack brought the apple to his mouth. What reason had Huckney with wanting to kill them. If he wanted them dead, he had the strength to kill them. Huckney's hammer would make a fine weapon. Inara's suspicion of him left Huckney looking haggard. The man's loneliness seeped into the wind at that moment, crushing Jack's resolve.

The juice exploded into Jack's mouth. It tasted wonderful, and to have something to finally crunch between his teeth brought a smile to his lips. Before he had time to swallow the morsel of fruit, Yang reappeared. His shadow had drifted behind Huckney, and growing big peered over the head of the large man. The apple stuck in Jack's throat, making him cough and gasp for air.

'You poisoned him,' accused Inara, reaching out for Jack's flailing arm.

'He's turning as red as the apple,' said Bill, standing still.

With his windpipe blocked, Jack fought for air. Clutching at his neck, he raked his fingertips across his skin. Crazed, he looked around for help, but all he saw was the world grown dark. Did Yang come for him? Was his shadow going to be his death shroud? His stomach clenched. Knowing he was about to die, the demon sought to escape. The Narmacil wrapped itself around his abdomen, pulling his muscles tight. Yang warned him death would be the only way he would be free. The pain in his stomach climbed higher, settling in under his ribs. The apple clogging his airway drifted to the back of his mind as he felt the demon rising up his body. He gave a jerk and the apple shot from his mouth. Gasping, he sucked in the morning air, letting it fill his lungs. Coughing weakly, he felt the pressure the demon had exerted ease.

'That's it boy, breath in. The apple is on the ground now, your throat is clear.'

Jack, recognising Huckney's voice twisted around to see the blacksmith behind him. Looking down he gasped as Huckney's arms began to loosen their embrace.

'You tried to kill him.'

'I saved the boy's life.'

Only half listening to Inara's and Huckney's exchange Jack looked for Yang. His shadow, having drifted from where it had resided, now stood far off looking toward to the Hanging Tree. Jack had felt certain the tightening bands around his body were the struggles from the demon within him.

'Look.' Huckney marched over to where Jack had dropped the apple. 'If this apple were poison, would I take a bite?' Sinking his teeth into the red fruit, he chewed and swallowed. 'Your talk of poison scared him half to death. No wonder he choked.'

'Thanks for helping him,' Inara said, grudgingly.

CRIK

'Don't be so quick to judge,' said Huckney. 'There're those here that lay down too much judgement already.'

Looking embarrassed, Bill stepped forward to pat Jack's shoulder. 'You ok now Ying?'

'Don't call me that,' said Jack throwing off Bill's arm.

Bill shrugged. 'Now that we all know you aren't trying to kill us, how about you show them what you can do Huckney?'

Huckney wore woollen green trousers with many deep pockets. He put a hand into one of them and withdrew a small lump of tin. The smooth round metal sat in his palm like a river tossed pebble. From another pocket, the blacksmith retrieved a book, which had a small hammer wedged between its pages.

'He can read, I didn't expect that,' said Inara, chewing her lip.

'This book hasn't got any words,' said the blacksmith. He opened the book to the page the hammer bookmarked. Tipping the leather bound cover; he showed them all an exquisite pencilled drawing of a field mouse. Every drawn hair leapt from the page. It would be easy to imagine the tiny ears listening to them from the sheaf of paper.

'My apologies, your Narmacil is an artist,' carried on Inara, pushing herself forward to study the drawing.

'I suppose that's true,' replied Huckney.

Setting the drawing down, Huckney took his hammer and started working the lump of tin. Jack watched in amazement as the blacksmith's large calloused hands moved around the metal with practiced ease. The tap of the hammer on the metal tickled his ears. Gradually the round tin began to flatten. It no longer appeared like a pebble, it now resembled a slipper. Again, the hammer went to work, denting the metal like a master baker kneading dough into a loaf of bread.

Bill, watching even more eagerly than Jack and Inara, clapped his hands. 'Look he's working on the head now. I can see it taking shape.'

Jack had to agree. Deft touches transformed the metal in swift stages. With a hard to follow rapidness, from the tin emerged the head of a mouse. The back end of the tool curved down to a point. Spinning the hammer around Huckney used the fine tip of the instrument to start laying on the detail. First, he tackled the hair on the head of the rodent, carving individual strands as shown in the drawing. Before forming the eyes, he tapered the end of the metal so that it resembled the nose and whiskers on the fluttering page. Once done with the round eyes Huckney carved out the mouth. After pulling the lips back from two large incisors, the mouse, coming to life, snapped the air in irritation. 'Hurry up and finish me,' it cried.

Falling back in shock, Jack knocked into the amazed Inara who sat behind him.

'Isn't it incredible,' said Bill.

A GLIMMER OF GOLD IN THE MORNING

'Of course I'm incredible, I'm me. The marvellous mouse trapped in a slab of metal. Look and stare at my lumpy behind, and wonder, will I ever be finished?' said the mouse, twitching its nose.

'Be patient or you'll remain as you are,' warned Huckney.

'If you were quicker, I wouldn't have reason to be impatient,' said the mouse.

As the mouse complained, Huckney continued to groove hair, and shape muscle on the rodent's body.

'It's alive, but it's metal,' said Jack.

'So was Herm,' pointed out Bill.

'Careful, that tickles,' said the mouse, as the blacksmith's tool shaped its feet. Flexing its new toes the mouse said, 'it's good to stretch after being cooped up for so long.'

The smooth tin gave way to individual hair and limbs. With ease, Huckney brought the rest of the mouse into being. 'Stop moving your legs or I'll drop you,' said Huckney.

'Can you blame me for wanting to run? I've been sitting in your pocket for days already.'

'If I didn't pull you from the slag of tin you'd still be there now, so be quiet until I've done your tail.'

'I don't want a tail, it'll catch on things,' complained the mouse. 'Why would I want a tail?'

'The book shows you having a tail, so I will give you a tail,' replied Huckney.

'If the drawing had butterfly wings on my back you'd put those on me too, wouldn't you?' moaned the mouse.

'I've never seen a real mouse,' said Huckney. 'So if the book tells me you had wings then you'd be flapping them by now.'

'I'm grateful you haven't given me a trunk instead of a nose then,' replied the mouse, twisting in Huckney's lap as the blacksmith put his hand into another pocket.

Watching the blacksmith talking with the argumentative mouse, turned Jack's thoughts to home and all the Talents in the Village. The carpenter's son Holst, who could hear the trees speak, and who eventually went mad from the screams the wood made as his father cut them with his saw. His mother told him of a girl who could fill an empty bucket with water by just looking at it. Grandpa Poulis had also mentioned the girl, and how after losing her baby she had flooded the Tristle River with her tears. How many demons were there? He wondered whether for every person there was a demon waiting to jump inside.

'You've given me a gold tail!' shouted the mouse, flicking the golden appendage around its round body. 'I'm tin, not gold.'

'I thought it would look nice,' said Huckney.

CRIK

Bill nodded in enthusiasm. 'It does,' he said. 'Why just be ordinary when you can have a tail that glimmers in the morning sun? Instead of Tin Mouse, everyone will know you as Gold Tail. I know which one I'd prefer.'

Gold Tail closed one eye before addressing Bill. 'That's original,' said the mouse. 'Should I call you Spectacle Boy, or Chubby Boy? Are we all named after how we look?'

'Well no,' said Bill, taken aback by the mouse. 'I thought it'd be a nice name.'

'Oh, you do think before speaking then,' said Gold Tail, now sitting on its haunches to shout up at Bill. 'I guess being called Gold Tail is the best I'm going to get. If I left it to this buffoon,' it pointed one tin paw up at Huckney, 'I'd probably get stuck with everyone calling me Mouse.'

Huckney smiled. 'I was thinking Grumpy would be a good fit.'

'I'm not grumpy,' said Gold Tail, 'just observant.' The mouse twitched its whiskers and turning its head toward the Hanging Tree said, 'Being sharp-eyed I know when it's time for me to leave. You've got some visitors, and I don't want to be around when they arrive.' Gold Tail climbed up Huckney's arm and then down the blacksmith's leg before running off. With a last flash of gold, the mouse disappeared.

In front of where Yang stood approached three figures. One crouched, walking toward them in a perpetual bow. The lead, a hulk of muscle, brushed the rough ground with its knuckles. Wisps of fabric, or perhaps smoke, followed; at its core burned a cold light.

30. NEW LIFE

JACK RECOGNISED THE CHIEFTAIN Raglor, First Fist of the Feylr Clan. Overlapping bronze plates crashed together as the Myrm marched up the hill. The clamour that reached them sounded like kettles hit with thousands of spoons. Only its powerful biceps lay free of the encumbering armour. An ornate helm, resembling a stag, complete with a rack of antlers, made the chieftain even more impressive. Raglor, and then Krimble, gave Yang a wide berth. Raglor grunted when he passed the shadow, and turned to keep Yang in sight. Kyla, drifting behind the pair, no longer shone, her ghostly appearance had grown dull and grey, like ash falling from a dirty chimney. At her approach, Yang shrank to Jack's side, coming to a halt to face the morning sun.

'Kyla's full of anger,' cautioned Huckney, 'be careful what you say. The least thing will cause her insult.'

Wiping his misted glasses, Bill said, 'We know, we've already met her. We'd be rotting from the highest branch of the Hanging Tree, if it weren't for Justice.'

Huckney nodded.

Inara gritted her teeth. 'I could make Krimble eat his own hand.'

'You would only upset the Ghost Walker,' said Jack.

'I think you should give it a try.' Bill's hands balled into fists.

'It seems Krimble has found himself a circle of friends, best not antagonise them until we know what they want,' said Jack. Inara gave him an ever-suffering look. Perhaps she was joking, but he didn't want to take that chance.

The Ghost Walker arrested Jack's attention. Flowers would wilt with her passing, his tremulous thought sighed. His mother would call Kyla a handsome woman, not pretty, but not unattractive. If her hard lined mouth softened, and her brow relaxed, she would be someone who would engender trust and comfort. Recognising what could have been, unsettled and saddened him. Had she lived, would she have had a family? Perhaps her grandson would now be his friend. Imagining a life without Bill brought sharp anxiety to his quickening pulse. A possibility if the village had known about Grandma Poulis's secret. Would Mr Gasthem have led the village to the Hanging Tree to see her swing from the hangman's noose? Mr Dash, the grave keeper, would then bury her in an unmarked grave with the other Ghost Walkers. Rushing into his mind came a vision too horrid to hold back. Grandma Poulis's rotted body peeking through

CRIK

the rain washed mud, watching him from blind white eyes. He tried to turn from what his mind conjured, but instead it tightened its focus. 'Look what you've done to my rosebush,' she screamed. Her clawing fingers churned the black stems and crushed the petals of her flowers into mush as she lifted herself from the rosebush that now served as her grave.

'Ying, are you okay?'

'I'm fine,' said Jack, grateful Bill couldn't share his nightmarish vision.

Raglor stood close enough to block out the sun, and for its musty odour to reach them. In the Myrm's wake came Krimble. The zombie had decayed further, he now showed more bone than skin, and the tendons standing out on his neck were like frayed rope about to snap.

'I have come for the seeds,' Kyla said, coming to a stop. She looked at Huckney with expectation.

'Justice wanted five silver Oaks and seven gold Maple trees for the Mere of Ashes.' Huckney delved into his pouch.

The Ghost Walker frowned, withholding more of her light. 'She wants them to grow faster. The trees you gave a few months back are still only saplings.'

The blacksmith produced five silver acorns and golden twin-winged maple seeds. 'The soil is poor, and trees take time to grow. I've also created ten River Birches. They'll grow quicker than the bigger trees and the copper leaves will bring the lake to life.'

'Justice didn't ask for River Birches,' snapped Kyla. 'Nor did she request Willow seeds when I came here last. We're making our Wold, and you'll do as we command. Your father listened to us. It would be wise for you to follow his example.'

Huckney's jaw hardened, until his muscle revealed itself as a ball through his cheek. 'Although a great blacksmith, my father could not create an entire wood by himself. Your precious Hanging Tree took him months to create. A solitary Oak or Redwood would keep him working for days at a time. With my seeds, I am sowing the Wold with shrubs and towering giants that don't rust like the first trees my father created. Here take them,' he pushed the hand holding the nuts and seeds toward the Ghost Walker.

'Give them to the Myrm,' said Kyla.

Standing so close to one another, Jack saw with surprise that Huckney's wiry muscles and dominant height overshadowed the more heavily muscled Myrm chieftain. The delicately carved acorns and the other seeds had every detail Jack would expect to see on a real acorn littering the floor of Crik Wood. They tinkled as Huckney dropped them into Raglor's gauntlet.

'We know about your gift.' Kyla addressed Inara. 'It is an extraordinary Talent. Though I feel your friend, doesn't appreciate it as much as he once did.'

'I'm no friend of the bitch,' said Krimble.

'Your rotted tongue hasn't improved your manners,' observed Bill.

'Nor my tolerance of you boy,' said Krimble, glowering.

'Enough of your petty squabbles,' said Kyla. 'Each of you has abilities that will serve us well. As long as you prove yourself useful, Justice will not allow me to show you the view from the topmost branch of the Hanging Tree.'

'What use is my ability to you?' asked Inara. 'I can only control one dead thing at a time. And I will not relinquish my hold over Krimble.'

Krimble cackled. 'You forget I can talk to your Narmacil,' he said. 'It tells me things. I told you when you were my guest that you were wasting your Talent. Still you believe you have limitations, that you have everything figured out.' The grey gums of the zombie showed as it grinned. 'I would have served you so much better than this cripple. Boy,' his hate filled gaze swept to Jack, 'you still believe you just have a shadow. A scheming conniving shadow, which double crosses those who only wanted to help. You know nothing of what it, you, are capable of.'

For now, Yang remained fixed, like every other shadow obeying the rules laid down by the sun. Always suspicious of his shadow, Jack kept one eye on Yang. Experience had taught him that Yang rarely stayed quiet for long. Kyla would end up disappointed if she wanted to control Yang through him. He tried for years to stop Yang from doing things that got him into trouble. The demon controlled his shadow; he didn't have a hand in Yang's actions. Krimble's implication, that Yang had more surprises, confused and scared him. What else was the demon capable of?

'Krimble has agreed to talk to your Narmacils, to help them become stronger,' said Kyla. 'By accepting his tutelage you will grow, and possibly prove your worth.' Her sneer left no doubt about her own misgivings.

Inara spat. 'He doesn't want to help you. Krimble only wants to control our Narmacils for his own end. If you let him speak to them, that will happen. I've seen him lie and seduce the Children of the Wood. He will corrupt them, make them bend to his will until they become as wicked as he is.'

Colour first blossomed across the Ghost Walker's grey lips, and then spread a strong amber glow. 'I don't care what he is, or wants.' Colour swept down her body burning away the shroud she wore into a dress of light. 'Obey and you won't see how the Wold looks from atop the Great Tree. You will remain here with the blacksmith and share his fruit. Disobey, or fight Krimble, and you will answer to me.' Her colour at once disappeared, transforming the floating dress back into dirty smoke. 'The choice is that simple. Allow Krimble to die and you will all follow him.' An expression of pure hatred flitted across her features.

When she turned to the Hanging Tree, Jack expelled the breath he had held since her final threat. Raglor, clutching the precious seeds to his chest, followed her, leaving the group staring at Krimble.

'Shall we start?' said Krimble.

CRIK

'You're lucky Inara doesn't make you impale yourself on a rusted spike,' said Bill, shifting his glasses, more out of anger than need. 'She could have you do it.'

Krimble shook his head. 'No she couldn't. Not unless she wants you and your friend to suffer at Kyla's hand. I'm quite safe from her petty torments.' Darkness showed behind the zombie's cracked lips. 'Besides, she knows she lacks my imagination. Do you recall my dear,' he said to Inara, 'how I punished poor Mr Thunnel for trying to escape?'

'He's dead, you can't harm him anymore.'

'Quite right,' agreed Krimble. 'It's a story to make these young lads leave their breakfast though isn't it? Let's just say it's incredibly hard to run without your toes.'

'You made him eat them.' Inara's eyes were pools of tar.

Krimble smiled. 'It was his choice.'

'You starved him for days, and then brought his toes back to him on a plate.'

'Smothered in gravy.'

'How're you going to train us?' asked Bill, shuffling his feet.

'I'm not training you,' said Krimble with a sneer. 'Your Narmacils are what's important. Your selfishness has locked them away for too long.' Smiling at Inara, he said, 'The Children of the Wood need their teacher. Kyla recognised my intentions, and though motivated by greed, at least she can see that I only wish to help the poor Narmacils. Now let's begin.'

The zombie walked closer to where Inara sat on the rough ground. 'There's something you may not be aware of my dear,' he said. 'The Wold is one huge graveyard. The Myrms not only destroyed the trees, they destroyed the homes of thousands of animals. Badgers could no longer use the roots of the trees to shelter from the rain and sleet. Worms died as the metal replacing the roots poisoned the ground. Without the worms, the birds fell hungry from the sky. The fox and wolf held prisoner behind the Hedge Wall lay down and starved like poor Mr Thunnel. They all rot beneath our feet. Your Narmacil can sense them. Not two feet in front of you lays a stag buried under the red dirt. Reach out and touch the ground girl.'

'I'm not going to listen to you,' said Inara. 'I didn't do what you wanted in the Marsh House, and this new prison will be no different.'

'Then you risk the lives of your new friends,' said Krimble. 'Or do you think the blacksmith will help you?'

Huckney, stepping forward, snatched Krimble's rotted shoulders and lifted him from the ground. 'The Ladies need me,' he said. 'You can't threaten me. I could crush your body and use my hammer to powder your bones.'

Krimble laughed. 'You are a powerful man. I know you can easily do what you say, but think. Were you to do that, could you then protect the children? Kyla would order the Myrms to grind them all into paste. If you could stand up

NEW LIFE

to her, you would've escaped the Red Wood a long time ago. And your father would now be alive, and not just a pile of bones feeding your apple tree.'

'The Ladies are fickle, and their affection dies fast,' said Huckney, bringing Krimble closer to his face. 'When they tire of your stench, I'll be here, waiting to carry on this conversation. Be careful how you treat the children, if I hear anything I don't like, I'll be back with my hammer.' He dropped Krimble.

Jack watched as the blacksmith stomped away. All they needed was for the wolves to turn up and the old gang would be complete.

'Now that the lummox has gone we can carry on,' said Krimble, climbing to his feet. 'The stag is before you, reach out and touch it, it won't bite.'

'What do you mean reach out and touch it?'

'Not you girl,' Krimble told Inara. 'I speak to one more important than you. Feel the contours of the bones. Remnants of sinew and flesh wrapping its frame still have life. Listen to its last moments. The stag is trying to tell you its story, to let you know it's here for you.'

'Do you feel anything Inara?' asked Bill.

The girl turned to him. 'It's strange; I know there's something in the ground. It's like a muffled drum, or the lapping of water at the shore of a lake. Whatever I'm sensing it's not just in front of me, it's beating at my back as well as my sides. I've never felt anything like this.'

She looked scared. Jack could see her pulse fluttering in her neck. Whatever Krimble attempted was working. A desire to go to her, and put his hand on her shoulder overcame him. He didn't. Before she could accept his help, she needed to understand what happened within her.

'Focus, I know all this is new to you,' said Krimble. 'If you came to me when I asked, I would've revealed your potential a long time ago. Listen to the beating of the Stag's decayed heart. You can still hear it if you are quiet enough. There, it's faint and can still falter and stop if you don't get a hold of it. Don't let it go. Demand it to get stronger. You are its master.'

'I can feel it moving within me,' said Inara. 'It's magnificent.'

When crossing the blue stones, Jack had felt the demon thrash about. The memory of the demon's movements in his stomach made him feel nauseous. His eyes drifted to Inara's top where the girl held her stomach. He tried to see if he could spy any movement under her hand, but saw nothing to reveal her demon.

'What's it doing?' asked Bill.

'It feels wonderful,' she said. 'I'm aware that I am part of something far greater than I ever thought possible.'

'Remember, it's your demon and Krimble who are making you feel so wonderful,' remarked Jack.

'I know exactly what's happening,' said Inara. 'I would prefer Krimble to be nowhere near me. His presence is vile; his communicating with my Narmacil

CRIK

leaves me cold. That doesn't stop me from recognising what is happening within me. It's as if my Narmacil is only now waking up. We aren't alone here; I hear bird song and the rustle of branches. If I close my eyes, I could be down by the brook near my home.'

'You're hearing ghosts,' said Jack. 'Everything is as dead as him,' he pointed to Krimble. 'Don't be fooled. It's not you who is hearing these things, it's your demon. Everything is gone Inara. The Ghost Walkers and the Myrms ruined it all.'

'You're wrong Jack. They are all still here, and I know I can bring them back. I can restore the Red Wood. All I have to do is concentrate and the deer will run again, the owl will wake at night and the fish will once more swim in the streams.'

'Not as they were,' argued Jack. 'The water is still poisoned by falling rust. What living thing could survive in that? No Inara, they won't be alive. They'll be like Krimble, shambling uncaring things.'

Inara's head snapped around. 'You know nothing. You don't want your Narmacil. What is happening is glorious, a gift I can share. For the first time since losing my legs, I feel as though I can run. Everything is alive. My Talent did not warp Krimble. His evil predates Silver ripping out his throat. The stag means no harm. I can hear them in the ground, calling to me. Like me, they want to run again.'

'The dead aren't meant to leave their graves,' continued Jack, recalling his vision of Grandma Poulis climbing out of her rosebush.

'So you think I'm an abomination,' accused Inara. 'Should your village also hang me, as they had Justice?'

Taken aback by her words, Jack floundered. He did not expect such a venomous reaction. Couldn't she see that Krimble was using her? A smile refused to leave Krimble's crooked mouth since he started to talk with the demon. Who's to say what they discussed. This was horrible; he won't allow Krimble to conspire with his own demon. Horrified, he discovered Yang had taken the shape of a stag over the stretch of ground where the dead animal resided. Huge shadowed antlers forked out in all directions. Following them, he felt cold as the shadow continued to outline other animals on the ground. Rabbits, a fox complete with a bushy tail, and over there a hawk with outspread wings. Although tempted to ask Inara if his shadow had located more dead animals, he was afraid of the answer. Did his demon commune with the other demons? Were they constantly chatting away, scheming against them? Feeling numb, he sat down.

'Don't trust them,' he meekly told Inara.

'You worry too much,' she said. 'I control my Narmacil. Only I'm now aware that I can make it do so much more than I ever thought possible. Keeping Krimble alive is like having dirt caked under my fingernails. No matter how hard I try, I always feel dirty. This,' her spread hands encompassed the valley with the shadowed outlines of the animals, 'feels right. With this at my control I feel more than I am.'

'You're great as you are,' said Jack.

'Easy for you to say,' said Inara. 'In the marsh you didn't so much as lose a finger.'

'You understand now, don't you girl,' said Krimble. 'When I told you every night and day that you were holding back, keeping your Narmacil imprisoned. You understand now, don't you? I've opened the world up to you. Now concentrate girl, make the stag run once more.'

Inara looked at the ground where Yang had taken the form of the stag. Her eyes opened wide and her thin lips showed her astonishment.

'It's moving,' she said.

'Yes, the muscles are tightening. Focus, you have nearly got him.'

The sight of Krimble's happiness appalled Jack. He wanted to hurl a rock at Krimble's head, to make him remember his only reason for living was for punishment for his crimes.

'Look, the ground is cracking,' said Bill, pointing. 'It's coming.'

'Don't let it go,' commanded Krimble. 'One more push and you will have done it.'

Sweat beaded Inara's brow, plastering her hair in darkened swirls. 'It's hard,' she said.

'Only because you've never done it before,' said Krimble, his rushed tone betraying his excitement.

Inara grunted, and Jack, believing her to be in pain, rushed to her side. 'Are you alright?' he asked, putting his arm around her, but she shoved him off.

The red earth split; Yang withdrew.

A spear of bone pierced the crust of earth. Barbed antlers materialised from the cracked ground like a magician's trick. Dirt and stone flew in the air as the stag broke the surface. The stag's horror-stricken scream hushed the morning. Its bleating call spoke of its outrage; its sunken sockets dripping soil-filled tears told its own story.

The breath caught in Jack's throat at hearing the anguished cries of the stag, and knew what Inara had done was an abomination.

31. WHEN THE DEAD WALK THE WOLD

WHAT FUR REMAINED, HUNG from the stag like a tattered cloak. The once proud animal struggled from the mud, its cracked hooves seeking purchase. As it rose, the meat hanging on the skeletal frame clung to the dirt, as though shamed by the watching eyes. Its bleats, more pitiful for its tongue had rotted away, could not articulate its horror. Sinew, like white jelly, still covered rounded joints, though this did nothing to dull the noise of the scraping bones. Taking its first steps in years, the stag brought Inara to tears. Limping, it moved from the gaping hole in the ground.

Staring in horror, Jack tried to turn away, yet the stag's tail, still white after all this time, held his attention.

'Magnificent, isn't it,' said Krimble, moving to the beast and laying his bone fingers on the bumps of the stag's spine. 'I've never seen anything more beautiful.'

'Beautiful?' said Bill, his face blanched white. 'It's horrible. It can barely walk on those sticks of bone.'

'The first steps are always the hardest,' said Krimble. 'This is his second birth, first a hind pushed him from her loins, now the earth has given him up to us. Look how he's taking in his new surroundings. When he last stood here, the Wold still had green leaves on its branches. You've brought life back to the Red Wood,' he said, turning to Inara.

'I know you aren't speaking to me,' she said. 'You've used the Child of the Wood that chose me. The sounds of the deer, the stag, and the other animals laid to rest here, weren't anything like the sounds this poor animal is now making. I don't want this, and I will return him to the ground.'

'The cries you hear are the same birthing cries you hear from any new-born,' argued Krimble. 'Air is swelling lungs that have not expanded in years. If you return it to the hole in the ground, you'll be killing it.'

'It's already dead,' said Bill.

'You're wrong,' said Krimble. 'I have free choice, to say what I want.' The zombie clicked its fingers. 'She didn't tell me to do that; did it myself.'

'You've wanted nothing more than for Inara to let you die,' said Jack. 'Why the change of heart?'

WHEN THE DEAD WALK THE WOLD

Smiling, Krimble circled the stag, brushing clots of soil from its hide. 'All I've ever wanted was to serve the Narmacils. When I took them in, I opened them up and showed them all what they could do. The girl is right when she calls them the Children of the Wood; they are children, and like all children, they need guidance. I can talk with them; I can teach them how to reach their full potential. They need me.'

'You tortured and cajoled to get them,' said Inara. 'Then held them imprisoned inside your black heart and used them for your own ends. You have no interest in helping them, you just want their Talents.'

'The Narmacils live far longer than any of you know. Hundreds of years, living without realising all what they can do. Think of what I offer them. Your Talent has grown this morning, and with it so has your Narmacil. You've connected with a world you didn't know existed. Listen, you can still hear the beat of bird wings; grounded for far too long.'

'I hear nothing but the screams of the stag,' replied Inara.

'Concentrate,' urged Krimble. 'They are all waiting for you to release them. Every one of the animals here died before their time. Populate the Wold like the Ladies desire. See life come back to the Red Wood.'

'I can't,' said Inara.

Jack knew if she had legs Inara would have fled from the valley, and kept running until the cries of the stag faded. Whatever Krimble had unlocked within her would forever haunt her, and no matter how far she ran she would always hear the sounds of those buried beneath her feet. Knowing she would never have a moments respite from that awful truth brought a lump to his throat. She had suffered enough.

'This place needs flesh and blood,' said Krimble, licking his lips. 'Bring life back and the Wold won't be such an empty place, filled with only metal and bugs.'

'You can't possibly be contemplating doing what he wants,' said Bill, having noticed how Inara struggled with herself, like a recovering alcoholic outside a pub's door. 'The stag can barely stand, it's a ruin. Look at it Inara.'

'I know that Bill,' she said. 'I can hear them all around me. Like phantoms, whispering to me from beneath the earth. I've seen so much death since leaving my home; this is my chance to bring something into this world.'

'Those cries aren't natural,' argued Bill, indicating the stag with a trembling finger. 'It doesn't want to be here.'

'Krimble didn't want me to raise him, only look at him now.' She drew quiet. 'Life will adapt.'

'It's not life,' said Jack. 'All I can see through its exposed ribs is dirt and stone. There's no beating heart. You raised Krimble to punish him. He's only happy now that he can control you through your demon, as he attempted to do back at the Marsh House.'

CRIK

Snapping her head back, her eyes blazing, she said, 'He's not controlling me. I brought back the stag, not him.'

'At his urging,' said Jack. 'Don't you see he's using you?'

'I don't want to listen to you Jack. You don't like it that I'm not afraid of my Narmacil. Wanting to discard the companionship of Yang is a mistake. Don't throw away your bond as though it were one of his,' she jerked a thumb in Krimble's direction, 'rats in a cage. We'd all now be home safe, if you only knew how good the Children of the Wood are. We'd be less than we are without them.'

He was the only one who had seen one of the forked tongued devils. It had changed shape back in his room, yet its eyes always remained cold. 'If they are so good then why do they slip into you without your knowing? I followed the demon into Bill's room; I saw it jump into him.'

'I'm glad it did,' said Bill. 'I wouldn't have had Black if it hadn't. Ying, you have no idea how horrible it was being the freak of the village. Everyone else had their Talent long before I had mine.'

'You all blame me for being here, but if you didn't want to show off and get yourself a wolf we never would've left the village in the first place,' said Jack. 'If we had,' he said to Inara, 'you'd never have escaped the room without windows.'

'I'm sorry Jack. This,' she pointed at her chest, 'is who I am. My Narmacil chose me, recognising something that was within me. The child is with me. As Yang is a part of you.'

His shadow moved over to caress the stag. Every one of Yang's strokes pulled loose another clump of hair. Couldn't his friends see how perverse this was? Black tears tumbled down the stag's rotted cheeks. Frustrated, he bit down on his tongue. The stag, like the stuffed animals back in his bedroom, was just another plaything for the demon.

'It isn't who I am,' he said. 'How many demons live inside Krimble's crooked body? Ten, fifty, a hundred, it doesn't matter. Inara, you say you and your Narmacil share a bond. We all live with that connection.'

Inara nodded. 'That's right.'

'An unbreakable bond,' said Jack. His hand's became animated, making his point as much as his mouth.

'Where are you going with this?'

'Every Narmacil, but yours, abandoned those imprisoned at the Marsh House. Left them to die. There is no special relationship between you and your demon. It will leave you as soon as it finds a better host.'

'You're wrong Jack,' said Inara. Her fingers raked the ground, making four parallel lines either side of her. 'If you placed your hand over a flame, would you be able to keep it there? No,' she said. 'The pain would get too much, eventually you'll flinch. The Narmacils endured far more pain than that before they recoiled from the torture inflicted upon them. Look at me. Krimble used a rusted saw to cut my legs. My Narmacil screamed with me, yet it refused to leave me alone. I'll let the stag live, and do what the Ghost Walkers want of me, not for them, for the child inside me. I owe it that much.'

Why argue, Jack could see by the set of her mouth that she would refuse to listen to him. Although Bill remained quiet, he could see that his friend agreed with Inara. For the chance to control more than just a wolf, he knew Bill would sit for hours in front of Krimble. Well he had no intention of allowing Krimble anywhere near Yang. His shadow had shown him more than enough surprises already, without entertaining anymore.

'What are you going to do Inara?' asked Bill, edging closer to the stag and the two figures already smoothing its fur.

'I'm not going to control it,' she answered. Instead, she looked farther afield. 'Other animals are waiting their turn to feel the breeze again.'

Shuddering, Jack remembered the bodies Yang had sketched on the valley floor.

'The stag has stopped screaming, perhaps Krimble was right when he said the screams were nothing more than birthing cries,' said Bill.

The screams had stopped; however, the quivering in its limbs had not abated one-bit.

'See,' answered Krimble, 'I told you. Give it time to regain its strength and it will run for you.'

'Only to get away from you,' said Jack.

Iron shards and dry earth layered the valley floor. Not even one weed took root in the jagged splits in the crust of the ground. Ringing the valley loomed silver and copper trees, mimicking those that had once stood in their place. Looking at the metal constructs turned Jack's stomach. The animals Inara wanted to raise would also parody what had come before. How could they ever look on that stag with the same sense of wonder as seeing a living animal? Justice and her sisters destroyed the Wold; they could not use them to rebuild it.

'If I close my eyes I can hear the rabbits thumping the ground.' Excitement laced her voice like rum in a cake. 'They still want to scamper around.'

Jack knew Yang heard them too, his shadow had moved away from the stag to stand expectantly over a patch of ground. His shadow sat on his haunches to study the bare earth between its feet.

'Do you think you can control anymore?' asked Bill.

'I don't know,' said Inara. 'Up until now I thought my Talent only allowed me to bring back on thing. Whatever Krimble showed my Narmacil, made it stronger. I'll try.'

They all looked at the ground under Yang, waiting for some sign of movement. A layer of sweat glistened on Inara's brow and upper lip. Licking the salt from her lips, she narrowed her eyes and leant forward. She focused so hard on the valley floor that Jack expected her to clench her fists, or grit her teeth, and then the floor split. Small pockets along the length of the valley floor tore open. Some ruptures were close, others opened up yards away.

'What's happening,' said Bill, jumping back from a patch of vibrating earth.

'I can hear them, they're all so excited,' said Inara, who still only looked at the ground by Yang.

Most of the disturbed patches of ground formed triangles as the dirt rose. A few larger areas shook more violently, throwing up loose stone and shards of metal as far as the huddled group. Running to Inara's side Jack shielded her from the falling debris.

A rabbit with missing ears bounded from the ground first, making Yang jump back from the hole. Its mewling cries, though quieter than the stag's, wrenched at the heart. It jumped around on browned bones. Not much fur or flesh remained. Sitting tenaciously on its skull was a thick thatch of hair, looking like a wig. Flexing its hind legs the rabbit scampered, with a series of awkward jumps, to a wire bush. They watched the fleeing rabbit pass the bush and disappear out of the valley.

Other cries soon rent the morning, taking the place of the departed rabbit. Other rabbits, in varying states of decomposition, left the ground of their dead warren. One unfortunate rabbit dragged itself from its hole. A predator had cracked and gnawed at its bones to get at its marrow, leaving little left of the rabbit. Only a few still had their ears intact, and they stabbed at Jack's heart the most.

'So many rabbits,' said Bill. He shook his head annoyed. 'I can't feel any of them. Not like I could with Black.'

'Your Talent only works on the living.' For now, Jack almost added. Who knew what feats their demons were now capable of? Turning from Bill's disappointment, he followed his wandering shadow as his twin ran after the dead rabbits with a worrisome fervour.

The largest animal since the stag's rebirth scrambled out of its grave. The once bushy tail of the fox, now hung limp and sodden between its trembling legs. It yelped constantly, ignoring the fluttering of a bird who tried to take flight on broken wings.

'Wonderful,' shouted Krimble, just as the stag bolted, knocking him from his feet.

Ignoring the laughs coming from Krimble's savaged throat Jack watched the stag. He saw it no longer trembled as it sped toward the edge of the valley. Dirt rained from its ruined coat in dirty clouds, revealing hair that remained brown.

More animals rose, crowding the valley. A badger, after rising and taking a quick look around, burrowed back into the ground. Farther infield a fawn, retaining its spots, struggled to stay upright on spindly legs. While a pack of small wild dogs snarled at each other from bleached skulls.

WHEN THE DEAD WALK THE WOLD

Yelps, barks, and faint cries filled the morning. None of them wants to be here, reflected Jack. Looking down he saw the strain on Inara's face. 'Stop this Inara,' he pleaded.

She shook her head. 'It's wonderful Jack. I can feel them all. Scared and confused as they are, I'm sure that will pass. They have a chance to live again, to run and explore.'

He could not share her enthusiasm. Stepping around, what he believed was the moving skeleton of a mole; he walked away from his friends. He carried on walking toward the trees that did not move with the wind, ignoring the cries that the wind carried. His shadow remained, stretching behind him on tapered legs, anchoring him to the valley he wanted so desperately to leave.

32. SHADOW MIMES

LIGHT FROM THREE LANTERNS woke Jack from a deep slumber. He stirred, unwilling to leave the sun drenched glade of his dream. When his dream sun turned blue, he prised his eyes open and stared in incredulity at a blue lantern. It sat a few feet from him. A red light also shone to his left, and standing a little farther off, on his opposite side, stood a green beacon. Beside the blue light sat Krimble. The light etched the scars deep on the old man's face, making him appear like a charcoal drawing.

'What's going on?' He rubbed the sleep from his eyes as he rose onto one arm.

'Quiet Ying,' said Bill, 'this is incredible.'

'What's...?'

Disbelieving what he saw, Jack finally took notice of his shadow performing a handstand to his right. Yang also danced to his left. Twisting with ferocious speed, he saw Yang behind him with his arms folded. Three Yangs, how could there be three of him?

'After talking with Yang for awhile, Krimble came up with the idea of lighting the different coloured lanterns,' said Bill. 'When they were lit Yang split into three.'

'You let him talk to my demon.' Outraged anger escaped him in a torrent. 'How could you allow him to use me?'

'I watched him the entire time,' said Bill, defensively. 'I would've stopped him if he tried anything suspicious. You were so tired I didn't want to wake you.'

'You didn't wake me because you knew I wouldn't have allowed Krimble anywhere near me, or my demon.' He jumped to his feet. As though having one troublesome shadow wasn't bad enough, he now had to contend with three. Bending at the waist, the shadow cast in blue, blew Jack's hair over his eyes.

'Did he just blow your hair?' asked Bill.

Ignoring his friend's wonder, Jack turned to the shadow behind him. His heart raced. Yang had always moved things. According to his mother, Yang started picking things up before Jack was old enough to play. He had never felt his shadow's breath. It was cold, like the keening wind on a winter's night. Every time he thought he understood the demon, it did something unexpected.

SHADOW MIMES

'There's more to our Narmacils than we ever imagined,' said Inara.

Looking at the girl cradling a rabbit that only had one ear and a hole in its cheek, sent a second cold chill down his spine.

'I see you've been enjoying the show too,' said Jack. 'Did any of you think to wake me up? What's happening is happening to me not you. And you,' he addressed Krimble for the first time, 'have no right to do this.'

All the blood had left the old man's gums a long time ago, leaving them sallow. A few shown teeth reminded Jack of lone trees sticking out of the mud of the marsh. 'Yang gave me the right. He's tired of you trying your best to get rid of him. At least your friends aren't afraid of what's inside them. The girl is far happier having her pets. It seems, not having your legs isn't that important when you can raise the dead.'

Jack hurt his hand as he struck the zombie in the face, rocking Krimble's head back. He tried to block out the sound of Krimble's laugh as he moved to douse the blue light.

'Ying, don't,' cried Bill. 'Aren't you curious to know what Yang can do?'

'No I'm not.' The last thing he wanted was to find out what else the demon could do; the morning's discoveries had left him shaken and scared.

'He just blew on your neck. All the years he's been with you, you never knew he could do that. What else can he do? If you turn off the light you'll never know.'

'I want him gone Bill, you know how I feel. Why should I be at all interested in what the demon can do?'

'He helped us escape the Marsh House, didn't he? Perhaps he can do something to get us away from the Red Wood.'

Looking at Inara, cradling her pet dead rabbit, Jack said, 'It seems some of us no longer mind it here.'

'You know nothing Jack. You're still the same little boy who wants to hide behind your mother's skirt and ignore what's happening. By letting my Narmacil grow, I've opened myself up to so much. Throughout the wood, I can feel all the animals exploring their new lives.'

'Are they still screaming Inara?'

'You know nothing,' she retorted, but Jack could see his words stung. 'This is Mylo.' She looked down at the rabbit in her lap. 'He died when the Myrms filled in his burrow. He didn't have a chance to live. I've given him a second chance.'

'You've cursed him,' said Jack.

'Is living now a curse?' She threw up her mangled legs. 'Perhaps you're right. Living isn't easy. Sometimes you can't replace what you lose. What I found I could do yesterday, has given me a chance to become more than just a cripple. I can't walk, but if I close my eyes and concentrate, I know what it's like to run like the stag, or climb a tree as though I was a squirrel. Just because you find out

CRIK

something new about yourself, doesn't automatically make it wrong. Why deny yourself a chance to become better? Don't be so scared.'

'After losing contract with Black I no longer know where he is. Can you look through the dead creature's eyes like I can with the animals?' asked Bill.

She shook her head. 'I feel the sensation of running, the thud of the hoof on the ground, the stretching of the limbs, but I don't see what they see.'

'That's a shame; you could've looked for Black and Silver. I worry about them,' said Bill. 'I hope they are alright.'

'I'm sure they're fine,' said Jack.

'How would you know?' asked Bill.

'The Myrms, or Kyla, would've shown us their bodies if they had caught them. The Ghost Walkers want to frighten us, so that we'll do what they want. They are still out there'

'I thought I sensed Black yesterday when Kyla came to us. Only a fleeting touch, but I'm sure it was the ol' dog. I didn't want to say anything, in case I was wrong, and they are dead somewhere out there.'

'They survived Crik Wood without our help,' said Inara. 'They'll be able to look after themselves.'

'Yeah,' agreed Bill with a glint in his eye, 'any Myrm that gets too close to Black will regret it. Silver too, she'd tear out their throats. Isn't that right Krimble.'

Instead of answering, Krimble turned to the Yang highlighted in green. He stumbled closer on legs that shouldn't be able to support him. 'You're a beautiful thing,' he said, reaching out to grip Yang's arm. The shadow didn't flinch as the fingers locked, holding him firm.

'He doesn't let anyone keep hold of him,' said Bill. 'Why isn't he turning to smoke, like he does when I've tried to catch him?'

Moving forward, Jack halted before Yang. Could he grip him too? He had never touched Yang as he would a living person. Although times existed when he had felt Yang, it was more Yang touching him than the other way around. Many times his shadow had wrestled with him, locking his arm behind his back, or tying his legs in an uncomfortable knot. Yet, whenever he attempted to fight back Yang disappeared through his fingers. Firm, unyielding muscle met his probing fingers. The contour of the developing triceps, the curvature of the bicep played out beneath his hand. Everything felt solid to the touch. His twin even shared the pimple on Jack's shoulder. Pinching Yang made his shadow recoil. I hurt him, he thought in wonder. A fierce desire to punch and kick his shadow overcame him. How much pain could he inflict on, what until this moment, had been an incorporeal phantom? An opportunity now existed to show physically how much he despised the deception he had uncovered. Yang mirrored him, no spiky hair, no elongated legs or anvil shaped fists. Only himself, looking so small. Even Krimble, with his bent back, towered over

SHADOW MIMES

them. It would be so easy to strike out, to punch Yang. Oddly, his desire to hurt Yang dissipated now that his shadow was so defenceless. Why couldn't his shadow always just mirror him? Turning, he looked down to discover Bill's outline didn't actually match Bill. Bill was shorter than Jack, yet his shadow stretched along the ground to at least twice his height. Long skinny legs travelled from Bill's stodgy looking ones. Looking as Yang did, showing every curl of hair standing out from Jack's head, revealing his every imperfection was unnatural.

Stepping up, Bill patted Yang on the back, making the shadow stumble forward. 'He feels cold.'

He did. If you left your fingers on Yang for too long, the coldness sank into your bones. Removing his hand from Yang's arm, Jack clenched his fingers into a fist to warm them.

'Of course he isn't warm,' said Inara. 'What shadow do you know that has blood?'

Its reflecting the cold heart of the demon, mused Jack. Everything about the thing hiding in the warmth of his stomach felt insidious. Suddenly the green light vanished, and with it the solid Yang. Looking he saw the Yang highlighted in blue leaning in front of the doused lantern.

'Did he just blow out the light?'

'I think he did,' Inara answered Bill. 'I guess he doesn't like being handled.'

It's showing a weakness. The green light made Yang solid, made him vulnerable. When Jack pinched him, he hurt the demon; the notion that he could wound his shadow quickened his heart. He didn't fail to notice Yang turn and look at him while he pondered over what he now knew. How much did the demon know about him? Not for the first time he questioned whether it could read his thoughts as easily as it changed shape. With that thought in his head, no doubt, if Bill patted his back, Jack would feel as cold as his shadow.

'You scared him,' accused Krimble. 'Prodding and fondling him like a piece of meat at a butcher's shop. You should show him more respect.'

'Didn't you call him a scheming conniving shadow not too long ago?' said Bill. 'Strange how quickly you changed your tune. Could it be, thanks to the Ghost Walkers making us give you access to our Narmacils, that you're trying to befriend them once more?'

'Like you tried in the windowless room,' added Inara, stroking Mylo's surviving ear. 'You'll never get them you know. The Ladies may command us to allow you to remain close, but there are limits to what I'll allow you to do.'

'What power you think you have over me is waning,' said Krimble, edging closer to where Inara sat. 'I called you a bitch, but you can't even be that. What man would ever want to lie with a cripple like you?'

CRIK

Swelling up to thrice his size Yang seized Krimble by the arm and lifted the zombie high into the sky. The cries Krimble made grew faint as Yang took him higher.

'Do you think he'll drop him?' asked Bill.

'I know I would like him to fall,' said Inara. 'The Ghost Walkers' threat remains over us all though. Yang knows he can't do Krimble too much damage, no matter how much we all may wish otherwise.'

'It's a shame it's so dark, I'd like to see him struggle up there. I can't hear him any longer,' said Bill. 'I wonder how high he is.'

Ignoring what Yang did with Krimble, Jack had turned to the sole remaining shadow. Bathed in red light Yang looked more ominous than at any other time he had seen him. 'So what's different about you?' His question only whispered passed his lips, yet he knew Yang heard him. 'What secret does the red light reveal? Is it something you don't want me to know?'

With a finger, Yang beckoned him forward.

Turning, Jack saw Krimble's plight still held his friends attention. With a thunderous sound pounding his ears, he approached Yang. He needed to do this, to find out what the red light did. As Yang enveloped him in a sweep of his dark arms, he wondered about the rain he heard.

33. THE HANGMAN'S NOOSE

SUFFOCATING DARKNESS wrapped Jack. The absence of light did not disturb him as much as the knowledge that the darkness itself was alive.

The sound of rain grew louder, invading the dark, before he felt the raindrops dampen his hair and clothes. First only a few spots hit him, then so much rain came down he felt saturated, clogging his pores like cold wax. The rain filled his senses, making it difficult to breathe as the torrent drove into his face. Raising his hands against the downpour, he spied shades of grey mixed with the black, to reveal hard outlines. They stood square and looming. Everywhere he looked more shapes came into slow focus. At first, the animals appeared as blurred circles and sickles atop defined squares. An owl, larger than any bird he had ever seen, sat looking over his head, its wings folded behind its back in quiet contemplation. Standing with one paw raised stood a wolf and farther back a dog with a stone bone in its mouth. He recognised them at once.

Turning about he came face to face with Yang. His shadow, reaching forward, pinched his arm. Flinching, Jack pulled away. Yang mirrored him; he even held the same arm as Jack. Although they stood the same height, and shared the same width, for the first time Yang, having feet, stood separate from Jack.

'I know these gravestones.' said Jack. 'This is Long Sleep cemetery.' He knew he was right. The owl headstone belonged to Willow Temper, the old woman who left Bill a ton of books when she died.

Lightning lit up the world in a blinding flash. He remembered how Yang had stood in his bedroom, with his hair standing on end during the last electrical storm he had seen. Another lightning bolt lit up the sky.

Looming behind Yang stood another tomb. This burial place was both larger and more ominous than the other graves atop the hill. A hooded figure stood holding aloft a stone noose. The Hangman, he thought with a stab of fear.

'Am I really here?' Could he run down the hill away from the graveyard? If so, what would stop him from sprinting home to surprise his mother? Had Yang brought him home?

Yang shook his head, as a misshapen form walked passed. The smell of earth and rotten vegetables assailed Jack's nostrils. Holding his nose, he looked up at the huge frame of the figure as it approached the hangman's tomb.

CRIK

One huge hand lifted high. Its fingers, appearing more like tree roots than flesh and bone, slipped free from the overhanging sleeve of the white shirt that covered its humped back. Standing only as tall as the Giant's waist Jack felt panicked. Hitherto, the Giant had failed to see him, yet at any moment that could change.

The tomb's stone door shattered in a loud explosion of dust and marble as the Giant brought his hand crashing down. The roots and leaves dangling from the Giant's head shook at the impact. Striding forward, the darkness inside the tomb swallowed the Giant whole.

The rain thrummed around Jack, bouncing as high as his knee. Scared, he remained still, unsure of what to do. Dare he also enter the tomb? Remembering the cramped interior, he knew he would crowd the Giant. Somehow, Yang had brought him back to the night the Giant had buried the egg. By remaining in the rain he won't understand Yang's purpose. Wiping the water from his eyes, he walked over the rubble-strewn entryway.

The lid of the coffin creaked on rusted hinges as the Giant, with clumsy hands, yanked it open. Sound of tearing cloth cut through the air as the Giant's shirt caught on the wooden lid. Watching the white fabric drift into the coffin brought Jack face to face with Mr Hasseltope. He looked fresher than Krimble. The cheeks were sunken, and Mr Hasseltope's eyes were two dark pits above a grin that showed too much teeth; it would not have surprised him if the old hangman sat up.

The same dead fox Jack had noticed the first time he entered the tomb lay curled on Mr Hasseltope. That morning he had carried the egg of the demon in his pocket. He checked to see whether he somehow still had the golden egg. Relief at only finding a smooth pebble and a piece of string left him lightheaded. Lifting the fox from the hangman, the Giant laid down the animal with reverential care. Seeing the hangman in silent repose brought back Grandpa Poulis's words, "He liked to see 'em twitch."

'You should've waited.' The voice came from behind Jack, making him jump.

The Giant twisted around, looking through Jack, with its many eyes, at the newcomer.

Jack gasped as Mr Dash, Long Sleep's grave keeper, entered the tomb.

The grave keeper twirled a set of large keys around his bony hand. 'It's hard with the storm; if you had a bit more light you'd have seen that the door had a keyhole. Now this will stir everyone up tomorrow, that's for damn sure.' The grave keeper shook his head as though he had dropped a pie he had spent two hours preparing and stepped into the crypt. 'I'm guessing, after the initial ruckus, the girls wouldn't want anything to do with this business. The boys on the other hand. He may even be among them. He's smart; I hope he doesn't tie tonight's event with his change in a couple of days.' Mr Dash lit a lantern. 'Mr

THE HANGMAN'S NOOSE

Hasseltope was always good to me,' he said. 'I never sat idle for long when he was about.'

The largest eyes, dotted around the face of the Giant, reflected Mr Dash, yet Jack saw neither he nor Yang in those black orbs.

'Well this is a messy business,' said the grave keeper. 'Best get it done.'

Hunching over, the Giant tore open the dead man's burial shirt. Pulling back his huge hand, a stray finger caught the coffin's red lining. Jack watched as the lining folded to cover the fox. Bloodless, the skin had grown purple and black over the hangman's stomach.

'I'd rather do this inside the tomb than at one of the graves down beside the river,' muttered Mr Dash. 'Dirty business down there. Though blaming the river for washing out the dead folk, always satisfies the curiosity of the children,' he conceded. 'Where is it?'

The roots, covering the Giant's mouth, twitched, making its leaves rattle. Jack found the sound rather harmonious.

Mr Dash nodded. 'Fine.'

Reaching out, the Giant let its hand hover over Mr Hasseltope's stomach. The hangman's bruised abdomen moved, reminding Jack of fish swimming just beneath the surface of water. A bulge formed beneath the suspended hand.

'It's waited a long time,' said Mr Dash.

The Giant's leaves rustled in response.

'I know,' said Mr Dash. 'It had to regain its strength. Still, this one has taken its merry time.'

The hangman's stomach burst, releasing gases that had lain trapped for years. Craning forward Jack gasped as he saw a golden egg rise from the ruptured innards. Both Mr Dash and Jack gagged on the foul smell, while the Giant continued to peer down at the egg. Jack started to retreat, when a firm hand held his back. Turning he saw Yang barred his way.

The egg continued to rise, revolving as it gained height. A flap of skin had roped itself across the circumference of the egg. It rose higher and then the skin fell back with a plop. Jack paled at the sound. Patiently the Giant waited for the rising egg to touch his hand, when it did, a light flashed across the Giant's palm. The light faded to reveal, zigzagging across the egg, a silver line.

'We can't leave him here like this,' said Mr Dash looking down at Mr Hasseltope. 'The tomb has kept our old executioner rather fresh all these years.' The grave keeper stroked his chin as he contemplated what to do. 'You'd best carry him to the river. The water will carry him away, or the fish will gorge themselves before any of the kids can discover him.'

After placing the egg in the sack, the Giant hoisted Mr Hasseltope easily over its shoulder.

A soft thud drew Jack's attention to the floor, where he discovered the hangman's noose lying on the cracked marble. Mr Dash hunched down to

CRIK

retrieve the rope. To Jack it seemed as though the grave keeper wanted to keep the killing tool, but then, with a delicate touch, he lay the noose on the silk pillow.

If Mr Dash knew about the Giant and the demon, who else knew? The Village Elder, Mr Gasthem, with all his bugs scurrying through the village, he must know. Who else knew about the Giant fetching demons into the village? His neighbour Miss Mistletoe? Perhaps Dr Threshum, who knew more about the inner workings of a body than anyone else. With all his stories, could Grandpa Poulis remain oblivious to this most damning secret? Would his mother keep this from him? Not wanting to believe his suspicions, he nevertheless suspected her. Violated by the thought of someone he trusted bringing the egg into his home, when he was a baby, made him want to cry. Let them all love their inner demons, he thought, gritting his teeth until his jaw ached. Refusing to allow the creature's supplicating Talent to beguile him, gave him strength to fight his unwelcome guest.

Turning from the empty coffin, Yang walked through Jack. Shuddering, as though he had jumped into a lake during November, Jack gasped in shock. Standing close, his shadow had pulled back its eyelids, fixing him with golden eyes, dissected by a jagged silver line. The shine of the eyes defined Yang's cheeks, giving them form for the first time.

'This is who you are,' said Jack. 'Hatched from an egg the Giant brought to my house. You aren't my shadow.' He looked down. 'How can you be, you have feet and the ability to do what you want. Everything you do is what you want,' he sighed. 'You're your own creature, to go and do as you please. Why don't you leave me alone? I don't want you. All my life, you and those who know in my village, have used my ignorance.' Clutching the coffin with a cold hand, he continued, 'When I die, will the grave keeper meet the Giant in my tomb? To give an unsuspecting kid a troublesome shadow so that you may live. How many other boys and girls have you lived in before me? Will there be others after me?' His voice broke with emotion. Would the cycle ever end? 'I call you Yang, what did the others name you? Black, like Bill's wolf, or Inky, or perhaps you were always so bothersome they just wanted you to Disappear.' He laughed. 'I should start calling you Go Away instead of Yang. What do you think?'

As the lightning lit up the night, Yang pointed to the far wall of the tomb. Drawn on the stone was the drawing Jack had first seen with Bill.

'I've seen it before.'

Yang insisted, pointing at the drawing.

Crudely drawn, the worn sketch had much of its prior detail rubbed away. Cracks had intruded on the pictures, cutting the drawn boy in the first picture in two. The drawings remained as Jack had recalled. First, the boy standing

THE HANGMAN'S NOOSE

amongst the trees waving, the second showed the arrival of the demon and the boy's fear. 'There's nothing new here,' he said.

Yang stabbed the final image with an elongated finger.

Passing over the two pictures, he settled on the third image of the boy happily carrying the demon on his shoulder. 'I told you,' said Jack, 'I remember seeing this before.' Then, through Yang's finger, he saw something he had missed the first time he had been here. On the ground, waving up at him lay the shadow of the boy. The boy had his arms at his side. Whoever this boy was, he had also had a living shadow.

'Is that you?'

The golden stare did not flicker as Yang continued to study Jack. Then when Jack was about to repeat the question, Yang gave him a wave.

Taking a hurried step back, Jack tripped against the coffin and fell inside with a scream.

Krimble's angry calls for Yang to release him, replaced the sound of the rain against the walls of the tomb.

'I don't know why you're screaming so much,' said Bill, 'Yang could've let you drop when you were up there amongst the clouds.'

Wiping furiously at his eyes, Jack found his skin was no longer damp from the rain. Dumbfounded, he looked around at the glade in the Wold, where Inara and Bill crowded Krimble, who Yang held upside-down by his shoe. The Giant, Mr Dash, and the tomb, on that long ago night, had vanished.

Looking behind him, he saw the Yang highlighted by the red lantern light waving at him.

34. THE GHOSTS AMONGST US

Soot stained lanterns, with coloured glass, lay strewn at Jack's feet. Rubbing away his sleep with a hurried hand, he sat up. Cursing the sun glinting off the red glass, he turned aside to find a herd of deer surrounding them. That they were dead didn't seem to affect anyone, but him. The one Bill chose to pet at least had fur, some roaming the field were little more than skeletons.

'You've been busy,' he said to Inara.

'It's not that hard to know where they're buried,' said the girl, holding Mylo close. 'Now that I know what I'm capable of it's only a matter of concentrating.'

He chose not to ask whether they had screamed like the others; he already knew the answer. He noted a number of fawns amongst the deer. They remained close to their mothers, who in turn kept a wary vigil. Did the dead fear predators? A fox had risen, and no doubt other predators since then. Although the open cavities under them suggested the dead didn't eat, other instincts must govern them.

A small shape hurried amongst the returned denizens of the Red Wood. Watching, Jack spotted a flash of gold. He tried to catch another glimpse of the precious metal as it danced between the hooves of the dead animals. It raced amongst the deer so fast he only saw a glimmer of gold.

'The Ghost Walkers will want to know where these have all come from.' Jack raised his gaze. 'I'm surprised they haven't already investigated.' After experimenting with his demon, he didn't want to tell the others what Yang had shown him last night. Still fuming at their lack of caution, he tried to put their betrayal to the back of his mind. What Yang could do scared him. How powerful were their demons? He could try to hide the full extent of his Talent from the Ghost Walkers, whereas Inara's power was everywhere. 'Will the Ladies look kindly on having a herd of dead animals running through their metal wood?'

'They're dead themselves,' Inara pointed out.

Shaking his head Bill said, 'No they're not. Just because they leave their bodies doesn't mean they died during the night. It's just their Talent, like Yang, or me controlling Black.'

'But they are dead,' said Inara. 'The villagers killed their bodies while they walked in the woods. They hung them from the tree before they could return and wake, leaving them with nowhere to go. The Ladies were once Ghost Walkers, now they are only ghosts. I don't think they'll object to seeing animals return to the Wold, do you?'

Long Sleep cemetery had many graves. Some, like Mr Hasseltope, rested within tombs, some dotted the hill, with poems written on headstones, to mark their place. Another, older site, lay within a basin of dirt, nothing grew over those graves. Despite time having faded the chalk on a single standing stone set amongst the clearing, the words "Ghost Walker", still declared its damnation. The Village of Crik had always had secrets, Jack thought with disgust. Did his mother know about the demon? That question haunted him. He pictured her sitting over his cot, humming a lullaby, while the Giant laid a golden egg on his blanket. Did she wait to see it hatch? Had she seen the demon wriggle into his toothless mouth?

'They smell, and each one of them tried their damnedest to squish me under their hooves.'

Looking down Jack saw Gold Tail. Wrapping his tail about himself, the mouse didn't look happy. 'A fox chased me,' said the mouse. 'Lucky for me it limped, or I would've had a very short life. Everywhere I go I see more animals. I spent last night defending my hole from unwanted intruders. The rabbits are the worse; you'd think they'd make their own burrows instead of trying to kick me out of my home.'

'Perhaps you're living in what used to be their home,' Inara told the mouse, who sat close to her on a rock. 'I'm sure there're plenty of holes for everyone.'

'I don't care about plenty of holes, I want mine. It's been my home all my life; I'm not going to give it up to some filthy rabbit.' That the mouse had only lived for a day went unsaid.

'They'd have found other places to burrow by now,' said Inara.

'I hope so,' said Gold Tail. 'I get cranky if I don't get any sleep.'

'You get cranky, come on, you're the most even-tempered mouse I've ever met,' said Bill, shifting his glasses. 'In fact, I'd go as far to say that you're always delightful company. You never whinge, moan, or complain about anything.'

Gold Tail's tin whiskers twitched. 'That's right. I don't moan or complain, I just point things out. Like how the morning stinks of rotting meat. It's enough to dull my tail.'

'Talking of rotting meat, where's Krimble?' said Bill. 'I haven't seen him at all. Do you think Yang's stunt finally rid us of the old git?'

He probably ran to the Ghost Walkers to tell them what has happened, thought Jack. He knew the Ladies would be coming. Not wishing to have five Yangs around him next time he awoke, made him want to hide the lanterns before they arrived. His shadow sat astride a deer, riding the animal through the middle of the vale. The deer carried Yang so far he appeared as a small speck, yet his legs still connected them. Unlike last night, he mused, remembering the dark feet of his twin.

'Why don't you turn the dead animals against the Myrms,' suggested Bill. 'I bet, after what the Myrms did here, that this entire place is one giant graveyard. I'd like to see those brutes stand up against thousands of undead animals.'

Her fingers thrummed on the ground as Inara listened. 'These woods had a few packs of wolves,' she said. 'Perhaps a couple of lone bears made their home amongst the trees. Most are small rodents and deer; no good in a fight.'

'Make them,' said Bill. 'We need to escape. I want to get Black and Silver and leave this Red Wood for good.'

'There is no point,' she said. 'Armoured as they are, the Myrms won't be troubled by anything I can raise here. Besides, I am not sure of my limits.'

'Well we have to think of something,' said Bill. 'I don't fancy growing old here like Huckney.' Slapping the rump of the nearest deer sent the startled animal running down the vale. 'We only have Justice's word that the Blackthorn Tunnel is the only way in or out of the Wold. Inara, you told us you could feel the animals running through the Red Wood. If they won't fight, then send them out to search for other ways to leave this place.'

Jack watched as Inara shook her head, fanning her face with her dirty, blonde hair. 'I share the sensation of running with the animals, of feeling the wind rush across my face and the stretch of their limb, but I don't see what they see. I told you before, you can do that with the animals you control, that's not something I can do.'

'Try reaching out for Black,' said Jack. 'He's out there somewhere.'

'I'll try again,' said Bill.

Closing his eyes, Bill sank to the ground. His brow furrowed in concentration as he reached out with his mind. Jack wasn't surprised to see sweat beading Bill's face. Bill's eyes shifted beneath his closed lids, as he searched for the only animals still alive in the entire Wold.

'Nothing,' Bill finally gasped. 'I couldn't feel them anywhere.'

Knowing how disappointed he felt, Jack could only imagine the dejection Bill experienced. He missed having the added safety of the wolves. 'Try again later,' he said. 'They're probably too far away for you to feel.'

'Don't worry Bill. I'm sure Jack is right.'

'It's alright for you two,' said Bill. 'You have your Talents with you. What can I offer the Ladies to stop them taking me to the Hanging Tree? We need to scram.'

'If they try to take you, they'll have to take me with you,' said Jack. The thought of the Ghost Walkers marching them to the tree with the bowed branches wasn't exactly appealing, but he meant every word. He wouldn't let them take Bill away from him.

'And me,' said Inara. 'We won't let anyone face the Ghost Walkers alone.'

THE GHOSTS AMONGST US

'I preferred it when the wolves were hunting us,' said Bill, falling back against the rough ground. 'At least we knew what they wanted to do with us. My grandfather told me a story once about a little boy who kept a hamster in his room. Everyday the boy fed and cared for his pet. He started feeding the hamster cake instead of seeds. Fruit cake, even cake smothered in chocolate. Eventually, the hamster grew so fat he stopped running on his wheel. The day he stopped spinning the wheel, the boy took him out of his cage and fed him to his cat.'

'Nice story,' said Inara.

'I just hope we can sneak away before our wheel stops,' said Jack.

'I'd give that cat indigestion,' said Gold Tail. 'Though I'm glad the lummox is away tinkering in the wood. I saw him carting away huge shards of metal before the rabbits appeared. He'd no doubt enjoy making a cat with that hammer of his.'

Having the new denizens taking over the Wold won't please Huckney. The Red Wood was his home, and in one night, they had changed it. Jack wondered whether animals had still roamed the Wold when the Myrms brought Huckney and his father here.

'We've got a visitor,' said Bill. He looked toward the Hanging Tree, telling Jack before he looked that the Ghost Walkers were on their way. Turning he saw a solitary Ghost Walker drifting over the coarse ground. Her light burned a deep amber, with wisps of yellow and blue along the ends of her floating dress.

'I hope that's not Kyla,' said Jack. He looked down at the discarded lamps, certain the Ghost Walker would see them.

As the figure grew closer, they recognised Justice. She held aloft a squirming rabbit. The rabbit, in worse repair than Mylo, looked a horror of rotted flesh and bone. Even with its wasted muscles the rabbit continued to kick out at the Ghost Walker, something Jack couldn't blame the critter for doing.

'These things surround the Rainbow Lake,' said Justice, reaching them. 'Hundreds of them hopping around, making a nuisance of themselves. This loathsome creature,' she held out the rabbit with no ears, 'is incapable of hopping, it instead drags itself around. They seem to seek something; what that is no one knows. Perhaps a home that isn't there anymore.'

'A home taken away from them,' said Inara.

Jack held his breath, waiting for Justice's reaction to Inara's rebuke. The Ghost Walker's smile didn't lessen his anxiety. In fact, his nerves tightened further as Justice's smile spread.

'No doubt they had a warren around the lake many years ago,' agreed Justice. 'Times, however, change, and with it those who once ran amongst the grass and trees will find themselves – displaced. The Wold is no place for rabbits and deer.' She looked around at the stumbling herd. 'This tin mouse is what the Wold has become.'

CRIK

'The rabbits tried kicking me out of my home last night,' repeated Gold Tail.

'As they would,' agreed Justice. 'They remember, but they don't understand.'

If Inara could stand she would have shouted in Justice's face as she said, 'You killed them when you came here. This entire place has suffered under your control. You took away the trees, and the grass these animals needed to survive. With the Hedge Wall surrounding the wood, they had nowhere to run. Those who died an unnatural death at your hands deserve a second chance at life.'

Justice's lingering smile wriggled like a worm caught in the sun. 'This is no way for them to live, child. They can't eat or feel their hearts beat as they run.'

'Do you?' asked Inara.

'Your fathers killed us.'

'And you killed them,' said Inara pointing an accusing finger at the surrounding deer. 'Do you want me to return them to the graves you dug for them? Will that be enough to hide your shame? You're no better than those men who took your body to hang from the tree.'

'Inara,' cautioned Bill.

'No Bill, she needs to hear this,' said Inara. 'You made the Red Wood. There's no life here, just an imitation of what lies beyond the Hedge. Everything here is cold and harsh. The rust may paint the Wold red, but the blood is on your hands.'

'Look at this rabbit,' said Justice, lifting the rabbit higher. 'Without any ears does it hear? Half its ligaments have decayed, making it impossible for it to run. Its eyes are sunken. Do you envisage this as life?'

'The Red Wood is a graveyard,' said Inara, scratching Mylo's one remaining ear. Jack noticed the rabbit leant into her hand. Did the rabbit enjoy having its ear stroked? 'There're thousands of residents under our feet,' she continued to say. 'You wanted me to use my power, and so I have. I'll continue to use it. I don't intend to stop until all those killed by you, and your pets, have returned.'

Justice laughed. 'You are a delicious child, to accuse me of doing the unnatural. Of creating a world around me that shouldn't exist. Yes, the trees have gone, replaced with hard metal and twisted spires that offer little warmth. Huckney creates animals, like the swans on the lake and the tin mouse at your side. Yet you have gone one-step further. Raising your captor is a harsh punishment. Watching him decay with a pitiless heart you ignored his pleas of mercy; just as you overlook the screams of these tortured animals. Keep them around you. Enjoy the sights and sounds as the deer stumble and fall in the dust. Laugh as the rabbits lie down and wait for a death that will not return. Welcome Inara, you are truly at home here in the Red Wood.'

The answering smile from Inara was just as cold as the Ghost Walker's. Jack found himself wondering, as he saw that mirthless grin, and not for the first time, whether the girl he had rescued from the Marsh House was insane.

35. ANGRY WORDS

THE MOON STILL BATHED the ground in a silver glow when Jack ran to where Inara screamed. She shook, gripping her blanket tightly beneath her chin, unaware that he stood over her.

'Inara?' He shook her shoulder.

Bill came over to them, his round face, a second moon above him. 'What's upset her?' he asked. 'Is she having another nightmare?'

'I don't know,' said Jack. 'Her eyes are open, but she's not seeing us.' He demonstrated by waving his hand before Inara's unblinking eyes. 'She's trembling.' Holding her, he could feel her body violently shaking.

Inara cried out, her face contorted in agony.

Cringing, Bill covered his mouth. 'Look at her.'

Jack saw his friend's hands shake. Another cry, almost a shriek of pain tore from her mouth. Feeling her body tense against him, she then jerked backward out of his grasp and landed hard on the stone strewn ground. She writhed, twisting the blanket around her body.

'Help me hold her,' Jack called, gripping her shoulders. 'If she keeps moving like this, she'll tear herself open on the rocks.' He couldn't believe her strength; even with Bill's help, he had a job to hold her still.

'Her cries are horrible,' said Bill. 'What's happening to her?'

She spat unintelligible words at them through gritted teeth. Another spasm contorted her body. Her ruined legs kicked out feebly, smacking Jack's arm. He didn't notice until then that Yang had thrown himself across Inara's midsection. The weak light didn't give his shadow enough strength to hold her firm.

'Teeth, I can feel them....'

Jack almost let go as he heard her tired strained words.

'Make 'em stop,' she cried.

'What's happening to her?' Bill, awakened so suddenly, did not have time to put on his glasses. Without them, he looked younger. Both boys watched, caught in hopeless inaction.

What was Inara feeling? Pain spread from her, making Jack's fingers tingle. Hot and clammy sweat waxed her skin, making holding her difficult. Her cries rose into a heart-wrenching scream.

CRIK

'Keep her quiet,' said Bill. 'I don't want the Ladies coming over to investigate.'

'How're we going to keep her quiet, when we don't know what she's going through?'

'Put your hand over her mouth.'

Looking at him in aghast, Jack said, 'I'm not going to do that.' Her next scream was louder. When Bill put his hand over Inara's mouth, stifling her scream, he didn't argue.

'She's crying. I can feel her tears on my hand.'

He didn't need Bill to tell him, he had seen her tears glistening in the moonlight.

Suddenly, Bill let go of Inara. A scream spilled out into the cold night as she tore from Jack's grasp.

'Bill, what do you think you're doing? Help me.'

Sitting back, Bill looked out into the Red Wood. At first Jack thought his friend was about to start screaming like Inara. What is going on?

'I can feel him,' said Bill.

'She's hurting Bill, come back here and help me.'

'You don't understand Ying,' said Bill. 'Black is alive. He's out there.'

'That's great Bill, but we have to help Inara now.'

The girl's struggles abruptly stopped. She still breathed hard beneath Jack, and Yang stayed stretched over her stomach.

'I've stopped him eating,' said Bill.

'What?'

'Black had caught the stag,' said Bill. 'The animal drew Black, bringing him close enough for me to feel him.'

Realisation dawned as a horrified expression twisted Bill features. Do you think Inara was inside the stag when Black caught it? Was she feeling Black's teeth when he bit into the stag?'

'Inara,' said Jack, holding her close, not waiting for Bill to respond. 'Inara, it's okay, Bill has taken control of Black. Inara.'

The pained look on the girl's face slowly abated, leaving her exhausted and drenched in sweat. Her breath rasped through cracked lips. Slowly, she raised her hand to hide her sobs.

Jack wanted to turn his head while she wept. She had gone through too much already, without having to experience any more suffering. His mother always had a knack of making everything better with a touch and a soft word. Although he didn't share his mother's nurturing touch, he still patted Inara's shoulder to let her know he was close.

'He's starving,' said Bill. 'I don't think Black has fed for days. Despite the stag having only a little meat left on its bones, Black couldn't resist the meal.'

ANGRY WORDS

'I know Bill. It's alright,' said Jack. Inara felt everything. That she had experienced the wolf's jaws clamp down to eat the stag, twisted his bowels into tight cramping knots.

'Why didn't she just leave the stag when Black caught it?' asked Bill.

'I couldn't, the attack caught me by surprise.' Inara sucked in a deep quivering breath. 'I like to run with the stag; because I can't,' she said. 'When inside the stag I feel exhilarated, when it leaps over dirty streams, or outruns the smaller deer and foxes I'm more alive than ever.' She took a moment to collect herself. Refusing to lower her hand from her raw eyes she said, 'It happened so fast. Sensing danger the stag's momentum faltered. Fearing, perhaps a Myrm, the stag veered to the left; Black leapt from cover tearing out its rear leg. Hamstrung, it still tried in vain to flee. I shared its terror, its pain. The intensity of the attack took over, stopping me from thinking. All I could do as Black bit the stag's throat was gag as I fought for breath. He didn't release his hold until Silver came...' Inara's mouth crumpled up as a fresh wave of tears took over.

Smoothing her arm, Jack said, 'It's over Inara, you're back safe with us.'

'It's not over though Jack,' she said. 'The stag is still alive. They are eating something that will not die.'

The realisation of what was happening somewhere in the Red Wood hit Jack. The stag, being already dead, didn't draw in breath; it wouldn't die like a normal animal. It would experience the torture of the wolf attack until nothing remained but bone.

'Let it die,' said Bill. 'I've stopped Black from eating. But I can't stop Silver too.'

Inara shook her head. 'I have to slip into the stag to turn it off.'

Turn it off, like gas in a lantern, thought Jack.

'Take Black away from the stag,' Jack told Bill.

'He's starving,' said Bill. 'The stag hasn't much meat on it, but some meat is better than none.'

'Do it Bill,' said Jack.

Bill shook his head, ignoring Jack's deepening frown. 'The stag is dead, it shouldn't be here. My wolf is alive and needs to feed. I won't let him starve.'

'Bill...'

'No, let him eat,' said Inara. Her drawn face became unyielding. 'Part of me is in every creature I bring back. They exist only as vague passing sensations. By concentrating on any one of them, I can jump into them, take control, or share their awareness. My Talent is growing; there is more I can do with my Narmacil. Controlling two, or more animals, is easy, and if I was to push myself, I am sure I could inhabit every creature raised in the Wold. Only,' she paused, to draw in a shaky breath, 'where those animals, who I only share a surface connection with, can come to harm without hurting me, those creatures I fully inhabit relay

CRIK

everything back. If I can't suppress that I will not be able to jump into another animal.'

'What're you saying Inara?' asked Jack. His mouth had lost all moisture as he predicted her answer.

'I will control it,' she said.

'Control the stag,' cried Bill. 'You can't, they are still eating.'

'I must find a way to shut off the pain. To set up a barrier between me and the hurt the animal is going through, or it will take away a Talent that makes me whole again.'

'Krimble...'

'Damn him Bill. He only unlocked our gifts, showed us some of what we are capable of. There is more we can do, and we don't need his help to find it. I'm returning to the stag.'

'No,' Jack began, when Inara stopped him with a look.

'This time I'm prepared, I won't be caught off guard. If it gets too much for me, Bill can stop the wolves. I must try.' Without further discussion, she closed her eyes and grimaced.

Watching in horrified silence, Jack saw her hands clench as jolts of fresh pain slammed into her.

'Bill,' he whispered.

'She told me not to stop the wolves.'

'Don't you dare,' Inara said through tight lips. A moment later, she gasped, wiping stubbornly at fresh tears that trickled down her cheeks. 'I'm in the stag. It is scared. My presence is soothing him.' She grunted.

Jack tightened his grip on her arm.

Her face relaxed. 'Although Black and Silver are still eating, by directing the stag's consciousness away from his body, into his mind, I can shut off the pain.' Long moments passed in silence. 'I'm aware of the bites, but they no longer hurt me or the stag. Taking control has freed the animal from any pain.' Frequently she tossed her head to the side as though she smelt a foul odour, but she never screamed. At last, closing her eyes, she said, 'I'm sorry you had to suffer, it is over now. Thank you for letting me run with you.'

Jack felt embarrassed hearing Inara's last words to the stag. He felt as though he eavesdropped on a private conversation. Standing away from her, he looked up to the moon. It looked the same as when he stared at it from his bedroom window, only now it seemed colder. An uncaring eye, set high in the sky. Another night it will wink at him. When it did, he would tip his head, as though meeting a long known, but untrustworthy, acquaintance.

'I knew the Myrms wouldn't catch Black,' whispered Bill. 'I knew it.'

'Now you control Black again, don't let him go,' said Jack. 'We need the wolf if we are to escape the Wold.'

ANGRY WORDS

'What can Black do against the Myrms?' asked Bill. 'I won't sacrifice him in a hopeless fight.'

'He can carry Inara,' snapped Jack. 'We can't stay here. We live on the whim of the Ghost Walkers. Inara upset Justice. The Ghost Walker may now listen to Krimble's poison. If Justice heeds him, as she now might, we will hang.'

'Send Black to the Hedge Wall,' urged Inara, still hurting from her ordeal. 'Have him look for a way out. The Blackthorn Tunnel can't be the only escape.'

'Yes, of course,' said Bill, eager to please. 'I'll look for a gap in the wall. There'll be another exit. I'll do it now.'

Exhausted, Inara slumped to the floor. She stared blankly into the valley. Jack let her be, unsure how to engage her. Off to his left Bill took up position to listen and learn from the wolf. A serene expression overcame Bill, now that he was once more in contact with Black. He sat upright, highlighted by the silver light of the cruel moon. All night he concentrated on his wolf.

The ground stuck pins in Jack every time he moved, and yet Bill had not fidgeted all night. Yang, roused by dawn's arrival, sat beside Bill, mirroring the boy's posture. His shadow spied on everything they did. Turning his shoulder and mind from Yang, Jack wondered about the blacksmith. Huckney had not made an appearance in days. Gold Tail told them the blacksmith had taken large sheets of metal into the Red Wood. Liking Huckney, he hoped the blacksmith was safe. Would he come with them when they made their escape?

Rousing herself, Inara visibly shook off her fatigue as she addressed Bill. 'Has Black found anything yet?'

Bill shook his head. 'Nothing so far. Black flowers cover the hedge, as they did within the tunnel. Where they don't grow, deadly thorns sprout like tangled hair. I took Black to the top of a large hill; even tilting his head back, I could not see where the wall ended. It is so huge I doubt it ever ends. He's now skirting the hedge to the east.' He pointed off into the distance.

'Have you seen Huckney?' asked Jack.

'I heard ringing; it sounded like his hammer, from within a deep valley. Whether that was him, I don't know. Not wanting to risk running into any Myrms, I changed direction.'

'Probably for the best that we don't see the blacksmith again,' said Inara. 'We don't want him getting into trouble with the Ghost Walkers once we escape.'

'He could escape with us,' said Jack.

Inara shook her head. 'He won't come. This place isn't perfect, but it's his home. Would he leave what he helped to create? I don't think he will. He won't leave Gold Tail, Herm, or any of the others behind.'

'He'll help us,' said Bill. 'He gave us apples to eat, didn't he?'

CRIK

The memory of choking on the fruit brought tears to Jack's eyes. 'We can't tell him anything,' he said, keenly feeling his own disappointment. 'If he doesn't know of our escape, the Ghost Walkers can't accuse him of helping us.'

'Hush,' said Bill, waving his arm. 'Black sees something.'

'What?' asked Jack.

Looking cross, Bill said, 'What does hush mean to you? Ask questions. There're two Ladies in front of Black. They haven't seen him or Silver. I'm trying to hear what they're saying.'

Jack found himself leaning forward, straining to hear something that he couldn't possibly hear. With intense curiosity, he moved closer to Bill. Yang followed, his ear was the size of a dinner plate.

Listening to a conversation taking place miles from where Bill sat made the chubby boy pensive. His lips moved, articulating the words he overheard.

'Come on Bill, what're they saying?' asked Jack, tired of trying to lip read.

'It's not good,' said Bill. A bead of perspiration ran from his hairline over his cheekbone. 'I don't recognise either of them. Both are taller than Justice, with a strong red light obscuring their faces. One called the other a "Red Sister", and both carry a wooden staff with bones tied to its length. Black heard the clattering of the bones before he saw the Ladies. He's right to be scared of them; Silver too is lying low. Her nose is in the dirt. They're arguing about us.'

'Is it about the animals?' asked Inara.

'That's only part of it,' answered Bill. 'They don't like us being here. They think Justice was wrong by imprisoning us.'

'So they want us to go,' said Jack in a hurried whisper. 'They can help us leave. If they let us go, there's no chance of us returning.'

Bill shook his head. 'No Ying,' he said, 'they want to take us to the Tree to kill us. Our coming has convinced them that they aren't safe.'

'Why?' asked Jack.

'We're from Crik Village. They are angrier than even Kyla. They are biting off their words. They mistrust anyone outside the Wold. They talk about protecting those within the Red Wood. We aren't safe here.'

'I thought they wanted us for our Talents,' said Inara.

Yang nodded.

'They are angry, they don't want the animals in the Red Wood,' said Bill. 'They say they made the Wold how they wanted it. Every living thing reminds them of the past. That's why they uprooted the trees. They don't want any reminders of the time they were alive. Oh my, they called Justice a foolish little girl. How old are they? We're in trouble Ying; we've got to get out of here.'

'We can't just up and go,' said Inara. 'Without the Syll the creatures in the tunnel will tear us to pieces.' She rubbed her arms. 'They would plant those flowers on us.'

'We'll die if we wait here,' said Bill.

ANGRY WORDS

'What's the point of rushing from one death to another,' she argued.

'Look at Yang,' said Bill.

All turned to see Yang standing away from the group with his arm stretching toward the east. His finger stretched until it disappeared into the distance.

'Isn't that where the wolves are?' asked Inara.

'Close,' said Bill. 'They passed that way a few hours ago. There's no way through the hedge; I looked.'

'There's something down there,' said Inara. 'Do you think Yang wants us to go that way?'

Yang nodded, and then clapped.

'You want to trust him?' asked Jack. 'A demon is telling us to follow him, and you want to go with him?'

'We've been through this a hundred times Jack,' said Inara. 'Yang isn't a demon. If your Narmacil is telling you we need to go in that direction then I'm going.'

'How? You can't walk, and neither of us is strong enough to carry you.'

'Then I'll crawl,' said Inara. 'I'm not staying here any longer.'

'Bring a deer over, you can ride that,' said Bill.

'We can all ride one,' she said. 'Yang, can you bring us three of the strongest deer from the herd.'

While Yang spread out through the herd to capture them mounts Jack sat down. 'How can we outrun the Myrms on the backs of animals that are years dead,' he said. 'I want to leave here too, but its suicide to leave without a plan.'

'We followed you into the Red Wood, Jack,' said Inara. 'It's your turn to follow us out.'

'Shouldn't we at least wait until dark?'

Inara shook her head. 'The Ghost Walkers seem more active during the night, so why wait?'

'Besides,' said Bill, 'I don't fancy riding into a rusty shard. I want to see what's in front of me.'

The three deer Yang brought to them at least had meat on their bones. One only had one eye; the deer given to Jack had none, and its dirty skull poked through loose fur. Yang lifted Inara onto the fittest animal, which sported an impressive array of antlers. Grabbing a clump of fur, she righted herself.

'This is crazy,' said Jack. He smacked his mount and a cloud of dust and dirt filled the air around him, making him cough. 'All the Myrms need to do to find us is follow the cloud of dirt.'

'Where's Mylo?' Bill asked, looking around for Inara's pet rabbit.

'He ran off during the night,' she said. 'I suppose to find a home.' She looked worried.

CRIK

We are planning on running for our lives, and a dead rabbit has her concerned. Jack shook his head. I must be crazy. He vaulted onto the deer. He expected the deer to collapse under him, but the animal took his weight.

'We have to hold onto their necks,' said Bill, when his deer trotted forward. 'If we don't, we'll fall off as soon as we get going.'

Great, thought Jack, circling his arm around the decayed throat of the dead animal. He had the maddening urge to cough and sneeze, as the musty smell of the rotted fur assailed his nostrils.

'Well let's not wait around.' Inara smacked her mount, making the deer run forward.

'They'll kill us for sure if they capture us,' said Jack.

Bill, looking over at him, gave a tight nod. 'I guess they will. Then you'd best not get caught.' He followed Inara.

Sighing, Jack dug his heels into the exposed bones of his mount. With Yang holding onto his back, he followed the others, sneezing as the wind carried the dust back into his face.

36. STAMPEDE

WITH THE DUST BILLOWING off the deer, showing no sign of abating, Jack believed his coughing fit would never end. Added to that, the jostling motion of the deer's awkward run almost dismounted him at every turn. Both he and Bill struggled to keep hold of their mount's necks; ahead Inara laughed with abandon.

The other deer had scattered before them as they started their escape. Peeling away from the startled herd, Inara led them eastward. Ahead the rusted foliage that bordered the barren valley grew to become a foreboding barrier.

'Come on,' cried Inara, eager to leave the valley.

They easily avoided the towering metal trees, yet the smaller plants, tore at the running deer, scoring their flesh with short barbs and bundles of wire wool. Watching a daisy with razor sharp petals slice into his mount's hoof, Jack could only marvel at the beast's tenacity. Despite the obstacles, the swift deer carried them through the Red Wood. Inara laughed loudest when her deer leapt a copper bush, or one of the few red streams running like arteries throughout the Wold. Looking behind, Jack could no longer see the valley. Deliberating whether leaving their prison was the best course of action, and coming up with no answer; he swung forward, knowing the need for haste.

Inara led them into a grove of silver oaks. The orderly rows of trees allowed the deer to run faster, slipping passed the giants with ease. Silver trunks rose cathedral-like around them, shepherding them farther away from the Hanging Tree and their captors. Even Jack's coughs became hushed as they threaded their way down the long corridors. Unsettled by the unnatural neat rows, Jack kept his gaze averted. Where was the diversity in this quiet wood? They moved in silence, only an occasional directional arm from Yang broke the monotony of the ride.

In time, they cleared the oaks and stumbled upon a monstrous beast with a bronze horn rising from a large head. The immense size of its body, supported by four sturdy iron legs, brought the deer up short, halting their run. Gnawing at a tin plant, the horned creature stared at them with deep-set steel eyes. It was in no hurry to finish its meal, chewing slowly it grinded the metal between blunt teeth. Under Jack, his deer pranced nervously as the metal beast snorted through its nostrils, making the sound of a blacksmith's bellows.

CRIK

'Ahh, you cannot beat a bit of tin in your diet,' said the horned beast, after swallowing its meal. 'And I thought Huckney was squishy looking. You three would not be able to dent my hide with a hammer. What brings you to my grove? Speak quickly; I want to finish my breakfast.'

Jack wanted to speak; only his tongue had glued itself to the roof of his mouth. Thankfully, Bill rescued the moment by saying, 'You're a rhinoceros.'

'I have never met anyone who knew what I am. Some call me a unicorn.' The rhino sniggered. 'I wonder whether my winning smile makes them think I am something I am not.' Grey metal slabs, lumped on its gums, showed as the rhino opened its mouth.

'I've seen pictures of you in a book,' said Bill. 'I thought you didn't exist. Like dragons and,' he paused, looking awkward.

'Unicorns,' laughed the rhino. 'I am prettier than a unicorn, do you not agree?'

'Huckney made you,' said Bill.

'No doubt from the same book you read. I have no way of knowing whether there are any others like me,' said the rhino. 'If they do exist, they are not here in the Wold. Beyond the Hedge Wall perhaps – I do not know.'

'What're you doing all the way out here by yourself?' asked Inara.

'Trying to enjoy my breakfast,' replied the rhino. 'I have seen more squishy things during the last few days. Rising from the ground, they interrupt my mealtimes. They do not talk to me. I trampled one by mistake. Being so very small, I did not notice it until I felt the crack of bones beneath my hoof. When I stepped away, the little thing I stepped on, did not hop like the others, only dragged itself away. Watching I could not understand how something so soft did not die.' The rhino sounded sad.

Shifting uncomfortably, Jack observed Yang sitting in silence. His shadow returned his look. Satisfied his demon would cause no mischief, he returned his attention to the rhino, who rubbed its horn against a steel trunk. The rhino grinned as sparks flew from its horn.

'Do you know where the blacksmith is?' asked Jack.

'I have not seen him since he took his wagon through here a few days ago. He gave me a piece of tin from the load he carried and then he went. Have you got any tin to give to me?' asked the rhino.

'I'm sorry we haven't got anything,' said Jack.

'Thought I would ask, you never know.' The rhino bent down to find something else to eat.

'We'd best go,' said Bill. 'The Ladies could discover us missing at any time.'

Looking back, Jack tried to gauge the distance they had travelled. Not far enough, he was sure. He had not forgotten the speed the Myrms travelled through the metal branches.

'Do you know a way through the Hedge Wall?' Bill asked the rhino.

STAMPEDE

The great horn swayed to the side. 'There is no way through the Hedge Wall. I tried running through it once, only to get my horn stuck.' The rhino began to munch on what little tin remained on the plant.

'Come on,' urged Jack, steering his deer around the metal rhinoceros.

They left the rhino to eat the rest of his breakfast in peace. They moved quickly through the glade, only Jack knew once the brutes started the chase they would never outrun them. The Myrms would spring through the trees, using the magnets to keep from falling. Casting his eye over his shoulder, he scouted the treetops for any sign of pursuit; nothing followed them. How much longer could they expect not to see anything? An hour, two at the most, if lucky they would reach wherever Yang was leading them before the Ghost Walkers caught up with them. Yang swept his arm forward and to the left of where they were running. Altering their course to follow the shadowed arm, the group naturally bunched together as boulders hedged them on both sides.

'I wonder what else Huckney has made,' said Bill, riding to Jack's right. 'How wonderful, I can't wait to tell my grandfather that I've seen a rhinoceros.'

If you see Grandpa Poulis again, was the gloomy thought that immediately sprang to Jack's mind. Bill looked so content, almost happy riding his withered deer, and Inara rode with absolute glee. Don't they realise we have yet to escape. At least he had stopped coughing. He sneezed. 'Damn it,' he cursed. 'Where's Black?'

Bill let go of the deer's neck and with one arm pointed. 'Straight ahead,' he said. 'They're still quite a way in front of us.'

'And the Ghost Walkers?' asked Inara.

'The Red Sisters,' added Jack.

'Nowhere near the wolves,' said Bill, pushing back his glasses. 'Before moving the wolves away I heard them say they want to share the Wold with Huckney's beasts, but your animals Inara. That's very different. They don't like what you've done here at all.'

'That's tough,' she replied. 'These animals were here before they came. It's more their home than the Ghost Walkers, no matter what they've altered here since they came.'

'I'm not arguing,' said Bill. 'They won't listen to you if they catch us.'

'I don't care.' She spurred her mount to greater speed.

They followed her into tight passages that led through overbearing rocks. A swarm of insects crowded the tight route hovering higher than the deer's hooves. The children instinctively lifted their legs.

'I forgot how disgusting having all these insects around you is,' said Bill.

Although Inara remained quiet, Jack noticed her looking at her shortened legs with trepidation anytime the brown haze drew close.

'The swarm will cover our tracks,' shouted Jack. He listened to his echo, hearing his hollow words of comfort career around them.

CRIK

The canyon twisted and turned. Sometimes the valley opened up, allowing the group to build up greater speed, other times the stone walls closed in, making progress painfully slow. Always the steady hum of the swarm pressed in.

The canyon ended at a red lake surrounded by iron birches. Jack paused to look at the rusting trees. Split trunks, and splintered limbs, lay submerged in the polluted water that lapped the stony shore.

'It's blood,' said Bill, as the hooves of his deer sent ripples across the lake.

'This entire place is bleeding,' said Inara, studying the old plants. 'If this is the heart of the Wold then it's rotten.'

'Huckney's father must've made these trees,' said Jack, knowing the trees grown from the metal seeds Huckney made, would last longer than those crafted by the blacksmith's father, who had relied on just his hammer and skill to create the trees.

'They should've used silver.' A puff of rust exploded as Inara strode along the shore. 'Silver doesn't rust.'

'Shame silver doesn't grow on trees,' said Bill.

'You can smell the iron in the air,' said Jack.

He noted, as they picked their way around the lake, that the fallen trees still held crudely crafted leaves on their broken branches. The entire place felt rushed. Was Inara right; was this the birthplace of the Red Wood?

Saddened by so much decay, the group wound their way through piles of rust. Vigilant of the protruding shards littering their way, they slowed their pace. As they neared the far edge of the lake, they glimpsed silver and gold amongst the rusted sentinels. These thin saplings, arranged around the lake, only just managed to clear the thick layer of insects.

'I know where we are,' said Jack. 'Look.' He pointed at the silver sprouts, and then the gold maple trees mingled throughout the oak. Raising his sights higher, he saw copper trees, already half-grown sending spindly branches, full of leaves, over the water. 'These must've grown from the seeds Huckney made.' He counted five oaks and seven maples, while the more mature birches outnumbered them at ten. 'This is the Mere of Ashes,' he said. 'The last time we saw him, Huckney gave Raglor the seeds for these trees.'

'He gave the Myrm the seeds to plant,' said Bill, glancing at the burgeoning wood. 'I don't like this. What if Raglor is still here?'

'He won't,' said Jack. 'It would take time for the seeds to sprout.' He still looked around, suspicious of every tree and dark place. Just knowing the Myrm chieftain had come here made the lakeshore more ominous. 'I think we best carry on.'

'Which way do we go from here, Yang?' asked Inara.

The shadow had spread across the red water, disturbing the surface as he curiously delved its depths. Finding nothing of interest Yang rushed back to the group. Forming himself into the shape of an arrow, he pointed to the northeast.

STAMPEDE

'What's out there?' said Jack. 'We already know there's no way through the Hedge. Unless our demons can make us fly, the Ghost Walkers will eventually catch us.'

'He brought us out here for a reason,' said Inara. 'If we had stayed in the valley the Red Sisters would have killed us. You know that. What choice did we have? We couldn't sit and wait for them to take us to the Hanging Tree. Unless you have a better plan, we'll carry on following Yang.'

'Alright,' said Jack, as his shadow urged them to move away from the Mere of Ashes and its blood red water.

They travelled a further twenty minutes through the rusted foliage when they heard a roar to their rear. Twisting around, the group waited to hear the cry again; when with a fright each heard the distant ringing of magnets striking metal.

'They're coming,' said Bill.

'Then let's not wait here for them,' said Inara, spurring her deer forward.

The others followed, unmindful of the dangers peppering their path. Jack's arms ached as he furiously gripped the neck of his mount. With his face planted into the decayed back of the deer, he prayed the animal knew where it was going. Remembering his mount had no eyes filled him with dread.

In counterpoint to the clip of their mounts' hooves, rang the clap of magnets striking trees. They urged the dead deer to ever greater speed. The deer responded, leaping over rusted logs and dancing deftly around other obstacles with a grace that defied their frightful appearance. All the time the sounds of pursuit grew closer. Harried, the group dared not slow down for an instant, fearful that their pursuers would descend from the trees and capture them once more.

'Which way?' shouted Inara to Yang, as a fork in the track slowed her headlong flight. The shadow sent an arm down the right trail.

The path declined, sending the group careering wildly down into a dark dell. Each amazingly held onto their mounts as the deer kept their feet. Jack heard Inara laugh as their speed doubled down the slope. They entered a passage where even the bugs refused to enter. The entwining branches overhead made a latticed roof. Only a few stray beams of sunshine got through the dense network. In the gloom, they relied on the instincts of the deer to keep them moving. Their momentum kept up well into the path. When their pace lessened, the sounds of pursuit had grown quieter. Sneaking a backward glance, Jack's heart faltered as the sun spearing through the latticed roof flickered as bodies raced atop the canopy.

'They're right behind us,' cried Jack. 'They're running on top of the branches.'

CRIK

Instead of answering, all three dug their heels into the flanks of their mounts, demanding more haste. The end of the tree-lined tunnel came into view.

A Myrm leapt for Jack as he exited. The brute had come within arm's reach of him when Yang batted the armoured figure away. Jack didn't watch the Myrm crumple against the iron bole of a giant sequoia. Other muscled forms appeared on the lip of the tunnel exit. Each roared. They wore eagle or wolf masks, distorting their challenging cries.

The Hedge Wall rose ahead. Clouds eddied against the looming barrier, creating a layer of swirling mist. Beyond the thin cover, the wall continued to an immeasurable height. Bolstered, by finally seeing the wall, the group sped onward. The Myrms leapt after them. Jack counted at least twenty in pursuit, and he was sure more armour-clad figures followed.

'We're almost there,' cried Bill, just as a thrown iron club missed his head by inches. Hugging his deer tighter, he squeezed his eyes shut.

Behind Jack Yang had spread himself out into a dark vapour, catching four of the nearest Myrms. The Myrms roared as the black mist enveloped them, bringing them crashing to the ground. Others leapt over, or skirted around Yang.

'They keep coming,' said Jack into the neck of his mount.

They could now see the individual leaves of the Hedge Wall. The triangular leaves with their serrated edges fluttered in the breeze. Brown wood peaked through the foliage, it was the first time Jack had seen the colours brown and green since entering the Red Wood, the sight made his heart yearn for the world on the far side. He missed Crik Wood; all he wanted was to hear birds sing in the branches of a normal oak tree. Instead, the sounds of struck metal and grunted cries entertained his ears.

Taking the form of an immense cat, with razor sharp claws, Yang sprang for the Myrms. The ferociousness of his attack slowed the pursuit. Dropping a mangled corpse Yang sprang for the foremost Myrm, tearing through its fox helm with foot long sabres.

Watching as his demon tore chunks from a pursuer's arm, Jack could not hide his horror. Pained cries mingled with the angry calls around them. He had never seen his shadow kill. That it could scare him to his core, making him shiver despite his sweat. If his demon decided to kill his friends, or his mother, how could he stop it?

Another Myrm fell lifeless to the ground when amber light appeared amongst the metal trees driving Yang back.

When his shadow retreated to the deer, Jack shouted, 'Ghost Walkers.'

Gossamer strands of light filtered through the tightly packed trees, illuminating all with sensuous ease. Remembering the love he had for Grandma Poulis, when her light had touched him, made Jack yearn to experience the

STAMPEDE

spreading amber glow. Needing to recapture that feeling of protection Bill's grandmother had given him, he slowed his mount. Quickly the radiance that had marked the Ghost Walkers' arrival reached him. Frozen brilliance, like damp November air, struck him as the amber light travelled up his body. Any attempt to control his shaking fell apart with the Ghost Walker's arrival. Twisting her lips into a cruel sneer, the lead woman shattered any hope he still had for mercy.

Rough hands forcibly spun him around from the stranger. Bill leaned across the gap between their mounts, screaming for him to run. The spell broken, Jack pulled the neck of his deer away from the woman and galloped after his retreating friends.

The Hedge Wall darkened the world as they rode close to its base. Yang threw out his arm to the right, and they followed. Where was their escape? Despair started to seep into Jack, making his mind race with panic. They followed his demon here, yet the wall remained impenetrable. If a rhinoceros made from iron and steel could not barge his way through, what hope had they to get to the other side?

The Ghost Walkers converged on them. Kyla led the chase, her features contorted into a mask of hate. Jack watched as her eyes sank deeper and deeper into her face to leave two tar pits peering out from a bleached skull. Her hair became lank, its golden colour bleached white.

She will kill us. While the terror commanding Jack's mind took hold, Inara, with a scream, fell from her rearing deer.

In their way stood the Red Sisters. Both had their arms raised, holding aloft staffs with rattling bones. Jack had thought Kyla's face showed hatred, yet the two women bathed in red light revealed a horror beyond anything he had yet experienced. Whereas Kyla chose to show her skeletal face, the two before them showed faces ravaged by time. Skin hung from them in sagging folds. Their cracked, sneering mouths, appeared like badly healed scars.

'You dare try to escape,' shouted Kyla as the group came to a hurried stop. 'I'll hang you. I'll watch as your eyes bulge and your tongues loll from your mouths as you choke to death.'

'You've no right to keep us prisoner,' said Inara, pushing against the floor. Stumbling away, its legs flayed to the bone, went her deer.

'We have every right,' said one of the Red Sisters. 'You came to our home, and you altered it. You have done more than trespass.'

'We should take them back,' said Justice, coming forward. Unlike the others, her face remained serene.

'Tell us child,' said the second Red Sister, 'why should we let these three live?'

CRIK

Ignoring the Red Sister, Justice stopped before Inara. 'They are children. What happened to us was not their doing. Cadhla, if we kill them, then we're no better than the villagers who carried me to the Hanging Tree.'

'Children grow to become men and women who carry torches in the night,' said the Red Sister named Cadhla. 'If we leave them go, they'll return and destroy our home. We can't allow them to leave.'

'Then they remain with us, like Huckney,' said Justice.

'The blacksmith has his uses,' said Cadhla. 'This one,' she said pointing at Inara, 'has raised abominations throughout our wood. Who's to say what else she will make happen if we allow her to live.'

The Myrms, keeping back from the Ghost Walkers, growled and beat the floor. No doubt, they want to kill us as well, thought Jack. A few of the beasts carried cuts and bite marks from Yang's attack.

'What else can she do,' replied Justice. 'Having already raised the animals buried in the Wold, she is powerless to make any more changes.'

Cadhla shook her head. 'The Narmacils in these children are strong. Bring him forward,' she commanded the Myrms clustered behind the group.

Jack's heart faltered upon seeing Krimble stumble forward. The old man cackled as he approached.

'You say you can speak with the Narmacils,' said Cadhla.

'Yes,' replied Krimble. 'They share their secrets with me.'

'Then tell us,' instructed Cadhla, 'has this girl reached her full potential?'

Inara cringed as Krimble took a faltering step forward. 'Each of them house a Narmacil of power,' he said. His ruined visage crinkled back into a horrific grin. 'They tell me much; yet even the Narmacil don't know the full extent of their power. It falls to me to educate them. The children have no idea what lives within them, or the full capability of the Children of the Wood.'

'You see Justice,' replied the other Red Sister. 'We can't allow them to live. In time, they could wreak havoc on the Wold. I have run before, I will not flee again.'

Cadhla shook her staff, making the bones rattle loudly. 'The sins of their fathers are on their head. Your innocence went unheeded. They took each of you to that wretched tree, and so shall we now take them.'

'Let me talk to them,' said Krimble, walking into the red glow of the sisters. 'I can control the Narmacil, they are my friends. With me controlling them, I will do what you want. Let me free the Narmacils and you can then kill the children.'

'We don't trust you,' said Justice. 'You stink of deceit. We should bury you so that we don't have to listen to your conniving tongue any longer.'

'He can help us sister,' said Kyla, from her bleached skull. 'We can use him to spread our influence beyond the Wold.'

'Which will only bring us more unwanted attention,' argued Justice.

STAMPEDE

'The Narmacils are dangerous,' said Cadhla. 'We can't allow them to exist here amongst us. Justice is right; they will bring unwanted attention to our home. Even now the parents of the children hunt for them.'

'Then we hang them from the Hanging Tree,' cried Kyla with cruel glee.

'No sister,' said Cadhla, 'we won't hang them from the Hanging Tree.'

Kyla swung around to face the Red Sister. 'I want them to die,' she cried.

'They wanted to reach the Hedge Wall,' said Cadhla, 'and they have. We will hang them in its shadow.' As she spoke, she pointed to a gnarled iron tree set a few feet from the group. 'Bring us rope.'

Turning, Jack watched with dread as Raglor, wearing his owl helmet, carried forward a length of rope.

CRIK

37. AS THE NOOSE TIGHTENS

When Raglor pulled the rope taught, the iron branch refused to break. It creaked and groaned, the iron limb bowed under the pressure, only the reprieve Jack sought evaporated as the chieftain let go of the thick rope. Counting the seconds in conjunction with the swinging rope, drove home his despair. Looking down he saw Yang huddled close to his leg, hiding from the Ghost Walkers' light. Where was his shadow when he needed him the most? Disgust rose up his throat like steam. Transforming into the giant cat, Yang, baring long sabres, snarled. Positive the demon wanted to bite him, made Jack flinch away. The change lasted mere seconds, yet his shadow's threat left him shaken. Yang wanted to kill him. Well, let the demon do its worst, he will be dead within minutes anyway.

'The girl should die first,' said Kyla. 'She brought the decayed things into our garden. Everywhere I turn, there's another pitiful creature wandering across my path. Yesterday a duck with half a bill swam across the Rainbow Lake. The golden swans scattered from it, and have yet to return to the water. Kill her, and all those things will return to the ground where they belong.'

'They look horrible to you,' said Inara, 'because you put them in the ground. Why don't you die, and see what returns to the Wold.'

'You would be such a pretty girl if you had legs,' said Kyla, with a sneer. 'I would've guessed a cripple like you, would welcome the noose. What's a moment of pain against the anguish of living as you are?'

'Enough sister,' said Justice. 'If we're to do this, then let us do it quickly. I will not taunt them as the villagers mocked me. Raglor, take the girl. Only,' she added, her features softening, as a golden light spread from her, 'be gentle with her.'

Laughing, Inara said, 'How can a rope, snapping the bones in my neck, be gentle? I misunderstood, all this time I thought you wanted to hurt me.'

'Leave us go,' repeated Jack, looking up at the looming Hedge Wall. Crik Wood lay on the other side, with clear streams, and animals that didn't limp and claw their way out from the dirt. Most of all, on the other side of the wall he wouldn't have to see metal everywhere he looked.

Cadhla drifted over to the gnarled tree, bathing the crooked metal in her fell light. Kyla joined her on the other side of the tree. 'We have wasted enough time with these children,' said Cadhla. 'Foolish things, did you truly believe you could escape? The Wall surrounds the Wold. You cannot dig under it; you cannot wriggle through its barbed fence. Knowing you had no way through the hedge, why bother to come here? Were you hoping to find another tunnel? Are you hiding other gifts from us? Can that shadow of yours do more than attack my Myrms?'

Krimble shuffled forward, until the red light from the two elder sisters covered him. 'Let me talk to them,' he said. 'In her attempt to ruin your home, the bitch went against your wishes. I can talk to the Narmacil, coax them out and let them live inside me. Within me, their powers will serve you.'

'Listen to him sisters,' said Kyla. 'Krimble told me that the fat boy can control animals. With such a gift we can go out into Crik Wood, and widen our influence.'

'The Wold is our home,' said Cadhla. 'If these children had somehow managed to escape we would not be safe. Others would discover our secret sanctuary. The life you seek sister, the life beyond the Hedge Wall, is not for us. We burnt the trees to stop you from remembering the life they ripped from you. Fixing her stare on Krimble she continued, her voice a whispered threat. 'Your pet, Kyla, is no different to one of those wretched husks that now contaminate the Rainbow Lake. He is a deceased creature that is better off dead.'

'I can serve you,' cried Krimble. 'Look.' Straightening his crooked back, he pointed to the clear sky. Within moments, threatening clouds gathered, billowing together as though caught in the eye of a storm. When the heavy clouds burst, a torrential deluge descended. Rain drummed off the metal armour of the Myrms in a jarring musical litany. 'This is but one of my Talents,' he cried, triumphant. 'Give me a chance to extract the Narmacil from the girl. With her gift, I will continue to live beyond her death.'

'He will be of use to us,' said Kyla. 'Give him what he wants.'

'No Kyla,' said Cadhla, 'I will have the Wold back to the way we envisaged.'

'You allow the blacksmith to live,' said Krimble. 'Why not me? With my babies, I can swell your lakes with the rain. I can have you bask in the heat of the sun. Let the girl die without me taking her Narmacil and you will lose everything.'

'What use is the sun to us, when we cannot feel its warmth,' said Cadhla. The downpour that soaked Krimble slipped through the Ghost Walkers. 'The blacksmith continues to build our Wold. Huckney's father,' she studied the bent branches, dotted with rust, 'created these trees. They are rotten. Like so much of his work. Seeds sown by the son grow without risk of rust. Same with the creatures he creates.'

The noose swayed, buffeted by the storm. 'By killing us you only prove the villagers were right,' said Jack. 'They feared you, believing that you were unnatural creatures from the darkest wood to steal their wives' souls. Bill's grandmother is one of you. She hides in her house. If you hang us from that branch, you are only confirming the villagers' suspicions of you.'

'Justice has told me of your grandmother,' Cadhla told Bill. 'Sons have turned against their mothers before. Amongst us, some have learnt that hard lesson first hand. I will not give you the chance to do the same to your grandmother.'

Bill strode forward, splashing mud up his leg, and scaring the one remaining deer into the wood. 'I would never hurt my grandmother. Anyone who tried to hurt her would have to come through me first.'

'Cheap words.' Cadhla scowled. 'Raglor take the girl.'

'No,' both Jack and Bill screamed as the massive chieftain grabbed Inara's shoulders and hoisted her over his head.

'Leave her alone,' said Jack, running toward Raglor.

The Myrm chieftain causally knocked Jack back with his free hand. Jack landed hard in the mud. Paralyzed by the ghost light, Yang could not aid Inara.

'Get off her.'

A wolf's howl answered Bill's shout, and from behind the tree leapt Black. Black attacked Raglor, knocking the Myrm and Inara to the ground. The ferociousness of the wolf attack tore the owl helmet from the chieftain, exposing the older Myrm's white hair and wide eyes. Huge gnarled hands tore hunks of hair from Black's back. Snarling, the wolf clamped its long fangs onto his prey's neck. Immediately a fountain of red blood met the rain, swelling the puddles with its crimson tide. Raglor, killed by the bite, collapsed to the floor.

Black released his hold. Gore dripped from his open maw as he circled Inara, staring at the other Myrms with his blue eyes. The wolf, leaner since entering the Wold, remained a formidable hunter. Steam rose from his raised back.

'Black,' cried Inara, reaching a hand up to pet the wolf's shaggy coat.

'Kill the wolf,' said Cadhla.

'Rip it to shreds,' cried Kyla, turning to the Myrms with her skeleton face.

The reluctant Myrms roared and beat the ground with their fists. One with an eagle helmet charged. Holding a metal club, he brought it down to strike Black's head. The large wolf, evading the cumbersome attack, bit into the arm of his attacker, severing the limb in two.

Inara crawled away from the fallen Myrm. Mud covered her from head to foot, and her clothes became paper thin in the downpour. When she reached Jack, they clutched each other, shaking as the other Myrms leapt forward in attack.

'He can't take on five at once,' said Jack, as Black barrelled into the chest of the first Myrm.

AS THE NOOSE TIGHTENS

A silver streak came from behind the group as Silver, with teeth bared, entered the fray. Quicker than the larger black wolf, she tore into the legs of the attacking Myrms. Pain filled cries answered her snapping jaws.

'Kill the boy,' cried Kyla. 'He is controlling the beasts.'

The metal face of a snarling dog fixed Bill with a deadly stare. Leaving the group to fight the wolves, he ran toward Bill. He held a cruel metal shard in two hands. Its jagged edge, capable of cutting Bill in two, came up as he reached the cowering boy.

Advancing, Yang enveloped the Myrm. Raising his hands to his face the Myrm dropped its weapon.

Kyla drifted toward the struggle. Spreading her light she touched Yang, who shied away to reveal the Myrm. In despair, Bill picked up the weapon, and with a cry, stabbed upwards, spearing the Myrm through its stomach.

A pained yelp, high and pitiful, rent the air. Another cry, torn from the throat of a wolf, stole the groups' attention. Behind them lay Silver. Blood coated her white and grey coat. She yelped again as another strike from a cudgel broke her back. Lying in a pool of rainwater, the female wolf lifted her head toward Black.

Jack, trying to raise himself, cried, 'No,' as Silver's attacker smashed his weapon into her skull; instantly killing the wolf.

Disengaging from the fight, Black, tilting back his head, gave a long mournful howl. When his cry went unanswered, the black wolf rolled back his lips exposing his red sabres.

'He can't fight them all off,' said Bill. 'He's so wild; I'm finding it hard to control him. They killed Silver,' he whispered, falling to his knees.

'So this is how we die,' said Inara. 'Better than dying alone in the windowless room. Thank you for taking me from there.'

'Anytime,' said Jack, holding Inara firm as Black attacked the four remaining Myrms.

Jack at first mistook the loud booming for thunder. A second crash, closely followed by a third, rolled out from the Red Wood. The ground shook each time the sound came. 'What's happening,' he said, as in the distance the sound of a falling metal tree punctuated the steady rumble.

'Look,' cried Inara, seeing the top of a silver oak shake.

Everyone watched in awe as the tree toppled. Spectators to the frightful display, all fighting had ceased. After witnessing another tree crash to the floor, the Myrms scattered into the wood. What followed was a series of ground shaking impacts that grew more forceful as it approached. Wary of what would appear from out of the Red Wood, the Ghost Walkers drew together. Another tree crashed to the ground. The solid thud of the copper smacking the earth sent forth a powerful shudder, rippling the pools of water. Snapping iron retorted piercingly, jarring the ears of the listeners.

CRIK

'What's coming?' said Bill.

Black, nuzzling Silver's body with his wet nose, paid no attention to what approached. He lay down beside his fallen partner. The only sign he showed that he heeded the world around him were his pricked ears.

Through the rain, an indistinct shape began to materialise. As tall as the highest tree, the creature strode on purposefully. The rain drubbed the skin of the metal giant, as with one hand it uprooted the rusted tree that held the hangman's noose. Tossing it aside the giant stepped into the Ghost Walkers' light.

Immensely broad, the giant turned its boulder-sized eyes to the Ladies drifting close in blooms of colour. The two feet supporting its weight, had three toes, two to the front, and another growing from its heel. Its bowed legs were as powerful as the trunk of an oak tree.

'Look at the size of it,' said Bill. 'Its hands are bigger than the three of us.'

Jack had noted the hands of the giant were disproportionate to the rest of its immense body. Like his own, the Giant's hands contained four fingers with a thumb, which took root further from the fingers than Jack's own. Extending from thick wrists extended arms bristling with coarse copper swirls. Arching upward its mighty biceps led to powerful steel shoulders, where dark metal strips hung from it like coarse hair. Rain swept over its bare chest, and distended stomach, in glistening rivulets. Unhurried, the giant placed its arms on the ground, resting its weight on its knuckles.

'Look at how high its head rises above its face,' said Bill. 'And see how its mandibles protrude. I'm sure this is a gorilla.'

'You've seen one of these in your book?' asked Jack.

'Not quite like this, but pretty close. The hands are far larger than the pictures I've seen, and the giant only has three toes on each foot; but the rest of it matches.'

'Well I don't care if you've seen it in one of your books,' said Inara. 'Can either one of you tell me what it's doing here?'

As though to answer Inara's question, the metal ape extended a hand out to the children. Everyone froze; with the hollow clang of the torrent sweeping across the enormous palm the only intrusion on the prevailing stillness.

'If you try to leave, we will follow you,' said Kyla, her face still showing bone. She drifted to the side of the giant gorilla. 'There is no way to leave the Wold.'

'I think he wants us to step into his hand,' said Bill, ignoring the Ghost Walker's threat.

'If we do, it could crush us by just curling its fingers,' said Jack.

'Is there another option I'm missing here,' said Inara. 'We either go with the gorilla, or stay here and wait for the Myrms to regain their courage and come back to kill us all. Now, help me onto the hand.'

AS THE NOOSE TIGHTENS

With Bill taking Inara's legs and Jack holding onto her shoulders, the children climbed onto the iron palm. Effortlessly, the hand lifted them into the sky. Once they were in the air, the giant closed his fingers around the children. To Jack, sitting between the cracks criss-crossing the Giant's palm, it seemed they had made a mistake trusting the giant. Drawing in the metal fingers the ape produced a scream of working joints that assaulted the children's ears. Inara, screaming, held her hands against the sound. Suddenly the fingers stopped moving. Cradling them gently, the powerful giant took them higher.

Peeking through the curled fingers, Jack saw the Ghost Walkers looking back at him. Standing closest to the giant the two Red Sisters waved their staffs above their heads. The other Ghost Walkers drifted clear of the giant as the bones on Cadhla's staff rattled in the wind and rain.

With a challenging roar, the giant gorilla turned, and clutching the children to its bronze chest, returned to the Red Wood.

38. A HELPING HAND

FOLLOWING ITS OWN TRAIL of destruction, the gorilla backtracked through the Red Wood. Imitations of what had once existed inside the Hedge Wall lay twisted at every turn. Through the ape's fingers, Jack saw a large bronze dome, the apex of which had buckled inward. If he had to hazard a guess, he'd say the gorilla had sat on the huge dome. Even that funny idea did nothing to alleviate his terror. Jostled by every crashing footfall did not improve his demeanour. New bruises coloured his entire body, and poor Inara, unable to use her legs to steady herself, fared even worse.

Bill had started to cry as soon as the light from the Ghost Walkers faded behind them. 'I can't believe they killed her,' he said, clinging to a finger wider than the span of his arms. 'She didn't have to attack the Myrms. I made Black attack them. Silver acted by herself. She left where she lay hidden to help us out, and we let that brute crush her head in with his club.' He pressed his face tight against the mixed metal.

'Where's Black?' asked Inara. She had her fingers wedged into the cracks lining the Giant's palm, stopping herself from sliding across the hand. 'He's alright isn't he? Everything happened so fast I don't know what happened to him.'

'He's following us,' said Jack. Black's unmistakable form slipped through the metal foliage.

'Of course he is,' said Bill, sniffing loudly. 'You don't think I'd let him fend for himself do you? Wherever we're going, Black's coming too. He's one of us, and I won't leave him behind again.'

'Can you see anything following us, Jack?' asked Inara.

The torrential rain obscured much of the route they had taken through the rusting jungle. Twisted trees bordered the giant footprints that caught the downpour to make muddy pools. Wiping the water from his face, Jack scanned the upper branches, but he failed to see any chase. Frustrated he cursed the storm; for all he knew the Myrms could be leaping through the trees after them. The combined noise of the giant gorilla and the storm Krimble had brewed up, masked any sounds the Myrms would make as they leapt from tree to tree. 'If they are behind us, I can't see them.'

A HELPING HAND

'Good,' said Inara. 'You wouldn't see the Myrms, but if the Ghost Walkers pursued us they would light up the wood.'

'They aren't going to forget about us,' said Jack. 'We may have escaped one hanging, but there're plenty more branches to sling a rope over in the Wold. Unless this gorilla knows of a way through the Hedge Wall;' he cast his hands up, 'well, I hate to say it, the Ghost Walkers still have us trapped. Same as we were back in the valley, only this time we don't know where we are.'

'I want to bury her,' said Bill. 'She deserves that much.'

'You don't bury animals,' said Jack.

Inara glared at him. 'I can raise her if you like?' she said to Bill.

Bill shook his head. 'I prefer her as she was. If you raise her, she'd be like the others.'

'Others?' asked Inara, swiping her hair away from her eyes. 'What do you mean by others? Do you mean like the deer that helped us escape?'

'I'm not saying what you did was wrong,' said Bill. 'It's just that, if Silver were to return to us, she'd smell different.'

'What does that have to do with anything?' asked Inara.

'When I share Black's skin, I smell things like he does. I know when a Myrm is close, by lifting my nose to the wind. Back in Crik Wood, Black could sniff out a deer trail and follow it for miles. Since finding Black again, I've smelt the animals you've raised. They smell wrong. It's not just the smell of decaying flesh and dirty hair.' Bill looked between the fingers holding them aloft.

'What else can you smell?'

'They smell wrong Inara,' he said. 'The stench coming off them turns my stomach. Everywhere reeks of rot. I don't want Silver to smell wrong. Neither does Black. That's what he was doing when the gorilla came marching through the trees. He was remembering Silver's scent.'

'When Dwayne's dog died,' said Jack, 'your grandfather told him that his dog would always be close. That his dog could smell him on the wind, and would wait for him like a good dog should.'

Nodding, Bill said, 'That's how animals remember.'

'You can worry about what something smells like when we know what this giant wants with us,' said Inara.

'You were the first to want to trust it,' said Bill.

'Only because we had no other choice,' said Inara. 'For the moment we don't have to worry about the Ghost Walkers. We do have to worry what's about to happen to us.'

The gorilla crashed through bronze branches that scored its metal skin with a loud screech. It carried on, allowing no obstacle to slow its steps. Tearing a few trees from its path the giant entered a deep gorge. Valley walls echoed its crashing gait. Using its free hand to support itself, the gorilla stooped forward,

CRIK

picking up speed as it went deeper into the valley. The cries from the children mingled with the thunderous steps of the metal ape.

'This is crazy,' called Jack, clutching Bill. His teeth snapped together as another jolt hit his body.

When the gorilla increased its pace, Inara had gone from one end of the hand to the other. Her fingers bled, and her sleeve had torn away from her thin arm. 'Careful, you stupid ape,' she cried.

'Hush Inara,' cried Bill, 'He might hear you.'

'Hear me? How can he hear me when he's crashing through the Red Wood, snapping iron as though it were kindling? My ears ring every time it takes a step.'

Silence.

The children stopped talking. They looked at one another. Bill mouthed the words 'He heard you,' when they realised the gorilla had come to an abrupt stop.

Looking between the imprisoning fingers revealed the bottom of the deep valley. Sheets of grey rain washed the stone that surrounded them. Iron wool bushes, dotted the landscape, shivering in the downpour. Day had darkened into night with the passing over of the clouds. Jagged bolts danced through the cloud, exposing the world in instant brilliant white. Below ran Black, keeping to a winding path parallel to them. In the moment of the lightning strike, Jack noted Yang had retained the shape of the cat. Crashing thunder swallowed his frightened gasp.

Gripping the creased palm, Inara sat too far from the edge to see the land. 'Where are we?'

Sonorous, metal digits began to open; the tortured joints pummelled their ears. The rain fell on them as the sky opened up. Looking up the children saw the gorilla looking down at them. Copper lips spread, revealing large iron teeth. Its squashed nose flared, blowing cold water away in a mist.

'It's going to eat us,' said Bill.

'Don't be silly,' said Jack. 'If it wanted to chew us up, it would've eaten us by now.' He wished he believed his own words.

The gorilla brought its face closer to its open hand. Its eyes were both wider and taller than were the children. 'Sorry if I hurt you,' its voice boomed, ruffling the children's hair. 'I tried to be careful; it's just that you are so soft.'

'You can talk,' said Bill.

'Of course he can talk,' called out a voice from below.

Scrambling to the edge Jack looked down on Huckney, who waved up at him. 'Huckney,' he cried.

'Of course it's me,' said the blacksmith as the giant gorilla lowered the group to the ground. 'I'd have thought you would've known Gashnite belonged to me.'

A HELPING HAND

'I don't belong to anyone,' said Gashnite, beetling its brow.

'Sorry,' said Huckney. 'I should've said, who else could create something as marvellous as Gashnite. Isn't he incredible? It took me days, and more metal than I have ever used before, to create him.'

'How could you make something so big in secret? The wolves heard you working, surely the Ghost Walkers would have found you.' said Bill, following Jack off the palm.

Huckney grinned and his eyes sparkled as he said, 'Not only did they know, they gave me their blessing!'

'How?' asked Bill.

Indicating the massive hands of the gorilla the blacksmith answered. 'The Wold is a jungle of rot and decay. The rusting trees give this place another name.'

'The Red Wood,' whispered Jack.

Huckney nodded. 'I proposed making Gashnite to uproot the old trees my father built, so that I may plant my living trees in their stead.'

'Living,' said Jack, looking up at the iron trunks crowning the ravine. Cut from hard metal, those trees were cold, not at all like living trees.

Huckney saw the doubt in his eyes. 'Everything that grows is alive. It does not matter that they came into being from the pages of my book. Each one is independent of me.'

'Doesn't your Talent give your animals their personalities,' said Bill, interested despite his fear of pursuit.

'Wish that I could, if so I wouldn't have made a quarrelsome mouse. No, they are who they are and as long as I am close, they will remain that way. I bring life to this wretched place; which is why I will not leave.'

Inara remained quiet, pensive, thinking of all she had brought into the Wold.

'You rescued us,' said Jack, ignorant of Inara's concerns.

'I know the Ladies; more importantly, I know the Red Sisters. It was fortunate that Justice met you. If Cadhla or Evangeline had attended when the Myrms brought you to the tree, you'd have hanged that day. Kyla is bad enough,' said the blacksmith, 'but those two are far worse.'

'You put yourself in danger for us,' said Inara, from the gorilla's hand.

The blacksmith shook his head. 'I don't think so. The Wold is my home; I've lived here for most of my life. Besides, the Ladies need me. Who else can finish off the Wold? No, they'll be angry with me, but I know they won't do anything.'

'How'd you create the gorilla?' asked Jack.

'Gashnite,' said Gashnite.

'Sorry,' said Jack.

The blacksmith smiled. 'Gashnite is by far the largest creature I have ever made. It took days of hard labour to bring him to life. If you notice, many different types of metal went into his making. Copper, bronze, iron, steel, zinc,

CRIK

and silver covers his back. Although I didn't have enough of one type, I think I did a good job with what I had.'

'He's perfect,' said Bill.

'What goes, crash, crash, boom, boom, stomp, stomp?'

Looking behind Gashnite, Jack spied Herm running toward them. The metal squirrel clutched his acorn to his chest.

'Hello, Herm,' said Jack.

Herm leapt onto Gashnite's arm, clutching the copper curling up the forearm of the gorilla. 'My head is still rattling, after you came running into the valley,' said the squirrel, knocking the acorn it held against the giant. 'It's lucky with all this noise that I don't need to hibernate.'

'Quiet Herm,' said Huckney.

'What has two legs, and a head of lead?' asked the squirrel.

'Shush,' said the blacksmith.

'What's harder, your hammer or your head,' retorted Herm. 'You have no time, yet you waste it, which is a crime. The Myrms are at my back, they are so near, and yet you show no fear.'

'They recovered quicker than I had expected,' said Huckney, addressing the children. 'Gashnite isn't the subtlest of creatures, and they have followed his path to us.'

'Where can we go?' asked Jack. 'There's no way through the Hedge Wall.'

'You won't be going through the hedge, you'll be going over it,' said the blacksmith grinning.

'Have you made a giant bird to fly us over?' asked Bill, excited.

Tapping his chin, Huckney said, 'Wish that I had considered it. Well it's now too late to craft such a bird.'

'I'll be taking you over the Hedge Wall,' said Gashnite.

'You,' said Jack.

'Gashnite can climb the hedge,' said Huckney. 'He'll carry you over, using his feet as a second pair of hands.'

'What goes splat after a great fall?' asked Herm.

The same notion occurred to Jack as he looked up at the immense gorilla. The Hedge Wall loomed over the valley. 'Can the hedge take Gashnite's weight?'

'The wood in the hedge is stronger than any metal,' said the blacksmith.

'How high is the Hedge Wall?' asked Bill, tilting his head back to look at the Wold's barrier. 'Does it even have a top?'

'You'll find out,' said Huckney. The blacksmith held his hand out to Jack.

Taking his hand, Jack said, 'Thank you.'

Bill also shook Huckney's hand, while Inara hugged the blacksmith. 'The Ladies aren't evil,' said Huckney, disengaging from Inara. 'What happened to them when they lived in your village haunts them every moment.'

A HELPING HAND

'So that excuses them,' said Bill.

'They are wrong in wanting to hurt you,' said Huckney. 'That's why I'm helping you. Well my friends, this is goodbye. Look after one another, and get home as quickly as you can.'

'Come here Black,' said Bill, calling to the big wolf. Black ran onto the metal palm. Up close, the group could see the wolf's injuries. Blood as well as rain dampened his side. Holding him close, Bill pressed his face into the wolf's coarse hair. 'I'm sorry,' he whispered.

'Goodbye Huckney,' said Jack, as Gashnite lifted them away from the big man. Jack watched Huckney wave, while Gashnite's fingers rose around him. Herm scampered onto the blacksmith's shoulder, waving his nut above his head.

Knowing Gashnite was not intending to harm them, put the children at ease. Swaying with the motion instead of fighting against the gorilla helped. Taken back through the valley they all felt calmer. Black lay across Inara, with the boys sitting before her.

'Did Yang know what Huckney was doing?' she wondered.

'How could he,' said Bill, shifting his glasses. 'Yang never leaves Ying's side.'

'Krimble told us that the Narmacils speak to one another,' said Inara. 'Perhaps Jack's Narmacil spoke to Huckney's, or at least knew the blacksmith's intent from afar.'

The dark day only allowed Yang to appear as a weak outline beside Jack. Did his demon communicate with the other demons? Reflecting on the question troubled him. What secrets did the demons talk about amongst themselves?

'Well Yang did point toward this valley,' said Bill. 'See Ying, I knew following Yang was a good idea.'

Jack didn't answer. He didn't trust his shadow. Let Bill and Inara think what they liked, as soon as he found Knell he would no longer have to worry what his shadow schemed.

'There's trouble ahead,' Gashnite's voice boomed from above them.

Rushing forward, Jack looked at the rain swept world to see the head of the valley ablaze with Ghost Walkers' light. Through that light, ran the Myrms, appearing warped and misshapen in the glow. 'They're waiting for us,' he told the others. Roars of defiance from the head of the valley strengthened his warning. The Myrms no longer looked scared. Cadhla drifted through the rabble, colouring the storm with her red light.

'There's no way around them,' said Gashnite. 'We've got to go through them.'

'Great,' said Bill, clinging tighter to Black's fur.

The roar Gashnite gave dwarfed the sound of the storm. Charging forward, the giant gorilla scattered the Myrms. He turned to where the Hedge Wall stood tall before him.

CRIK

'They're coming up your legs,' warned Jack, spying the Myrms using their magnets to climb the giant.

A colossal hand lowered, picking off the first Myrm. The roar from the Myrm suddenly cut off as Gashnite closed his hand into a tight fist. Dropping the crushed Myrm the gorilla reached for another.

'There must be at least ten Myrms climbing up Gashnite,' Jack told the others. 'He's hitting them off, but it'll only be a matter of time before one reaches us.'

Screams filled the air as Gashnite batted two Myrms off his thigh. Another struck the Giant's knee with a menacing club, and fell back as the weapon bounced off the bronze to strike its bearer in the face.

'That'll teach him,' cried Jack, watching the Myrm fall.

'Jack, what's happening?' asked Inara, clinging to the wolf just as fiercely as did Bill.

Gashnite was far quicker than Jack expected, but he saw a few of the Myrms had reached the Giant's midriff, with more jumping onto the gorilla's legs all the time. 'Gashnite's trying his best,' he called back.

Another roar from Gashnite broke thunderously from above as he threw three more brutes into the Red Wood.

The magnets of the Myrms clanged against Gashnite's skin. Looking down Jack could see the faces of the nearest attackers. Their small eyes fixed on him as they climbed. The nearest wore a mask of an eagle, its sharp beak appearing even more threatening with the rain sluicing down to its point.

'Get ready,' cried Jack.

Black rose and stepped away from Inara and Bill. With the wolf beside him, Jack felt braver.

More screams.

The foremost pursuer raised itself between Gashnite's forefinger and thumb; it wore the eagle mask. In its hand, the Myrm carried a rusted blade, which it brought up to defend itself from the wolf's attack. Black bit into the Myrm's shoulder, wrenching a roar of pain from the monster. While the wolf sank its fangs into the nest of muscle and nerves, the Myrm brought up its weapon, ready to deliver its own wicked bite. Seeing the raised blade, Bill screamed and rushed forward. The weapon was coming down when Bill threw his body against the Myrm's arm, stopping the sword from reaching the wolf. Tearing out a chunk of flesh, Black tore his mouth free, before shredding the Myrm's throat in an explosion of gore. The Myrm went limp. Leaving go of the arm, Bill let the Myrm fall back and out of sight.

Braving another look, Jack saw two other attackers almost upon them. Suddenly, the day lit up as two forks of lightning speared down from the dark cloud. Somehow, the lightning missed Gashnite to strike the two Myrms sending their smoking, ruined bodies back to the ground.

A HELPING HAND

'What just happened?' asked Bill, squeezing his eyes tight. 'The world just lit up.'

Another lightning strike hit a pair of Myrms climbing over the Giant's stomach.

A deep rumble of thunder met Gashnite's roar, as the giant looked up at the swirling clouds.

Far below, stood a lone figure set far behind the Ghost Walkers. Jack hadn't noticed Krimble until then, but as another fork of lightning struck, he saw the man from the marsh holding his hands up to the sky.

'Krimble's calling down the lightning,' said Jack.

'Krimble, are you serious?' asked Bill.

'I can see him,' said Jack, hearing his own incredulity. 'I don't know why he's helping us, but the Myrms are abandoning the fight. They're fleeing back into the Red Wood.'

'He doesn't want us to die,' said Inara.

'Why not,' said Bill.

'If I die, he'll die,' she answered. 'His only chance of ever getting our Narmacils would die with me. If we live, he still has hope of one day taking our power for himself.'

'Fat chance of that happening,' said Bill.

'A small gamble is better than none,' said Jack.

After lowering his arms, Krimble watched as Gashnite turn his back on the Wold to face the Hedge Wall. Hoping it would be the last occasion he would see Krimble, Jack looked at the hedge.

Holding the children to his breast, Gashnite reached for the Hedge Wall.

CRIK

39. WHAT GOES UP, MUST EVENTUALLY COME DOWN

WET LEAVES CASCADED down wherever Gashnite's metal fingers gripped the Hedge Wall. Already the Ghost Walkers' screams grew distant as the giant gorilla tirelessly climbed. The storm raged, lashing the iron, bronze, and the silver covering Gashnite with enough rain to break a river's bank. As Gashnite rose, he held the children close to his breast, shielding them from the elements.

'I don't know how you can look,' Bill told Jack.

The Wold grew smaller all the time. 'From up here the Red Wood isn't so threatening,' said Jack, over the storm. Even the light from those wanting to kill them appeared small, drawing comparison with a candle's flame, flickering in the wind. Huckney had mentioned Gashnite would climb using his feet as a second pair of hands, and he saw the blacksmith had not exaggerated. Every time the gorilla stretched out with his free hand to grip the hedge, the feet rose to push them higher. Gashnite climbed the hedge as though it was a ladder. Still, Herm's words haunted him. They would go splat if the gorilla made a mistake.

'You should step away from the edge,' repeated Bill for the fourth time. 'The metal is slick with rain.'

Jack wanted to ignore Bill's words, to tell his friend to stop worrying, but when he turned his feet slid on the bronze. Breathing hard he clutched a giant forefinger.

'Ying, be careful,' cried Bill, rising in alarm.

'I'm alright,' said Jack, annoyed; he would not have slipped if he weren't turning around to answer Bill. Biting his tongue, he stubbornly remained where the rain wet his sandy hair. He wanted to watch the Wold disappear, only then would he accept their escape.

'Leave him Bill,' said Inara. 'If he wants the thrill of looking out as Gashnite carries us into the sky, let him.'

'And if he falls?'

'I won't fall,' said Jack, still fiercely gripping the metal digit. 'Don't worry Bill; I won't blame you if I do.'

'You don't have to be so hostile,' said Bill, crossing his arms. 'It'd be a shame if you died after everything we survived.'

WHAT GOES UP, MUST EVENTUALLY COME DOWN

The Red Wood spread out beneath the stormy sky. Every structure, from spinneret, to silver and dark ironed tree, looked small, like a miniature map rising from crumpled brown paper. Jack couldn't help remembering the small forts and tiny men he had left sprawled across his bedroom floor. Imagining the Wold as a toy left him feeling empowered. They had managed the impossible by escaping the Red Wood.

'I hope Huckney is alright,' said Bill, immediately bringing Jack's mood down. 'They won't be happy with him for helping us.'

'He said they can't do anything to him,' said Jack. 'Without him, their precious Red Wood will fall into ruin. You saw how his father's trees were crumbling away. He'll be alright.' He hoped so. After having only met the blacksmith a few times, the man had risked everything to save their lives.

'It's fortunate Huckney had that Talent, isn't it,' said Inara. 'Without it, he'd only be a blacksmith; easily replaced.'

'I think he was the one the Ghost Walkers wanted all along,' said Bill. 'Perhaps they needed his father only until Huckney grew into his Talent. It's a good thing he's so useful, or Cadhla would kill him for sure.'

Remaining quiet, Jack continued to watch the storm. Let them believe having a demon living inside them was a good idea. If Huckney could not create life from metal then the Myrms would not have kidnapped him or his father. When he reached Knell, they didn't have to follow him. Yet, Yang had helped them escape. Without his shadow, they would still be in the glade, or hanging from the Hanging Tree. Reflecting on Yang's actions, he looked down on the faint outline moving across the giant palm. Had the demon saved him and his friends? Or, had it only acted out of self-preservation? He hadn't forgotten how his shadow had attacked him. No, the demon was using him, as it had used him his entire life. Only, the demon had the chance to enter Krimble. It didn't need him to live. Doubts nagged at him as Gashnite entered the clouds.

Rain gave way to a thick mist, obscuring everything. Jack couldn't see his friends, and the giant fingers rising over him were only dark smudges in a sea of white. He heard Bill cough, and Black whine. The wolf likes this as much as he did, and he would prefer almost anything to this white purgatory. Tortured working joints squealed in protest as Gashnite carried them through the clouds.

What would they see beyond the clouds? Jack began to wonder whether he would ever find out, when the mist began to dissipate around them. First he noted Black's bulk, and then as the mist continued to thin the slender forms of his friends.

'We're higher than the clouds.'

Recognising the note of fear in Bill's voice, Jack ruminated on how high they had come? Tilting back his head, he looked through the giant fingers that framed the sky. The wall still towered over them. Did it have an end?

CRIK

Something of flesh and blood would have tired by now; yet, Gashnite's metal limbs carried them inexorably higher.

'At least the rain has stopped,' said Inara. 'Gashnite, shielded us from most of the downpour, but I'm still dripping.'

Standing at the edge of the hand Jack had caught most of the rain. Water trickled from his damp hair down his spine. With no storm clouds the sun once more appeared, and with it so did Yang. Immediately, Jack's shadow rushed to ruffle Black's fur.

Inara laughed. 'He hasn't played with Black for a long time.'

'Careful of his injuries Yang,' said Bill, looking with concern at Black's wounds.

'I don't think the wounds are that serious,' said Inara. She smoothed away Black's hair to inspect a long gash running along the wolf's ribcage. 'The cuts aren't deep. He'll be tender for awhile. Give him a day or two and he'll be back to fighting strength.'

'I don't want him fighting anymore,' said Bill. 'What if I lose him, like I lost Silver?'

'Is he strong enough to carry you Inara?' asked Jack. 'We won't be climbing forever.' At least he hoped they wouldn't.

Inara nodded. 'If I'm careful, he'll be alright.'

'Good,' said Jack, having no idea how far Gashnite would carry them once they crossed over the Hedge Wall. He guessed, when they were safe, the giant gorilla would return to the Wold. Perhaps the returning giant will be enough to keep Huckney safe. When Gashnite left them, they would need Black to again carry Inara.

The group grew quiet as they rose ever higher. Each looked upward, willing an end to the climb.

'I wonder what lies ahead of us. Up there.' Bill pointed up the steep side of the Hedge Wall.

The same question riveted Jack, to such an extent that he found it impossible to tear his eyes away from the Hedge Wall, and to where, eventually, Gashnite must take them. The Wold's barrier didn't seem to have an end. As far as he could see, the wall continued uniformly upward, neither bulging outward, nor sinking away from the sheer side of the wall. It is perfect, he thought, glancing down at the storm clouds that had dwindled to a fine layer of white mist.

An occasional bough broke through the layer of roping vines, and nests of dagger length thorns, which gave the Hedge Wall its other name, Thorn Hedge. Gashnite used the extended branches to pull himself up, leaving the wood scored by the gorilla's rough treatment. One branch, bereft of its bark, came close enough for Jack to note that Huckney's remark that the wood lining the Hedge Wall was stronger than any metal was not just a flight of fantasy.

WHAT GOES UP, MUST EVENTUALLY COME DOWN

Standing up, Bill asked, 'How long have we been climbing?'

'At least an hour, maybe two,' said Inara. 'It's hard to tell.'

'We left the storm behind about an hour ago,' said Jack. 'The sun has moved that much.'

'What suddenly made you such an expert?'

'You asked, I told you,' said Jack. 'If you don't believe me, why don't you ask Yang? He seems to have all the answers.'

'He led us to Huckney,' said Inara. 'Without him, we'd...'

'We'd be dead,' interrupted Jack. 'I know. He showed us where to go. But you forget, Huckney was the one who rescued us, not my shadow.'

'Ying, Yang knew where Huckney was. He took us to him.'

'Or did he expect to find the Red Sisters?' said Jack. 'They were there too. Or are you so in love with my demon, that you overlooked that fact?'

'You're not being reasonable,' said Inara. 'While we ran, Yang fought off the Myrms. If he wanted the Red Sisters to capture us, then why did he help?'

'That's right, my fantastic shadow turned into a big cat with claws and large teeth,' said Jack. 'Did you know he tried to use those teeth to bite me? If the lightning flash lasted more than a second, my demon would've killed me before Cadhla had a chance.'

'You probably offended him,' said Inara.

'How could I upset him?'

'Of course you upset Yang. You have spent the last few weeks lost, going from one danger to the next, just to purge him, as though he was a virulent disease. If I were Yang I'd do more than just try to bite you,' said Inara.

'So you think it's alright for my shadow to attack me, is that it.' He rushed over to her.

'Calm down Ying,' said Bill, standing up.

'No Bill, if Jack wants to hit me, let him.'

'I'm not going to hit you,' said Jack, stepping back. 'I would never hurt you, or Bill. I just wish you could see what I know.'

'You're one view has blinded you to any other possibility,' said Inara. 'You saw the Narmacil jump into Bill, and you immediately thought that it was evil. Only ask yourself this. In all the time you've lived with Yang, has he ever hurt you? Has your shadow ever harmed your mother, or tried to get others to hurt you?'

'He was always getting me into trouble,' said Jack. All his life he had battled with people blaming him for something Yang had done.

'Getting you into scrapes; isn't the same as harming you Jack.'

'If we didn't have demons, inside us, we wouldn't be here in the first place. I'd be playing in my room, while a book would have Bill enthralled. Inara,' he said, 'you wouldn't have left home.'

'Krimble hurt me; the Narmacils had nothing to do with it.'

CRIK

'They gave him the power to hurt you,' said Jack. 'And who's to say that the demons inside Krimble didn't alter him. Without them, he would just be a lonely old man living in the marsh. He's the only one who can hear them, understand what they are saying. Did they whisper to him? Can you be sure, they didn't want him to do what he has done? We can't hear what they are saying.'

'No Jack, I won't believe that.'

'You may not want to believe it, but you can't disprove it either,' said Jack, walking back to the edge of the hand. He shook his head. Did his shadow mean them harm? A question he couldn't answer, perhaps Knell would tell him.

'We're almost at the top,' Gashnite's voice bellowed out.

Shielding his eyes, Jack saw an innocuous dark line marking the top of the hedge. After such a monumental effort to scale to the summit, he felt slighted. Flags, flapping in the wind, or some celestial blown trumpet, to herald their coming, wouldn't have gone amiss. Excitement quickly overcame his initial disappointment. Once they reached the dark line, their ascent, and their escape from the Wold, would be complete.

Gashnite gave a grunt as he threw the elbow of his leading arm over the lip of the Hedge Wall, before pulling himself over. Having travelled through the Blackthorn Tunnel, the immense width of the summit came as no surprise.

'Well done, Gashnite,' said Jack. He smiled up at the giant, who blew out his copper and bronze cheeks in response.

'I thought I was tall,' said Gashnite. 'That hedge was much higher than I expected.'

'Are you tired?' asked Inara. 'Would you like to rest, before continuing?'

The gorilla shook his head. 'I don't tire. The height of the Hedge Wall came as a surprise, that's all.' To demonstrate his continued strength, Gashnite rose to his full height and took two purposeful strides forward.

'Look Ying,' cried Bill, rushing to stand between two of Gashnite's fingers. 'I can see the marsh from up here.'

'Are you sure,' said Jack, rushing to his side.

The Wold sat within the encircling reach of the Hedge Wall. Storm clouds covered the corroded jungle, making it appear as though they stood on the lip of a gigantic cauldron. Lightning flickered like glow-worms within the churning depths, casting phantasmagorical shapes within the soup. Beyond the encompassing arms of the Thorn Hedge Jack spotted sunlight skating on grey water. His excitement bubbled as he caught sight of the marsh. 'You're right, I can see it,' he exclaimed. Straining his eyes, he tried in vain to discern more detail, but his vision was not that keen.

'It so far away,' said Bill, leaning precariously through the Giant's fingers.

'Be careful,' said Jack. Yang took hold of Bill and pulled him gently back into the hand.

WHAT GOES UP, MUST EVENTUALLY COME DOWN

'Thanks,' said Bill, once Yang released him. 'I guess it was my turn to take a foolish risk. If we can see the marsh, I bet we can also spot our home.'

'I doubt it,' said Jack. 'Deep wood surrounds the village; and without any tell-tale landmark to guide us we will never find it.'

'I guess you're right,' conceded Bill. 'Can't harm to look though can it.' Bending forward he narrowed his eyes, trying to spy anything familiar.

How far had they travelled, mused Jack as he looked over the miles of dense woodland, sprawling grass fields, and hills. He wondered which ones they had crossed. Under which trees did Black's pack now hunt? If he shouted from up here, would his voice carry all the way back home, or would the wind whip it away before it even left his lips? These and more questions rushed to mind. Never would he have believed he would ever see such a sight as this.

'I don't know where my home is either,' said Inara. She had pulled herself to the edge of the hand. 'It felt like I wandered for days before finding the marsh. I think I came to Krimble's house from the west, or possibly from the east. I don't know.' She shook her head in dismay. 'Krimble didn't make a straight route for me to follow. Pink blossomed trees grow close to my home.'

Knowing she looked for any pink amongst the browns and greens of the landscape made Jack hunt for them as well. Dense vegetation blanketed everything, and each plant sported a different hue. Searching for the obscure pink trees reminded him of trying to locate a particular jigsaw piece amongst thousands.

'My house sits alongside a wide lake,' she whispered.

Jack saw hundreds of lakes dotted around the countryside. Any one of them could be the one she remembered.

'I'm sorry Inara,' he said, rubbing his eye with a knuckle.

'One of the village hunters will know where you live,' said Bill. 'When we get back home, they'll take you to your parents.'

'Yes, when,' said Inara, as she continued to look out at Crik Wood.

After long minutes of silence, Gashnite turned and took them across the summit of the Hedge Wall. His long stride covered the distance quickly, making short work of the walk. Snow-capped mountains, and woodland, met them on the far side.

'Well Ying,' said Bill. 'I doubt we'll find home on this side of the wall.'

Of that, Jack had no doubt, only, for now, he didn't seek home.

'Didn't you say heather covered the Scorn Scar?' asked Inara.

Jack nodded.

'Well, the only purple I see, lies in the cleft at the foot of that mountain.' Inara gestured forward.

With eager eyes, Jack followed her direction and found what he sought. 'That must be it,' he cried. 'It doesn't look that far away.'

CRIK

'The marsh didn't seem that far away on the other side,' said Bill, 'yet it took an age to reach the hedge.'

'You're exaggerating, Bill,' said Jack. Though, thick woodland did fill the terrain before the Scorn Scar. Shaking his head, he wondered what dangers hid amongst all that greenery. They had survived the Red Wood, with its Myrms and Red Sisters; they will survive whatever Crik Wood had in store for them. Besides, he smiled; they had Black to protect them.

'Hope we don't cross another pack of wolves,' said Bill.

Jack scowled at him.

'Will you take us as far as that mountain?' Inara asked Gashnite.

Metal squealed as the giant gorilla shook his head. 'I have yet to explore my home,' said Gashnite. 'I will get you to the foot of the hedge and then return. I already miss the metal trees and the iron bushes. Huckney has told me of what lies within the Wold, and I am eager to discover the Golden Glade with its glittering fronds, and to see my reflection in Chrome Hill.'

'Well I've seen enough metal to last me a lifetime,' said Bill.

'Bill,' said Inara, raising her eyes to the metal gorilla that held them in his bronze hand.

Bill gulped. 'No offense, Gashnite.'

Gashnite's laugh shook the thick layer of thorns under his feet. 'You are soft things, it is only right that you long to return to softer lands.'

Atop the Hedge Wall, the Scorn Scar appeared so close; Jack fancied he could reach out and grab it. Heather emerged from the base of the mountain like a birthmark on the landscape. Almost there, he mused, knowing Knell's home waited for him close to the purple swathe.

The hedge effectively contained Krimble's storm, so the descent remained clear, making them fretful at how frighteningly far away the floor beneath them was. Captivated with the view, Jack drank in every detail. He spied a lake close to the Scorn Scar; crystal blue water lapped a stony shore.

Did she expect him? When the Lindre took him to Knell, she had been waiting for him. Again, Jack wondered what the hooded woman knew.

Gashnite descended faster than he had climbed, and Crik Wood revealed more of its detail the closer they got to the woodland floor. The lofty, Birch, Hazel and Hawthorn trees, soon hid the Scorn Scar from Jack's keen sight.

Birds, startled into flight by Gashnite's arrival, soared into the sky. Unconcerned, the metal gorilla came to a sudden screeching halt as he placed one foot on the ground. 'Here we are children,' he said. 'I hope you enjoyed the ride.' Bending down, Gashnite allowed the children to step off onto the grass.

Laughing, Bill rolled on the ground, smelling the weeds and small white flowers as though he had never seen them before. Jack breathed in deep, letting the smells of the wood fill his chest to bursting.

'Gashnite?' Inara said, looking up at the gorilla with concern.

WHAT GOES UP, MUST EVENTUALLY COME DOWN

Looking behind, Jack asked, 'What's the matter?'

Gashnite still knelt down, with his extended hand outstretched before him. He didn't move.

'Why isn't he getting up?' asked Bill, walking up to place a hand on the copper swirls running up Gashnite's massive arm.

'Answer us, Gashnite,' said Inara.

'Look at his eyes,' said Jack. What had once danced with brilliance now held inscrutable dullness. Only the reflected sun offered any contrast to Gashnite's dormant features.

'Is he dead,' asked Bill.

Climbing back on the giant hand Jack knew Gashnite was no longer with them. 'What happened?'

'He must have gone too far from Huckney,' said Inara. 'He lost contact, the same way Bill lost contact with Black when they were apart.'

'Is it the same for you?' asked Jack. 'Are all the animals you raised in the Red Wood gone?'

Shaking her head, Inara said, 'I can still feel them. My Talent must work differently from Bill's and Huckney's.'

Or something has happened to Huckney. Jack pushed away the dreadful implication of that thought as though it were a deadly disease.

'Do you think either Gashnite or Huckney knew what would happen once Gashnite got us to the other side of the Hedge Wall?' asked Bill.

No one answered as they looked upon the silent giant.

40. WHAT CAME NEXT

WHERE HAD THE HEDGE WALL GONE? The question nagged Jack throughout the third day of walking through the lush woodland. No sign of the colossal barrier remained through the foliage. For a couple of days, they couldn't escape its oppressive presence, and then it vanished. Sat within the glow of a campfire he recalled the same phenomena on the other side of the wall, where the hedge only appeared as they grew near. From its summit, they had seen the entire wood spread out before them, so why couldn't they see it from everywhere in Crik Wood? He didn't bother posing the question to his friends; no doubt, they'd blame some protective spell; he had enough of spells and Talents to last him two lifetimes.

Fat sizzled from a roasting pig they had suspended over the fire. Absently he turned the spit, savouring the smell of Black's latest kill. Inara stared at the crackling flames in silent contemplation. Bill had his eyes closed, sharing Black's skin as the wolf hunted. Since having Black back with them, Bill had entered the big wolf's mind every night, and grew more distant during the day. If Bill's withdrawal concerned Inara she didn't show it; it troubled Jack. He didn't want his best friend relying on his demon.

'It's lucky we've got Black with us,' said Inara, breaking the silence. 'I doubt any of us would make good hunters.'

Sometimes, Inara's unerring way of talking about what was on his mind spooked Jack. Could she read him so well, that she knew what he was thinking? Or was he wrong, did Bill's growing reliance on Black also trouble her? Probably unlikely; Inara loved everything about the demons. She'd no doubt jump for joy if she saw him dance with Yang. Imagining dancing with his shadow left a bad taste in his mouth.

'The woods are full of game,' he said. 'All this noise has given me a nervous twitch. When something crawls or slithers through the underbrush I keep expecting an attack.'

'I know what you mean,' said Inara. 'The Red Wood was so quiet. Out here, everything is alive.' A twig broke in the darkness as though to underline her words. 'Do you think the Myrms will follow us?'

WHAT CAME NEXT

Jack, though sharing her fear, tried to calm her. 'I don't think so. The Blackthorn Tunnel is on the opposite side of the hedge. They won't come after us.'

'I won't go back,' she said, staring into the flames. 'I'd prefer to die.'

'No one is going to capture us. The Scorn Scar is only a few days away. Once we get there, all this will end and we can return home.'

'Will my parents still love me?'

The question stunned him. 'Of course they'll love you. They haven't given up on you, Inara. Your parents search for you everyday.'

'Look at me,' she said, jabbing a finger at her legs that ended at her knees. 'I'm not the same girl that left home. I'm a cripple, how can I help around the farm when I haven't got any legs?'

'You're their daughter; of course they'll welcome you back.'

'A daughter that has seen too much death,' she said. 'My time in Krimble's house changed me. I don't see much hope or joy in the world anymore. Everything is dull, lifeless. On the sunniest day, it feels overcast. When it rains, I hear blood splatter falling against a wooden floor. Screams from those tortured haunt me everyday. Only sometimes, I hear my screams. Do you know what I think when I hear my screams?'

Jack shook his head.

'I have heard enough dying people to recognise when death has come.' She stared harder into the fire. 'I don't think death has forgotten about me; I'm still waiting for my fate to catch up. My Talent is death; raising the dead from the ground so that they may live again. Not something a parent would want their little girl to do. Growing plants, as does your mother, is an envious ability. Mother is fond of flowers, and I could help my dad grow his crop in the field.' Forcing a smile made her cracked lips bleed. 'Can you imagine my mother's face if I brought back our old dog Huxter? We buried him beneath one of those pink trees I looked for atop the Hedge Wall. He'd only be gristle and bone now. A good dog, he was softer than mud. Mice would spook him, and send him running for cover. Huxter's return would not be a good idea.'

'No matter what trouble I was in, my mother always loved me,' said Jack. 'Your parents love you, there's nothing you can do that'll ever change that. Instead of riding Black, they'll give you a horse with a comfortable saddle. Riding a mare you'll be able to go anywhere on your farm.'

'I'm fourteen years old, yet my reflection tells the truth. I've aged since leaving home. I'm closer to forty than I should be. You're only twelve, and yet you look younger. Nothing has touched you Jack. I hope nothing will.'

Nothing had touched him; how can she think that? Everything affected him. He had accepted Yang before this all started, desiring his shadow's company. When Dwayne picked a fight, Yang was always there to stop him. Joined with Yang he had never lost a scrap. Hilarious, standing out here in the unknown

CRIK

wood, to think weather was his biggest concern back at the village. Long days stuck in his room looking out on the rain no longer seemed such a chore. At least in his bedroom he had his toys for company. The laughter that had threatened to spill from him dried up in his throat like spit on a hot griddle. What he now saw when he closed his eyes was not the rain beating against his bedroom window, but the Giant standing in the downpour. A cold wave swept up his back as he recollected the Giant watching him with its cluster of eyes. Stretching toward the flames, he tried to control his shivers.

'Careful, you'll burn your fingers,' Inara said.

The heat didn't touch him; a deep cold wrapped his innards like a strangling weed that crushed his will. The inescapable knowledge that he carried a demon had erected a barrier between him and the solace offered by the fire.

'I can still feel Krimble,' said Inara suddenly. Ignoring her own warning, she spread her hands toward the inviting flames. 'They hurt him for helping us escape.'

'Did you feel it, like when Black killed the stag?'

She nodded. 'Only with him I didn't turn his mind away from the pain. Staying with him, I relished every slice from their blades, though they hurt me too. Each time they bludgeoned him I gave small thanks; he deserves to suffer. Although I could only manage the connection for a few minutes, I know they attacked him mercilessly for hours.'

'Is he alive?'

'Of course,' she said, cracking a frightening smile. 'He is still getting off too easy. I cannot forgive his inhuman crimes against me, and especially the others. Torturous weeks, months, years for all the windowless room told me, we spent under his vacant mercies. Every unheard cry, every unanswered prayer, rings in my head. His every movement is a struggle, and yet, I want to inflict more pain on him. Do you think that is bad of me? Tell me Jack, should I let him die?'

Jack knew his mother would want him to urge her to forgive Krimble. He could hear her voice now, "Holding onto your hate, will make you as bad as him," she would say. Jack was not his mother. 'Let him suffer,' he answered. 'Given the chance, he would have let those rats eat our faces.'

'If it wasn't for Yang knocking him out,' said Inara.

Wisps flowed upward from Yang's back as he imitated the smoke rising from the roast. It looks so evil, thought Jack, staring at his dark twin. Would he feel differently if the demon that had jumped into Bill had looked friendlier? The question stumped him. Had he taken his friends into peril just because of the way the demon had looked? Naming the demon a Narmacil softened its inherent horror. Then, if benign, why had it kept itself secret? If it was kind, why did the Giant sneak it into the village during a storm? Mr Dash knew about it, yet he kept it secret. When the Village Elders dragged Mr Hasseltope from the river, the grave keeper didn't say a word. Again he wondered whether Mr

WHAT CAME NEXT

Dash needed to say anything. Bugs would have told Mr Gasthem, and if he knew, others would surely know the secret.

Opening his eyes, Bill said, 'There's a deep hole in the woods. It's not an animal burrow.'

'What's so strange about that?' asked Inara.

'It smells odd.'

Jack recalled the hole behind Knell's house. Krimble had destroyed the Lindre before he had discovered what lay at the bottom of that hole. Were the two holes somehow connected? 'Where is it?'

'Not far,' said Bill.

'We'd best wait for morning,' said Inara. 'Traipsing through the woods during the night isn't the best idea.'

'She's right,' said Bill. 'In the dark we won't be able to see what's in the hole.'

Despite the good reasons to wait, Jack wanted nothing more than to peer into the depression. He looked away from the fire to see only blackness. What waited out there for him to discover? Both Inara and Bill didn't share his eagerness to find out. Inara withdrew from the flame, while Bill busied himself with cutting into the cooked meat. Jack's growling stomach forced his attentions to the roasting pig. After handing a leg to Inara they all devoured their supper with relish.

'Why don't you bring Black back to camp,' said Inara. 'I'm sure he'll welcome the warmth of the fire, and we'll feel safer for having him close.'

'He's on his way back.'

'Did he look closer at the hole?' asked Jack.

'After taking one sniff he left it alone,' answered Bill. 'I think it's probably for the best if we walk around it tomorrow. Black has a nose for trouble, and if he doesn't like it, then neither do I.'

'We're going to the hole,' said Jack. 'Remember, I told you Knell had one in her garden.'

'You think the two holes are connected?' said Bill. 'Knell lives miles away.'

'Much of what we've seen doesn't make sense,' said Jack. 'If it's dangerous then we'll go.'

'If it's dangerous, we may not be able to leave,' said Bill. 'Good night Ying.' Turning his shoulder he fell immediately to sleep.

Hours passed before Jack stopped watching his sleeping friends. Curling up on his side, he tried to make himself comfortable on the lumpy ground. He tossed and turned until the black night sky turned lighter. Black watched him with his blue eyes. Jack wondered what the wolf didn't like about the hole. No matter what it was, he would find out soon.

Only a few wisps of smoke drifted up from the remains of the fire as Jack stood. Yang stretched beside him, before running into the trees. Stay out there, thought Jack, when Yang disappeared.

CRIK

'Come on, wake up,' said Jack, nudging Bill with his foot.

'What's the rush,' said Bill, covering his face.

'You too Inara, its morning.'

'Already,' she said.

'Ying, you can be really annoying,' said Bill, rising. 'Wish I hadn't mentioned that hole.'

'The sooner we find it, the quicker we'll be on our way,' said Jack.

With Bill's help, Jack got Inara onto Black. The wolf tossed his great head as Inara shifted her weight. 'Which way to the hole?' she asked.

Pointing, Bill said, 'About an hour's walk that way.'

'Then let's go, before Jack suffers a heart attack,' she said, gripping the coarse wolf hair.

Crowding the wolf's head, Jack led the group, with an occasional shout from Bill telling him he had gone the wrong way. Meandering through the bush, they found fresh water to fill the skins from Black's latest kill. Slinging one sloshing bag over his shoulder, Jack pushed through drooping vines and almost stumbled into a large hole.

Black shied away from the lip of the depression, jostling Inara, who patted his side with a calming hand. 'Careful Jack,' she said. 'I don't think you want to fall in there, Black's afraid of the hole.'

'Told you,' said Bill. 'Whatever this place is, Black can smell it's not right. Are you sure you want to look inside that thing?'

Regarding his friend, Jack gave a nod. 'I'm not just going to walk away. Whatever's at the bottom of that thing,' he said pointing at the hole, 'I'm going to see it. I don't care if a bird suddenly bursts into flames.'

'What?'

'Nothing,' replied Jack, edging toward the broken ground. Now closer, he could smell what had upset the wolf. It smelt like walking into a long disused room, occupied by bats and desiccated spiders. Deep rents tore the lip of the depression, some of which were wide enough to enclose his foot. Taking care where he tread he edged along the hole. Square-cut stone littered the blackened earth, like tombstones. He scanned the woods for signs of a dwelling. No abode sat nearby, the woods remained untouched.

'What do you see?' Bill called out.

What am I seeing, Jack wondered. Hanging over the edge, the overpowering smell made him light-headed. Carefully, he lowered himself onto his knees. Moist earth crumbled like freshly baked cake. Whatever made the hole had done it recently. Fearfully he returned his gaze to the dense wood. Was something out there watching him? The tightly packed Hawthorn trees could hide an army. A silent deadly army if one existed. No, he shook his head, Black would know if something watched them, but the wolf regarded him, as eager as Bill and Inara

WHAT CAME NEXT

to know what he had discovered. Although the depth of the hole would swallow him whole, he realised it would only reach Gashnite's giant calf.

'It's too dark to see what lies at the bottom,' said Jack. 'I'm going to climb inside.'

'Are you nuts,' cried Bill. 'Would you jump into a monster's mouth to pull its tonsils?'

'There's nothing in here, I just need a closer look. That's all.'

'And I suppose if you start screaming you expect me to rush in after you,' said Bill.

'Don't worry Bill, you can stay up here. I don't expect you to come in after me.'

'Good,' said Bill, crossing his arms. 'I'm glad we got that sorted.'

After leaping into the hole, the earth disintegrated before Jack's rushing shoes. Placing his feet side onto the crumbling ground, he tried to slow his descent. Each time his trailing fingers dug into the ground, they met little resistance, and the roots he did clutch snapped like fine hair. Something shattered beneath his heel as he reached the bottom. Looking down he expected to find an earthenware pot, such as the ones his mother kept her plants in, what he discovered astounded him. An egg, or more precisely, half an egg, lay under his foot. Recognition made him nauseous. Beneath his heel rested the remains of a golden egg, dissected by a jagged silver line. A Hatchling's egg. Another three broken shells were only a few feet from where he stood. Comprehending that he stood inside a demon's nest made his heart patter like a caged animal. Immediately he scanned the ground for any demons still lurking in the shadows. If they were here, they disguised themselves as brick and dirt. Sure the demons were about to attack he spun around and spied tracks leading from the broken eggs. Two-toed footprints trampled the ground. Staring at the imprints, he recalled their duplicate in his own garden. Serpentine tracks crossed the other prints, slithering its way through the moist ground before changing into small mouse tracks. They led away from the hole.

Following the demon tracks, Jack climbed out of the hole. Earth caked his fingers by the time he got to the top of the depression.

'What'd you find?' asked Bill, coming forward to help Jack.

Ignoring the question, Jack followed the two-toed prints. Every few feet the stride of the creature grew, as though the demon had both grown and increased its pace. The bare earth at the crest of the hole made it easy for him to see the prints, and when it entered the wood, the bent grass continued to tease him forward.

'Are those footprints?'

Jack only nodded.

'Those tracks lead in the direction where we want to go,' said Inara, walking Black up to them.

CRIK

A fifth and larger set of footprints met the four trails leading from the hole at the tree line. The new prints dwarfed Jack's own. He knew, by the two-inch depressions left in the soil, that something heavy had made the tracks.

'What do you want to do, Jack?' asked Inara.

The demon trails ended where they met the larger footprints, so whatever made those prints had carried the demons into the wood.

Looking ahead, Jack said, 'We follow the tracks.'

Bill's groan joined Black's whine as Jack led them into the trees.

41. THE CAT AND THE MOUSE

BIRD SONG FOLLOWED THEM into the woods. Tall grass whipped at their legs, dampening them with the dew that still clung to the green blades. Approaching a river Jack spotted a Heron standing on the bank, peering ever vigilant into the clear water. Everything hunted something, he mused. Fish ate the insects skating on the glassy river surface, the Heron waited for its chance, and Jack followed his quarry. Only, in his case, who hunted whom? The tracks following the winding river, carried them ever forward. Dense foliage crowded them, with red flowers colouring the undergrowth. Bill pointed out small animals the others missed. He was the first to notice a family of river voles. For a time the voles kept pace with them, before diving into the water.

The tracks remained fresh, so when the group spoke they did so in whispered tones that travelled no farther than their ears. Still, each spoken word ratcheted up Jack's nerves. When Bill discovered a badger's burrow, his shout almost had Jack follow the voles into the river.

'Be quiet,' said Jack. 'Whatever made these tracks is nearby.'

Bill muttered something, but left the burrow undisturbed.

Despite following an unknown danger, Jack still appreciated the variety of wildlife on offer. Even the blue dragonflies, hovering just above the swaying grass, enthralled him.

'This is stupid,' said Bill, forgetting to be quiet. 'Why are we following these footprints anyway? You want to see Knell, not rush into the woods to follow mysterious tracks.'

'Those were demon eggs we found,' whispered Jack. 'We need to see what they're up to.'

'We? Don't you mean you,' said Bill.

'There's a demon inside you as well.'

'It doesn't bother me half as much as it does to you.'

'Then you don't mind finding out what they're doing out here, do you?'

'As a matter of fact, I don't.' Bill crossed his arms.

'Then why argue?'

'It's what's carrying the Narmacils that concerns me.'

Jack had attempted, with little success, to match the stride of the maker of the footprints. Igneous Fowlt, who rode his multi-coloured wagon into Crik

CRIK

Village to sell his clocks, was the tallest man he knew. When the salesman tried to sell his wares to Jack's mother he always ducked to enter the house. Bill called him the Scarecrow, but even the Scarecrow couldn't match the wide stride they now followed.

'It crunched that log pretty good,' said Bill, pointed to where a splintered length of timber crossed their path. 'Do you see the impression it left.'

'The wood is rotten,' said Jack.

'You would have to be very big to make a dent that size,' said Bill.

'Black hasn't eased since discovering that hole in the ground,' said Inara. 'He's jumping at every sound. It's a wonder he hasn't thrown me off.'

'He doesn't like it here, that's for sure,' said Bill, patting the side of the big black wolf.

'If you're so scared of what's out there,' said Jack, stabbing his finger forward, 'then keep your voices down.'

'We aren't exactly inconspicuous out here, Jack,' said Inara. 'The river is keeping us out in the open. If that thing retraces its steps it will spot us, as surely as you can see me.'

'We can't enter the woods,' said Jack. 'We'd lose the tracks if we did.'

'Quiet, both of you,' said Bill. 'Do you hear that?'

Jack listened. At first, all he heard was the buzzing of the insects, and the occasional bird singing from the branches; then a continuous roar met his ears. A low rumble from ahead underscored every other sound in the wood. The question of whether a demon produced that noise struck a nerve in him. 'We'd better hide in the trees until we know what's making that sound.'

'So now you want to enter the woods,' said Inara.

'We can follow the sound as easily in the woods as out here,' said Jack, heading for the nearest tree.

The roar became a clamour the closer they got to the source. Hopping over a fallen branch Jack peered out to see a large waterfall. Water clashed against rocks, sending spray up in a white mist.

'It's only a waterfall,' said Bill, smiling with relief.

'What's that,' said Inara, cutting their reprieve short.

Within the mist moved an immense shape. Jack saw one huge hand, with roots for fingers, escaping a white shirtsleeve. Spying the Wood Giant, he threw himself against the ground, pulling Bill down with him. Could this be the same Giant he had seen burying the egg in front of Bill's house? It wore the same clothing, and the leaves falling from its high-rise brow were the same size and shape as the one he had seen.

'It's old,' whispered Inara, who kept back in the shadows. 'Look how broad its leaves are. I'd say it's at least two hundred years old.'

In the daylight, Jack noticed more detail than he had during that long ago stormy night. Tufts of moss grew out of the cracked brown skin of the Giant.

THE CAT AND THE MOUSE

The green and yellow moss concentrated mainly around the Giant's neck, gave the appearance of a thick scarf. Its humped back had split the white shirt fabric to reveal a patchwork of leaves, branches. Grey stone rose unevenly on its back, pushing aside red and brown leaves.

'It's heavy enough to have totally demolished the log it stepped on,' said Bill. 'It looks powerful enough to walk through a wall.'

A fact Jack had noted when he had watched the Giant from his bedroom window. At first, he thought the Giant hunched over to the drink the water, when the roots covering the Giant's mouth clutched at a wet stone. Within moments, the rock cracked and fell to pieces. His mother had told him the wood folk ate rock minerals. Whilst it devoured a second stone slab, movement at the back of the falls drew the attention of the trio.

'Do you see that,' said Bill, fixing his sights behind the feeding Giant.

Two immense spiders skittered across the wet stone. Each had grown to the size of a large dog. One had thick hair covering its long legs, with cruel fangs that no doubt oozed venom. A black carapace covered its swaying abdomen. Knuckles of twisted bone grew along the larger arachnid's carapace and legs. Their slow movements promised a creeping death. With its back turned to the spiders, the Giant was oblivious to the approaching danger.

'Those spiders will kill the Giant, for sure,' said Bill, watching the drama unfold with an intentness that concerned Jack.

'Do you want me to shout out a warning?' asked Inara.

'Are you crazy?' said Bill. 'Given the chance those spiders would be happy to snack on us too. No, let's see what happens.'

Did Bill want to see something die? Such bloodlust unsettled Jack more than the scuttling spider legs. Yang shared the dreadful fascination that excited them both. He almost threw up when Yang transformed into a spider. Trust his demon to share an affinity with these foul creatures. Turning back, he saw a huge thick centipede join the two spiders. The newcomer's, flattened, segmented body rushed across the rock, its long antennae twitching in the air as it located the spiders.

'There's something not right here,' said Bill. 'Arthropods don't grow to that size.'

'We're in a strange place Bill,' said Inara. 'We've never been this far away from home before. Who's to say what lives out here?'

The entrance of the centipede had stopped the spiders. The Giant still refused to look away from its meal.

'Will you stop it,' whispered Jack, swiping his shadow's spider legs off his arm. 'Why can't you just be normal? You don't always have to join in, and change your shape.' His internal temperature had plummeted at Yang's touch. Ignoring his shadow's antics, he turned back to the falls. 'Can either of you see the eyes of the spiders, or the centipede?'

CRIK

'Why?' asked Inara.

'If I'm right, I think I know what we're looking at.'

The falling water obscured his view, shielding the arthropod and the arachnids in its rising wall of mist. When he saw the golden eyes, dissected by a silver gash, between the centipede's antennae, Jack knew them as Hatchlings.

'The demons that live inside us,' he said, pointing forward, 'that's what they are.'

'You said it had two legs,' said Bill.

'I told you it changed its shape,' said Jack. 'Those are the things that hatched from the eggs. Do you see now why I want it gone? I don't want one of those things living inside me.'

'You're lying, Ying,' said Bill. 'I haven't got a spider crawling around inside me.'

'No, you've something worse than that. Every time they choose a new shape, they decide on something more grotesque. It mirrors the twisted, obscene creatures that they are. Look, Yang has changed its form to that of a spider.'

'Yang's only playing around,' said Inara. 'What he's doing is harmless.'

'Would you go down to the waterfall and cuddle one of those spiders?' asked Jack. 'Of course you wouldn't, you don't know what they would do to you.'

'You don't know that they're evil,' said Inara.

'Look at them Inara,' said Bill. 'They look pretty grim to me. The spider with the bones growing from it has fangs as long as my forearm.'

'So you're joining Jack now,' she said.

'I'm not saying that,' said Bill. 'But you've got to admit, they look scary.'

'That's a pretty shallow view Bill,' said Inara. 'You love Black, and he's not the friendliest looking beast in the woods.'

Leaving a pile of rubble behind, the Giant turned toward the Hatchlings. In anticipation, Jack hunched toward the tableau. The waterfall, sounding like the laughter of small children, drowned out the Giant's words; the Hatchlings rushed forward. Hanging from the ceiling the centipede transformed into a leaping frog with huge golden eyes, complete with its tell-tale silver lightning bolt. Both spiders kept their shape, though the hairy spider altered its hair into twigs and leaves.

'They're going to eat the Giant,' said Bill.

Instead of attacking the Wood Giant, the large frog leapt into its outstretched arms. Immediately it changed into a long snake and wrapped itself around the Giant's neck, nestling down amongst the moss that grew there. Carrying the snake, the Wood Giant retreated to the back of the waterfall.

'It's drawing something,' said Bill. 'Look, its holding a piece of chalk.'

The Giant busied itself with its sketch, and the Hatchlings paid attention. Jack wished he could see what the Giant drew. 'It looks like its teaching them.'

THE CAT AND THE MOUSE

'What do you mean, teaching them?' said Bill, not taking his eyes away from the strange classroom under the falls.

'How should I know,' said Jack. 'It reminds me of sitting in class though. Look, the spiders aren't moving; they're studying the wall.'

'Perhaps it's teaching them the best way to kill,' said Bill.

'That's something I expect to hear from Jack, not you Bill,' said Inara.

'Who's to say he's not right,' said Jack. 'I wouldn't pit Black against any one of those spiders. Out here in the woods, far away from the village, the Hatchlings don't have to hide what they are.'

'They never have,' argued Inara. 'Just because you don't understand them, doesn't automatically make what they're doing wrong.'

'You don't know what they're doing either,' said Jack. 'Why are you so scared to find out?'

'I refuse to damn them out of hand,' said Inara.

What more proof of the demon's nature, did she need? He wanted to get under the falls to discover what the Giant scrawled on the rock. Could he risk sneaking in closer? The trees thinned at the falls, cutting down his chances of remaining hidden. With a sigh, he settled down to wait for the Giant to finish.

Whatever it drew, it took the Giant a long time to complete. Roots seemed a poor alternative to fingers, making holding the chalk cumbersome and drawing with them an arduous task. The Hatchlings showed more patience than Jack did, with each sitting in rapt attention until the Giant finally stood back from the wall.

'I'm sure Dwayne would be able to see the drawing.' Bill fixed his glasses higher up his nose, perhaps in the hope of seeing beyond the Giant.

'You two will just have to be patient,' said Inara. 'The Giant will move eventually.'

'So now you're an expert on Wood Giants,' said Bill.

'I know a lot more about Crik Wood than you two,' she said. 'Until you met me you had never heard of the Lindre. And let's not forget, you had no idea about the Narmacil until I told you. You still don't understand them.'

'It seems,' said Jack, 'that the Narmacils have a few surprises that you weren't expecting either.'

'Everything has different sides to it. A dog might bite a stranger; does that make the dog mean? Or, was it protecting its master?'

'A dog isn't capable of turning into a monstrous spider,' replied Jack.

Yang mirrored the form of the Wood Giant, only smaller than the one who stood beneath the falls. Jack's shadow even mimicked the Giant's gestures, throwing up his large hands. After waving at each child, Yang turned to indicate the far mountain.

'We're going to the mountain,' said Inara. 'Once Jack is through with this foolishness,' she added under her breath.

CRIK

Morning lapsed into afternoon, and evening threatened before the Giant finally turned from the wall. Both spiders taking the form of ravens perched themselves on the hunched shoulders of the Wood Giant.

'Looks like it's going,' said Bill.

'Let's be patient a little longer,' said Jack. Cramp had settled into his legs whilst the Giant conducted the strange classroom, and he took a moment to rub his muscle. 'It's taking the demons toward the mountain.'

'Towards Knell,' said Bill.

Jack remained silent. Was the hole behind Knell's house, somehow connected to the hole the demons had vacated? If so, did the Giant's move toward the mountain indicate it had business with the woman with the crying baby. Were the two, cohorts? Had the Giant risen from the ground to hurt him? He wanted Knell to tell him how to kill his demon, or at least expel it from himself. Something he doubted she would do, if she were friendly with them.

Bill jumped into Black, and took the wolf down to the river's edge. Jack watched as the wolf entered the falls and appeared on the far side. 'Make sure it is safe.'

'Why do you think I'm doing this,' said Bill, opening his eyes.

What seemed an hour of waiting, only took a few minutes, when Bill said, 'The Giant is still walking. He's not coming back.'

'Then let's go,' said Jack, rising to his feet.

After waiting for Black to return to carry Inara, the three, led by Jack, walked down to the waterfall.

The sound of the crashing water was thunderous as they entered the falls. Deafened by the roar, the three approached the far wall, where the chalk shone brightly on the brown rock, which quickly revealed itself as a map. They knew many of the locations featured in the drawing.

'It's a map of Crik Woods,' shouted Jack. 'Look, there's the Hedge Wall.' He stabbed his finger at a large oval set in the middle of the drawing. The Giant had filled the inside of the oval with the broadside of the chalk. 'We must be here,' he said, indicating a series of three lines, which he presumed marked the waterfall.

'Look up here,' said Bill, moving forward. 'That's the mountain range, look how far it stretches.'

'And there, at the base of the mountain,' said Jack, 'is that a house?' A crude square stood where Jack looked. It was at the point where he expected to find Knell's house.

'There're more over here,' said Bill, indicating another three squares, with the third square being much larger than the others.

'Is that larger square a town?' Jack mused.

THE CAT AND THE MOUSE

'Look Ying, home,' said Bill, hunching down toward the base of the map. 'The Giant even drew the Hanging Tree; there's the noose hanging from its branch.'

Jack looked with amazement; it even showed the marsh with its solitary abode. 'This shows us the way home. Look, we don't have to go back through the Wold.' His finger traced a dotted path that connected each settlement on the map. 'Krimble lied; we could have gone around the Red Wood.' He saw how each dotted line gave the Wold a wide berth, with Knell's house being the closest dwelling to that foul place.

Inara remained quiet, until, with a cry, she jabbed the map with her cracked fingernail. 'I think this is my home.' The square she pointed out resided to the east of the marsh. 'It's beside a river, and not too far from the marsh. This must be it. And these,' she exclaimed with excitement, pointing at a series of sticks with round heads, 'must be the pink blossom trees I tried to see from atop the Wall.'

'If that's your house,' said Bill, 'it's close to our village. The line that follows from the Hanging Tree, that's Brandy Road, which connects directly to your house.'

'It must only be a day's ride from your village.' A shadow of concern swept aside her broad smile.

Jack held her shoulder and gave her a warm smile. 'They'll be happy to see you,' he said.

Inara nodded.

'I don't understand these markings.' Bill indicated what he could only discern as letters above three disparate squares. A fourth lay closer to their location, near the edge of a lake. 'Did the Giant name something?'

'How many broken eggs did you see in the hole, Jack?' The roar of the cascading water smothered Inara's words.

About to answer three, Jack stopped himself. Two belonged to the spiders, another to the centipede, but four sets of tracks led from the hole. Above the sound of the waterfall, he heard something scrape along the stone roof.

42. HERE'S LOOKING AT YOU KIDS

A GOLDEN EYE, PEERING DOWN from a sail of black barbs and flapping skin, twitched from Inara to Jack. Nests of bubbling worms tethered the sail to the roof of the waterfall with little hooks that found even the smallest cracks in the rock. Moving, the creature's hooks scraped the ceiling, emitting the tell-tale sound that had first alerted Jack to its presence.

Black snarled up at the Hatchling, showing his long fangs. Inara wrestled with the wolf to stop it from leaping for the Narmacil.

'What's it supposed to be?' asked Bill, craning his neck.

'I guess, a mixture of things it's seen,' said Jack. 'Or perhaps something it conjured in its sick mind. Before the one that jumped into you took the shape of a two-legged demon it looked like a dragon. Only it then had two mouths. That night, the demon copied Yang.' He looked at his shadow, who studied the demon clinging to the ceiling. 'Yang decided to play with it. Though I now believe my demon taught the Hatchling.'

'We know the Narmacils are old,' said Inara. 'What makes you think Yang had to teach it anything?'

'I don't know.'

'Perhaps, when they go into the egg, they forget things,' said Bill. 'When I wake up, I always forget my dreams. When the Narmacils find someone new to join, they may draw a blank when it comes to their past lives.'

Pulling itself along, the Hatchling stopped above Yang. An incomplete hand separated itself from the canvass of skin.

'It's waving at Yang,' said Bill.

'They're saying hello to each other,' said Inara.

'Let's hope my shadow doesn't decide to transform into a bear, or we'll have a real problem on our hands.'

Jack wished he had kept quiet. Instead of a bear, Yang took the shape of the ferocious cat it had used to thwart the Myrms' ambush. The razor sharp claws, the long muzzle filled with curved sabres that snapped at the air, were enough to entice the Hatchling to follow Yang's example. Instead of worms with their little hooks, the Hatchling now dug into the rock with nine-inch long claws

'That's wonderful,' said Bill. 'Now we're screwed.'

HERE'S LOOKING AT YOU KIDS

Skin bubbled as the Hatchling formed the cat's tail and a mane of hair that writhed as though brushed by a gale.

'Don't mention anything else Ying,' said Bill, backing away from the cat. 'I don't want you giving this thing the idea to bite us.'

'That isn't a thing,' said Inara. 'The Narmacil is copying Yang; it doesn't mean us any harm.'

Jack detected a quiver in her voice. The demons were showing Inara a side of themselves that she never knew existed. She still fought against the idea that the demon inside her could be evil. He only hoped that it wouldn't be too late when she understood the threat the demons posed. Looking at the cat, with its switching tail, he hoped that time wasn't now.

'Do we run?' asked Bill.

'We won't outrun that,' replied Jack. 'But I think we best get back to the trees. Eventually the Giant will notice he's missing one demon, and come back for it.'

'Wait,' said Inara, pointing up at the Hatchling.

Turning from Bill, Jack saw the demon waved at them with a hand extending from its chest.

'It's saying hello,' said Inara. She enthusiastically returned the wave.

'It's trying to keep us here,' said Jack, moving toward the curtain of water. 'It wants to delay us, so that the Giant can catch us.'

'It's trying to communicate with us,' said Inara.

'There's only one person that I know of that can talk with the demons,' said Jack.

'Krimble would be evil with or without his Narmacil's Talent,' said Inara.

'You can't be certain of that,' said Jack. 'If we stay here and try to play pantomime with this thing, we'll get caught. I don't fancy escaping the Ghost Walkers, to just get captured by the Wood Giant.'

'I think Ying's right,' said Bill.

'Stop calling me that. My name's Jack. Now come on, before we run out of time.' He leapt through the curtain of water to the other side of the falls.

Bill left without taking his eyes from the Hatchling and his steps were ponderous as he passed through the water.

'Is Inara coming?' asked Jack.

'She was still waving her hand when I left. She waved so fast; you'd swear she was trying to fan a fire.'

Great, now she's trying to befriend the demon. Through the falling water, Jack saw her silhouette atop Black. He couldn't see the demon, its black skin blended perfectly with the dark roof of the falls. He noticed, without surprise, that Yang had also remained behind. The only thing he could see of his shadow was its two legs extending before him. No doubt, Yang enticed the Hatchling with the delights it would enjoy when it found a host. The demon may grant a

CRIK

little girl with the Talent to make her dolls move, or give a boy the power to breathe under water. Who would care where they got it? Would they be troubled if they knew that spiders as large as dogs could jump into their sleeping mouths? Disappearing like a puff of smoke in a blizzard. Until now, Bill couldn't care less where he got his Talent to command animals. Looking at his friend, he knew Bill's attitude had changed since seeing the demons for himself. Inara's hadn't, the demon excited her.

'Inara, come on. We have to go.' The roar of the falls drowned out his words.

'She's not going to leave,' said Bill. 'She thinks it's wonderful.'

'How wonderful will she think it is when it jumps down and bites her?'

Each minute Inara remained behind the falls the more impatient Jack became. First, he tapped his palm against the side of his leg, and then his foot kicked the wet stone. 'You'll have to bring her out,' said Jack. 'The Wood Giant will be here any minute.'

'How can I bring her out if she doesn't want to leave?'

'She's riding Black isn't she,' said Jack. 'Command Black to follow us, and he'll carry her with him.'

'She's not going to like that.' Bill looked worried.

'I don't care. Just do it.'

'Ok, but when she starts shouting I'm going to tell her you made me.'

Still flapping her hand Inara came closer to the falls. Jack realised, to his horror, that Inara wasn't waving at the demon, she was beaconing for it to follow her. Beyond her, a dark outline dropped to the ground.

'What do you think you're doing?' said Jack as Inara joined them.

'It's by itself,' said Inara, looking back as the large cat followed her through the water. 'We can't leave it here.'

'Yes we can,' said Bill.

'The Wood Giant will come looking for it,' said Jack. 'We can't have that thing with us.'

'Can't Jack?' said Inara. 'When have you ever listened to us when we told you that you couldn't do something? We entered the Wold for you. We're here now because of your hunt to discover more about the Narmacil. Well, we have one.'

Jack shook his head. 'It's too dangerous. We can't go up against the Wood Giant. By drawing that map, it showed it knows Crik Wood better than anyone.' He pointed back into the falls. 'And remember, Yang guided us to Huckney, by talking with the other demon. They're connected. The other three will always know where this one is. We can't take it with us.'

'This is your chance to see that the Narmacil aren't something to fear,' said Inara. 'If the Narmacil wanted to hurt us, all it had to do was attack us when our backs were turned. Look at it, it hasn't even growled.'

HERE'S LOOKING AT YOU KIDS

Looking at the Hatchling, with its gaping mouth, showing rows of fangs, made Jack believe the demon was grinning at them. He had no doubt the demon had enough intelligence to follow the argument, or at least understand that they talked about it. The demon hadn't formed any eyelids, making its stare unbearable.

'What do you think Bill?' asked Inara, turning to face Bill. 'Do you think the Narmacil is a demon? Should we fear what's inside us? Remember, before the Giant brought the Narmacil to you, the village regarded you as a freak. Do you want to go back to having no Talent? Without it, you'll lose Black.'

'I don't fear the Narmacil.' Bill took off his glasses, and busied himself by wiping the lenses on his shirtsleeve, which left them more smeared than before. 'Ying is right about one thing. Why have they kept themselves secret? By hiding from us, they make me suspicious of what they're doing.'

'What they are doing,' said Inara, 'is helping you. Jack doesn't want to see how Yang has helped us. Krimble would have killed us all back in his house if Yang hadn't struck him. If you didn't control Black, Silver wouldn't have been in the marsh when we needed her. Without his Narmacil, Huckney couldn't have made Gashnite, leaving us to fend for ourselves against the Ghost Walkers. At every turn, our Narmacils have helped us. Can you tell me of one occasion where they have not been there for us?'

'What of the Giant?' said Jack. 'Do you trust that as well? By taking that thing with us, we run the risk of angering the Giant. Do you want to invite more danger, after everything we've gone through?'

'If the Giant is helping the Narmacil, then the Giant is helping us,' said Inara. 'Why didn't the Giant attack you Jack? We've all seen it now; your front door wouldn't have stood up against one blow from the Giant's hand. If your knowing was so dangerous, it would have silenced you that night.'

Jack knew Mr Dash knew about the demon. He had seen that too, though he hadn't told the others of his vision. Everyone and everything had secrets, even him.

Yang played with the other demon, tugging on its wriggling mane. The two demons acted like children, playing in the garden. The Hatchling now ignored the conversation, giving Jack's shadow its undivided attention. Looking at them, Jack almost smiled. No, he thought, they are acting innocent to fool me again.

'It can't come,' Jack said again. 'I'm trying to find Knell, for the reason of getting rid of my demon. I'm not going to invite another one into my life.'

'Getting rid of,' said Inara. 'That's so final Jack. Do you want to kill Yang?'

'If that's the only way to be free,' replied Jack.

'And you Bill?' asked Inara. 'You've only had your Talent for a short time. You remember how excited you were when you discovered you could control an animal. How excited you must have felt to tell Jack, and to show the others in the village what you could now do. Without the Narmacil, none of that would have been possible.'

'If the demons didn't exist,' said Jack, 'Bill wouldn't have ever felt singled out in the first place. Tommen Guild wouldn't be able to ice things by just touching it. Tracey wouldn't dance in the air.'

'Why would that be a good thing?' asked Inara. 'She must love the feeling of rising in the air. Your Talent is not what defines you. I see you Jack, not what your shadow is doing. Bill,' she said, focusing on Bill, 'when I think of you, I think about how smart you are. The books you've read. The relationship I know you have with your grandparents. Your grandmother is a Ghost Walker, yet she isn't evil like Kyla, or the Red Sisters.'

'No, she's not,' said Bill.

'It's you who defines who you are. What you chose to do with the gift that the Narmacil has given you, not what it does.'

'This is nonsense,' said Jack. 'We're wasting time here. Bring the demon if you must. But, at the first sign of the Wood Giant, we'll leave the demon behind. Agreed?'

'Ok, Jack, that sounds fair,' said Inara. 'Which way do you want to go? The Giant set off in the direction we need to follow. Do you want to set off after it, or should we head back into the woods and hope to find our way through the trees?'

'We follow,' said Jack. 'Only this time, we keep far back. I don't want any more surprises.'

Taking the lead, Jack skipped over the wet stones to the other side of the river. Looking behind he watched as the demon, with a forked tongue dangling from its black lips, followed him across. He didn't trust the demon, it would betray them the first chance it got; of that he had no doubt.

43. THE WRITINGS ON THE WALL

THE FIRST THING TO ANNOY Jack was having the demon with them. The second was that the demon seemed fond of him. The bouncing cat, with its snake-like hair, had refused to leave his side since departing the falls. The cat's exuberance left him cold and sick. He wished the demon would aggravate someone else. Irritating him almost as much as the demon's affection was the smile fixed on Inara's lips. Sat atop Black she towered over him, with Bill taking up the rear. Cruel black teeth extended from the demon's quivering lips. One bite from those powerful jaws would snap his bones as easily as a stick would break rhubarb.

The mountain rising above the trees made their direction easy, though the bracken they fought through was hell-bent on trying to stop them from reaching it. Jack beat the brush aside with a long stick, clearing the worst obstacles from his path. Roping vines and twisted reeds ensnared his feet at every step. To combat the underbrush, he noticed the demon constantly changed the cat's paws into different shapes. Stilted legs picked through nests of thorns. Tackling low hanging branches, the demon transformed its legs into crab-like claws that scrambled under such obstruction. He was almost glad that Bill had a harder time picking his way through the woods than he did.

'I haven't seen any sign of the Giant passing through here,' said Inara.

'Good,' replied Jack. 'We know which way we have to go. Hopefully,' he added, 'the Giant struck off somewhere else.'

'Unless he returned to the falls to find the Narmacil, and is now following our footsteps,' said Bill.

Great, something else to worry about. 'We'll get through the trees soon,' said Jack, pulling his foot from a muddy puddle.

Trudging on for a further hour, Jack constantly cast his eyes back, afraid that he would spy the Giant lumbering up behind them. Again, he cursed Bill for planting the idea into his head.

'I'm exhausted,' said Bill.

'There weren't any tracks marked on the map this close to the falls,' said Inara. 'I'm afraid we'll have to battle through until we reach the lake.'

Jack had forgotten about the large body of water he had seen from atop the Hedge Wall. The Giant had drawn it, making the lake appear as a moth splashed on the rock just above the falls. He would worry how they would get across the lake when they reached its shore.

'How're we going to cross the lake?' asked Bill.

Wonderful, thought Jack. His friend struggled through the mud behind him. 'We've got difficulties already, without thinking ahead to anymore.'

'Well I can't swim,' said Bill. 'I suppose Black can carry us across, one at a time.'

Inara shook her head. 'We aren't talking about a small pond. Black doesn't have the strength to carry us across. Jack's right, we can't worry about every obstacle ahead of us, we must focus on where we are.'

'If you say so,' said Bill. 'Only, we haven't got any tools to make a boat.'

'Bill,' cried Jack and Inara together.

The demon beside Jack began to bubble and shrink before his eyes.

'What's it doing,' said Jack, taking a step from the demon.

Looking at the Narmacil from atop Black, Inara said, 'It's changing shape.'

'Into what?' wondered Jack.

The demon shrank to the height of Jack's knee. Its mane disappeared, as did the cat's large fangs and razor sharp claws. The demon's hind legs grew powerful; with a low joint bending the leg back in on itself. Small bristles appeared along the length of the legs. Overlapping plates along its elongated body reminded Jack of the Myrm's armour. Golden eyes watched from an alien head; two short antennae struck out from its brow.

'What is it?' said Jack. He didn't try to disguise his disgust at the form the demon chose. 'Do you think its preparing to attack?'

'Don't be silly; if the Narmacil wanted to attack us, why change from the cat?' said Inara.

'Look at its square head,' said Bill, moving in closer. 'It's weird.'

Rubbing its hind legs together, the Narmacil emitted a rasping sound.

'It's calling out to the Giant,' cried Jack.

Twitching, the Narmacil leapt high into the sky. It bounded again, to disappear into a hedge with blue leaves. They waited in stunned silence, and then they heard the Narmacil rub its legs together from within the bush.

'It's a grasshopper,' said Bill, clapping his hands.

Around them, they heard a sea of singing, crackling from within the tall grass. The grasshoppers hidden around them, answered the demon, reinforcing Bill's recognition of its chosen form.

'I think Yang wants to play with his new friend,' said Inara. Yang taking the form of a giant ant scurried into the brush after the Narmacil. 'It's good to see him happy.'

Jack knew Inara was attempting to goad him into arguing with her. It seemed she wanted to defend the demons at every turn. Let her, it wouldn't be too long now until this whole adventure came to an end. A duck broke from hiding with a flap of its wings, breaking his train of thought. The demon leaped after the duck, chasing it with Yang in tow.

'Those two are like children,' said Inara, watching the grasshopper and the ant. 'They like to play all the time.'

'Well their play is making a racket,' said Jack. 'It's not only the Wood Giant we have to worry about. This is a dangerous place. We escaped a pack of wolves once already; I don't fancy trying it a second time. What if they wake a bear,' he added, seeing Yang crash into a tree.

'There're always what ifs, with you,' said Inara. 'Let them play. We've been dragging ourselves through the woods for hours. We daren't speak, in case we stir some unknown thing from cover. Well I've had enough. Bill,' she said, turning around to see Bill tripping over a looping vine, 'why don't you tell us one of your grandfather's tales. It will cheer me up.'

'A story, here, now?' said Bill.

'Why not,' said Inara. 'It may lift our mood.'

'I'll give it a go,' said Bill. 'Though I'm not the storyteller my grandfather is.'

'Just tell the story,' said Inara, her patience exhausted.

'Okay,' said Bill. 'Here goes.

'There was a boy, all skinny and fair,
Not like the other boys, who always gave him a glare.
For the Hunters and sportsman, would often swear,
What use was the boy with the mop of fair hair?

There was a bear, big and strong,
Who would often do wrong.
He wore his winter's coat, grown grizzled and long,
Back in his cave he slept where he belonged.

Hunters and sportsmen teased the boy, all skinny and fair.
He couldn't run fast, against them he hadn't a prayer.
He gleaned, from what he could read,
How best to win a measure of their esteem.

Everybody is scared of the big, mean bear,
Not our boy, who slipped away without a care.
With whistle and sling he only carried,
To the cave, to see the big, mean bear.

The bear's snores made the cave rumble,
From without it seemed the rock would crumble.
In crept the boy, taking care where he tread,

CRIK

and then the cave echoed to his whistle instead.

A terrible roar,
Magnificent and raw,
Awoke with the terrible bear.
A boy entering his cave was rare.

The bear sought to scare,
With his terrible, stare.
For the boy with the fair hair,
Didn't belong in the bear's lair.

With a scamper and jump,
The skinny, fair boy fled,
To the village he led,
The terrible mean bear.

The huntsmen hid,
The sportsmen fled,
From the terrible bear,
The young fair boy led.

From his book,
The young fair-haired boy read,
The bear had a soft head,
He smiled, for this he had read.

He swung, overhead,
A fistful of stone,
Which when sped,
Struck the bear on his soft head.

With a moan and groan,
the big mean bear,
All ten feet tall,
Fell with a stone imbedded in his head.

With the bear put abed,
The huntsman and sportsmen, filled with dread,
Weary of the boy, all skinny and fair,
And what he had read.

THE WRITINGS ON THE WALL

'Told you, it wasn't any good,' said Bill, looking embarrassed.

'I thought I knew all your grandfather's tales and poems,' said Jack. 'I never heard that one.'

Bill, looking even more uncomfortable, said, 'It's not one of my grandfather's. I made it up. I've done some more, and I'm afraid they're all just as bad.'

'I thought it was fantastic,' said Inara. 'Brain over brawn, every time.'

Inara's smile was so infectious the two boys joined her. Jack was enjoying the feel of the smile on his lips; he couldn't recall the last time he had something to smile about, when a cry from beyond the hedge cut his mood short.

'The demon attacked someone,' said Jack.

'The cry came from over there,' said Inara, pointing toward a bush that stood away from the Narmacil and Yang. 'Whatever made it, sounded human.'

'It could be a trap,' said Jack. 'Laying bait, the same as a hunter would do to get his kill.' He strained to hear anymore sound from beyond the line of bushes. He thought he heard a muffled cry. The wind rattled the leaves on the bush, making it look for a moment as though someone, or something, fought their way through. Yang headed toward the plant, curious as ever to see what lay beyond the green screen.

'I don't want my shadow to stir up anymore trouble,' said Jack, moving toward the hedge himself. 'I think we'd best see what made that cry, someone could be hurt.'

Without another word, the trio moved forward, with Inara, having dismounted Black, using her arms to pull herself across the uneven ground. Mud sucked at their knees, and the grass tickled their faces. Each one listened for any sound. A creak, as though from tortured wood, intruded the hushed silence as they approached. The groan of wood repeated, as Jack, with a wavering hand, pulled the covering foliage aside to see a wagon resting on the shore of a large lake.

Flaking paint covered the four wheels of the wagon; one wheel had a thin coat of yellow, another red, the third blue, and the fourth wheel had a faded layer of green paint, with long strips missing to reveal the cracked wood beneath. All four colours covered the wagon. Two round windows peered out from its side like two holes cut into a scary mask.

A wiry man, wearing what would have once been a bright shirt, yet was now as faded as the wagon wheels, whittled away at a wood figure in his lap. Working quickly he shaped a small figurine of a girl; her upraised arms locked in a dance pose. The small knife, the man held between forefinger and thumb, cut the cheeks and carved a smile on the face of the little figure. Before the man stood a woman, with thick black hair tied into braids. She wore a yellow skirt, with a red sash around her waist, and a second scarf, draped over her arms.

CRIK

'Ajenda,' said the wiry man. 'I have made you this figurine, to give to your daughter.'

'Jess is our daughter,' said Ajenda, looking to the wagon with an arched eye. 'You may not like having one. Perhaps you're still feeling the sting of me giving birth to a girl, and not the boy you so desperately wanted.'

Yang pointed, and the three cowering within the cover of the foliage saw a young girl with a tear streaked face cowering under the wagon.

'It's not the disappointment of having a daughter that troubles me,' said the man, finishing the wooden figure by separating the fingers on the upraised hands.

'Then what is it Jankal?'

'You are a fine woman Ajenda. I feel honoured to have you with me. You are useful. With a flick of your wrist you command the wagon to move.' Jankal indicated the wagon with a toss of his head. 'I don't have to have horses pull the wagon, so I don't have to worry about feeding them. By making the trees step from our path, you speed out travel. Make this figurine dance for Jess.' He handed over the doll.

'And you can make one fish turn into two, and then four,' said Ajenda. 'So that's it. You don't think your daughter is of use to you.'

'Don't put it so harshly,' said Jankal, wincing from the raven-haired woman's words. 'How will she attract a man without a Talent?'

'She can cook, and mend your clothes already,' said Ajenda. 'And isn't she beautiful. That would be enough for most men.'

Jankal shook his head. 'Life out here in the woods is hard. A man needs his wife to be of use. Without a Talent, Jess will only ever be a man's acquaintance. No one will take her seriously.'

'Is that how you see me, Jankal?' asked Ajenda. 'If I couldn't move wood, would I have just been your plaything?'

'You know what will happen,' said Jankal, ignoring the fire in Ajenda's eyes.

'With your tests, you have made our daughter cry again,' said Ajenda. 'She's still young; it's not unheard of for someone older than Jess to gain their Talent.'

'It's my duty as a father to help her discover her gift.'

'Making her stare at a fish for hours isn't helping,' said Ajenda. She snatched the wooden figure from Jankal's grasp. 'No wonder she cried out. Having you tell her she isn't good enough is upsetting her.'

Ajenda placed the wooden figure on the ground. The raven-haired woman stared at the doll, and then with a tilt of her hand she made the doll dance. The doll's stiff movement accentuated her performance. Pirouetting over the ground, the doll leapt over the leaves. Kicking her heels high into the air, she danced under the wagon to where Jess still cried.

Jack watched as the girl reached out to the dancing figurine. He could see the girl was still clearly distraught, and yet her mother's present made her smile

THE WRITINGS ON THE WALL

as the dancer twirled under her outstretched hand. Playing with her new toy, Jess didn't see the pair of golden eyes slinking closer to her beneath the wagon.

Jack saw the demon. His mouth dried. He knew the demon wanted the little girl. Suddenly he knew the meaning of the writing on the wall beneath the falls. The Giant had marked this spot, knowing Jess would be here. Jess would play host to the demon.

With a rush, Jack bounded to his feet, breaking his cover.

44. THE DEMONS WITHIN US

As Jack ran from the hedge, a forest of twig, branch, and logs, rose into the air, causing his steps to falter. Jankal stood in front of Ajenda; he now carried two knives instead of one. Both sets of eyes watched with narrowed suspicion. A snapped twig, with a sharp end, revolved in the air a few inches from Jack's temple. He had no doubt Ajenda would throw the wood with deadly accuracy if he tried anything rash.

'Speak quickly, and be careful what you say,' said Jankal. 'Who are you, and what do you want?'

Noticing maroon splashes on the faded yellow shirt, increased Jack's trepidation of the man. Was that blood? He wanted to look toward the wagon to discover how far away from the little girl, Jess, the demon was.

'There's something under the wagon with your daughter,' he said, holding up his hands.

'It's her doll,' said Jankal. 'I made it for her.'

'No, not that,' said Jack. 'A devil is under the caravan; it wants your daughter.'

'Jess,' said Ajenda. 'Come out here, quickly.'

Managing to wrestle his eyes from the spinning wooden projectile, Jack looked to the wagon. Cloaked in shadow it took him a moment to find the girl and the animated doll. He failed to see the demon.

'Listen to your mother,' said Jankal. 'Come out here where we can see you.'

Jess crawled out between the wagon wheels. Her white dress, stained black and brown, hung on her skinny frame. The muddy bank of the river had also coated her hands and face; tears had left clean streaks down her cheeks.

'Quickly now,' said Jankal.

The girl scampered to Ajenda. The wooden doll, with its rickety steps, tried to keep up with Jess.

'You okay Jess?'

Jess nodded at her mother.

'What's the meaning of scaring us like that?' said Jankal. 'My girl is fine, there's nothing under the wagon.'

THE DEMONS WITHIN US

Still looking under the wagon for the golden eyes, Jack said, 'The demon that followed me here crept under the wagon. The last time I saw it, it was behind your daughter.'

'Are you alone?' asked Jankal, tossing the knife in his left hand.

The bush behind Jack rustled as Bill, with Inara clinging to his back, broke cover. Jack was happy to see that Bill had enough sense not to bring Black with them. As the pair joined them, Ajenda threatened them with more wood.

'You were spying on me and my family,' said Jankal.

'We heard someone crying, and came over to see if someone needed our help,' said Inara. 'Is the girl alright?'

'My daughter's condition isn't any of your business,' said Jankal.

'You three aren't travelling folk,' said Ajenda. 'Where're you from?'

'The village of Crik,' said Bill. 'Lost in the woods, we have travelled far.'

'Seems to me that you're still lost,' said Jankal. 'Your village is a long way from here. I have met a few of your hunters. One stole a deer I had tracked for hours.'

'You still had the deer,' said Ajenda. 'You doubled the carcass so that both you and the hunter had meat.'

'That's not my point,' said Jankal. 'I had followed the deer through the wood, down deep dells, and across flowing streams. She was mine to kill.'

'The demon,' said Jack. Their lack of questions concerning the demon had him wondering whether they had heard him. The demon had crept up on their daughter, and he still couldn't see where the monstrous grasshopper had gone. Yang still held the ant form it had taken when it played with the demon, thankfully his shadow remained flat against the ground. So far, the travelling troupe hadn't seen him.

'If there is a demon here, why'd you bring it to us?' asked Jankal. 'You brought danger to my family. For that, I should have my wife stick you with the wood.'

Did the wood by Jack's head spin faster? He thought so, but he dared not step away from it. 'We didn't know you were here,' he said. 'We want to travel across the lake.'

'Why'd you want to cross the Kratch? Nothing lies beyond there; only mountains,' said Ajenda.

'You want to get to the Scorn Scar,' said Jankal.

Despite himself, Jack took a forward step. 'You know of the Scar?'

'And of the witch that lives there,' said Jankal. 'She consorts with demons. Is that why you travel with one?'

Jack wanted to yell at Jankal, to shake the man in his faded shirt. Why would he put himself at risk to warn Jankal about the demon, if the demon belonged to him? Shaking his head ruffled his nest of sandy hair that had grown unruly as the days passed. 'We're going to see Knell, so that she may free me from a demon.'

'The one you saw under my wagon,' said Jankal.

'No,' said Jack, 'there's another I want gone.'

'You have more than one demon with you?' asked Ajenda.

Inara, living in a normal house, knew about the Narmacil. A family spending their lives in the wood would surely know of them. Their apparent naivety perplexed him.

Jankal noted his confusion. 'What aren't you telling me, boy?'

Jess, without joining with a demon, would never show a Talent, no matter how hard her father pressed her. As that notion registered, he looked to the little girl clinging to her mother's skirt.

'Ask your daughter if she can do anything she couldn't before,' said Jack. 'If I'm right, she'll now be able to show you her Talent.'

'You spied on us; you know she hasn't got a Talent. Are you taunting us?' said Jankal, edging forward with a glower-darkened face.

'Ask her,' repeated Jack. 'If I'm right then she'll show you her Talent.'

As Jankal turned his attention to his daughter, Jess reached up and pulled on the red sash tied around her mother's waist. The doll in turn clung to Jess's leg.

'It's alright,' said Ajenda, smoothing her daughter's dark hair. 'The boy is scaring her,' she said to Jankal.

'The boy is nothing to be afraid of,' said Jankal.

'Ask her to try,' said Jack. 'If I'm wrong, I'll be happier for my mistake.'

'Don't try anything,' said Jankal, waving a knife toward Jack. 'Jess,' he said, turning to his daughter. 'I'm sorry I shouted earlier. I was only trying to help you. Your mother is right, you don't have the same Talent as me, and you can't lift the wood and make trees walk like your mother. Something remains hidden within you; you have to coax it out.' When Jess refused to pull her face from Ajenda's skirt, Jankal reached out to her. 'Baby girl, do you feel any different? Is the world speaking to you, guiding you to your own special Talent? Show us Jess.'

The girl shook her head. 'I tried, I can't do anything.'

'Do as your father says,' said Ajenda. 'Reach out, and try once more. I promise no one will be angry if nothing happens.'

Looking at Jess's father, holding his two knives and a scowl, Jack doubted whether Jankal would be happy if his daughter failed to show her Talent.

The wooden figure of the dancer sprang away from Jess's leg. With her wooden arms upraised, the dancer spun, scattering brown and red leaves as she rushed away from the little girl. Abject horror twisted the dancer's face as she ran from Jess. What was the little girl doing? Looking up from the doll, Jack saw Jess's hair rise. Pirouetting, the doll leapt through the air, when her wooden tresses caught alight. Fire spread slowly across the carved face of the dancer,

THE DEMONS WITHIN US

blackening the wood, before spreading, setting the maple dress on fire. Jack stumbled back as the doll danced closer. Spreading her fingers, the dancer tried to catch the rising embers, as though wanting to keep hold of every part that burned away. Blackened legs crumbled under her, toppling her to the ground where she lay twitching as the fire raged.

The parents watched the smouldering remains in shocked silence.

'I wouldn't fancy sleeping in that wagon if she can do that,' whispered Bill.

'Hush,' said Inara, smacking Bill's arm. 'Unlocking her Talent has terrified her.'

'Why is she frightened? She started the fire.'

'It's all new to her. A minute ago, she couldn't do a thing; now she can make things burst into flame with her mind. Such power would terrify anyone. Can she control her Talent?'

'If she can't, we should be afraid of her,' said Bill. 'I'm only glad that we're standing beside a lake.'

Jess's hair had fallen once more about her slender shoulders. She turned from her mother's skirt and looked at the remains of the doll she had burnt. Unshed tears sparkled in her dark eyes, offering a clue as to what the girl thought about her new power.

'Did you do that?' asked Ajenda, holding her daughter's shoulders.

'I knew I could do it,' said Jess. 'I didn't want to hurt her.'

'Don't worry, I'll make you another doll,' said Jankal.

'Something inside told me I could do it,' said Jess.

Jack knew she talked about the demon that had entered her. It had unlocked something in Jess, giving her a destructive Talent. He again looked down at the pile of charcoal at his feet. She could set them all ablaze. Would the demon want her to do that? Her demon knew his intent, get to the Scorn Scar and kill his demon. Feeling unsafe, he wanted nothing more than to flee from the travelling family.

'You've done something wonderful Jess,' said Jankal, with enough pride to burst his brass buttons. 'From now on, you can light the cooking fire for your mother. You can keep us warm during the winter.'

A look of concern on her daughter's face, prompted Ajenda to say, 'Jess, you have a gift. With it you can help your father and I. Your Talent will grow with you. When I was your age, I could only lift a single branch. Now look at what I can do.' The smile Ajenda gave her daughter was as warm as the smoking remains of the doll.

'I'm happy for you Jess,' said Inara. 'Discovering your Talent is a wonderful thing.'

'It was the demon,' said Jack. 'It entered your daughter, allowing her to destroy the doll. Come with us across the Kratch, there Knell will help your daughter.'

CRIK

'I won't take my daughter to that witch.' Jankal's face filled with anger. 'You talk as though finding her Talent has cursed my daughter. What she can do is cause of celebration, not something to fear.'

'We all have demons inside of us,' said Jack.

'You, with your moving shadow, may have a demon inside of you.' Jankal smiled as he nodded. 'Yes,' he said through a snort, 'I saw your shadow rush to the flame. My daughter can do something beautiful.'

'Beautiful? She killed that doll,' said Jack. Didn't they see the horror on the dancer's face? Why was he the only one who saw the tragedy of what had just unfolded?

The wood floating around Jack's head spun faster as they drew close. Closest spun a gnarled log. Dark smoke rose from the suspended projectile.

'He didn't mean to upset you,' said Inara. 'If you can tell us a way to cross the lake, we'll be on our way.'

'The Kratch is wide and deep,' said Jankal. 'You wouldn't be able to swim its waters, even if you had your legs.'

More smoke rose from the other pieces of wood Ajenda held in the air.

Jack felt the rising temperature. Was it the girl or the demon doing this? Yang acted separately from himself, could the giant grasshopper, which had jumped into Jess, be trying to scare him? If it did, it was succeeding.

'Is there a boat around here?' asked Inara, trying her best to ignore the smouldering wood.

'There're no boats on the Kratch,' said Jankal. 'Why would there be? I told you, there's nothing on the other side worth getting to.'

'A road or track we can follow around the lake, then?' said Bill.

'The country is too wild,' said Ajenda. 'We're only here because of my Talent. All other families have to stick to the roads that ended miles from here.' She smoothed her daughter's hair. 'If I got you across the water, do you promise not to set the witch onto my family?'

'Ajenda, don't,' said Jankal, turning on his wife.

'They're children,' said Ajenda. 'The boys are only a little older than Jess. They have parents who care for them. If they have to get to the Scorn Scar before they turn back home, then I'll help them on their way.'

'Damn woman, the witch will smell us on them, and come after us,' said Jankal, making Jess whimper against her mother's skirt.

Jack noticed the first finger of flame on the log. If they waited here any longer, the demon would set the entire clearing ablaze. Running sweat fell into his eyes. Pressing a knuckle against his right eye to stop the stinging, he heard a creak from behind. Spinning around, he saw the branches of a large oak move through the hedge where he had lain hidden. As he watched, the tree grew larger as it neared the clearing. The groan and creak of the oak enveloped the group. Leaves and smaller branches rained down on the floor as the tree lumbered forward.

'Ajenda, stop making the tree walk,' said Jankal.

'Wouldn't you want strangers to help Jess if they found her in the wood?' said Ajenda.

Snaking roots, covered in mud and lodged stones, crashed through the hedge. Leaves continued to cascade down as the oak walked toward the water's edge. Creaking, the tree came to a shuddering stop.

'This will get you to the other side of the lake,' said Ajenda. The tree standing to the side of her, gave an almighty groan as Ajenda made it topple forward.

The spray of water that shot into the air, as the tree hit the lake's surface, swept over the clearing, dousing the fire that licked the floating wood and drenching the people on the shore. Ever widening circles spread across the flat surface of the Kratch.

Jack tried to keep the waves in sight, when the wood, that Ajenda held in the air, crashed to the ground about them.

'You have your boat,' said Jankal, pointing toward the tree bobbing in the water.

'That's not a boat,' said Bill. 'We won't be able to paddle that, it's too heavy.'

'You won't need a paddle,' said Ajenda. 'I will send the tree to the other side of the lake. All you have to do is sit and enjoy the ride.'

'Bill, call Black,' said Inara. 'We have a wolf with us. Don't worry Bill keeps him on a tight leash.'

On seeing the black wolf following the ground that the tree had rent open, Jack felt braver than at any other time since entering the clearing. Black looked ferocious as his large muscles played under his fur. His gaping mouth displayed deadly teeth that extended from his blood red gums.

'Keep the wolf away from my family,' said Jankal, who had suddenly grown pale.

'He won't harm you,' said Inara, as she climbed onto Black.

Bill massaged his shoulder. 'I've got him under control,' he said. 'He's my friend.'

'Friend or not, he has big teeth,' said Jankal.

Jess waved at the wolf. Her dark eyes were clear as she watched Black carry Inara to the floating tree.

Setting his foot on the rough bark, Jack felt the sway of the lake move the tree. Lowering himself to his hands and knees, he crawled along the trunk, not trusting his balance on their makeshift boat. When he finally sat down, he held onto a branch that was as thick as Huckney's thigh, and refused to leave go. Bill joined him, while Inara, on Black, brought up the rear. Camped amongst the branches they looked back at the travelling family with their painted wagon.

CRIK

'Make sure you don't mention us to the witch,' called Jankal.

Jack just wanted to be away from the little girl, before the demon inside of her decided to set their tree ablaze.

'Thanks for you help.' Inara waved as Ajenda, with a flick of her wrist, cast the tree out onto the lake.

Jack gasped as he saw Jess's hair rise. Then he relaxed as the same breeze that had ruffled the little girl's hair reached him. Sickened by the family's compliance in harbouring a third demon had him turn his back on them. Across the lake towered expectant mountains.

45. WITHOUT A PADDLE

JACK DIDN'T RELAX UNTIL the family, still standing on the shore, dropped out of sight. Even then, the water lapping against the tree kept him gripping the branch with his entire strength. The lake, though placid, continued to rock the oak. Bill stood astern, unconcerned with the hidden depths beneath them.

'You wouldn't be so scared if you learned to swim,' said Bill.

'In the Tristle?' said Jack. 'I've seen too many bodies drift down that river to want to join them.'

'They were already dead,' said Bill. 'Like Mr Hasseltope.'

'Not like Mr Hasseltope,' said Jack. 'Someone broke into his tomb and dumped him in the river, for the Elders to fish out.'

'He was as dead as the others,' replied Bill, snapping off a chunk of bark and throwing it into the lake. When the ripples died, Bill turned to the mountains. 'Soon we'll reach the Scorn Scar.'

'I guess,' replied Jack.

'You didn't tell us that Knell's a witch,' said Bill. 'I don't fancy meeting a witch.'

'Jankal warned us that Knell consorts with demons,' said Jack. 'Demons like the one that followed us through the wood, and leapt into his daughter. The same demons that live in us. Knell's knowledge about the demons has brought us to her.'

'Grandfather distrusts witches and their spells.'

'Like how my shadow moves around, and Inara raises the dead, or how you control Black. Spells are the Talents the demons give us so that we'll close our eyes to them. We allow them to live inside us as long as we have something in return.'

'They aren't demons,' said Inara. 'The Narmacil help us.'

'I can do without their help,' said Jack. Hanging over the side of the tree Yang caught a fish. The silver body squirmed in the shadowed hands. Quickly Yang tossed the fish to the hungry wolf, who snapped the fish out of the air. Revolted, Jack ignored the slavering wolf. Death surrounded him. Could he have imagined the wooden doll's terror, transposing his own horror at what transpired onto the carven features? Had Ajenda given the doll life, or only commanded it to move? If alive, Jess had murdered the dancer. Shuddering he

CRIK

remembered the doll leaping for the ash rising from her diminishing body. Such a heinous crime went unnoticed by his companions. Would Yang have to kill someone for them to recognise the danger the demons posed? Bill strode confidently along the tree. Bill's attitude toward the demons had changed since seeing them beneath the waterfall. Jack didn't know whether he could trust his friend to do the right thing once they met Knell. Nevertheless, for now, he was happy that Bill no longer saw the demons as harmless.

Again, the question arose in his mind: would someone who befriended the demons free him from his? Inara tried to talk him around; if she could, she wouldn't give him the knowledge to destroy Yang, then why should Knell? Did the witch recognise the dangers the demons possessed? So many questions; he hoped he would find the answers at the Scorn Scar.

Sitting beside Jack, Inara scratched the cloth bandaging her legs. Noticing Jack's attention increased her discomfort. Her slack mouth revealed a chipped tooth that Jack had never noticed. 'All this talk of spells and Talents has me thinking.'

'Of what?'

'We each have something that is unique to us. Krimble had collected many Talents. I'm certain we didn't see all of his powers. Bones already filled the casket outside his house when I arrived.'

'What're you trying to say?'

Inara's hands continued to rub her ruined legs, massaging the rounded stumps. 'With all these abilities, there must be someone out there,' she lifted her eyes to the trees ringing the lake, 'who can help me regain my legs. Maybe it's a stupid dream.'

Jack recognised only the destructive nature of the demons. Yang collected dead things. Stuffed animals packed his bedroom. Jess's demon demonstrated its power by burning the doll. Could Inara be right to hope that a demon might help her walk? He shifted his gaze to Crik Wood, where they had encountered mysteries beyond count, and yet imagining an egg hatching forth a creature that could help Inara was beyond him. 'Since escaping Krimble's house, you've managed well enough,' he said.

Inara's face clouded over. 'What do you know about me managing anything? If not for Bill commanding Black to carry me night and day, I'd still be crawling through the marsh. You're so afraid of falling into the water you won't stand up. You clutch that branch as though it keeps you from falling into a deep chasm. I guess Black is my branch, without his help where would I be?'

'I'm sorry, Inara. I only meant…'

'I know what you meant. Look, you can keep thinking the Narmacil are evil, that they only have the power to hurt, and I'll hold onto the hope that there's one out there who can help me.'

WITHOUT A PADDLE

Water splashed against the trunk punctuating the tense silence. Jack wanted to alleviate the tension, only he couldn't think of anything to say. Inara still rubbed her legs. Looking at the bloodstains on the bandages made him want to comfort her, only, if he told her what she wanted to hear, he 'd be lying. Knowing she would hear the lie, made him close his mouth. Bill stood at the far end of the tree throwing more pieces of bark into the water. When the intolerable silence stretched from seconds into minutes, Jack loosened his hold on the branch. Water lapped against the tree's underbelly rocking them. Although he wanted to tighten his hold on the bough, one look at Inara's blank face strengthened his resolve to get to his feet.

Stooped over he walked, ready to throw himself flat against the tree trunk. This way he inched toward Bill. The tree's width could hold four people standing shoulder to shoulder, only this knowledge did nothing to calm his fraught nerves. By the time he reached Bill, sweat bathed his brow.

'What was that all about?' asked Bill, looking back to where Inara sat amongst the branches.

'Nothing,' said Jack. He sat down, eager to get off his feet.

'If you say so,' said Bill. 'It's good to see a lake without a film of rust. Blue water beats the multi-coloured water of the Rainbow Lake.'

Jack nodded. 'I agree with you there. There's nothing I miss from the Red Wood.'

'There's Huckney.' Bill sat, and flicked dirt from a long root.

Jack remained silent.

Ajenda's command kept the tree moving toward the mountains. Jack saw a splash of purple heather on the low-lying hills. Not far now. The shore was still out of Bill's swimming distance, another hour on the log and they'll all be ashore. Anxiety cramped his stomach. Resting his hand on his stomach, he wondered whether his demon felt nervous. Yang looked to hook another fish; he didn't seem affected by the Scorn Scar's proximity.

'When we get back to the village, we can tell my grandfather our story,' said Bill. 'He won't believe we entered the Red Wood.'

'Or that a metal ape carried us over the Hedge Wall,' replied Jack, offering a lopsided grin. 'I don't think we should tell him about the Ghost Walkers.'

'My grandmother isn't like them.'

'I'm sure Justice and Kyla weren't so bad when they lived. Their deaths made them bitter. Besides, your grandmother kept the fact that she's a Ghost Walker a secret for a reason. I don't think they'll appreciate me knowing what she is.'

'Yeah, they'll kill you for breaking into our house in the middle of the night.'

'Only to protect you.'

Bill held his hand up. 'I know Ying, I was joking. Still, you know how harsh my grandmother's tongue is. Best not mention it. The heather, is it the same as your vision?'

CRIK

Heather clung to the side of the hills like lichen on wet stone. Fewer trees dotted the landscape closer to the mountains. The land, though not as dry as the one he had seen in his vision, was the same place the Lindre had transported Jack too. He confirmed this to Bill.

'A bleak place,' said Bill. 'I wouldn't choose to live here.'

'Better than the marsh,' said Jack. 'Some people prefer to live by themselves.'

'The Giant drew a road at the foot of the mountains. There wouldn't be a road if no one to used it. Perhaps others share the Scorn Scar with Knell.'

Remembered cries from the cot still disturbed Jack's sleep. Knell didn't live alone, only he didn't know what kept her company. A cowl hid Knell's face, concealing her age. Was the crying infant her child? Discovering the second crater in the woods convinced him that the hole in her garden contained demon eggs. The Scorn Scar had many secrets to share. Looking again at the gaining shore, he hoped the secrets he discovered amongst the rock and heather would help him, and not harm him, or his friends. The unease, settling into his stomach, no longer had anything to do with the boat ride. Under an hour and they would be ashore.

46. SCORN SCAR

WHEN THE TREE CRASHED into the shore, the log continued to move up the pebbled bank, driving inland. For one horrifying moment, Jack feared Ajenda's flick of a wrist, would send the tree all the way to the looming mountain. The impact of the makeshift boat's landing threw both he and Bill onto the bank. Entwined in the branches, Inara screamed. Driven forward the oak slammed into a young birch, snapping the leaner trunk, before coming to a complete stop.

'You alright?' shouted Jack, running alongside the gulley left in the tree's wake.

Cradling her head, Inara winced as a cascade of leaves showered her. Seeing Jack, her face became inscrutable, obliterating all signs of her earlier fright. 'Bill, call Black to me. I've had enough of this tree.'

While Bill pulled Black away from the wolf's investigation of the new shore, Jack took the opportunity to do some investigating for himself. Compared to the lush woodland they had traversed the land was barren. What scant foliage existed offered little concealment. Since leaving the Wold, the constant threat of a wolf attack, or ambush, had beset him. At least here, no hunter would creep up on them unawares. Grey pebbles littered the ground. Sometimes a swirl patterned the smooth stone at his feet. After pocketing a perfectly round pebble, he left the lake by climbing the steep bank. Cries of blackbirds, flitting across the sky, failed to surprise him. He expected to find the birds. When the Lindre had taken him here, hundreds of the feathered creatures had lined the road leading toward Knell's house. In the stillness, he heard the clap of their wings. Yang watched them as well. No doubt his shadow wanted to stuff a few for his collection back home.

'Don't run off like that,' said Bill, leading Inara into the trees. 'We don't know what we'll find out here.'

'I do,' said Jack, following the birds.

'All is fine then,' said Bill, crossing his arms. 'Are you willing to share what you know?'

'A baby will be crying in a crib,' said Jack. He strode forward, not waiting to provide any further information. Let them find out for themselves. 'A path, or beaten track, must run through here,' he mumbled.

CRIK

Instead of showing reluctance, Yang sprang forward, as impatient as Jack to find Knell. Watching his shadow snatch a tree and propel itself forward, made Jack wonder whether his demon knew some secret about Knell.

'There's a dog barking,' said Inara. 'Can't you hear it?'

Stopping to listen, Jack waited until in the distance his ears picked up the faint sound of a dog's bark. He had forgotten the tethered dog, harassed by the birds. Picking up his pace, he followed the bark, no longer needing a road to find his way.

'I don't like the idea of crashing through the wood,' said Bill. 'The witch will be waiting, ready to cast a spell on us.'

'Would you prefer to surprise her?' said Inara. 'Accidents happen when you startle a person.'

'Good point,' said Bill.

'She knows we're here,' said Jack. 'When the Lindre sent me here, she was expecting me. I don't think creeping through the woods will make any difference. Besides, we want to talk to her. Not sneak up and scare her.'

The dog's barking grew louder, causing Jack to quicken his steps. Tramping through the low-lying underbrush, he took no notice of the browning fauna. His shoe crunched heather, trampled white flowers, and the browning ferns, without a care. If Bill saw any animals hiding amongst the coarse grass, he never brought attention to them. With the mongrel's barking filling their ears, Black lowered his nose to the ground.

When the expected road cut in front of them, Jack intently studied the packed earth. The track was wider than he remembered, wide enough for two wagons riding abreast. At the centre of the road, two deep-set lines, a few metres apart, wound away in both directions. Taking a moment to study the tracks, he said, 'Heavy wagons made these, perhaps there's a quarry nearby.' Craning his neck, he looked at the mountain that dominated the wilderness with a godlike presence. Nothing moved on the rock. His eyes rushed passed the heather to settle on the suspected quarry, filled with square cut stone. Stone from here may have reached Crik Village; the stone shared the same pale characteristic as the tombs in Long Sleep Cemetery.

'Are you sure you want to see Knell?' said Inara.

'We can all follow this road back home,' said Bill, shuffling his feet.

'Jack?' said Inara, when Jack ignored them.

Yang stood scratching his head. Jack remembered trying to work out crossword puzzles by lantern light, with Yang perplexedly scratching his head just as now.

'Don't look to Yang for help,' said Inara. 'You're so close to your goal; hours may only remain until you destroy him.'

'It hid from me,' said Jack. 'My insides crawl with the thought of it.'

SCORN SCAR

His eyes misted as he looked at Yang. Yang had gotten him into trouble, but his shadow got him out of a few scrapes too. He had come all this way; he would see it to its conclusion. Resuming the trek his legs ate up the distance to Knell's home and the dog's beckoning call.

As he turned a bend in the road, more houses than expected met his gaze. Every stonewalled home lay abandoned. Dirty curtains and spread cobwebs filled the windows. Thin trees grew from open doorways, their limbs curled like arthritic fingers. Here and there, weeds grew from forgotten chimneystacks. Even the insects had abandoned the small town. A well, with a broken hand pump, and a discarded bucket to the side of its crumbling wall, drew his attention. At some point, the well had been the centre of the town; people would have come here to talk. Children would have played while their mothers drew up the water. Disconcerted, he noted Yang staring down the well. What curiosity had his shadow found? Passing weed filled gardens and broken fences, he reached the well; he peered through his shadow into the dark depths. An old grime encrusted rope, plunged into the well, leading the way to hundreds of dead birds. The dark plumage of the blackbirds still clung to broken frames, and snapped wings. Pushing himself back, he stumbled, desperate to distance himself from the rising stench of decay.

'What's down there?' asked Bill.

'You are pale Jack,' said Inara, moving Black with a touch of her legs.

'Dead birds fill the well.' He bit his hand to stop from vomiting.

'Why kill birds?' said Inara.

'Only blackbirds,' replied Jack, rubbing the back of his hand against his mouth. 'When I was here last, hundreds of birds waited outside Knell's house.'

'We all saw the birds flying this way when we first entered the trees,' said Bill. 'I wondered where birds went to die.' Inara and Jack exchanged a quizzical look. 'Think about it,' said Bill, 'when was the last time you saw a dead bird? Sure, you'll see a cat catch one or two, but you never find them dead on the ground. With the hundreds flying in the skies, we should be picking our away through dead birds everyday. Maybe there're other deserted towns, each with their own well full of birds.'

'I don't know about that, but something's drawing them here,' said Inara. 'This is all very strange. If I paid better attention to the bones outside Krimble's house, I wouldn't have drank his tea. Perhaps the birds in the well are a warning.'

'Listen to her,' said Bill. 'We know this road leads back home. We can tell everyone about the Narmacil.'

Jack wanted to shout that the Village Elders, Mr Gasthem, Mr Dash, perhaps even Bill's own Grandfather, already knew everything. Revealing Mr Dash's collusion with the Giant would mean divulging his secret. 'I'm not going to turn back,' he said, 'not when we're so close. I have to hear what Knell has to say.'

'We've come all this way with you Jack, we won't let you face Knell by yourself,' said Inara.

'Then let's find her, before my shadow decides to jump into the well,' said Jack, eyeing Yang with distaste.

Leaving the cluster of houses circling the well, they strode up a hill. Away from the centre of town, the homes became elaborate; some had porches and balconies that extended from upstairs windows. One house had stone pillars outside its door with a welcoming stone ribbon wrapping the white marble. Reading the script brought a pang of sorrow for the once thriving community that had lived here.

'This whole town reminds me of the spook house,' said Bill.

The spook house was what the children back home named the deserted house that sat on the far side of town. Jack never walked passed the spook house in the dark, afraid of what would give chase from its dilapidated door. 'It's not like the spook house,' he said. 'Sometimes people just move on.'

'Jankal warned us to keep away from the Scorn Scar,' said Bill, denying Jack the opportunity to brush aside his remark. 'People don't get up and leave their homes. There's a doll on that stoop,' he pointed to a rag doll with red knitted hair. 'What girl would leave behind her toy?'

'You're spooking yourself,' said Jack, impatient to crest the hill. Bird chirps mingled with the dog's bark.

Cresting the brow of the hill with Jack, Bill saw blackbirds perched on trees, fences, and old swings. 'Must be thousands,' he whispered. 'Why are they here?'

The sheer volume of birds confronting them, made Jack take a backward step. When he had last visited The Scorn Scar, blackbirds had loitered outside Knell's home, but nothing prepared him for this sea of birds. Birds had turned the trees black, hiding the lofty branches with pinion and tail feathers. They occupied every inch bordering the two houses at the bottom of the road. Blending together, the monstrous flock formed a lake of tar, rippling with constant movement. From atop the hill, Jack saw four islands from which that black lake receded. Two homes, the pit in Knell's garden, and the tethered dog also had his own patch. Thousands of birdcalls, emitted from yellow beaks, incessantly taunting their target, giving the birds the demeanour of bullies. Drawing its leash taught, the dog snapped at the feathered fiends in a frenzied assault.

'That's Knell's home,' said Jack, pointing to the house with the billowing net.

'I've always found birds passive creatures,' said Inara. 'These remind me of vermin.'

'They're only blackbirds. They flap over the village all the time. Miss Mistletoe's cat, Gesma, catches them,' said Bill.

SCORN SCAR

'No, Inara's right. These birds are acting queer.'

'Well, we've got Black with us,' said Bill. 'If they try anything, he'll crunch them up and spit them out.'

'I don't fancy getting into a fight with a thousand birds,' said Jack. 'I have no doubt Black will kill a few...'

'Which only leaves a few hundred for us to contend with,' interrupted Inara. 'But, we're here now. There's nothing for it, we have to get to Knell.' Her pointing finger traced an invisible line through the birds and passed the dog. 'We can stand around and debate for hours, or end our journey.' Biting her chapped lips, Inara urged forward the big wolf.

Bill raised his hands. 'Come on Ying, you aren't afraid of a few birds are you?'

With his stomach clenched tight, Jack followed his friends down the road.

The first birds they passed threw them dark glances, they then returned their attention to the house with the caved in side. Those in Jack's way, hopped from his scuffling shoes, only to return once he had passed. A few fanned their wings in annoyance, trilling their spite. One he kicked from his shoe, scaring a dozen others into the air.

'They don't seem at all interested in us,' said Inara.

'They're watching the net on the side of the house,' said Bill.

Or waiting for the woman behind the net, mused Jack.

'Aren't blackbirds an ill omen?' asked Bill.

'You're thinking of ravens,' said Inara. 'My father hates ravens. He told me that they eat the dead, or those too weak to defend themselves. These are blackbirds, quite different.'

Yang had taken the form of a large dark bird, reminding Jack more of the Lindre's rook than the small birds surrounding them. Instinctively he looked at the large tree where he had first spotted the rook cawing at him. Blackbirds by their hundreds ignored his gaze.

'That's odd,' said Inara, looking toward the houses. 'Neither house has windows, just white boards.'

'I can't see any doors either,' said Bill. 'If it wasn't for that large hole in the side of Knell's house, I wouldn't know how to enter. This is most peculiar. The haunted houses my grandfather mentioned in his stories, always had windows. Remember the tale of the face frozen in the glass?' he asked Jack.

Heather rose beyond the houses, reminding them of the world outside this strange town. A cold breeze rattled the rusted chains of a broken swing, admonishing them for their lack of attention.

The birds continued to ignore the group moving through their midst, preferring to keep their rapt attention on the house. A few blackbirds took flight to find food, only to resume their vigil once fed. The dog, for the first time, noticed the children, or more importantly, he became aware of the large black wolf. Instead of cowering, the dog raised its bark, hushing the birds gathered just beyond the range of its rope.

'Do you think it'll bite?' asked Inara.

'That little thing,' said Bill. 'I'd like to see it try.' He strode forward, scattering the birds with impatient kicks. The dog, baring its needle sharp teeth, rolled its eyes back into its head.

'We should leave him alone,' decided Bill. Stepping back, he trod on a bird wing; the bird, raising a flute-like protest, pecked the offending boot. 'It could have rabies.'

'There's a sign,' said Inara, pointing to the post that held the dog's leash. 'It's a little troubling, "Knell tells no lies, so don't ask."'

'There's more,' said Bill, shifting his glasses. 'The chalk has faded, it's hard to read.' He stepped closer. 'It says, "The truth has a high price to pay".'

'Do you have any idea what that means?' asked Inara. Her sparkling dark eyes regarded Jack.

'I guess that Knell knows the answers to our questions,' replied Jack.

'And the price?' asked Bill. 'What will the witch want in return for answering your question?'

'We won't discover that by nattering out here,' said Jack. 'Anyway, it's my question, so the price, if any, is mine to pay. Now come on, we don't want these birds taking an interest in us.'

Ruffling the dog's fur, Yang put a stop to the barking, and had the dog wag its tail in delight. The shadow continued to play with the dog as Jack and the others moved toward the house. Meeting the mongrel's brown stare, Jack wondered whether the dog recalled him from his last visit. As far as he knew, the dog never saw him, or at least it took no interest in him, when the Lindre had transported him here.

The fluttering net, coated in dust and grime, draped the open cavity leading into the house like a funeral shroud. The sombre sound it made as the breeze stirred its roping, whispered its own warning. Jack's mouth dried up as he looked into the gloom beyond the net. His eyes hunted for any movement. Any telling sign that Knell still lived here.

'That looks like the hole we found the Narmacil eggs in, back in the woods,' said Bill. The gaping hole, ringed by broken red brick, lay at the centre of the garden.

'Do you want to look in the hole before we go into the house, Jack?' asked Inara.

'Why, it's just another demon's nest,' said Jack, more impatient than ever to enter the house.

The netting felt spongy in Jack's hand, making him want to snatch back his hand as though he touched the hair of a living creature. Steeling his nerve, he lifted aside the rope, as he did he heard a loud crash. Horrified, he observed the blackbirds flying toward them.

'Hurry.' He pulled Bill through the opening, and urged Black and Inara impatiently into the house.

The air bristled with falling feathers as the birds swooped for the opening. Underlying their thunderous assault was the sound of the maddened growls from the enraged dog.

Jack screamed as a bird struck his neck. Warm blood flowed down his back as the beak penetrated his skin. Taking a stance between Jack and the deadly flock stood Yang, striking the winged fiends with hands as large as shovels. Sneaking beneath the shadow's defence a few birds dove for a breach in the netting. More struck Jack, scoring his hands and head with painful cuts that drew blood. Turning, he snatched a bird clinging to his collar, and rung its body in his hands. Enraged he reached for another bird when a pair of hands gripped his flailing arm and pulled him inside the house.

Outside the net, the birds had turned day into an impregnable wall of black feathers and sharp beaks. Surging inward, the net threatened to collapse. Jack took a step into the house, he was sure the blackbirds would bring down the flimsy barrier. Bulging, like a balloon with too much air, the net held. The holes between the ropes barely allowed through a few yellow beaks.

Sighing with relief, Jack took note of his exhausted friends, when from within the house he heard a dreadful scream.

CRIK

47. BEHIND THE VEIL

THE SCREAMED WORDS, "Close the net, close the net", repeated at such a high volume, and at such a high rate, that it took Jack a few moments to decipher them. Without windows to dispel the dusty interior, any attempt to locate the originator of the frantic calls was hopeless. The wings beating against the net sent Bill scurrying deeper into the house. Black growled and Inara clung to the wolf as though her life depended on staying on his back.

'Is that you, Knell?' asked Jack.

The reply, 'Tie the rope to the pedestal,' came from the gloom.

'There Jack,' Inara said, pointing to a coil of rope by his feet.

Taking the rope, Jack secured the line around the indicated stone pedestal. Immediately the blackbirds lost interest in wanting to enter the house, and as one, took flight to resume their eerie vigil.

An oppressive hush wrapped the group who stood staring into the dark passage, wondering about the open doorways that dotted its length. No one wanted to move. They sensed that if they took a step, they would never escape the house. With the net secure, the owner of the house remained quiet. Jack looked from one pale expectant face to the other. Inara loomed above him, her fringe sweeping down across her brow in jagged cuts. An unspoken plea shone from her eyes, begging him to make the first move.

'I came here before,' Jack cried out, for Knell to hear him. 'You told me that you were expecting me to come.' Again, he waited, and again not a breath of wind stirred the dust motes hanging in the air.

'I can send Black in to check out the rooms,' said Bill.

'Not with me sitting on him you won't,' was Inara's immediate reply. 'Jack wanted us to come here; he can lead us into the house.'

Dry swallowing, Jack said, 'Okay, I'll go first; stay close.' Now that he had finally arrived at Knell's house all he wanted to do was leave. The air itself felt ominous.

'I'll be behind you all the way,' said Bill.

The first step took more courage than Jack knew he possessed. His foot felt heavy, almost as though he dragged a body across the dusty floorboards. An indistinct Yang pressed his finger against his lips in a hush when he noticed Jack paying him attention.

BEHIND THE VEIL

Above the first doorway, coloured glass portrayed the mountain looming over the Scorn Scar at sunset. Rustic reds coloured the glass, reminding Jack of the paintings hung in Krimble's house. Hoping this wasn't another trap he edged toward the room's gaping entrance.

He flinched as he noticed white forms clustered within the small room. Big shapes and a myriad of smaller ones crowded him as he pushed passed the door. Showing no fear, Yang, with a flourish, threw aside a white sheet from a cupboard. Not expecting to find a cupboard, perhaps a hulking troll instead, had him take a hurried backward step.

'Watch it,' cried Bill, as Jack backed into him.

'Why cover all the furniture?' said Inara. 'Seems rather pointless to have all this stuff and not use it.'

'I don't think Knell gets many visitors,' said Bill.

Amongst the furniture, Yang uncovered, was a small cot fitted with a tiny ruffled mattress. Whether Jack had seen the same cot when he last came to the house he couldn't be sure. He had expected to hear the baby cry; perhaps the baby slept in a different crib. With a cursory inspection of the other cabinets and tables, he stepped back into the passage. An old clock, with a face crawling with spiders, kept the midnight hour.

'Hello,' said Jack. Knell's stubborn silence troubled him. Did she wait to pounce on him and toss him into an oven to eat him? With his imagination swirling with Grandpa Poulis's wild stories, he approached the second door and stopped. A figure swaddled in layers of clothes stood a couple of feet into the room. Amongst the folds of cloth, were bags of leather and purple coloured suede pouches. An old rope tied at the hip carried other purses and a few corked bottles swimming with brown liquid.

'Knell, I've come to ask you a question,' said Jack.

'Of course you have, no one comes here if they already know the answer,' replied Knell, shuffling across the room. She refused to turn and face the group plugging up her doorway. 'You almost let those disgusting birds in my house. That net is there for a reason.'

'I'm sorry,' said Jack.

'None got in I suppose,' replied Knell. The rasp in her voice was sharp enough to cut the flaking plaster on the walls. 'The last time you came here, you came alone.'

'This is Bill, and Inara,' said Jack.

'I don't mean the cowering children.' Her green hood turned toward Jack, and in the darkness, he discerned a blindfold drawn tight against parchment skin. 'You came without your shadow, as it is now.' Stray sunbeams stole through the netting, revealing Yang.

'He haunts my every step,' said Jack.

CRIK

'Haunts,' replied Knell, moving to a chair with balls of stuffing escaping from worn seams. 'I wouldn't say your shadow haunts you child. No, it accompanies you. It goes where you take it, and no farther.' The chair creaked as it took Knell's weight. 'Your Talent is unique to you. A Talent others have sought for themselves.'

'Krimble wanted our Talents,' said Inara.

'You don't have to remain by your wolf, like a little girl clinging to her mother's apron,' said Knell. 'Come in and make yourselves comfortable. The chairs outnumber people in this house.'

'I'll stay on Black,' said Inara.

'Do as you will. Though being the eldest of your group I'd have credited you with more compassion for your animal. The wolf needs to rest.'

'I'll stay on Black,' repeated Inara.

Bill passed Jack and sat in a wooden chair adorned with carved grinning faces on its arms. Moving his head like an owl on the hunt, Bill studied every corner of the room.

'If you're looking for cookies, you are out of luck,' said Knell, noting Bill's interest in his surroundings.

'I wasn't,' said Bill, fumbling over his words. 'You have the same dolls as my grandmother.' He pointed to a doll with a red dress and floppy hat. 'That's one of her favourites,' he indicated a blonde doll carrying a folded umbrella beneath her arm.

'Such things are common,' said Knell. 'Some are gifts, others I bought myself, when this was still a town.'

'What happened here?' asked Jack. 'Whoever lived in this town deserted it in a rush.'

Knell laughed so hard she began to cough. Hunched in her chair, she covered her mouth with a closed fist. Pulling the cork from a bottle at her hip, she brought the brown bottle to her lips. After hesitating, she drank its contents, gagging on the sweet taste.

'You should've seen the mayor herding everyone up like cattle. The wagon train stopped at every house; every house bar mine.' Her breath whistled between compressed lips.

'Why'd they leave?' asked Jack.

'And why'd they leave without you?' asked Inara.

'I normally ask for something in return for answering questions,' said Knell. 'This time I'll answer you for free.

'They left because of the birds. Yes, those little winged fiends you nearly invited into my house. Time was the townspeople liked having me around. My Talent for answering those questions that trouble people had brought many to the Scorn Scar. When people arrive, they bring money with them. The quarry provided men with work, and the women sold what they had to the strangers who passed through my door. Helen Jacon sold lemon cakes and cups of tea. Miss Strapply offered pups, or kittens, I never remember which, to the strangers' children. Mrs Turnorlay had her own wares to sell, while her poor unknowing husband worked the stone on the hill.' Knell's mouth tightened. 'I lost count how many sat in that chair,' she pointed to where Bill sat, 'eager to hear what I had to say. Most were idle questions, things they should've known for themselves. I once told a farmer how to irrigate his fields. Another time a new Mother came to me with wet eyes begging me to tell her how to stop her new-born from crying.'

'What did you say to her?' asked Inara.

'I told her to dangle her baby by the feet over the highest cliff, and when the baby stopped crying take it home for it would've cried its tears dry.'

'You didn't,' said Inara.

Knell cracked another smile. 'Didn't I? Perhaps I told her to care for the child, to feed it when hungry and to change it when it soiled itself. That's all that babies do, eat and poo. Eat and poo.'

'I remember a baby crying here,' said Jack. 'In the other room dust sheets cover unused furniture, including a cot.'

'Are you so impatient to know everything,' snapped Knell, taking another swig from the brown bottle. Her knuckles protruded hard and white as she fiercely gripped the arm of her chair. 'Once in a while a visitor would arrive seeking the answer to a problem that haunted them.' Her blindfold twitched to Jack. With her skin drawn tight against her cheekbones, and with the cloth masking her eyes, it was impossible to guess her age. 'I demand a high price for answering such burning questions,' continued Knell, savouring her words in long drooling tones. 'Not everyone paid what I asked in return for my help, preferring to live with their burden. Those willing to pay, I sent out to perform a task for me.'

'A task?' asked Inara, frightened by the implication of further trouble.

'One that I cannot perform myself,' said Knell. 'Some had a Talent that helped them achieve what I requested of them. Others did it by hook or crook. I never asked how they did it, nor cared as long as I had my price.'

'You wanted more than a doll with a frilly hat,' said Inara.

'Depends on the question asked,' responded Knell, easing back in her chair. Dust rose into the air like ghosts, catching sunlight that speared between slatted boards.

'You must've angered a few of those you turned away,' said Jack.

The creases lining the blindfold shifted as Knell's face dropped. 'It was common for me to have threats. Some didn't like the answers I gave. Others tried to force me into telling them what they wanted to hear. I never paid them any attention. Until the man with the bird perched on his shoulder arrived.

CRIK

'I had a door back then, and his knock reminded me of a woodpecker tapping the bole of a tree. Tap, tap, tap.' Knell mimicked the knock with a closed fist, her teeth bared. 'I wasn't accustomed to having visitors at night. It took me awhile to rouse myself. Not that he waited for me to answer the door. He let himself in, while his blackbird flapped its wings on his shoulder. Wearing a long black coat, and with his hands clasped behind his back, he resembled one of his diseased birds. Perched himself in that corner,' she pointed to a shadowed recess, 'well away from the lit lamps. Sorrow scarred men have always sought my advice, hungry for any way to improve their lot. This Birdman felt different. His sadness wafted from him like gases from a bog.'

Desperate to know what the Birdman wanted, Jack leaned in closer to Knell. Alarmingly he found that he clasped his hands behind his back, in the same manner as she had described. Going a step further, Yang transformed himself into a large bird, mimicking the cocked head of a raven. Ignoring Jack's accusatory scowl, the shadow remained rapt on Knell and her tale. Straightening, Jack retreated from the woman in the chair.

If Knell noticed Jack's distress, she declined to mention it. A crackle in her parched throat coloured her words. 'I found it difficult to hear what he asked, the baby cried something awful. Most of the time I know the question before my visitor utters it. This time I waited to hear it like any other.'

Jack's ears perked up at mention of the baby. He guessed what happened between Knell and the Birdman had something to do with the empty cot. Clustered shadows obscured the woman's face. Yang, only inches from Knell, fed into the shadows. She ignored the demon's intrusion as she resumed her tale.

'He wanted to know how to create a perpetual night.'

'If he did that, there would never be another day,' said Jack, not believing what he had heard.

'Snub out the sun, like you would douse a gas lamp,' said Knell, sagely nodding her head.

'That's impossible,' said Bill. 'You can't stop the sun from rising.'

'Everything is possible,' said Knell. 'You just need to know how.'

'There's no reason,' said Inara, rubbing the back of her neck in incredulity. 'Who would wish for a night that never ends?'

'Exposure to the sun burnt his hands and face. The great fireball in the sky imprisoned him to dark rooms and blacker caves. Alienated during the day and shunned by his people, the man took the company of the birds. In time, he grew to hate those who enjoyed what had denied him his freedom. I have speculated that he loved someone, no doubt a fair girl with sun in her hair and fire in her eyes. Another thing he could never possess. Deprive someone of what they desire the most and it will blacken their soul.'

BEHIND THE VEIL

'Couldn't you reason with him,' asked Jack. 'If you befriended him, he may have given up his mad quest.'

Cold emotion washed over Knell's unsympathetic face. Were others right to name her a witch? She grew still. 'I would sooner befriend a marsh rat,' she said. 'I told you, his soul had turned wicked. You cannot reason with such as him.'

'What did he do when you refused him?' asked Inara.

'You know that already,' said Knell. 'He sent the birds. At first, he only sent a few extra blackbirds to decrease the worm population in my garden. Soon, entire flocks of the foul creatures arrived to torment me. They attacked me when I tried to leave my home. The disgusting things would cluster around my face, pecking me with their yellow beaks. It soon became impossible for me to leave these rooms. Some of those living in the town attempted to kill the birds. In retaliation for trying to help me, the Birdman called down more birds and turned them against the mayor and his flock. That's when they abandoned their homes.'

'They didn't try to take you with them?' asked Bill, pushing his glasses up his nose.

'They knew the Birdman had cursed me,' said Knell. 'They forsook me and the child to fend for ourselves. At first people still came with their questions, braving the birds. My fee remained the same for every answer.'

'Kill the blackbirds,' said Inara.

'We saw the well,' added Bill.

'It didn't matter how many they killed,' continued Knell, 'more birds always arrived. Each night the Birdman would wrap on my door, asking his question, and each night I kept the door barred. This kept up for weeks, then months, until he suddenly stopped knocking my door.'

'You didn't hear him again?' asked Jack.

'I heard him knocking one night,' said Knell. 'Only he didn't come to my door. Peering outside, I saw him at the old Pearson place, boarding up the windows and door. All night he worked with his hammer and nails, until he had enclosed the house.'

The neighbouring house without windows, Jack realised.

'The following night he returned to block my windows.' Knell pointed to her wall. For the first time the children noted boards of pale wood adorning the wall where the window should be. 'He repeated his question in time with his hammer. To keep the baby from crying I played the Syll.' Knell withdrew the same fluted instrument Llast had given Jack when they were about to enter the Blackthorn Tunnel.

'We had one of those,' said Bill, leaping from his chair.

'It lulls things to sleep,' said Knell. 'A very useful instrument to have.'

'I remember you playing it when I came here before,' said Jack.

CRIK

Knell nodded, shifting her hood so that it tipped forward into Yang. Yang remained close as she said, 'Without windows the Birdman sought to deprive me of the sun.'

'How'd you lose your door?' asked Inara, looking back to the gaping hole at the front of the house.

'He did that too,' said Knell. 'The night he came for the baby. I always stayed awake during the night and slept during the day. Only without windows to see, I lost track of the time. My clock,' she pointed to the large clock still clustered with spiders, 'hasn't worked in years. This one night I fell asleep. When I failed to rouse at his knock at my door, he wrenched it off its hinge, creating that gaping hole. In swept the birds, attacking me with their flapping wings and pecking beaks. Although the child screamed for me, I could not fight off the birds. Helpless, I listened to her cries as the Birdman took her from me. He left with her, taking his birds with him.'

'That's horrible,' said Inara, covering her mouth with her hands.

'That is what happened,' said Knell. 'Now boy, you came here to ask me a question.'

Jack's heart beat faster as Knell turned her blindfold to him. He knew she would ask him to kill the birds. Even with Black helping, he would never kill them all.

'Ask away boy,' said Knell. 'You've travelled far enough to ask me the question.'

Yang remained by Knell, only now the shadow observed Jack. With his dark twin watching, Jack felt his mouth tighten. His lips were as hard as bone as he uttered the words, 'How do I kill Yang?'

48. THE PRICE

'YING,' CRIED BILL rushing forward to face Jack. 'What're you saying? Stop this now. You don't want to kill Yang.'

'What else can I do?' said Jack. What else could he do? Having wrestled with the question since learning the truth, he saw no other course open to him. A malicious cat-eyed creature, with its evil look and forked tongue, could only have evil intentions. Why else did it choose to hide away? To free himself from his curse demanded swift, and terrible, action. Both his friends called them Narmacil, yet neither had seen the demon hatch in his room. 'You witnessed the demons with your own eyes under the waterfall; how it possessed the little girl.'

'Did you miss the joy and relief exhibited by Jess's parents after their daughter had found a useful Talent? A gift that would make her life, and the lives of those she travelled with, easier,' said Inara.

'She killed that doll,' said Jack.

'It was a doll,' said Bill. 'It wasn't alive.'

'Then why did it run from Jess?' retorted Jack. 'You didn't trust the demon when it travelled with us.'

'This is Yang,' said Bill. 'Not some random creature we picked up at a waterfall. Yang has helped us every step of the way. He is part of you. Do you realise how jealous of you I am. Both of us have no brothers or sisters, but in Yang you had the company I have always craved.'

'You can have him,' said Jack. 'He's nothing but trouble.'

'There's a price for asking me your heart's desire,' said Knell, breaking into the conversation. She peered through the erect shadow separating them.

Did his shadow look sad? Without features, it was hard to tell what emotion his shadow portrayed, yet Jack knew his words must be like daggers. No, he must be strong. 'I'll kill as many of the birds as you want,' he said.

The woman cackled. 'If only it were so easy. I have had others kill the birds for me, only for the feathered fiends to double in number the following day.'

Apprehension coloured Jack's words when he asked, 'If you don't want me to kill the birds, what do you want?'

Knell eased herself back into her chair. 'There is a way to split you from your Narmacil. Although I can tell you how, your question has many prices, not the least of which is your shadow's death. I require you to bring back the child from the Birdman.' She spoke quickly, with only a slight shake of her hood betraying her need. 'He lives in that house.' She indicated the boarded up building. 'Inside those walls he cowers from the sun. Retrieve her and you will have your answer.'

'How do you expect us to enter that house?' asked Jack.

'Us?' said Knell. 'You seek the answer, no other. Your friends cannot help you.'

How could he go up against the Birdman without any help? In that moment he realised how much he relied on Bill and Inara. Without Bill, he could not call on Black. Feeling desperate, he said, 'They've come all this way with me. We travelled through the Red Wood to find you.'

'Neither wanted to come here,' said Knell. 'Though in coming, the girl has grown hopeful of a resolution to her own problem.' Knell waved her hand when Inara opened her mouth to speak. 'It is not your time girl; the boy has my attention.'

'I won't let Ying go into that house alone,' said Bill, leaping from his chair. 'With Black at our side we won't have to worry about the birds.'

'Mistrust has wormed its way into your heart,' said Knell, regarding Bill with a hard-set jaw. 'Since observing the Wood Giant and the Narmacil by the waterfall you have grown wary of them. The appearance chosen by the Narmacils alarmed and disgusted you. Nevertheless, you do not regard them as demons, as this one does,' she indicated Jack with a hooked finger. 'This is Jack's task; only he can find his answer.'

'What if I need help to retrieve your daughter?' said Jack. 'Denying me the help of my friends puts her life in as much danger as mine.'

'She isn't my daughter,' said Knell. 'I care for her as though she was of my blood, but that doesn't change that she didn't come from me.'

Feeling bereft, Jack turned to Yang.

'Don't expect your shadow to help you,' said Knell, cackling. 'After all, your success would seal his fate.'

Yang's shape grew denser, hiding Knell behind his form. If contending with the Birdman and his flock was not enough, he also had to keep one eye on his demon.

'You will find no door to his house,' said Knell. 'The Birdman is paranoid of allowing light into his hideaway. Having sealed the door, you will find no trace of it.'

'Then how do you expect me to enter?'

'There's a tunnel leading from his house to my garden.'

'The hole in the garden,' said Jack. He had presumed the crater surrounded by red brick and clay was the same as the Narmacil nest back in the woods.

'Take this to find your way through the darkness,' said Knell, unhooking a small silver lantern from her rope belt. The precious metal grew in tangled vines

THE PRICE

that ringed the handle she grasped. Within the casing sat a long purple candle. 'Light this to find your way.'

Taking the lantern Jack's finger brushed Knell's hand. Shocked at her ice cold skin had him pull back his hand, taking the silver cage with him. 'It has no weight,' he said, hefting the casing holding the purple candle over his head.

'Yet its importance weighs heavily,' said Knell. 'Do not lose it, or you will not be able to see.'

A fine looping script ringed the base of the casing in a language Jack didn't recognise. Tilting it toward the light revealed a second finer line written in an additional unknown language.

'I don't have to tell you how dangerous this is,' said Inara. 'Every time I try to talk you out of this foolishness, you stubbornly refuse to listen to my advice. Nothing we say or do will alter your mind.' She bit her lip hard enough to draw blood. 'Keep that lantern safe, it may save you.'

'Yeah Ying, don't go doing anything dumb, like dying,' said Bill. 'I don't want to be the one to tell your mother.'

With his back turned from his friends, Jack said, in a weak voice, 'Don't call me Ying, it is not my name.'

'You don't have to do this,' said Inara. 'You've lived all your life with Yang.'

'Not all my life,' said Jack. 'I wasn't born with him. He crept into my room and jumped inside me, just as Bill's and Jess's demon did with them.'

'I hope Jack sees differently when the time comes Yang,' said Inara. She held her hand out to Yang. Jack's shadow enclosed her hand in shade. 'If not for you we would never have escaped Krimble. During our travels you have become a true friend, someone I could always rely on to do the right thing.' She let go, praying it was not the last time she would see Jack's independent shadow.

Anger rose like steam in Jack. He had come all this way to free himself from his demon. Housing the demons had decayed Krimble's mind, they had all seen this, and yet they persisted in tormenting him by loving his shadow. 'My task won't become easier by standing here,' he said.

'Wait,' said Bill. 'Without my Talent the others in the village looked down on me and called me a freak.'

'I never did,' replied Jack.

He strode from the room, allowing Bill and Inara to say goodbye to Yang. Let them, after today he would be free of his demon. Halting, he focused on the floor where his shadow should be in relation to the light. When had his shadow started disobeying that rule? Although he couldn't remember being without Yang, how far back could he actually remember? His earliest memory was looking through the bars of his cot to where his mother cleaned the upstairs passage. Had Yang possessed him while he slept in that crib? 'When I bring back the child, you'll free me from my demon,' he said to Knell.

'Bring her back to me and you will have your heart's desire,' replied Knell.

CRIK

Black's whine accompanied Jack as he spied the blackbirds through the net. His friends watched him, waiting to see if he had the courage to lift the net and leave the safety of the house. Did they doubt his resolve? His fingers brushed the billowing rope. If he lifted the net, the birds would come and there would be no turning back. Bill stood in the doorway of the room, his face drawn and pale. Jack wished they were back at Long Sleep, hiding amongst the gravestones, scaring each other with ghost stories. Well this wasn't a story. Squeezing the rope's coarse fibres burnt his fingers, yet he tightened his grip.

'Are you still my friend?' asked Jack with hesitation.

'Always,' replied Bill.

'Even without Yang?'

Bill didn't have time to answer. With a flick of his hand, Jack untied the rope tethering the net to the pedestal and threw aside the net. Silent and fast, the birds came. Stepping through, he turned his back to the blackbirds flocking around him. Hunching his shoulders, he refastened the rope, anchoring the net in place. Once the house was secure, he braved the beating wings around him. Let them peck, he thought as a jabbing beak drew blood. Ignoring their screeching and flapping wings, he trudged forward, he had a task to do and nothing would stop him. Clutching the lantern against his stomach, he pushed through the shifting feathered wall. A bird struck his ear, causing him to cry out. Disgust welled up inside when he trod on another; the little body popped under his heel. 'That's one for you to stuff,' he said to his shadow in tow.

The ground became uneven with loose bricks and tossed up earth. Taking heart from his proximity to the tunnel renewed his efforts. One hole-riddled shoe caught the edge of a brick sticking up from the mud, sending him sprawling to the ground. Birds swarmed over him, tearing into his back with yellow beaks and raking his exposed skin with talons that felt like wire. Wailing his derision at the combined weight squirming over his back, he attempted to dislodge the birds. Beneath him, the soft mud crumbled, defeating his efforts; exhausted, he collapsed against the ground. Viciously the flock continued their assault. 'I'm so close,' he cried into the cold peat. 'It's not fair.' Strength ebbed from him. A beak scoring his cheek raised no cry; he had given into his fate. Suddenly, the pressure on his back eased. Grown numb to the pain it took him a moment to realise that he could move. Curling his fingers he scrunched the mud into his palm, and with it, a wave of pain assaulted him. In the time it took him to take an inward breath, he fooled himself into believing Inara had used her Talent on him. Twisting, he screamed, he didn't want to rise from the mud like the stag. Looking up he saw Yang had formed a protective bubble, shielding him from the birds.

'Why are you helping?' cried Jack. 'Stop it. Don't you know I mean to kill you?'

THE PRICE

He waved his hand up and through Yang, where a bird struck his finger. With a cry, he brought his hand back within the shadow where it was safe. Blood and earth mingled to coat his skin and torn clothing. The tunnel entrance lay only a few yards away; its black hole gave the impression of an open mouth, just waiting for someone foolish enough to enter. Scrambling to his knees, and with the lantern held tight, he stumbled for the opening, letting it devour him.

The sounds of the birds evaporated as he entered the tunnel. Pitch-blackness enveloped him. Scared the birds would follow him, he moved deeper into the tunnel. Feeling safer, he leaned against the rough earthen wall, listening to his ragged breath echo down the shaft. Why did Yang help him? 'Because if I die, he dies,' he said. Yes, that was it. As always, his shadow looked out for itself.

Striking a match against the dry stone, jutting from the mud, brought Yang blooming into life.

'You're always there. Aren't you,' said Jack. 'I can't see you in the dark, but you're always with me.'

Jack lit the lantern as the match burned down to his thumb. The candlelight that escaped through the silver cage threw out a strange purple haze, almost as though the light was a mist. It illuminated the tunnel. Intruding upon the curved walls, he spotted dangling hair-like roots from small plants and thick tree roots. Mole holes dotted the wall, and here and there, the lantern light reflected off the glistening bodies of worms and a few underground insects, that no doubt could tell Mr Gasthem a story or two. Not following a straight course, a few feet ahead the passage turned to the right.

'There can't be that much distance between Knell's house and the Birdman's hideout,' he said.

'That depends on how many twists and turns this tunnel takes.'

Hearing the unexpected voice, Jack dropped the lantern, plunging him back into darkness. His breath whistled from his throat, and he noted the tap of his shoe as he took a step, but he heard nothing more from the mysterious voice. Pressing his back against the wall, he waited. Someone had followed him underground. He did not recognise the voice; it had sounded hollow, as though the speaker had spoken into a bucket.

'Who's there?' he dared to whisper. No answer came. 'I know you're down here, you may as well tell me who you are.'

Blind, he knelt down, and with fumbling hands hunted for the lantern. He strained his ears to listen beyond his own noise to locate the person who shared the tunnel with him. When his fingernails touched the silver housing of the lantern, he snatched it to himself. Only two matches remained in his pocket; fishing one out he hesitated to strike the match. The absence of light also blinded the stranger. Unless the stranger belonged in the dark, the Birdman had built the tunnel to hide from the light. Even now, the Birdman could be creeping up on him. Feeling the need to dispel the darkness persuaded him to light the candle. Although Yang once more leapt to life with the struck match, as Jack expected, there was no sign of the stranger.

'Reveal yourself,' said Jack. No reply met his command. He regarded the bend in the passage with suspicion. The Birdman could be standing to the right of that outcrop of rock, waiting for him. Who else but the Birdman would be down here with him?

'Give the child back to Knell,' said Jack.

Yang sprang forward, twisting his body down the tunnel beyond Jack's vision. Returning the shadow shook its head.

Jack could not trust the duplicitous nature of his shadow. Yang could have looked directly into the eyes of the Birdman for all he knew. With the match almost burnt out, he touched the flame to the candlewick. Purple haze infused the Birdman's burrow. Behind, the tunnel carried on straight; if anyone followed from the garden, he would see them. No, he knew the speaker with the hollow voice had come from ahead. Grey stone, spotted with fungi, obstructed the passage. He imagined the Birdman clinging to the rock behind the bend, waiting for him to approach. Without his birds, he is only a man, became a mantra in his head. That he was only a boy didn't escape him either. Would Yang help him again? What did the shadow see? The soles of his shoes scraped against the rough-hewn floor, leaving a trail in the dry earth. Edging closer to the grey stone, the lantern light painted the depressions within the rock. Realising the purple haze would alert the Birdman to his approach made his heart beat like a torn jugular. Ornate silver bit into his hand as he reached the stone outcrop. Could he hear someone breathing around the bend? Taking root, the thought paralyzed him. It took twenty flickers of the candle flame for him to realise that he listened to his own tortured breath. His muscles eased at the realisation, allowing him to shuffle forward. Standing to his left, Yang continued to look where he could not. If he reached out, he would touch the opposite wall; the narrow confines restricted his movements. Like a badger in a trap, he thought sullenly. Knowing he couldn't go back, he turned the corner, bracing himself for an ambush. None came, the light revealed a longer passage ahead, as unremarkable as the one he had just left.

'I did hear someone,' said Jack, as much to test his hearing as to voice his quandary.

Suspecting someone raced toward him from the garden, he darted his head around the corner. Only earth and stone met his questing eyes.

Had the speaker retreated deeper into the tunnel? The passage continued straight, yet the purple light only managed to illuminate part of the tunnel ahead. Another bend in the tunnel, or even a depression in the shaft's wall, could conceal the Birdman. Raising the lantern spilled racing shadows across the tunnel, like leaves blown on an autumn wind.

'The tunnel is empty. We are alone,' said the hollow voice.

THE PRICE

Spinning around, he managed to hold onto the lantern. He didn't see anyone, only Yang, staring at him from the opposite wall. Again, he checked the passage he had just left, and again it stood empty.

'Who are you?' asked Jack.

'Why, I'm you, and you're me,' answered the mysterious voice.

Jack's brow furrowed as he said, 'That doesn't make any sense. What do you mean, you're me?'

'You aren't normally this dense,' said the voice. 'You're looking straight at me.'

The only thing standing ahead of Jack was his shadow. Yang had looped himself into the corner of the tunnel roof. 'There is nothing but my shadow,' said Jack.

Yang clapped his hands together. 'I've wanted to speak with you for a long time Jack.'

Dumbfounded, Jack realised the hollow voice he had heard earlier, emitted from Yang. His demon spoke to him.

49. A HUSHED EXCHANGE

JACK OBSERVED THE SHADOW coiled into the roof of the tunnel with despair. Clapping his shadowed hands, Yang dislodged a trickle of dirt from the earthen ceiling. Concerned that the sound could affect the stability of the newly dug tunnel drove Jack back against the supporting beam. Despite this very real fear, his mind refused to concentrate on anything other than Yang's whispers. Wind entering from the garden buffeted the purple hue, swirling the lantern light around his shadow as a cadaver drew flies. Correlating the odd colour to Yang's ability to speak, as the different coloured lanterns back in the Wold had bestowed his shadow with different attributes, amplified his misery. How many more mysteries did the demon possess? The lantern gave the shadow a solid appearance, giving the impression that if he were to throw a stone it would hit the opaque form. Every contour lining Yang's face was hard and sharply angled. Pronounced cheekbones, though mirroring Jack's own, belonged to someone older. He distrusted Yang, who had transformed into something utterly alien. Edging away from the beam, he preferred to brave the birds rather than remain underground with his shadow.

'Don't you want to hear what I have to say?' asked Yang. Each utterance sounded like an indrawn breath. Its movement disturbed the coloured mist. 'Do you want to know why I saved your life outside, when you only wish to destroy me?'

When Jack fell back, Yang slithered down from the roof to clutch his arm in an ice-cold grip. Fingers extended around Jack's bicep, pinching the muscle, making him drop the lantern. Struggling to break the demon's grip, he threw himself toward the garden exit. Snatching his other arm, Yang forced him up against the back wall, immobilising him against slick stone.

'Consternation, trepidation, some even experience dismay when they first discover they have a Narmacil living inside them,' said Yang. 'You aren't alone in your struggle with the truth. I lived with one girl who named me Giggles, because the thought of me moving around inside of her made her laugh. Paige was a nice girl, always happy to see me. Invariably boys have the most trouble adapting to the knowledge about my existence; that their Talent comes from me.'

'You have no right to use me,' said Jack.

A HUSHED EXCHANGE

'Use you?' said Yang. The shadow stuck out his face to a few inches from Jack. 'Most people use their Talents. Your mother wouldn't be able to grow all those plants without the help of her "demon".'

'Don't talk about her.'

'She knows what I am,' said Yang, tilting his head to the side. 'I showed you the meeting between the grave keeper and the Giant. Everyone knows we share a special bond. You are angry; it's hard accepting people have kept a secret from you.'

'I don't care what others know. You jumped into my body without my permission. When that thing hatched from the egg in my bedroom, you knew what it was when you spoke with it. No doubt telling it where it could find Bill. How much fun you had, playing me for a fool.'

'A part that you've grown into,' replied Yang. 'You put your friends at risk by taking them into the Wold.'

'They were already at risk,' retorted Jack. 'It's not natural to have you inside us.' Avoiding his shadow, he diverted his gaze to his stomach. 'What are you doing in there anyway? Why do you need to hide?' The lightest touch from the demon pimpled his skin, straightening the hair lining his arms. Shivering, he wanted to rub his arms and stamp his feet. His shadow had never been this cold. Looking into the blank orbs set into their sunken sockets, he pondered what Yang concluded from this, their first proper exchange. The depths of those eyes made him feel younger still, as though he was looking up at the night sky where time became irrelevant. 'What happened to Paige?' he asked, expecting the demon to have turned on the girl.

A sudden sadness overtook the shadow, softening the hard ridges and turning down his mouth. 'She died a long time ago. She always left a candle burning in the night, afraid that I would vanish and never come back. When her final night came, she never reached for the match. I heard her giggle, once, as the life ebbed from her; in the dark I said my own goodbye.'

The emotion in the demon's voice caught Jack unaware. Could it feel love for those it used? He forgot about the grip leaching the warmth from his body as he observed the girl's passing. In his mind, the silver haired woman lay under a chequered blanket; Yang sat motionless in a bedside chair as the first morning light filled the room. Despite the strong sun, Yang grew faint and disappeared. Jack lurched back against Yang's restraint. His shadow entered his mind to show him Paige. 'Get out of my head,' he said, through gritted teeth.

He had never known anything as old as the demon. With one glimpse, his shadow revealed shared lives going back generations. The demon could be ancient, older than the Hanging Tree with its gnarled roots. Apart from Paige, it had mentioned "boys". How many lives did that plural indicate? Had the demon hitched a ride with, two, three, four, or lives so numerous as to travel back hundreds of years? His own life paled in comparison to those accounted years. Other features swam across Yang's visage. A furrowed brow over small eyes gave way to an open face with a large bulbous nose. It transmogrified into a good looking youth, followed by a haggard man with roping black spirals painting long straggly hair.

'What're you doing?' demanded Jack.

'It pains me to show you these faces. Each one has given me a lifetime of joy and doubt. Some liked walking in the rain. Others preferred dusty rooms with stacks of books.' Yang shifted form from male to female, passing so fast they blurred like a hundred animated pictures. One moment he appeared as a young girl, and then took on the guise of an old man with a hair-lip.

'So you hid inside them too,' remarked Jack. 'Did they want to have you? Did you ask permission to use their bodies? I wouldn't take food from my mother's table without asking her first, and yet you jumped inside of me when I was still a baby.' His anger grew as new shadowed faces emerged. 'I can't be the first one who wanted you gone. Perhaps they didn't come as far as I have. They may have only wanted you to stop getting them into mischief. My life would be so much simpler if you didn't exist.' He was shouting now, spittle flew from his lips.

A third hand grew from Yang's chest to cover Jack's mouth. 'Hush.' The shadow warned. 'Remember, we aren't alone down here.'

Jack didn't care. He tossed his head to the side in an attempt to throw off the hand keeping him silent.

Paige's face came to the surface, younger than when Jack had seen her, and in that now familiar inhaled breath voice, Yang said, 'He's a killer Jack. You don't want to meet him down here.' Yang contemplated the tunnel to where the purple light diffused in trailing smoke. 'We need to be careful.'

It's you I'm afraid of, not some Birdman lurking in the dark. The demon, with devilish golden eyes, could tear open his stomach at any moment. Defenceless to stop such a reprisal for any affront silenced his remark. If confronted by the Birdman he could run away; how could he escape something that lived inside his guts? Despite his immediate fright, his eyes did stray, from Paige's likeness, down the long tunnel. Light from the dropped lantern illuminated the Birdman's burrow, highlighting dangling vegetation until cloistered darkness reclaimed the shaft. Briefly he mistook the thrown shapes of the dying purple mist, as it tried in vain to spread its light deeper into the tunnel, as that of the Birdman. His breath frosted the air as Yang withdrew his hand.

'You didn't let the birds kill me,' said Jack, 'and you won't allow the birds' master to harm me now.'

'I wouldn't be so sure of that Jack,' said Yang. Paige's young face aged into the weathered countenance of the old woman Jack had seen lying under the chequered blanket. 'If you die, I will sleep for ten years. While I rest, I will remember you Jack; perhaps regret my decision not to defend you. I will look

A HUSHED EXCHANGE

back upon our time and find new meaning in every shared moment. Each action I will scrutinise, seeking new understanding, much as a poet returning to a half-forgotten verse. Recollecting us playing with toy catapults on your bedroom floor, watching as you fed pebbles into the wooden cup of the throwing arm. Relishing those good times would also bring hurtful reproach. By abandoning you, you will die here, miles from your mother.' Jack's likeness replaced Paige's face; the shadow copied him down to his mussed hair. 'You incessantly complained about what you called "the dead things" I kept in your room. You forgot; you presented me with my first stuffed animal. It was the owl, which I keep on the top shelf. We helped Miss Mistletoe find Gesma, only a kitten at the time. Hours passed, but you would not stop until we returned her to Miss Mistletoe. Eventually, muddy and bruised, you found Gesma down at the river. Mesmerised by the swimming fish, the kitten had forgotten to go home. Miss Mistletoe gave you the owl for returning Gesma.'

Five years old, Jack remembered scouring the village for the cat. He had climbed trees and hunted under bushes for the kitten. Recalling that day, he realised Yang had omitted to mention something important. Gesma, not content with just watching the fish, jumped after them, into the rushing water. The swift current was too strong for the cat. 'Frantic, I tried everything to pull the cat ashore. A stick, anything would have done.' He recalled his shadow slipping into the water to retrieve Gesma from certain death. Yang had held the mewling kitten up to Jack. 'Believing I had rescued Gesma, Miss Mistletoe gave me the owl. Only you did,' he said. 'I had forgotten that's why I gave the owl to you.'

'You have forgotten much,' said Yang. 'So have I. If you were to die here, you will never recall all the things we have shared. Only I, in my dreams can rediscover them,' said the shadow. 'Bit by bit, I can fit small fragments together and form memories. However, if you died, I would find no joy in those memories. Each day that comes back to me will be a poisoned kiss. I would mourn you.' Yang's face sagged with sorrow. 'I will not die for you.' Yang's grip tightened on Jack's arms, making Jack gasp in pain. 'By killing me, all the memories I have built up from those I have loved before you, will vanish. You would silence Paige's giggling laugh. That will not happen, I will not allow it.'

'This is my life,' said Jack, tensing himself against Yang's hold. He leaned forward, his frosted breath mingling with the eddying purple swirl. 'If I want to live without you, I will. You only exist to catalogue lives, an ever-watching observer. It's my choice to let you live within me, not yours. You're just like one of those spiders under the waterfall, waiting to ensnare someone new.'

'If I wanted someone else, I could've jumped into Krimble, he wanted me.'

'Others had,' said Jack. 'The casket full of bones, outside the marsh house, reveals their abandonment.'

CRIK

'No, those bones are a testament to those who refused to give up their Narmacil. Each suffered unbearable torture; until the Narmacil could no longer bear for those they loved to experience anymore hurt. They sacrificed themselves for Krimble to put an end to the suffering. Memory of those days will forever haunt those poor Narmacil, who will replay every cut, each whimpered plea, a thousand times over. They spoke to me when Krimble brought the rats into the room, telling me what he would do. Voices implored me to give you up, to save you from torture, to save myself the anguish of witnessing your suffering.'

'Why didn't you?'

'Inara has a very old Narmacil. Amongst the choir screaming inside Krimble, her voice came through strongest. Her one question asked whether I would fight for you. Krimble's ability is intoxicating; we believed we had lost the ability to communicate with a human. A host sometimes travels from Crik Wood, taking the Narmacil with them. Not only could Krimble talk with us, and to an extent control us, he opened us up to greater Talent. He knew about the coloured light, as he worked out that Inara could raise an entire forest of dead animals. Power is exhilarating. If I knew lanterns such as this existed,' he looked down at the fallen lamp, 'I could've spoken with Paige, told her how much I loved her.'

'I remember you playing with the rats,' said Jack. 'You weren't concerned for me then.'

'I tricked Krimble into believing he had more power over me than he did. The rat diverted his attention from what was important. Krimble let his attention drift; Inara's Narmacil took that opportunity to whisper to me, giving me the power I needed to resist him.'

'You still haven't said why you need me,' said Jack. 'Those Narmacil with the Giant didn't have anyone, until one leapt into the Traveller's daughter. Inara called you a Wood Sprite; live amongst the trees, haunt the deep dells, change shape as you wish; I don't care. Grandpa Poulis told us stories about shape shifters living deep in the woods.'

A cry drifted down the passage; the same cry Jack heard when he had first visited Knell. 'The baby,' he said, peering into the dark.

'The Birdman is up there too,' said Yang.

When Yang released his arms, Jack controlled his shiver, while the warmth seeped back into his muscles. His vantage allowed him to view both the passage back to the garden and his friends, and onward to the Birdman. Faint daylight turned the underground route behind him grey, whereas darkness swathed the way to the crying baby. Comparing the way ahead with an open cage, set to slam shut when he entered, did nothing to alleviate his trepidation.

'Time is short,' said Yang. 'Down here the baby won't survive long.'

A HUSHED EXCHANGE

Jack picked up the lantern. The casing, which had felt so light when Knell passed it to him, pulled down his arm. 'You will still have to tell me why you need to live inside me.'

'You will know soon enough,' said Yang. Placing a finger to Paige's lips, Yang sprang forward.

After a brooding moment's pause, Jack followed his Narmacil toward the Birdman's lair.

50. FADE TO BLACK

FOLLOWING IN THE WAKE of his shadow Jack heard the baby's cries grow louder. Fiercely holding onto the lantern he ran through the faces Yang had shown him. Each was familiar, not as well-known as the faces back in the village, more fragments of forgotten dreams. He once owned a game made from small wooden squares, with a painted face and an accompanying name written on the bottom. His mother would describe a feature, perhaps the man had a moustache or a woman wore a hat, and he would guess who it was. Having played the game so often, he could name the character from two or three clues. That was how he identified with Paige and the others, he didn't know them, but he could pick them out of a crowd.

The silver handle cut into his palm as he edged down the passage. A beetle's shell glinted a sly wink before it scurried into a hole. Wishing he could also find a bolthole, he came to a twist in the passage. Ahead the ground rose in a sharp incline. Familiar red brick packed the rising floor. Spread out on the stones like a bathing lizard waited Yang. Yang dared go no farther; could he step beyond his shadow? Each wail from baby reminded him of wind passing through trees on a lonely night. His heart tripped with each new howl. It's a baby, he told himself, trying to shake off his nerves. She needs me.

Paige's face peeled up from the floor.

'You didn't want to come here; now you want me to go into the house?' said Jack to the upraised face.

'She's crying Jack.'

'Fine, if we die, remember you told me to go forward.'

'I will,' said Yang.

He considered the dark opening at the top of the slope rather than Paige's solemn face. Steeling himself, he swallowed his fear, only for it to catch in his throat like a fishing hook as a chair scraped across bare boards.

The baby cried louder.

Spurred on by that desperate cry he stepped over his shadow. On all fours, he scrambled up the incline. Smells of old curtains and disused rooms wafted down from the boarded up house. Thinking of how ghosts haunted houses like this increased his anxiety. Why had he listened so keenly to Grandpa Poulis's stories? He had worries enough without conjuring images of skeletons hanging from hooks on the wall. Yang kept close to his side as they crept forward with forced control. His heel pulled a brick loose and sent it tumbling down to the tunnel. The baby matched the stone's raucous fall; he hoped her cries masked the tell-tale sign of his approach.

Cracked stone, caked in dust and cobwebs, took the place of the now recognizable earthen surroundings. The floor levelled off; a few feet ahead stood a closed four-panelled door. A hole left by a missing door handle formed a surprised mouth from which escaped the baby's cries. Free of the confining tunnel, the lantern light spread through the house. His light would alert the Birdman to his presence, yet without it, he would be blind. Tightening his already ferocious hold on the small silver lantern, he rose and stepped into the house. An old carpet, with more holes than a rabbit's warren, and thinner than dry skin, tracked through to a staircase. Thankfully, no ghostly apparition stepped down those lonely stairs. White paint, long turned to yellow and spotted black with damp, coated the intervening door between Jack, Yang, the baby, and the Birdman.

Yang gave a nod as Jack raised his palm to the door. Wet wooden panels yielded against his touch. Hinges groaned like an old man getting out of a chair as the door swung inward, opening to a room devoid of warmth. Floral wallpaper clung forlornly to the walls, its design amplifying the house's fall into disrepair. In one corner stood a bookcase filled with forgotten titles. A cot stood on bare boards in the middle of the room, eerily rocking back and forth. An empty armchair and a small table were the room's only other residents.

'Behind the door,' said Yang, pointing to the yellowed coloured wood inches from Jack's face.

Expecting the kidnapper waited behind the flimsy barrier weakened Jack's fingers; he anticipated the Birdman to wrestle the door from his grasp. If the baby ceased her cries, he had no doubt he'd be able to hear the man breathing like a dehydrated dog. Tremulously he eased open the door, waiting for it to come to a sudden stop. Different wallpaper swept into view; someone had drawn a happy family in crayon on the wall. Childish scrawls painted them with garish red grins and balloons over their heads. The door continued unabated to the sidewall.

'Where is he?' whispered Jack. Dumbfounded, Yang gave an exaggerated shrug.

Passed his shadow, Jack spied movement from down the corridor. The swirling purple light could have tricked him again; candle light moved like smoke, creating shapes out of air. Yang refused to budge from his side; was his shadow scared to investigate? Reaching out he prodded Yang with his finger. He wasn't surprised to find his finger hitting solid mass, as though he was in the presence of a person, and not a shadow.

'You're firm,' said Jack.

CRIK

'I appreciate it if you didn't poke me.' His shadow rubbed where Jack had stabbed him with his finger.

'Did I hurt you?'

Movement down the hall stopped Yang from answering. A pale smudge, renewing Jack's fears of haunted houses, edged away from the wall. Dust rose from the old carpet as a heavy foot thumped down onto its faded pattern.

Jolted into action Jack and Yang threw themselves into the room with the cot. When the fallen foot's echo swept through the house, the baby fell silent. Hinges groaned as Jack, with Yang's help, swung the door shut. The doorjamb vibrated as the two leant their weight against the wood.

Silence pervaded the house. Jack held his breath, not even a ticking clock offset the quiet. With his nerve ready to break, heavy steps started up the hallway. Following the stillness, each step snapped the air like exploding fireworks. The floor thrummed with the kidnapper's approach, making the balls of Jack's feet jump in his shoes. Creaking wood, as the Birdman levied his foot from the floor, alerting them to his proximity to the door.

Seeking a means of escape, Jack turned from the door to find thick wooden planks nailed into the wall blocking the window. Without any other egress, he lowered himself to the hole in the door. Enough purple light seeped through the hole for him to see the outside corridor. His steps were so loud; the Birdman must be crashing down with his entire weight. Convinced he would see the kidnapper arrive at the door, didn't prepare him for when it happened. The Birdman's pale skin shone white; Jack had seen duller white paint. Transfixed, he could not move as the man lowered himself to the peephole. Expecting a wild eye to stare back at him, the Birdman surprised him by covering the round hole with his open mouth. Breath hissed through the aperture, making Jack gag against the rotten smell. A bloated tongue licked broken brown teeth, like a kid with a mouthful of sticky toffee.

'You wanna hur' me,' whispered the Birdman. He kissed his teeth as he leaned in closer. 'Da Witch sen' you with burning ligh' to hur' me. It won' save you. You're not safe in 'ere.'

'We came for the baby,' said Jack.

'No baby.'

While they spoke, a shrill cry rose from the crib. Yang went to soothe her. A story of a boy and his dog unfolded in mime atop the shadow's hand. Rising smoke formed the boy casting a stick for the dog. Giggles escaped the crib as the boy tripped after trying to wrestle the stick off the dog.

The Birdman's fingertips thrummed the wood. 'Birdies should keep you 'way from my house. Should a no' gone into ground. Now won' leave.' His tapping subsided moments before he exerted pressure against the wood.

'Yang, help,' cried Jack as the doorway widened. He tried to push back against the Birdman's strength. Hinges did not groan this time, they screamed.

Yang left the baby to add his weight to bar the Birdman entry. Faltering, the kidnapper redoubling his efforts eased the door open.

Defeated, Jack stumbled back into the room. The man framed in the doorway resembled a clay model made by an amateur. From his sloping brow, to the absurd length of his arms, nothing fit. Burns covered every limb, creating a weird tapestry of melted skin. He stood breathing heavily while his bloodshot eyes roamed from Jack to Yang.

'We curse'.' The Birdman pointed at his scars, saying, 'My 'ere -' he lifted his hand to Yang. '- 'is fault.' The man's clubfoot led the way into the room.

Noticing the man flinch against the purple light, Jack raised the lantern like a shield. 'Let us take the baby; we don't want to harm you.'

Whimpering, the Birdman shied away from the light. 'Hur' me boy, all life odders hur' me, always hurding me. Sun mel' me like your candle. He's ta blame.' He jabbed an accusing finger at Yang. 'Demon, in 'ere.' Slapping his stomach left behind a red handprint. 'Keep me in dark, in tunnel, like worms.'

From his broken speech, Jack ascertained the Birdman referred to the Narmacil. Jack had also called it a demon everyday since discovering the thing inside him. Had the Narmacil made the Birdman as he was? They shared the same distrust of the demons. Not all the scars on the man's body had come from exposure to the sun; long criss-crossing knife cuts covered his stomach. He had tried to cut the Narmacil out of his belly. A shudder ran through him; the man was insane.

Without realising, Jack had backed into the room as far as the crib. He only became aware of it when his foot hit the crescent shaped feet. Yang stood to his side. To his surprise, Yang had taken on the guise of Inara, complete with whole legs.

'He blames his affliction on us,' said Yang.

'Is he right,' asked Jack. 'Would he be alright if a Narmacil hadn't leapt inside of him?'

Yang shook his head, fanning Inara's fringe. 'The Narmacil trapped in his body, gave the Birdman control over the blackbirds. His Talent brought the birds to the Scorn Scar, destroying this town.'

'Look at him.' Disgust filled Jack's voice as the Birdman flinched from the lantern light. 'If your kind left him alone, he wouldn't be like this. His Narmacil did this to him.'

'No Jack, the Narmacil did not cause his suffering. His condition stems from a rare, and cruel, skin disease.'

'How do I know you're speaking the truth,' asked Jack. 'If his demon did curse him, you wouldn't tell me. You'd keep that to yourself, wouldn't you?' He prised his eyes from the whimpering man to look at his shadow. 'You can't prove that you wouldn't do the same to me, if I continue to try to separate us.'

CRIK

'Keep the light up Jack,' warned Yang, noticing Jack's arm waiver. 'The lantern is the only thing keeping the Birdman from us. Given the opportunity he will kill us all.'

Cowering from the purple haze the man had lost his sinister persona to become someone Jack pitied. The Birdman went to Knell in the hope of extinguishing the cause of his pain. If he blotted out the sun, could he go back to his family? Did he have anyone who would welcome him? Without the sun, there would be no reason to board up the windows. He could leave the tunnel behind. Covering the candle with a spread hand allowed the man to drop his defensive arm. Jack's sympathy for the man died with a single sideways look from the Birdman's deep-set eyes. Transparent madness gleamed within his glance, teasing with horrors beyond imagining. Feeling faint, he backtracked, extending the lantern above his head.

The baby started to cry as he came abreast the cot. Assured the light kept the Birdman from charging him, he turned his attention to the baby and gave a gasping cry of his own. Swaddled in rags, so dirty you wouldn't clean your floor with them; lay the familiar black form of a Narmacil. Resembling a baby only in that it was both small and had two arms and legs. When the Hatchling had spilled from the egg, he had suffered overwhelming disgust for the Narmacil, a distaste that had driven him all the way to the Scorn Scar. Again, the same sense of violation for the creature swept through him. The Narmacil differed in one aspect from the others he had seen, the eyes of this Narmacil were pure gold, missing the characteristic silver lightning bolt.

Reeling from his discovery, Jack backed into the faded wallpaper.

'Jack, it's a baby,' said Yang.

'He's right,' said Jack, pointing to the Birdman, 'that's no baby. It's another demon. To escape harm all it has to do is transform into a moth and fly away.'

Yang, taking the form of Bill, shook his head. 'The baby can't change shape. It's different. I haven't seen a Narmacil this young. It doesn't know how.'

'Do you have to go to school to learn?'

Pushing spectacles up his nose Yang stepped toward Jack, only for Jack to edge away.

'You know I care for you,' said Yang. 'I have often proven it. I've stuck by you through all this adventure.' Yang's voice cracked with emotion. 'All I want is to see you grow, and to grow with you. To help you in everything you try. You're also inside me.' Yang tapped his chest.

The only visible part of the Birdman was his bone white hands as they spread like crab claws around Yang's neck. The shadow gasped as the man with the patchwork scars hoisted him backward.

Jack screamed. The purple light had made Yang solid, protecting the Birdman from the harmful light, and hiding him from Jack's sight. His shadow, gasping for air, locked his hands about his assailant's wrists.

'Leave him alone,' cried Jack. He jumped to the left, swinging the lantern in an attempt to throw light onto the man. The Birdman kept Yang facing the light with a turn of his body.

'Demon die,' growled the Birdman. His fingers dug deeper into Yang's neck.

Horrified, Jack watched as Yang tried to alter his form from Bill's into something that would allow him to escape the man's clutches. Each time the shadow tried to free himself the man squeezed harder, defeating Yang's every effort.

'Leave him alone,' said Jack.

'Kill demon.' Grunting with effort the man drove his fingers into Yang's black flesh.

A cold flutter in Jack's stomach had him press a hand against his shirt. Movement pulsed under his skin. The Birdman was killing his demon. Jack shook his head, it wasn't a demon, nor was it his Narmacil, the Birdman was killing Yang. Never again would his shadow pull up Liza Manfry's skirt. He would never wake up to find a stuffed animal on his pillow, placed there to scare him. His mother would only lay one plate for him on the kitchen table. Faced with losing Yang he knew he couldn't live without him. Yang said he remembered Jack's life; Jack also remembered each day with Yang. Having Yang meant he was never alone. Without Yang, his life would be less than it is. It would be as empty as a shadow that followed the sun.

Jack's sudden dart to the side scored light across the man's arm. Flinching against the searing pain, the Birdman blocked the light with Yang's weakening body. Yang hung limp in the man's rough grasp, another minute and he would die. A cold shudder twisted through Jack's stomach.

'Yang,' he shouted.

'Kill you.' The Birdman looked over Yang's sagging head at Jack.

'Yang!'

Yang lifted his head; he tried to speak, his mouth formed a word only for a choke to mingle with the baby's startling cry.

Jack brought the lantern up to his face. The purple haze made his tears sparkle on his cheeks. Yang still held onto the Birdman's wrists. Another minute and those hands will drop and his shadow would disappear. To save Yang, he would have to sacrifice himself. 'I'm sorry Yang.' He extinguished the candle.

CRIK

51. THE CURTAIN CALL

ONE DAMP AUTUMNAL DAY Jack had witnessed Farmer Goldsmith lead a pig to slaughter. The squealing animal had spawned a thousand nightmares, from which he awoke bathed in a lather of sweat. Now, cowering in the dark, he listened to the Birdman make the same horrific sound. Unable to see, made the man's cries take on phantasmagorical shapes. In his mind, the man's clubfoot became a cloven hoof.

Amongst the inane babble, the man said, 'It gone. Where'd it go?' The frantic words tumbled from him as he screamed his outrage at Yang's escape. Another few seconds and the Birdman would have crushed the life from Jack's Narmacil. Fearing he had extinguished the candle too late, drove Jack almost to the point of calling out Yang's name. Without light, he had no way of knowing if Yang lived. Rubbing his stomach gave no clue as to the Narmacil's condition. By lighting the lantern he would land Yang back in trouble - he could not risk the Birdman getting another hold on Yang.

Stumbling against the cot, the Birdman revived the baby Narmacil's cries. Instinct led Jack to the boarded up window. Paradoxically he stood in pitch darkness while a few feet from him blazed a hot sun. Reaching up he discovered square-headed nails held the wooden barrier fast against the wall. To allow sunlight into the room he would require a crowbar. Alone in the dark he wanted to join his own cry to that of the baby. The Birdman was closer. A quiet shuffle, reminding him of someone shrugging on a heavy coat, took the place of the man's wails. Jack preferred the outraged cries to the closing furtive movement. No need to pierce the dark to know the Birdman sought him with animal cunning. Without doubt, one large hand, with hair sprouting from pale knuckles, reached toward the corner where he stood. If Knell had allowed Bill to come with him, Black would protect him. He shook his head; this was his fault, no one but him had wanted to come here. This was his problem.

The man's stench assailed his nostrils as he closed to within a few yards. Trying to remember the layout of the room, conjured an image of the cot, an armchair, and a table. Dropping to a crouch, seconds ahead of the Birdman lunging forward, saved him from capture. An annoyed grunt from the Birdman provoked a laugh from the crib.

THE CURTAIN CALL

Keeping low Jack manoeuvred away from the cot and the irate kidnapper. Desperate to keep silent restricted his movements. Hugging the wall, he moved, aware of the killer's dangerous proximity. Picking up a splinter from the floorboard had him snatch back his hand. Wood bit into the meat of his thumb, tearing from him a murmur of pain. The Birdman's hands were on him before he had time to pick out the wooden spear. Lifted into the air and pushed against the wall knocked the air from his lungs. Strong hands crushed his thin arms, pinioning them to his side. Imprisoned in the Birdman's vice-like hold, his defence relied solely on ineffective kicks to the kidnapper's chest.

'Leave me go,' cried Jack, throwing out another kick. 'Killing Yang has punished me for coming to your damn house.'

'Shadow man escape,' moaned the Birdman. 'He disappear. I know where he is.'

He moved in closer, forcing Jack to straighten his legs. Confined by the mad man's weight, Jack gagged against the putrescent odour. When he didn't return, would his friend's follow him to a similar fate? Ignoring Knell's command not to pursue him, the Birdman would kill them.

Using his malformed body to imprison Jack against the wall, the Birdman lowered one clammy hand down to the boy's stomach. 'I know where he hid.' Exerting pressure, he made Jack groan in pain.

Gritting his teeth, Jack said, 'Yang hasn't done anything to you.' Becoming used to the dark he could discern the Birdman's pale body and even the evil leer on his face. Gagging against the Birdman's stench, he recognised the enjoyment the man got by hurting him. Wanting to throw up he turned his head away from the hissing fetid breath. 'Leave me go. You won't ever see me again.'

The Birdman ignored him. 'I won' let Shadow Man hide from me.' A rasp of metal against hardened leather cut through the room.

'What are you doing?' said Jack. A moment later, an ice-cold knife pressed into his stomach. Gasping, he flinched back from the weapon. 'Get it off me!'

'Tried to cut my curse out,' whispered the Birdman. 'Lots of blood, lots of pain. The demon hid deeper.'

Recalling the scars, criss-crossing the Birdman's stomach, drove Jack insane with fear. Driven crazy by the tortuous sun, the man wanted to cut Yang out of him. The knife was about to open him up like a steaming meat pie pulled apart on a dinner plate.

His high scream drowned out the baby Narmacil, and the Birdman's mounting excitement. When the knife cut his skin, the shock stopped his screams. Absently he felt a trail of hot blood run down to his leg. The sharp blade, as cold as an icicle, cut him without effort.

'Cut your curse out,' said the Birdman.

'No.' Jack tossed his head to the side. 'You cannot take Yang from me, he is part of me; he is my friend.'

CRIK

'Demon inside curse you,' said the Birdman. 'Keep you from sun. Live in cave.'

'You're wrong; the Narmacil isn't what makes the sun hurt you. You have a terrible disease that has nothing to do with the Narmacil.'

'I help you. You'll be free, no more demon. I cut out, no scared anymore.'

Jack howled as the knife bit deeper. 'Yang!'

The Birdman's grin spread as he turned the knife, readying to deal a savage cut. 'Demon die. Will drag it out and sta...' His words faltered, as did his smile, as the hand holding the knife withdrew. Incredulous, the big man wrestled with the blade; fear rushed into his eyes. The pressure holding Jack tight against the wall eased as something grabbed a hold of the Birdman.

Coughing, Jack fell to the ground. Relief washed over him when he discovered only a single shallow cut along his stomach. Looking up he saw the Birdman struggle in the dark. The bloodied knife lay on the floor.

'Shadow man,' shouted the Birdman. 'I found you.' An instant later, before his exuberance had time to die, a loud crack resonated through the room. Howling in pain, the Birdman cradled his arm. 'Kill you!' Ignoring his pain, the Birdman rushed his invisible assailant. Unable to locate his attacker, the Birdman's headlong attack soon faltered, and then, as something took hold of him, he sped from view.

Wincing, Jack covered his ears, when a terrific clap of bone against plaster reverberated from the far wall. Snapping bone punctuated each scream from across the room. What happened a few feet from him in the dark was something he never wished to see. Getting to his feet, he took a few unsteady steps toward the cot. He lowered an arm to locate the crib just as the screams in the corner came to an abrupt and final end.

'It's alright, I've got you,' said Jack, lifting the baby Narmacil from the dirty sheets. Its rough skin was searing hot. Adjusting himself so he could carry the baby in one hand, he moved back to the corner where the Birdman had held him and located the dropped silver lantern. 'I think I'll light this when we're out of the room.'

With the baby nuzzling against his chest, he hurriedly passed the cot. When his foot skidded on a wet patch, he expected to fall. Surmising that spilt blood drenched the floor carried him quickly through the darkness. Hitting the table with his hip saved him from crashing to the ground. The metallic smell of blood filled the room. Though shallow, the cut on his stomach, bled profusely, so he couldn't tell whether the room reeked of his blood or whether it mingled with that of the Birdman to create a heady perfume. Thankfully, darkness hid the far corner.

The baby giggled against him. Had she assaulted the kidnapper? Each Narmacil had a unique power. Could the baby have used its Talent to

THE CURTAIN CALL

overpower and kill the Birdman? Shivering, he stepped into the corridor, and refused to strike a match until he had reached the tunnel entrance.

Yellow flame flaring to life from the sulphur head illuminated his shadow. Lifting his arm had a corresponding effect on his outline. Scared, he kicked a stone, which clanged against the brick under his shade, and still Yang showed no sign that he was with him. 'Come on Yang, you can't be dead.' He spoke the words low, afraid to voice his prayer, in case he would curse himself. 'I am so sorry for everything I have said and done. Show me a sign; not knowing is driving me crazy.' Ignoring the tears streaming down his cheeks, he lit the candlewick. 'Say something,' he urged. Despair pulled at him like a strong current until his hope died. When Yang waved, he laughed in relief.

'You had me scared there,' he said.

'You didn't think I'd leave Ying,' replied his shadow.

'I thought the Birdman had killed you. I was sure I had hesitated too long before blowing out the light.'

In the purple light Yang took on Jack's form. With hands on hips, the shadow breathed hard. 'Any longer and he would have choked the life out of me. As it was, it took me a long time to recover from the attack. I'm sorry you had to wait for my help.'

Confused, Jack looked into the room where the cot still rocked from side to side. His bloodied footprints led across the floor from a spreading pool of blood. 'Did you kill him?'

Yang hung his head. 'I couldn't let him stab you. When I regained my strength, I pulled him away. I knew if I didn't kill him he would keep on coming and wouldn't stop until he had murdered us all.'

'But without light,' said Jack, 'the room was in pitch black.'

Yang gave a wan smile. 'Paige had it wrong. She didn't need a burning candle to keep me close. I never left her side, nor do I disappear when you fall asleep. Although you cannot see me, I always watch out for you Jack.'

'I suspected,' said Jack, ' though I couldn't be sure.'

'Light imprisons me,' said Yang, pointing at the lantern. 'I alter my shape by bending the laws that govern other shadows. I cheat those laws only so far, the light paints a definite boundary. Without this constraint I take on no form, I am everywhere and everything, and yet that lack of form makes it hard for me to control things.'

'How come?' asked Jack. 'If the darkness makes you more powerful you should be able to do anything you want.'

Yang shook his head. 'How can I move things without hands to move them?'

'But you pulled the Birdman off me?'

'Only with great effort. The light gives me shape, without that source I have to use my mind to coalesce. Hands afford incredible degrees of manipulation.

CRIK

With them, I can pick petals from a rose or hit a punch bag. That is not how the mind works. I cannot do delicate things in the dark; it is like using a hammer to wash a cup. Every time you blow out the candle for the night, I stay still, terrified of losing control and hurting you. Unable to sleep, I remain motionless, waiting for dawn to give me form. After losing me, I knew the Birdman would kill you; he left me with no choice. You have no idea how relieved I am that I did not hurt you.'

They moved down the tunnel, both desperate to leave behind the bloodied room. Without the threat of the Birdman, the tunnel felt shorter to Jack. He passed the stone outcrop where Yang had first spoken a short time ago; then he had seen his shadow as a threat, an alien entity hiding nefarious secrets, now as he passed the same stretch of ground he looked at his shadow as a friend, as a brother. How could he have mistrusted Yang for so long? All his life Yang was someone he had trusted. No one was closer to him than his shadow, not even his mother could hope to know him as well as Yang.

'I'm sorry.' The apology was inadequate, and he knew it. Embarrassed, he waited for Yang to respond.

Yang studied him for a long time. A smile formed and he slapped Jack on the back. 'I'll tell you one day about Tom. I never thought anyone could distrust me more than that boy, but you gave him a run for his money.'

The sunlight shining into the tunnel from the opening in the garden lifted Jack's spirits. It painted the tunnel a light blue, diffusing the purple light spilling from the lantern.

'This won't be much use out there.' Jack held aloft the lantern.

Yang nodded. 'It was a pleasure to speak with you. Knowing lights like this exist has opened up so many possibilities for me, for us to explore. Using the candle, we can talk to one another so there will no longer be any secrets between us. Coming here and making this discovery has opened up a whole new world for me.'

Reaching out, Jack placed his hand on Yang's shoulder. His shadow still felt cold, only this time the touch warmed him. 'Next time I try to pat you on the back my hand will slip right through you.'

Laughing, Yang said, 'Best blow out the candle, I have taken enough blows for one day.' Leaning forward Yang blew, dousing the candle.

The baby Narmacil, clinging to Jack, playfully tugged his hair. 'Alright, you're almost home.' He laughed.

The familiar red brick took the place of the soft earthen tunnel floor and led him once more into the sun. The sun on his face felt good. Yang rushed ahead, growing in size as daylight returned to their world. Fearing the birds still waited for him, Jack held the baby close as he clawed his way up from the hole. Spying a few stragglers perched on the swing, and another group of blackbirds in the

THE CURTAIN CALL

garden, froze him to the spot. When they ignored his arrival, he cautiously proceeded toward the house.

A deathly hush had fallen over the scene as though he was about to find something horrible. Limping through the garden, he kept expecting to see his friends. Where were they? Surely they kept watch for him from within the safety of the net. Fearing the worst, he jogged passed the watching birds, with their predatory gaze.

52. HOMECOMING

BLACKBIRDS WHEELED IN THE SKY above Jack. The Birdman's death had taken the fight out of them, but what had the birds done during Jack's absence. He told himself repeatedly that his friends were safe, he just wished he believed himself. His confrontation with the deranged man could not have resulted in putting his friends in further danger. Dead birds piled up against the house like dirty snow, paying proof of his delusion. Blood glued feathers to the stone. Hesitating, he noticed clumps of black fur amongst the carnage. Although he knew the hair belonged to Black, he didn't know how much of the blood belonged to the wolf.

'Bill. Bill can you hear me? Answer me damnit!'

The trail of dead birds led into the house. The amount of feathers covering the passage made it difficult to tell how many bodies littered the floor; he estimated hundreds of blackbirds had passed the net. Frail bird bones crunched under his heel like crackling. Where were his friends? Frantic, he called out their names. Gripping his shoulder, the baby answered with a shrill cry. Entering the vacant room where he had left his friends amplified his terror. Clumps of bloodied dark hair clung to the armchair. Tasting the blood in the air curdled his stomach; he spat on the floor in distaste.

'Inara!'

He ran back to the passageway. Heart hammering he stopped at the foot of the stairs. Resting one foot on the first step, he prepared to climb, when he noticed a heap of bodies covering a small downstairs door. Threaded amongst the half-chewed birds, like ribbons on wrapped presents, were old bandages, spotted with old blood. Recognising the strips of cloth as belonging to Inara, he leapt down the corridor.

Yang scooped away the dead birds, while he kicked them from the door. Once clear he tried the handle, the door rattled against its jam. Studying the wood, he found no sign of an outside lock; the door had no keyhole. 'Secured from the inside,' he muttered. Allowing his hopes to rise he banged the door.

'Hey it's me, open up!'

He hit the door so hard he hurt his hand.

'Yang, you could slip under the door and open it from the inside.'

Yang shook his head.

HOMECOMING

'If you're afraid of blowing the door off its hinges and hurting me, don't, I'll stand well back.'

Giving a quick nod, Yang shooed Jack and the baby back with a flap of his hand. Spreading himself flat against the floor, Yang slipped under the door. The wood creaked, then bulged outward, and finally exploded into the passage. Jack shielded the baby from the flying wood.

'You weren't kidding when you said you can't control yourself in the dark.'

The broken entryway framed Yang, who beckoned him to follow. Dust filled the air as Jack took after his disappearing shadow down a flight of stairs. He almost tripped on a twisted deadbolt lying on the fifth step. Someone had pulled that lock shut. The baby Narmacil scurried over his shoulder to grip his back. It was like taking a plunge into a midnight lake as he descended the dark stairs.

'I can't see, is anyone down here? Bill, Inara, anyone, answer me.'

The floor echoed his steps when he hit it. Shuffling forward he tried to listen to anything beyond himself and the Narmacil clinging to him. When he heard a creak, he suspected someone had followed him down the stairs. Had the Birdman survived? Was he following him down here? A sliver of light appeared across the room as a second door opened. Yang materialised at his side as the door swept wider, spilling a warm glow into what must be Knell's cellar.

'Is that you Ying?'

'Bill!' cried Jack as his friend stuck out his head.

Both boys rushed across the cellar floor and flew into each other's arms. Bill's glasses fell off as he laughed. Yang caught the spectacles. Jack slapped his friend on the back.

'Why didn't you answer me when I called your name?'

Bill appeared sheepish. 'Well, we've had a time of it since you left. Those birds attacked the house in one mad rush. It was like being inside a hurricane. In case a bad storm ever hit the village, Grandpa insisted on building a storm cellar. Knell had the same idea.' He grinned. 'When the birds broke through the net, Knell led us down here. We couldn't hear what happened in the house.'

'Jack,' cried Inara. She clung to the injured wolf. Slick with blood and with hair missing on both sides Black never looked more fearsome. Overjoyed, Jack rushed to greet them.

'Are you hurt? I saw your bandages on the floor.'

Inara flicked back her hair. 'Nothing can hurt me while I'm with my protector.' She smoothed the wolf's head.

'A few of the birds flapped around her legs, pecking at the bandages. Black beat them back, no problem, he killed hundreds of them.' Bill said with pride.

'People called me crazy for wanting to put the deadbolt on this side of the door; I knew what I was doing,' said Knell joining them. Stray feathers clung to her robes. 'The Birdman sent his filthy creatures into my home when he found

CRIK

you in his. They'd still be here now, pestering me, if you and Yang didn't come to an understanding.'

'Yang, I didn't know if I would ever see you again,' said Bill.

The shadow handed Bill his glasses, before enveloping the boy in a big hug. Yang then turned his attention to Inara, sweeping her off Black and holding her up in the air. She laughed, but for Jack, seeing her ghastly leg wounds uncovered for the first time, tempered the happy moment.

'Hey, what's that,' cried Bill.

The baby Narmacil had circled around and clung to Jack's back when he climbed down the stairs; only now, that Knell stood amongst them, did the baby feel confident in revealing herself. Her golden eyes shone.

'Hello baby,' said Knell. She reached forward and the Narmacil leapt from Jack to her waiting arms. 'I missed you.' Those few words held more emotion from the woman than any of the children had seen from her.

'That's your baby?' asked Bill, gawping at the Narmacil.

'I care for her as though she was,' said Knell. 'In that respect I am her mother.'

'It's a Narmacil.'

'And you are as dull as a donkey suffering from sun stroke,' said Inara.

'Each Narmacil lives for hundreds of years,' said Jack. Recalling all the faces Yang showed him he added, 'Perhaps more than a thousand. How can you call the Narmacil a baby?'

'You witnessed a Narmacil hatch from an egg, and then you all saw the Narmacils under the waterfall,' replied Knell. 'Do any of you notice anything different about this child?' Her hands trembled as she lovingly held forward the Narmacil.

It shared all the same characteristics as the Narmacil Jack encountered in his bedroom. Yang's information concerned the Narmacil's inability to change its form, but Knell indicated another oddity.

'Its golden eyes,' said Inara, pointing. 'Where's the silver bolt. Every other Narmacil has that zigzag line.'

'Well done,' said Knell, offering a smile. 'If more people used their own wits, they wouldn't keep coming to my doorstep. The boy is correct; there are ancient Narmacil within Crik wood. Becoming an ancient is a long process, fraught with danger. An elder Narmacil, called a Dintraise, lives in Inara.' They turned to Inara. 'Never mind that,' snapped the woman, returning their attention to her. 'Every Narmacil is old, living far beyond our lifespan, always bestowing its Talent to the chosen.' she regarded Jack sombrely. He could not lift his head for shame. 'When you die, your Narmacil will rest. A Narmacil sleeps for ten years, and in that time they form a protective shell about themselves.'

'Why?' asked Jack.

HOMECOMING

'While you live your bodies protect them,' said Knell. 'A Narmacil cannot survive long without that protection. It is for this reason that the Lindre granted the union between the Narmacil and us. We benefit each other. The Narmacil grants you a Talent, in return for your body's defence.'

Remembering the figure in the storm that had started his adventure, Jack asked, 'Where does the Giant come into this?'

'Ysgor, a Woodland Giant, is a friend. He looks after the sleeping Narmacil, and when they awaken he takes them to the one they will join.'

'I saw him in Mr Hasseltope's tomb.'

'The people of your village sealed the tomb ten years ago. Protected within the stone, the egg matured. Retrieval of the egg before maturity is hazardous, and only undertaken if the egg is in danger. When it was time for the Narmacil to awaken, Ysgor went to the tomb.' Knell turned to Bill. 'You carry that Narmacil. Mr Hasseltope also had the Talent to control animals.'

Jack remembered the body of the fox inside the grave. 'So that's what the Giant was doing with the Hatchlings at the waterfall. He was taking them to the children who waited to have their Talent.'

'Like the gypsy girl, Jess,' said Inara.

'Ysgor works tirelessly. The other three Hatchlings have now granted their Talents to children who live within the wood.'

'Wait a second,' said Bill, shifting his glasses. 'You say that we protect the Narmacil, that without our bodies they won't survive.'

'Then how come your child isn't dying?' asked Inara.

'Narmacil become vulnerable at maturity,' answered Knell. 'Gaining the ability to transform stretches their skin, making it thin. At that juncture any exposure to the outside elements will eventually kill them.'

'How old is she?' asked Jack.

'Five years,' said Knell. 'She has yet to find the gift that will grant her Talent to another. The Birdman hoped his need would influence the formation of her power. A Narmacil is full of potential; he was not mistaken in that. When the day arrives, when she finds her gift, her eyes will appear like all the rest.' Indicating the golden eyes, she said, 'It is the power, such as your shadow, that bestows the silver line through the eyes. Once she has reached maturity, Ysgor will arrive to take her from me.'

'I doubt there are many Narmacil this young,' said Jack.

'The next youngest Narmacil is five hundred years old,' stated Knell.

Moving passed the children; Knell began to climb the stairs. She carried the crying Narmacil in the crook of her arm. Taking a Syll from her rope belt, she began to play, colouring the cellar with the light that whispered through its many holes. The baby listened for a few moments, her eyes wide before they began to droop closed.

CRIK

An outstretched hand stopped Jack from following the blindfolded woman. Turning he saw Bill holding his arm. 'What's going on?'

Bill waited for Knell to disappear. 'Yang is still here.'

'He is.'

'You didn't demand your answer from Knell,' said Inara. 'You rescued her child from the Birdman. She will have to tell you what you want to know.' She balled her hands into tights fists. 'Do you still want to kill the Narmacil inside of you?'

'Knell said you two came to an understanding,' said Bill. 'You heard her say that didn't you Inara? I heard it loud and clear.'

Wanting to smile, Jack looked up at Inara, suspended in the air by his shadow. Nothing would give him more pleasure than to hold her, and Bill too, to laugh and apologise for being a fool. 'Knell gave me a light, so that I would be able to see clearly. Blindly I went into the tunnel, refusing to see what was in front of me. Stupidity almost cost me Yang, and my obsession put you both in danger. Everyday you told me what a friend I had in him, but I couldn't see it. He was a monster I needed to destroy - only when faced with his destruction I realised his true nature. Yang is my brother; through him, my life is richer. Losing him is unthinkable, a horrendous crime. How we survived the Red Wood, is a miracle in itself. I have taken us far from home. Inara, you should now be back with your parents, not here with us. Bill, my oldest, closest friend, you only wanted to enter the wood to get your wolf.' He laughed. 'There's no better wolf in Crik than Black. You will have the honour of bringing him into the village, to show everyone what a fabulous Talent you have. It was worth the wait. I owe you both a huge apology. To answer your question then, no I will not be asking Knell how I can destroy Yang. We will be together all my life and Yang will carry me with him to his next.'

Bill clapped his hands. 'That's great.'

'Yes Jack, that's wonderful news,' said Inara, relaxing.

'There is something else Knell may be able to help us with,' said Jack, looking up the stairs. 'I think she will answer.'

'What?' Bill asked.

'The quickest way home,' Jack said smiling.

'About time.'

Black, carrying a slight limp from his tussle with the birds, led the way back up the stairs. Jack took two steps at a time, eager to see Knell. He remembered the map Ysgor had drawn behind the waterfall; it had shown a long winding road leading from the Scorn Scar all the way to Crik Village. Knell may have a couple of horses, he thought, excited. A few more days and he would end his mother's misery. Jumping over the dead birds, he followed Black into the room where Knell sat. The baby Narmacil lay in the cot at her side.

HOMECOMING

'How do we get home?' he asked before his friends had time to catch him up.

Knell wore the hood of her cloak up, hiding her face apart from the tip of her nose. 'Speak softly,' she said, pointing to the resting Narmacil. 'You already know the way home.' Yang carried Inara on his shoulder; Bill stepped through the shadow to stand beside Jack. 'The long road will take you away from the foot of the mountain, through the wood and eventually you will see your homes again.'

'Is there a faster way?' asked Jack.

'There is always another way,' said Knell. 'Different paths to the same spot. A bird will fly over the mountain; a fish would swim down the river. Most people take the road.'

'Is the road the quickest way we can travel?' asked Inara.

'You have already asked me your question,' said Knell.

'What question?' asked Jack, perplexed.

Inara looked down at her destroyed legs. 'I told you on the lake.' She stopped, overcome with emotion.

'Your legs,' said Jack, recalling her dearest wish. He regarded Knell with hope. 'There is no one in my village with the Talent to help Inara, but there are others living within the woods. One of the gypsies or perhaps someone in another village can help her?'

'No,' replied Inara. 'Knell said no one exists with the Talent to make me whole again.'

'I said, no such Talent exists, yet,' said Knell. 'That does not mean such a Talent will not appear in the future. Mayhap when that time arrives, you would not want to have your legs back. You will be that much older. Time has a way to alter perceptions.'

'I can never see me not wanting to walk on my own two feet again.'

'If you want, we can discuss it again in a few years. Perhaps by then I will have a different answer for you.' Knell checked to see whether the baby still slept. Satisfied, she continued, 'As always the solution to your problem will not be free.'

'I'll be willing to pay anything,' said Inara.

'We'll see.'

'Don't worry Inara, when the time comes for you to return, I'll be with you.'

'Thanks Jack.'

'Me too,' added Bill. 'Black will be even bigger by then.'

'Is there a quicker route than the road back to our home?' repeated Jack, impatient to get going.

'You came to me asking how to kill your Narmacil,' said Knell. 'By giving you the purple candle I gave you the means to destroy Yang. Your shadow became solid, making him mortal. A thrown knife, or hands around his throat, would be enough to kill him. The real question, the question you hid from yourself, was whether you wanted to be without Yang. Even when you found out about the "demon" living inside you, you still wanted him. When you first visited me, you came without Yang. Remember how you felt when you discovered your shadow remained fixed to the ground?'

Thinking back to when the Lindre had transported him to the Scorn Scar, Jack remembered feeling lonely. Without Yang stretching ahead, to look at what lay around the next corner, he had felt lost, abandoned.

'You had your answer then,' continued Knell. 'I will only answer a single question. If I answered every query a person had, I would spend my entire life with that person. Now leave me, I wish to return my home into some semblance of order.'

'I guess we follow the road back,' said Jack. 'At least it will keep us away from the Wold.'

Stepping from the room with Inara and Yang, Jack failed to notice Black and Bill remaining behind.

'Jack, wait,' said Inara, watching Bill take a step closer to Knell.

'I haven't asked my question,' said Bill. He could not keep a tremor from his voice.

'What question would you ask of me?' said Knell.

'I want to know the quickest route home?'

'There is always a price,' said Knell.

Bill gave a firm nod. 'Ask. If I can, I will pay your price.'

Lowering her head Knell appeared to be in deep thought. When she raised her head, she pointed to an adjoining room. Following her finger the group saw a set of dolls standing on a small cupboard. Some of the dolls wore frilly hats; others carried a basket, or flowers.

'You told me that your grandmother owns dolls like mine.'

Bill paled. 'She does.'

'Promise to return to me with one of her dolls, and I will give you your answer.'

'Grandma Poulis will never give up one of her dolls,' said Bill. 'She's already going to give me a hiding for running away to find my wolf. There'd be nothing left of me if I told her I promised away one of her babies.'

'Then you best put on your walking shoes,' said Knell, leaning back in her armchair.

'I think she cares more about her dolls than she does me,' said Bill, looking back at Jack in despair. 'She'll ground me for a week.'

'Is that such a bad thing?' asked Jack. 'I just want to get home.'

Chewing on his lip, Bill turned to Knell. 'There isn't another tunnel you want me to go down is there.' He looked at Jack. 'Alright,' he said, throwing his hands up in defeat. 'I promise to give you a doll. Grandma won't like it.'

HOMECOMING

'To the rear of my garden grows a tree. One of you will recognise its like.' She stood; her hand knocked a bottle on her hip making it chime. Moving past the children, she said, 'Many unique things exist in this world. I know of no other with a moving shadow. You boy,' she pointed to Bill, 'are the only one who can control your wolf.' The kitchen she led them through had a bird flapping by a glass window. 'Shoo, get out.' Knell told the bird. She opened the backdoor and away the bird flew. 'Sometimes a twin exists; when this happens they form a connection; an unbroken bond. When Ysgor comes across twins, the Narmacil splits in two, bestowing both siblings with its Talent. Diluting that Talent.' She climbed up a series of chipped stone steps, overgrown with vine and moss. Night bruised the sky, placing the garden in a deep gloom. 'Watch your step up here, the ground is more unkempt than a boy's hair.' Jack raked his fingers through his mop of hair; his finger snagged a knot, making his eyes water. 'There are, of course, twin animals.' She picked her way through the overgrown garden. 'Though there are few twinned trees, they do exist.' The garden stopped rising and became level. Standing at the centre of the grass stood a grey tree.

'It has hair,' said Bill, noticing how the wind ruffled the grey hair growing on the tree's trunk.

'It can't be,' said Jack, running forward. Reaching the tree, he passed his hand over the bark's familiar warmth. Again, the tree reminded him of the supple back of a rabbit.

'What is it Jack?' asked Inara, as she floated across the garden on Yang's shoulder.

'You recognise the tree,' said Knell.

Jack nodded. 'Yes,' he said. 'The same morning I found the Narmacil egg, my mother found a strange seed. She grew it into a tree that sits in my garden. It's the same tree as this.'

'Not the same,' said Knell, 'its twin.'

Turning from the grey tree, Jack looked at Knell. 'How did the twin of this tree find its way to my house?'

'I had Ysgor leave it there,' said Knell.

'Why?'

'Before the occurrence that forms the future question, my Talent already knows the answers. I knew I had to give Ysgor the seed when he travelled to the tomb. Your mother's Talent allowed her to grow the tree, forming a connection between your garden and mine.'

'What do you mean?' Jack asked.

'The tree in your garden and this one came from the same seed, forming a bridge between them,' said Knell. Passing Jack, she moved aside the tree's long hair to reveal a hole.

CRIK

'Are you saying by stepping into that hole we will find ourselves in Jack's garden?' Inara asked.

When Knell nodded, Bill gasped. 'You are joking.'

Knell moved aside for Jack, who pulled back the tree's hanging hair and felt a rush of warm air coming through the hole. 'Impossible,' he whispered.

'Step though and find out,' said Bill.

'Is it a tunnel?'

'No,' replied Knell. 'Your passage home will feel instantaneous, though in actuality it will take a number of hours.'

They had travelled for days, perhaps weeks since leaving home. Now standing before the tree he found it hard to believe he was only moments away from seeing his mother again. 'The warm air I can feel...'

'Blows from your garden,' said Knell.

Spots of rain touched Jack's hand as he pushed it though the tree. Pulling back his hand he laughed. 'It's raining back home.' He lifted up his wet hand, marvelling at the rainwater that sluiced down his arm.

'It is always raining back home,' said Bill, shaking his head.

'Thank you,' Jack told Knell.

'No need,' she replied. 'I have my price.'

'What are you waiting for,' called Bill. 'Jump through the hole, we'll be right behind you.'

Separating the strands of hair, Jack discovered the size of the hole would allow them all to step through the tree. 'Goodbye.'

'Goodbye,' said Knell. 'Thank you for returning the child to me.'

Smiling, Jack stepped into the tree.

The tree's hair tickled his face as he fell through the hole and into his garden. The rain thrummed the ground around him. He laughed at the absurdity at arriving back home. Looking up he saw his house and began to cry. Glass from the shattered windows littered the garden, while smoke, from a raging fire, billowed out from the open apertures.

53. ON THE OTHER SIDE

WHEN INARA RODE BLACK through the hole, the fire inside Jack's home had become a furnace; charring the wooden window frames as black as tar and sending ferocious orange flames skyward. The air crackled with heat making the rain hiss. Jack, lying on the ground, stunned into immobility, let out a strangled cry. Surrounded by shards of glass and wild honeysuckle, that was a constant denizen of his garden, he felt adrift. He supposed, as he looked up to the kitchen window with its cascading smoke, that this fire was his fault. No, he hadn't lit a match, or rubbed together two sticks to start the blaze, only in his heart he knew if he had stayed home this would not have happened.

Bill shouted something; he could see his friend's mouth opening and closing like a drowning fish caught in a net, and his wild gestures toward the inferno a few feet away. He guessed he should move, if he could only get to his feet. The cold mud squishing through his fingers offered a stark contrast to the heated air. Wishing he could escape the horror he had found, he wanted to burrow into the soil; let it bury him. When he rose, his legs felt like two wickets hit by a fast spinner; he would've fallen without Yang's support. Biting back a hoarse sob, he became aware of other houses ablaze. Miss Mistletoe's, and the large tree in her garden, looked worst than his own, and farther along, he noticed Dwayne Blizzard's house leaning as though it too wanted to bury itself in the wet soil. Bill's house at the opposite end of the street was conspicuous in its normality. Every other home was a furnace; the Poulis household had taken no damage. Another thing struck Jack, something extremely odd, and in its own way, more alarming than the burning homes. Looking around, he scanned the road and the gardens to make sure. No one was in sight. Where were the people fighting the fires? There should be a line stretching to the Tristle River, with each person holding a bucket, pan, or cup, anything that would hold water to fight the conflagration. Mr Dash talked of people dying in their beds during a fire. "Died of breathing in too much smoke," he had said. Jack guessed if anyone would know it'd be the grave keeper.

Mad fear took hold, shaking him out of his nervous shock. His mother, please don't let her be in the house. Sprinting passed Bill, who now gazed with dumb awe at the licking flames, and then Inara, who wore the same troubled expression as anyone faced with a calamity they felt powerless to stop. Skidding to a halt, he felt the incredible furnace heat singe his hair. Intent of finding a way into the house, he skirted the building to the main entrance. Air shimmered in the heat, bathing him in a sick orange glow. The sight of the melted doorknob dashed any ambition of entering his home from the front. Defeated, he fell to his knees. Sucking in a searing breath, he prepared to call for his mother, when a horrendous crash came from his home. First the roof sagged, and then, in a cloud of smoke and fiery embers, it collapsed into his attic bedroom.

Bill shared his dumbstruck terror; he came to his side, laying a silent hand on his shoulder. There were no comforting words spoken. What could any of them do?

'What happened?' said Jack, knowing Bill had as much idea about what had started the fire as he did.

'Where's Yang going,' cried Inara.

Hot air fluttered the burnt remains of the plants Jack's mother had grown on his windowsill. Mesmerised, he watched the reeds, caught in the maelstrom they reminded him of kelp caught in a swirling current. Tearing his eyes from them, he spied Yang stretch toward the living room.

Heat and falling debris had no effect on Yang. Two shadowed lines connected Jack to his shadow as it vanished into the billowing smoke. Kneeling, he envied his shadow's ability to search the house, out here on the lawn he was no help to his mother.

'If she's still in there, Yang will find her,' said Bill.

'Why did it have to be a fire?' Jack offered a quiet curse. Since the accident that had disfigured her, his mother had grown deathly afraid of it. She dared light a fire only when frost crept up the windows like rising steam from a kettle. Suspicious of the burning coal, she refused to relax her vigil as she stood over the fireplace, clutching the poker in tight fists. Her fright, on those cold dark nights, mirrored his own silent condemnation of the stuffed animals Yang brought to his room when he was younger. An ever-constant dread, that the cold dead animal eyes would glint with new life and its head would turn on a neck stiff with sawdust, never left him. When she watched the glittering coals, she kept her body taught and her voice silent, standing with an inexpressible dread. Jack shivered despite the heat. Long minutes stretched on, lengthening his painful wait. Not wanting Yang to find his mother, he knew if she were still in the house, she would surely be dead. He thought he spotted Yang upstairs, passing by with a hunched back; it could easily have been the smoke tricking his mind. Switching from one side of the house to the other, the shadowed legs gave away Yang's location.

A loud explosion thumped Jack in the chest, pushing him backward. Bracing himself with an arm, he watched a pillar of fire explode through the front door. He tried to draw breath only for the heat to scorch his throat.

ON THE OTHER SIDE

'There's Yang!' cried Inara, stabbing her finger toward the kitchen.

Amongst the boiling smoke, Jack saw his shadow. Yang ran toward the rear right of the kitchen, to where Jack knew stood the pantry door. Realising the small cupboard could hold his mother, he dared hope she cowered inside against the fire. He jumped to his feet as Yang wrenched debris away from the door. The smoke parted, allowing him to watch Yang open the door. Inside laid only blackened bread and smoking vegetables. Sighing with relief, he considered where his mother could have gone.

'She's not in the house,' said Bill as Yang jumped from the kitchen and raced across the lawn. 'Yang would've found her for sure.'

Shaking his head Yang stepped in front of Jack.

'Thanks for looking,' said Jack, feeling both relief and despair vying to overcome him.

'What're you holding Yang?' asked Inara.

Focusing on his shadow Jack noticed Yang held something in cupped hands. Reaching out Yang opened his hands to reveal the charcoal drawing of Jack's father. Strangling back a cry, Jack read the familiar words "To Jack" written at the bottom of the curled paper. He took the paper and studied the only picture he had of his father. Tears fell from his eyes.

'Thank you,' Jack said simply, slipping the picture into his pocket.

'If your mother isn't here, where is she?' asked Bill.

'Where is everyone?' said Inara, regarding the deserted street bordered by burning homes.

'We best check on your grandparents,' Jack said to Bill. 'Your house is the only one not on fire, perhaps everyone is up there with them.'

'Let's hope so,' said Bill.

They all knew, even Inara, who stared at the strange burning village, that no one would hole themselves up in the end house while their own homes burned to the ground. Still, at least they could enter Bill's house, and perhaps inside find a clue as to the location of the townspeople.

They drifted away from Jack's home. They expected the crumbling foundations to fall at any moment. Bringing up the rear Jack touched the picture of his father in his pocket. Staring up at the shattered windows, he half-expected his mother to appear. In his mind, her hair would be aflame as the fire finished off the job it had started ten years ago. He pulled his eyes away from his home; his friends already filed out in the street. The burning tree in Miss Mistletoe's garden put Bill in a trance. Jack wondered if Bill searched the branches for Gesma.

The white picket fence ringing Jack's home laid unscathed, with each stick standing brilliant in the dark, like soldiers on parade. A footprint on the wet ground stopped Jack from reaching for the gate. He hunkered down to his knees. Black had stepped through the print, and Bill's smaller shoe had stepped around the heavy tread. Pressed a few inches into the soil, the print, characterised by a large circle at its centre, paralyzed him.

'Jack, what have you found?' asked Inara, seeing his troubled look.

Jack fingered the ground, not believing what he saw.

'Ying?' said Bill, peering over the gate.

Jack peered up at the mention of his name. 'This track belongs to a Myrm.'

'A Myrm. Are you sure?' said Bill.

'See for yourself.' He pointed down at the print. 'I bet you that round imprint is from a magnet.'

Bill looked long and hard at the footprint. Rainwater had collected in the circular depression, mirroring back his wide-eyed face. 'What is a Myrm's footprint doing in your garden?'

'They knew where you lived,' said Inara. 'Back in the Wold you recognised the Hanging Tree. When we escaped over the hedge they must've come here to get us.'

'But Grandpa said we were safe from the Myrms in the village.'

'When the Myrms took Huckney and his father from their forge they lived outside the village,' said Jack. 'Would they attack the entire village?'

'It would explain the fires,' said Inara.

Yes, it would, thought Jack with growing unease. If the Myrms attacked the village, no one would be able to stop them. Few of the villagers could offer any resistance. Sure, Mr Gasthem would send his bugs, thousands of them, but what chance did ants and moths have against the Myrms wearing their metal armour. Hunters, like Hank Swath, who had the strength of five men, would have some defence against the Wold's brutes. What about his mother, what hope had she when they came for her? Growing plants and flowers was very nice...he broke off his train of thought. The idea of a Myrm carrying off his mother was too much.

Lifting his gaze, he spotted a second print and a third beyond the tapered heads of his fence. He looked around for any sign of his mother's passing. A footprint, a piece of her skirt caught as she fled the house, anything to settle his trepidation. No, trepidation was too mild a word for what he experienced. Cold terror had him, shaking his mind and tossing his emotions around his body like pebbles in a tin can. The shock at finding his house on fire threatened to take hold of him again, only this time he saw it coming and managed to put on the brakes. His cold fingers ran through his hair, casually, not hurried. Knowing if he let his hand speed up, as he wanted it too, he would let in too much emotion and panic would take a hold of him, shake him some more and toss him away. To think, he would have to remain calm. Breathing through his mouth, in long drawn out sighs, helped. Still shaking, his legs became stronger when he stood up straighter. Light cast from the fire that devoured Miss Mistletoe's house revealed another track on the grass bordering her garden, daring him to follow.

ON THE OTHER SIDE

Stepping past Bill; he walked with purpose toward the shining footprint. He kept a sharp eye for any other prints. The smoke pouring onto the street from the burning houses wrapped him in a suffocating hug. His friends, only a step behind, coughed as the fumes caught in their throats. Yang spread himself out in a large dark swathe, looking for a sign of the missing villagers.

'Can Black smell which way my mother went?' asked Jack, still hoping she had escaped before the Myrm had arrived. Fled to the meadow or hid amongst the tombstones of Long Sleep until it was safe for her to move.

'He doesn't know her scent,' answered Bill. 'Besides, all this smoke would mask any trace of her.'

Resolute, Jack strode up to the print the Myrm had left behind; only to flinch as he spied the tracks of a second Myrm meet it. Two furrowed lines in the baked earth trailed the footprints of the second Myrm. They came from Miss Mistletoe's stoop. He knew what he saw; the Myrm had dragged poor Miss Mistletoe behind it. From the straight, unaltered lines, her feet had left in the dirt; he knew Miss Mistletoe was either unconscious, or dead.

The oppressive heat from both sides of the street hurried them along. The tracks took them to the fork in the road and turned right toward the Tristle River. Jack took a step in that direction when Bill, ignoring the footprints, stepped across the road to his house.

Bill's house was soon before them. If you could ignore the rest of the street crumbling away into mounds of ash, you would believe everything was okay. By the full-bloomed roses and violets filling her garden, Grandma Poulis had spent Bill's absence tending to them with an unusual vigour. The grass remained short and the bushes neatly trimmed. White, heart shaped, flowers now bordered the bed of roses where Jack had dug up the Narmacil egg.

'It's dark,' said Bill, peering at the windows.

'Do we enter?' asked Inara.

Jack looked. It did not seem as though anyone was home. 'I think we must,' he said, his mouth tight against his teeth. 'If there's even a chance that someone is hiding in one of the rooms; we have to try.'

'Yes,' Inara said quietly.

'Whoever it is that Black has smelt, has unsettled him,' said Bill, without looking at the wolf.

'The Myrms,' said Jack.

'No, he can smell the others.'

Without further explanation, Bill strode up to the front door to his house. The last time he had touched the polished wood he had only just discovered his Talent. That morning he had felt so energized. He had run down the street, ignoring the other children, eager to see Ying. Excitement had kept the air bottled in his lungs, waiting to explode with his news. Now, as he pushed the door open and saw the familiar green carpet and his grandfather's thick woollen jumper hanging from the brass hook on the wall, he felt his lungs contract again, this time it threatened to suffocate him. This time fear, not excitement, pressed its hand on his chest.

After the smoke filled street, the house felt cool and lightly fragranced with polish and a few houseplants lining the cupboards.

'Hello, Grandma, Grandpa, it's me I'm back.' Bill's voice shot out in a gasping breath.

Deafening silence sank into their bones, making them throb with anticipation, as they predicted an immediate attack from a hidden Myrm. A low rumble in the wolf's chest foreshadowed the lowering of his shaggy head. Trusting Black's instinct, the group halted. Raising his blue eyes, Black looked up the stairs, baring his teeth in an almost human grimace.

'He smells something upstairs,' said Bill.

'I know,' said Jack, watching the black wolf.

'Should we look downstairs first?' asked Inara, her face chalk white beneath the black smears from the smoke on her cheeks and brow.

'No need,' answered Bill. 'Black knows there's nothing to fear down here.'

'And up there,' said Inara. 'What has Black so spooked?'

The mahogany vines, twisting over the banister, brought back the night to Jack when he had followed the Hatchling up to Bill's room. Placing his fingers on the wood, he regarded the dark stairs. He half-expected to see a Narmacil appear on the upper landing, poking its forked tongue at them. Not for the first time he wished he had stayed home that night. Yang took the lead, climbing the stairs in utter silence. Jack came next, with Bill only a step behind, Black, with Inara riding his back, came last. Orange light spilt from the yawning front door, flickered across the wall. This light mingled with furnace red, creating warped shadows and monstrous faces that wore lurid grins and watchful eyes. Those faces swept over the framed paintings, and followed them as they mounted the stairs one-step at a time.

'The third step from the top creaks,' warned Bill.

The sense of dread grew in Jack. A cold sweat dampened his upper lip. He stepped over the creaky step and his eyes moved toward the master bedroom. The door stood ajar, the fires from the street eddied on the wall like snakes. His friends also ignored the other two rooms on the upper landing. They knew, as he did, that it was inside the far bedroom where they would find out what had happened here.

Jack seized the banister, fastening upon the roping vines that seemed to come alive and wrap themselves over his wrist. He looked over at Yang, who gave a thumbs up. His fingers let go; his hand drifted to his side.

The carpet cushioned Jack's feet as he stepped onto the landing and turned toward the end of the hall. Bill crowded his back.

'Do you want to go first?'

ON THE OTHER SIDE

Bill shrank away. 'I'm afraid of what I'll find.'

Jack understood; he had experienced the same feeling in the pit of his stomach when Yang had swung open the pantry door. Stairs creaked; Black had stepped on the suspect step making Jack grasp for the banister that was no longer at his side. His head sank to his chest; he wanted to turn and run, to get as far away from the half open door as he could. He needed to stay; if he fled, Bill would step into his grandparent's bedroom to find… The answer to that question slowed his hand.

The door widened at his touch revealing more of the room. Ten dolls, frozen in place on small black pedestals, looked toward the king-size bed. Jack followed the glass expressionless eyes and let out a choking cry. Beneath the neat blankets lay Grandma Poulis. She was dead.

CRIK

54. REUNION

JACK STOOD PARALYSED in the doorway. Two steps forward and he would reach the bed, another step and he would be able to touch the cold skin of Bill's grandmother. She looked serene; a slight smile curved her mouth, crinkling the skin of her cheeks into a network of fine hash marks. Her silver hair spread out on the pillow picked up the flickering firelight pouring in through the window, turning it a deep auburn. Around her, the bedding remained orderly, with the upper blanket turned at chest height. Grandpa Poulis's blanket was a tangled mess, with the twisted under sheet pulled loose from the sprung mattress. Jack snapped his head away from the bed, he expected, and dreaded, to see the crumpled body of Grandpa Poulis sprawled on the floor. Dolls had fallen from the shelves still clutching an assortment of accessories. Firelight sparked in their glass eyes, giving the appearance of life. Sickened, he viewed them not as clutter, but as though they were the bodies of little girls, rather than plastic melded over wireframe. His chest expanded to let out a sigh of relief at not finding Grandpa Poulis amongst them, when Bill pushed passed him to see his grandmother.

Jack took a step toward the wall, unsure what to do. If he had found his mother dead would he have welcomed a friendly arm over his shoulder, or would he have seen that as an intrusion of a private moment? Debating with himself, he opted to watch Bill, his body poised to rush forward should Bill show any sign of needing him. He had forgotten about Inara on the upstairs landing, until she and Black crowded the doorway. Inara had seen enough dead bodies to recognise another. Only, and he saw this with the clarity of a young boy, she showed no sign of fear, or revulsion. Her dark gaze swam over the body in the bed. She stood as though death to her was as commonplace as puddles after a downpour. His skin puckered up in thick clustering gooseflesh. Later, he would think of her lack of emotion at finding Grandma Poulis; she only softened her gaze when she observed Bill.

Bill stood over his grandmother, his face contorted into a frown. Reaching out he pulled aside a stray hair that curled across her brow. His hand lowered down to her clasped hands.

Bill's voice shook as he said, 'I'm sorry I went away. Finding my Talent was the best thing that has ever happened to me. No one could ever call me a freak

REUNION

again. At last I could show off what I could do, and the ability to control animals is better than most. Wanting to test myself, I begged Ying to come with me to the woods. The last thing I wanted was to hurt you and Grandpa. Grandma, I missed you.' He squeezed her hand. 'If I knew the trouble this would bring I would never have gone looking for a wolf. I should've made ol' Wolf stand on his hind legs, like I did in the kitchen.'

'Are you alright?' Jack asked.

'Not really,' Bill said, wiping at a hanging tear. 'It's because of me that all this happened. You never wanted to go into the woods; afraid your mother would ground you. I insisted that we should go, it is my fault.'

'Grandpa Poulis isn't here,' said Jack. 'When we find out where the Myrms took him, we will rescue him and then we can both tell him sorry. I know he'll understand why you had to leave.'

'I know Grandpa will understand,' said Bill. He pulled back his hands in a rush as though he held a bunch of nettles. 'It's what my grandmother will say that concerns me. You know her Ying; her lectures last for hours. More than anything else, she enjoys seeing me squirm.' He confided in a hushed voice. 'It'll take me weeks to get back into her good books, and I've yet to ask her for one of her precious dolls.' He let his shoulders sag.

'She's dead,' said Inara. 'Can't you see she's not breathing?'

'I know she's not breathing,' said Bill. 'She never does when she goes walking in her sleep.'

'Walking in her sleep?' said Inara.

'Of course,' shouted Jack. He stepped away from the wall, his body felt lighter, no longer fearful of his discovery. 'It's like what it says in the poem.'

'What poem?'

Her quizzical look made Jack want to laugh. 'The poem Mr Dash told me one night:

On blackest night, she roams,
Stepping from her house of bones.
She schemes and hides,
While her house falls and dies.'

'I don't like that poem,' said Bill.

'You know that Bill's grandmother is a Ghost Walker.' Jack told the puzzled girl. 'When her spirit walks from her body, her body appears dead; only she isn't.' Relief made him feel faint.

'Then she's not dead,' said Inara.

'No, just angry,' said Bill. 'A few years ago I rushed in here after having a bad dream. Grandpa woke with a start and tried to console me when he saw I couldn't wake Grandma. I screamed, not understanding why he didn't care that Grandma was dead. That's when she came back into the room. You'd call her a Ghost Walker; she was so beautiful. Her light, unlike Justice and Kyla, is warm and comforting.' Jack, remembering the freezing touch of the Ghost Walkers, shuddered. 'Light wrapped her,' said Bill, 'making her appear young. She sat with me, and with a hand on my shoulder, told me that she was safe. The next morning Grandma was making eggs as normal. Appearing as she always did, she greeted me with an appraising glance. You know that look Ying,' said Bill, 'the one she uses when she suspects you or Yang have been up to no good.' Jack knew that look all right; he had seen it all too often. 'That morning I had to promise not to tell anyone what she could do. Although I never understood why she wanted it kept a secret. Until now,' he said.

'What do you guys want to do now?' asked Inara, after Bill had fallen silent. She had waited, what had felt to her to be a few minutes, but had in fact only lasted a few seconds. Her question, cutting through the quiet, had the considerable effect of stealing back the good mood that had filled the room when Bill explained his grandmother's condition.

'We follow those tracks and find everyone,' said Jack. Peering out the window his eyes sparkled like rubies. 'We brought the Myrms here; we have to send them back.'

Each felt the weight of Jack's words. Neither Bill nor Inara asked how they were to achieve what Jack had so boldly spoken. Gripping Black's hair Inara prepared to turn and exit the room when she noticed Yang spreading himself over the wall. 'What's Yang doing?' she said.

They all turned. Moving colours of reds and yellows still splashed the wall, like a kid's wild creative outpouring on a blank canvass. Yang began to etch out a picture on the wall. From his torso emerged black thread, spreading out over the room. Altering his shape, Yang reminded Jack of clouds blurring into recognisable forms before the wind dispelled the brief illusion. Concentrating on his shadow, he attempted to grasp the message. Dropping a vertical finger, Yang formed an "O", and began swinging it like a pendulum. Horrified, Jack realised his shadow had drawn the Hanging Tree. Stepping back, he took in the entire prophetic etch. The hangman's noose Yang animated continued to swing, just like a ticking arm of a big Grandfather clock.

'If they took them to the tree, they mean to kill everyone,' said Jack through a throat compressed with fear.

He did not wait for the others to respond, the knowledge of his mother's peril was enough to drive him from the room. He had reached the top of the staircase before he realised Inara called his name. 'What,' he replied with impatience. 'It'll take us ten minutes to run to the Hanging Tree.'

'So what,' she said. 'You arrive just to say goodbye to your mother, before Kyla slips a noose over your neck. What good is there in running out there without a plan?'

'We can't just stay here, slinking through the village, hoping for inspiration.'

REUNION

Bill and Inara stood on either side of the open door. Bill had his arms crossed, and Inara, with the same emotionless face she had shown him on so many occasions, waited for him to answer.

'Yang will take care of...' Before he could finish, and his idea had time to take hold in his mind, he saw Inara shake her head. 'Why not,' he said. 'Yang took Raglor, had him beaten so bad that monster wouldn't look sideways at my shadow.'

'Raglor was one,' said Inara. 'How many Myrms are there?'

Her slow voice frustrated him, if she hadn't called him back he'd be down on the road by now, running passed the bed of roses and up toward the stone bridge that crossed the Tristle River. 'Yang could fight them all.' Even his ears didn't believe him.

'Even if Yang could best all the Myrms, the Ghost Walkers' amber glow drives Yang back,' said Bill.

'Then you propose we do nothing,' said Jack. 'Shall we hop back through the hole in the tree and live with Knell? To pretend none of this is happening. Is that what you want to do?'

'Now you are being foolish,' said Inara. 'We have to think about our next step, all the rushing in the world won't help your families.'

'The longer we stay here doing nothing,' said Jack, losing his temper, 'the more chance that a Myrm will hang my mother from the tree. I will gladly die in her place.'

'Your death won't save your mother,' said Inara.

'We can argue about this on the way,' said Bill. 'The cemetery lies on a hill. We can see the Hanging Tree from up there and what we're up against.'

Jack hesitated. Picking his way through Long Sleep's graves and tombs would take time. He kept remembering the swinging circle tipping Yang's finger, and imagining his mother jerking at the end of the rope.

'Jack,' said Inara. 'Your mother may have hid in the cemetery.'

The idea that his mother had escaped the village prior to the Myrms setting upon his home had earlier crossed his mind. Would he find her, frightened, but alive, amongst the gravestones, or inside one of the stone tombs cresting the top of the hill? Improbable, his pessimistic mind snapped at him. Since her accident, she hardly ever left the house. Likelihood was she would be the last to leave at any sign of danger. He recalled the lines dug into the baked ground that led from Miss Mistletoe's house. The Myrms got those who remained in their homes.

'It's worth searching,' said Bill.

'Okay, we'll have a look around,' said Jack. 'If I spot my mother standing by the tree when we're up there, I'm going to help her. I won't wait around to see if you two are with me.'

'If Grandpa is in trouble I'll be right behind you.'

CRIK

The stairs thundered under his feet as Jack sped down to the gaping front door. Hearing the others following him, his mind calculated the distance to the cemetery and then the time it would take him to travel from the cemetery to the Hanging Tree. Far too long - if Kyla had her way, the villagers, and his mother, would be dead already, punished for crimes they had no hand in. The heat from the burning homes stung his face as he exited Bill's house. He glanced down the street; his house smouldered in a ruined pile of brick and blackened beams. Its only material, he told himself, paper comics, leather chairs, wooden cabinets and wilting flowers; only they were not just fuel for the fire, each item consumed was now a priceless memory, something that he would never have again. His toys, melted into shapeless piles of lead, were forever beyond him. That fire consumed memories. Then I will make new memories, he thought, furious with himself for pausing to contemplate what he had lost, his mother needed him and together they will make a new life.

Yang raced ahead, following the road and then veered off to the right behind the houses. Following, Jack hit the beaten track, through the ferns and bramble the kids used instead of the cobbled lane, at a dead run. His shadow flickered amongst the surrounding trees and hedges that blocked off most of the light from the burning village. Scrambling, he passed a tree house he had made the year before, its boards hanging on rusted nails threatened to collapse, and probably would the next time a high wind hit it. In his eagerness to reach Long Sleep and climb its high hill, he ignored his childhood relic.

He breached the thicket like a bird taking its first flight. Arriving at the bank of the Tristle River, with its assortment of leaning crosses, he stopped. Observing the first unaltered scene since his return, filled him with relief, but also anger that the only thing not destroyed were the graves of those who had started this cycle. Those buried under the headstones and sticks had executed Justice, Kyla, and the others for being Ghost Walkers. If they had left them alone the warped spirits of those women would not have hid themselves in the Wold, and they would not have now returned seeking vengeance. Yanking the first cross from its wet moorings, he thrust it from him. The ancient wood clattered to the saturated bank. His harsh intake of breath met the sound. He indicated the crooked crosses. 'Our ancestors committed crimes against the women who had called this place home.'

He turned to see Bill watching him; Inara remained unseen behind, wrestling Black through the narrow path. 'Come on,' he said, knowing he must look insane, panting over a grave and covered in mud. Although the rain fell with less intensity than it had, it was still heavy enough to make footing treacherous and he slipped on the slick mud.

Bill rushed to help pull him back to his feet. 'What are you doing?' cried Bill, his face a melody of conflicting emotion; confusion at seeing Jack desecrating a grave when he should already be halfway up the hill, and fright at the night's

REUNION

horrific turn of events. What would he find once they reached the topmost tombs? Would he look across and see his grandfather hanging from a broken neck? 'They need us to keep calm. We are the only ones who can rescue them.'

'How can we rescue anyone?' said Jack. 'What can we do against Ghost Walkers? We are only children.'

'We're children,' answered Bill, 'with Talents.'

'You just told me my Talent,' he pointed at the faint outline moving along the floor, 'has no chance against the Myrms. You can only control one animal at a time. They already killed Silver; Black won't last long against them.'

'Then we come up with a plan.'

The sound of snapping wood rose above their voices. The boys stopped arguing when the great wolf burst through into the cemetery. Inara, white faced, clung onto Black with tenuous strength. Red marks scored her skin from the bramble. She looked over her shoulder, her mouth turned down into a rigid snarl. From within the overgrown track, large shapes blundered through, beating through the underbrush with unstoppable power.

'They're coming!' she shouted.

Her warning was unnecessary; both the boys recognised the danger and the dusty rank odour of the nearing Myrms. The leaping wolf flitted between the graves with agility beyond that of the following boys. Taken uphill by the loping wolf, Inara waved encouragement.

Jack turned and spotted a metal hawk's face looking up at him. Matted hair dangled from the arms of the Myrm like stalactites. A second and third monster crashed through the bramble. One wore a boar's helm; fastening cold eyes onto him, it let out a blood-curdling cry.

Repeatedly Jack's shoes skidded on the slick grass. He had overtaken Bill by the time they reached the fourth marked grave; Bill's face showed the strain of his effort. The heavy strides of their pursuers haunted their backs. Daring to look behind Jack saw the extra joint in the legs of the Myrms made running difficult. The beasts were more at home in the iron branches of their home.

'Come on Bill,' shouted Jack. 'We can lose them.'

Then Jack fell. Age had eaten away at the headstone, leaving only a humped stone rising a few inches above the level of the grass. His feet smacked into the stone sending him sprawling across the grass and mud. Blazing agony shot through his legs.

'Ying.' Bill stopped to put his hands around Jack.

'Leave me alone,' said Jack, pushing Bill's hands away. 'If you stay with me they will catch both of us.'

'I'm not going on without you.'

Gritting his teeth, Jack, with the help of Bill, pulled himself back to his feet. He saw Black transport Inara over the crest of the hill. She had looked back. Goodbye Inara, he whispered as the three chasing monsters caught up to them.

CRIK

55. CONVERGENCE

A CALLOUSED HAND CAME down hard on Jack's shoulder, hard enough to rattle his teeth and jangle his nerves. He would have let out a gasp, only when his mouth parted the hand gripping his collar yanked him from his feet, and threw him into the air. When he found himself flying backward, he noted, with an odd fascination, at how time appeared to slow down. Marvelling at the fat beads of rain falling around him, he admired their lucent quality. Casting his eye up the hill, he wondered whether his new vantage would allow him to see Inara fleeing from these monsters. He landed, hard. The rain saturating the ground softened the blow enough to knock the breath from his lungs instead of breaking his back. He arched his back anyway, perhaps checking to see if he was still in one piece. Screaming, his body yelled for him to quit it, to lie still, just don't move. Shit, he thought and collapsed. Dirty puddle water lapped his calves, chilling his skin and cramping his muscles. Listening to his body, he suffered the discomfort without moving.

The world had drifted from night black to a dull grey, as though he surveyed the scene through soaped up windows. His assailant, stepping over the crumbling gravestones, appeared as a lumbering shape within this grey world. Tossing his head to the side, he tried to clear it. Blackness seeped into the edge of his vision, spreading welcome dark branches that promised relief from the pain. Allowing his eyelids to close he started to drift. The thrumming sounds of the rain grew distant, muted as though he listened to a storm from inside his house. I no longer have a house, the bitter thought searing his mind with hot fire, its flames coaxed by his mounting anger, made his eyes fly open. 'No,' he cried out, his teeth gritted together in a fierce grimace.

The Myrm stood before him; its bestial form huge and terrifying. Misted breath swirled around its metal boar tusks in tight circles, like the smoke rings Bill's grandfather blew when he smoked his pipe. A tangled mass of reddish fur covered arms that hung idiotically at the beast's sides. Jack wondered whether this creature had pulled his mother from her house, had she screamed for him, desperate to remain in her home, waiting for his return.

Behind the monster, which bore down on him with as much ferocity as a rabid dog, Jack saw Bill. Bill had his arms up to his neck, trying to prise loose the two hands that gripped him in a vice-like hold. Jack snapped. He flung his

CONVERGENCE

hand up, not realising he held a stone until he had thrown it. The egg-sized projectile rang against the helmet of his assailant. Sunken yellow eyes widened in surprise, and he felt a momentary swell of triumphant glee at that look.

'Leave him alone,' he screamed, scooping up another muddy rock and hurling it this time at the creature that held Bill. It struck the beast's shoulder with a hollow thunk and sprang up into the air as straight as a dart.

The beast dropped Bill, who lay gasping for air; his face had gone the colour of faded November sunlight. Forgetting Bill, the Myrm turned toward Jack. It wore the face of an eagle; the rain sluicing down the sharp beak spread out like blood splatter. Jack now wanted to get away; only the creature with the boar helm had taken hold of his shirt, tenting the fabric from his sunken stomach, stopping him cold. After everything he had survived, he feared this was how he was finally going to die, torn apart by these animals. The faint outline of his shadow, stapled to his feet, expanded. If the Myrms noticed Yang, they may remember what had happened to their chieftain and back off; leave him alone to look elsewhere for easier sport. That hope evaporated as the eagle helmed Myrm stepped over Yang without pause.

Its massive shoulders, bunched into two hillocks of bristling fur, rose above its lowered head. Tightening its grip, the boar picked Jack off the floor. Depleted of all strength, he dangled from the hoisting hand. His panting breath mingled with the steam billowing out of the boar mask. The other beast emerged behind the one that held him, and now he could see how sharp that metal beak was, sharp enough to puncture his neck, he thought, letting out a shallow breath.

Bill screamed hoarsely, shouting out Ying. Quickly the hands of another Myrm wrestled him to the ground. Jack wanted to answer that cry with a shout of his own. He felt alone, and if he could somehow communicate with Bill, to let him know he was still here, then he would not be so scared. That was what he believed, until dirty fingernails reached for his face.

No, no, his mind repeated in a frantic, silent plea. Those fingers extended toward his face, they were going to drive themselves into his sockets and pluck out his eyes! The eagle's face, which had appeared passive until then, now seemed to leer at him. Not my eyes, he wanted to shout. Leave me alone, I didn't mean to throw the stone at you; you were just hurting my friend. No words echoed his conscious plea. He could not breathe. You had to release him or he was going to die, his mind shrieked.

The creature behind the boar mask growled, knocking away the hand reaching for Jack with its free hand. The Myrm that had choked Bill let out an answering growl, and reached out again. Forestalling the beast again, the Myrm with the red fur waved a hand over the lapping water of the river. Understanding the importance of that gesture intruded upon Jack. Across the Tristle lay the Hanging Tree. Thwarted from having its fun, the eagle-faced beast seethed with rage. He guessed the Ghost Walkers had given them orders to bring anyone they found to the tree. *They want to see us hang.* Trading one death for another, he thought, yet his overwhelming emotion, as the bird's face pulled back into the wet night, was one of relief. *It would have gouged out my eyes,* an inner voice whispered. A spray of ice struck his spine, and sank in deeper, making his entire body shudder.

The hand holding him let go of his shirt and he toppled forward. He managed to catch himself and stand on legs that felt as sturdy as a rope bridge held together by a slipknot. The brute barged passed him in the direction of the stone bridge that crossed the Tristle River. Panting, Jack almost fell for a third time.

Limping, Bill approached. 'I was sure they would kill one of us, if not both of us.' He rubbed his reddened neck. 'Who knows how far they would have taken things if you hadn't thrown that stone.'

'They do what Kyla and Justice tell them.'

'I struggle to keep control of Black during a hunt. The scent of blood drives him wild.' Bill's eyes moved to the beasts crowding the foot of the cemetery. 'They wanted to kill us. Still do, I suppose.'

'The Ghost Walkers scare them.' Jack remembered how the Myrms had scattered to the trees when Justice and the others appeared after their capture. 'Nothing demands obedience more than fear.'

'I guess you're right. If one of these things suddenly spoke and told me to jump down a well I'd be hip deep in water before I had time to think.'

The eagle faced Myrm stepped closer, making the pair take a few hurried steps toward the rain fattened river. Ten yards ahead, they saw the shape of the lead Myrm, walking along the crumbling shoreline. It did not look back to see if anyone followed it.

'I think we best keep up with him,' said Jack, pointing ahead. 'I don't want to be alone with bird brain.'

'You got that right.' Bill cast a fearful glance behind; his feet picking up the pace before his head had turned back.

Now that they were moving, Jack felt the invisible bands binding his chest ease. The light had all but gone; he could no longer see Yang, though he knew his shadow was with him. Sandwiched between the leading Myrms, they marched ahead of the raucous knot. They stayed beside the river; a piece of land both he and Bill knew expertly. Even blindfolded he would be able to walk without stumbling. His feet automatically rose, missing hazardous rocks and roots breaking through the muddy banks. Coming to a smooth verge, where both he and Bill had sat on hot days fishing, or skipping stones, filled him with sadness. Looking to his right he saw a well-known headstone; seasons had robbed the stone of its name, but the epitaph read, "She died too young, for some, she lived too long for others."

CONVERGENCE

'I didn't imagine my homecoming would be more dangerous than my going,' said Bill. 'I hope everyone is alive. I don't know what I'd do if I saw Grandpa hanging from the tree.'

'I think Justice and Kyla will find their match in your grandmother.'

'I don't know. Scaring us kids is one thing,' Bill hiked back his finger, 'these monsters won't care what she says.'

Bill's fear jolted his own, making his breath wheeze in fits and starts. 'Where's Black?' he asked, between hitching breaths.

'They aren't in any immediate danger. Black carried Inara to the top of the hill; they are hiding amongst the tombs. The wind is coming from the direction of the Hanging Tree, so Black will smell any approaching Myrm.'

'Good.' Jack failed to mention his fear; if the Ghost Walkers killed Bill, no one would control the wolf, and Black, in a frenzy of gnashing teeth, would turn on Inara, devouring her. 'Let's hope they remain safe,' he said, his heart sank, as though submerged in the water that rushed beside them.

'You know how hard it is to find anyone up there; every tomb or stone offers a hiding place. Never mind them, the Myrms already have us.'

'They are taking us where we want to go,' said Jack.

Despite his assurance to Bill, his fear crystallised at the thought of seeing someone he loved hanging limp from a branch. Although he tried to detach his fear, it tormented him, a dreadful pulsing tattoo that refused to leave him alone. His stride widened, taking him, and Bill, closer to the Myrm captain. Cutting through the murky night loomed the ashen profile of the Tristle Bridge. Growing impatience swept through him like a broom sweeping a dust-filled room, throwing up more emotion than he could handle. The need to spring forward overcame him, to reach the Hanging Tree in seconds, not the long ticking minutes forced upon them by the slow-paced Myrms. Damn them and their stupid jointed legs, he thought bitterly. He wanted to scream, 'come on, move it, run!' He did not, knowing with certainty that the brute would wheel on him; only this time perhaps the Ghost Walker's words would not be enough to save him.

'Slow down, any faster and you'll be leading this party,' said Bill, gasping to keep up with Jack. He looked ahead and the frightening boar masked turned in annoyance. 'There's the bridge, it's not much farther to go.'

Jack wanted to say, 'what if they are at this moment slipping the noose over my mother's neck?' He had told Bill not to think of the worst; he should follow his own advice. He forced himself to slow down, to relax his breathing.

They crossed the bridge. The Myrms still wore magnets on their feet, and these clipped the stone like hooves. Their trip trapping set Jack's teeth on edge, so by the time they left the bridge he stepped out onto the grassy shore with relish.

CRIK

A steep bank stretched ahead, hiding the Hanging Tree; if the Myrms had followed the old Harmon Road, they would have seen the tree. Streams of colour suffused the crown of the hill, amber, blue, and red shot the sky. The colour promised both warmth and coldness; the sound of raised voices mingled with this riotous blend of colour. Jack shot forward, passing the surprised Myrm, in his eagerness to see the owners of those voices.

What he saw brought him to a sudden stop.

The colour brought Yang back into focus, and he shared the boy's horror. They only viewed the topmost branches of the large tree, and from these hung five bodies. Three men, and two women, still wearing their nightclothes. Rope acted as the awful punctuation to their ghastly expressions of pain. Their death throes had turned their faces a terrible black, making identification difficult; unfortunately, Jack recognised Miss Mistletoe. She hung from the highest branch that could support a person's weight. The light spotlighted her white clothes, with stark shadows fanning the birdlike bones standing out from her clenched fists.

Jack wanted to fall to his knees and cover his face. Fearing the executions of those people he knew, had not prepared him for its awful fact. Shame at not being able to identify all the bodies crippled him. They had died because he had entered the Wold; the least he could do was mourn them. Feeling sick, he welcomed the distraction of the bile burning his throat. Stumbling forward, the tree grew in his eyes, revealing more branches bowing under the weight of hung bodies. These too wore the clothes they had gone to bed wearing before the fires and the Myrms had roused them in frightful alarm. He recognised people amongst the grisly exhibit. Karl Guild had torn at his shirt, leaving bloody streaks on his chest. Aghast, he looked in terror for Tommen Guild, but saw no children amongst the dead. Alongside Karl, hung the hunter brothers, Mark and John Alefeet. Mark's Talent brought drawings to life, while John summoned any bird in the wood, just by whistling.

Lower, beneath the roots of the aged tree that rested on two stone horns of land, stood two groups. Immediately Jack regarded the two clusters as them and us. The "them" group, comprised of ten Myrms. At their centre issued roping strands of colour from three Ghost Walkers. Ignoring the Myrms, awash in amber, he instead focused on the three tall figures. Justice serenely stood before her sisters. Amber light wrapped her frame. She appeared to be talking. Kyla stood there too, her green eyes staring from a skull she no longer hid. Aged bone no longer had the power to overwhelm him. It still unnerved him, made his stomach flop like a caught fish on the deck of a boat, but he no longer wanted to reel back and hide. A third Ghost Walker drifted through the pack of Myrms, letting her diaphanous hands caress the beasts' armour in twisted affection.

CONVERGENCE

Bill ran up, his wide horrified eyes travelling over the executed villagers. He kept mumbling incoherently while touching his bruised neck. Jack gripped him, pulling him close.

'Look,' Jack said, pointing to the group facing the Ghost Walkers. 'Bill,' he shouted when Bill refused to lower his eyes from the tree. 'There they are.'

Bill's gaze fell at slow increments down the huge tree, his iris darkened eyes counting each of the bodies hanging from a rope. Jack realised his friend's mumbles were the names of those hung. He shook him, knowing the approaching Myrms were almost on top of them. 'Damnit, there's your grandpa.'

Bill's face broke into a smile.

Grandpa Poulis stood at the front of the large group of villagers, leaning on his wolf-headed cane. Wolf was at heel, barking at the Myrms. Striking a resolute figure, Mr Gasthem stood with Grandpa Poulis. Jack noted the swarm of flies and moths circling the Village Elder's head with an aching familiarity. Most of the adults stayed with the children. Liza Manfry touched a piece of her torn nightgown to a bleeding gash across Dwayne's temple. Via and Cassie stayed close beside Liza, crying in each other's arms.

Jack saw all this with absent interest. There were two points of particular importance that drew his eyes. The first stood before the group. Wreathed in blue fire, her hair caught in an updraft of hot air, stood Grandma Poulis, just as he had once seen her when he had entered her house. Her beauty struck him anew, and in that moment, he loved her. She possessed so much life; he wondered how he could have ever feared her. Unlike the other Ghost Walkers, her light emitted warmth that drove away the chill of the night. Villagers crowded within her light, and cringed from Justice's amber glow with fearful urgency. Compelling his attention away from Grandma Poulis was the lone figure of Dr Threshum stepping amongst two rows of bodies. Holding a black bag in one hand, in the other he held aloft a roll of bandages as though it were a talisman. Men and women groaned at his feet, most had blood on some body part or held their heads in great pain. All called out for the doctor's attention. A few lay still. His mother was one of those who lay without moving.

CRIK

56. THEM AND US

IF JACK SAW THE SNARLING FACE of the boar bearing down on him, he could have prepared himself for the imprisoning fingers. Instead, the hand locking around his bicep tore a scream from his already sore throat. So high and shrill was his scream that the Myrm flinched, and those down at the bottom of the descent turned in shocked dismay. Jack could not stop the horror erupting from his throat. The sight of his mother; dead, even the possibility of her death was more than he could bear; sent waves of despair through him. His voice rose higher, as though a great bellows blew into a toy whistle. Letting go of his arm the Myrm shrank back, startled by his grief stricken outcry. Bill too took a stumbling backward step, his own relief at finding both his grandparents alive, dissolved, allowing the horror to come crashing back.

Each intimately known face watched Jack from down the slope. How he had longed to see them. Tommen Guild sat close to Jack's mother, his eyes huge with the same terror that stamped every face. Jack knew the fears that trampled through their minds. When he had gone to the Wold, it had felt like a dream world, disconnected from his reality. Seeing the Myrms there, where creatures lived in a hedge as tall as a mountain and metal swans swam across muddy lakes, though shocking, was not the terrifying encounter they had now become. Lost in that world had kept him from his mother; in turn that meant his mother was safe from the creatures he encountered. Only there she now laid, just another body amongst rows of bodies. Her plants, his inner voice cried out, won't grow without her! The prospect of having a seed, without his mother's ability to grow in seconds, what nature would take weeks, months, even longer to accomplish, smacked him as an awful damnation of his world's order. Without her, he had nothing.

Exhaustion, not acceptance of the scene, stopped Jack's scream; like a leaking tap, a few last strangled cries escaped his sore throat in a stuttering falsetto. Yang had his arms around him. Wrapped in despair, Jack had missed the shadow, now, his emotions still raw, but for the moment spent, he collapsed gratefully into Yang's arms, sobbing into his shoulder. Remaining solid, Yang allowed Jack to hold him and for him to hold the boy.

'Ying,' said Bill, moving up on urgent feet. 'Your scream spooked the Myrms.' He looked fearfully back a few feet to where the Myrms stood in a ring.

THEM AND US

'They won't stay back for long. If they grab us now they will take us to the Ghost Walkers. I prefer to stand behind my grandma. Eagle face is looking as though he's about to charge us. We can escape them, if we run now, and be amongst our friends.' He almost said family; he slung that word to the back of his throat, to speak it now would be blasphemous. Jack's grief was too raw. 'What do you say, are you ready to run?'

'I don't think I can,' said Jack. He felt so tired. Every limb carried extra weight.

'I won't do this without you. I need you to try.'

Bill had always been there for him. When he had built a den on the wooded outskirts, only Bill and Yang knew of it. Unlike everyone else, who kept a wary distance from his troublesome shadow, Bill always wanted to play; he accepted Yang more than had any other kid in the village. After discovering his Talent Bill's first impulse was to go to him, and since that day, they had grown closer. He had never had a brother, but in Bill, he knew that love.

'Take my hand.' Jack's hand passed through Yang, the shadow becoming incorporeal to allow the connection to take place. 'If I falter, or stumble, carry on, don't dare stop until you're standing with your grandpa.'

'Not on your life. You would never leave me behind, and I won't let them get you either.'

It felt as though wood splinters, not legs, supported Jack as he struggled to match Bill's pace. With help from the downward gradient, he managed to hold onto his friend's hand; he feared that if they had to run across more treacherous, or strenuous, ground, he would trip. Yang ran with him, the shadow finding the going far easier. Howling for their blood the Myrms took up the chase. For the moment, Jack did not fear them, with his head start, together with the creatures' awkward stance; he knew the beasts had little chance of recapturing them. Ahead, once the rolling slope flattened out, it stretched toward the ribbon of road and the Hanging Tree, where the two companies, frozen in their observation of the chase, stood. Bill headed east toward the line of blackberry hedges, and then cut back in a long arc. Immediately Jack saw how Bill had cleverly placed Grandma Poulis and the people of Crik between them and Justice.

Drawing them on were the recognisable voices of the villagers. Loudest of all was Grandpa Poulis, who in his excitement had turned into his accustomed youthful guise. He waved for them to hurry, his arms flapping over his head as though they were flags caught in a gale. Every one of the faces, save Grandma Poulis, who never let her gaze stray from the other group, beckoned them with surprised cries and broad, however tired, smiles. Wolf joined in the excitement, howling like his namesake.

The hand enclosing Jack's own grew tighter, pulling him along with irresistible force. He wondered why the Myrms gathered about the Ghost

CRIK

Walkers had not intercepted them. Although it would take little effort, they remained beside the three Ghost Walkers, at heel like a master's hounds. Not daring to meet Justice's dark gaze, he kept his focus on the back of Grandma Poulis. His love for her overrode all other thought, even his emotions for his mother began to dwindle as he reached the warm blue haze. The power of his emotion unsettled him. At the first touch of the blue light any attempt to focus on anything other than Grandma Poulis faltered, and died. Her allure only grew the closer he got to the group. A shameful undercurrent ran through him when he realised his mother's death had diminished to no more than a spluttering candle next to Grandma Poulis's blazing light. Chancing a look behind he saw, without surprise, that the group of Myrms had broken off their pursuit. The brutes had veered toward the road to join the rest of their vicious company.

'Grandpa!' Bill, having let go of Jack's hand, rushed his grandfather, sweeping him up in a titanic hug. He spun him around as their old dog wagged his tail.

Grandpa Poulis laughed, smacking his grandson's back. 'I thought wolves had eaten you two.' He gave Jack a warm smile over Bill's shoulder.

'We escaped,' said Jack as other hands clapped him on the back or ruffled his hair. His eyes still lingered on Grandma Poulis. She was so beautiful; it was hard to correlate her with the old woman with the razor sharp tongue.

'It is great to see you two,' said Mr Gasthem. Even the moths circling his head flew faster, caught up in the moment. 'I only wish you had returned at a better time. This night it is safer in the woods.'

'Put me down lad,' Bill's grandfather told Bill. Back on his feet, the old man grew back to full size. 'The Village Elder speaks the truth. It seems my stories have come back to haunt me. These beasts are...'

'Myrms,' interrupted Bill, 'from the Wold.'

'We've seen them before,' said Jack, disengaging from Beth Hulme's suffocating hug. 'They are here because of us.'

'You want to explain yourself, boy,' said Mr Dash. A blood soaked bandage bound his arm and he walked with a limp. His serious face looked graver than ever as he marched away from the injured. 'What do you mean, this is your fault? What have you two done?'

A cold whispering laugh fell over the group, making the children shiver and hold onto one another. Mouths opened to form hollow circles. Their faces at once turned toward Grandma Poulis for protection.

Beyond Grandma Poulis, Justice had drifted closer, two Myrms trotted beside her; they both wore stag masks with barbed antlers. They stopped shy of the blue swathe of colour. Where Justice's amber light touched this blue haze the air sizzled with energy.

THEM AND US

'I see your spies have returned,' said Justice. 'I had expected to find them when we emptied the village.' Her appraisal of both Jack and Bill was cursory, she, like everyone else, waited for Grandma Poulis to speak.

Jack recognised the old woman's authority, and knew their survival depended on her resolve. When she spoke, the familiar voice that had berated him on numerous occasions had mellowed. 'My grandson and Jack are part of this community; as were you at one time.'

'I ceased to be part of this community when they killed me,' said Justice.

'A sin no one here was part of. If you will share your full name I am sure you will find your descendants still live here.'

'It was my family that gave me up to the others.' Justice's eyes grew distant as she lifted them to the overhead branches. 'I watched as my husband gave me over to the hangman's noose.'

'So you in turn want to see others hang,' said Grandma Poulis, a touch of her old self, roughening her softened tones. She also looked up, seeing the bodies swaying in the cold night winds.

'As they would hang you, sister,' said Kyla. Two Myrms accompanied her as she floated closer. 'Everyone now knows what you are. If we left you, your dear husband will do the same as what Justice's husband had done to her. In their mourning, they will say they released you from an evil spirit. Believing, as did those before them, how the woods crept into your house one night and took you away from them. You are a stranger to them. Each person here will mistrust you from this day until your last.'

'My husband has known since before our wedding day, what I am. He did not care then, and he does not care now. Only you hold onto the past - sister.'

The filaments of amber light stirred around Justice, obscuring her ivory skin. 'Then your husband is an exception,' she said. 'If you have no reason to fear, why then do you lock yourself up in your house each night? Your light is a gift, given to you to share with the woods.'

Grandma Poulis's following hesitation gave the two approaching Ghost Walkers strength; they bore down on her, surrounding her warm light with their cold touch. Jack, feeling the chill, wrapped his arms across his chest. Others around him did the same, and even Mr Dash looked perturbed at the drop in temperature.

'They love you now, but what will happen when the morning sun extinguishes your warm light? Will they still love you? Or will the harsh light of day bring mistrust?' said Justice, solemnly. 'Some will think you bewitched them, not trusting their adoration for you was real. Others, bereft of your love, will feel abandoned in the daytime when you are once again only an old woman.'

When important matters arose in the village, Mr Gasthem, being the Village Elder, spoke, or in his absence Grandpa Poulis, or Dr Threshum, all three remained silent. Their unusual deferment to Grandma Poulis disquieted Jack.

CRIK

Looking around he saw Mr Gasthem captivated by Grandma Poulis; his eyes had a strange vacancy. Others shared this look, the children in particular watched the old woman with reverence; even Liza, he noted, and she always looked down her nose on the Poulis family. Only Bill and his grandfather were exempt, they watched with love, not with enrapture. Grandma Poulis had earned their love, what they feel is real, not forced upon them. Mr Dash watched him; his piercing eyes sparkled beneath a stormy brow. Jack recalled what the grave keeper had told the Giant when he had seen them in the tomb, "I liked Mr Hasseltope, he always kept me busy." He had said this whilst holding the hangman's noose. Would the grave keeper turn on Grandma Poulis? The thought was unsettling, even more so because he wondered how he would react if they lived beyond this night. He tried not to dwell on his misgivings; after all, he had known Bill's grandmother all his life. Or had he; how much did he actually know about her? She had kept such a large part of herself hidden. Perhaps keeping her secret was justifiable in light of what had happened in the past. Although to keep her secret for so many years in the village, spoke volumes about her duplicity. What power did she have? Could he ever again fully trust her?

When Grandma Poulis spoke, her voice was heavier, carrying tension with each uttered syllable. 'Everyone here knows me. Each cares for me in their own way. You murdered the only person who could claim to be older than me.' Her eyes lifted to Miss Mistletoe. 'When you have been part of a village, as long as I have, you earn people's trust.'

'Trust and duty are poor substitute for love,' said Justice. She stood so close her amber light bled into the blue, creating currents of purples and browns. Although the air still crackled with energy, it no longer sparked, as though the two colliding colours were no longer at odds with one another.

'Come back with us,' said Kyla, seeing a chance to capitalise on their advantage. 'We will take you away from those who wish you harm.' A spreading patchwork of skin covered her skull like lichen growing over smooth stone. 'Leave this world behind.'

'I don't wish to leave it,' answered Grandma Poulis. 'If they decide to harm me, it is their sin, not mine.'

'It is you who will pay the price,' said Justice. 'Don't trust them.' She stood nearer now, her influence taking hold as the cold seeped into the protection Grandma Poulis provided the group.

'Esmelda.' Grandpa Poulis let go of Bill's hand and stepped forward. His assured walk was at odds with the strain on his weather beaten face. When he stood facing his wife, he said, 'Although you and I were both young when the hangings took place, we both remember those nights. Witnessing the line of fire snaking through the village gave you nightmares for years. You thought if I knew about your secret I would give you over to the Elders, that I would allow them to hang you. Well,' he smiled, 'I've known for many years, and not once during our time together have I ever thought you had an affliction that needed a cure.' As he spoke the blue colour surrounding him and his wife became stronger, pushing back the other colours. Once more, the air began to spark with energy.

'I know many stories,' said Grandpa Poulis. 'I bore people with them all the time. I scare Bill with tales of Bone Doctors, creatures of the wood, ghosts, and bandits. I have even told him a story about a group of bandits that were ghosts. I do so, not just to make him wary of running off without a care into the woods, not that it did any good, but because they are good stories. There are stories about Ghost Walkers too,' he said. 'Bill hasn't heard them from me.' He looked back, and for an instant, his eye lingered on Mr Dash. 'Not because they don't make a good yarn when around a campfire on some cold night, they do. Those tales come from misunderstanding and distrust. It's right to warn the youngsters about Bone Doctors, if one found you they would take you and do everything an old man like me tells you they would do; I have no doubt they would do more besides. My telling serves two good purposes, entertainment and a warning.

'My uncle first told me about the Ladies of Light when I was younger than Bill. He refused to name them Ghost Walkers. I got that name from the planks of wood marking their graves.' His remark brought a sour twist to his mouth. 'He believed the trees spoke. They did not whisper or connive, as some would have us believe. According to my uncle, who knew Crik Wood better than any tracker who has ever lived in this village, the trees cared for us. Saw us as their children. Most here know we receive our Talents on the night of the Pairing. It is the Narmacil, another woodland creature, who gives us our Talent. When old enough to understand every person finds this out.' Many of the adults muttered agreement, and not a few of the children looked confused. 'The Ladies of Light don't come by their Talents in this way,' Grandpa Poulis continued. 'My Uncle believed, as do I, that the trees, wanting to connect us with the world, bequeathed you with the purpose of protector. Your light brings hope and love. You would soothe the wild things that hunt the night woods around our homes. When people find their loved ones in bed, appearing to be dead, they presume an evil spirit had stolen their wife or mother's soul. Only,' Grandpa Poulis paused, first looking toward the people of his village and then to Justice and her sisters, 'I know it is your soul I now see. It is why,' he said, taking Grandma Poulis's hand, 'everyone here loves you. Every person sees who you are. Lack of this understanding has bred mistrust in the past. If we could see them, we would know others possess souls as bright and as beautiful as your own.'

He pointed at Kyla. 'These, through the actions of scared people, have turned into what those people had feared. Their souls are dead and cold, turning

CRIK

their light into a shroud. They have proven this by killing our friends and neighbours.

'Esmelda, please do not go with them. The boy is back and we can rebuild the village that these Ghost Walkers,' his deliberate use of the cursed name, sent a ripple of black through Justice's figure, 'can go back to wherever they call home. You belong here with Bill, all your friends, and me. I need you my love.'

'You foolish old man, I am not going anywhere.'

Jack's heart leapt in his chest. He watched Bill's grandparents hold each other. While Grandpa Poulis spoke, the light around them had grown steadily brighter, driving back the Ghost Walkers. The huddled Myrms lowered their masks; each one a parody of the life they had destroyed in the Wold.

'They will betray you,' said Justice.

'No.' Grandma Poulis stepped away from her husband to face the group from the Red Wood. Her eyes blazed with anger. 'You killed my friends. You would kill my family if I were to allow it. I am no sister of yours. Leave these woods; hide behind your wall of thorns and don't ever trouble us again.'

'We came to rescue you from your imprisonment,' said Kyla. 'When the boy told us there was another like us in the village we had to come.'

'You came to avenge the wrongs made against you,' said Grandma Poulis. 'Although what happened to you is beyond forgiveness, you cannot blame any here for those crimes. Those who carried your bodies to this tree are long gone. If you seek them they are at rest in the ground.' She pointed toward Long Sleep. 'By coming here you threaten the future. The children behind me, including my grandson, knew nothing of what had transpired here. This night will start new nightmares. Go now, so that we can rebuild our village and bury our dead.' Her commanding voice drove into the three Ghost Walkers with a power that reverberated in Jack's chest.

Justice grinned, her lips scythed open across bone white skin, peeling back to reveal only darkness. Madness had taken her as Grandma Poulis spoke, and all her pretence slipped away. She no longer attempted to cajole the old woman into following her back to the Wold. Turning to the Myrms, her hair, now white, flew up, surrounding her with a terrible halo. The Myrms shrank away as their mistress strode into their midst.

'If you came back with me, I would have left your people alone.' Justice's teeth bit each word with a snap of her jaws. 'The Red Sisters told me to do this, and I would have obeyed. We wanted to share our world, with all its wonders with you.' She turned her deadly gaze back on the villagers; her skin had retreated, leaving behind only a screaming skull. Kyla and the third Ghost Walker had also shed their skin. The three horrors came together. Justice kept her eyes, whereas her sisters stared from hollow dark sockets. 'Since you are not returning with us, you leave me with no choice. You already sent spies into our lands to scout out any weakness. We always knew you would come looking to finish what you started. The Red Sisters were right to send me to stop that from happening.'

'None here has any interest in the Red Wood,' said Grandpa Poulis. 'We know where it is, and we have always shunned it. Our hunters and explorers know to stay well clear of that accursed place.'

'Not everyone.' The Ghost Walker fixed her eyes on Jack, sending a cold shiver through him. 'We placed blue stones to stop any trespass. They were not enough to dissuade you. No,' she said, 'the only way for us to remain safe is to kill you all.'

'You will find that harder than you think,' said Mr Gasthem. A haze of flies heralded the Village Elder as he picked his way to the front of the group. 'Your Myrms caught us by surprise when they attacked us in our beds. Now we are together, and some of us have surprising Talents.'

Graham Belson transformed his top half into a bear, while his brother changed his legs into the giant paws of the same fearsome beast. Under his feet hundreds of beetles pushed up through the ground. No, Jack thought, there were thousands of the multi-legged crawlers, oozing out of every crack. Even with an abacus, or ten others each with their own counting device, he would never be able to count all of Mr Gasthem's little charges. Yang changed his form into the same formidable cat he had used back in the Wold, snarling back his lips to show rows of wicked fangs.

'It will not be enough,' said Justice. 'My Myrms outnumber you.'

Then the bodies hanging from the trees began to twitch and fight against the ropes holding their necks. From Long Sleep Cemetery, shuffled into sight freshly raised bodies; the earth from their graves fell from them in clumps. At their head, sat upon a huge wolf, was a girl.

57. THEM OR US: PART ONE

COLD WHITE FINGERS CLUTCHED at the rope's coarse fibres like climbing ivy. They scrabbled higher, cutting themselves on the rough spun as they sought the knot. Sounds of fighting drifted from below, a scream, a roar, and a whistle that pierced the night with a frightening blast. The fingers did not slow at the sounds; they had found the knot and busied themselves with untying it.

Deafening roars from the gathered Wold army made Beth Hulme scream out in fright and snatch her sister's arm. Every beast wore a mask of a slain animal, eagles, trout, bulls, and a woodpecker with a dangerous sharp beak. Their continued parody of those creatures they had eliminated from the Red Wood turned Jack's stomach. To the front of the snarling horde stood five Myrms, their hair, a reddish thatch, covered exceptionally large shoulders; the other Myrms watched these five intently.

'Raglor would be amongst those five if Silver hadn't ripped out his throat.'

Jack found Bill speaking at his shoulder. 'It doesn't matter; if they attack amass they'll finish us off before Inara can reach us.' Like a fortune-teller's death card, his statement left behind an air of despondency.

'I wish they'd hurry up. They sure do move slowly,' said Bill, looking at the hill where the zombies moved as though they were hip deep in his grandmother's thickest winter stew. 'The fighting will be over before they arrive.'

'If Justice gets her way it will.'

Grandma Poulis turned her serene face to them. For the first time since Bill had returned, she smiled down at her grandson. 'You have much to explain,' she said, sounding more than ever like her old self.

'Great,' said Bill, 'even if I live through this I'm dead meat tomorrow when she gets hold of me.'

Grandma Poulis, either not hearing Bill, or ignoring his comment, looked toward the scared faces. She began to speak, intimately and urgently, aware of the coalescing threat behind her. 'Mr Gasthem is right, we can fight them.' She assured the people of Crik Village. 'You possess formidable Talents. I call on you now to use what you have to defend those that you love.'

THEM OR US: PART ONE

'Some do,' said Liza Manfry, her flaxen hair fanned across her pallid cheeks. 'Only,' she paused, taking the time to look around, 'not everyone has a Talent that can fight those creatures.' Love for Grandma Poulis glazed her eyes; it was apparent how much courage it took for her to speak to Grandma Poulis, let alone question her.

'I know you; I have seen you play in the village.' Grandma Poulis favoured the scared girl with a smile. 'You aren't one of my grandson's friends, so I don't know you very well. What is your Talent?'

'I hide, the air becomes misty, and when I am within it no one can find me.'

'Then hide child, and if you can spread your mist, keep others safe with you. Move to where Dr Threshum is taking care of the injured. You will find shelter beneath the arm of rock where the tree has anchored its roots.' She pointed to the side of the path where a horn of rock formed a dark earthen alcove. Its twin, that helped support the Hanging Tree, loomed impassively over a cluster of Myrms. 'Those who can confront these beasts will draw around you, to form a protective ring. Go, now,' she shouted, knowing the horde at her back were about to charge.

The command broke the spell that had held the group; they ran toward Dr Threshum. First went the children, screaming with outstretched arms, following them ran the adults, who had no offensive or defensive skills, the ones that preferred to stay close to home rather than go hunting in the woods. Last of all strode the hunters and trackers, backing to form a line before the children and the wounded. Jack went with this last group, confident that Yang would protect him.

Noticing Bill a step behind, he snatched the other's shirt. 'Go with the children; Black can't help you here.' He searched the hill and saw Inara at the head of her army; that was still perilously far away. Come on Inara.

'I'm not leaving you,' Bill cried, shaking off Jack's grip.

Jack could see the resolution on his friend's face; he had witnessed it too many times to try to argue. The hard faced hunters only spared him a quick glance before seeing the black shadow cat prowling a few paces ahead, and let him stay. Everyone in the village knew his Talent, Yang had pulled a prank on everyone at one point or another. Jeff Swizleback stood beside the boys, his large form dwarfing them. Jack was trying to remember the old tracker's Talent when the Myrms rushed forward.

'Boys, get behind the line.'

Hurling themselves across the ground the creatures roared, drowning out the recognisable voice of Grandpa Poulis. Blue light from Grandma Poulis bathed the metal masks, and to Jack, the created shadows brought the masquerade to life. Bears snarled, boars ground enormous tusks, owls twitted, and eagles screeched - a whole jungle to fight. In the face of this onslaught, his bowels turned to water. What was he doing standing out here? Doubt riddled him; he

CRIK

should be behind the men, with his mother. Thoughts of his mother cramped his stomach. The Myrms had already gotten to her, doubtless whilst he spoke with Knell. Raw feelings he had, before love for Grandma Poulis took them away, like a magpie snatching a brass ring, resurfaced. He felt adrift, alone. That was how things were now; knowing he was an orphan, without a home or any security, made him look at his feet, where a cluster of beetles, ants, and roaches, scrabbled over his laces; he bit back the need to cry and lifted his chin. They went into our home and killed her. Snatching the up-swell of dark emotion, he used it to stop from turning and fleeing, as he suspected he should do. With his anger rekindled, he cried out in defiance, only for a furious buzzing sound to swallow his shout. Looking up he saw thousands of flies, hornets, and mosquitoes, flying overhead in a dark cloud. Mr Gasthem had sent the insects ahead, a flying squadron to intersect the Myrm's frontline. Grinning, he watched as the swarm collided with the beasts from the Red Wood. Best of all the hornets attacked them with their stingers, making them cry out in dismay.

'They're hurting them,' said Bill in triumph.

The winged menace slowed the progress of the Myrms. The hairy brutes swatted at the air, at their arms and legs. A few of the hunters laughed and jeered, knowing how painful a hornet's sting was.

'It's a shame there aren't any giant hornets for Mr Gasthem to command,' said Jeff Swizleback. 'Then we'd have something to cheer about.' He paused, a contemplative expression swept over his darkened features. 'Do you boys know that girl on the wolf? Do we have to worry about her?' The tracker hiked a thumb to where Inara led the reanimated bodies down the embankment.

For the first time Jack noticed how the hunters watched the zombie army with as much alarm as they showed toward the army from the Wold. A few of the men even ignored the Myrms, choosing to protect the flank facing Inara's approach. He should have foreseen that the dead villagers would scare the men; why hadn't he thought of their reaction to Inara's gift until now. During their time together Inara's Talent had become almost commonplace; something he accepted, despite its discomforting nature. Yet, remembering Krimble's reanimation still made him shudder in abhorrence.

'That's Inara,' Bill answered Jeff Swizleback, oblivious to the fear her appearance had caused. 'She's our friend. She can raise the dead.'

'I can see that lad. With her fighting with us, we will outnumber these beasts. We have to hold on until she arrives. She better hurry, things are about to get ugly.' Snapping his fingers, the tracker gained the attention of the men. Quickly his digits flowed into a series of crooked gestures with such rapidity that Jack could not follow. Those watching the moving fingers began copying the complicated movement with well-practiced dexterity. It's a code, Jack realised. Like butterflies, the dancing fingers leapt from one hand to the other. Without a

THEM OR US: PART ONE

word, those facing Inara swung around to face the threat posed by the Myrms. They all ignored the walking dead as though they were not even there.

In that instant, Jack spotted two of the red furred Myrms take note of the reformation. They bent close, grating out their speech from between blunt teeth. When they parted, they called out, gesturing toward Inara. A third of the fighting force facing the villagers separated from the main horde and raced toward the reanimated dead. They howled as they cut into Inara's force, stabbing with swords and bludgeoning the corpses with metal clubs.

Jack only saw the initial collision, and prayed Inara would be all right. The beasts beset by Mr Gasthem's insects became his focus. Crawling insects created a living tapestry of flailing arms, falling bodies, and stamping feet. Shimmering wings glinted in the Ghost Walkers' glow like thousands of gold coins.

A few of the more ferocious Myrms crashed through to the front, knocking over their besieged companions. A haze of mosquitoes clung to their fur, halting a few, and turning others aside. Despite this small victory, the insects only managed to slow down the attack, not stop it.

'Here's where we find out if your shadow is as fierce as he looks,' said the old tracker.

'He knows what to do, he hasn't let me down yet,' said Jack, happy to feel a swell of pride. A day before he would have only felt dread or disgust for his shadow. Despite his renewed faith in Yang, the sight of the charging Myrms formed a hard knot of tension in his chest. Beside him, Bill now looked as white as cotton. *Yang has to protect us both*; the thought doubled his fear.

A badger faced Myrm came straight for them. From the mask's mouth lolled a copper tongue. A twisted shard of metal, held tight in the beast's enclosing fist, stabbed the air. It would only take a single swipe from the sword to cut him in two, thought Jack, with mounting horror.

Yang, seeing the immediate threat, rose up on his hind legs, sprouted a spear from his chest, and struck the beast high in the neck. Thick blood flew as the beast fell.

'I wasn't expecting that,' said the old tracker with admiration. 'A few more tricks like that and we may even live through this.'

Jack was not sure how many more tricks his shadow could perform. Not enough to protect them all, he knew that, they faced too many. A scream from down the line; a Myrm had thrown an anvil-sized rock into Mr Karne. There were few adults in the village who tolerated Yang, Mr Karne was rare, in that he actually liked the shadow; even joined in with a prank or two. It hurt to see the man rolling on the floor, and Jack fancied that if he kept watching the injured man, he would feel his own leg hurt, like catching a cold, or someone else's fear. He brought his hand to his face, yet he still heard the screams, and felt awful. Unable to bear not knowing his fate, Jack peeked through his fingers. Before

CRIK

the Myrm closed the distance on Mr. Karne, the ground heaved upward, hurling the creature off its feet.

'Dwayne Chancer did that,' said Jeff Swizleback. He elaborated when he saw the incomprehensive stares thrown back at him, 'A hunter visiting from Grenville. That trick of his scares rabbits to death.'

A Myrm sidestepping Yang, prevented any response they may have given, and Bill looked desperate to speak, eager to concentrate on anything other than the coming assault. Hurling itself forward the beast barrelled straight toward the old tracker. Jeff did not flinch; he only stood still with his mouth agape. Had the shock at seeing the attack focused on him rendered the man motionless? Tossing his head Jack searched for aid; the men standing nearest to him engaged the enemy with their assorted Talents, fighting for their lives. Surrounding them, the Myrms squeezed them into a tight circle. Mr Gasthem's winged menace had dissipated, leaving only a few lone hornets to bother the oncoming tide of armoured beasts. Inara's army, at first looked decimated by the ferocious attack. Bodies lay strewn across the ground, their limbs twisted and cut. Only, the screams coming from that quarter issued from the Myrms, not the risen dead. The hacked bodies still moved intent on pulling down the armoured beasts. A body of a woman, her backbone showing through a silk burial dress, clung onto a Myrm. She tore off its fox helm to expose a face crazed in fright. Jack wished he had the woman beside him.

'Mr Swizleback,' Bill cried, reaching out a hand to shake the tracker.

Mr Swizleback brought to mind the stone statues overlooking the village cemetery. Jack, convinced, that if Bill touched the tracker's arm, his friend would feel marble under his fingertips.

The Myrm, bathed in warm blue light, threw up its weapon and prepared to kill Mr Swizleback. Although Yang had twisted around when the Myrm had evaded his attack, he had no time to stop the descent of the metal hammer.

He is going to die; the words drove repeatedly in Jack's head, a frantic gallop that picked up speed with the falling hammer.

Mr Swizleback, standing still, with his mouth still open, his breath misting before his lips, whistled. The sound, both high and piercing, punched into the Myrm's armour, buckling the bronze chest plate, as though the man had shot a high-powered dart from his mouth. With a thud, the hammer fell to the ground, forming a deep depression in the grass. Falling, the Myrm's dying eyes registered shock.

The tracker's surprising defence afforded Jack a momentary respite, in which he saw the onrushing army of armoured creatures divide around Bill's grandmother. They flinched from the blue light, as though, yes, he knew, they are afraid of her. Pouring around her as an island splits a river in two. He saw too how the creatures' eyes could not bear looking at her; they turned their heavy masks aside and rushed on, almost as though even being close to

THEM OR US: PART ONE

Grandma Poulis hurt. Nevertheless, the sheer numbers besetting them dwarfed her presence. Marooned from the people of Crik, she attempted to push through the fighting, when Kyla and the unnamed Ghost Walker cut her off.

Eager, Jack wanted to see what was about to happen, when Yang bowled an attacking Myrm to the ground and sank his sabres into the exposed neck. Although he wanted to thank his shadow, another high whistle blast from Jeff Swizleback stopped him. Bill screamed, jamming his hands over his ears. The Myrms pressed in hard, desperate to end the battle. Men, and a few women, screamed as clubs and swords smashed into the defensive circle. A series of bangs and lights tore through the night as the retaliating villager's threw their Narmacil given Talents into the fray. In this turmoil he spotted Malcolm Belson, who had changed the lower portion of his body into that of an enormous snake, the coils of which strangled an eagle faced Myrm. His brother finished off the Myrm with a snapping bite from a hooded cobra's head. Graham saw him watching and winked a black eye, spreading back his scaly lips in a smile that revealed curved narrow fangs that dripped with venom. Shuddering, he was grateful the twins were his friends. Beside him, Bill had grown quiet; concerned he turned to check on his friend.

Bill faced neither the fight nor where two Ghost Walkers accosted his grandmother. He ignored the zombies pulling down the screaming Myrms. Instead, the injured villagers lying on the ground had him transfixed. Noticing his friend's puzzlement had Jack hunt around for its cause. A low stationary mist hung in the darkest reaches beneath the spur of land rising above the path. The thin mist, Liza conjured, swaddled a group of small children. Stretched to cover the infants negated the mist's effectiveness; he could see the children and Liza as indistinct shapes amongst the billowing vapour. He doubted her Talent would be enough to protect them. Continuing with his search, he noticed that the Doctor was kneeling beside his mother. Why would the doctor care about someone who was dead when others cried out for his skills? Confused he took a step away from the defensive ring. First one-step, and then another.

'Ying,' said Bill.

Despite the battling bodies, the night was still ice cold. Great plumes of steam billowed from the Myrms' bodies, almost as though fires smouldered beneath their worn armour. Jack's own breath froze in the air. The Doctor laid a hand on his mother's forehead and consulted his timepiece. A small stream of frosted breath rose to meet the Doctor's brass watch. Everything, sounds of fighting, the Belson twins snatching another victim, Bill shouting at his side, pointing frantically at the injured villagers, seemed so distant. Reminding him of smoke drifting up from a lit candle, he saw his mother take another breath. She was alive.

58. THEM OR US: PART TWO

THE MOMENT OF PARALYSIS Jack experienced at the revelation that his mother lived, slowly left him. Now running, he weaved his way through the panicked villagers, passing Grandpa Poulis without a glance, desperate to reach her. That she lived was beyond any hope, a dream taken form. Vaguely he was aware of Bill at his side pointing a stiff arm at his mother. He never heard Bill's words, either because of the chaos of the battle, or the greater turmoil within his own head.

Doctor Threshum stood at his approach. 'Slow down young Jack.' The Doctor held up a hand like a stop sign.

'She's not dead.' Jack's statement came out sounding like a question, or an accusation; he needed the Doctor to reassure him before he could totally accept the fantasy, that he was not too late to help her after all. He looked down at his mother's pale cheeks, then to her sealed eyes. Desperate, almost frantic, he looked again for the misted breath that had given him hope. She looks dead; the thought hit him so hard he felt his legs wobble.

The Doctor steadied him with a firm grip. 'Your mother has a nasty bang on the head. I suppose her injury saved her life.' Jack's quizzical look brought a sardonic smile to Doctor Threshum's bloodless lips. 'Your mother was among the first these monsters captured, and of those she remains the only one not hanging from a branch. Mistaking her for dead, they left her. Not much fun in stringing up someone who can't feel any pain.' The Doctor confided this grisly fact without emotion.

Jack had stopped listening. Blood seeped through his mother's bandage, turning the white cloth a dull maroon. Apart from a single speck of brilliant crimson, appearing like ink glistening in its pot. The blotch of colour absorbed him more than the cloth had soaked up the blood, fixing him to the spot. Darkness spread around his vision in a swirling tide.

The Doctor gave him a hard shake. 'Don't you faint,' he warned. 'Given half a chance these beasts will kill every one of us.' He sounds scared thought Jack. Hate for the man's cowardice mustered in his throat like a clod of phlegm. Then he realised, the Doctor did not fear for himself, but for the people under his protection. Anger left him as suddenly as it had come. 'We need you and your shadow.'

THEM OR US: PART TWO

Jack blinked, dumbstruck. 'What can I do?'

'By surviving the woods you have proven yourself capable,' said the gaunt man, turning to the children behind them. 'The outer defence is beginning to buckle under the attack. When they fail, as they surely must, you will have to act.'

'Inara will help when she breaks through,' said Jack, seeking an avenue to slink away from any responsibility beyond helping his mother.

'She's busy with her own fighting,' said Bill, his eyes anxious. 'Ying, listen to Doctor Threshum, the hunters are losing ground. They won't collapse all at once, but it will only take one of those things to get behind the men to kill the children.'

Jack wanted to say the children had Talents; they could defend themselves, only he knew how foolish, and selfish, that would sound. The youngsters may in fact have formidable abilities, some deadlier than those used by the hunters, however, would a child stand and face the menace that had come out of the Red Wood? If they ran in an attempt to escape, then the rampaging beasts would strike them down before the thought even occurred to them to use their Talent.

Trembling, his eyes suddenly wet, he looked away from his mother. Wiping irritably at the tears, he faced his fear. Stay here and do nothing while others died, or leave her, the choice lay before him like a cruel jape. 'Look after my mother.' The words, escaping his throat in a croak, betrayed his feelings. He could only glance at the Doctor's deep lined face. All he wanted was breakfast with his mother, him having burnt toast while she arranged a few new houseplants into the corners of the kitchen. With the blaze from the burning village still colouring the sky, there was no chance of his daydream becoming a reality any time soon.

Doctor Threshum, never one to give false hope, whispered, his hushed tones carried his hesitant words like a cold breeze intruding into a warming room: 'I can only administer what aid I can. Head injuries are tricky to deal with at the best of times.'

Jack looked from the sorrowful face of the Doctor to the children. They stood nestled beneath the old gold and green sentinel, huddled within Liza's mist. The tree will not offer them sanctuary; the Ghost Walkers had uprooted every tree in the Wold. He refused to look higher than the children's cowering heads; he did not want to see Miss Mistletoe.

Bending down he touched his mother lightly on the head and brushed his lips against her cheek. 'I am home,' he told her in a whisper. He wanted to say more, to apologise for what he had done, to beg for forgiveness; only he knew she would not hear him. The coldness of her skin made him bite back a rising cry. Straightening, he strode away from the injured people, leaving the Doctor, without another word, to take care of them, holding back tears as he went.

CRIK

Bill trotted to keep up with Jack's lengthening strides. 'Where are you going?' he asked.

Jack pointed ahead to a raised mound.

'Why? The children are by the tree, not out there.'

'That's right,' said Jack. 'Pick up all the stones you can carry.'

Without further argument, Bill did, and before long, both his and Jack's arms were laden with sharp rocks. 'Yang can take on one of the Myrms,' said Jack, 'we saw him defeat Raglor. He may take on two or three at once; I don't know.' Despite Bill standing at his shoulder, he had to shout over the clamour. 'We can't get the children to safety. Even if we could sneak them through the surrounding beasts, the Myrms would hunt us down. The hunters will be their focus; wanting them gone before Inara joins us.'

'She is almost here,' answered Bill.

The corpses filling out Inara's army were, for the most part, shambling wrecks. Bone and sinew showed like the inedible remains of a chicken on a dinner plate. They crept inexorably through the ranks of Myrms sent against them, as unrelenting as ground frost, a death as bitter as winter. Fresher bodies amongst the throng, those who had not died too long ago and who had escaped the worst of the ground decay, were ugly things. Most wore skin that had now turned green and sallow yellow, with their extremities eaten away by the things that lived in the ground. As was the custom, a sewn representation of the person's Talent adorned the burial clothes. Guessing his would show a shadow, Jack prayed, a long time from now, that his mother would have a badge with painted flowers. From these badges, sewn onto sleeves and jacket breasts, he fancied he recognised a few of the old villagers. He studied the badges more than their faces, for those who had not yet moulded in the underground graves had visages too horrid to study. Spotting Inara upon Black, laughing, and whirling her hands over her head, delirious, had him biting his lip. Grouped about her, screaming, their armoured helms discarded, and their pelts matted with blood, were those Myrms who had already fallen. Screams of the raised Myrms froze the blood. Driven by madness these wretched things descended upon their own, clawing them with their bare hands. One grey furred Myrm, with a howling wolf mask, sank to the floor beneath dozens of mud-splattered bodies. After its struggles had abated the frenzied mob lost interest in the bloodied corpse. There it lay still, forgotten amongst the carnage. Only a fly hovering over its congealing blood witnessed the eyelids close then open. Screaming, it tore off the wolf head and joined its fellows as they targeted someone new.

'We'll stay here,' he said, feeling sick. Rain, having abated, left behind pools of water scattered over the pocked crown of the mound. His and Bill's arsenal of stones now filled the puddles. The knoll, which rose to the height of a man, allowed a better vantage of the battle. From atop the elevation he saw the entire tumult. Standing back, keeping away from the fighting, stood three of the five commanding Myrms; the other two had joined the force fighting Inara. Each wore a stag helm, hiding their features with a magnificent rack of antlers and impassive stares. They looked so formidable; their presence made Jack quake in fear.

'If anything breaks through the line, start throwing the rocks. Get its attention on us and away from the children.'

Bill listened in silence. On the mound, it seemed as though they were separate from the battle, transformed into observers. The twins had now turned into a scorpion, snapping with sharp claws, while the other struck with a poisonous tail. Other Talents beat at the pressing Myrms, sending back the hairy brutes with flashes of colour and loud shrieks. A tear split the ground, swallowing two denizens of the Wold before a plump girl, who Jack recognised from an outlying farm; her mother made the best lemon cakes. Jeff having appropriated a sword dealt a deadly riposte to a clumsy attack. Three Myrms lay clutching their bellies at his feet, with another four beyond his blade's range with punctured chests. Despite the Doctor's foreboding, Jack clutched at the idea that they could win.

Then he saw Justice join her sisters, completing a triangle around Grandma Poulis. Pale blue light, appearing like ice, had shrunk to encompass only the four women. The Ghost Walkers joined hands, siphoning off the blue light while their own cold colours deepened. Grandma Poulis dropped to her knees.

'Grandma,' cried Bill.

Jack held Bill's arm, stopping him from leaving the mound. 'We can't get to her,' he said. The fighting line separated them; she may as well be on the other side of the Wold for all the good they could do.

'Send Yang through the line to help her,' Bill cried.

'Don't you remember,' said Jack, his heart heavy in his chest, 'Yang can't do anything against the Ghost Walkers.'

'What're you talking about? She needs our help. Yang can slip through the line.'

'The Ghost Walker's power drives Yang away. When he fought Raglor back in the Wold, their light had pushed him from the Myrm Chieftain. My shadow can't help her.'

Standing to his side Yang gave an affirming nod, his shadow hair falling in a flop over his eyes.

'If it was your mother over there, you'd try.'

If his mother was in danger, he had little doubt that he would command Yang forward; his panicked mind would allow him to do nothing else, discarding all rationale in a futile hope. He had a moment to ponder why he did not feel that way now; after all, a few minutes ago he had loved Grandma Poulis with an all-encompassing passion, one that precluded even thoughts of his own

CRIK

Mother. Then he realised he no longer stood within the blue hue. The night felt colder without it, sinking into the marrow of his bones. If not for the realisation that he could help his mother, he would surely feel bereft. Understanding made him look around at the stark faces huddled in groups. Their palpable fear nourished the sense of abandonment they all felt. Without Grandma Poulis they lost heart, without her warmth they became vulnerable.

The line creaked as a hunter fell; and broke when a second fair haired man from Grenville fell with a sword thrust to the belly. The Myrms spilled through the gap with howls of triumph.

Jack snatched Bill, turning his friend to face him. 'We will go to your grandmother when we can,' he promised. 'Now we must protect those we can help.'

Jack let go and hunkered down to fish rocks from the puddles at his feet. When he brought out a handful, Bill stooped down to gather his own supply. He could have hugged Bill in that moment. As he surmised, the Myrms largely ignored the old men and women, and paid little attention to the cries of the youngsters who found themselves outside Liza's protective mist, in favour of beating the hunters into submission.

'Don't throw any rocks until we have to,' he said.

A small boy scampered past, his white pyjamas shining bright. A bronze eagle caught sight of the movement, as a bird of prey spots a frightened rabbit. The eagle staring after the boy could be the same one that had brought Bill and him to the tree. Great mounds of muscle bunched on its back when it turned on the small boy. Jack recognised the boy as the Delver's kid, the one who could find anything. One autumn day Bill had rolled his favourite marble; the one with the red cat's eye; down a gutter clogged with dead leaves and fallen twigs. Hitting the obstruction the marble had disappeared. Bill had looked for nearly half an hour for the little glass ball when up strolled the Delver's boy. He could not have been more than five at the time, must be seven by now, thought Jack. Having asked Bill what he was looking for, the boy at once pointed down the street to Betty Granger's house. Being the heaviest in the set the marble had bulled through the blockage and rolled all the way down the street. Eventually it had rebounded off the granite slab, which served as Betty's front stoop, and dropped into another, larger, nest of brown leaves. Although Jack knew the boy's Talent had merit, he also knew it amounted to little in the face of the Myrm's strength.

A stone struck metal with a sharp crack, breaking off the threatening growl and turning the beast from the boy. Bill threw a second stone, striking the round beak. Bloodshot eyes, peering from the eyeholes, grew larger as they spied them standing atop their mound. The boy stood rooted to the spot behind the hulking menace. Jack wanted to scream at him to run away; instead he flung his own rock. Enraged, the beast charged forward. In its haste to reach them it did not see the pool, as dark as tar, on the floor. As soon as its feet struck him, Yang sprang upward, swamping the Myrm in roping black lines. Entangled, the arms fought against the bonds, trying to heft its weapon and strike at its assailant, and yet the more it struggled the more knotted Yang became. Black ropes rose up the chest, coating the breastplate and filling the gaps in the armour. Shock snapped the eyes wider as it felt the cold touch rise higher, and then, with a sudden jolt, Yang snapped its neck. Finally, the body fell to the ground.

Sweat bathed Jack's back; making his muddy rags cling to him like a second skin. Although the fight had only lasted a few seconds his emotional investment into the outcome left him exhausted. He didn't notice the Delver's kid still standing over the fallen Myrm until the boy shrieked. Aghast, Jack saw the boy, his face paper white, cringe as Yang placed a hand on his shoulder.

'No,' Jack cried, jumping down from the mound. 'He's your friend, he won't hurt you.' He knew, no matter what he said, the boy had watched Yang wrap himself around the Myrm before breaking its neck, and would think the shadow also meant him harm. 'Yang, get off him.'

Flinching from the cowering boy, Yang changed shape to a large sparrow, and flew a few yards away. From high, the shadow kept watch on the surrounding violence.

'I got you,' said Jack; he dropped to his knees and took the boy's hand. The boy was shivering. Ignoring the desperate struggle only a few feet away, he asked, 'You're Dean Delver's boy aren't you?'

The boy's glance reminded Jack of balloons buffeted by wind. The large pupils shone darkly. A moment passed when Jack thought the boy's shock had rendered him mute, and then the boy spoke. 'I was looking for him.'

Most farmers, living outside the protection of the village, had formidable abilities. Dean Delver was no different; he patrolled his farmstead in the form of a massive badger. Most of the trees ringing the Delver farm had deep scratches on their trunks. Mr Gasthem had told Jack that Dean Delver did that to keep wolves and big cats from troubling his cattle. Looking around Jack knew he had no chance of spotting the badger in the darkness. 'Come on, I'll take you back to the other children. Your father will know where you are when he comes looking for you.'

'Will he?'

The pathos held within that simple question aroused such emotion in him that Jack took a moment to answer. He hoped the boy's father would come looking for him. So many had died that it was not certain whether Dean would survive to see his son again. 'He knows all the children are by the tree. You will frighten your father if he doesn't see you with them.'

'You don't want that to happen do you Michael,' said Bill as he joined them.

CRIK

Of course, his name was Michael, how could he have forgotten? He gave a sour shrug at the vagaries of his mind. 'We'll take you back to the tree. Liza will look after you.'

'What about the mound?' Bill asked.

'Yang has to stay close to protect Michael, and with him gone who will protect you when you start throwing stones?'

'I see your point.'

The bones in Michael's hand felt like a collection of loose twigs. Jack gave a gentle squeeze. 'Yang will protect us.' Looking scared at the mention of the shadow Michael made to pull away. Remembering a stuffed toy Michael at one time carried with him, Yang took its form. Reassured by Yang's resemblance to a badger, the boy allowed Jack to lead him away from the mound.

With Yang trailing behind, the three of them began pushing their way through the throng. The tight press at once jostled them. Jack tightened his grip on Michael's hand.

'I'd have thought the farmers would be far enough away from the village to escape this mess,' said Bill as they broke through to a clear area no larger than a front stoop.

'It must be Friday night,' Jack answered. 'They always come the night before the street market so that they can set up their stalls early.'

'Were you at the Crik Inn?' asked Bill, looking down at Michael.

The boy gave a quick nod at the name of the only inn in Crik village. 'My father hid me in the cupboard when the monsters came.' Bright tears formed in his eyes.

'Don't worry; our friend is beating the monsters. It won't be long before they are all gone.'

'Her name is Inara,' added Bill. 'And that's Black, my pet wolf.'

'You have a pet wolf,' Michael exclaimed, his fear forgotten in his excitement.

Bill's answering grin grew wide, as though someone had pushed a plate into his mouth.

Huddling close they drove into the crowd, eager to enter the comparative safety of Liza's concealing mist. As they squeezed passed Mr Scorch's fat belly, who Grandma Poulis always said ate more of his own bread than he ever sold, came the first screams of terror from the crowd. Those without a defensive Talent broke and ran, as the stag helmed chieftains altered the focus of the attack to them. Jack almost fell, and knew the fleeing crowd would have trampled him underfoot if not for his fast reflexes. The Hanging Tree lay ahead. With Bill in tow, he darted toward the looming wood, desperate to escape the maddening press.

Jack bundled Michael up into his arms. The boy let out a cry, 'Let go,' in a shrill voice that rose above the other screams.

THEM OR US: PART TWO

Ignoring the pleas of the boy, they broke through to the deep obscuring mist. The smudged shapes within became more distinct as they entered the shroud.

'Liza,' called Jack.

'I'm here,' Liza said. She sat on a looping root, with boys and girls sitting around her. Dwayne stood behind, holding a stick in his good hand.

The mist dampened the sounds of alarm from outside; tricking the senses into believing the danger was distant. People and Myrms alike were no more than shades, flickering by like smoke. Still, everyone within Liza's boundary stood rigid, ready to flee at the least provocation.

'They are attacking Mr Dash,' said Dwayne, his large eyes peering through the mist as though it was clear glass.

'I know,' said Jack.

He lowered Michael to the ground. The boy ran to where the other children welcomed him back with tired smiles.

'Should we stay where we are?' Liza asked. She cringed against the wood, her eyes darting at every movement beyond her veil. The haughty girl Jack knew had disappeared, leaving Liza looking vulnerable, and for the first time he thought she looked pretty.

Briefly, he considered asking Liza to carry her mist to where the injured lay, concealing his mother from the terrible rout. The heightened risk of discovery involved in moving the children stopped him from suggesting that to Liza. 'No, you have to stay here; it's not safe to move.' The words left his mouth tasting of copper pennies.

'What's happening out there?' Bill asked Dwayne.

Dwayne took a moment, scanning the field the rest could not see, from one end to the other. 'The girl on the wolf has broken though; the creatures are fleeing in terror.' His voice rose in incredulity. 'Some of the monsters are fighting for her, attacking their own kind.' His face grew pensive. 'Mr Dash is with her; I saw him die?'

'It's her Talent,' said Bill, distracted. 'If the Myrms are running away does that mean we've won?'

'Can you see Dr Threshum?' asked Jack, desperate to hear news about his mother.

'Oh no,' said Dwayne.

'What?' Jack was about to run back through the mist when the fear in Dwayne's voice stopped him.

Dwayne pointed as four shadows coalesced into stark relief against the vapour. Leading the company strode a creature with a carven mask supporting a rack of antlers. Jack looked to Yang to tell him to protect the children, only to discover that within the mist he cast no shadow.

CRIK

59. WITHIN THE SHROUD

GOLD-FLECKED EYES, peering from the stag mask, betrayed more emotion than any other of the foul creatures that had come from the Wold. Revealing not anger, nor hatred, only a need to escape. The cautionary turn of its body amplified the desire trapped within its fleeting eyes. Intent on what lay beyond the mist, the chieftain, and the creatures under its control, missed the children. Blood caked the arms of the Myrms, whether the blood belonged to them, or some unlucky villager, Jack could only speculate with feverish concern. Passing shapes waxed against the shifting backdrop, heightening the clarity of the four beasts. Each notch on the naked sword blades, etched themselves in vivid relief against the white vapour.

Confronted by the Myrms, the children let out gasps of horror. One child, her hair a brown nest with so much twigs and dirt in it that Jack would not have batted an eyelid if he saw three chicks amongst its growth, screamed. Too late: 'Quiet, Kari,' scolded her brother, wrapping his hand over her mouth to muffle the noise - her raised cry had snapped the Myrms attention to them.

Even without the added height afforded by the antlers, the chieftain stood a head taller than the other Myrms. Its fear made Jack think of a cornered animal, and like a trapped badger the Myrm was ready to fight. Slicing its wicked sword blade through the billowing vapour created swirls of lazy smoke around its point.

The children cringed at the sight, huddling against the bole of the tree as though it would protect them. Liza backed away until she stood rooted amongst them. Dwayne stood before her, shaking as a leaf caught in a draught.

'Stand with me,' Jack told Bill. Bill settled in beside him, clutching a rock in his right hand, while his left sought another in his trouser pocket.

'Get out of here,' said Jack, stabbing a finger at the lead Myrm. His face felt as stiff as slate. 'You have seen the Talents we possess here in Crik; if you want to live, go now. None here will stop you.'

He knew his words meant nothing to the Myrms; only Krimble had the ability to speak with them, yet, after seeing Inara's gift, they were cautious. Every person in the village had a unique Talent; these creatures had no way to know what abilities this group possessed. Even the smallest child may have the power to defend himself - who was to say one of them did not have a power more terrible than Inara? Faced with such unknown dangers must frighten the beasts. Taking heart, Jack took a step toward them brandishing his own stone as though it were a talisman of great power, and then threw it away. 'I don't need a weapon,' he said, taking another step, trying his best to ignore the flutters that took flight in his stomach. It is a mummer's farce, he thought, his words made as much sense as a dog's bark, and yet by moving closer to the beasts he had brought them to a halt. The trailing Myrm looked set to run.

The chieftain spat out a guttural word; spittle flew from its blubbery lips in a fat spray. The fog, as thick as a stew, swirled around its legs, giving the beast an ethereal quality. Jack could almost believe this was all a dream. More words sprang from the chieftain's mouth to echo around its metal helm.

'Don't show any fear, and they'll think we've got the power to stop them,' Jack told Bill.

'Who's scared? I'm done running from them. This is our home; these are our people.' He jerked a thumb to the children. To Jack's surprise Bill threw the stone he held. Although the projectile missed his target by a few feet, the rearmost Myrm disappeared into the mist with a frightened snarl. 'Must've reckoned I missed on purpose,' said Bill, astounded by the result his thrown stone had on the fleeing beast.

'It doesn't recognise you, so doesn't know your Talent. Perhaps it feared the cast stone would transform into a gargoyle and squash it.'

'First time someone regarded my throwing arm as a talent.'

'Dwayne, can you get the children safely away?' Jack dared not take his eyes from the Myrms; sure, if he lost contact for even an instant they would be upon them. He was about to repeat the question when Dwayne shouted, 'Its chaos out there, those dead things are...'

'Never mind those dead things, they are fighting for us,' cried Bill.

Time was Dwayne and Liza had bullied Bill for not having a Talent, calling him a freak; now both boy and girl jumped at the whip of his voice. 'It's too dangerous,' Dwayne resumed. 'The Ghost Walkers have left your grandmother to help with the fighting. No one's Talents can hurt them; when touched even the raised bodies under your friend's control fall to the ground.'

That did not sound good. Since light affected Yang, he had hoped the Ghost Walkers mastery over the Narmacils stopped with him. With this evidently not the case, the outcome of the battle remained uncertain. 'Stay with the children,' he ordered Dwayne. 'Our words are gibberish to the Myrms so they can't tell how vulnerable we are. Their wariness is close to turning into panic.'

'My grandmother is out there.'

Jack ignored Bill's whisper; he had to focus on the chieftain. He noticed the skittish behaviour of the Myrms, loitering behind their chief; he knew he had only to give them a shove and they would break and run. The world within the

CRIK

mist was alien and unfriendly; no doubt, the rising vapours brought their own terrors to them that knew nothing of Liza's gift.

'Liza,' he called back. 'How much control do you have over this mist?'

'I can't stretch it any farther.' Her voice sounded strained and weak.

'I don't want it stretched,' he replied, keeping his impatience hidden. 'This is your world Liza. Are you able to make the mist act?'

'Act?' she queried. Then she understood. 'I can make the mist dance, push it against the wind.'

'Do it,' Jack ordered. 'Have it dance around them.' His pointing finger created its own current in the mist.

The three remaining Myrms stood still, their wariness making them uncertain. When the first Myrm had fled from the mist, the two others behind the stag helmed chief had looked at one another. Despite the iron covering each face, it was easy to see they wanted to flee the mist, only the hulking presence of their leader stopped them from escaping. Each held their weapon as though they bore a torch in some underground cavern, frightened to lower the steel for what might attack them. Outside, the conflict, though muted, still played all around them. Loudest of all were the screams of the killed Myrms raised to attack their own kind. Every scream intensified the fretful Myrms' anxiety. Tired of the impasse, the chieftain growled from deep within its throat. Striking its fist at the nearest Myrm, the antlered brute strode forward, swinging its weapon. Only a few feet separated it from Jack when the mists began to swirl. The beast slashed the billowing clouds that wrapped its armour, only for its blade to disappear in the smoke.

The whipping fog swirled like ghosts. Both hind Myrms copied their chief and stabbed the speeding damp air. Liza pulled back the mist as the swords descended, only to return the white wall in a rush, making the brutes flinch and backtrack. Faster and faster, the fog swirled, first going one way and then the other. Each time the chief took a step, she increased the speed. Sweat dripped down her face. She compressed her lips so tight they had lost all colour, but her eyes blazed with vigour.

'Look,' cried Bill as one of the Myrms fell back, dropping its weapon.

Antlers rose above the cyclone, their barbed lengths marking the location of the chieftain as the mists rose higher. The blurred outline marched closer, unafraid of the moving mist.

'That one is the last of them,' cried Dwayne, his huge unblinking eyes staring into the cloud. 'The other ran away.'

As Dwayne's words died, the enormous creature plated in steel, iron, and copper, sprang through the mist. It did not care that it stood alone; it brandished its weapon high above its antlered head. Ignoring the huddled children, the Myrm raced across the open ground, intent on Jack.

WITHIN THE SHROUD

Recognising the savagery of the charging beast, Jack pushed Bill away. Bill shouted in surprise at the shove an instant before the chieftain barrelled into Jack. The impact expelled Jack's breath in rush. Crashing into the ground, he felt every snarl and root. He had time to wish for Yang to be with him, but not to ponder where his erstwhile twin and gone in this white world. Raising the sword up, the Myrm prepared to bring the weapon down, severing Jack in two. Faintly, Jack heard Bill scream out his name. A desire to laugh overcame him; he had come all this way back to the Hanging Tree, and for what? Reflecting on his craving to expel Yang only brought bitter remembrance. His quest alone had brought this killer to his village. Deserving of his fate, he lay down. Here he would remain, under the great tree's shading branches; he would not go on any more adventures.

Liza yanked back the mist, collecting the vapour into a surround shining white wall, with Jack at its centre. The world above Jack grew clear, allowing him to spy movement in the trees. Hung bodies writhed against taught ropes. High above, Mark Alefeet, the hunter who had beguiled Jack with his drawings that sprang from the page, had managed to loosen the noose about his neck. Others, who the Ghost Walkers had executed, struggled on yet higher branches. Miss Mistletoe, horrid in her frailty, was amongst them, bucking against the hanging branch that anchored her in the sky.

The Myrm's sword stayed up, wavering in the air, as the beast looked up at Mark with fear crazed eyes.

The white walls collapsed in, popping Jack's ears. Damp air hit him as hard as a fist, plastering his hair to one side. Above him, the sword went spinning through the air to land, point first, a few inches from Bill's staring face. Reeling back from the unexpected blow, the Myrm tumbled into the cloying cloud. Jack could only discern a blurred shape where had stood his assailant. A shadowed outline dropped from above to cling to the Myrm's back while it staggered in terror. The sound of ripping cloth mingled with the clang of fists beating against metal. Twirling together the two combatants embraced each other in a deadly dance.

The strange governing winds whipped the mist into frenzy. Standing against the storm Liza wrought, Jack pushed toward Bill.

'I have to help her,' Bill cried as Jack drew close.

Seeing how frightened he was Jack hunkered down with a thought of putting his arm over Bill, but Bill shoved him aside with a brusque swat of his arm. 'I have to go,' Bill repeated.

'Where do you want to go? The Myrm chieftain can't harm us.' Even as Jack said the words, he knew them to be true. Although smaller, Mark Alefeet had both surprise of his attack, and the fear of what he was, against the Myrm. The chieftain howled, not in pain, he screamed in terror and outrage at what Inara had brought back here tonight. With Mark staying within Liza's cover, he knew the children would remain safe.

Bill was no longer thinking of the children. He had come to the same conclusion as Jack, allowing him to turn his mind to other matters. 'They were killing my grandmother,' Bill said in a half a sob. 'The Ghost Walkers had her on the ground.'

Behind them, the Myrm had dropped to one knee as a second shadowed figure dropped from the tree.

'Come on,' Bill urged. 'The children no longer need us.'

Turning, Jack saw the blank expressions of the children. It hurt to leave them, yet by remaining with them meant hiding, while those beyond the mist fought and died for his mistake. 'Alright,' he relented.

Dragging the sword from the ground Bill took off in a clumsy run. Jack wanted to tell Liza where they were going, but Bill did not spare him the time. Liza slumped against the tree, with her limp hair covering her exhausted face. Driving the mist as a physical force against the Myrm had taken it out of her. As different coloured light revealed surprising aspects to Yang, Liza had discovered a new trick when she attacked with her Talent. Raising his hand to the girl, he tried to reassure her. She only stared back, uncomprehending. The children too beseeched him to remain with them, not with words; they communicated their need through scared, hopeless faces that did not understand. They are safe now, he told himself. No Myrm remained to threaten them. Upset, he followed Bill, rushing through the damp air, hoping the children would remain safe.

The sight that assaulted him as he broke from the white barrier had brought Bill to a standstill and astounded him. The shambling bodies of the fallen were everywhere. Scores of wounds covered each as they stumbled over the ground. Almost all fighting had stopped; a few Myrms had retreated to the top of the rise, where long rotted bodies, freshly killed people, and Myrms that had already succumbed, besieged them. Not a single body remained undisturbed; Inara would not let them rest. Frantic, he searched for survivors. Dr Threshum struck a determined figure, as he remained steadfast beside the wounded. He hoped his mother still lived. No, he told himself, she is safe, if she had died then she would be one of those attacking the hill and he saw no sign of her. Mr Dash walked amongst his onetime charges. The grave keeper had appropriated a shovel, which he held close to the ground as though he was about to dig a grave. Jack saw other recognisable faces amongst the throng, and each one hurt him to see.

'There's grandpa.'

From where he stood, Jack could not say for sure whether Grandpa Poulis was amongst the living, or another foot soldier in Inara's ever growing army. The old man stood to one side of the track that had once served to separate the two factions. Dropped weapons, abandoned armour, blood drenched cobbles, and scorch marks from a fire that still blazed close to the trees, lay about him. At his feet, wrapped in grey cloth, lay Grandma Poulis. Wisps of feeble blue light seeped into the air around her, fighting the black night. Where is everyone? Jack wondered. They could not all be dead. He fought back his rising dread with great effort.

Bill had taken a few unsteady steps forward. One of the bodies that had risen from its grave wandered before him, dripping mud and gore. Behind this first strode a young girl, whose skeletal face wore an askance grin as she cradled a clump of sodden grass to her chest as though it were a favoured doll. Bill took one look at the grisly pair and picked up his speed toward his grandparents.

'Bill,' cried Grandpa Poulis when he saw his grandson. 'My boy.' He grabbed Bill and pulled him tight to his chest. 'I've missed you, I've missed you.' He went to repeat the words again when Bill pulled away.

'What's wrong with Grandma?'

The punitive treatment by the hands of the Ghost Walkers had left the once radiant Grandma Poulis looking old and weary. She had not transformed back into the accustomed wizened woman, her physical body remained in her upstairs bedroom, yet deep-set lines marred her smooth features and shadows pooled under her closed eyes. The meagre light coming from her managed to spread some warmth, a promising sign that Jack held onto as he joined Bill.

The smile slipped from Grandpa Poulis. 'They tried to steal her light. If not for that girl on the wolf drawing them away they would've succeeded.'

'Did they mean to kill her?' Jack knew it was a dumb question as soon as he uttered it.

'I don't know if they could,' said Grandpa Poulis, looking down at his wife. 'The one calling herself Justice,' he scoffed, 'strode through fire without harm. Benjin drove a sword through her; she only paused long enough to reach into his chest and stop his heart. I saw more try to stop the other Ghost Walkers with their Talents. Formidable powers, such as Jeff Swizleback's mouth dart, passed right through them without effect.'

'Where are they now?'

'They went to the river after the girl. They knew while she remained their pet beasts had no chance.'

Without Inara, the dead would remain dead, and the surviving Myrms atop the hill would regroup and kill the rest of the villagers. Then the village would belong to the Ghost Walkers, and Grandma Poulis would bend to their will.

Jack moved away from Grandpa Poulis. 'Stay with your family,' he said as Bill followed him.

'You can't go after Inara by yourself. They'll kill you for sure.'

'I'm not alone, I have Yang.' The shadow had sprung back to life when the light from the fires swept over the field. 'I need you to stay here with your family, you can do more good here than with me.'

CRIK

Bill looked torn and tired, not just physical exhaustion, but soul weary; he had seen and done too much. 'If my grandfather and I can move my grandmother to Dr Threshum, I'll stand guard over your mother too.'

Jack gave Bill a hug. 'I will be back, with Inara; you can then show everyone Black.'

Bill brightened at the mention of his wolf. 'Make sure you look after him - I don't fancy going to look for another. Besides,' he said, 'Black is one of us, he's my friend.'

'He is our friend.' Jack wished he could promise to keep the wolf safe. 'Keep that sword to hand, there're still Myrms around.'

Jack broke away from the hug and ran toward the river. His headlong flight saved him from seeing the worst sights of the fighting, dismembered limbs, and enough blood to fill a river dampened the ground. Come daybreak the sun would sparkle on crimson pools; until then he paid the plasma splashing up his calves no heed. Skirting the hill, where the conflict still waged, he looked up to the silver Tristle River that reflected moonlight and starlight. Yang, strong and ink black, led the way. The shadow directed them from the worst of the carnage, for which he was immensely grateful; Bill was not the only one who had seen too much horror. Walking in Yang's wake, he feared that despite their route he would see more evil before the end of the night.

60. GRAVES END

Once Yang led him to the banks of the Tristle, Jack could almost trick himself into believing the horrors of the night had ended. The waters lapping the steep slope sounded the same, as ever, there was even a frog croaking amongst the tall reeds. If he concentrated on the passing water, its flow and eddying currents, he could allow his mind to escape from everything that had happened. However, as he watched the running water take a meandering path toward the bridge, the first glint of red firelight danced across its surface. The sky was aflame, and even down here he felt the heat touch the back of his neck. Then there was his mission; he had to find Inara before Justice grabbed her. Not only to save a dear friend, but also someone who in all likelihood would prove to be the pivot that swung the village from survival, to a sure death at the hands of the Ghost Walkers. He had never counted any girl amongst his close friends; a few, like Betty Hulme, were pleasant company, in small doses. Inara was different; he wanted her around, and missed her when she was not. This realisation scared him; it in fact frightened him to his shivering core.

'Are you sure they came this way? I see no wolf prints.' His voice came out fast and hoarse.

Yang gave a curt nod to the impatient enquiry, the shadow then pointed down the river away from the bridge. Although Jack looked, he could see nothing of interest along the length of the bank. He had supposed Inara must have escaped to the cemetery; there she may find more bodies to aid her - why then did she head downstream? Her choice of direction perplexed him. She did not know Crik as he knew it, he reminded himself. Perhaps she made a mistake in choosing her route, or the Ghost Walkers had herded her away from the graves, where Inara may escape amongst the labyrinth of tombs and figureheads.

He walked at a brisk trot, all the time fighting the urge to break into a run. What good would it do to arrive at Inara's side too exhausted to stand? Despite his rationale, the feeling persisted and grew as Yang drew him away from the cemetery. Where was his shadow leading him? Scanning the coarse brush for any sign of Inara's passing, he wished he had either Dwayne's night vision or a tracker's skill to locate what he sought. He didn't want to second-guess Yang; after all, the Narmacil had located Huckney back in the Red Wood. The

CRIK

Narmacils had some connection tying them together; perhaps they called to one another by some secret means, a communication only they heard.

He wracked his brain trying to understand the strange path Inara had taken. Something at the back of his mind, teased him. He supposed he had forgotten something, which at a less fraught time, would be obvious. Although he knew this side of the river well, when he ventured this far from home, he was apt to climb the tree, not spend his time beside the river. Intrigued by his partial memory, that had sown a seed of understanding as to Inara's flight; he stopped questioning where his Narmacil led him.

'Do the Ghost Walkers have her?' The fear of being too late to help Inara made him wish he had brought along Bill. Justice would kill the wolf that protected Inara, and Bill would know if anything happened to Black. The doubt niggled at him like a bad tooth. Yang didn't answer, he only infuriatingly stretched ahead.

Only the soft rustle of the grass against his legs, and the soothing water beside him, met his straining ears. Though he had left the fight, atop the hill, far behind, he was still amongst the grounds the Elders counted amongst the boundary of the village. He passed a lover's bench, its pale wood shaped into the likeness of a leaf. A few yards farther, he noted a familiar leaning fence that allowed a splendid vantage of the river as it dove down a clutter of rocks in a mini-waterfall. The cascading water hid copper pennies on the riverbed. Nostalgia tightened his throat, as he strayed from his path for only a moment to take in the well-known sight. If he had a penny, he would have thrown it into the water, to make a wish for Inara's safety.

The river moved from the woods that threatened to the west. Its meandering course would take it through boggy fields, that come spring would have daisies, bluebells, and clusters of clover. Taking a sharp turn, the Tristle would eventually enter Crik Wood, near to where he and Bill had entered the trees to look for Bill's wolf.

Ahead he spotted the tell-tale amber glow of the Ghost Walkers. Piles of jagged rock partially obscured their light from him; and, he hoped, him from them. Yang had retreated to his side on sight of Justice and her party. Their light reminded Jack of a sun, paled by passing clouds, when you could look directly at the rising star and see its entire opaque sphere. Like that winter sun, the Ghost Walkers promised only a chill touch.

The purple candle, Knell had given him, lay secure in his pocket, but he dare not light it for fear of Kyla or one of the others seeing him. Feeling alone, and unsure of his next step, his fingers traced the cylindrical object; he would have done much to hear his Narmacil's advice. He considered hanging back to hear the raised voices that tumbled from dead lips like soot from a dirty chimney. To discern the angry words required him to sneak in closer. From here, he only heard their high pitch, swatting at the night like mothers beating a rug. Now that he was so close to the Ghost Walkers, he asked the question that he had not dared face since leaving Bill. What could he do against Justice and her sisters? They had nothing to fear from Yang. His shadow shrank from them, like any other shadow confronted by light. Grandpa Poulis had told how a sword passed harmlessly through Justice's chest, only for her to kill the weapon bearer where he stood. Deprived of a sword, he decided not to dwell on its absence.

Despite his fears, he took an unsteady step forward. Although he could still not understand a word, the sound increased enough for him to differentiate between those ahead. Kyla's voice cracked like a whip, while the mollifying tone of Justice carried its own weight. No, he thought with a sudden fierce heat. Justice did not wish to appease, only to cajole Inara, like a cruel boy calling a cat, only to hit the animal when in range of his stick. Tantalised, by what transpired beyond the stones, brought him two quick strides closer.

Kyla sounded like an out of tune piano, punching at every syllable. He had no doubt her rushed sentences would remain incomprehensible, even if the wall, which acted as a sound barrier, were not there. Even with the obstacle, he knew the Ghost Walker, who had wanted to execute them back in the Wold, had lost it.

The ghost lights moved, stretching the shadows as they did. Not wanting them to catch him in the open, he sprinted for the piled stone. If Yang, lit by starlight, did not brace his shoulders, he would have collided with the sharp rocks hidden in darkness. Stifling a cry, he saw the tip of a Ghost Walker's dress slip by the edge of the rocks. The transparent cloth floated close enough for him to reach out and touch. Its tattered ends sailed against the wind, moving by its own accord. Cautious of the ghostly garment, he moved from Yang's embrace. As he was turning toward the wall, he thought he spied a silhouette, beyond the billowing fabric, well away from the Ghost Walkers. Searching for the shape, he saw nothing. Perhaps there was nothing to see, a tired and scared mind was apt to create tricks for the eyes. Unable to explore further, he began his ascent. Sharp rocks scored his hands a hundred times before he gained the top. He always figured someone, long ago, had piled the stone one atop another, with such expert precision that it had withstood the test of time and elements.

He knew the floor of the basin as a dust bowl, hard packed earth with no grass, and good for nothing other than a few ball games. Now as he peered over the top of the wall he saw that the rain had transformed the floor into an ankle deep muddy lake. The wall circled the dirty water in two protruding arms, like the horns of a ram. Within the crook of the stone arms, gripping Black's wiry hair was Inara. She slumped over the great wolf, one hand gripping her opposite shoulder. Shivering, she jerked as though shocked by the soft whispering wind. Another spasm twisted her, making the wolf growl. When the seizure passed,

CRIK

she tilted her face to reveal gritted teeth and lips etched into a gruesome grin. Deep pain lines furrowed her white skin, making her look like another corpse. This time Jack shivered. Incredulous, he watched as she threw back her head and laughed. He could not help but think that she had gone insane. Justice watched; her hollow cheeks clove to her skull like plaque on teeth. Circlets of cold sweat coated his arms, and a damp crown peppered his head, as another peal of mirthless amusement cut the night.

'Why are you laughing?' Kyla, unlike her impassive sisters, strode partway across the water. Her reflection threw back a once beautiful face. A deep loathing curdled her lips. 'You should not scoff at an offer to spare your life.'

'It is her choice to make,' said Justice.

Against the wall, Black bared his fangs. Jack heard the threatening growl with a heavy heart, Black could no longer protect Inara; the wolf's teeth were useless against the dead women. Inara, swaying with the wolf's motion, fell silent and fixed her dark heavy eyes on Kyla. 'The Red Sisters want me dead.' Her guttural broken voice only just managed to find Jack's straining ears.

'No,' answered Justice. 'We never wanted to eradicate all life in the Wold. Our fear, of what had happened to us, made us blind and rash. The Red Sisters closed us off from the rest of the world, to protect us. To make a haven for our kind, somewhere we could be safe from persecution.'

'Isabelle,' said Justice, looking at the third Ghost Walker, 'was your age when her mother took her to the tree.'

Isabelle nodded. 'I promised to leave the village, to go into the woods and never return. She refused to listen, and waited for me to leave my body before tying the rope around my neck.'

'We all have sorrowful tales,' snapped Kyla. 'Each of us trusted someone, who in the end betrayed us. This girl will be no different. We should only trust in our own kind. The village has not changed; the Hanging Tree still stands at its entry, with rope tied to its branches.'

Jack stared open mouthed. That was not fair, he and his friends played on that rope, it had been years since the last execution.

Justice spoke, ignorant of Jack's impotent rage: 'We came to Crik to rescue your friend's grandmother. She refuses to see their fear and hate; in time her beloved village will turn on her.' A sympathetic smile smoothed her hard contours. 'You are also an outcast. They will come to fear your Talent; others will call you an abomination. They will distrust you, and fear what you can do.'

Inara shook her head. 'They will thank me for what I have done tonight.'

'Tomorrow they will,' answered Justice, with a sad tilt to her mouth. 'In time they will forget the debt they owe you. They will see how you alone turned the battle, and knowing that they will fear you will turn on them. They live beside a large graveyard, filled with the bodies of their mothers, fathers, wives, husbands, and their lost children. The burial ground is a constant reminder of your capabilities. All it would take for it to spread is for one person to speak of his trepidation. They will lay aspersions against you; how you fornicate with the dead, and use their loved ones to poison their land when their crops do not grow. At first, the stories will only be there to disturb, or to entertain the listener. Those hearing the tale will tell their own lies; people will begin to believe those lies, and when there are enough believers, they will turn on you. Each will carry a burning torch, and in the flame, you will see triumph in their eyes.'

'Listen to her,' said Isabelle. 'I was much loved in the village before they discovered my secret. Half the boys wanted to be my boyfriend, and the other half wanted to be my friend. As I was without a Talent, they pitied me, but never made fun of me. I used to dream of being like them, envying even the most frivolous Talent. Each time a young child woke to tell the world that they had found their Talent my heart sank. Being much older than they are, I yet waited, and waited. Then one night, to my horror, I left my body. All my life I had heard warnings about Ghost Walkers; evil spirits from the woods come to invade a person's body to take it over. Only that did not happen. I was still me. I watched my sleeping self for a long time, waiting to see if something would possess me, to stop me from going back into my body. Nothing happened. When I wandered the woods, I befriended the animals. Returning to my body, I returned to the terror that someone would find out my secret. Whenever I heard the stories and warnings about Ghost Walkers, I had to bite my tongue from shouting down the lies.'

'Lies are their religion,' spat Kyla. Angry, she glided over the dark pools, her fingers drawn toward her palms like twisted thorns.

'I thought my mother would listen to me. We were very close; best friends as well as mother and daughter. I thought if anyone would listen to me, it would be her. She could then speak on my behalf to the Elders. They respected her. You know how that ended.' The light fell from Isabelle to reveal her ash grey skin; she looked forlorn at Inara. 'We will be your friends. Come back with us and you can exercise your gift without fear of persecution.'

'You can bring back life to the Wold. It does not have to remain only a place of metal and dust,' said Justice. 'With your power you can give the land back to nature.'

With hands clammy with sweat, Jack clutched the top of the wall. Gripping the rough-hewn stone with his leg pressed against sharp protrusions, he bit back a cry of agony. He had to shift his weight, or his leg would go numb, and up this high that could be disastrous. Gritting his teeth he pushed the pain away, he needed to hear Inara's response. She could not seriously be contemplating the Ghost Walkers' offer. The Red Sisters had sent Justice to Crik Village for revenge; they had used Grandma Poulis as an excuse to come, a smokescreen to commit murder. Inara had told him at the Red Wood that she had given the animals a second chance of life. Blind to the desiccated husks that roamed aimlessly across barren fields; to her the animated rabbits lived. That day, her Talent, which Inara had seen as something perverse, had opened up with new possibilities. Now she could create life, sustaining it with her will alone. That is what Justice offered, a chance to use her Narmacil, to bring the Wold's dead heart to life.

Inara's pain wracked body livened as the Ghost Walkers laid out their plans for her. Her face had regained some of its colour, and her back straightened. 'I am a part of each creature I bring back,' she said. 'They open themselves up to me. To others, the animals I raised in the Wold displayed no conscious thought,' she regarded Justice with a cool expression, 'they were wrong, I sensed their needs, a place to shelter, something to eat. It doesn't matter whether this instinct is biological or memory induced, it is part of them, proof then of life. They were attempting to reconnect with what they once were, before the Red Sisters came. I gave them a chance to find themselves, to inhabit new homes, and experience life others had stolen from them.'

'We will help you to help them,' said Isabelle, her smile widened as light wrapped her body.

Feeling dread, Jack eased forward. His leg shifted away from the wall; despite the movement being slight, it was enough to send his foot shooting into the open air. He wanted to cry out, he was falling, and his mind did shout with alarm; perhaps his mouth gave vent to that horrible encompassing realisation. His fingers scrabbled across the slick stone, breaking fingernails as they skittered over the rough surface. The fall would kill him. Trailing his fingers to the lip of the wall, the pressure turned his flesh white, and then he felt hands catch him under his elbows and lift him up. Yang? Cold seeped into his joints. Twisting against the grip, he saw Kyla, not Yang holding him. Her face crowded over his, her visage carved into a hateful mask of decay and corruption. She carried him up over the ancient wall and into the basin, where the others watched him. Horror stamped Inara's face. Closer now, he saw how she had aged since their parting.

'The trespasser has become a spy,' said Kyla.

Jack wanted to cry out, it felt as though the Ghost Walker had sank her digits into his elbows, twisting his nerves around shards of ice. 'Don't listen to them, they want to use you,' he shouted. Kyla tightened her hold on his arm, making him scream.

Justice drifted close to Jack, her expression one of compassion. 'Don't hurt him. He is Inara's friend.'

'Jack,' said Inara.

Her renewed strength had abandoned Inara, as sudden as a stone shot from a sling. Cradling her shoulder, her once vibrant eyes clouded over. 'Don't worry about me,' he said. 'Because of you, we are winning the fight.'

'The fight is over,' said Inara. 'We have taken the hill.'

Both Isabelle and Kyla bristled at this revelation. Jack sensed Kyla's doubt and anger like a poisonous fume. Only Justice retained her composure to say, 'This village is a monument to death. The graveyard has expanded its boundary, in time it will cover everything. Depart this place; share your Talent so that we may put the past behind us.'

'You brought death to my home,' said Jack. 'Those creatures were yours to command. You took people from their beds, driving them to the tree.' His finger shook with venomous accusation. 'You had every intention of hanging every soul in Crik.'

'The people who live here are a pestilence,' said Kyla. 'If they will kill us, their own children, then no one is safe from them. The Hedge Wall could only shield us for so long from the torches that would eventually come.'

Jack realised the terror that lived within Kyla. She constantly relived the night the villagers had killed her. Even behind the Hedge Wall, she did not feel safe. Her entire existence was one of expecting hunters to find her, and finish the job their fathers had started. How many years has that fright festered, warping everything, until nothing remained but it and the need to survive. An unpleasant thought occurred then, had Miss Mistletoe been party to the executions. The old woman had been old enough to have witnessed the cruelties, and perhaps agree with the sentence. Had Mr Hasseltope drawn the noose around Kyla's neck while she watched from the woods? Isabelle, who had died so young, had she dated Mr Gasthem, or someone else Jack knew? Crik collected secrets like shipwrecks at the mouth of a harbour. Desperate, he wanted to tell them that they were safe from any reprisals for this night. He just wanted them to go, to leave them alone to rebuild their homes and their lives. Only, he knew, he could not promise anything. Fear made the Ghost Walkers return here; would fear in turn make the people of the village turn their weapons toward the Wold? Imagining snaking torchlight, winding through the woods, snagged in his mind. Another vision came crashing through, of armoured Myrms trekking through the same woods on their way to finish the job they had started here tonight. Next time they would not give the villagers a chance to defend themselves; they would murder everyone in their beds, including his mother. It's them, or us. Whoever made the first strike would survive. The realisation made him want to weep.

'Prove to me that you are better than them,' said Inara. She lifted a finger to point at Jack. 'Release him.'

Kyla tightened her grip sending waves of pain up Jack's arm. 'Next time this one comes to the Wold he will bring others.'

'Jack will not harm you,' assured Inara. 'He turned away from his home, when he had the chance to return, because they had kept secrets from him. He

CRIK

values the power of truth, if he promises not to return to the Red Wood in vengeance, you can believe him.'

The dead woman's cold bosom pillowed Jack's head. Revulsion at the touch clutched his stomach. He would never feel warm or safe again.

'We do not wish him harm,' said Justice.

'No,' Kyla hissed through withered lips. She forced Jack tighter against herself. 'This child brought the others. They know the secret of our sanctuary. If we allow him to live, we will never be secure. We must kill them all; even the girl must die. The Myrms have failed us; we are wasting time. Kill the children and then the rest of them.'

'There will always be others,' said Justice. Her light grew brighter, swallowing her sister's light in her brilliance.

The feeling of love Jack had felt within Grandma Poulis's blue light crept into him, warming his body. Traces of blue now mingled with the cold amber surrounding the Ghost Walker.

'We can't trust them.'

'Come to me.' Justice spoke to Jack, ignoring Kyla's protestations.

The cold fingers slipped reluctantly from Jack's arms. Free, he stumbled from Kyla's grasp. Justice stood to his right and Inara to his left. Hesitant with indecision, he cast about for a solution. Should he run to Inara, or to the woman who now exuded such warm love? His foot trailed to the right, and his eyes lifted to Justice's eyes, that were so alike his mother's own. Through her colour, he spotted the red haze of the fire, still burning, and thought of Bill. Bill now stood over a woman who had refused to listen to the Ghost Walkers' offer, a woman who could have died for her decision. Refusing to love someone who had caused so much misery and death, he turned from Justice and ran to join Inara.

Kyla laughed. 'He rejects you sister.'

Jack hugged Inara. Her body felt so frail, like an old woman. Afraid his embrace would hurt her, he let go, and patted Black's shaggy head. Beside him, Yang appeared in the likeness of Bill.

'Will you come with us?' Justice asked Inara.

Jack felt a shiver course through Inara's frame. She is so tired. The defence of the village had left her with no strength. What could he do to help her? Without any weapon he could use against the three Ghost Walkers, all he could do was stand beside his friend. Then Yang began to grow. From Bill's chubby frame grew broad shoulders and arms as big as boulders. Yang's chest developed while corded muscles roped his lengthening thighs. Both he and Inara stared, wondering what Yang grew into, and then they both realised.

'What happened to Huckney after we left?' asked Jack. He stood beside the likeness of the blacksmith. 'He helped us escape. Did you punish him for sending Gashnite to carry us over the Hedge Wall?'

'He betrayed us,' said Kyla, stopping Justice from speaking.

'We punished him,' said Justice, drifting closer. 'The Red Sisters do not take betrayal lightly.'

'Is he dead?'

Inara had asked the question Jack could not bear to utter himself. His heart beat as fast as though he had just run a marathon. The idea that the blacksmith had died for them made him want to hide. Everything was his fault. They would never have entered the Wold if he had not forced them into it.

'Dead?' The blue had left Justice, leaving behind emptiness and a sense of something that could not last. 'No,' she said, 'he lives.'

'What did you do to him?' Jack asked the question before it had time to form in his mind.

'You will not believe it from our lips,' said Justice. Her hand beaconed to the darkness, outside the ring of stone, where something stirred.

With his heart stampeding in his chest, Jack waited to see the blacksmith. Was Huckney here? Although he could not dare contemplate such a hope, someone did approach.

'Huckney is part of the Red Wood,' said Justice as the shape ebbed slowly closer. 'He is part of our family, we could no more kill him than cut off a healthy limb.'

'Lies,' whispered Jack.

A brown blanket spread over the humped back of the skeleton that limped into the basin. The blanket gathered over something round that the desiccated body clutched to its ribs. Bone fingers, held together by the last of its sinew, cradled the object protectively.

'Come closer,' said Kyla with disdain.

The shambling wreck edged closer, until it spotted Inara watching him. The skeleton reeled back in alarm, almost dropping its treasure. Turning, it revealed a twisted spine. At the base of the back, a few fused vertebrae made the body hunch forward at a harsh angle.

It cannot be him. Jack reeled in distress.

Inara gasped. 'You.'

'Leave me alone,' croaked Krimble. 'Let me go, I don't want to see you.' The man from the marsh shied away from Inara's stare. His hands fumbled at the blanket for a moment, before looking up at Kyla. 'Don't let her take it from me.'

'You betrayed us, you tricked me,' said Kyla. 'When you sent the lightning to protect the children, you condemned yourself.'

Krimble whimpered under the Ghost Walker's harsh gaze. 'No,' he said. 'I knew how valuable the girl is. I told the Red Sisters that they were making a mistake in wanting to kill her. You should have left her to me. In time I would have had her power, and then the Wold would remain secure.'

CRIK

'By aiding them you compromised our home.'

Bones trembled along Krimble's body as though Kyla hurled stones not words. 'I wanted to help you,' he now pleaded to Justice. 'Don't you see it's not the girl you want, it's her Narmacil; the girl is nothing without her Talent.'

'She doesn't need her Talent to be special,' said Jack, balling his hands into tight fists.

'And neither did anyone else you killed,' added Inara. The pain lines, so deeply cut into her face, appeared like the scars that had once criss-crossed Krimble's own features. 'I should have sensed you.' She shook her head. 'Lost amongst the crowd,' she muttered in a low rasping whisper.

'Tell them what became of Huckney,' ordered Justice.

'The blacksmith, why do you want to hear about him?' said Krimble, forming a sneer even without the lips to do so.

'Damnit, tell us,' said Jack, scared, but determined to hear what had happened to his friend once they had escaped.

'He lives,' said Krimble. 'The Red Sisters still need him to build their forest. They did, however, take away his beloved pet.'

'What are you saying?' Inara hunched herself over the great wolf's head.

Brown teeth gnashed together. The skull turned up to Justice in silent appeal.

'Tell her,' said Justice.

'That infuriating squirrel of his, the one with all the riddles,' answered Krimble, clutching his blanket tighter against himself.

Jack took a forward step, he felt as though someone had thrown a bucket of ice-cold water over him. 'What about Herm?'

'They built a fire and melted him down.' A sense of glee slipped by Krimble's, otherwise impassive, exterior.

He loves that they killed Herm, thought Jack. Even stripped down to nothing, the man, who had kidnapped them in the marsh, had not changed. Given half a chance and this rogue would kill them all. The knowledge of Herm, melted down into a puddle of bronze, made him hate Krimble even more. 'You enjoyed it.'

Krimble's only reply was the clatter of his teeth coming together in a hard bite.

'What are you holding?' asked Inara, spying the bundle of brown wool with suspicion.

'Nothing,' snapped Krimble.

'Show me.' Inara commanded the zombie. 'Drop the blanket and show me what you hold with such reverence. I wonder what it is that you prize.'

'No.' Krimble sounded like a small child asked to give up his favourite toy. 'I told you what happened after you left. You owe me for saving your life. Don't take this from me.'

'Drop the blanket,' Inara said, implacable.

A cry of such anguish lifted from Krimble that Jack believed something had hurt the zombie. The cries crescendo rose to such a sorrowful pitch Jack would have put his hands over his ears, if anyone, but Krimble, had issued it. Instead, he had no pity for the man. His mother would want him to feel something, anything, but the fact that he could not, only made his jaw hang wider, turning the grin that had formed, wolfish. Glittering, his eyes watched the blanket fall away to reveal a golden egg. 'A Narmacil egg,' he said.

'It's mine,' said Krimble.

'That's your Narmacil,' said Inara.

'That's right.'

'The one that gave you the Talent to speak to the other Narmacils,' said Inara. 'It imbued you with the ability to coax and steal the Talent from others. Gave you the means to capture and destroy those who came to the marsh. With it, you stole the Talent to alter a path's course, to lure people to your house. I followed one of your paths; it led me away from my parents.'

'His body can no longer sustain a Narmacil,' said Justice. 'This is the last of the eggs. He will not part with it.'

'That Narmacil is for the living,' said Inara, her eyes glittered darkly. 'Give it to me.'

'I won't. Have satisfaction that you have taken everything from me.'

'Not everything.' Inara lifted her arms so that her palms spread out before her. 'Give me the egg.'

Despite his tortured cries Krimble took a step, and then another. His skull, split at the mouth, mewled like a wounded animal. Yellow bone digits cradled the egg, stroking its shell as though it would protect him. Yards turned into metres and then the distance dwindled to a mere few feet and still Inara held her arms outstretched, waiting to take the egg.

'You have punished me enough.'

'Not yet,' was her whispered reply.

The clack of bare bone rang in Jack's head as Krimble drew closer. He remembered the cask of bones outside this man's home. How many had died to sate Krimble's desire for more power? Not even Inara knew that number. Jack watched, with a sense of justice, as Krimble pushed the egg away from his chest. The holes in the marsh man's skull watched as his hands betrayed him by dropping the Narmacil egg into Inara's waiting embrace.

'Now I have everything from you,' said Inara, and smiled.

The wind carried off the moan of loss that escaped Krimble's jawbone as his bones fell lifeless to the damp floor.

Inara's shoulders relaxed as though she had dropped a heavy weight as she stared at the stack of bones. Jack studied her, hoping to see a flicker of emotion. She showed none.

CRIK

'The vile creature deserved to live in limbo,' said Kyla. 'His betrayals deserved a harsher fate.'

Once more Inara laughed. Tears streamed down her face, cutting rivulets through the grime on her cheeks. 'He tried so long to win my Narmacil from me.' Her voice cracked, dissecting her laugh, turning it into a growl. 'We sat at a table; I don't know for how long, the room had no windows. People came and went; only I refused to give in to him. He begged, threatened, and carried out those threats to have what is mine. Now, at the end,' she lifted the egg, divided by a silver line, 'it is I who took what was his.' The smile that scythed her mouth was terrible. 'He is nothing, and before I released him, he knew it too.'

'He was yours to punish,' said Justice. 'Come back with us.' She glanced at the sky, now serene after the storm. 'The hour is late.' Her hand, which reached out to Inara, could not distract from the impatience in her voice.

Glancing from the egg to Justice, Inara shook her head. 'You want the same thing as he did. He wanted to use my Narmacil for his own ends. If I returned with you, then I would be like Huckney, a prisoner within your Wold. I would exist only to serve you. My animals would run through an ever-expanding metal forest. Their hooves would send up clouds of red rust and you would have your world under your control. I want to see my parents again.' She looked down at the old bandages wrapping her knees.

'Enough.' The harsh cry from Kyla stilled the night. 'Sisters, we must leave. Take the girl by force if you want her. We must kill the boy.'

The light billowing around Justice had lost all warmth. Amber frosted the air, dropping the night temperature by a few more degrees. A grimace replaced her comely smile. 'Take her,' she ordered.

The pool of muddy water mirrored Kyla's leering skull. White hair fanned out like cobwebs in a tomb. Decayed flesh showed on her arms and legs as she floated over the basin toward them.

Beside Jack, Yang had turned into a cat. Hair bristled along the shadow cat's strong shoulders. Teeth, as long as butcher knives, bit the air as Yang snarled at the approaching woman. The cat doubled in size as it bounded toward Kyla, and then Yang sprang at the Ghost Walker. Jack held his breath, pride for Yang wrestled with his fear. A few feet before Kyla, Yang touched the amber light, and disappeared.

'He can't penetrate their light,' said Jack through numb lips.

Pulling back on Black's neck, Inara said, 'No Black, stay here.'

They heard the black wolf's snarls and the clash of his teeth. Did Black recognise the Ghost Walkers, and remembered what had happened to Silver back in the Red Wood. Jack could see the wolf straining not to jump forward in attack. He knew Bill watched the scene through Black's eyes. Would Bill, now with his grandparents, see the Ghost Walkers kill them.

'Take my hand,' he said to Inara, holding out his. She took it without comment.

When she was only a few feet from them, Kyla came to a sudden, jolting, stop. Her bone mask, with its splattering of decayed flesh, opened up in surprise. Spiralling, her dress flew around her, caught in a whirlwind of her own making. Twisting, she looked as though she fought against a patch of quicksand. The skin spreading over the bridge of her nose filled her cheeks, adding more expression. Amongst the flickering emotion, the most prevalent was raw horror. Kyla looked down to the muddy water to where a skeletal hand had risen from the muck to seize her ankle. She screamed.

At the entrance to the basin, the muddy water swelled upward as something below the surface began to rise. Water ran from the black earth as a shape formed.

'What's happening?' Jack shouted over Kyla's anguish.

Inara watched the hand that crept up Kyla's leg, revealing a withered arm, dressed in rotted laced fabric. 'They've come home,' she said.

A back, its spine clotted with the dirt of its grave, broke through the ground. Riveted on Kyla, Isabelle pulled her face down in fright and disbelief. Unaware of the body behind her that pulled itself from the sucking mire. The nightclothes the corpse wore were a present from her mother. Faded pink flowers, which Isabelle had adored, showed through the clinging mud. Clods of dirt fell from the raised body to strike the pool of water, sending small waves to lap at Isabelle's feet.

The arm, now revealed to its shoulder, drank in Kyla's light. Streams of amber threaded its way into the aged bone, imbuing the body with greater strength. Kyla, struggling to free her leg, fell. Her ghost-like form caused no splash. When the gaping skull, so like the face Kyla often chose to wear, surfaced, the Ghost Walker howled in despair.

'Stop this,' cried Justice. 'We only wanted to help you.'

Inara shook her head. 'You despise life. That is why you cut down the trees, and killed every living thing in the Wold. You even force your precious Myrms to wear masks, to hide their flesh from your eyes.'

'You are wrong,' said Justice. 'We came to protect the boy's grandmother, and to offer you a better life.'

'A life of servitude is not a better life,' replied Inara.

'I wished to be your friend,' spoke Isabelle. 'We are the same age. We are so alike.'

'We are not the same.'

Behind Isabelle, the corpse in the nightgown, wrapped her arms around Isabelle's chest. Unlike Kyla, Isabelle did not scream, as the body, her mother had taken to the tree, reclaimed her soul. The light fled swiftly from Isabelle, deserting her body like embers escaping a fire.

CRIK

Jack was sure he saw a ghost of a smile on Isabelle's face as she disappeared into her skeletal remains.

Now half emerged from the muddy pool, Kyla's body pulled itself up to Kyla's heaving chest. Most of the Ghost Walker's light had vanished, leaving behind grey skin. 'Get it off of me,' she screamed. 'I don't want to go into the ground. I promise to leave this place and never come back,' she pleaded with Inara, though she never looked away from the skeleton slouching out of the mud.

The pressure in Jack's hand increased as Inara tightened her grip. Her haggard appearance again wrenched at him. How much energy was it taking her, first to bring these bodies up, and then to fight for control of the Ghost Walkers' souls. He squeezed her hand, hoping to give her the strength to continue.

Kyla's voice broke when the dirt-caked skull leant down atop her face and drank the last of her light. Without her light, Kyla disappeared, and the relaxed body began to sink back into the soil.

'You tricked us by bringing us here,' said Justice.

Then Jack remembered what this place was. People believed that the woodland spirit by possessing the woman had cursed her. Not wishing to contaminate the graves on the hill, they had erected a second graveyard. He looked around at the enclosing walls. Mr Dash never tended this place; he only cared for the headstones on the hill. A few crosses, with the scrawl, "Ghost Walker," written on aged wood, stood near the river, but they buried the bodies here.

'How many years have you wanted peace?' asked Inara. 'You did not find it behind the Hedge Wall. There you only hid from your fears. Here, I can offer you a peace without fear. The village committed a hideous crime against you, and through that act, you became what they presumed you were. By killing the villagers here tonight you betrayed yourself.' Inara indicated the waiting body at the entrance to the graveyard. 'The woman you once were waits to take you back. Those who did you wrong are long gone. You cannot hold onto your hatred forever; by continuing as you have, all you spread are new hatreds and fears.'

Justice, looking at the figure of her own self, waiting besides the crumbling wall, let her arms fall to her side. 'I wanted to make a world free of persecution. When you came into the Wold, you awoke old fears. I suppose our fears are so deeply ingrained that we are nothing without them. There are those in the Wold who harbour even deeper distrust.'

'The Red Sisters,' said Jack.

Justice gave a nod.

'I will return to protect the village if I have to,' replied Inara.

GRAVES END

Justice smiled. 'The Red Sisters are not from this village. No one knows where they came from. Without the Red Sisters' graves, how do you propose to protect anyone? For now, you are safe. I will not fight you; my time has come and gone; and the Red Sisters have not left the Wold for hundreds of years. Who knows,' she said, and gave them a wink, 'they may not come here at all.'

Tendrils of amber spread forward to touch the waiting body. The light caressed the bone structure with longing. A stream of light touched the swell of a cheekbone, like a hand cupping a child's face.

'Rest in peace,' said Inara.

Justice disappeared into herself and Jack watched as her body slowly sank back into her grave, and, he hoped, the woman Justice once was could now find the rest she could not find in life.

'Oh Jack,' said Inara, 'I am so tired.' She slumped forward and Jack took her weight. He pulled her from Black and cradled her head against his chest. 'I just want to sleep,' she confided.

Warm tears sprang at the corners of Jack's eyes. 'Don't worry,' he said, smoothing her hair as she closed her eyes. 'Bill,' he said to the watching wolf, 'if you can hear me, bring Dr Threshum; hurry.' Inara felt so light in his arms, he drew her closer, keeping her body away from the dirty water. The cold clamour of her skin made the fright jump up into his throat. Bending closer he heard her soft whispering breaths. 'If I had a bed to offer you, you could have it,' he said. 'I'm sure Bill won't mind giving his up for you. Rest now Inara, you've earned it.' As her breathing deepened into the steady pattern of sleep, he relaxed. She was going to be all right.

61. EXODUS

CURLING HIS FINGERS, Jack watched the sun dried mud on his hand crack. Rubbing together his forefinger and thumb powdered the dirt. His trailing hand dragged a heavy shovel; its metal head scuffed the earthen track in a snaking line, which if followed, would lead all the way back to Long Sleep. Another day of filling in graves had left him exhausted; his back ached, his hands had splinters from working the shovel, and his shoulders refused to bend. Beside him Yang strode effortlessly along, the shadow carried his own shovel, this one slung over his shoulder. Jack cast a sullen glance over to his twin. He would like to have shadow limbs instead of aching muscles and sore joints. The knowledge that without Yang's help he would still be ankle deep in the boggy ground beside the Tristle alleviated none of his envy. Although the dead had obeyed Inara to return to their graves, the villagers had to fill in those graves, and dig new ones. In the two weeks since the battle, the grave detail had managed to inter all those Inara had called forth, until only a few remained. Some of the adults had spoken against his being part of the crew working the graveyard. Needing the distraction the work offered he had feared they would stop him. His mother had yet to come out of her coma. Dr Threshum kept assuring him of the likelihood of his mother waking up, stating, in his mellow voice, her injuries were not as serious as he had once feared. Then why were her eyes still closed? It baffled him, and in time, his confusion had turned to frustration and annoyance.

They burnt the bodies of the Myrms in a large pyre, well away from the village. The black billowing smoke from that conflagration had inked the sky for almost two days. Closer to home sat a new, smaller cemetery, for those who had fallen during the fighting. Jack did not like to think of how many headstones had sprung up in that patch of ground. Again, he gave thanks to the volunteers for taking on such a difficult task. He had not raised his hand to help them.

Stepping from the well-trodden path, he cut into the high grass to follow a second path, only the children knew about, or at the least used. This new path took him passed a number of hiding places that had hid a number of children two weeks prior. He noticed a place where the impression of a hunkered body still bent the grass out of shape. Perhaps Buckleseed - the boy had told him how he had laid low during that night. The boy's parents, thinking him dead, were

EXODUS

frantic with worry, when the scamp ran from cover at midmorning. Admiring Buckleseed's quick action, he almost didn't hear the familiar voice carry through the grass. Picking up his speed he almost crashed into Bill and Inara; both rested against a wheelbarrow.

Bill, his hair mussed up, and his clothes covered in stone dust, appraised Jack's sudden appearance with a start. Dust filled the air, making Black sneeze.

'You almost made me drop my stones,' accused Bill. Pale stone filled the wheelbarrow to its brim.

'Hey Jack, Yang,' said Inara.

She looks better, thought Jack. He had feared the exertion of raising all those bodies had messed her up for good. She slept for almost four days, making him panic that she would follow his mother into a coma. Colour had returned to her cheeks, and the marks of strain, though still apparent on her face, were no longer deep.

'Hi Inara,' he said in greeting. 'You having another break?' he asked Bill, eyeing the stationary wheelbarrow with an upraised eyebrow.

Bill almost tripped over his words. 'I've pushed these stones from one end of town to the other. If you don't believe me the wheel has left a furrow so deep in your garden you can shoot marbles down it.'

'When you took the doll to Knell I bet you never expected it would lead to this,' said Jack.

'I blame my grandfather. He just had to come through the tree with me. Thought I'd run away or something.'

'You did once,' pointed out Inara.

'That's not true,' said Bill, indignantly. He ruffled Black's shaggy coat. 'I did not run away; I went to get my wolf. When Grandpa spoke with Knell, I played on the swing in her yard. Later, Knell led Grandpa out of the house and into the Scorn Scar. She took him through the town to the quarry. It was his idea to bring back the quarry stone to help rebuild the village. I had nothing to do with it.'

'I hear Dwayne's parents have decided to remain in the Scorn Scar,' said Jack. 'Before long there won't be enough people left in Crik to need houses.'

Inara shrugged. 'Those who lived in the shadow of the mountain moved on when the birds arrived. Your people may as well use the houses they abandoned. Bill's home is the only one left standing after the fire.'

'There's plenty of room in my house for others,' said Bill. 'Apart from you two, no one else wants to stay with my grandmother. There is your mother of course.' He cast a guilty glance at Jack.

'They'll come around,' said Jack.

'After what Justice and her sisters did to them you can't blame them for being wary.'

CRIK

Bill winced at Inara's words. 'If not for my grandmother you would have arrived too late to help us. No one says anything to her face; they just keep their distance. I have no doubt that some went through the tree to get away from her.'

'If they did, they can stay at the Scorn Scar,' said Inara. 'Good riddance to them. I don't care what people think about me, and neither does your Gran.'

'I don't know,' said Bill. 'By coming here the Ghost Walkers revealed my grandmother's secret. All her life she feared people knowing what she is.' Falling quiet, he looked through the tall grass in the direction of his home. 'The Ghost Walkers sucked more than her light when they attacked, they stole her secret. She's now so old and frail'

Jack laughed. 'I saw her shout at Mr Gasthem for dumping a pile of stones atop her lilies. The Elder almost skipped out of his trousers; he looked like a small boy reprimanded for stealing a hot cake. Although your Gran is many things, frail is not one of them.'

'There are times I catch sight of her standing in silence; sometimes for minutes at a time. Each time I try to talk to Grandpa about it, he just tells me to stop worrying. Even Wolf looks older since our return.'

'He was always an old dog,' said Jack, trying to lift Bill's dipping mood. He had hoped his friend would lift his own disposition, not pull it to the ground.

'Well, he's here.' Bill regarded Inara with impatience. 'Are you going to tell me your big secret, or do we have to wait for someone else?'

Perplexed, Jack looked from Bill to Inara. Her fingers coiled in Black's wiry hair. Whatever she has to say is making her nervous. Yang, also aware of her anxiety, dropped his shovel, straddled the wolf, and crossed his arms around her waist.

Her fingernails, nibbled down to the quick, drummed against Yang's arms. 'It is happening so fast I don't know how to say it,' she began, now hesitant. 'Did you notice how many people were here during the attack? There were far more than what you led me to believe. Crik is a small village.'

'There are always people coming in,' replied Jack. 'Some come to the market to sell their wares. Others come to buy the best beef for a hundred miles.'

'My grandfather says we have the darkest ale,' boasted Bill, though both he and Jack, who having tasted the foul stuff for themselves, could never understand how anyone could enjoy the drink, let alone make a special trip to get it.

'The village attracts people,' agreed Inara. 'There are many reasons why they come. I heard that this is the oldest village in Crik Wood.'

Jack, knowing the patter of Igneous Fowlt, an ancient merchant, who sold even older clocks, gave a nod. He still did not grasp where Inara was going with this.

EXODUS

'There are a lot of different reasons why people come here.' She grew more pensive. 'Yet, there are even more reasons to move on. The woods are larger than what we know. Wondrous things grow and live outside the boundary of your home. Discovering the Wold taught us that much.'

'It taught us how dangerous the woods are,' countered Bill.

'Impressions are more treacherous. Until he found out his Narmacil was not a demon, Jack wanted to kill Yang. Misguided notions started this entire mess. Fearing the Ghost Walkers led your village to do cruel things to those they loved. In turn, the Ghost Walkers of the Red Wood wanted to destroy this village, to erase any threat to them. If we always choose to mistrust before accepting the differences in others, we will have learnt nothing from our experiences.'

'What are you saying? Do you want to leave, to go on another adventure?'

Inara shook her head at Jack's question. 'No. At least not yet,' she quickly amended, cryptically. She chewed her lower lip. 'The old man who sells the clocks, the one who said this is the oldest village in Crik.' Her hands clutched Yang for support. 'He says he knows the mouth of Silvertree River. My parents live along its bank. Most days father fishes its waters. Massive salmon swim with rainbow trout, and whitefish.' Tears collected on her chin, held, and then fell to her chest. 'Igneous, promised to take me to the river. He's travelling with a hunter named Oslen.'

'I know them both.' Emotion raged inside Jack. Was he going to lose Inara, as he was losing his mother? With her gone, the village would become hollow indeed. 'Oslen is a good man, he carves small figurines. He helped out at Long Sleep.' He rambled to buy more time.

'When are you thinking of going?'

Jack wanted to strike Bill for asking the question he dreaded. She would now have to tell them. His chest contracted as though instead of him shovelling dirt on the dead at Long Sleep, he lay at the bottom of a deep hole, with a leering corpse shovelling clods of dirt atop him.

'They want to leave today.'

The words clamoured in Jack's head. Today, she cannot go today, she hasn't prepared for the journey. Where were her provisions, food, drink, warm clothes for the cold weather? All his objections remained trapped in his throat. How could he deny her the opportunity of reuniting with her family? He would give anything for his mother to recover, to show her that he was safe. He could not, would not, stop Inara from having her wish. Not again, he scolded himself. Still, protests wanted to spill from him. She had not recovered from the rigours of confronting the Ghost Walkers. She had yet to speak to his mother. His jaws clamped shut, hard.

'I know this has come as a shock,' she said. 'Two days ago I was too weak to leave the house.' Biting down on her lip, she noted Jack's sullen silence. 'When

CRIK

will I get a better chance than this? The trackers are leaving with the rest through the tree. The Scorn Scar is a lot farther from home than it is from here. Igneous promises to have me home within a week.'

'I know...' Jack started to say, and then stopped. 'Will you need to take Black?' His heart hammered. 'Bill will have to go with you if you do.' He did not want them both to go. Fear took hold. If Bill went away, he would have no one.

'Calm down Ying, I'm not going anywhere.' Bill laughed. 'It'd be a toss up who would stop me first, Gran or Grandpa. These days Grandpa rarely leaves me alone.' Anxious, he looked through the tall weeds for the silver-haired man. 'No, Black is staying with me. At least until things settle down. Eventually I'll take him back to the woods and set him free. Perhaps he'll find his pack. All this talk about families has made me feel guilty for taking him away from his life.'

Patting Black, Inara said, 'Black is as much a part of our family as any he left behind.'

Family. With his mother in a coma, that word had taken on special resonance. Looking at Bill's dusty face, and the troubled expression on Inara's, Jack knew she was right. 'We are family,' he said. 'Me, Bill, Black, Inara,' he regarded Yang, lingering before stating his name with affection. 'I made you go through so much, and in the process almost got everyone killed.'

'Secrets,' said Inara, 'make people lose trust. Without that, they question everything.'

'Mr Gasthem promises to tell every child in the village how they get their Talents,' said Bill.

'According to him, everyone knows on their eighteenth birthday,' said Jack. Why the Elders wanted to wait so long, he could not understand. If everyone knew when they were small kids, they'd swallow the idea like chicks flying from the nest. No big deal. Finding out as he did, no wonder he had gone crazy. Remembering Bill's Narmacil transforming on his desk, still unnerved him.

'You should've listened to me Jack,' said Inara. 'I am older than you and quite obviously wiser as well.'

Grinning, Jack told the time by the sun. 'Only a few hours left until sunset. When's Igneous leaving?'

'An hour,' said Inara. 'I can ride in his wagon. The sound of all those ticking clocks will drive me nuts, but it beats crawling home.'

'You'll be safe there,' said Jack. 'The Red Sisters don't know where you live.'

'They won't dare leave the Wold,' said Inara. 'Let them rot behind their Hedge Wall.'

'What about Huckney?' asked Bill. 'He's behind that wall too.'

'His Talent keeps him safe.'

EXODUS

'Perhaps, but he's still a prisoner. Krimble told you that they destroyed Herm because Huckney helped us. Nothing will stop them doing the same to Gold Tail.'

'I have enough problems,' said Jack, rubbing his forehead in agitation. 'My mother is comatose; I don't know if she'll wake up. The village is still mourning for those the Myrms killed. We can't ask them to storm the Wold for one man. No matter how much we want to free Huckney, we are powerless to help him. At least for now,' he said, forestalling any more arguments. 'Things may be different in the future. He's my friend as well.'

'Jack's right,' said Inara. 'Although none of us likes the idea of leaving him, we have our own pieces to pick up. Your grandmother needs you Bill; and Jack's mother will want to see him when she wakes.'

Tears burned Jack's eyes. 'Come on, let's go back. We'll help you pack your things. Liza gave you so many dresses; it'll take two chests to take them all.'

'She likes her frills,' said Inara, making a wry face.

His shadow walked with them as they stepped into the deserted road, at least twenty feet long. Not even Yang's black swathe could fill in the void left by the villagers who had abandoned Crik. Although a few men remained, busy tearing down the blackened beams that had supported the roofs of their homes, most of the village remained empty. No one spoke. The home Jack and Bill had travelled back to no longer existed. Charcoal littered the pavement amongst broken stone, and scattered fences. Across the street, the Hulme house leaned to the left. Its gutted interior showed through the gaping hole left by the front wall's collapse. Rubble clogged the scorched garden like pimples on a bearded face. Husks, not homes, framed the road. No wonder people distrusted Grandma Poulis, her house was the only one untouched by the carnage that had swept through the village. Looking down the street, Jack saw the shelled ruin of his own home. As Bill had said, he observed a furrowed line cut from the tree across his lawn. Truth told there was no lawn anymore; a few sparse clumps of grass still stood, but traffic from the tree had left his mother's pride in bald ruin.

'Will one of you help me with this,' said Bill, wrestling with the wheelbarrow. Dust rose from the bricks like smoke. The sound of his complaint scared three blackbirds from cover. Jack had time to wonder if those birds had attacked him at the command of the Birdman; and then their dark wings bore them away.

'Where are you taking the stone?'

Bill indicated a pile of rubble behind a burnt tree. Rustic gold leaves still clung to the branches, having miraculously survived the inferno that had engulfed the trunk. White marble slabs baked in the sun.

'Is there anyone in the village who knows how to use that stone?' asked Inara, eyeing the mound with scepticism. 'It's one thing getting the stone here from the quarry, but another to cut stone and shape it. Has someone got a Talent to bend stone to their will?'

CRIK

'Kresta always repaired any damage to our homes. He knows what he's doing,' said Bill, pushing the squeaking barrow once more. 'His Talent has something to do with water, doesn't it Ying?'

'Can't remember,' said Jack, preoccupied with thoughts of Inara's imminent departure.

Bill carried on undeterred. 'Anytime a flood damaged the bridge over the Tristle, Kresta made it good as new in a hurry. Without that bridge the farmers would have no way of bringing their crops to market.'

Still not convinced, Inara waved at the devastation. 'Is one man going to rebuild the entire village?'

'Of course not.' Bill was now blowing hard from the pushing his load. 'He tells everyone else what to do. Jack is part of the grave detail, helping to fill in the graves. I help with getting the stone from the tree to here. Kresta and his gang are the builders. He'll get Crik Village back on its feet.'

Jack doubted that. Fewer men each day returned from the Scorn Scar. Kresta began with twenty men, only the seven men across the way helped him today. Tomorrow he may have less. A week from now and Kresta may be the only man who cares about restoring the village. Was life in the Scorn Scar so appealing? Even the men who worked the graveyard with him hurried back through the tree once their work was complete. To him the place felt haunted. Mr Gasthem had ordered the well clear of the dead birds. Bucketfuls of small-feathered bodies pulled up from the drinking water had not stopped anyone from dipping their cups.

Upending the wheelbarrow, Bill dumped his stones onto the bigger pile under the tree. Discarding his shovel Jack walked with them to the only intact house in the village. Stopping, he regarded them both. 'If you don't mind, I'll wait here,' he said. His voice sounded as thin as a dying breath. Standing in the sun, the windows facing them felt ominous, as though death waited inside. Every time he walked through the house to his mother, he wished to see her open her eyes, to smile and greet him. However, each time the fear that she would never open her eyes grew more insistent. The idea that his mother had passed away since this morning crystallised into a certain dread.

'Why?' asked Bill. 'Gran promised to bake cakes for us for when we got home.'

Unsure what to say, Jack shrugged. 'I won't drift off.' He pointed to the stoop. 'I'll wait for you there.'

'Is everything alright?' Inara looked concerned.

'Sure. You don't need me to pick through the dresses.'

'I guess not,' she replied. 'We won't be long. Now don't move from this stoop. I haven't got much time, and I can't go hunting you down if you wander off.'

EXODUS

Promising that he would not, Jack took a seat in the shade. When his friends entered the house, he picked up an old blue ball Wolf had chewed and tossed it to Yang. Playing catch with his shadow took his mind off his premonition that something had happened in the Poulis house. Yang kept changing the direction of his throw, one going high, the other fast and low. Before long, Jack was sweating.

'No matter who leaves, I'll always have you with me,' he told Yang. His shadow dropped the blue ball. It drummed on the stoop with a hollow patter.

From time to time, he heard voices inside, and Grandma Poulis - after chasing Black out the house - brought him out a current cake and a lemon slice. He gulped the cakes down, and paid little heed to the talk. Distracted he almost missed the ticking of many clocks as a red and blue wagon rolled down to the crossroad. Igneous, perched on a small black seat, guided two white ponies to the rosebush and stopped the wagon.

'Right on time,' said Jack.

Sunlight caught the thin man's round spectacles, turning them gold like two new pennies. 'With all these timepieces, I have no excuse to be late.' He first indicated a watch on his wrist, and then a myriad of old clocks set within his wagon. Sand trickled from an hourglass above him.

'Your clocks may be wrong.'

'Ha,' said the man looking offended. 'I have a Sythson and Wu timepiece on my wrist.' He held aloft a watch with a soft leather strap. A small brass triangle extended from its face. 'This Sythson and Wu is older than you lad. Having carried it for years, I can assure you I always know the exact time. I set these timepieces,' he indicated the collection behind his back, 'twice a day. Now, listen.' Holding up a finger as scrawny as a bird's foot, he demanded silence. 'Do you hear?'

'All I hear is ticking.'

'Ah, but the ticking is together. In precisely eight minutes, every timepiece will chime a symphonic demonstration of the accuracy of my wares. Are you looking for a clock?' His head twitched, surveying the wrecked village. 'Time changes everything. In time, this place will be as it once was, or better. Only time will tell. Then you'll be happy to have a clock'

Remembering Miss Mistletoe strung up on the Hanging Tree, Jack disagreed. Nothing will be the same ever again. 'I don't have a home.'

'Did you know, this is the oldest village in the woods,' said the clock seller, ignoring Jack's words. 'I sold my first timepiece here.' Pausing, he looked at the Poulis house. 'A fine freestanding Candre house clock; a wonderful design. It had the most delightful motif.' A large clock with clouds painted on its face sat in the Poulis downstairs passage. Grandma Poulis polished it each day without fail. 'Ever since that first sale I've always made time to come back here.'

CRIK

Igneous looked ready to continue when the front door crashed open. Bill hefted a large suitcase with bright straps through the doorway. 'Help me Ying,' he cried. 'Inara decided she liked all the dresses.'

Taking one end of the large case Jack helped Bill to the wagon. His body, already aching from the day's labour, screamed at this new exertion. It was so heavy he suspected Inara hid a body, not clothes, inside.

'Put it in the back lads,' said Igneous, not offering to help.

Together they loaded the case into the tightly packed interior. All the while, a pendulum shaped like a crescent moon jabbed Jack in the shoulder. The sound of all the clocks threatened to split his head open before he and Bill backed out of the wagon.

'Inara's saying goodbye to my grandparents, she won't be long.'

'Time is of the essence lad.'

'Where's Oslen? Isn't he travelling with you?' asked Bill.

Jack had forgotten about the hunter.

'Afraid of getting soot on his fine blue cloak, he decided to meet me at the Hanging Tree.' Neighing, the ponies pulled at the harness. 'Hey, calm down,' Igneous cried pulling back on the leather straps twisted over his fists.

'Black, to me,' said Bill. Smelling the small horses brought the large wolf slavering from the cover of the same bushes that had once hid the Hatchling.

'That's the biggest beast I've ever laid eyes on,' cried Igneous. In a flash, he retrieved a staff from his wagon. 'The smell of all the bodies must have brought him down from the woods. Don't move lads; by his look I say the dinner bell is clanging in his head loud and clear.'

Laughing, Bill ran up to Black and gave the wolf a big hug.

Dumbfounded, the merchant dropped his staff. 'Well, I never,' he exclaimed. 'Is he your pet?'

'No,' Bill answered, ruffling Black's fur. 'No wolf is a pet. This is our friend. He won't harm you.'

'Not unless you hurt Inara,' said Jack, levelling his gaze at the old man. 'Black knows your scent and will catch and eat you if you harm her.'

Thin lips parted as Igneous cackled. 'A poor meal I'd make. My old bones will make fine toothpicks, but that's their only worth. Sheila and Neb,' he nodded at the nervous ponies, 'would make up for my lack of meat.' He winked. 'I have no doubt you speak truly lad, but I have nothing to fear. Selling clocks is all I do, and do not intend to harm the young lass. The way she tells it, she has been away from her parents for long enough.'

'Hello Igneous,' cried Grandpa Poulis. The old man stepped from the porch holding Inara in his arms. 'The boys keeping you company?'

'They were just warning me to watch my step on the road.'

EXODUS

'Woods are dangerous, as you know,' agreed Bill's grandfather. 'It's a good thing you are here. Inara is keen to get going. Says you will take her to Silvertree River, where she lives.'

'A poorly named river,' confided the merchant. 'The trees have pink blossoms, not silver branches. I once set up a stall at a fair, where the kids couldn't get enough of balls of sugar. They ran hither and thither wagging their sticks of pink clouds over their heads.' Laughing, the clock seller wiped at his watering eyes. 'Perhaps I should rename the river Candyfloss River. It would avoid disappointing those seeking silver trees.'

Jack, having enough of silver trees, approached Inara. 'I will visit when I can,' he promised.

Lifting her dark eyes, Inara regarded him sombrely. 'We don't live worlds apart; I will expect your visit before year's end. You too Bill,' she lifted her voice. 'Without you I would not be going home. It took longer than expected, but you kept your promise to see me back to my parents.' Leaning forward, she kissed Jack's cheek, making him blush. 'Thank you. Take care of him Yang.' The shadow standing at Jack's shoulder puffed out his chest.

A sob threatened to escape Jack's aching chest. Why was he so upset, she was going home, not heading into danger. He would see her again, and soon.

'Bill,' said Inara, 'bring Black over.'

The great wolf strode across to where Grandpa Poulis lowered Inara to the ground. She wore a light green dress, which hid her mangled legs. Mud dirtied the laced hem. Wrapping her arms around Black's neck, she wept. 'Oh Black,' she cried. 'What can I say to you? I relied on you most of all. Soon Bill will take you into the woods, and you too will go back home.' The wolf's blue eyes did not waver from the girl. When Inara released her hold, the wolf stepped back and then stopped. Stretching his neck Black licked tears from her cheeks.

'I didn't make him do that,' said Bill, incredulous. 'He did that by himself!'

Again, the wolf extended his tongue, and took away the last of the girl's tears.

'Happy hunting,' she whispered. Nodding to Grandpa Poulis, the old man lifted her back up. 'Make sure you take him deep into the wood,' Inara told Bill. 'I don't want him stumbling across a hunter's path and getting himself shot.'

'It'll take more than an arrow to hurt him,' said Bill.

'Promise,' she urged.

'Don't worry,' said Grandpa Poulis. 'I'll make sure my grandson releases the wolf well away from here. This village already has one wolf, it doesn't need another.' The old dog at his heel gave a tired bark.

Bill stepped forward and gave Inara a fierce hug. A long moment passed as they clung to one another. They parted without a word, yet the emotion of their farewell suffused the air. Jealousy stabbed Jack at their parting, a bitter barb that drove into his chest.

CRIK

'Where'd you like to sit?' asked Igneous. 'There's enough room next to me, or you can make yourself comfortable in the back.'

Inara eyed the narrow seat Igneous perched himself on dubiously. The worn leather padding titled forward at a precarious angle. 'If there's room in the wagon I'll travel there,' she said. 'I'm still weak and would welcome a lie down.'

'Your call lass. Take care not to knock over any of the clocks, they are fragile.'

Assuring the seller she would be careful, Inara allowed Grandpa Poulis to place her into the covered wagon. She sat amongst the ticking arms of a thousand clocks, looking older than her years. The dress she wore looked odd on her after the rough spun tunic, but she seemed happy to have lace against her skin. Her mother will be so happy seeing her looking so pretty thought Jack. He recalled Inara's concern that her folks would love her less for her having lost her legs, and knew she had nothing to fear. Who could not love her?

Grandma Poulis came bustling from the house carrying a basket full of food. Brushing past her husband, she passed bread, cookies, and cake to Inara.

'Those are for you,' said Grandma Poulis. 'You may share with Igneous, that's up to you. I won't have you going hungry.'

'Are those cookies chocolate?' asked Igneous Fowlt, craning his neck to peek at the wrapped goods.

'Chocolate gives a girl spots,' said the old woman. 'There are hazelnuts, and almond biscuits. You liked the lemon slice,' she addressed Inara, 'so I packed a few extra for you. Clock seller, you make sure you take care of this one.'

'I've already promised to treat her like my daughter.'

'Treat her better,' snapped Grandma Poulis. 'If you have a daughter I've never seen her.'

'It's time we were off,' said the old man, bristling under Grandma Poulis's rough tongue. As though agreeing with him the wagon erupted in chimes. Seven small birds sprang from wooden trapdoors, chirping at the end of bending springs. A wooden figure walked around a track under a glass domed carriage clock and struck a small hammer against a tiny anvil. Ignoring the chaos, Igneous reached over his head and turned the hourglass as the last grains of sand ran out.

Happy to get away from the black wolf that watched them hungrily, the ponies pulled the wagon forward. Painted wheel spokes revolved, first slow and then picked up speed until they began to blur. Jostled, Inara waved with one arm while she secured a precarious clock with the other. As the last bell clanged, the wagon drifted from view, taking Inara away.

Jack stood with Bill and Yang long after the wagon disappeared. All three remained silent, lost in their own thoughts. The near deserted village felt morose, as though it too lamented the departure of the girl that had saved it from total destruction.

EXODUS

'I can still hear the clocks ticking,' said Bill.

The noise had faded a long time ago, but Jack didn't argue, let him believe Inara is still close. At least for a few minutes longer.

'Better clean that grave dirt off,' said Bill, looking down at Jack's clothes. 'Gran won't like you traipsing it through the house.'

***

When Jack stepped from the bath the water was a grey sludge, and his skin was rosy pink. He continued to breathe in the steam, hoping it would clear his head. Depressed, he reflected on Inara's trip home, he felt as though he had a limb severed when she left. Disgusted, he shook himself. Towelling himself vigorously, he slipped into the clothes Grandma Poulis had provided. Although the dim light only afforded Yang a dim outline, he could see his shadow shared his downcast demeanour. The certainty that his mother's condition had worsened lingered like the scum the lowering water revealed on the iron tub. Perhaps he dwelled on Inara so he would not have to face what was happening to his mother. Yang's loping arms and bowed head only reinforced his dread. Steam clouded the mirror, saving him from seeing his own haggard appearance.

Leaving the bathroom, he paused to study the painting lying lengthways on the landing. Grandma Poulis had moved her easel out of the spare room to make space for his mother. Looking up from the painted field of blackened trees, he saw the door beyond the stairs was ajar. His heart lurched. No doubt, Bill or his grandparents had checked on his mother whilst he bathed, yet that crack, coated by flickering amber candlelight, set his heart pounding in his chest. Scrunching his toes in the carpet, he perceived the landing to stretch, doubling its length. Swooning, he touched the cold wall. Closing his eyes, he tried to collect his thoughts; only his thudding heart shattered all clarity. Cold fingers gripped his arm; startled, his eyes flew open. Yang held him.

'You think I should go in there,' said Jack.

His shadow did not have to make a reply; he knew he would have to check on his mother. Dr Threshum assured him that his mother's coma would not last. What the doctor did not mention was what came after the coma, life or death? Even if she woke, would she be herself? Others had injured their heads in accidents, and some could no longer speak. Some could not look after themselves. Cringing from such a possibility, he pushed away from the wall. Bill shouted for Black in the garden. Jack wanted nothing more than to jump down the stairs and play with his best friend and the fierce wolf. His fingers traced the wooden vines looping the banister; the rough texture beckoned him to follow its rope down to the ground floor. Snatching his hand back, he hurried on, blocking out everything but the open door.

Hinges creaked as the door swung inward. The flickering candle illuminated a large four-poster bed. Chestnut oil aroma filled the room. Dr Threshum advised the oil would help his mother breathe, so Jack had scavenged all the jars he could find, until they lined every shelf. Patting him on the back Yang urged him forward. Wooden flooring met his foot. Applying his weight the wood creaked, making him catch his breath as though he was a thief stealing into the room. His mother did not stir at the sound; her chest rose and fell rhythmically, stirring the blankets covering her only slightly. Her every breath is a struggle, he reflected. Thankful for the support, he allowed Yang to take hold of his arm. A stool sat close to the bed, which he used. Meagre light painted the burns on her face, casting a play of shadows across her cheeks and forehead. He had never seen anyone look so beautiful. Guilt for leaving her hit him again.

'I no longer think she was angry at me for leaving the village,' he confided to Yang. 'Frightened and lonely, yes; I betrayed her and left her alone. Farmer Vine told me how frantic she was that no one could find me.' He wiped away at the hot tears that spilled unbidden down his cheek. 'She would've wrapped me in her arms and welcomed me home.' He sobbed into his chest.

When he took her hand, he gasped at the warmth. He expected hands as cold as Yang's. Every time he had touched her skin, it had felt ice cold. Hope bloomed suddenly in his chest, robbing his fear of its potency. Quickly he touched her face, and almost cried when his fingers warmed at the gentle caress.

'Yang.' His excitement threatened to send him into another swoon. Could she be getting better? After so long, could he dare hope the impossible. All other cares left him. Her pulse beat strong against his fingers as he probed her neck.

'Mother,' he said, though emotion strangled the word. He repeated, this time with more urgency. 'Can you hear me? Mother, it's Jack. I've come home.'

Though she made no reply, he now listened with renewed hope and found her breathing was stronger. A week back Grandma Poulis had placed a mirror before his mother's face; concern had etched new lines into her withered face. Finally, a thin layer of mist clouded the glass and the old woman had breathed a sigh of relief. That sigh had haunted him. Had Grandma Poulis expected his mother to die? Wanting to laugh he instead restrained himself, wanting to listen to each sound his mother made.

Threading his fingers into Jack's trouser pocket Yang grasped the purple candle Knell had given the boy. Retrieving the candle, he extended the cool wax to the lit wick that resided on the bedside table. Before he could light the candle, Jack saw him.

'You want to speak,' said Jack.

Nodding, Yang lit the strange candle; a moment later thick tendrils of purple cloud filled the room.

'She is fighting hard,' said Yang, in his hollow voice. 'But Jack, your mother is weaker than you think.'

EXODUS

Alarmed, Jack stood, knocking the stool to the floor. 'What're you saying? Is she going to die?' The possibility that he could actually lose his mother after this new hope was too cruel. 'Tell me Yang?'

'We must help her,' answered the shadow.

In disbelief, Jack watched Yang clamber onto the bed. Bedsprings groaned under the added weight. His mother remained unmoved as the shadow pressed its now solid frame atop her. Pushing his weight down Yang brought his angled face to within inches of the unconscious woman.

'No,' said Jack. He reached out and gripped an arm as cold as an icicle. 'She's struggling to breathe; with you atop her she won't be able to draw a breath.' Pulling with all his strength, he could not budge his shadow. 'Please, she is getting better.'

'She is not out of danger yet,' replied Yang. The shadow's echoing voice sounded as though it came from deep within a cave. 'If I don't help her, I fear she will not have the strength to break free and will slip further into this coma and never awaken.'

'What are you planning on doing?'

'Do you trust me?'

That question had taken them from one end of Crik Wood to the other. When faced with Yang's demise he realised what he would lose. Together with his mother, Yang was the only family he had. Yet he could not understand what Yang intended. Would the Narmacil's actions cause his mother harm? Neither of them were doctors. Was it possible that Yang's meddling could halt his mother's recovery? Since Yang climbed on the bed, her breathing had become shallower. Yang was ice cold, would that rob her of the warmth that had so infused him with hope for the first time since the battle? Hundreds of questions and concerns rifled through his mind.

'I trust you,' he said, knowing that was the only answer he had.

Black lips parted in a sigh. 'Thank you Jack.'

Leaning forward Yang pressed his face to Jack's mother and breathed into her. Her entire body lurched upward, pushing Yang from the mattress. Jack lurched forward, snagging the bedclothes with fingers as stiff as pegs. Cold sweat dampened his brow. Roving patterns of thick purple smoke obscured the bed. When the smoke dissipated his shadow breathed, and again his mother's body swelled under the dark form that pinned her to the bed. Once more dark cheeks expanded with air that then filled her lungs. She shuddered as though assailed. Compressing his lips, Jack kept still; he had to believe in Yang or he would lose everything. Time lapsed, with only the eddying purple light marking its passage. Relaxing her taught body, his mother sank into the soft blanket. Dark lips parted from pale lips with an almost inaudible murmur.

CRIK

Exhausted, Yang slipped from the bed. His head hit the bedpost with a load thump, but the shadow did not seem to care. Short breaths hitched his chest as he slumped to the floor amongst the swirling clouds that made him corporeal.

'What did you do?' demanded Jack.

'I had to give her my strength,' said the shadow in a weedy voice. 'When that happened, she took from me.'

'Took what?' All Jack could think of was two flippers slipping into Bill's open mouth.

'There were two lives at risk,' answered Yang. 'Your mother suffered an injury that would have killed her if not for her Narmacil's efforts to keep her alive. My kin's essence saved her, and battled to restore her to you. Such efforts exhausted them both. Hearing her Narmacil's cries for assistance, I had to act.' Yang slumped against the bed like an old man after an arduous run. 'Do you understand?' he gasped.

Jack nodded dully. 'How much of yourself did you give?'

'I will recover.'

If the shadow had anything more to say, the groan from the bed stopped him. Both boy and shadow turned at the sound. Colour had blossomed in cheeks that for days had stubbornly remained chalk white, turning them a faint pink. Her eyelids fluttered.

'Mother, come back to me.' This time Jack's words were strong, and he repeated them as though they could wrestle his mother back from the brink. 'I am home, I'm here for you.'

An arm lifted from the rumpled blanket to wipe away a dark curl that clung to a temple damp with sweat. Jack stared in awe as his mother's arm fell back. He could scarce believe what he saw. His mother had moved her arm.

'Jack.'

The softly spoken word did not have a hollow tint. It took a long moment before Jack realised it was not his shadow that spoke. Excited, he waved away the thick cloud that billowed from the candle. Through the parting mist, he saw his mother appraising him with two bright eyes. A smile softened her face as she looked upon him.

'My son, you have come home to me.'

THE END